May 1, 2001

To Patricia Gwilliam

I hope you enjoy this story that came from my heart — and my past.

Remembering the way the she lived — and the way he called me Rose.

Patricia Berington

The Famous Rose Callahan

by Patricia Berrington

THE FAMOUS ROSE CALLAHAN

A Silver Rose Book/July 1997

All rights reserved.
Copyright (c) 1996 by Patricia Berrington

ISBN 0-9658379-0-4

Library of Congress Catalog Card Number 97-91989

Published by Silver Rose Productions
P.O. Box 3326, Las Cruces, New Mexico 88003

Trademark Registered in the office of the
New Mexico Secretary of State, Santa Fe, New Mexico, U.S.A.

PRINTED IN THE UNITED STATES OF AMERICA

TO MIKE ....

For keeping the promise.

ACKNOWLEDGEMENTS

For his insight, generosity and dedication of time and spirit, my love and gratitude to Mike Steffey, without whose inspiration this story would never have been told.

Sincere thanks to Ben Traywick, historian, author, and friend, for his expert advice and kind encouragement to take the "alternate route," and to a grand lady called Red Marie, for assisting my efforts to recover the little gray house and save the rose tree.

Heartfelt appreciation to Bill Hunley, owner of the Bird Cage Theatre, Tombstone, Arizona, and Paula Jean Reed, for their gracious hospitality and generous promotional efforts in connection with my music and this book.

For technical assistance, many thanks to Sherry Curtis, John Davis, and the staff of Arizona Lithographers, Tucson, Arizona for their commitment to excellence; to my technical editor, Tom Custer; and to Lana Schaff.

With artistic expertise from a friend who created an authentic impression of a lady from another place in Time, an element of a bygone era was captured on the cover. It is with the highest regard for her talent and attention to detail that I give all credit for historical costume research and design to couturière extraordinaire, Elizabeth Heuisler.

...and for her portrayal of the "ghost" of Rose Callahan on the cover and title page, bouquets to Mimi Boynton.

There are those who awaited the printing of this book, but could not stay to read it. Publication came in the same year of their passing from this world. Until we meet again...

Remembering Elizabeth Snyder, 1941–1997
Remembering Marie Traywick, 1923–1997
Remembering Dorothy Briggs, 1916–1997

FOREWORD

If you've ever wondered about the possibility of past lives and whether you might have passed this way before, you're not alone. Reincarnation has been a subject of great speculation and wonderment throughout the ages. Existence of a spirit world and those connected with it have always been a fascination regardless of whether you choose to believe it. Reports of hauntings and ghosts who appear to relay a message or tell a story are nothing new. Messages have been passed from the other side to one of us by virtue of a channel or, in some cases, channel writing. There are plenty of unexplained phenomena that make even hard-core skeptics scratch their heads and admit they have no idea how such things might have occurred. This is one of those stories. The best part is, it really happened.

After experiencing unexplained events and emotions triggered by an antique music box in the 113 year-old Bird Cage Theatre in Tombstone, Arizona, the author was swept back to another place in time. Over the following two and a half years, recurring dreams revealing dates, events, and people of another era took the form of a story. References are made to old-time medicinal remedies, Indian names and a way of life far removed from Twentieth-Century medicine and space-age technology we know today, but which were previously unknown to the author. Detailed descriptions of the construction of buildings and the drawing of a house floor plan the way it was in 1881, without ever having seen the place; a date of the opening of a business; a child's name, described as having lived over a hundred years ago — all verified more than a year after the initial writing. Strange messages dictated into a recorder without a clue as to their meaning were discovered as relevant information at a later date. The mention of a silver rose, found in a subsequent visit to the Bird Cage Theatre, on the floor in front of the old music box, linked the telling of the story to the theory of spirit influences. If there was any doubt as to the source from which this story emanated, it disappeared with finding the silver rose.

Connection to a spirit world is a primary element in this story about a woman who the author is convinced lived more than a hundred years ago during the heyday of the wildest mining camp and silver boomtown in Western history. Even more incredible is the recognition and reunion of those with whom there is unfinished business from another time. It was not by accident that the author was drawn to Tombstone, but rather by predetermined destiny for the purpose of resolving unfinished business from a past life. Without realizing it, the person who led her there did so because he was part of the unfinished business; a promise made in 1882 that they would meet again; a promise kept in 1994. Neither was it by accident that the story led to others who felt a similar connection to the place. Nothing about the writing of this story has been an accident.

Although some of what is written has been confirmed by credible sources, no trace of Rose Callahan has been found, but as a notable historian has pointed out, "...just because you can't find her, it doesn't mean she wasn't here." Not everything made the history books. The search continues for the Irish prostitute and entertainer who lived in Tombstone and worked at the Bird Cage Theatre from 1881 to 1889. They called her the Silver Rose.

True wealth is not measured in gold, but in gifts of greater value. This story was neither contrived nor researched, nor the product of a wild imagination, but rather a gift from the other side. Although she knew some famous people, it's not about them. It's the story of a connection between two lifetimes; Rose Callahan's and Patricia Berrington's. The crossover is closer than we think.

How often are we given a second chance? How many truly rare opportunities are offered to us? How many times do we know love? And when it is given to us, how do we recognize it for what it is?

It is rare that love is found and recognized once in any lifetime, but practically unheard of that it would be found in two places in Time, and shared by the same two spirits. Two travelers in Time; one and the same; a recognition of memories long asleep. Memories awakened by spirits searching throughout the Universe to find their counterparts; soul mates for eternity.

A simple message to those who believe.

TIME CANNOT ERASE
THE MEMORIES THAT LOVE
HAS MADE

Chapter 1

DENVER, COLORADO – JANUARY, 1994

The alarm crashed into her senses and threw her violently into consciousness. Eyes closed, she instinctively reached out and thumped the noisy culprit. Everyone said this would be a cold winter in Colorado. She shivered at the accuracy of the prediction and pulled the comforter over her head. Five-thirty a.m. Even the birds weren't awake at such an ungodly hour, but she was. Determined not to let the warm comforter win, she threw it off and waited for her eyes to adjust in the dark. It would be so easy to crawl under the covers and go back to sleep. Better get moving before she changed her mind. She sat up and put her feet on the floor. The rest of her body followed reluctantly. It was still dark outside, but the streetlamp lit up the yard enough to show how much snow had fallen during the night. One glance out the window told her the usual twenty-minute drive downtown would take at least an hour this morning, maybe more. Temptation to fall back and pull the covers over her head was strong. Willpower! She'd have to get an early start. Streets would be slick. Ice skates would be a more appropriate mode of travel. Just pray some idiot wouldn't run into her car; one of those fools who drove 4-wheel drive trucks and thought they owned the road.

Tying the sash on her bathrobe, she shivered and checked the thermostat. Couldn't hurt to turn it up a notch or two. Ever since her lung collapsed a couple of years ago, she had to be especially careful about catching cold. Mornings like this reminded her all too well how she suffered that year; two weeks in the hospital and six more recuperating with respiratory therapy every day. She never wanted to go through that again. Doctors told her to move to a warmer climate. Easy for them to say. They could afford it. She'd like nothing better than to be lying in the sun on some white, sandy beach in the South Pacific with palm trees swaying in the breeze. Tahiti would be nice. Reality kicked in. She wouldn't be going to Polynesia any time soon, least of all, today. Today, it'd be a bloody miracle if she survived the drive down Seventeenth Avenue to get to work.

It was exceptionally cold this morning; one of those bitter, sub-zero days where Old Man Winter forced his freezing breath through the tiniest crack around a window or under a door to bite you even when the heater was on. No matter what you did, there was no getting toasty warm on a day like this. As an afterthought, she turned up the thermostat another degree on her way to the kitchen. Icicles hanging from the edge of the roof outside the window were proof of how cold it was. She poured a cup of coffee and inhaled the rich aroma before taking a drink. Thank God for timers. She set it before she went to bed and the coffee was made when the morning alarm went off. Holding the cup with both hands, she sipped the hot liquid and closed her eyes, savoring the first taste and reaffirming her choice. Colombian was definitely the best. Strong and rich. She'd make a point to remember not to ever buy some other kind.

Now that the house was warming up and the first cup of coffee was down, she had to think about getting ready for work. Into the bathroom to light the morning candle. She never could stand bright lights first thing in the morning. Every day when she stood in the glow of the candlelight, hot water from the shower careening over her body, the same thought sent a twinge of longing through her. Wouldn't it be nice to have someone to share this romantic morning eye-opener with? Was she the only one who had these little ideas? Was there no one out there who appreciated the opportunity to share special moments like this? Despite heartaches of relationships over the years, she was still a hopeless romantic. When her marriage ended, she lost herself in her work. She watched the shampoo bubbles rush down the drain. Nine years of her life down the drain. What a sad admission. After this last failure, she made a conscious decision to stop looking for someone to share her life with. She wasn't bitter. She had simply given up the search. There was no one now. Nevertheless, the dream was still there. It was a private dream she never talked about. Everyone thought she was so professional, so logical, so together. She was all of those things. She never allowed the pain inside to show. Who would ever suspect that someone like her carried the deepest of hurt? No one had ever loved her. A profound, but true statement of fact. The missing link in the chain that would make her life complete — love. It wasn't there. Such a small word. Such monumental definition. Far too much to hope for.

A few tears mixed in with the shower water at the total sense of loss and the possibility of spending the rest of her life alone. Not a very encouraging prospect to think about first thing in the morning. The candle flame sputtered in the steamy bathroom and the shower washed the tears away. There couldn't be any trace of them by the time she showed up at the office. Reality was a cruel companion sometimes, but she looked him square in the eye every day. Some days were just worse than others.

An arctic cold front moved in a few days earlier and the temperature this Monday morning was eleven degrees below zero. Everything was frozen solid. She wondered why she ever left California. Well, she knew why. At least she thought she did at the time. She believed there was a better life waiting in Denver. After all the years of searching for love, she really thought she found it. The "Cosmic Cowboy." That's what they called him because his business was satellite communications. What a joke that was. Looking back, she couldn't believe she'd been such a fool. Nine years of her life thrown away on a man who never cared anything about her. Like a naive, gullible schoolgirl, she fell for his con — hook, line and sinker. Of course, she knew why it happened. Life had been a constant struggle. Divorced at twenty-one with two kids, alone for eighteen years, she was hungry for love and companionship. He promised her a home, a real home, and convinced her life would be easier, better. He promised a lot of things that never materialized. Looking back, she realized he never gave her the only thing she wanted. He never loved her, and because of that, there was no sense of loss at his leaving. It was doubtful she'd ever know why she stayed with him so long. All he wanted was her money, and he got it. Every penny. She left a business and thirty years of her life in San Diego and moved to Denver with him. She set him up in business and threw herself into making a home. Her reward was that he spent her life savings and treated her like dirt. He cheated on her, lied to her, insulted her. He used her and when the money was gone, he threw her away like yesterday's newspaper. To add insult to injury, he told her she'd gotten too old for him and he needed a younger woman. That was the day he moved out.

It was pointless to blame him. He was a slick one alright, but she was a big girl. There were no excuses. She allowed it to happen, so she couldn't blame anyone but herself. It was a familiar scenario. Her life was a series of mistakes and disappointments, not to mention looking for love in all the wrong places. More than once, the thought occurred to her that she'd been born under a bad sign. How much worse could it have been? Come to think of it, a lot worse. She could have been dead, but by some inexplicable stroke of luck, she wasn't. Not many happy times to recall, but at least she was alive to tell the story. As for the love part, she finally decided to stop looking and abandon what had always been an exercise in futility. The search was over.

Why was she thinking about all this now? It was history and she wanted to leave it that way. She'd turned the bad memories loose a long time ago and didn't often think about the past anymore. After what she'd been through, she ought to be thankful to be alive. She was thankful. She'd made a lot of mistakes, and although she didn't have a sense for the direction to take, she knew she was being given another chance to do it right this time. A recurring nightmare over several years finally disappeared. In fact, it stopped right about the time he moved out, a severing of ties to a relationship that should have ended years ago. She imagined it was a form of relief. In the dream, the house was burning and she could never find a way out. She always woke up in a cold sweat, feeling trapped and scared. For the moment, the fire was out, a possible indication she might be making headway toward a new beginning. In recent days, she had a feeling she was on the brink of discovering something important. It was kind of like standing on the edge of a cliff without a life jacket, watching a raging river rush by below and seeing calm water up ahead, almost within reach, but not quite. All she had to do was figure out how to get past the white water, but there always managed to be an obstacle between her and smooth sailing. If she jumped, she might drown. On the other hand, there was the possibility that if she jumped, she just might make it. Reaching peaceful waters would be worth fighting the rapids, but if she didn't jump, she'd never know if she could have made it. She didn't know how to swim.

Listening to the icy, January wind whistling around the building and echoing through the parking garage made her thankful for underground parking. She felt sorry for people who had to park in outdoor lots a few blocks away and walk through the freezing morning air and blowing snow. She punched the "UP" button on the elevator and rested her briefcase on the concrete floor to remove her gloves. Bundled up for the frigid temperature outside, it was almost too warm in the heated garage. She loosened her scarf and checked her watch — seven thirty-five. She made better time than she expected.

Two men boarding the elevator moved behind her and commenced a familiar conversation, lamenting their fate at having to visit their lawyer and whining about the exorbitant fees. They complained that for the sake of image and ego, attorneys located themselves on the top floors of tall buildings in high rent districts to justify charging big fees for the luxury of extravagant decor. The higher the offices, the more expensive the lawyer. She knew the type well. They expected you to drop everything when they called and were never satisfied with anything you did. Everything was an emergency. Believing whatever ailed them to be the only problem on the planet, they were the first to call in a panic, and the last to pay their bill. They were takers, the kind who always wanted something for nothing. It's the way they lived.

Listening to them complain, she wondered how much of their time they gave away. Not much, judging from the expensive suits and fancy cars. Upstairs, they'd whine and try to cajole their lawyer into discounting his fee and if he stuck to his guns, they'd revert to finding fault with the service even when they knew he'd done a fine job. Eventually, they'd succeed in getting something written off. How many times had she heard one of them say, "How about some free legal advice?" And how many times had they called her to ask a question, thinking they might circumvent the attorney to avoid paying for an answer? Even if she knew the answer, she couldn't give it. On those occasions, she loved to give the standard response, "I can't give you legal advice, but I'll make an appointment for you to see the attorney." Invariably, they decided the question wasn't so important after all. Anything to get out of paying. She thought to herself, "They get what they pay for, and then some." Free legal advice wasn't worth anything and you could get it anywhere from your brother-in-law to your hairdresser. You could also pay the price and suffer the consequences when you followed it and things blew up in your face. If you wanted a good lawyer, you paid for his advice. It was no different than any other business. If either of them needed an appendectomy, they'd go to a surgeon and pay for the operation. They wouldn't try to get the doctor to take less money. They'd pay the bill and thank him. People had a funny idea about the value of professional services. In a legal crisis, they sought the advice of their lawyer with a sense of urgency comparable to that of their doctor in a medical emergency, but when it came time to pay the lawyer's bill, not only did they not thank him, they argued about it. She considered it an insult because it implied her skills and those of her associates were of lesser value than other professionals. She had to laugh about a magazine ad she saw where a number was painted on a tag hanging from the pin of a hand grenade. A sign on the stand said, "Free legal advice. Take a number."

All the way to the thirty-eighth floor, the two men complained about their lawyers, yet they were on their way to consult with the shysters at that very moment. She wondered if they understood the irony in that and how foolish it made them look. The lighted numbers flashed upward as the elevator approached her destination and the men continued to expound on the unscrupulous dirty deeds they knew awaited them upstairs. She wanted to say something like, "If you really believe your lawyer is a crook, don't you feel a little stupid coming back for more worthless, expensive advice?" She had to bite her tongue. It'd be her luck they were going to the same place she was going. A lesson learned long ago from witnessing repercussions of someone else's mistake was knowing when to keep her mouth shut. You never knew what the results of a careless comment might be.

The high-speed elevator stopped abruptly as the lighted, digital number above the door blinked to thirty-eight. No matter how often she made the trip, she was never ready for the stop and it always left her with momentary vertigo. Same thing happened every time. Her feet left the floor for a split second when the hydraulic system reversed to slow the car and threw her slightly off balance before the moving room came to a complete stop. It was that breathless moment where you knew if the cable you were dangling from was ever going to snap and send you plunging to your death thirty-eight stories below, it was now. She glanced at the elevator inspection record posted beside the buttons. Was it current? She rode these cars every day and never noticed. Without her glasses, she couldn't see the date. No time for a close look, she made a mental note to check it later. The men behind her didn't wait for her to recover from the stop. They didn't even wait for her to get out of the car ahead of them, but pushed rudely by, bumping into her with no apology. At a time like this, she wished she had the nerve to stick out her foot and watch them go sprawling on the carpet in front of her. Instead, she muttered a sarcastic, "Excuse me." One of them turned and looked at her briefly, but didn't acknowledge her comment. The other one walked on as if she were invisible. They were the kind who made you believe chivalry was dead. No gentlemen. They probably cheated on their wives too.

She held her briefcase to the edge of the elevator door to break the electronic beam as it began to close. The door immediately opened and she stepped out onto the plush green and gold carpet in the hall. When it closed behind her, she looked back. As usual, the cable held. Defied death, again! She'd live to ride the moving room to the thirty-eighth floor another day. Just ahead, the two complainers disappeared through the double oak doors, the topic of conversation having switched from the dastardly deeds they imagined being contrived by their lawyers to the recently ended football season and their predictions for the Broncos' future. She waited a few seconds before entering the office behind them, thankful she hadn't said what was on her mind in the elevator. Sometimes, discretion truly was the better part of valor or, if nothing else, that consummate moment of self-restraint that kept you from being fired.

The smoked glass and brass marquis listed the names of the partners of the most prestigious law firm in town. You were blessed with instant status and implied success if you enjoyed membership in this influential organization of legal beagles. Some of the most brilliant minds in the country practiced law from behind the heavy Florentine doors. A side thought; some were not so brilliant. She shifted her briefcase to the other hand and turned the brass knob. Expensive furnishings and art in the reception area shouted success and longevity; a third generation law firm, long-established and well-respected. Every time she passed through those doors, she entered a world separate and apart from the one outside in the hallway. There was a surrealism about the inordinately too-perfect setting, an intense, irrational reality of a dream even though she knew she was wide-awake. It was always the same. Skipping down the yellow brick road and finding herself smack in the middle of the Emerald City. Even Dorothy would have been amazed. Some people called the staff and associates snooty. She disagreed. It was a professional organization full of hardworking people; the best legal team in town. She preferred to think of herself as intelligent and successful, and if anyone interpreted those merits as snooty, so be it. Concentrated effort and long hours earned her the position of senior paralegal, and she didn't care what anyone said.

Not expecting anything to the contrary, her office was exactly as she left it yesterday; yesterday being Sunday, and a purported day of rest. She couldn't remember the last time she had a weekend off. This one had been no exception. She paused in the doorway long enough to survey an all too familiar Monday-morning aftermath of the Sunday work explosion. The damage was more extensive than she remembered last night. Did she really drag all those books down here from the library? She dropped her briefcase beside the desk and hung her coat on the back of the door. When she turned around, she spoke out loud, emphasizing each word. "What a mess!" There was a desk somewhere under all the books and papers. By the time she went home yesterday, housekeeping had been the furthest thing from her mind. Case files were stacked on the desk and piles of folders overflowed onto the floor. It looked like a bomb went off and the fallout was nothing but paper. Open law books, pages marked with psychedelic-pink sticky notes, were spread out two deep on the desk. Sometimes she wondered how anything got done on time, but the crisis of the moment was always met. Once the trivia was out of the way, she returned to the priority case, the one that took most of her time these days. It was the reason she was here late every night and weekends, and it was why she was here again yesterday. Plenty of times, she'd asked herself if she didn't make it more difficult than it had to be just to have an excuse not to stay home alone. This case helped her maintain some semblance of sanity over the past two years when everything else in her life was disintegrating. For a lot of years, the law had been her refuge and this case was her escape from recent personal pressures. She checked the calendar, then did an instant assessment of the condition of her office. The smart thing would be to spend an hour, maybe two, cleaning it up. There was no alternative plan unless she wanted to find herself buried under a mountain of paper by the end of the day. First things first though. Coffee.

She left her office and started down the hall to the kitchen. When a yawn snuck up on her, one of the attorneys shook his finger and made a comment to the effect that she shouldn't stay out partying so late. That was funnier than he knew. It wasn't worth explaining she'd spent her entire Sunday right here at the office and topped it off by doing laundry and reading thirty pages of case-law research in bed last night. She ignored the remark and kept walking. She was tired this morning and she knew it showed; a little on the grumpy side too, so it was better not to say something she might regret later. One of these days, she'd stay home on a Monday and sleep all day. Famous last words. One of these days! She rounded the bend to the kitchen, hoping no one made that French vanilla stuff so early in the morning. All she wanted was a cup of good old-fashioned black coffee, the stronger, the better.

Abandoning the idea of calling in the haz-mat team for clean-up, she tackled the wreckage, starting with the big chunks. Once the books were lugged back to the library and a week's worth of filing stacked in her outbasket, patches of the desk top and credenza reappeared. A little improvement in housekeeping gave way to the light at the end of the tunnel and got her motivated to finish the job. She carried an armload of files out and dropped them on her secretary's desk, receiving a "thank you" for the delivery she was certain came straight from the heart. "Don't thank me yet. There's more." A minute later, she returned with a second stack and the out-basket full of papers perched on top. Setting the basket on the desk, she leaned on the pile of file folders. "I apologize for dumping all this on you at once, Teri, but I promise not to give you another thing to do until you get the filing caught up." The other woman slid her glasses down her nose and crossed her arms. She'd heard that one before. They'd worked together for two years and in the process, had become friends. Teri Eldridge was an outstanding legal secretary and a genuinely nice person. She also knew the Monday-morning housecleaning routine including what the realistic chance was that she wouldn't get another thing to do until the filing was done. Arms folded and no hint of expression on her face, she sat back and responded to the promise. "Do you know if you tell a lie, your nose will grow? Your nose is growing."

Friday's leftover messages were arranged in order of priority and stacked in a neat little pile next to the telephone. One of them was sure to be a problem designed to disrupt her plan for the day. She tapped the pile of messages thoughtfully with one finger. They could wait a few more minutes. A clean office provided a sense of accomplishment, so maybe she'd just sit and enjoy it for a while. It wouldn't last long. Most Mondays, she had to whip the office into shape and dive right into a project somebody wanted yesterday. So far, the phone hadn't rung once. Things were pretty quiet for a Monday. The storm slowed everything down, including the desire to work. Teri brought in a fresh cup of coffee and set it on the desk in front of her, exchanging it for the old cup. This was where she got her dose of Monday-morning advice on the state of her health and her love life, or lack thereof. It was a ritual they went through as part of beginning every week. She leaned forward and folded her hands on the desk, giving her full attention to the lecture she knew was coming. Right on cue, Teri stopped at the door and turned around. "You drink too much coffee, Pat. You look tired too. Why don't you go home early today? If you'd ever stop being a workaholic and take a day off, you might find yourself a good man to relieve some of the stress." When no response was offered, Teri put her hand on the door knob. "I'll hold your calls a few minutes." She closed the door on her way out. No point waiting any longer for an answer to the "Why don't you go home early today?" because she knew there wasn't so much as a remote possibility of it happening. Taking better care of herself was certainly good advice, and the concern of a friend was appreciated, but there was a lot more to being a workaholic than Teri knew. As far as finding a man was concerned, Teri didn't understand that wasn't even a consideration under present circumstances.

Now, for a minute of quiet before the first bomb of the day went off. She didn't know how she got so lucky. She had a corner office with a wraparound window that provided a fantastic view for miles. Inspirational actually. Holding the coffee cup with both hands, she swung her chair around to face southwest. In the distance, the snow-capped Rockies emitted an essence of peace and on a clear day, you could see all the way to Pike's Peak. Unfortunately, this morning, she was met with instant disappointment. Winter enveloped the city in a shroud of cloudy vapor that obscured her view of the mountains. So much for inspiration. She sipped the hot coffee, glad it was the real stuff. A heavy snow was falling. A bad sign so early in the day. If it kept up, the drive home tonight would be more treacherous than the one coming in. Maybe she'd avoid rush-hour traffic at five o'clock and stay a little late. The idea made her smile. She always stayed late. Weather conditions had nothing to do with her hours. Teri was right. She was tired, but there was too much to do to go home early. Right now, she couldn't think as far ahead as the end of the day and gazing out the window wouldn't get the work done. She swallowed the last drop of coffee and set the empty cup on the desk extension. Then, she spun her chair one and a half revolutions and ended up facing the computer. She flipped the switch to "on" and the monitor sprang to life. She thought about science fiction movies she'd seen where computers took over humanity. The screen flashed, "Good Morning, Ms. Berrington. Don't forget to bill your hours." Right! That was Rafferty's idea of funny. Time was billed by the minute around here and she was notorious for failing to complete the mandatory daily time sheets. The morning message was intended to refresh her memory. Teri had already set up the clipboard beside the phone stocked with enough time sheets for the week. All she had to do was write it down. She smiled. It was good having Teri around to keep her organized, and to make her think about taking a day off — soon. She hit the "Enter" key and called up the crisis of the moment.

Just another Monday morning. Years ago when she started in this business, it sounded so exciting, even glamorous. Early on, she watched too many episodes of Perry Mason, but when she really started work as a paralegal, it didn't take long to figure out it wasn't anywhere near as glamorous as she thought it would be. Still, she believed it was where she belonged. She liked the work, but despite the comfortable niche she enjoyed in the firm and the confidence they placed in her, fact remained, she was not an attorney. Because of that, she was prevented from doing the things she wanted most to do. Someone else carried the ultimate responsibility for decisions. She couldn't give legal advice or represent a client in court. Bottom line was, she didn't have a license to practice law, which invariably brought on another familiar twinge of frustration. How many times had she regretted not having gone to law school? She thought about going, but never did. She even sat for the entrance exam once, and passed. It was nobody's fault but her own that she didn't go. She could have been making some real money today if she'd followed through with her plan. The plan started when she was in the fifth grade, but by the time she finally got around to starting college at twenty-seven years old, the plan lost it's fizzle. She never went to law school. Instead, she did what she thought was the next best thing and became a paralegal, but it wasn't the same. She did the tedious research and the attorneys took credit for the results of her efforts. When she was up to her nose in law books at five o'clock on Friday afternoon and the attorney handling the case came in and said, "I'm taking off for the weekend, but don't give up on that. I know you'll find what we need," or "When we win this one, all your hard work will pay off. Keep pluggin'. No pain, no gain!" — it was hard to remember how glamorous she used to think this work would be when she watched Perry Mason. Needless to say, she'd been greatly deluded by Della Street's role as Perry's indispensable sidekick. Watching Della's exciting career with a super-sleuth lawyer who cracked every case and treated her more like his partner than an employee was enough to make any girl want to be a legal secretary. Her job was filled with an endless array of investigative tasks and at the end of the day, she always went home with a smile on her face, looking like she just walked out of the beauty salon. Did Della ever have a hair out of place or a broken fingernail? Did she ever once get frazzled and want to throw a typewriter at her boss? Why should she? She had the perfect job. Only in the movies.

No pain, no gain! That was a bunch of crap. She suffered through the frustration and they got the recognition for success of a case. If only she had that piece of paper to hang on the wall. She knew she could manage a case and take it all the way through trial. She could present the evidence and examine a witness on cross, confusing him to the point where the poor soul wished he'd never been born. During mock trials in the conference room, the attorneys had a tough time with her as the opposition. Full of fire and determination to win, she could have been a great litigator. They all said so, but the chance to prove it would never come. Instead, she had to be content to spend her time in the paper trenches and turn the war table over to the lawyers when it came time for trial. Many times, it was hard to sit quietly in the courtroom and watch them present a case she'd spent weeks working on. They always kept her handy at counsel table to confer on an issue she might be more familiar with and she made sure they looked good when they needed something. They never had to risk trying the court's patience while they fumbled for a document as long as she was there. She made a point of knowing where to put her hand on what they needed when they needed it. She was good at making sure they never broke stride in the middle of an effective run. Frustration was the understatement of the day though. How many times had they missed a pertinent point and she gripped the arm of the chair so tightly her knuckles went white from lack of circulation? It would have been completely unacceptable for her to say anything. She had to sit still and keep quiet. More times than she could remember, she clutched the arm of a chair as an anchor to keep from jumping up and saying something stupid that would suffice in getting herself ejected from the courtroom. They always cut their argument too short to suit her and they always left something out, something she felt was critical. No one knew the facts as she did because no one did the research and dug up the obscure cases the way she did. No one except Tom. Countless times, she saw him in the library poring over the books. He had a phenomenal memory for the smallest details and he was a walking encyclopedia of case law. He always listened to her opinion and he never brushed off anything she believed was important. When he asked her to do research, he read every page she brought to him. The rest of them couldn't be bothered. All they wanted was a synopsis and pertinent points highlighted with a yellow marker. Plenty of times, she knew they weren't listening when she tried to show them something, and she knew they threw out things she believed were useful.

During what Teri referred to as her three M's (Monday morning meditation), this precious little time when the door was closed, Teri ran interference to keep people out for as long as she could get away with it. With the door shut, it was quiet and she realized she'd been staring into the computer monitor for quite awhile, thinking. She wondered what brought on the complaining episode this morning. Things really were not bad at all. She just suffered from her own little ego problem of having to turn over the work she did to someone else who usually took the credit. It wasn't that she needed a pat on the back for every little thing, but it would be nice to receive credit where credit was due once in awhile. Her grandmother said if you weren't thankful for what you had, the good Lord would take it away and you might not get it back. She was thankful for the job and wouldn't want to lose it. There wasn't anything to complain about. She had a great position with the best law firm in town. She got paid well and should be counting her blessings instead of finding fault. The only person she was angry with was herself. She wasn't a lawyer because she'd chosen not to be. No other reason.

Notwithstanding the resignation to being forever plagued with that frustration, she never justified the stupidity of those who were supposed to be better informed than she was. They were a constant source of aggravation. All except Tom. He was a perfectionist. Too bad they weren't all like him, but that was too much to hope for. Nevertheless, she really wasn't being fair. The people she worked with were far from stupid or incompetent. There was only one who might fall within that category and she knew he was the reason for the current mode of thinking. It was one of those days where stress created by a recent announcement had thrown her into a bad mood. The result was that events she considered personal failures all surfaced at once even though none of them were important anymore and had nothing to do with the work announcement. They were in the past and all she could do was try not to make the same mistakes. Leaning close to the window, the street below was barely visible through the falling snow. Concentration wasn't going to be easy to come by today. Maybe Teri was right. A few days off might be just what the doctor ordered. She didn't like it when she was cranky, but she couldn't shake it.

Next week would be the high point of her career, but this week, the push was on to get ready for trial. The case was as good as won. A sure thing. She rapped her knuckles on the desk. Knock on wood. She reminded herself it was bad luck to be over-confident, but she didn't know how they could possibly lose. She'd lived and breathed this case for two years. Late nights and weekends spent in research and compiling facts, days of sitting through depositions, meticulously scrutinizing volumes of paper, and drafting she couldn't remember how many pleadings. All of it to convince a jury that after a preponderance of the evidence, they should reach a verdict in favor of the client; emotionally charged statements that would be part of both sides' closing arguments. Considering the way the facts had come down, she hadn't even thought about losing. There was no reasonable doubt as to what the verdict should be. Despite attempts at reaching a settlement, the other side balked and continued to be unreasonable. It didn't matter though. They were going to win. The verdict was a given and the award would be a big one, probably in the neighborhood of six million; a small price to pay for a man's life. There was plenty of motivation to win and she was more than pleased with the work she'd done. She was proud of it. She'd committed herself to winning this case. It was the way she confirmed her faith in the judicial system. Not just winning, winning for the right reasons. Their client suffered a tragic loss when her husband died at the hands of a doctor who should never have been admitted to the practice of medicine. The crime was so bizarre that it was Tom's opinion the doctor should have been brought up on murder charges for performing what amounted to grotesque medical experiments on a patient who believed the radical procedures would save his life. By the end of the final operation, medical bills had exceeded one hundred and fifty thousand dollars. Saying there was nothing more he could do and pronouncing the man terminal, the doc took an extended European vacation, essentially abandoning his patient to suffer an excruciatingly painful death. That's why Tom initially turned the information over to the District Attorney, but was disappointed when the investigation fizzled out and no criminal charges were filed. Lack of an indictment didn't stop Tom. He couldn't get a murder conviction, but he could win a medical malpractice suit and might succeed in yanking the doctor's license. They had to win to keep the butcher from destroying more lives.

Staring at Tom's message on the computer monitor, she was hit with an anxiety attack. She enjoyed working with Tom Rafferty. He was the senior partner in the firm and one of the best litigators she'd ever known. Other paralegals, and some of the attorneys, cringed whenever they had to work closely with him. Not her. She remembered how she'd been thrilled when they told her she was chosen to assist him with this case. Tom picked her for obvious reasons, but she still felt privileged to work with him and she couldn't wait to get started. He was a virtual wealth of legal knowledge and she'd learned a lot from him. He never became irritated when she asked a question and he never made her feel stupid for asking. Those who plowed ahead without asking for guidance and made mistakes as a result were the ones he got irritated with. Funny, they were the same ones who were afraid of him. He was tough, but that was part of his character. In reality, he demanded far more of himself than his associates. However, those expectations were heavy and not many could keep up with him. Although he presented a stern facade, he was a good man. He had a good heart. Not everyone took the time to look close enough to see that in him. He never offered much in the way of compliments. You were expected to do the work, and do it right. If you didn't understand that, you better pack it in. He rarely smiled, but she managed to catch him off guard once when he asked her what she wanted for Christmas. She knew how he was always testing people for quick responses, so she didn't bat an eye when she answered, "a nickel's worth of hundred-dollar bills." She remembered how he raised his eyebrows and squinted his eyes ever so slightly. He didn't say a word, but when he turned to walk away, she detected the hint of a smile at one corner of his mouth under the mustache. He'd never admit it, but they both knew her answer caught him by surprise and he thought it was good.

She respected Tom and he knew it. The respect was mutual. He appreciated the work she did and said so, although only occasionally. Most people were intimidated by his broad-shouldered, six-foot, four-inch frame and severe demeanor. Maybe it was the mustache. She liked it. She thought he looked like Wyatt Earp. If that didn't do it, the fact that he graduated magna cum laude from Harvard was enough to create inferiority complexes in lesser associates. He was a force to be reckoned with and everyone knew it. If you were honest and worked hard, he respected you. If you were lazy or hesitated the least little bit when he demanded a response to a direct question, you knew you were in for the verbal ass-kicking of your life. When the man looked you in the eye, you just knew he could see inside your mind. He practiced law with a vengeance and one goal in mind, the prevalence of justice. He was hard-driving and ethical, with a fierce sense of commitment to the cause of law and order, relentless in his pursuit of it. Nothing less than absolute truth was acceptable to him and there was never a time when he considered stretching it to suit his own purpose. He detested prevaricators and shirkers and there was no hesitation on his part to confront those he believed failed in their responsibility to represent their clients professionally and with due diligence in the interest of what was right. His sense of honesty and fair play intimidated those of lesser character, and he could drag the truth from the most seasoned of liars. There was no sympathy for criminals and because of his ardent advocacy for capital punishment, the mere mention of his name instilled instant fear in the hearts of those he prosecuted in the early days as a deputy district attorney. He was a brilliant trial lawyer and she had seen the hypnotic effect he had on judges and juries alike. Courtroom spectators were spellbound by his presentations. Opposing counsel knew they better do their homework if they expected to have one iota of their case stand up against him in court. Sloppy opposition drew a bad lot. Few had been successful in attempts to outwit him, and even those who managed to come away with some partial victory were never able to claim they won the war. He stood his ground when he knew he was right and unless you were damn sure you could prove him wrong, backing away gracefully was your only hope of leaving without a new anal orifice. When you saw him in action, the one thing you were absolutely certain of was that you were glad he was on your side.

Unfortunately, the cost of genius and devotion to cause came high. He was only fifty-two years old, but long hours for years finally caught up with him. Three weeks earlier, Tom suffered a coronary and stroke that left him partially paralyzed, a devastating setback personally and for the case. Recovery would extend far beyond the trial scheduled to begin in little more than a week. When he was taken ill, they were four weeks away from trial. An immediate replacement should have been assigned to learn every aspect of the case. Even three weeks out, it would have been tight, but they might have had a chance. They waited too long and with only one week to go, she didn't think it could be done. There was a lot of material to cover on such short notice and time was running out.

She was more than a little apprehensive when the decision was announced Friday afternoon. The partners assigned a younger, less experienced attorney to take over the litigation, not exactly the cream of the crop, in her opinion. The news came as a complete shock and ruined her weekend. She didn't understand why one of the other partners hadn't taken it. There were several experienced at handling this kind of trial. Surely, a case of this magnitude deserved a much more seasoned and sophisticated barrister to see it to judgment. Knowing how to work a jury was crucial. Just because they thought they had it in the bag, now was not the time to get careless. She didn't believe the best interests of the client or the firm could be served by allowing Don Griffin to try the case. Prayers for the win would be futile unless they received an absolute miracle. She'd have to make certain this guy knew what he was supposed to do. How she'd manage to pull that one off, she hadn't a clue. A fellow attorney might have a chance of getting through to him, but she wasn't a lawyer and there was no common ground between them. She was dreaming if she thought he'd listen to her suggestions. No use worrying about it. His ego would get in the way of better judgment. He wouldn't be particularly inclined to listen to someone he considered beneath his status, and she was one of those people. He had an irritating way of saying "only" the paralegal, implying it was an inferior position to his own. In truth, she and half the secretaries in the firm had probably forgotten more about the law than he'd ever learn, not for lack of intelligence, but rather, lack of motivation. He had what she identified in less than professional terms as a "low give-a-shit factor." He just plain didn't care. Notwithstanding that, the mere fact she was a woman was sufficient grounds for rejection of her opinion. He was the epitome of male chauvinism, never referring to his secretary by her given name. Instead, he called her "my girl" as if she were his personal slave. She smiled. Griffin's secretary had him pegged for the nincompoop he was and didn't make any bones about what she thought of him, quite adeptly dubbing him "the little jackass prince." A more than fair rebuttal.

Right now, she'd think positive and in the interest of positive thinking, she'd try to emphasize his good points. He was young, but not that young. Thirty-three. Since joining the firm, his work kept him in the office. He'd never taken a case to trial, but he was extremely bright. That was good. Over time, he generated some pretty impressive briefs and he worked on this case a little, so he wasn't a complete stranger to the issues. When he put his mind to it, he could be a pretty good lawyer. An encouraging thought. He always managed to crank out enough billable hours to keep Tom off his back, although she knew his secretary was, in large part, responsible for the number of hours he billed. Janie was old enough to be his mother and, like a mother, constantly pushed him to get things done. Guess she figured he'd wake up one day and appreciate all she did for him when he settled down to seriously practice law, but that day was probably a long way off. In the spirit of fairness, everyone deserved a chance to show their stuff. Maybe this was his chance. She just wished his trial debut could have been with some other case. Despite the fact his attitude irritated her, she'd given him the benefit of a doubt for the simple reason that he was young and spoiled. Neither was a legitimate excuse for his actions, but there was always the chance he'd improve with age. He was smart and when he applied himself, he could produce quality work. Problem was, he didn't do it often enough. She tried to remember some of his better efforts. A few things came to mind that were actually quite remarkable and it made her feel a little better to think about what he was capable of producing when the urge to earn his paycheck struck him.

There was, unfortunately, another side of the coin; definite negative factors to be considered. Griffin's significant accomplishments were not of any great number and his moments of inspiration were few and far between. She drew a line down the center of a yellow pad and labeled the columns, Positive and Negative. Some things required immediate attention, not the least of which was a cocky, self-centered attitude and overrated opinion of himself. Her year-long assessment of him hadn't changed and the less desirable components of his character started to override the positive attributes she'd been trying to credit him with. The list "against" was getting longer than the list "for." Not that she was perfect by any means, but at least she admitted her shortcomings and recognized her own flaws. She worked on improving herself. He, on the other hand, was way too self-centered and egotistical and would never admit to any imperfection in his character or work habits. It was his unabashed belief that he was the answer to every woman's prayer and he spent more time at the secretaries' desks than he did at his own, reinforcing that contention. Humility was not his strong suit. He spent a ridiculous amount of time in front of mirrors too. It was a wonder the man had any hair left judging from the frequency with which he combed it. He was a smart alec — a joker. She lost track of his positive side altogether. No matter how you looked at it, items in the negative column outweighed the other list ten to one. She leaned her elbows on the desk and dropped her face into her hands. Oh, God! He was an impudent little dickhead and she was dreaming if she thought the Wizard would step from behind the curtain and give this guy motivation to handle this case the right way. A mental picture of him strutting his stuff in front of the jury made her head spin. He'd never listen to her admonitions to eliminate the sarcasm and cutsie quips that were part of his usual routine. He was a clown! It wouldn't take much of his foolishness to turn this trial into a circus and make a farce of two years worth of very hard work. With so much at stake and the verdict riding on presentation, the jury would hang them if his attitude came across as even the slightest bit unprofessional or frivolous. She could feel the noose tightening already. Might as well release the trap door now and let her swing. What was the line everyone quoted when they knew Tom had the opposition on the run? "Bend over, put your head between your legs and kiss your ass good-bye." Somehow, the humor was lost when directed inwardly and she had the sinking feeling the line would apply to her this time. It wasn't the least bit funny. Griffin was her partner in this case, but she couldn't shake her adversarial attitude toward him. She'd have to work at not losing her temper. She still couldn't believe the partners dumped him on her. If one of them didn't ride herd on him, it'd be a disaster they'd never forget.

With her head resting on her hands, she thought about Tom. She hoped he'd get well soon and be spared a permanent disability. Of all people, he didn't deserve to suffer. Tears filled her eyes as she considered the tragedy of his medical condition. Why did these things always happen to the good guys? A tear dropped onto the Griffin pros and cons list and she simultaneously flashed on the response she gave Tom when he asked what she wanted for Christmas. At the firm's party that year, he greeted each member of the staff at the door, wished them a happy holiday and handed them an envelope. Everyone received their annual bonus check. Everyone but her. There was no check in her envelope. Her envelope contained five, one hundred-dollar bills — "a nickel's worth." She brushed away the tears and blotted the wet spot on the paper with another paper. The ink smeared and she crumpled them both up and tossed them in the basket under the desk.

Back to Griffin. There were plenty of reasons to be worried, but a fatalist attitude could lead to destruction in the long run. No sense dwelling on the downside. The power of positive thinking was needed to prevail. Like it or not, she was stuck with him and there was no choice but to make the best of a bad situation. She hoped she'd find the strength, but by the time this trial was over, Griffin would probably be a dead man and she'd be in jail for murder. She sat back in the chair, a delightfully morbid fantasy running through her mind. The defense would be a snap. She'd plead temporary insanity and be acquitted. If they knew him, they'd find her not guilty even if the charge was premeditated murder. She could think of several dozen people who'd thank her.

The entire week consisted of fourteen-hour days, except Friday. Friday morning, she was in the office at seven o'clock. At six that evening, they ordered pizza. Everyone went home at eight. Everyone but her. By midnight, she was exhausted. She felt like a sponge, squeezed dry one time too often, and her energy level had dropped to something below nonexistent. Her eyes were so tired, they refused to focus anymore. She desperately needed sleep, but she was not about to go thirty-eight floors down into the parking garage at this hour. Her own bed would be great, but not worth the trouble to get there. If that elevator cable was ever going to snap, it would likely be tonight, and if that didn't get her, the drive across town on icy streets would. She decided this wasn't a good night to die. She double-checked the locks on the front door and turned the dead bolt on the entrance to the inner sanctum. Even without setting the alarm, the place was a fortress. It'd take dynamite to get in when the doors were locked. In the lobby and security office, armed guards manned banks of tv monitors fed by closed-circuit cameras on every floor of the building including the garage. It'd be safe to stay right where she was. Down the hall, she stretched out on the couch in Tom's office and pulled the familiar crocheted afghan over her shoulders. She'd been here before, nights she worked until nine or ten and found staying here easier than going home to an empty house. She wondered how Tom was doing. She said a prayer for him and closed her eyes. She had to get some sleep or she wouldn't be worth anything tomorrow. She wanted to see Tom before the trial. Maybe she'd give his wife a call in the morning and stop by with some flowers in the afternoon.

She nearly jumped out of her skin at the gentle shaking. Still not completely awake, she sat up too fast and her aching body mercilessly reminded her of where it spent the night. She winced and blinked her eyes. Morning already? Couldn't be. She didn't even remember lying down. She found herself staring into two, oversized brown eyes. The smiley face attached to the bouncy body in the Broncos tee shirt was informing her it was eight o'clock and the staff was in. They were ready to help with whatever she and Don needed. Was she "ready to rock and roll?" She scowled at the girl. A heck of a question for someone who wasn't sure if she was alive yet. In response, she rubbed her eyes and counted to ten. Patience was a thin virtue at the moment and she didn't want to say the wrong thing and hurt the girl's feelings. Yesterday, she asked for volunteers to make copies and put trial notebooks together and this is what she got, more help than she needed. Any other time, she'd appreciate the girl's eagerness to help. This morning, however, that kind of enthusiasm was too much to take. Oh, to be twenty again.

Satisfied the sleeping beast had indeed awakened, the bearer of good tidings bounced away to join the group in the kitchen. When she was alone again, she answered the question out loud. "No. I am not ready to rock and roll!" She released the breath she'd been holding since being shell shocked into consciousness. Laughter poured down the hall from the kitchen where the staff gathered around the coffee pot and donuts. A radio blasted country music and a sing-a-long was in progress. She put both hands over her ears. She needed a few more minutes of peace and quiet, but knew she wouldn't get them. Spirits were high and excitement of the upcoming trial had reached a crescendo. They were gearing up early for the anticipated celebration of the verdict. From the sound of the party down the hall, it seemed everyone else enjoyed a good night's sleep and were refreshed. As for herself, she felt like yesterday's warmed-over scrambled eggs. She'd slept in her clothes, her hair looked like she styled it with an electric mixer, and the taste of last night's pizza and coffee made her hope she hadn't breathed on the secretary who woke her up to happily announce the arrival of volunteers. This wasn't the first time she'd grabbed a few badly needed hours of sleep on this sofa and experience taught her to be prepared for the eventuality of a repeat performance. Backup essentials kept in the credenza for such occasions would at least render her presentable.

She sat on the edge of the couch, staring at the swirls in the carpet. Burgundy and navy with rose and colonial-blue accents, and a touch of ivory. Verlene Rafferty did the decorating and everything matched perfectly, from carpet and cherrywood-paneled walls with tasteful touches of wallcovering to brass-accented furniture and Tom's favorite pieces of art. It was a comfortable room. Even had a surround-sound stereo system. The whole concept was indicative of the way the Raffertys did everything; unpretentious, but elegant.

When she was satisfied she was sufficiently awake, she stood up, yawned and bent over to touch her toes. Her back popped loudly and she held the position, afraid to move for fear something had broken. Tentatively straightening up, she stretched her arms above her head. Everything popped. To hell with exercise this morning. She yawned again and ran her hands through her hair in a feeble attempt to stimulate brain activity. Still yawning, she stumbled around the corner into her own office.

She opened the sliding door in the credenza and removed a small cosmetic case containing a toothbrush, toothpaste, soap, and deodorant. A clean sweatshirt on the shelf would replace the one she slept in. One glance in the mirror told her she looked about as bad as she felt. Fifteen minutes in the ladies' room and a cup of strong, black coffee and she'd be ready to jump into the final hours of trial prep. Well, maybe jump was a little too strenuous. Crawl was probably more like it. She hoped the girls hadn't decided to spice up the Saturday-morning work event with their French vanilla coffee. They liked it, but she just couldn't take that stuff so early.

Griffin promised faithfully to be there by nine. It was no surprise when someone announced at nine-thirty that he wasn't there yet. At ten, she called his house. When his answering machine spat some imbecilic greeting at her, she hung up without leaving a message, shaking her head at the telephone. Would this guy ever grow up? He was thirty-three years old and had been a practicing attorney for seven years, but he still acted like a kid. The only reason he became a lawyer in the first place was because his father threatened to disinherit him if he didn't land a real job. He had some kind of misconceived notion that being a lawyer was the career requiring the least amount of work for the most money. He didn't take anything seriously. Life was one big party. She wished she'd been a fly on the wall during his interview with the partners. He must have said something right because Tom hired him, but it was beyond her why they kept him around. More than once, the thought occurred to her they might have made a place for him with the firm because one of the partners was a friend of his father. Not like Tom to do something like that, but sometimes things happened in business that had no logical explanation. Whatever the reason, they must have thought he was worth something because here he was, handling a very important case.

Thirty minutes after she made the call, Griffin strolled into the conference room where everyone had assembled to run through the final checklist. After the girls made their usual fuss over him, he swaggered over to her and started to put his arm around her. Before he touched her, she slid her glasses halfway down her nose and shot him a look that said, "Touch me and you're dead." The implied threat worked. He raised his hands in surrender, reconsidered his position and withdrew the advance. Never quite sure what her capabilities were, he was just smart enough to know that physical contact would probably be fatal. The other girls reinforced his theatrics, but she didn't think he was funny. She pushed her glasses back in place with one finger and returned her attention to the stacks of documents on the conference table. Lack of appreciation for his brand of humor didn't discourage him and he never gave up trying to aggravate her. He stuck his thumbs in his front pockets and leaned as close as he dared, whispering so the others couldn't hear. "You'll never know what you're missing." She didn't look at him and she didn't flinch. She continued the paper shuffle with no obvious reaction to his comment, but he knew she heard him. He retreated slowly to the doorway, knowing he was the center of attention. As he walked away, she rolled her eyes up and watched him. The little creep did know how to make a pair of blue jeans and cowboy boots look pretty darn good. She understood why the girls liked him. Six feet tall, blonde, blue eyes, cute smile, great body, nice clothes — even a Rolex. The guy had style. If she were fifteen years younger, he might affect her too. She couldn't condemn him for being young or having money. Good Lord! Where was her mind? This was Don Griffin. She shook it off and continued with the checklist, hoping no one noticed her looking at him and thinking to herself, "You're right. I'll never know."

She could tell he had something up his sleeve by the way he walked. Slinking. That's what Janie labeled his walk when he was up to something or knew he was being watched. The wheels were always turning in his devious little mind. He wasn't finished with her yet. Nothing he said or did ever surprised her, so she was ready for whatever he was preparing to throw at her. He always had to have the last word. At the doorway, he hesitated with his back to the room. She looked up at him again. Thumbs still in his pockets, he turned around and gave her one of his dopey Clark Gable looks, the one that was his idea of sexy; droopy eyelids and a sideways smile. She thought to herself, "Here it comes." She was right. "Next time, Berrington, leave a message. You know I'll return the call." Damn. He must have one of those things on his phone to identify the caller. She stared at him. There was no way she'd give him the satisfaction of a retaliatory comment. Her glasses slipped a little and she pushed them in place, turning her back to him and pretending to read the paper in her hand. She'd never known anyone quite so antagonistic. He just didn't know when to quit. He waited at the door for her to fire a round back. She had the ammunition and the motivation to use it, but there were more important things demanding her attention than the target in the doorway. Failure to attack would be construed as surrender, but if she opened fire on him, the ensuing volley would use up valuable time that was not expendable right now. Not only that, she'd feel like a fool later if she let him force her into losing her temper and reverting to name-calling in front of other people. There'd be plenty of chances to tell him what she thought of him. She was sure he still had that ridiculous grin on his face. Better judgment prevailed and she decided to forego the battle and direct her efforts to the business at hand. Without turning around, she got her point across. "The documents you need to review are on your desk and time is running out. I finished them last night around midnight, about the time you were ushering some unsuspecting, sweet young thing into your boudoir." He snapped to attention and proffered a mock salute in her direction. "Touché." The girls giggled. It infuriated her the way they encouraged his antics. She didn't have to turn around to know he'd done something he thought was cute. Having to work with him seemed to be a sentence with no chance of parole. She wished he'd go away, to his office, or anywhere. She checked her watch. Ten forty-five. In a few hours, she'd be rid of her nemesis until Monday morning.

For the rest of the afternoon, Griffin actually put forth a reasonable effort to complete the work. He even had some good ideas. Maybe her remark embarrassed him into working. Not likely, but maybe. She was cautiously impressed. She might have to alter her opinion of him, slightly. At five p.m. on the dot, they were done. Expecting him to say good-night and leave like everyone else was out of the question. The entire secretarial crew was there. What better audience for his grand finale? He announced that he had a hot date. She shook her head in disgust and muttered under her breath, "Naturally." He didn't say anything back, but he gave her the idiotic, sideways smile when he positioned a black cowboy hat on his head. Without a word, he turned and walked away. She was in shock. He was leaving without his usual slam. She breathed a sigh of relief. For a minute, she was off guard, thinking the day hadn't been too bad after all. Halfway to the front door, he called to her, "Hey, Berrington. Call me tomorrow night." The girls looked from him to her, waiting for her response. Any decent thoughts she might have had about him during the day were instantly retracted. She clenched her teeth together so hard her jaw cramped. It was hard to keep from calling him the names he deserved, but she wasn't about to give him the satisfaction of knowing he'd gotten to her, not after she managed to hold it back all day.

A combination of fatigue and excitement contributed to a sleepless night. Sunday was equally as restless. She tried to relax, but all she could think about was the trial. She managed to get a few hours sleep Sunday night, but the adrenaline was pumping overtime and before the five-thirty alarm went off Monday morning, she was already out of the shower and half-dressed. Weeks ago, she had carefully chosen the right thing to wear the first day of trial; a navy-blue power suit with a white silk blouse, subtle gold necklace and earrings, and the gold watch she only wore on special occasions. She wanted to look as "lawyerly" as possible. The mirror reflection told her she made the right choice. At seven, she was punching the "UP" button to the thirty-eighth floor.

Monday morning, seven-thirty. Where the devil was Griffin? He was supposed to be there at seven-thirty, sharp! At seven forty-five, she went hunting and found him combing his hair in the mirror behind the kitchen door. She shook her head in disgust. No class. Par for the course. She walked out as soon as she saw him and on her way down the hall to her office, she announced she was leaving for court in five minutes. She wanted to get there early. If he wanted a ride, he'd better stop primping and get moving. Otherwise, he could take his own car. She wouldn't wait for him.

All the way to the courthouse, he carried on a one-sided conversation about the weekend's latest conquest of the opposite sex. When he reached the juicy part, she raised a gloved hand and told him to spare her the details. His expression became quite serious when he told her what she already knew. "You don't like me much." She looked at him like he'd just answered the sixty-four thousand-dollar question. "Very observant." He opened his mouth to elaborate on his observation, but the look she gave him told him to stifle it. She was in no mood for his foolishness this morning. When she parked the car, she turned to him. "Lock the car." Before he could say a word, she got out and slammed the door, walking ahead of him into the building. People would know soon enough that she was with him, but for now, she'd pretend she'd never seen him before. He was such a nuisance. When he called to her and ran to catch up, she wished she could become invisible. She didn't acknowledge the exaggerated steps he took, pretending to try to keep up with her. She kept walking. "I hope you locked my car."

Inside the courthouse, Griffin disappeared. She turned around to say something to him about not letting Tom down and embarrassing them both, but never got the chance. He was gone. Probably combing his hair in the nearest mirror was her guess. No use worrying about it. She knew he did these things on purpose to aggravate her, and she also knew he'd show up just before the Judge came in. Even he didn't have the nerve not to be in court on time. She went on into the courtroom alone to get organized. One of them had to be ready. A few minutes later, the client arrived, nervous and anxious. She tried to assure the woman there was nothing to worry about. They were well-prepared. She couldn't say what she really thought; that she was extremely worried about Griffin's conduct.

They'd been seated at counsel table for fifteen minutes by the time Griffin sashayed past the spectators and through the gate. He always had to make a production of his entrance and a spectacle of himself. If he happened to take a bow, she wouldn't be a bit surprised. She clenched her teeth together to control her contempt and handed him the list of questions he was to ask the prospective jurors. When he reached for the papers, she held onto them and looked him square in the eye in an attempt to telepathically convey her message, that being, he better do this right. He gave her an exaggerated smile and jerked the papers from her hand. The message had been noted, and rejected.

Preliminary examination to determine the competency and possible prejudices of the jurors was underway. More than a little apprehensive observing voir dire, she glanced over at opposing counsel. He was an old friend of Tom's, a top-notch insurance defense lawyer who really knew his stuff. He was watching Griffin. The movement was barely detectable, but she saw him shaking his head. She knew exactly what he was thinking. No competition here. The first clue that the circus was in town was when she saw Bozo wink at one of the jurors. The other attorney saw it too. All she could do was stare straight ahead and pretend she hadn't noticed. Like watching a child's balloon drift out of sight in the clouds, hope for winning floated away right in front of her and the chance to grab a string and pull it back was already gone. The writing was on the wall. All of her work, all of Tom's work was wasted. Griffin was going to screw the whole thing up and because she was there, she'd be guilty by association. If they dispensed with the trial at this point, the result would be the same.

She was right on target with her prediction that Griffin would be true to form. In direct contradiction to the way the partners instructed him to present the case, he was acting like a baby Perry Mason. She closed her eyes. "Oh, Perry! Where are you when I need you?" She said a silent prayer that somehow, Griffin would receive guidance from the Universe and clean up his act before trial commenced. Failing that, a bolt of lightning would be an acceptable alternative. For a second, she considered faking a faint, but that would prolong the misery. If only Tom were here. She knew what he'd do. He'd shake the living daylights out of this pompous little ass. It should have been an interesting trial. With Tom here and his friend on the other side, they'd have had a real battle of wits. She looked over at the other attorney. He was sitting back in his chair with his arms folded, not taking down a single note. Once again, she knew what he was thinking. There wasn't going to be any battle. He was right. The sense of foreboding increased and she knew this week was not going to be fun at all. This week was going to be like having a root canal on the day your dentist got the notification of his IRS audit. It would be Hell Week, and she had to live it with the Lawyer from Hell.

Griffin's opening statement sufficed to confirm her worse fears. The small voice inside her told her to hold on tight because this was going to be a very rough ride. To say he didn't present well to the Court was being kind. To say he was committing judicial suicide was more accurate. From the onset, the signs weren't good. She watched the faces of the judge and the jury. Right off the bat, they didn't like him. Why didn't that surprise her? From the beginning, he was in big trouble and didn't recognize the danger. He missed all the warning signs and plowed blindly forward. The truly pitiful thing was that the damn fool thought he was brilliant.

The next four and a half days went from bad to worse. Griffin did everything wrong. No one had to tell her he blew it from the minute he opened his mouth. He had his facts mixed up. He had the people mixed up. He tried to be dramatic in his presentation. As soon as he knew the press was there, he stepped up the performance, standing in one place longer than necessary to pose for the sketch artist. He was showboating, waving his arms in the air and making smart remarks that were severely out of line and quite obviously not appreciated by the judge or the jury. He was irritating and arrogant. She wished she could tattoo the words across his

forehead. If it was the last thing she ever did, she'd see to it they were part
of his epitaph. The other side gave him all the rope he needed to hang and
he even kicked the stool out from under himself. She prayed the old adage
about being judged by the company you kept wouldn't apply in this
instance. Heaven forbid anyone think she was here with him of her own
free will. In truth, she was here under vehement protest. Although not visible to the naked eye, she'd come silently kicking and screaming all the
way. The media was going to rip him apart. Tom's name and the name of
the firm would be plastered all over the front page of the newspaper. After
the trial, they'd interview Griffin and the embarrassment would be tenfold.
By the time the press was finished distorting the facts, the verdict relating
to her participation would be perfectly clear in print. Guilty by association.

Granted, he didn't have much time to prepare for trial, but it wasn't as
if he didn't know the facts. He'd been in on the case for a long time and
done work on it periodically. Everyone in the office knew what it was
about. Why didn't he stick to the strategy they'd worked on for two years?
What in the world was he thinking? She'd probably never know. He failed
to present critical facts which would have left no reasonable person doubt-
ing the validity of the claims. It was so simple. The script was written
months ago. All he had to do was recite it. They must have rehearsed it
two hundred times. For him to be so caught up in his own theatrical debut
rather than focusing on the best interests of their client was unbelievable.
Leaving so much as a fragment of doubt in the minds of the jury would be
a fatal mistake. Where was his mind? She retracted every good thing she
tried to say about him in the earlier decision to put aside her personal opinion and give him a chance to prove he might actually be a good lawyer.
When the realization hit him that the outcome of the trial depended on how
well he did his job, she thought he might come through with flying colors.
She was wrong. He couldn't have helped the opposition more if he'd been
sitting in their lap. Like a quarterback who hadn't the foggiest notion
which way he was supposed to throw the ball, he kept scoring for the other
side. The only consolation was in knowing that by Monday, he'd be looking for another job. By the time he tendered his closing argument, she
couldn't look at the jurors and she kept her face turned away from the
sketch artist. She'd been publicly humiliated enough. They'd already
gotten one picture of her in the paper simply by virtue of her presence at
counsel table, but she didn't want to be included in the scathing article that
would ultimately tell about the defeat. The doctor's lawyer concluded his
summation to the jury and both sides rested their case. Everything that was

going to be said was said. All she felt was relief that it was finally over.

At three-thirty, Friday afternoon, the jury retired. Not expecting a verdict until the following week, the spectators left the courthouse. Only the attorneys and their clients remained seated at opposite tables. She fought back tears of embarrassment as Griffin made an animated attempt to talk with the other lawyer and his client. He jabbered incessantly and gave her a headache. She let out an exasperated sigh and shoved her chair back. Enough was enough. The judge hadn't officially dismissed the jury, so they'd stick around until five o'clock to see what happened, just in case. She had to stay, but she didn't have to sit there and listen to Griffin hammer nails into his own coffin. She stuffed the last of her notes into her briefcase and slammed it harder than she meant to. Griffin rolled his eyes at her, drumming his pen on the table and making fun of her obvious irritation. "A little testy, are we?" She glared at him, hoping he felt the daggers she shot his way with her eyes. He did. "Relax, Berrington. You worry too much." She stood up and jerked the briefcase off the table. She was perfectly relaxed. She walked around behind his chair, leaning close, so only he could hear what she said. "You're an idiot, Don, and I hope Tom cans you for this fiasco. Let's see you slink your way out of this one." By the way she was smiling, no one guessed what she'd said to him, but when she turned away, he wasn't laughing anymore.

The bailiff left the judge's chambers. "All rise." She froze. Armageddon! The Judge resumed his seat on the bench and the jury filed in. She searched the six faces for a hint of what was coming next. The Judge asked if the jury had reached a verdict and the foreman answered, "Yes, Your Honor, we have." She stared at the jury, then, at the clock on the wall above the jury box. Not possible. Four forty-five. They'd only deliberated an hour and fifteen minutes. They couldn't possibly have... She panicked, still on her feet with her briefcase in her hand. The judge told her to sit down. Her response was an audible reflex out of pure shock. "What?" The jury foreman's affirmative answer knocked the wind out of her and she made a funny gurgling sound taking a deep breath. She hadn't meant to say it and was embarrassed by her reaction. She rested the briefcase on the floor gently and resumed her seat, glancing up at the judge in apology for the gasp. Over the top of his wire-rimmed glasses, she could see he understood her shock completely and overlooked the "what?" that inadvertently slipped out. He cleared his throat and calmly read the jury's decision as to each claim by the plaintiff. The verdict threw her into a spin and she felt like she'd been run over by a train. She took a deep breath and tried to appear unaffected by the impact. It wasn't as if it was unexpected, not after Griffin's week-long exhibition of monumental stupidity, but it certainly was a far cry from the desired outcome. Not only had they lost, they lost on every single claim. The jury didn't even throw them a crumb. The doctor was guilty as hell — and free to go, to murder some other trusting, unsuspecting patient and ruin more lives.

She fought hard to maintain her composure and dignity in the wake of what had just been the most disastrous blow of her career. She tried to keep a poker face. She'd been on the losing side before, but at least they'd always had a fighting chance. This time, they had no chance. They should not have lost. The other side had no case until Griffin gave them one. She couldn't allow anyone to see that she'd come undone inside and she reached for the client who stared at the judge in disbelief, hoping she hadn't heard right. The poor woman was devastated and while tears streamed down her face, she didn't utter a sound. Justice most certainly had not been served.

It took all her strength to keep from bolting from the courtroom and throwing herself headfirst into a snowbank. The champagne in the office refrigerator would not be opened tonight. There'd be no victory celebration. The verdict marked the end of an exhausting two-year effort with no reward, rather, total disappointment and painful defeat. That was an understatement. A nuclear explosion had blown her off the face of the earth. She just witnessed what had to have been, undeniably, the grossest miscarriage of justice she'd seen in nearly thirty years of practicing law. When a reporter shoved a microphone in Griffin's face outside the courtroom, it was apparent he hadn't been the least bit humbled by the loss. He'd get himself on the six o'clock news tonight and his supreme, asinine comment quite possibly would be the newspaper headline in the morning. "Somebody wins, somebody loses. That's the way it goes in this business." Unbelievable!

At the blast of a horn, she snapped back to reality. She hit the brakes and slid sideways into the curb. Someone shouting obscenities; something about women drivers. She rubbed her forehead. How long had she been driving? She didn't remember getting into the car.

She tossed and turned all night. Sleep finally came around five a.m. The phone rang at eight. She rolled over and dragged the receiver to her ear. She felt awful. The voice on the other end didn't wait for her to say hello. The partners were calling an emergency meeting to discuss work on the inevitable appeal. "Can you be here by nine?" She didn't believe what she was hearing. Were they nuts? Didn't they understand what she'd just been through? Apparently not. Mindful of the old "consequences of your actions" lesson, she closed her eyes and restrained herself from yelling into the phone. Her voice was calm. "No, I can't be there by nine. I'm exhausted. Can we talk about it Monday?" Without waiting for an answer, she dropped the receiver onto its cradle and closed her eyes. They didn't need her to tell them they lost. They wanted her to tell them what happened, but she couldn't drag herself down to the office today. Besides, if they really got a blow-by-blow account of his performance, she was sure the thought would cross their minds to throw Griffin out the thirty-eighth floor window and send the arrogant, incompetent little jackass prince crashing to the street below. Seeing his brains splattered all over Broadway would definitely make the trip downtown worthwhile. She couldn't believe she was thinking such a thing. It was the frustration coming out.

She didn't have to wonder what Tom said when he saw the six o'clock news. She knew exactly what his reaction was. It was the same as hers. With everything that happened to him recently, he didn't need this upset. They'd have him in on a conference call and she ought to talk to him, but it would be difficult to do that with other people around. A face-to-face conversation was the way it had to be. She was expected to be there with the rest of them to talk about filing an appeal, but she didn't want to see Don Griffin and right now, she couldn't think about the office. It wasn't her decision to make anyway. She wasn't a partner. She wasn't even an attorney. If she had been, she'd have won, and they'd have popped the champagne last night. There it was again, the old anxiety attack and the words she said so often. If only. Of all the places she'd like to be today, the office was not one of them and thinking about the case was the last thing she wanted to do. In fact, she didn't want to go back there — ever. This would be the first Saturday she hadn't gone to the office in two years.

Saturday afternoon, she soaked in a hot bubble bath to wash away the disappointment of the day before. No luck. All she got from the soaking was wrinkled fingers. She put on a pair of sweats and unplugged the phone. Snow was falling fast and heavy. She built a fire and made some tea. A shot of brandy would have been better, but she had a lot of thinking to do tonight and she wanted to keep a clear head. There was no escape from the real world, but she was standing on that cliff again with the white water swirling below. The rapids were closer and her little voice was telling her it was time to sink or swim. She threw a blanket and pillow on the floor in front of the fire and watched the sparks fly up the chimney in the draft, wishing she could fly away that easily; out the chimney to some tropical destination where she could find warmth and happiness — maybe love. It was a scarce commodity in her life. Worse than that. She never found it, but not for lack of trying. She wondered how she'd recognize it if it ever did come her way. Tears restrained yesterday broke free, releasing the frustrations of the past week until she finally cried herself to sleep.

When she woke up, it was dark outside. Where had the time gone? Her pillow was wet and cold and she felt like the weight of the world lifted from her shoulders while she slept. She must have cried for several hours in her sleep. She opened the drapes and watched the snow sparkle as it fell through the streetlight beam out front. She thought about a lot of things that night. Her life never had any real direction. The only constant was her burning desire to practice law, the one thing that never changed and kept her going all these years. Life had been chaotic otherwise. Raising two kids alone had been anything but easy. Easy? She didn't know the meaning of the word. There was an ongoing struggle for survival within her. She survived family pressures and beat overwhelming odds in a fight against cancer. She got through the devastating death of her dearest friend, the only real friend she ever had. Her thoughts drifted back thirty years. She was the kind of friend you could tell anything to. Since her death, there'd been no one to listen. Over the years, there hadn't been a lot of time for friendships anyway. Every minute was taken up by work or school or raising kids. Despite her longing to become a lawyer, she settled for a paralegal career, but that wasn't handed to her. She paid her dues and she was respected by the best attorneys in town. She was good at what she did. She knew that much. She ran her fingers through her hair and closed her eyes. Why was she recycling this stuff all over again? It was time to put it to rest and move on.

If only that friend were here, the friend who listened and understood what was in her heart of hearts. Her death was so unexpected, sudden and tragic. They were young. Twenty. There was no warning. One afternoon, they were shopping and the next morning, she was gone. It was so unfair.

She'd been dead for twenty-eight years. Hard to believe. Only yesterday, she could pick up the phone and call. She'd never stopped grieving and probably never would. She counted herself among the lucky ones to have had such a friend, if only for a few years, and she'd always be grateful for that time and memories created by friendship. Somehow, she knew that gentle spirit watched over her, helped her over the rough spots. She'd felt the presence many times when life became seemingly unbearable. When she was down, something lifted her up and there were times when she could have sworn she caught a fleeting glimpse of someone very close out the corner of her eye. On those occasions, she had an amazingly clear picture of the person for a split second and it was a sense of more than just a flash of memory. She knew they'd meet again someday, on the other side. In fact, they promised.

They were thirteen when they met and their first conversation consisted of trying to remember where they knew each other from. Up to that time, they lived on opposite sides of the country; one in New York, the other in California. Neither had been to the other coast, but they both had a strong sense of connection. They hadn't met. Not in this life anyway. For the next seven and a half years, they talked about it often. They were convinced they'd met somewhere before, but didn't know why. In all the years since her friend died, she never lost track of that idea and believed if they had a little more time, they would have figured it out. It was an eerie sense of not quite being able to remember something tucked far back in her memory, yet very close to being recognized. In life, they promised each other that the one who left this world first would be there to help the other one into what-ever waited in the world beyond. They had no way of knowing if it was possible to keep the promise, but they made it anyway and they never told anyone about it. They believed the one who went first could come back to visit the one who stayed behind, and that being the case, they decided they needed a code word so the other one would recognize the spirit visitor. Her friend picked the word and they agreed if the time ever came when they had to be certain of the sign, it was a word not likely to be confused with any other. The word was "Abigail."

Sitting alone in the dark watching the snow fall, she had the distinct impression something was trying to get her attention. It was a strange pulling, not in a physical sense; more like a subtle message coming through as a thought, not necessarily her own. Her little voice was whispering, but the message was inaudible. A tapping on her shoulder. Someone standing behind her. She turned around. No one there. Just a shadow created by the streetlight shining through the big pine tree outside.

She felt a chill and realized she'd been absorbed in thought for a long time. The fire was out. A few crackling embers was all that remained of the former blaze. They made a popping sound, like a reminder the clock was ticking down and some sort of decision must be reached, soon. A decision about what? She was standing on the cliff without a life jacket again and the urge to throw herself over the edge was powerful. She had that feeling a lot lately. Maybe the decision was to find a better way to live or spend the rest of her life in a rut. To go for a new life meant she'd have to take a chance and jump off the illusory cliff. There were a lot of maybes, but sink or swim seemed to be the only choices. She curled up in the blanket. Answers always came more readily in the morning when the mind and body were rested, but first, she'd have to understand the question. Tomorrow.

Sunday morning. A heavy overnight snow not only blanketed the yard, but piled a foot of the white stuff on the sidewalk and back deck. The wind had sculpted it into curly drifts in the driveway like fluffy whipped cream and piled it against the garage door. The garage! She'd have to shovel the driveway to get the car out. When it snowed, she wished she'd bought a 4-wheel drive truck instead of the little red sports car parked in the garage. The poor little thing would never make it out to the street without a clear path. It was cute, but not very practical in a winter wonderland. She turned on the radio long enough to hear the bad news. No break in the cold temperatures was expected. She switched it off and looked out the living room window. The front-patio thermometer indicated a below-zero temperature again today. Once it got down to zero, it didn't matter how much lower it went. It was freezing and she'd have to bundle up and be careful not to overexert herself shoveling. Days like this were constant reminders of her dysfunctional breathing apparatus, but somebody had to clear the driveway. Her ex-husband would never think to offer. She thought about calling him to ask for a little help, but quickly canceled the idea. He wouldn't do it anyway. Might as well save herself the trouble of asking and face it. She was alone. She'd do whatever needed to be done and stop feeling sorry for herself. That's all it was, of course — self-pity. It was disgusting and she hated the feeling. All her life, she never asked for help with anything, so what was the problem now? She wasn't going to dwell on past mistakes and bad experiences. She couldn't stand whiners and she refused to become one. It was time to move on. She put on two sweaters and a pair of ski pants over her jeans. From the hall closet, she pulled out a down jacket and insulated moon boots. By the time she added a knit hat and gloves and wrapped a scarf around her face, she was ready for the North Pole. Thirty minutes later, she stood at the end of the sidewalk and laughed out loud. The entire walk and driveway had gotten shoveled with enthusiasm and she hadn't dropped dead doing it. Imagining how funny she looked with so many layers of clothes, she leaned on the shovel and laughed again. Her nose was frozen. She hated the cold weather!

Sipping hot chocolate to warm up after the shoveling, she envisioned the cliff. Right on the edge. It was time. Time to make the jump, fatal or not. The subtle tapping on her shoulder was there again. Whatever the decision was that kept flitting through her mind was close to comprehension. Looking out at the big pine tree with its branches bent to the ground under the weight of snow, she had a mental picture of a sun-drenched land, some kind of optical illusion the equivalent of a lake in the middle of a barren desert. She wished she were in the middle of a desert, a warm place where she could breathe without ice crystals forming in her lungs and freezing her nose.

The answer was right there in front of her all the time. She didn't know what took her so long to figure it out. Clearly, she had to leave Denver for a warmer climate. All her life, she'd done what someone else wanted her to do. She never followed her own heart, but she was about to go chasing madly after it with no idea where it might lead her. Lately, her ears had been ringing. According to her grandmother, that meant someone was talking about her or, at the least, thinking about her. Some invisible magnet was pulling her away from the cold, drawing her to another place, a warm place. Where? Jamaica! Not likely. The desert? Maybe. Her mother lived in New Mexico. Funny how in past visits, she never liked it much, but now, the idea became very appealing. In fact, it was more than that. She felt compelled to go.

It was easier than she expected. Monday morning, she called the office and explained she had a personal emergency that required her to leave Denver immediately. She was careful to phrase her explanation so it came across as the truth. It was the truth. No interpretation was necessary. She knew Tom could accept anything as long as it was the truth. She decided to call him at home. His paralysis made speaking difficult, but he managed to tell her he understood. His speech was slow and faltering and she put her hand over her mouth to keep from crying at the pathetic sounds he made. He wished her luck. The door would always be open if she decided to come back to Denver. He'd miss her. She was the best paralegal he ever had. She was stunned. He didn't say things like that easily. Coming from Tom, she considered it the highest compliment she'd ever received. His words made all the years of work worthwhile. It had been the best job of her legal career. She wanted to tell him she admired and respected him. It wasn't necessary. He could tell by the way she did her job every day. She was beginning to choke up. All she could say was that she'd miss him too. She'd write. It was enough. He read between the lines. She hung up the phone and cried.

One week later, four-thirty a.m., the wind was beginning to whip the snow into dancing, white devils in a prelude to the blizzard of the year. She considered waiting out the storm, but that might delay her leaving by several days. The roads weren't bad yet, but by noon, the highway patrol would close Raton Pass. If she was going, she had to leave now. There was no reason to wait. She was stalling. The furniture was in storage and the house was empty. The storm was growing and the howling wind echoed through the empty rooms like a thousand mournful spirits crying out for help. Something was telling her it was time to go. She backed the car out and left it running in the driveway with the heater on full blast. The tugging sensation was stronger and there was a sense of urgency to get going. When she carried the dogs to the car, she noticed the thermometer still attached to the front-patio trellis. She went back for it and tried to scrape off the layer of ice covering the glass casing. The reading was fourteen below zero. She decided to leave it behind. With any luck, she wouldn't need it where she was going.

After seven years, she locked the front door for the last time. It snowed twice since the trial, but she hadn't bothered to shovel anything except the driveway since she made the decision to leave. In the dark, she trudged through knee-deep snow out to the car where the dogs were already curled up on their blanket in the back seat. She climbed in and sat staring at the house, crying; not because she'd miss the events that had taken place within those walls. It hadn't been a happy marriage, but that wasn't why she was crying. It was a little unnerving to think about a major move and starting over at this point in her life, more a fear of what lay ahead in unfamiliar territory than anything else. There wasn't a grain of sadness for what she was leaving behind. That was the truly sad part; to have lived here all this time and not feel any remorse walking away. Nine years altogether, seven in this house, all wasted. It occurred to her that leaving might be just another mistake in the long line of years of mistakes. Maybe she should stay. A last-minute idea. It was gone. The pulling was there again and her ears were ringing. She wondered who might be thinking about her; maybe someone who was waiting for her in New Mexico. Halfway down the driveway, she braked to look at the house one more time. She hadn't turned on the wipers yet and the snowflakes were piling up on the windshield. The streetlight gave them a spooky, iridescent appearance and she could decipher individual patterns. Each one had its own unique design, separate and distinct from all the rest. If the defroster had warmed the windshield more, they would have melted and changed into miniature, jiggly puddles, but it was fourteen below and so cold that each flake held its shape until it was covered by the next one to fall. She wished she could have some kind of sign to tell her whether or not she was doing the right thing. She released the brake gradually and the car began to roll down the driveway. When it reached the street, the wheels hit a patch of ice barely covered by a thin layer of snow. She lost control and the car spun three hundred sixty degrees. When it came to rest, it was facing due south. That was all the sign she needed. She didn't look back. Six hours later, she crossed the state line and left Colorado in the rearview mirror forever.

New Mexico was a culture shock, to say the least. The move from a major metropolis to a small city would take some adjusting. She took a position at the University, but realized it wasn't going to be what she wanted. She missed the law. It was part of her. She wasn't happy in the new workplace, yet something compelled her to stay. She couldn't put her finger on it, but she knew there was a reason to stay, and she believed everything happened for a reason. Sometimes it just took awhile to bring it into focus. It was clear she'd been drawn to this place by a powerful force even though she didn't know what it was or why she had to come. That was it, of course. She had to come. Crazy as it sounded, there was a feeling that someone or something was trying to get through to her from another dimension. Maybe it was her little voice. Intuition. Something like that. Some unseen entity, whispering a message to be patient, always seemed close by.

When she least expected it, there it was, right in front of her — the answer. The first time she saw him, he took her breath away. It was the same feeling of having the wind knocked out of her that she experienced when the jury verdict ran over her in Denver a few weeks earlier. She had to concentrate in order to maintain her composure. It wasn't easy. She was usually good at thinking on her feet and pulling herself together in a crisis. She'd hit the ground running plenty of times, but the day she met him, she had to fall back and regroup. There was something about him that drew her in; more than a physical attraction. It was hard to describe the feeling. Even under pressure, she'd never been at a loss for words, but her tongue felt as though it were tied in a knot every time she tried to talk to him. When they made eye contact, she stuttered and lost her train of thought. He must have thought she was a babbling idiot. She wanted to tell him about a light she saw around him. It was the light that left her breathless. She'd seen it twice before in her life. She couldn't tell him. He'd probably think she was crazy. And that smile! It was like sunshine bursting through the clouds to chase away her cares. She was intrigued. The words "love at first sight" occurred to her. That was neither logical nor feasible and since she was a creature of logic, she tried to dismiss the feeling, without much luck. A sense of connection was so strong she couldn't push it away; not unlike the kind of connection to the past that she and her friend believed they had. It'd been a long time, but she remembered and it was the same now.

For six months, she engaged in only casual conversation with him. She liked him more than a little, but deliberately avoided him, at the same time thinking she'd like to know him better. It didn't make sense. She was being drawn to him like a moth to a flame, yet she dared not have an encounter that might lead to any meaningful relationship for fear of being hurt again. She was contradicting her own feelings. She'd been through too much, too many failures. There were walls around her emotions, built with care and guaranteed to protect against further injury. All her life, she desperately wanted to be loved, but received only abuse. Hope for a happy relationship ended long ago and she was not about to become vulnerable to an assault on her heart. Besides, she was trying to deal with another crisis not of her doing. What point would there be in pursuing a relationship while so many negative elements dominated her life? Something always happened to drag her away from her own desires and pursuits of happiness. She'd have to push aside her attraction to him. That's all there was to it. The timing was all wrong. She'd save herself the aggravation of trying to explain circumstances and avoid contact with him. Then again, maybe she was using all of that as an excuse for not allowing herself the chance to explore the possibility of happiness. As a result of previous wounds, she was gun shy. Truth was, she was afraid to try again.

Contrary to her expectations, the move to New Mexico had been anything but uneventful. Outside pressures resulted in constant aggravation and then, she received word that her position at the University would be eliminated in a couple of months. Concern for the ability to meet financial obligations prompted another decision. With limited job opportunities available, she was faced with deciding whether to stay in New Mexico or return to Denver. She called Tom and he confirmed her job was still waiting. The little voice was louder, telling her to stay. Sleepless nights became routine. When she did sleep, the dream was always the same. She was standing in the desert with coyotes all around. They were growling and snarling, ready to attack, and there was nowhere to run, no one to call for help. A young Indian woman was standing beside her, speaking a language she didn't understand. The woman seemed to be telling her not to be afraid and pointed toward the desert. In the distance, she could see him walking toward her, this man she wanted to know, but had been avoiding. An Indian was walking with him, a young man wearing a breastplate of bone and beads and a single Eagle feather in his long, black hair. The Indian was a striking figure and he made a lasting impression on her, dream or no dream. When the two men came closer, the coyotes ran away. She always woke up with a feeling that he was trying to reach her, but it was taking a long time for him to walk the distance. Maybe she'd been wrong to stay away from him. The attraction was still strong, but she didn't think there was much chance to get to know him now. She'd be leaving for Denver soon and the chance would be gone forever.

Time was running out on the job and the outlook for finding a new one was grim. Tossing and turning for hours from stress, sleep was a scarce commodity. She ignored the little voice that told her to stay in New Mexico. Against her better judgment, she made plans to return to Denver without really knowing why she was going back. Colorado winters wreaked havoc on her health. Pollution was heavy. Roads were dangerous. The influx of people from California had created overcrowding. Crime was increasing by the minute. The decision to go back was not a comfortable one. The old, familiar cloud of uncertainty cast it's shadow of doubt and she flopped around all night from one side of the bed to the other. No relief was in sight and the return trip to Denver, though unwanted, appeared to be inevitable. Wide-awake at three in the morning, she stared at the ceiling, thinking about her friend who'd been dead for so many years. She whispered her name in the dark. Maybe some friendly, spiritual guidance could be summoned. She listened. No answer. She closed her eyes and concentrated, whispering the name again. All she needed to hear was one word to know she wasn't alone. "Abigail."

When she looked up, he was standing at her desk. How long had he been there? She must have been daydreaming. So many sleepless nights were interfering with her concentration and she caught herself drifting off a lot lately. His presence took her completely off guard. There was that incredible smile. He made her smile too. He was like a rainbow on a gloomy, rainy day. Correction. Double rainbow. And that aura — it never went away. Did he suspect that he directed energy into her? Maybe he knew exactly what he was doing. Without laying a hand on her, he was sending electrical impulses through her body. He was some kind of Merlin. She could only guess how those impulses would be magnified if he ever really touched her. Her defenses were down. He had a great voice, strong and gentle all at once. Strangely familiar. She felt as though she'd known him forever. She tried to appear calm while her heart pounded so hard she was certain he must hear the thumping reverberating throughout the room. She wished it would be silent. He said something. What was it? Lunch? He was walking away. She was in shock. Had she answered? She must have said something. She hoped it was "yes."

Two days later, to her great relief, she discovered she'd said yes to his lunch invitation. She never thought of lunch in terms of excitement, but one hour with him triggered something in her that she could describe no other way but exciting. She would have settled for the hour and been grateful for it and then, he suggested a Sunday-afternoon hike in the mountains. She said yes to that too. Efforts to push him out of her mind ran into a stone wall and attempts to convince herself he'd be only a casual date failed miserably. During the next two days, he was all she could think about. Sleepless nights previously caused by stress became the result of anticipation. He was on her mind constantly. The invisible magnet that drew her to this place was no longer a mystery. He was the reason she had to be here. Logic went right out the window with the first "yes."

Sunday morning, she was up at five-thirty. She felt a little silly getting so excited over a Sunday-afternoon walk with a man she hardly knew. She changed her clothes three times. The third look in the mirror made her laugh. It was just a walk for Heaven's sake. All she had to do was throw on shorts and tennis shoes. No! That wasn't all she had to do. It had to be just right. She thought ten o'clock would never come. When it did, he was right on time. She knew he would be. He looked great. Better than great. He had the sexiest legs she'd ever seen. It'd been a long time since she paid attention to a man's legs, or anything else. She caught herself biting her lower lip and hoped she hadn't been staring at him too hard. She wouldn't want to be so obvious, but he was certainly worth staring at. And that smile. She couldn't get over what a great smile he had. From the minute she climbed into the truck beside him, she had the feeling she was about to embark on an adventure. Maybe just a Sunday-afternoon adventure. Maybe much more. Whatever it was, the exhilaration had her heart pumping overtime. The feeling was comparable to a theme-park ride that once scared the living daylights out of her; going from zero to eighty on that high-speed centrifuge and rolling the loop upside down, nothing between you and death but centrifugal force! For the first time in years, she felt alive. The whole day was that way. They couldn't have picked a prettier autumn day for a hike up the mountain. The sun was warm and the view at the top was spectacular. He even packed a picnic lunch. How many men did she know who'd go to the trouble? The answer was easy. None. She couldn't believe he'd done that for her. She said it over and over in her mind. She felt alive. He touched something in that secret place deep inside where she'd buried all hope of ever finding love. It couldn't be love. She barely knew him. She tried to act cool and calm. Act was the right word. Inside, she was a nervous wreck. She knew she didn't fool him a bit. He saw right through her. She also knew he was doing his best to penetrate the walls she spent so much time building around herself. He had a few of his own. She wondered what it would take to break through and decided Joshua probably had an easier time bringing down the walls at Jericho. Even so, it seemed important to think about and if it was worth having, it was worth being patient.

She suspected they'd been brought together for a definite purpose. A force beyond their comprehension directed them to this meeting place at a predesignated time. The words stuck in her mind. Meeting place. An extraordinary plan was being executed at precisely the right moment, a plan formulated a very long time ago. He was thinking the same thing. He didn't have to say it. She could see it in his eyes.

They were talking, enjoying the sunshine and scenery. A break in the conversation. Silence. Only the birds singing and the trickling of water down the rocks dripping into a small pool. Without a word, he picked her up and held her for several minutes. She wrapped her arms around his neck to keep from falling. There was the surge of energy again. She'd felt the same kind of energy before. Not here. A familiar touch. Distant, but familiar. Some forgotten emotion restored to consciousness by his touch was making her heart pound wildly with the sensation of his body next to hers, like quiet thunder inside her, keeping time with a faraway drum, a rhythm from another time. He told her they were being given a rare opportunity. He didn't say it, but it had something to do with what she'd been feeling about this being a preplanned meeting for them. Maybe he didn't understand it either — or maybe he did. He asked if she'd ever had a perfect relationship. Serious question for a first date. At first she laughed, but when she saw the intensity of the question in his eyes, she realized he asked because he expected an answer. She was being drawn closer to him by the minute. He was searching for something in her eyes.

Crazy as it sounded, she knew there was a connection. Memory flashed on and off like a traffic signal at a four-way stop, but she couldn't focus on the picture. Everything moved too fast. She wasn't able to identify the source and details were blurred. What was the connection? She watched him. Who was he? She'd never met him before she moved to New Mexico, but she couldn't shake the overpowering feeling that she knew him from someplace. There was no logical explanation for the way she felt and she was, after all, a logical person. She kept reminding herself of that. She was a finder of fact, and fact was based on empirical evidence, something that could be proven. There was no evidence of any kind to justify these feelings of familiarity. There was only a man. No, he wasn't ordinary by any means. He was an exceptionally intriguing man — a puzzle. A mystery. Even when there was no physical contact, she could feel his touch. Some invisible aspect of his being was reaching out and holding her with an absolute generation of energy and life from him into her. What was on his mind? He watched her a lot and she had the distinct impression he was reading her thoughts. So much for logic.

Maybe it was the place that made her feel they weren't alone on the mountain. Dripping Springs. The atmosphere was charged with emotion; kindness first, then, violence. A sense of a tragic death of a kind soul, a good man. It was the strangest thing she'd ever felt. He was watching her. She didn't dare tell him what just went through her mind.

At the end of the day, when he walked her to the door, she impulsively reached up and kissed him. A brief kiss, like two silent spirits passing in the dark, in Time, unseen yet touching. A spark! The kiss electrified her. It was the elevator feeling all over again. Momentary vertigo. It took her breath away and the hair on the back of her neck stood straight up. She saw him shake his shoulders as if a sudden chill hit him. It was the same kind of feeling she had. An unrecognizable flash of memory carried her away at incredible speed as if she were being propelled backward in Time. Something in the distance caught her mind's eye. Recognition. On the mountain, he asked her to go away with him to Ruidoso the following weekend. Without hesitation, she said "yes," knowing instinctively it was the right answer. She was saying "yes" to him a lot lately. She didn't even know this man, but she said yes to spending an entire weekend with him, in the same bed no doubt. She hadn't considered that when she blurted out the "yes." Maybe she should have thought before she answered. One-night stands were not something she'd ever been prone to, or one-weekend stands for that matter, and in two weeks, she'd be going back to Denver. What was the point in spending a weekend with him if she'd never see him again? The only answer she could come up with was, "because I want to."

The past five years had been lonely and empty. She was married, but they occupied separate bedrooms. The relationship was a disaster. After all those years alone, she was afraid she wouldn't live up to expectations he might have of her performance next weekend. She hadn't had an anxiety attack in a long time, but one was in full swing now. Physically, he was in great shape. All the women in the office were in agreement on that. She wished she could say the same for herself. He was probably an exciting lover too. She hoped he didn't have unreasonable expectations. Maybe she should have declined the invitation and saved herself the embarrassment.

Anticipation of the upcoming weekend held back the hands of the clock. Monday and Tuesday dragged on. When the middle of the week rolled around and he told her there were no hotel vacancies in the moun-tains, she assumed he changed his mind. She hoped not, but she was prepared for it. She learned a long time ago not to expect anything. No expectations, no disappointments. A couple days later, he met her in the hall and said he decided where they'd go. Miracles really did happen. They'd leave at noon Friday — for Arizona. Tombstone. The weather had been unbearably hot and she was looking forward to cool relief in the mountains, but they were going to Arizona. More desert and more heat. That was okay. It didn't matter where they went. She was looking forward to three days, and nights, alone with him — anywhere. One thing she knew for sure was that she'd finally jumped off the cliff she'd been standing on for so long — without a life jacket. Time to dog paddle like crazy.

Chapter 2

...for the emerald hills of County Kerry; sweet heather swayin' in a summer breeze, and God's sun shinin' on the deep blue lakes of Killarney; Like the twinkle in an angel's eye 'tis; as near to Heaven as you'll ever get.

CALLAY, IRELAND – DECEMBER, 1857

On the outskirts of the city, camp fires burned in the evening mist and the faint echo of a guitar drifted across the steamy bog. Through the haze, several wagons with tattered canopies could be seen parked in a half-circle around the fires. Sporadic laughter erupted every so often then, died out like embers of the fires smothered by the rolling mist. A bristled-hair old dog rolled in the dirt outside a small, ragged tent where a woman's voice was heard softly singing a lullaby to her child.

Gypsies were social outcasts. True to their reputation as drunkards and thieves for the most part, they were banned from entering city limits. Roving bands of uneducated, poor nomads moved around the countryside in dilapidated wagons, frequently begging or stealing the bare necessities of life. Most drank too much to kill the pain of an unhappy existence. Local crimes were usually associated with the close proximity of the camps and the unlucky ones who strayed too near the city were often hung without benefit of a trial. They were considered the dregs of the earth. If you were born to Gypsies, you had no hope for the future. If you were a Gypsy, there was no hope for anything. They were the persecuted rejects of Ireland.

Although the camp fire was fueled during the night, it provided no warmth inside the thin, old tent. There was no heat, no doctor. The mid-wives could do nothing to relieve the suffering of nineteen year-old Annie Callahan as she struggled for two days to bring her baby into the world. Shortly before dawn on the third day, the baby took her first breath. Frosty mist hung heavy over the camp, and as the sun appeared on the horizon separating night from day, Annie Callahan died. Her spirit left the ravaged young body and wrapped itself gently around the tiny life sleeping peacefully on Annie's arm, her newborn daughter, Rose.

COUNTY KERRY, IRELAND – 1873

By no means was Joseph Callahan a saint. Far from it. He was a gifted liar and in his time, even stole a penny or two. He was a poor man, a Gypsy. Old beyond his thirty-five years, hard living and too much whiskey having taken their toll, his hair was completely white. The only light in his life went out the day his wife died in childbirth sixteen years earlier. He tried to care for the child, but never quite knew what to do for her. There was a time when he believed his Annie would take care of raising any children. Instead, she gave him the baby and left this world, leaving him behind with the little girl. In sixteen years, he hadn't stopped grieving.

Material riches were not part of a Gypsy's life and the barest of necessities were hard to come by. Joe had no money, no home; only the rickety old wagon. His prize possessions were his daughter and his guitar. He had a great love of music. Despite his shaking hands, he played the instrument like a master and spent countless hours teaching the child where to place her slender fingers on the strings. As the years went by, Joe weakened and didn't play the music anymore. Most nights before the sun set, he was asleep and Rose was left alone. When the cold mist crept over the camp, she'd sit by the fire with her father's guitar, playing the sweet lullaby the mothers sang to their children. There was no mother to sing to her and she sang the song softly to herself. Sometimes she felt a presence nearby, a gentle arm around her. Joe said her mother watched over her. He seemed very sure of it. She closed her eyes and tried to imagine what her mother looked like. Joe said she was beautiful. Whenever he talked about Annie, his face looked younger. He loved her so much. When she returned from the fire, she'd find her father fast asleep, his pillow wet with tears. She'd tuck the blankets around him and kiss him on the forehead, the way a mother would kiss her sleeping child. For a young man, his face was old and tired. With his eyes closed, she saw the pain on his face and wondered how he'd lived this long with a broken heart. She knew he wouldn't be with her much longer.

As she did every night, Rose sat by the fire, softly humming to the sound of the strings. She drifted off to a place she often went when no one was around; a green meadow, full of wildflowers and butterflies. She walked barefoot through the grass, looking up at the blue sky and listening to the sweet song of a meadowlark. It was a peaceful place. Maybe it was Heaven.

She was startled by two men standing in front of her. She hadn't heard them approach. Strangers, not from the camp. They told her they'd seen the fire through the trees. In the heavy mist along the bog, they'd lost their way and needed directions back to the road. She didn't know the way, but she knew someone who did. Stepping closer to the fire, they warmed themselves and said her music was very pretty. When she stood up, they asked where her father was and she told them he was asleep. They seemed friendly enough, but there was something about them that made her uncomfortable. The hills were full of freebooters and highwaymen, many well-versed in the art of deception. On the road, you never knew who was an honest traveler and who was a brigand intending to slit your throat and steal whatever you had. Sad truth was, it happened all too often. Might be well to see these two on their way, the sooner, the better. She told them to wait by the fire and she'd bring someone to give them the directions they were asking. Their smiles made her nervous and she backed away from the fire, thinking to herself, for sure she'd be glad to see them go. She thought about running, but changed her mind. All they needed was directions back to the road. It was alright. She'd get a couple of men to send them on their way.

As she reached the last wagon, she realized they were behind her. Again, she told them to wait by the fire, but they held her arms and began to walk with her toward the bog. She tried to tell them they were going the wrong way. When they kept pushing her forward, she didn't know what to do. They were talking as if nothing was happening, moving her further away from the camp. It was all so unexpected. She didn't even know enough to scream. She was only a child, sixteen and trusting. Once out of range of the camp, they laid their hands on her and ripped her clothes. She was frightened and began to cry, clutching at her clothes and trying to cover herself. They told her if she screamed, they'd kill her and throw her body to the wild dogs, and then they'd return to kill her father while he slept. She believed them and stopped fighting. They dragged her through the thorny underbrush and into the woods. There, they ripped the rest of her clothes away and raped her. She didn't make a sound the whole time, believing that if she did, they'd kill her father. It wasn't in fear of her own life that she kept quiet, but only for him. When they were done, they threw her into the slimy bog and left her choking and gasping in the muck. As she fought for breath, she heard them on the bank. She'd never forget the sound of their laughter as long as she lived.

She awoke on the edge of the swamp, cut from the thorns and soaking wet, shivering convulsively in the damp night air. She tried to focus on where she was. The last thing she remembered was choking in the gritty water and didn't know how she managed to get out. Why hadn't she drowned? She couldn't swim. The only conclusion she could reach was that her good angel must have pulled her out. She never told her father what happened. There was nothing he could have done anyway and knowing would have hurt him. She endured the painful memory of that night in silence, promising herself she'd never tell a soul.

Over the years, Rose cared for her father. Each day, she watched him getting weaker. He was thin and frail, and looked like an old man twice his age. He rarely left his bed and he was cold all the time. She kept blankets over him, trying to keep him warm. Food had no appeal and he wasn't eating much anymore. She was lucky to get a few spoonfuls of broth down him and even luckier to get him to take a bite of bread. For days, he'd been saying he wasn't hungry, that he'd eat tomorrow. When tomorrow came, it was always the same. The women told her he'd be leaving soon. The will to live was gone. They'd seen the old ones die when they gave up on living. Joe wasn't old, but he had given up. It was no longer possible for him to go on without his Annie. She was prepared for the end and her prayer was that he wouldn't suffer in his final hours.

On the day she turned eighteen years, she awoke to find him gasping for breath and clutching a small, green velvet bag close to his heart. There were tears in his eyes when he told her he was sorry he hadn't been able to give her finer things in life, but those things were not to be had as long as she lived with him. He said he loved her dearly, but the time had come for him to be with his Annie. He'd waited so long to see her again. There was a sense of peace about him and he smiled as he placed the velvet bag in her hand. He told her the bag belonged to her mother and she was to use its contents to make a better life. America offered opportunities she'd never have in Ireland. She must follow her heart across the sea. Before he closed his eyes, he whispered a. request to the angels to take care of his child. Then, he drifted off to sleep for good. She laid her head on her father's chest and listened to the last beats of his fragile heart. When it was silent, she knew he was finally with his Annie. She pictured them embracing on the other side, in Heaven. A face so tired and furrowed with pain in life was peaceful in death, lines caused by years of grief now gone. For the first time in eighteen years, he was happy, and when she cried, she cried only for herself.

After Joe's funeral, she returned to the wagon for the velvet bag. She opened it slowly. Inside was a handful of coins and a gold locket on a fine gold chain, the tiny case containing a lock of her mother's hair. Joe carried it with him for eighteen years. She had to do the right thing with the money. All this time, he'd saved it so she could have that better life he talked about. The thought of traveling across the sea to a new world was frightening, but Joe was right. There was nothing for a Gypsy in Ireland but a lifetime of poverty and hardship. In America, things would be better. She turned the locket over in her hand. It was the key to a new world, a new life. She had to find a way to get to America, to the land of promise. Remembering the stories he told gave her a smile. He said the streets were paved with gold and when the rain fell, the drops turned into diamonds when they hit the ground, there for the scooping up, as many as you could carry. It'd be just like Joe Callahan to say that. Then again, maybe there was truth in his story. The only way to find out was to go.

Chapter 3

Angels don't have wings.

      She never felt so alone as during the trip across the Irish Sea. She was leaving behind the only home she'd ever known, but the first step to reaching the streets of gold had been taken and there was no turning back. In England, she booked passage on a steamer bound for America. She was deathly afraid of water, but travel by boat was the only way to get there. Unfortunately, fear of the water was not the only problem to face. Alarmed at first discovering the extent of accommodations her money bought, she resigned herself to the conditions under which she'd have to live during the trip. There was no stateroom with a bed and private porthole through which to see the ocean and other ships passing by. When she boarded, a young seaman pointed to a ladder that disappeared into a hole leading to a lower level. Once there, she realized it was the cargo hold. Beneath the waterline, the belly of the ship was damp and musty-smelling and she decided the seaman made a mistake. Some of the people inside were coughing and moaning like they were dying, and she cringed when a rat scurried along the edge of the wall. Surely, they didn't expect her to sleep with sick people and rats! She climbed back up the ladder, lugging her bag with her, and found the seaman. She showed him her ticket again, insisting there'd been a mistake. Where was her room? He checked it and said there was no mistake. Her ticket was for steerage. She stood on the deck, watching the activity on the dock below and wondering if she ought to run away before the ship cast off and try to get back to Ireland. From the way the boat was creaking and groaning with the motion of the water, she questioned its seaworthiness and wondered if it would stay afloat all the way to America. If she stayed on board, she might never see land again. She closed her eyes. She couldn't go back to Ireland, not after she'd come this far and spent a goodly portion of the money in the velvet bag. Joe would be disappointed if she didn't go to America. Remembering how sure her father had been that the streets of America were covered in gold, a single tear slid down her face. She'd never know if he was right unless she went there and saw it for herself.

Movement of her bag startled her and she reached for it with both hands. It was the young seaman. He was smiling and offering to carry it back down the ladder for her. At first, she hung on tight. Still torn between staying and running away, she looked over the rail again. The gangplank was being hauled up. If she was planning on running off the boat, she'd missed her chance. In a matter of minutes, they'd be leaving the pier and heading out to sea. She was going to America. More than one tear was running down her face now and she looked at the young man beside her. He smiled and said his name was Christopher. He convinced her he wasn't going to steal her things. He only wanted to help. She finally let go of the bag and let him take it, following him down the steps and into the hold where he found her a place to sit between some wooden crates. When he left, she rearranged the crates around the area that was to be her home for the next few weeks. He returned with two blankets, hanging one over the boxes to keep out the draft and making the other into a cushion for her to sit on. At night, she could use it to keep warm. He told her not to leave her things for even a minute and to sleep with her head on her bag. Later, he brought her a piece of canvas folded over several times and laid it down for a bed. It was rough, but a far site better than sleeping on the damp floor. He told her not to be afraid, that he'd be back as soon as he could. He'd bring her some dried fruit and jerky and he'd show her where to wash. He held up his finger to his lips and whispered it must be their secret. There was fresh water on board and he'd bring her some every day for drinking. If she was very careful, she'd get by without a case of scurvy or body sores. He touched her hand and told her she'd survive the voyage if she trusted him. She'd make it to America. When he was gone, she looked around the dimly-lit hold and breathed a deep sigh of resignation. No one told her to bring blankets or dried fruit, or anything else. If she'd had to rely on herself, she never would have seen land again. Even with the help of the kind seaman, getting to America was going to be much harder than she expected, and she prayed her good angel would make the trip at her side. Perhaps the young sailor was an angel come to help her get there.

The ship pitched and rolled on the high sea and it was freezing in the cargo hold. More than once, she thought she'd die from the cold before she got close to New York. When her fingers and toes were nearly frozen and she was about to give up hope, shivering in her space between the crates, the seaman would come to her with a cup of hot broth or an extra blanket. Then, he'd rub her hands and blow on them until the circulation returned. She felt rejuvenated and warm when he was around. He gave her strength in many ways. On days when the weather was tolerable, he'd take her up to the deck for fresh air. They'd stand at the rail and he'd wrap a blanket around her. He kept his promise and brought her dried fruit and jerky every day, and fresh water to drink. There were times when she wanted to share what he gave her with the other passengers, but he told her to be wise and keep the extra food for herself. Further into the trip, when their rations of fruit gave out, the others would fight over the little she had if they knew it was more than they were given and she might get killed for a piece of dried apple. Cruel as it seemed, it was a matter of survival and she must eat the fruit and dried meat herself when no one was watching. He assured her the others would not go hungry.

When only rations of bread and potato soup were left for the other people riding in steerage, his pockets yielded the precious extra food and he gave it to her whenever he took her to the deck for air. While she ate, they talked about America. She'd heard there were wealthy men in America who could provide a pretty young woman with fine clothes and a home; perhaps take her to the theatre or opera. She'd never been to a theatre, but she listened to stories about those places around the fires in the Gypsy camp. It all sounded so exciting and fun. She wanted to be a lady and wear beautiful clothes made of silk and fine linen, not the rags she had on. She wanted to be noticed. He took a piece of fruit from his pocket and told her to eat it. There was some dried beef too. If she wanted all those things, she had to keep up her strength and eat every extra bit of food he gave her. The jerky was tough and he laughed at the way she tore a piece off like a wild animal tearing at its kill. He wrapped the blanket around her, pulling it over her head and holding her close to keep her warm. He told her to take her time eating the meat. They weren't going back down until it was all gone. Even with the coldest time of the year upon them, she was warm when she was with him. She peeked out from under the blanket. "Christopher, are you an angel?" He laughed and pulled the blanket back over her head. "Do I look like an angel? I don't have wings." She stuck her head out and stared at him. "Yes. I know you're an angel."

An ocean voyage in January faced frightful odds. Winter gales whipped the sea into waves taller than the ship and when the walls of water came crashing down onto the deck, the hull moaned heavily under the strain. The battering water echoed through the hold like rounds of canon fire and some people in the ship's belly screamed each time a wave hit the boat. They were riding beneath the waterline and if the hull split during one of those oceanic cannonades, they'd be doomed to a watery grave. Up top, there were lifeboats to help the high-priced ticket passengers in a disaster, but in the bottom, there wouldn't be a chance for survival if the hull broke apart. She tried not to think about the danger and occupied herself with trying to keep warm, moving around as much as possible and rubbing her hands together to keep her blood going. To leave her sleeping place and belongings unattended would mean returning to an empty spot, so she couldn't go far. Other passengers watched as she danced in circles, beating her arms with her hands, then folding and refolding her bedding; anything to keep moving without wandering away. She waited to use a water closet on the upper level until the sailor came to watch her bedding and posses-sions while she was away. Every couple of days, he helped her pack up her bag and canvas bed and blankets. On those times, he took her to a small room off the galley where she could wash as much of herself as she dared uncover in a short time while he stood guard at the door. The amount of washing depended on whether the water in the bowl was warm or cold and whether the sea was calm or rough. The room was nothing more than a storage closet with barely enough space to turn around, but she was grate-ful for the chance to wash any part of herself after being down in the smelly cargo hold.

She had only one change of clothes besides the ones she wore under the old wool coat. One day, he told her to put on her clean clothes and give him the soiled ones she'd been wearing. She was puzzled. Why did he want her dirty clothes? He told her to hurry, they didn't have much time. If they were discovered, there'd be trouble for both of them. She obeyed and took off the dirty clothes, handing them out to him, then quickly washing and putting on the clean things. It wasn't warm in the closet and her hands trembled while she carefully wrapped the piece of strong soap he'd given her in the scrubbing cloth and stuffed it in her pocket. Just as she was about to open the closet door, she heard voices in the passageway behind the galley. She held her breath. There was another man outside and the sailor was joking and laughing with him. He had to pretend he was only passing by and he kept walking with the other fellow so as not to raise suspicion about his being there or about the girl hiding in the closet. She pressed her ear against the door. Their voices became fainter as they got further away from the closet. Not knowing what to do next, she panicked. She didn't remember the way back. And where did Christopher put her things? The canvas she slept on and blankets? Her bag? And what had he done with her clothes? She needed the coat and blankets to stay warm. All of her scant, worldly belongings were in the valise. It was a dreadful state of affairs! She remained still for several more minutes, listening for footsteps in the narrow passageway. Someone was coming. She stayed quiet. Suddenly, the door opened and she let out a startled squeal. The seaman reached for her hand and pulled her out of the closet, telling her to hush. They had to hurry before someone else came along. He tugged at something stuffed behind a stack of burlap sacks full of potatoes — the canvas and blankets, and her traveling bag!

Each of them carrying part of the load, they walked as fast as they could until they reached the deck. Outside, their breath turned to clouds of frozen vapor in the icy, winter air as they let out sighs of relief at once again being in a safe zone. Only then did they laugh about the close call. They'd have to be careful from now on. It wouldn't do for her to be caught in a part of the ship where he knew she shouldn't be. Worse, he couldn't be caught there with her. One more time after today should do it. New York was just over the horizon, two days, at most.

Except for the few precious, warm minutes in the galley closet, she was chilled to the bone during the entire journey. Most of her time was spent in the steerage compartment or in the cold air on deck. Had it not been for sheer Irish stubbornness, she'd have died on the way. Some did, and their bodies were dropped overboard into the freezing waters of the North Atlantic. She thought it sad there would be no grave to mark their final resting place, nowhere to put flowers. She remembered the wildflowers and sweet heather she laid on her mother's grave, a lump of earth with a small, wooden cross crudely carved by her father, bearing the name Anne Katherine Callahan. The wild white rose Joe planted on the grave grew tall and thick over the years, the fragrant blooms a sad reminder of the mother she'd never known. It was her mother's favorite flower, the flower she was named for. The day she left Ireland, she picked a rose from the bush and laid it on her mother's grave. Rose knelt and kissed the name on the wooden cross, whispering they'd meet in Heaven someday. She picked a second rose and laid it on the rough mound beside her mother's grave, and said good-bye to her father. There was no cross to mark the fresh grave. She wondered if she'd ever see a cross with Joseph Callahan's name carved into it. She never asked him if he had a name in the middle as her mother did. It was too late now. She'd always think of him the way he was in his younger days, full of energy despite his sadness, with a never-ending story on his lips. She smiled remembering what someone said about Joe's story-telling. "If anyone ever kissed the Blarney Stone, sure and they had to shove Joe Callahan out of the way to get to it." The stories were over. The fairy tales were tucked away in her memory. Joe was gone. Walking away from the graves of her mother and father, she remembered thinking she'd never know if anyone placed a marker on Joe's grave because she'd never return to Ireland.

WINTER – 1876

With the seaman's help, she survived the dangerous ocean crossing in spite of the hardship, but as soon as the ship docked, he disappeared. She thought it strange that after having helped her throughout the trip, he vanished when they made land. He didn't even say good-bye. She wanted to thank him for all the dried fruit and jerky that kept her strength up and for the cups of broth that warmed her when she thought her insides were freezing, and for taking her to the secret closet behind the galley to wash and find a few minutes of warmth, and for the blankets and canvas bed — and so much more. She left the bedding behind for the next poor soul who'd need some help to survive the trip. It only seemed right. On the day they docked, she awoke with her arm resting on the clothes she'd handed him out the closet door a couple of days earlier. They'd been washed and folded to start her first day in America. She wouldn't have survived the trip without Christopher's help. Of that she was certain. She was convinced he was an angel.

Off the boat, she stood on the dock looking up to where passengers and crew waved from the rail. For a minute, she thought she saw him, smiling and waving to her. She waved back. Then, he was gone. She scanned the upper deck, person by person, but couldn't find him. With no idea where to go, she turned her back to the ship and faced the city, pulling her coat tight and holding it together at her throat to keep out the cutting wind.

America! She was here at last. In her wildest dreams of the new country, she never imagined it to be of such overwhelming proportions. She remembered her father telling a story about a wonderful land far across the sea with streets paved in gold and rain that turned to diamonds when the drops touched the earth. She looked at the grimy waterfront ground at her feet — not gold, and the icy rain that began to fall turned only to snow, not diamonds.

Setting foot on solid ground provided a sense of security, but her revelry was short-lived. New York in January was bitter cold and the wind cut through the old wool coat where the moths had feasted. The thin linen dress and sweater she wore underneath provided no insulation. She'd mended her only other pair of woolen stockings so many times they were nothing but a pile of tangled threads that finally gave out and were of no further good for wearing. Days ago, she'd tossed them overboard somewhere on the high seas and the pair she had on wasn't much better. Her toes were numb from the cold, but she walked as fast as she could, all the time thinking her nose and ears would soon freeze and fall off. Exhausted, she finally stopped, unable to take another step. She stared at the icy ground. It seemed she'd been walking for hours, lugging the bag that got heavier with every step, and not knowing what she was looking for or where she was going. How sad her efforts to reach this country would end in frozen death. Tears rolled down her cheeks and crystallized before they reached her chin. At that moment, Irish stubbornness overtook self-pity. It was true if she didn't find a place to warm up soon, she'd freeze to death. That being the case, she'd never know if America was the promised land of opportunity, or if streets of gold lay hidden beneath the snow. Joe would be disappointed if she let that happen. She'd be disappointed in herself. She had to do something, and do it fast.

She raised her head and looked around. Muffled behind windows, the faint sound of voices floated on the icy air. The two-story house sported a sign with black lettering, "Room and Board." She couldn't read, but it was a house and it was warm inside. Perhaps a kind soul within would take pity on a half-frozen immigrant and allow her to purchase a cup of tea and a few minutes in front of the fire. She jammed her hand inside her coat pocket. The velvet purse was still there, although considerably lighter now. Only four American dollars left. She wore the locket around her neck. She'd have to ask for help. She had no choice. It was a matter of survival. She studied the house. It was very big, white with gray shutters and stone steps leading up to a wide porch supported by rounded beams. All around the porch was a fence made of smaller rounded pieces of wood and covered the entire length with a railing. The front door displayed a piece of oval glass into which a border resembling a crystal had been cut. It was a most impressive house and she thought it must belong to someone of considerable wealth and position, maybe even royalty. Although she wasn't sure if there was royalty in America, now was not the time to wonder. It was too cold to think about anything except getting warm. With no sensation in her toes, she took care to place her feet solidly on each step so not to slip. At the front door, she swallowed hard and thumped the brass knocker.

The door was opened by a small woman whose dark skin was radiant with a copper glow. Her hair was black as ebony and piled on her head in a fashionable arrangement. She wore what Rose thought was the loveliest dress she'd ever seen, the golden-brown of a newborn fawn, with long sleeves gathered at the shoulders over something Rose knew could not possibly be part of the woman's natural anatomy. It would later be explained that the puffiness was the result of padding at the shoulders. The sleeves were pleated to the wrist with tight-fitting cuffs and tiny buttons on the inside halfway to the elbow. The yoke was covered with ivory lace and the skirt touched the floor. The woman wore earrings made not of gold or silver, but of a metal the color of a sunset at its brightest moment. The inlaid stones were a beautiful blue-green. At first, Rose thought she'd arrived at the gates of Heaven. Perhaps the woman was an angel. Her father used to say angels walked the earth and you couldn't always recognize them as angels because they left their wings in Heaven. He said when your troubles were so great that you didn't know which way to turn, one of those angels would find you and save you. If that was true, maybe she was face-to-face with her own good angel.

Half frozen and so tired she could barely walk, she had the wild-eyed look of a crazy person. She didn't know how long she'd been standing at the door when the woman took her arm and drew her inside. When the woman closed the door against the cold and steered her into the parlour, Rose tried to speak, but words were stifled by her frozen lips. Oil lamps lit the house and a roaring fire crackled in the biggest stone fireplace she had ever seen.

The woman removed Rose's coat and led her closer to the fire where she wrapped a soft blanket around her and removed her shoes. Rose stared in amazement as the woman massaged her frozen feet. Gradually, circulation returned feeling to her toes and they began to tingle. It was then she became aware of a small girl sitting beside her, offering a pair of slippers lined with fur. She'd never seen shoes like that and she laughed when she put them on. They felt like two rabbits wrapped around her feet. The child disappeared into the next room and returned with a steaming cup of a sweet, brown liquid. The puzzled look on Rose's face prompted the girl to happily explain the drink was hot cocoa.

Rose sat by the fire, sipping the hot chocolate drink. It had the most wonderful flavor she'd ever tasted. She held the cup with both hands, the heat from within warming her fingers. The woman sat beside her and introduced herself as Ann Merrick. She stopped sipping the cocoa. The angel even had an Irish name. This had to be a dream. She couldn't imagine how she stumbled into such good fortune and concluded this kind woman who rubbed her feet and warmed her half-frozen body by the fire must be an angel. The angel, whoever she was, most assuredly saved her life just as sure as the seaman had saved her on the ship. Her father was right. He said the angels would watch over her.

She spent her first night in a real bed, a bed with fluffy pillows and sweet-smelling sheets, and a curious blanket. She was fascinated by the blanket. It wasn't very heavy, but it was warm and cozy. Ann explained it was a down comforter, filled with the soft feathers from the goose's behind. It was the funniest thing she'd ever heard. Throughout her life, she'd laugh each time she thought of it.

Next morning, she awoke to the smell of food cooking. The small girl who brought her the fuzzy slippers and hot cocoa the night before entered the bedroom carrying a tray. Rose rubbed her eyes. It must be a dream. It was too good to really be happening. She pinched herself. It was real alright. The child placed the tray on a table and approached the bed. Rose studied the pretty face as the little girl fluffed the pillows behind her. Her skin was dark like her mother's and she had the same beautiful black hair, long and shining, and the most unusual blue eyes. The contrast was extraordinary. She chattered happily, a delightful bit of sunshine on a cold winter morning. When the pillows were fluffed to her satisfaction and Rose was sitting up in bed, the child returned for the tray. Before setting it down in front of Rose, she paused for a moment, tilting her head to one side. She was curious. She wanted to know why Rose talked so funny? "Not meaning to be rude, of course. Just wondering." Rose smiled. "I come from far across the great ocean and beyond the Irish Sea from a beautiful land called Ireland where grass is the color of emeralds and the hills are covered with sweet, purple heather and wild roses. My father used to tell me the angels wear sprigs of Irish heather in their hair because it smells so good. 'Tis a land of mysterious happenins' and many wonderful stories about fairies and leprechauns and if you like, I'll tell you about 'em." The little girl was drawn in by the words "mysterious" and "fairies." She laid the tray on Rose's lap and took up a perch on the edge of the bed. "Breakfast! Mother fixed it special for you because you're our guest. You can tell me a story later. Eat some food now."

The child was anxious to hear more. "Are there really fairies in Ireland?" Rose smiled at her captive audience and paused before answering. It was the way Joe did it to add excitement when he told a story. She began in a whisper, implying the fairies and leprechauns were listening. "Why, they're everywhere — fairies and leprechauns. They live underneath toadstools and play among the violets in the woods. They like flowers, mostly purple ones. 'Tis where you're most apt to be findin' 'em — skippin' through the purple heather and wood violets. But early in the mornin' when a heavy mist lays out over the bog, you can hear 'em ringin' the tiny white bells of lilies of the valley. At night, they ride on the backs of fireflies when they don't feel up to flyin' themselves." The little girl's eyes were wide. "Have you ever seen one — a fairy? Or a leprechaun?" Rose winked. "Well now, if you can catch a leprechaun, he'll give you his pot of gold and grant you three wishes, anythin' your heart desires. They're very clever, and fast, and they know a lot of magic, so catchin' one takes a bit of doin'."

Rose couldn't remember the last time she ate and she didn't have to be told twice. The little girl sat cross-legged on the bed, talking the whole while as Rose devoured the food. "I know where Ireland is. I learn about all the countries and oceans in school and I can show you where Ireland is on the globe of the world downstairs in the library. It's called geography. But I never learned about fairies or leprechauns. My teacher must not know about them." Rose nodded her head while she chewed. It wasn't necessary for her to speak and she didn't want to come right out and say she hadn't actually seen a fairy or a leprechaun herself. For the most part, it was a one-sided conversation. The child talked enough for both of them, asking questions and then going on without waiting for answers. When Rose finished eating, the girl took the tray and left the room. To be sure she wasn't dreaming, she pinched herself again. Her stomach was full for the first time since she left Ireland. In a few minutes, the little one was back, resuming her perch on the edge of the bed and picking up the conversation where she left off. Rose was captivated by the pretty face and the animated way she spoke. She was a ray of sunshine, a little pixie full of energy, and she talked a mile a minute. Rose couldn't help but smile at the way she talked with her hands, acting out the meaning of what she said.

Her name was Rebecca and she was ten years old. Almost eleven. Ann was her mother. "My father's name is Richard and he's a general in the Army. He's a very important man. He knows the President. He's away on Army business, but Mother says in a little while, he'll retire. That means he can stay home with us all the time. I'm marking the days on a calendar and telling Mother how many we have left until he comes home." A far-off place, a distant memory came to mind as the girl talked. Rose told the Pixie her mother's name was Anne too, but she was in Heaven. Her father's name was Joseph and he was in Heaven with her mother. Rebecca put her head down, trying to imagine what it would be like without a mother and father. She hugged Rose. "I'll share my mother with you, and when my father comes home, I'll share him too. He's wonderful. You'll like him a lot. I do." Rose laughed. "Well, I hope you like your father." The Pixie became oddly serious. "A family is people who love each other. You can be in our family." Another hug, longer than the first. She knew the child was trying to comfort her and she hugged the Pixie back. The bond was formed. The redhaired Gypsy and the Pixie would become much more than friends.

Rose propped the pillows to make room for two and the Pixie climbed onto the bed beside her. Rose was amazed the child attended school and could read and write. She knew numbers too. The little girl was exceptionally bright and witty. Someday, when she grew up, she'd be a doctor. Her plan was quite clear. She knew exactly what she would do with her life. Rose never heard of such a thing. She knew about the midwives in Ireland, but all they did was help the women with birthing the babies and patch up cuts or splint a broken bone now and then. You couldn't call them doctors. A woman doctor, on the other hand, was something new. What an exciting future. She wondered what her own future held. Her aspirations were not as high as Rebecca's, but she would like to be able to write her name and maybe learn to read someday. She'd never seen her name on paper. The Pixie jumped off the bed and ran out the door, returning with paper, pen and a book. Resuming her place beside Rose and laying the paper on top of the book, she wrote Rose's name and drew a flower beside it. Then, she handed the paper to Rose and told her now that she'd seen how easy it was, she would teach her to write it herself. They'd make a game of it. She'd be the teacher and Rose would be the student.

They sat on the bed and talked until they heard Ann's voice in the hallway. "Rebecca, are you making a nuisance of yourself, bothering our guest so early in the morning?" Rebecca jumped off the bed and peeked out the door. "No, Mother. We were just talking. I'm going to teach her to write her name and she's going to tell me stories about Ireland." She turned to Rose with a questioning look. "Am I being a nuisance?" Rose laughed. "No, you're not a nuisance at all. I'm likin' your company. Stay as long as it pleases you." Ann was in the room by then. She put her hands on her daughter's shoulders. "I think you have some chores to attend to downstairs, young lady. You can visit with Rose later." Rebecca stood on her toes and kissed her mother, then turned to Rose. "Hurry and get dressed. I'll get the paper and pen ready and I'll teach you to write your name when you come downstairs. Afterwards, you can tell me a story about fairies."

When Ann and Rebecca were gone, Rose slipped back under the covers. She closed her eyes and enjoyed the warmth a few more minutes. She finally decided she'd better get up and make herself presentable to properly thank Ann for taking her in. She got out of bed and looked around the room. It was beautiful. A real home. She wondered if she'd ever live in a house with lace curtains at the windows and down-filled comforters on the bed; comforters filled with feathers from a goose's behind! She laughed out loud. She turned and found herself facing an oval mirror. When she touched it, the mirror rocked on hinges to reveal her full length. Her red hair was a bright contrast to the soft, white flannel nightgown Ann had given her to sleep in. She wondered if she looked like her mother. Annie Callahan was only a few months older than she was now when Rose was born. She wondered if she'd ever have a daughter. She'd need a husband first, but where on earth would she find a man who understood why she wasn't a virgin? That was important to a man taking a wife. She'd have to tell him about the terrible night she was attacked by two men in Ireland. The memory of that awful night made her stomach turn. She prayed they'd burn in hell for what they did to her. It was a secret she could never tell anyone. Even though she was but sixteen then, what man would have her if he knew? Sometimes, she thought it would have been better if she drowned in the bog that fateful night.

She tipped the mirror forward to see herself from head to toe. She thought she was pretty. Christopher said she was pretty. In truth, she was a striking beauty. Her hair was thick and red like her mother's, falling to her hips in soft, silky waves. She wondered if she could learn to pin it up the way Ann wore hers. She'd like to be taller. A pair of shoes with higher heels would help. She stood on her tiptoes and pulled the nightgown tight around her body, swiveling from side-to-side. Her figure was slender, but with pertinent anatomical attributes in precisely the right order. Her hands and feet were small and delicate. She turned her hands over and grimaced. They hurt. Red and chafed from the cold weather, they'd take some time to heal. She approached the mirror and stared at her face up close. Her eyes were the strong point of her beauty. They were as green as emeralds and the lashes were long and curved. She made a funny face at herself and stepped back to survey the overall picture. She was more than pretty.

Ann interrupted Rose's trip into the looking glass. A bath was waiting, and when she was done soaking, Ann wanted to visit with her about a business proposition. Rose hadn't a clue what the word "proposition" meant, and she knew absolutely nothing about business of any kind. Perhaps it was time to simply disappear out the back door. She'd not been taught manners, but something inside told her she couldn't walk away from the kindness shown to her in this house. She held the lace curtains open. It was snowing. Recollection of the day before, her frozen feet; the cold January wind outside, gave rise to reconsideration of leaving without notice by the back door. She looked at her hands again. They did need time to heal. Remembering her father's words about America and opportunity, she wondered when another one might come along. This could very well be the only time. That did it. She'd stay and go to the bath.

Steam rose from the white porcelain tub and the fragrance of lavender drifting on the air tickled her nose. She sneezed. Sweet oil had been poured into the water. She wiggled her arms inside the nightgown and let it fall to the floor. Without thinking, she stuck one foot into the steaming water and immediately withdrew it, hopping on the other one to keep her balance. How in the world did they ever get that much water so hot? She approached the tub cautiously as if afraid some monster were lurking below the surface, waiting to jump out and pull her under. She tested the water with her hand. It wasn't so hot. It was just that the initial plunge had been a shock because she wasn't expecting to find warm water. As a matter-of-fact, she expected it to be cold. Carefully, she stepped into the tub and sat down, sliding under the water up to her neck. She closed her eyes. Heaven! From now on, her favorite thing would be a hot bath with lavender oil.

Ann entered the room carrying a tray full of strange paraphernalia and set it on a table next to the tub. Rose sat up and scowled at the things on the tray. When she saw Rose staring at the tray, Ann explained their function, picking up each object as she described it. "Soap is to clean the dirt away and the sponge and long-handled brush will aid in the scrubbing. You do know what soap is, don't you?" Rose shook her head, yes. Ann continued with the identification, demonstrating how to use the next item. "This little brush is for fingernails." She laid it down and picked up another one. "This stone is called pumice, and you use it to smooth away rough spots on the bottoms of your feet, but don't rub too hard." Rubbing it over the heel of her hand, she showed the way to use it. A lesson on use of the bath tools over, she handed the soap to Rose. "When you're done with the bath, there's more warm water to wash your hair." She picked up a glass bottle and pointed to the picture of a girl on the label. "This is a good-quality shampoo. It'll make your hair shine." Rose tried to repeat the word. "Shem... Shep..." Ann smiled. "Shampoo. Liquid soap for washing hair." She added, "...but you have to rinse it well. I'll help you." Rose never heard of such a thing before, but she didn't want Ann to think her stupid. She nodded her head, implying she understood the reason for shampoo.

When Ann left the room, she blew out a sigh of relief and sank back into the water up to her chin. She never knew taking a bath could be so complicated. Rolling the bar of soap between her hands, she worked up a lather. Soap wasn't a novelty, but this smelled a lot better and felt smoother than the strong, homemade lye soap she was used to. Baths in a Gypsy camp were never like this and on the boat crossing the ocean, she washed from a bucket in a closet. The sponge had a curious feel to it and she alternately soaked it and squeezed the water out. When she tired of that game, she picked up the brush with the long handle. Different from any she'd seen before, it's bristles were soft and tickled her skin; not the least bit hard or scratchy. Next, she stuck her foot out of the water and rubbed the pumice stone on the bottom. It tickled and she laughed out loud. What a silly thing. She couldn't imagine any reason to want to scrape the skin off the bottoms of her feet. The most unusual thing was the shampoo. She uncorked the bottle, sniffing the contents. It smelled nice, like a meadow full of wildflowers. Maybe she'd give it a try, as long as she was trying everything else. If this bath was a sign of things to come, she could hardly wait to see what came next. America was full of new things alright, even if the streets weren't paved with gold.

After the bath, she felt like a brand-new person. Her skin was soft and velvety from the sweet lotion Ann gave her to rub all over and her hair was shining clean from the wildflowers shampoo. Upon returning to her room, she found a dress, undergarments, shoes, and a hairbrush and pins laid out neatly on the bed. She must be dreaming. The dress was the color of a dove, gray with a white lace collar extending to her shoulders. The cuffs were also white and tiny pearl buttons ran down the front. The dress presented no problem getting into. The undergarments, on the other hand, were a different story. Although lacy and very pretty, she'd never seen anything so complicated in the way of clothing before. She studied them for awhile and after due contemplation, decided that rather than appear ignorant by asking for installation instructions, she would simply not wear them. She hid them under the bed and slipped into the dress that fit like it had been sewn perfectly for her dimensions.

She felt like a princess in an Irish fairy tale. Everything was perfect — except the shoes. They gave her fits, but she managed to keep them on her feet. The heels she predicted would make her taller did that alright, but every time she tried to take a step, she turned her ankle. Walking would take some practice. As with the undergarments, the struggle to fasten her hair on top of her head with the pins was quickly abandoned. She brushed her hair and tied it up behind her ears with a piece of faded blue ribbon from her case. When she was all put together, she faced the mirror, tipping it forward again to view the results of her effort, top to bottom. The outline of her nipples showed under the fabric and she tried to coax the material to hang a little more loosely. It didn't work. She sighed and made a funny face at herself. Maybe she ought to try again with the underthings. She clasped her hands together beneath her chin and rapidly fluttered her eyelashes. If she could maintain the pose, her arms would cover what was otherwise seen through the material. She held the pose another minute. No one would know, and if they did, it didn't matter. She didn't have to wear the silly things if she didn't want to. A pirouette in front of the mirror showed off the finished product and she winked at the girl looking back at her, stepping very close to the glass and staring her in the eye. Joe always said the Irish were blessed with luck. If he could see her now, he'd swear to it, and if he was watching from heaven, he'd be dancing a jig with the angels from sheer happiness.

Walking in the new shoes was awkward and precarious, bordering on dangerous. She took deliberate steps down the stairs to the parlour, careful not to turn an ankle and risk losing her footing to end up sprawled out on the floor at the bottom. Concentrating so hard on negotiating the stairs, Rose didn't realize how ridiculous she looked with her hands under her chin like an innocent cherub and she didn't fool Ann for a minute with what she was trying to cover up. The kind woman smiled as Rose made her entrance down the staircase. Later, she'd teach Rose how to put on intimate apparel and the importance of wearing it. She'd teach her a lot of things when the time was right, but for now, she'd let Rose enjoy the time in her new dress and surroundings. This was an important day for Rose Callahan; the day she acquired a home and a family, and a new life.

A delicious aroma drifted through the house. Bread. Rose stopped midway down the staircase, sniffing the air in quick breaths at first, then, inhaling deeply. She never smelled anything so wonderful. She could almost taste it. Ann invited her into the kitchen where she took the golden-brown loaves out of the oven and set them on a board to cool. Rose was fascinated by the black iron stove. Her home in Ireland consisted of a rickety old wagon and a tent. There was no stove. Her meals were cooked over an open fire wherever they set up camp. When local residents harassed them, they moved on. Her eighteen years had been spent moving around the countryside and she'd never known the comforts of a house. This home, with its bathtub and lace curtains and fireplace was beyond her comprehension. It even had comforters with feathers from a goose's behind. That was the funniest thing she ever heard. She still was not entirely convinced it wasn't a dream. With no mention of the missing undergarments, Ann said she looked very pretty. "The dress seems to be a perfect fit, and how is the size of the shoes?" Rose lifted her skirt to display the shoes. "They'll take some gettin' used to, but they do fit me feet and they're a far cry better than me old ones. I'll say that for 'em." She sat down and raised both feet off the ground, wiggling them around so Ann could see the fit of the shoes. "I'll be thankin' you for the lendin' of 'em." Ann looked surprised. "Oh, they're not a loan, dear. They're yours to keep, and the dress — and the undergarments too." Ann went to the stove to stir a warming pot and Rose twisted her lips to one side, wrinkling her nose behind Ann's back. So, Ann knew she'd done away with them. What she thought was a well-contrived deception hadn't been so foolproof. Ann returned to the table with two cups of hot cocoa and Rose felt she had to say something about the discarded personal pieces of clothing. "I didn't know what to do with the underthins'. They're under the bed. ...but I'll be learnin' and I'll wear 'em next time." Ann placed a cup of hot cocoa in front of Rose and pulled a chair up to the table. She smiled. "I understand. I'll show you how those things work and you'll get used to them. It is important for ladies to wear them." She dropped the subject and sipped her cocoa. "Drink your cocoa before it gets cold."

They talked about Ireland and Joe Callahan. She missed her father. He'd be very happy if he could see her now, wearing a pretty dress and sipping hot cocoa with an angel. Her mother died when she was born. Ann touched Rose's hand. That was very sad. Every girl should have a mother to help her grow to be a woman. She listened while Rose talked about Annie Callahan and the way she imagined the mother she never knew. She sat quietly when Rose drifted off. When the thoughts passed, Rose told Ann it was time for her to go. She didn't have much money, but she offered to pay for the room and food. Ann refused the offer. Rose would need her money. Besides, she had a better idea. Since Rose had no idea where to go, and it was winter, Ann proposed she stay and work at the boarding house, at least until Spring. Ann would teach her to make the beds and prepare meals. In exchange for work, she'd have a room of her own and a weekly wage. She had a home for as long as she wanted to stay and the money she earned would be hers to save or spend as she saw fit. Rebecca would gladly throw in reading and writing lessons, and there'd be time for numbers if she had a mind to learn. Rose didn't know what to say. Everything happened so fast. One minute she was about to freeze to death in the street and the next, she had a job and a home. More importantly, these people cared what happened to her. They wanted to help. If it was a dream as she still suspicioned, she never wanted to wake up. After years of struggling to survive, her luck had changed. The days of roaming the countryside and sleeping in a tent and bathing in a stream with lye soap were over. Where her life had been laden with rejection as a Gypsy, it was now filled with acceptance. These people didn't care where she came from or what she was. The streets weren't paved with gold and there were no diamonds falling out of the sky, but she was in America. Joe hadn't been wrong. It was a good place and life was better here.

She fit right in. Home was the magic word. She finally had a home. Ann was like a mother, and the Pixie — well, the Pixie was an incredible little sister. That one was a constant diversion and a never-ending source of fun. She made Rose laugh. The Merricks became her family and she loved them. They made her feel like she belonged. Ann taught her how to maintain the house and prepare meals. Diplomatically, but firmly, she stressed the importance of wearing a complete ensemble, including the underwear Rose had previously hidden under the bed. She made Rose stand up straight and practice walking in her high-heeled shoes with a book on her head. Rose felt silly, but she did it anyway to please Ann. Before long, she realized it wasn't so silly. She felt herself walking straighter and behaving more the way Ann said a lady should behave. Ann educated her in the social graces, teaching her table manners and polite words to use in social situations. Whenever a careless, slang word slipped out in conversation, Ann would wag a finger at her and she'd correct herself, sometimes mistakenly using another impropriety to fix the first. She knew the English language fairly well, but there were still many new words to learn and it was hard to remember the proper, refined way to speak all the time. After having spent eighteen years of her life with Gypsies, her speech was coarse and often vulgar. She'd always cursed without a second thought. It was the way she'd grown up, swearing for no reason as part of everyday talking. Ann said ladies didn't talk that way. Learning to be a lady was harder than she expected. There was a lot to remember and she felt clumsy. When she thought about it, she likened herself to a sow in a mud wallow with dreams of becoming a graceful swan and she wondered if there was any chance Ann's efforts would succeed in turning her into a lady. Even for an angel, teaching a pig to fly would be a miracle.

Whenever Ann caught Rose lifting her skirt to her knees and running up the stairs two at a time, she would sternly reprimand her. The penalty for such unladylike behavior was walking up and down the staircase in proper form ten times. Rose took the scoldings good-naturedly and made the ten trips without complaint. When she was done, there was always the promise that she'd try to remember not to act like a tomboy. Ann knew it was the one unladylike activity she'd never break Rose of and she also made note of the fact that Rose never promised not to do it again, only to "try to remember" not to. Once in awhile, she'd come around the corner just in time to catch Rose forgetting to remember when she thought no one was watching. As long as Rose didn't see her, Ann let it go and laughed to herself. On the outside, Rose looked a lady. Inside, she was still a tomboy. There were some traits that might never be taken out of the girl, and maybe that was alright because they were the things that made her who she was.

Rebecca provided the tutoring every evening when they sat by the big stone fireplace, and Rose slowly learned to read and write. She practiced the letters over and over until Rebecca said they were perfect. They were far from perfect and Rose knew it, but it was a beginning and she was determined to learn. Each time Rebecca approved the page of writing by drawing a star at the top of the paper and praising the work, Rose felt like a star was shining down on her. This was a good place, a comfortable place. Home. Gradually, with Ann's guidance, she was becoming the lady she dreamed about being and learning to read and write to boot. She owed Ann a debt that couldn't be measured in terms of money. She hoped the day would come when she'd have the means to repay the woman who had become a mother to her.

Rose was part of the Merrick family now. Even the day-to-day routine of running the boarding house was fun. It was a better life than she ever imagined. The Pixie was always up to something and provided non-stop amusement. It was all good, but the best part of living here was the conversation at the end of the day. She looked forward to her private talks with Ann. In the evening, when the Pixie finally ran out of steam and went to sleep, the two women sat by the fire, sipping a hot drink and talking. During those talks, Rose shared her dreams and secret desires with Ann. It was a mutual exchange of trust and private thoughts. Ann was counting the days until her husband returned home from the Army. She looked forward to serving him his morning coffee and sitting by the fire with him in the evenings. He'd been away a long time. Too long. She missed him. Rose saw the sparkle in Ann's eyes when she spoke of the man she'd loved for so many years. The story of their romance was wonderful — better than an Irish fairy tale.

When she first arrived in New York, Ann was more out of place than Rose had been when she got off the boat. She was an Indian, daughter of an Apache chief. In the city, she found herself in a different kind of hostile territory and completely out of her element. There'd been a lot of difficult adjustments to make, so much to learn in the white man's world. Much of living here meant understanding prejudices and coping with cruel rejection from people who looked upon Indians as inferior human beings. In the beginning, she wasn't treated with respect even though she was the wife of an Army officer. She recalled the wife of another officer screaming at her and calling her a savage. To this day, she never understood the cruelty white men were capable of. Everything was different from the world of an Indian; the language, customs, clothes. She'd grown up learning to peacefully coexist with nature, but it was not the way of the white man's world. It wasn't an easy transition and her saving grace was Marian Merrick, Richard's sister. Marian lived in New York at the time and helped Ann adjust to a so-called civilized society. She had no relatives in this part of the country and it was doubtful she'd ever see her only brother again. Richard offered to bring him along, but he stayed behind with Ann's father. That was a long time ago. He'd be the chief by now.

Marian Merrick became Ann's mentor and friend, staying with her through the early days when Richard was away and the children were little. She helped Ann with the language and taught her how to live in the world of the white man. Marian made her home in Louisiana today and they hadn't seen each other in years. Ann and Richard talked about moving to New Orleans when he retired from the Army in a few months. They thought it might be nice to live where there was no snow when they grew older. She hoped it would be a main topic of discussion when Richard came home.

Ann looked into the fire and a faint smile crossed her lips. She was drifting off with her memories and she spoke softly when she told the story. She met Richard Merrick twenty-five years ago during a military campaign in what was now the Arizona Territory. The handsome young soldier had fallen instantly in love with the beautiful Apache girl and she was so taken with him that she thought of nothing else from the moment she laid eyes on him. Her father viewed Richard as a brave man. He was a white soldier in a hostile land, but he showed no fear. His love for Ann had driven him to try to convince the chief that his daughter would have a better life with him in the East. The old Indian listened in silence, his face expressionless as

Richard asked for the hand of his daughter and made the promises to take care of her. When Richard finished, the chief sent him away with a wave of his hand. The next day, the young officer returned to tender a more convincing argument as to why the princess should go away with him and discovered his prayers had been answered. The princess was packed and waiting for him. No further argument was necessary.

Parting of father and daughter was not emotional. She knew her father loved her even though he showed no sign of emotion as they stood face-to-face in the final good-bye. He told her the White Buffalo would walk with her and the Great Spirit would protect her on her journey. It was his way of telling her he asked for divine blessing. His expression was solemn, but there was great sorrow in his eyes when he told her to teach his grandchildren well. He wanted them to know who he was and he wanted them to remember they were Apache. It was the last time he'd see her. He'd never see his grandchildren.

The chief made the decision to release her because he loved her. He was a wise man. He recognized the signs of change as the white man invaded Indian land and he knew the future would bring hardship. She'd have an easier life with this soldier; this young man who, in peril of his own life, disregarded the dangers of a wild land and its people and asked unfalteringly for the daughter of an Apache chief. He was either a fool or a very brave man. In the eyes of her people, bravery was everything and Richard Merrick's bravery had been acknowledged. As Ann looked back on that time, she recalled her father's weathered face before she rode away with the soldier. The tear in his eye would not fall while she watched, but she never forgot that she had seen it. She didn't have to look back to know he stood there until she was out of sight and she knew he saw the White Buffalo walking with her. She thought about her father often, and her brother, wondering if they were still alive or if the white soldiers destroyed them and the rest of her people. They wouldn't have given up easily. They would have fought to keep their land. She knew Richard went back to the Arizona Territory and she knew he'd fought many battles with the Indians, but she never asked and he never volunteered to tell her where the Army sent him. It would have been unbearable to think he might have engaged her father and brother in battle. Richard would have done his job and they would have fought to the death to keep their home. It was better not to know.

She smiled, remembering how Richard tried so hard to contain his excitement the day they moved out of the Indian encampment and headed east. It wasn't until they were several miles away that Richard stopped and looked at her. She'd never forget the love in his eyes. He was a passionate man. The way he lived and the way he loved his wife and family throughout their marriage was proof of that. Although the Army kept him away a lot over the years, they managed to compile some glorious memories. When he was home, they made every minute together count. Ann said she was the luckiest woman on earth to have been blessed with such a wonderful husband. It was a shame the chief didn't know Richard and it made her sad to know her father would never meet his grandchildren. They knew who he was though. From the time they were babies, she told them about a great and wise Apache chief, their grandfather, and she told them about their uncle who followed in his father's footsteps. Whenever Ann told the story, Rose put down what she was doing to listen. It made her sad to think about the father who gave up his daughter out of love and for love. She never tired of hearing the story. Through the eyes of Richard and Ann Merrick, each looked the same to the other as the day they met all those years ago. For twenty-five years, the Indian Princess and the Soldier had an ongoing love affair.

It was 1851 when Ann traveled to the East with Richard. When they reached Washington, they were married. Shortly afterward, they moved to New York. He made good on his promise to her father, providing her with an education and a secure home. They had three children, John, Arthur and Rebecca. She was devastated when Arthur died in 1863 of influenza. Richard was her strength when they lost the little boy. Rebecca was now ten and there was never any doubt about her presence. Keeping up with her was a full-time job. John was away at college. Ann was quite proud of him. Whenever she talked about him, she stood very straight and tilted her head back. He'd be a lawyer and in accordance with his father's wishes, would join the Army. His future held a promising career as a lawyer and Army officer. The best news was, he'd be home in the summer.

In April, a letter arrived from the War Department by courier. Rose saw Ann's face as she watched the two uniformed men climb the front-porch steps, in no hurry to fulfill their heavy-hearted mission. Ann stood perfectly still with her hands clasped in front of her when she saw them coming and opened the door before they knocked. She didn't have to be told why they were there. All the years she was married to Richard, she'd been prepared for this eventuality and prayed it would never come. They handed her the envelope and stood at attention while she broke the wax presidential seal and read the short message. "It is with great sadness that the President of the United States of America regretfully informs you General Richard Garrison Merrick died in service of God and Country on the Twenty-Eighth Day of March, Eighteen Hundred and Seventy-Six." Ann folded the paper and replaced it in the envelope. She thanked the men for delivering the message. They slowly saluted, then turned and left. She stood with the front door open for several minutes. When she closed it, she showed no sign of breaking down. Resting her hand on the handle, she stared at the lace curtains covering the beveled-glass inset. She turned to Rose and calmly announced that General Merrick would not be coming home. That was it. Her husband of twenty-five years was dead. In a few weeks, he was due to retire from the military and they would have been able to spend the time together they'd waited to have for so many years. She hadn't even told him good-bye. Rose thought it strange that Ann didn't cry. Instead, she smiled peacefully. She felt the pain within her own heart for Ann and was overcome with sadness at the tragedy. She didn't know the man, but she felt the loss and cried. Ann was the wife of a military officer and conducted herself accordingly. He'd expect nothing less. Rose admired Ann's courage in the face of this devastating moment and wished she possessed the same kind of strength. That night, Ann excused herself early and there was no fireside talk. Rebecca had been in her room since her mother told her the news. When Rose went upstairs, Rebecca was asleep, but she heard the muffled sobbing when she passed Ann's bedroom door.

By June, the initial shock of General Merrick's death subsided and household activity returned to as close to normal as could be under the circumstances. Although Ann never outwardly showed her grief, she was quiet these days and Rose saw the sorrow in her eyes. The weather was warm and preparations were underway for the long-awaited homecoming of John Merrick. The colorful welcome-home sign Rebecca made a month earlier was hung above the porch and ribbon streamers fluttered from the railing. All she could talk about was seeing her brother again.

John Garrison Merrick returned home from school for summer holiday in July, 1876. He arrived while Rose was away on errands. When she returned to the house, she was unaware of the handsome, dark-haired man lounging on the porch swing. Certain that Ann was busy with the home-coming dinner and wouldn't catch her at being a tomboy, she secured the bag she was carrying in one arm, held up her skirt with the other hand, and bounded up the stone steps, two at a time. She was eighteen and a half and still more of a child than a woman. Most girls were already married by the time they were her age, many with a baby or two. John saw her walking up the street, her red hair catching the sun. He stopped the motion of the swing and watched her skip every other step in her assent to the porch, thinking her to be the most beautiful girl he'd ever laid eyes on. She let out a star-tled squeak of surprise when she noticed him on the swing and lost her bal-ance as she reached the top step. Her arms flailed out for something to grasp to keep herself from falling, and in the process, she dropped the pack-age. John's reflexes were instantaneous. He jumped forward and caught her as she was about to tumble backward down the stone steps.

By the time she managed to steady her footing, she realized the hand-some stranger had both arms around her waist. Her face was hot, and not from the summer sun. She knew she was blushing. She brushed the tou-sled hair from her face and tried to regain her composure. When he was sure her footing was secure, he let go of her and took a step back. He was still much too close. She stopped breathing. Her heart pounded so loud she was certain he must be able to hear it. He was breathtakingly handsome. His hair was dark brown and his eyes were steel-blue, probably like his father's. His skin was dark, like his mother's. She couldn't believe her own eyes. There was a strange light around him and she felt a kind of energy coming from him. She tried to say something, but nothing came out. The polite thing to do would be to thank him for saving her from certain death on the stone steps, but she couldn't speak. Some unseen, mischievous lep-rechaun must have tied her tongue in a knot when she wasn't paying atten-tion. It was most irritating. Surely, he must think her to be an idiot. He sensed her discomfort and saved her from total humiliation by making an exaggerated, sweeping bow. She laughed. When he stood up, he held out his hand and announced that he was John Merrick, and very pleased to meet her. She couldn't manage to get a word out, so she stuck out her hand. Without warning, he raised it to his lips and kissed it. His touch sent a ripple of shivers through her. He leaned forward. Hesitating close to her face for effect, he wiggled his eyebrows in an elfish expression and said,

"And you are — Rose? I'd know you anywhere." His comment surprised her further. Still unable to make a sound, she shook her head affirmatively. She felt silly.

Holding her hand, he went on to say his mother had written to him about the new boarder and although she told him Rose was pretty, she failed to describe her beauty with definitive accuracy. As he spoke, she noticed that he glanced several times at the front of her dress, a mint-green lawn, quite thin actually. Against Ann's continued strict admonition about the necessity of proper ladies wearing all appropriate undergarments, Rose occasionally still hid those mandatory items under her bed. When the weather was hot and humid as it was today, she didn't give a second thought to tossing them aside. At this moment, with John Merrick holding her hand, she suddenly remembered. This was one of those days. Standing here, with her outstretched hand in his, she was painfully aware that he had an unobstructed view of what she failed to properly cover with the infamous underwear. The lesson learned too late to remedy this time, she made a silent vow to never discard it again. His touch generated a feeling in her she'd never known before and she realized her nipples had become hard. Their outline pushed against the sheer linen material and she knew the reason for his devilish smile. She felt herself blush as red as her hair. As soon as he let go of her hand, she'd have to hide herself under the bed with the underwear and stay there until he went back to school in two months. She could never look him in the eye again from the embarrassment.

Her anxiety was clear and not wishing to cause her further discomfort, he released her hand and descended the steps to the sidewalk the same way she made her assent, two at a time. At the bottom, he scooped up the contents of her bag that went flying through the air and spilled all over the sidewalk when she lost her balance. By the time he finished picking up the scattered groceries and was beside her again at the front door, her embarrassment had diminished somewhat and she finally found her tongue. She thanked him for his gallant rescue and suggested they go inside for a glass of Ann's lemonade. She needed something to squelch the heat of the day, and although she couldn't tell him, the passion of the moment.

Rose was glad she decided not to hide under the bed after the front-porch incident. The summer flew by and she and John spent every possible moment together, their affection for one another growing stronger by the day. Evenings found them walking in the moonlight or sitting on the front-porch swing, holding hands and wishing on an occasional falling star. She never tired of hearing John talk of his plans to become a lawyer and she was fascinated by the things he was learning at the university. She admired him and wished she were as smart as he, but she was having trouble just learning the letters from Rebecca and correct manners from Ann. He was like a diamond, polished and sparkling. She felt rough and dull next to him, like a piece of coal. When she looked at him, she wondered what he saw in her, an uneducated Irish girl from a poor tribe of Gypsies. She couldn't even speak proper English. His speech was that of a gentleman, smooth and refined. She spoke with a thick brogue and much of the old-country vernacular. When she couldn't think of the right word to use in English, she'd switch in mid-stream of a sentence to Gaelic. Sometimes, John would roll on the ground in an exaggerated display of uncontrollable laughing hysteria when she talked. "Say that again, Rose. I love to hear you talk." Doing her best to keep a straight face, she'd stand over him with her arms folded, lips pursed and eyes narrowed, reprimanding his theatrics. "Now, tell me sir, whatever in God's Heaven could be so funny 'twould make you roll on the floor like a ravin' lunatic? Is't any way for a grown man to behave? Why, to look at you, a body would think you're touched in the head." He'd stop laughing, pretending to acknowledge he'd been properly called down and making his next comment sound as convincingly sincere as possible — "Eloquently put." He was never able to restrain himself for long and the way she said "tootched" made him burst into a roaring guffaw louder than the first round. He'd hold his stomach and draw his knees to his chest, rolling around again, laughing harder and louder and twisting his face into the most grotesque contortions he could arrange. She'd shake her finger at him sternly. "You ought to be 'shamed of yourself, John Merrick, makin' fun at a poor, helpless waif such as meself." At that point, he'd jump to his feet and pass his hand in front of himself in a sweeping gesture that implied he was wiping the laughter from his face. It took every ounce of control he could muster to replace the laughter with facetious sincerity when he tried to mimic her Irish accent. "Helpless? God knows I'd never laugh at a poor, helpless waif, but then, He also knows you are anythin' but helpless." She'd give an exasperated sniff and turn on her heel, but before she got one step away, he'd grab her, tickling her and pulling her to the floor with him. She always struggled to get away, scolding and pretending to be angry. Then, he'd make her laugh. She couldn't help but laugh. She scolded him again, feigning anger and trying to restrain her giggles at the same time. What would his mother say if she caught them in such a position? The question was pointless. She knew he didn't care. She also knew Ann observed their antics more than once and turned her head the other way.

When the play was over, the mood changed. It was during these special moments that he became serious. He'd brush the few wild strands of hair away from her face and stare into her eyes. "There is a secret behind your eyes, Rose Callahan. I don't know what it is and I won't ask, but someday, maybe you'll tell me about it." She wanted to tell him, but never had the courage. It would take a great deal of courage to tell him the story. Sometimes, she thought if she told him what happened to her in Ireland, it might ease the burden and put it out of her mind forever; a cleansing of the soul. On the other hand, he might think she was tarnished by that dreadful event and banish her from his sight. She couldn't bear the thought of him turning away because of something that happened so long ago, something not of her doing. Keeping the secret was punishment for a crime she didn't commit, but she couldn't tell. The story was better left untold, for the time being anyway. She wished he didn't see the shadow of that hidden secret. She'd tell him someday, when the time was right; someday, when they were older. She'd have to.

The last Saturday before John went back to school, they walked to a neighborhood park for a band concert. It was a perfect summer night, a night she'd never forget. They spread a blanket under a big tree near the raised gazebo shell. John leaned against the tree and Rose sat close to him, her head resting on his shoulder. Near the end of the concert, the band began playing a waltz. They danced in the grass and when the music stopped, they kept dancing, oblivious to people walking past. Voices faded in the distance as spectators left the concert and they were alone in the park. He was more serious than she'd ever seen him. He raised her hand to his lips and deposited a lingering kiss in the palm. Then, he held her hand to his chest. He whispered, "My heart is in your hands, Rose Callahan. Will you spend the rest of life with me?" She could hardly believe what he was saying. If she was not mistaken, he was asking her to marry him. She was dizzy, overcome with emotion, feeling as though his spirit reached out and embraced hers. A tear trickled down her cheek. He wiped it away and kissed the remnants of its track. "I didn't mean to make you cry. You don't have to answer tonight." She didn't have to think about the answer. She'd spent the entire summer thinking about the question and hoping he'd ask, but never expecting he would. Now that he had, there was no hesitation in her voice. "Yes, John. I'll spend the rest of life with you and when life is done, I'll be with you in Heaven." He smiled at her perception of eternity and her expectation of spending it with him. To seal the engagement, he gave her a single strand of pearls. He kissed her cheek many times before. It was different tonight. This time, when their lips touched, she felt the passion. His kiss sent sparks through her and she felt the exhilaration of her spirit celebrating, soaring to heights she never dreamed possible.

Sunday morning, Ann watched the two of them at breakfast. She recognized the silent messages they passed back and forth across the table with their eyes. Subtlety was not a strong point for either of them. John caught his mother looking at him with an expression that told him he might as well spill the beans. He stopped with a forkful of food halfway to his mouth when she smiled at him. They planned to make the announcement when he graduated, but this was as good a time as any to tell her. He put down his fork and stood up, raising his glass toward Rose and clearing his throat. After extolling her beauty and temperament, he told his family he'd found the love of his life. "I've asked Rose to be my wife, and she has accepted." Rebecca squealed and ran to each of them with a hug. She'd start planning the wedding right away. "Mother, may I be excused? There's so much to do?" They all laughed and Ann pointed to the empty place at the table. "I think the plans can wait until you finish your breakfast, Rebecca. I'm sure you'll have the entire event planned by dinner." Ann reached for Rose's hand. "I couldn't be happier. I only wish my husband was here to share in the good news." In the midst of the celebration, Rose felt a sadness. She wished her mother and father were here too. Maybe they were. She closed her eyes and imagined two people smiling at her; a lovely redhaired woman and a man whose face no longer bore any sign of grief. Somehow, she knew Annie and Joe Callahan were there, and Richard Merrick.

When the time came for John to leave for school, she promised to wait for him. It was an easy promise to make. She'd keep very busy until he came back. There was the wedding to plan, linens to be sewn, letters to write. She wouldn't have time to be lonely. He said he'd write every day. In the beginning, she wouldn't be able to tell him any private thoughts in her letters because Rebecca would have to help her write them. He'd have to use his imagination for the parts she wasn't able to put down on paper. She promised to practice her writing and in a while, she'd try to write one without Rebecca's help, to say those special, private things.

Monday morning, she went with him to the train. Saying good-bye was much more difficult than she imagined. With all the excitement and anticipation of his graduation, joining the Army, and wedding plans, she hadn't had time to think about him leaving. The impact of the forthcoming separation hit her while they stood talking on the depot platform. The blast of a whistle brought the reality of the moment into focus. As he was about to board the train, he took her in his arms and held her so tight she could hear his heart beating. He whispered, "I love you, Rose. I'll always be yours. Remember that during the long months ahead while we are apart." A sound of grating metal sent a chill through her when the engineer released the brake and the train began moving slowly forward. Billows of black smoke belched from the stack as the fireman fed shovelsful of coal to the engine furnace. John waited with her as long as he could. The train was rolling. He had to go. One last, quick kiss and he ran for the moving steps. The conductor reached down and gave him a hand up. He hung onto the metal handle and blew a kiss in her direction. She reached up her hand to catch the kiss from the wind. Once caught, she placed her hand with the kiss in it on her own lips. Walking along the platform beside the moving train, she waved back, blowing kisses to him until he disappeared inside the coach. She finally stopped when the train picked up speed and pulled out of the station. Now she felt the full brunt of his leaving, watching the train roll down the tracks further and further away until it was out of sight.

While he was away at school, John wrote often and she read the letters over and over. He came home for Christmas, but to her great disappointment, didn't return home in the summer. Anxious to get his schooling out of the way, he postponed the wedding and continued with classes throughout the summer months. That way, he'd graduate much earlier than originally planned. With his father gone, he had to complete his education and get on with his career. As soon as he received his degree, he'd be joining the Army. He assured her the extra time spent in school for an early degree would pay off in the end for both of them. She was disappointed, but she had to be patient and encourage his efforts. By the time he came home for Christmas the following year, wedding plans were in full swing again; Rebecca's plans at least. She'd made a guest list and planned the food and the music and the flowers... Lilacs if it was in the spring, roses for summer. It was a full-time project for her. John laughed at his little sister's enthusiasm and joked with her about the way she persisted until she came up with whatever information she needed to complete the current planning phase. He told her she'd make a grand lawyer. She told him to be the lawyer, she'd be the doctor. After the holidays, he was gone again. Back to school. The time with him went too fast and it hardly seemed he was there at all. For Rose, the months went by slowly. With each passing day, she missed him more. When she promised to wait for him, she had no idea how hard it would be, but wait she would.

SPRING – 1878

On Easter Sunday, Ann Merrick was taken ill. She'd been losing weight at an alarming rate over the past few months and suddenly collapsed. She used to be full of life and vitality, but she hadn't been the same since her husband's death nearly two years earlier. Despite a valiant effort to hide her grief, there was a sadness about her that was evident to anyone who'd seen it before. Part of her died with him. Rose recognized the look. She'd watched her father fade away when he could no longer bear the loss of his wife. Ann's health declined noticeably since she lost Richard. The will to live was gone. There'd been several episodes of illness where she took to her bed for days, and each time when she came downstairs after being sick, she looked weaker. This time, she didn't leave her bed and the prognosis for recovery was not good. Rose wrote to John asking him to come home, the urgency of her message bitterly clear. The picture he carried of her in his mind was one of a laughing imp. He'd never seen her in one serious moment since he met her, except the night he asked her to marry him, but when she opened the front door, the look on her face told him things were much worse than he expected. He had precious little time to say good-bye to his mother. That night, they sat by Ann's bed holding her hands. She never complained and she still managed to smile. Sitting there, watching the woman who had become a mother to her dying, Rose's thoughts went back to a night in an old tattered tent in Ireland. That night, she held the hand of a man who was dying of a broken heart. She recognized the look in Ann's eyes. The doctor said the disease was killing her. Maybe so, but Rose knew it was more than that. Ann was dying of a broken heart. She was waiting patiently to see Richard again. A few days later, Ann Merrick died. Rose didn't cry because she knew Ann welcomed death as the way to be with Richard. She felt an inner peace thinking about the Indian princess and the soldier embracing on the other side, in Heaven, as she imagined her father and mother reuniting when her father passed into the next world.

After his mother's funeral, John plunged into settling family affairs. A buyer was found in a matter of days and the boarding house was sold. One day, life was smooth sailing — happy. In the blink of an eye, it all fell apart. Life as Rose had known it at the Merrick house was over. John was only a few months from graduation and enlistment in the Army. He had to return to school as soon as possible. There was no time for intimacies. No time to talk about their plans for the future. No one spoke of the wedding that would have been only a few months off if things had gone according to plan. It would have to be postponed again, indefinitely this time. Of primary concern was Rebecca. She was thirteen and needed the guidance and nurturing of a woman. Rose couldn't take care of her alone and John had to finish school. They didn't have to think about it very long. There was only one thing to do. Rose would have to take Rebecca to her Aunt Marian in New Orleans. At least there, she'd have a loving home and the desperately needed support of family during this time of crisis. His aunt was a good woman and would take Rebecca in. She'd see to Rebecca's education and tend to her needs, and Rose would be there to help. ...but New Orleans was so far away. Not knowing what to expect was unnerving. Her life had been so organized and happy with the Merricks. With Ann gone, her sense of security and peace of mind had been violently disrupted and she felt the way she did when she left Ireland, afraid and uncertain of the future.

It was hard enough being in New York while John was away at school, but New Orleans was much further. She didn't know exactly how far it was, but she knew he wouldn't get home as often. When would they see each other again? The separation implied uncertainty. She was afraid. John tried to alleviate her fears by describing New Orleans as a lovely city, full of southern charm and mystique. She could learn to speak French there. The climate was mild and she'd have fewer colds in winter. No matter how careful she was, the cold weather always brought with it the abominable illness that affected her lungs and drained her strength. John said people were friendly in New Orleans. She'd like his Aunt Marian. She was a lot like his mother. He did his best to assure her the separation was only temporary. He was nearly finished with school and his military commission would soon be secured. He promised they'd set a wedding date and things would be better once he was situated with the Army and the family crisis was behind them. She said she understood. It had to be this way. She owed it to Ann to take care of Rebecca while John went back to school. Besides, there wasn't anyone else. She'd make the move as easy as possible for John and Rebecca and be brave for their sakes, but in her heart, she wasn't nearly as brave as John thought she was. She couldn't let him know she was afraid. It was selfish to think of herself at a time like this. He had enough to worry about. She put her fears aside and committed to taking Rebecca to New Orleans and waiting for John there, no matter how long it took. The sooner they left, the sooner they'd be together.

One week later, the girls boarded a train in New York and once again, she found herself saying good-bye to John Merrick. She closed her eyes to hold back the tears when he kissed her. He said words of comfort, but it didn't make the parting any easier. Her heart was breaking and when his arms tightened around her, she concentrated on the feeling of being close to him. She'd never forget his touch, strong, but gentle at the same time. If only she had some of Ann's courage. He held her and whispered the words she lived for, "Remember, I love you Rose. I'll always be yours." In the past when he said them, they warmed her heart. This time, they made her shiver. He was doing his best to lessen her anxiety, but his efforts were in vain. There was a shadow over them. She choked back the tears and smiled. A sense of foreboding was building; a feeling of loss and sadness moving in around her.

Chills ran up her spine and she forced herself to board the train. It took all the willpower she had to climb the steps behind Rebecca. As soon as they were in their seats, the train began pulling away from the station and she watched him wave good-bye from the platform. He faded in the distance, but she'd never forget the way he looked that day. A terrible thought engulfed her. What if she never saw him again? She couldn't remember telling him she loved him. She did love him, but try as she would, she couldn't recall saying the words. She must have said it. She just couldn't remember when. Surely, he knew. He had to know. She closed her eyes and imprinted his face on her mind. It would be a long time until she saw him again. Maybe never. That was silly. Of course she'd see him again. It was only the present circumstances that made her feel this way. Everything happened so fast; Ann's death and having to resolve family matters in a hurry, postponing the wedding for the second time, and now, John going back to school and she to New Orleans, to a place she didn't know, to live with someone she didn't know. They hadn't any time to talk about what came next. Of necessity, they were going in opposite directions at the time when they should be preparing to come together. It was only temporary though. He promised. But what if something happened to keep them apart? What if he changed his mind? Events of the past few weeks caught up to her. She was tired and worried, unable to rid herself of the uneasiness about this separation. She had to stop allowing those ideas into her head. She knew he'd come for her as soon as he could. He had to finish school and she had to take Rebecca to Marian's. Then, they'd be married and live happily ever after. She always loved that fairy-tale ending. There was no logical explanation for the way she felt, but she couldn't block out the terrifying thought that he was gone out of her life. It was like a black cloud overhead, a subtle prediction of ominous events to come and an overshadowing of the plans they'd made. They were all trying to recover from the tragedy of losing Ann, but it was more than that. Somehow, she knew her life was about to change — forever.

She turned to Rebecca. The little girl was looking out the window and sniffling. Rose took Rebecca's hand. "Don't cry, Pixie. Everythin' will be alright. I promise." She wasn't sure she could make such a promise, but it was up to her to comfort the one whose fear of what lay ahead was greater than her own. They watched the city pass by as the train rolled into the country, holding tightly to one another, each silently wondering what the future held.

Settling into Marian's house was easy. Fears of never seeing John again disappeared and after a few months, Rebecca announced one morning at breakfast that she was working on the wedding plans set aside in New York when her mother died. A proper mourning time had been observed and she believed her mother would want them to go ahead with the wedding. Rose should write to John and tell him to let her know when he could come home. If it was going to be at Christmas, they could get married then.

No need to wait for Spring. The date would be set as soon as he wrote back. Rose watched Rebecca talk, determining the mourning of her mother's passing was over and their lives should return to normal. She was much less animated when she talked these days. The Pixie was no longer a little girl. Losing her father had been hard, but her mother's death was devastating. At the funeral, she looked like a grown woman in her long, black dress and her hair piled on top of her head the way Ann always wore hers. She wore her mother's hat with the veil across her face, the same veil her mother had worn at her father's funeral, and she maintained the same composure Ann showed the day she buried her husband. No tears were shed in public. Rebecca inherited her mother's strength of character and self-restraint, grieving in private. The only time Rose saw her cry was on the train when they left New York and even then, she controlled it. She was a little girl who, by her own decision, grew up overnight. She wasn't as boisterous and excited about planning the wedding as she had been in the beginning. Everything was orderly and precise this time. Unlike the formal event originally planned, the wedding would now be small and informal and Aunt Marian would provide the list of guests to attend a quiet ceremony. Rebecca convinced them it was the right thing to do and the matter was settled. Rose wrote the letter. As soon as she received an answer from John, she'd know the date of her wedding. Maybe Christmas was a good time because once he joined the Army, there was no telling when he'd be able to come home again and she didn't want to wait any longer. Christmas this year would be a season of mixed emotions.

Rose fell in love with New Orleans. It was a charmed place with its mixture of cultures. In particular, she thought the French influence was romantic. Everything about it had an air of romance and mystique exactly the way John described it. The architecture was fascinating. The food was wonderful and spicy. She loved the way people spoke. She could hardly wait until he came home for Christmas so she could show him around the city. It was a place they might want to live one day. Of course, the Army would decide where they lived for awhile, but they could come back later.

John's aunt made her feel welcome and she found comfort once more in a Merrick home. Marian Merrick was the sister of John's father and she had those magnetic, steel-blue Merrick eyes and same warm smile. Although she never married, she was far from being a typical old maid. She was about Ann's age and still very pretty, and fun to be with. She reminded Rose a lot of Ann. They could have been sisters rather than sisters-in-law.

She wondered why Marian had never been married. A picture of a young man on Marian's vanity probably held the answer to that question. When she gave Rose a tour of the house, she identified the people in all the other pictures, but never mentioned the man in the silver frame. By the way she passed by the photograph without a word, Rose knew it was a special picture, a very private matter. She imagined a romantic, sad secret was attached to him. He was probably the reason Marian moved to New Orleans. She didn't ask about him and Marian never offered to tell the story. There were some secrets you never shared with anyone.

Alone in a strange city, she was grateful for Marian's kind offer to live with her until John finished school and got situated with the Army. Even after the wedding, she could stay on if John had to be away. It seemed the Merrick family was always coming to her rescue. She was given the attic apartment with its sloped ceiling and cushioned window seat in the alcove. From that seat, she had a bird's-eye view of the whole neighborhood. In the evening, the sweet fragrance of jasmine drifted up to her and she silently thanked whoever planted it beneath her window. It was a cozy place, up near the tree tops, her own small world where she could be alone with her thoughts of John. She fantasized about their future, wondering what her wedding dress would be like when Marian finished sewing it; what their children would look like. She wished the fulfillment of those dreams was not so far off. She'd have to be patient. Ah, patience. Ann always said it was a sign of character. She whispered the word over and over to herself, hoping it might sink in. "Patience, Rose. Patience."

With Marian's introduction, she acquired work as a hostess at the distinctive Cordon Bleu Playhouse in the heart of the French Quarter. The whitewashed exterior with its white and gold awning gave the impression that royalty resided within. Inside, sky-blue velvet draperies and white French provincial furniture trimmed with gold presented an even greater sense of romance and mystique. Expensive paintings of early renaissance nymphs and nudes were displayed on every wall. In other circumstances, they might have been offensive to certain conservative ladies. Here, they were not only accepted, but admired by all who attended the performance. When you entered the place, you got the feeling you just walked from New Orleans into some exotic, old-world castle straight into French aristocracy, and you half expected to see Marie Antoinette herself walk through the door wearing a foot-high, ringlet wig and satin-brocade gown.

Working at the theatre, all she had to do was smile and look pretty. That was easy enough. At twenty, she was a beauty. She loved to talk to people and soon captured the attention, if not the hearts, of quite a few regular customers. The names of performers displayed on the marquis were not the only names patrons became familiar with at the Cordon Bleu. Actors and musicians were not the only reason some patrons frequented the establishment. She became an attraction in her own right. Her red hair and emerald eyes drew people like a magnet, especially the gentlemen. They loved her Irish brogue and contagious laugh. When she laughed, everyone laughed. She enjoyed the stage productions. She loved music and was attracted to theatre life. It was a place where exciting people gathered. She imagined herself on stage, singing to an appreciative audience and taking a bow when the applause erupted. Whether she ever got to perform or not, it was where she belonged.

NEW ORLEANS – SPRING, 1881

She'd been in New Orleans three years. John was out of school and in the Army, an officer and military lawyer. His handling of government cases had already made an impressive mark in Washington. She hoped General Merrick was looking down from Heaven to see that his son had far exceeded his expectations. The waiting was nearly over. John was coming home at the end of summer this year — for the wedding. Plans had been made and postponed so many times she couldn't remember the dates they'd set and canceled, but after all the delays, they were finally going to be married. Marian had worked on Rose's wedding dress for a long time, finishing what Ann started four and a half years ago and creating a masterpiece with needle and thread. She even managed to find several yards of Irish lace. It was so beautiful that Rose cried every time she looked at it and she wondered what John would think when he saw her wearing it on their wedding day. She never understood why so many blessings had been bestowed on her. She was truly blessed and she reminded herself of it every day. The Merrick family had been a godsend. First, Ann and Rebecca, John. Now, Marian. She had a home and family and work at the theatre to help pass the time. In a few weeks, she'd be married. Life was complete — perfect. She had everything. At night when she said her prayers, she gave thanks and never asked for anything for herself, only that God watch over her family and keep John safe. She'd never be so ungrateful as to ask for anything else as long as she lived. Anticipation of the long-awaited reunion kept her awake hours after Marian and Rebecca went to bed. Funny, how she never felt the loss of sleep. When she finally drifted off, she dreamed about him. Just as in the old Irish fairy tales, the handsome prince and his lady would live happily ever after.

This past year, he didn't come home for Christmas. She hadn't seen him in more than a year and he'd be surprised at what she'd learned. Marian picked up where Ann left off with Rose's education and training in social graces. Ann laid the foundation, but Marian added the polish. She'd come a long way. From a caterpillar to a butterfly. That's how Ann said it would be. She had become a real lady. She didn't run up the steps two at a time anymore, and she never hid her underwear under the bed these days. She smiled sometimes when she resisted the urge to do both. She could hardly wait to see him. When he didn't come home for Christmas, she experienced a twinge of anxiety and the thought occurred to her that maybe he'd changed his mind. No, he wouldn't change his mind. Not now. Not after all this time. She never doubted he'd keep his promise. She just had to be patient a little longer. A few more weeks and she'd be his wife.

Working at the playhouse provided a diversion from missing John and helped pass the time. She was grateful for Marian's intervention in helping her get the job. For an uneducated immigrant with no apparent skills or aptitudes, she was fortunate to have found work that paid as well as it did. Without Marian, she might have been a scrub maid. She liked the theatre. The atmosphere was so alive and fun. She was happy there. She even liked the man she worked for. He spoke with a most unusual accent that included what sounded like a clearing of his throat and made everything he said funny. He made her laugh. He was short, about five feet tall, and considerably overweight for his height. His face was always red, as if he'd been sitting in the hot sun all day with no umbrella. Although she concentrated on his good points, she was never able to say he was the least bit attractive. She tried to be kind in the way she thought of him, but he was, in truth, the homeliest man she'd ever seen. The oddest thing about him was his beard. It was not an ordinary beard. It reached his chest. In and of itself, the beard wouldn't have been so strange but for the fact his head was completely bald. She couldn't help wonder how he managed to grow that thing from his chin when he had no hair on the place he needed it most. He wheezed a lot and was constantly wiping perspiration from his face with a handkerchief. She estimated his age to be somewhere around fifty, but she couldn't be sure. She liked him well enough and meant no disrespect by the way she viewed him, but she did think he looked rather like a troll. He treated her very well, and rightly so. After all, she drew nearly as many customers to his establishment as did the entertainment. Customers liked her. She gave each one special attention when she greeted them at the door. She inherited the gift of storytelling from her father, amusing anyone who wanted to listen with her light-hearted, fairy-tale style humor, and they all listened. She had a good life here. Except for missing John, she was quite content.

One evening, the troll took her aside. Usually friendly and talkative, he seemed exceptionally nervous. He was sweating more than usual. When she asked if he was ill, he said his health was fine and thanked her for asking, but kept looking at the ground while he talked, deliberately avoiding having to look her in the eye. Patting his forehead with the handkerchief, he told her he'd been asked to extend a personal invitation. A prominent politician had seen her and inquired as to her availability to attend a political function with him. The troll looked at her only briefly, then directed his gaze back to the floor. He smiled sheepishly and said he would consider it a personal favor if she'd accept the invitation. The politician was a valued customer, one whose business he'd like to keep. It would be a shame if the man should choose to make the establishment of a competitor up the street the regular dinner place for himself and his associates. That could easily happen in the event he became displeased for any reason with the service at the Cordon Bleu. If she would consent to accompany this gentleman to the party, it might ensure his continued patronage. She watched him closely. He was stuttering and tripping over his words.

She knew he catered to gentlemen of wealth and political power. They were at the theatre all the time. It was no secret they used it as a place to solicit votes and conspire against their opponents. That kind always received preferential treatment as guests of the house and they never paid for anything. They took advantage of their social and political positions to get the best tables near the stage and free dinners. They indulged in good whiskey and high-priced Cuban cigars at the owner's expense. That bothered her. She thought it unfair to the regular, paying customers. If it were up to her, she'd just as soon see them go somewhere else. She didn't understand why they weren't asked to pay. The owner called them valued patrons, but in truth, they were nothing more than thieves and freeloaders.

Imposing on his generosity and hospitality, they cost him a goodly sum every time they set foot in the place. It didn't make sense. They arrived in fancy carriages wearing expensive clothes and silk hats and diamond pins in their ties. Outward appearances implied money and affluence, but with all the material elements of their makeup, they weren't comfortable. They were afraid of something, looking around like rats, nervous and ever-vigilant lest the cat sneak up from behind and put an end to them. A sign of men with enemies, they traveled in the company of armed bodyguards. She thought it must be awful to always be looking over your shoulder like that. There was more to it than she wanted to know.

She spoke to the troll. Why didn't the gentleman ask her? Politicians were never at a loss for words. Certainly, he could have made his own introduction. The troll laughed nervously, sweating more than ever. His answer was lame, but she accepted it. Considering the circumstances, it seemed he'd been put in an awkward position as the messenger and she decided not to make it any more difficult for him. Despite her opinion of politicians in general, she was flattered that such an affluent person would request the pleasure of her company to a formal event. She'd never been to a fancy party. It might be fun. As the wife of an Army officer, there'd be lots of parties to attend. It couldn't hurt to practice her etiquette by going to this one. She accepted the invitation and the troll breathed an obvious sigh of relief.

The next day, Marian began work on a black velvet evening gown. Next to her wedding dress, this one would be the prettiest dress she ever owned. Marian did it again, created another work of art with her needle. Rose stood on a stool in front of the mirror while Marian pinned the hem. She stared at the reflection of the woman in the mirror. She'd changed a lot in a year and the person looking back at her was definitely a woman. She brushed away a tear. If only Joe Callahan could see his ragged little Gypsy girl now. She'd grown up since the day she first saw herself in Ann Merrick's mirror, the day she donned the dove-gray dress and hid her corselet under the bed. She smiled remembering that morning and how she hadn't fooled Ann about the missing underthings. It seemed like a lifetime ago that she left Ireland in search of a dream and found herself in a new country, in the home of an angel. The image in the mirror was proof of the dream come true. She owed it all to Ann's patience and perseverance, and Marian's polishing. She missed Ann. She wondered if her own mother met Ann in Heaven, sure that Annie Callahan would have thanked Ann Merrick for the kindness she extended to her daughter. Rose didn't have a chance to repay Ann for all she'd done, but Ann never expected payment. Her reward was seeing Rose's life change.

During the days leading up to the party, Rose had some second thoughts about going. If she really wanted to, she could think of a way to back out gracefully. She could always get sick. She wondered what John would think if he knew she was going to a party with another man. It wasn't exactly a personal engagement. It was really a business arrangement for the benefit of her employer. A favor. She saw nothing wrong in it and was sure John would not object. Besides, the gentleman probably felt awkward without a wife to accompany him to the formal event. Of course, she assumed he had no wife. Most likely, he was homely and bashful and unable to acquire a wife, or perhaps he was a widower. Otherwise, why would he ask someone to speak for him? Poor man. Outside the political arena, he might be quite shy. She was happy to keep him company. With a mental picture of the man who'd come to call, she knew she had to be able to control herself from any reaction to his appalling appearance. He was probably downright ugly, but she wouldn't let on that she thought so. She'd concentrate on his positive features, his education and political expertise, his... whatever else she could find to take her mind off his ugliness.

The evening of the party, entirely prepared as she was for an absolute toad of a man to call for her, she was pleasantly surprised to discover the gentleman was considerably younger than she expected and quite handsome. He was impeccably dressed in formal attire, complete with silk hat and diamond tie pin. Although pleasing to the eye, his appearance fit exactly the general pattern of dressing in common with others of his social breed, a group all cast from the same mold and lacking individual originality. They used the same tailors and bought their shoes from the same haberdashery. Like others of his billet, he was a stereotyped politician. Her evaluation of his appearance was interrupted and she lost her train of thought. He was offering a bouquet of roses. What a lovely surprise! The flowers distracted her from the assessment of her escort. She took the roses and asked Rebecca to draw a vase of water. She could tell by the way he looked at her that he was pleased. Black velvet turned out to be the perfect choice in material for the dress. She thought he was charming when he told her she'd be the most beautiful woman at the party. He had no doubt that he would be the envy of every man there. A few years earlier, she would have blushed at such profuse flattery. Perhaps, this evening wouldn't be so bad after all. With any luck, he might even be a reasonably good dancer. That would certainly be a bonus. She liked to dance. Ann and Marian coached her well. She smiled and gracefully accepted the compliments without blushing. On her way out the door, Marian winked and Rose tried not to laugh. He offered his arm and they walked to a very expensive-looking carriage, fully equipped with enclosed canopy and a white-gloved driver. She was impressed. Her comfort had been provided for in a most stylish manner.

He was right. At the party, she was the object of every man's attention. She was dazzling in the black velvet gown, her red hair piled on her head and held in place by two sparkling, black-beaded combs. No one guessed she was a simple theatre hostess. She looked more like a star. She was a star. She'd come a long way since the day she climbed the stone steps to Merrick's Boarding House in her shabby, moth-eaten coat, a half-frozen ragamuffin with holes in her stockings. If not for the kindness of an angel, she'd have died that day. She'd never forget the angel, Ann Merrick. Her father would be proud of her. She'd done well with the handful of coins in the velvet bag.

She had a wonderful time at the party. It was attended by glamorous, exciting people. No one asked what she did. They just assumed she was an important lady. When the party was over, the politician asked if she would mind if he stopped for a short meeting with a business associate on the way home. It was late. Past midnight. An odd time to discuss business. The gentlemen at the party kept her dancing all night. She was tired and her feet hurt. She would have preferred to go directly home and take her shoes off. Marian would be waiting up to hear all about the party. He assured her the meeting would be brief. It was quite important he attend to a business matter tonight that really could not be held off until the next day. Rose had no reason to doubt his story. After all, he was obviously a very important man. She'd overheard conversations at the party in which he was the topic of discussion. He was a well-respected, upstanding pillar of the community. People actually stood in line to speak with him. He probably had meetings every night of the week because there simply were not enough hours in his days to accomplish everything. She failed to recognize his nervousness. He was pressuring her, trying much too hard to elaborate on his reasons for having to go to the meeting tonight, and repeatedly stressing that it couldn't wait until tomorrow. She missed the warning signs. She had no objection to the detour so long as it would be brief. An hour one way or the other wouldn't matter. She'd sleep late tomorrow morning.

The ride was taking a long time and she became uneasy as the carriage drove through a deserted part of the city. She questioned him. It seemed like an awfully long way to go. It was after midnight. Surely, there was a better place to conduct business at this hour. In truth, it was a strange time to conduct business at all. He tried to convince her it was a matter of great urgency and begged her indulgence. Her anxiety increased when the driver stopped in front of a dilapidated hotel. The street was deserted. Not a soul in sight. She didn't like the feeling of the old neighborhood. They should be in the financial district or somewhere near City Hall, any other place more conducive to transacting business. Surely, he associated with more sophisticated elements of society than were found here and she started to question him again. Then, her thoughts took a different direction. He was a politician and it was well-known that politicians did things that defied logic and common sense. He probably had his reasons for coming here even if she didn't understand what they were.

He didn't give her time to think. Before she realized his absence from the carriage, he was out of it and standing beside her. He opened the door and offered his hand to help her out. She kept her hands folded on her lap. It was obvious she was worried. Taking sufficient notice of her furrowed brow as she looked around, he pretended not to see her concerned expression. He smiled and asked if she would join him in the hotel. A red flag waved in front of her eyes. Something told her to stay right where she was. She declined his invitation, saying she'd stay with the driver. He had to come up with a convincing argument fast. Ordinarily, he'd have no trouble with persuasion. He was a politician and quick response was a practiced reflex. This was a different kind of pressure than he was used to, but a legitimate reason was quickly conjured up. Prevailing on her sense of self-preservation, he assured her that her safety was his only concern. It was not prudent for her to remain in the carriage at night in this neighborhood. The driver was armed and would take care of himself while he waited outside. However, he could not, in good conscience, go inside and leave her in the carriage knowing she was vulnerable to a possible attack by ruffians and criminals in the street at this hour. He'd never forgive himself if any harm came to her. As a gentleman with only her welfare and best interests in mind, he must insist she allow him to protect her. His argument was well-taken. All the way through the neighborhood, she'd been considering the possibility of such an attack. In fact, she was surprised it hadn't already happened. She studied the man's face. He was still smiling and his concern appeared to be genuine enough. She surveyed the dimly-lit street again. It looked empty, but there was no telling what kind of fiends or murderers might be lurking in the shadows. Her imagination got the best of her. She looked back at his imploring eyes. Should she take her chances with the invisible fiends and murderers or go inside the building with him? He certainly looked a lot safer than the street and he was very persuasive. Perhaps she was being overly suspicious, but she wasn't sure the inside of the old hotel was any better than the seemingly deserted street. Against her better judgment, she agreed to go inside, concluding it was safer than sitting outside in a carriage after midnight.

Entering the hotel, his nervousness escalated. She threw him off balance when she asked if he was worried about something. A warning! He said, "No" — three times. She stopped walking to look around the foyer. It'd been some time since the last cleaning. The walls were dingy and the place smelled like mildew and urine. She wrinkled her nose at the unpleasant odors. When he knew she was having second thoughts about going any further, he nudged her forward, none too gently. She pulled back, indicating he was squeezing her arm too tight. His smile was forced and nervous and his speech became more animated as he hurried her past the desk clerk. She thought it strange that the man had his nose stuck in a book and didn't look up as they passed him. She asked another question. How long would this take? Absentmindedly, he repeated his answer three times as he did earlier. For the second time, she complained he was hurting her arm. He apologized, but didn't let go, still guiding her forward up the stairs to the second floor, and then, the third. She asked again. Why so far? Was there no available room on the first floor at this time of night? The more she talked, the more agitated he became. The little voice inside her was telling her to change her mind, to insist on waiting downstairs, but she didn't say anything. She was being warned of impending danger and still kept moving on upstairs with him. She ignored the warning and brushed away the feeling that there was, indeed, danger in this place. She was being silly. It was nothing.

On the third floor, her uneasiness increased when she discovered he had a key to one of the rooms. She questioned him on her observation. Where did he get the key? He hadn't stopped at the desk downstairs. He mumbled some inaudible response and ignored her when she asked again, saying she didn't hear his answer. She noticed his hand shaking as he tried to insert the key. Inside the room, there was no business associate waiting. They were alone. He was notably uncomfortable with her questions and she decided there was something wrong. She told him she was leaving and would be downstairs. She preferred to wait there until he was finished with his meeting. When she started out the door, he closed it, pleading with her to stay and saying he hadn't meant to be rude. It had been a long day and he was tired. She stiffened. Immediately, he realized his actions in closing the door made her defensive. In order to make it appear he was not holding her against her will, he moved away from the door, indicating she was free to go if she wanted to. He apologized once more, saying she was correct. He was distressed about the meeting. He was not a convincing liar and she became more apprehensive as the minutes passed. The small voice was there again. She felt a tugging at her arm, but no one was there. A sense of urgency permeated the room. Something was telling her to listen to the warnings. She should run away, now!

She asked where his associate was and, for the third time, why the meeting was being held in a hotel room rather than an office. Why on the third floor of an old hotel, moreover, in such a bad part of the city? His answer was ready, but his attempt at appearing calm was unsuccessful. She listened carefully as he explained the subject matter of this conference was highly confidential and required the utmost privacy. His smile was unnatural and strained. He was concentrating too hard on being calm and he was not in control as he would have her believe. He was becoming steadily more agitated. She asked when he expected the other party to arrive. A clear warning! A slip of the tongue. He didn't think before he spoke. "They'll be along shortly." She blurted out, "They? Who are they?" Her body went rigid. Impending danger was closer, rapidly moving in around her. The warning signal was louder, like a firebell, incessantly clanging.

She was near the door. All she had to do was turn the handle and run out. With each second she remained here talking to him, she was losing ground. The firebell clanged in her head, louder. Then, a voice — "Get out!" She kept talking. It was her understanding he was to meet one person. That's what he said — a brief meeting with "a" business associate, not two. Her alarm was apparent and he recognized it. Hope for escape diminished. She had to think, try to mask her fear. She demanded he take her home immediately. Marian was waiting up and would be worried. His expression changed. The smile was gone and the look in his eyes frightened her. He lied to her and brought her here under false pretenses. The danger was clear. She had to get away. She stepped back and reached for the door. Too late! He locked his hand around her wrist and twisted her arm. At that moment, the door opened and two men entered the room. They realized what was happening and closed the door quickly, turning the lock. She pulled her arm away and reached for the knob. Even if she reached it, she couldn't get out. It was locked. She was panicking.

If there was any chance to get away, she had to keep her wits about her. She glanced at the window. They were on the third floor. If she jumped, she might survive the broken glass, but she'd break her neck for sure. He stepped between her and the door. The escape route was completely blocked. She demanded that he allow her to leave. He told her to calm down. One of the other men intervened. She knew the second one felt he had to get the situation under control before she started screaming. She should have screamed. He smiled and spoke softly, stepping closer and saying there was no need to be alarmed. They had simply come to discuss business and were delighted she agreed to join them. They watched her at the party and were quite taken by her beauty. He took her arm and pointed to the table. Would she like a glass of brandy to calm her nerves? He repeated there was absolutely no cause for alarm. He was guiding her toward the table, his attempt to calm her only succeeding in heightening her fear. She knew exactly why they were here and why he tricked her into coming. She had to get out of the room. Perhaps she could beat them at their own game. She smiled and thanked him for the invitation, but she really didn't care for the taste of brandy and she knew they'd prefer to transact their business privately. It was no inconvenience for her to wait downstairs until they concluded their meeting.

She made another move toward the door and the one she'd come with grabbed her and wheeled her around. She tried to free herself, but his grip tightened around her arm. He was hurting her. She struggled and he shook her, bumping her head against the wall. She tried to focus on his face, but the crack on her head made her dizzy. He was speaking, but she couldn't hear what he was saying. Panic overtook her ability to negotiate for release and everything became a blur. She felt like she was drowning. He told her to listen to what he was saying. He was telling her to be quiet. She began screaming and fighting frantically to get away from him. She kicked at him and the pointed toe of her shoe found its mark dead center on his shinbone. He yowled in pain and let her go, swearing at her. He was angry now. He pushed her backward toward the bed and she stumbled, trying to stay on her feet. She opened her mouth to scream again and he slapped her so hard the blow sent her sprawling onto the bed. Her head was reeling. She scrambled to the other side. It was no use. They were all around her, laughing. The next time she opened her mouth to scream, a hand closed over it. She lost her balance and fell back on the bed. Before she knew what happened, he was on top of her, straddling her, his weight preventing her from catching her breath. He held her down tight while she continued to fight. The wind had been knocked out of her and she was smothering. His knees were pushing her arms to her sides and she couldn't move. She saw a glint of steel and realized he had a knife. He held it to her throat and took his other hand off her mouth. She stopped fighting and felt the blade cut into her skin. A warm trickle of blood ran down her neck onto the bed and she started to cry. He laid the blade against her throat again. He spoke slowly and deliberately. If she made another sound, it would be her last. The next cut would be deep. The voice which earlier had been so complimentary and pleasant now had a demonic flatness to it, an ominous monotone. His words painted an ugly picture and left her with no doubt as to his intentions. She'd be dead, but they would have their way with her. It made no difference to them if she chose to be a corpse. The choice was hers. Dead or alive, her fate for the night was sealed. She could put up a fight and die, or she could go along with them and have some fun. Either way, they'd have their fun. The other two laughed. She heard the clink of glasses and smelled whiskey. There was no escape. Nothing she said would buy her freedom.

In a final, frantic effort to convince her captors to let her go, she told them she'd report the incident to the police and they'd all be arrested. The threat drew another round of laughter. She realized how ridiculous it sounded. No one would believe her. They'd see to that. They were upstanding members of the community, businessmen and politicians who commanded a great deal of respect. They had wives and children and position in society. Any charges she might levy against them would be dismissed as frivolous. She couldn't prove a thing. They each had twenty witnesses who would testify as to their whereabouts tonight, none of whom would place them in this room. It was more likely she'd be accused of some crime that could very possibly result in her incarceration. An accusation by any one of them that she was guilty of some petty theft would be entirely believable by the authorities. She could go to jail. Their reputations were impeccable, their credibility solid gold. She was a hostess. They asked, didn't she understand the implication of her line of work? Most "hostesses" were prostitutes, pure and simple. That was a fact of life where she worked and everyone who frequented the Cordon Bleu knew it. Wasn't that the reason she accepted the invitation to attend a party with a man she'd never met? She was here. Why else did she allow herself to be brought to this room? She hadn't been carried here bound and gagged. She walked up the stairs on her own two feet. She'd be hard-pressed to convince anyone she didn't know what she was getting into. A dingy hotel on the wrong side of town; a room on the third floor with a perfect stranger — with three strangers? How much money did she expect to get from them anyway? She was horrified. The idea never crossed her mind. They were wrong. That wasn't the reason she came. They had to listen. She wasn't a prostitute and she didn't want their money. She just wanted to go home and forget the whole thing ever happened. If they'd let her go, she promised not to tell a soul. It was all a terrible misunderstanding. She agreed to attend the party with this man as a favor to her employer, no other reason. She was only trying to help. What an absolutely cruel turn of fate. She suddenly realized every word they said was true. The desk clerk had seen her walk up the stairs of her own free will. He saw all of them, but he'd never tell the truth. The money they paid him would guaranty that. She had no defense. The reality of the situation was crystal clear. She wouldn't be allowed to leave until they did what they came to do. Maybe, in the end, they'd kill her anyway. Even if she lived through it, filing a complaint with the constable would not only be useless but, quite possibly, dangerous for her.

Her thoughts were violently interrupted. He was strong and he moved fast. He rolled her onto her stomach and shoved his hand down the back of her dress, ripping it and pulling it open. The beaded buttons Marian had so painstakingly sewn on went flying in every direction and clinked against the walls. Her skin was exposed and she shivered. They laughed again. He whispered in her ear that she'd be warm soon. She turned her head and pushed at him. His hand slammed the back of her head and buried her face in a pillow. She panicked. She was suffocating and frantically fought for a breath. She felt the cold blade against her skin as he cut away the lace next to her body. She had to breathe. He removed his hand from her head to release her face from the pillow and she gulped in the air. All that mattered was getting a breath. As soon as the air in her lungs was replenished, she realized she was completely naked. She fell back down, her face buried in the pillow. Dead silence. They were all staring at her naked body. One of them pulled the combs from her hair and let it spill over the bed. Suddenly, his hand was between her legs. He pushed them apart and her head began to spin. She was sixteen — Ireland. The horrible memory made her instantly sick. How could it be happening again? She fought harder. She had to fight even if it meant death. She was not afraid to die and she'd rather die than suffer the indignant torture of rape again. She was no match for his strength. Both hands on her hips, he pulled her back against him hard. She started to cry and begged him to kill her. He laughed and said he changed his mind. He much preferred a warm body to a cold one. The others concurred and glasses clinked together in unanimous agreement. Before she could get another breath, he lifted her off the bed on her knees. The realization of what was about to happen gave her strength. She pushed and kicked at him and he lost his hold on her. In one second he had her again, pulling her back so hard she heard her neck snap. He didn't wait this time. She cried out in pain, drawing a round of applause from the other two men. Her reaction only served to stimulate his excitement and he pushed harder. The others cheered him on as he grunted like a pig in the throes of animal pleasure. Her crying had no affect and he didn't stop until he was satisfied. When he was finished, he pushed her away. She rolled into a fetal position and lay in a crumpled heap, her hair falling across her face and cascading over the side of the bed. Before she could catch her breath, the second man took his turn, rougher than the first, then the last. It seemed like it went on for hours. They were beastly, perverted men, these law-abiding, upstanding pillars of society, having no pity as they raped and brutalized her. It was the ultimate degradation. The pain was unbearable and somewhere during the assault, she mercifully lost consciousness. When they were done, she was like a limp rag doll.

She was awake. She couldn't let them know. She was cold, but tried not to shiver. She kept her eyes closed, listening to them talking and laughing as they drank more whiskey. It was the same laughter she heard from two men at the edge of the bog all those years ago. These were the same kind of men. She couldn't cry. If she did, they'd know she was awake. She had to be still. She felt as though she were deep in a cave. The voices seemed far away, like echoes in a canyon. She tried to hear what they were saying. The door opened and closed. Were they leaving? Not daring to look and too weak to move, she lapsed into benevolent sleep.

For the first few seconds of consciousness, she didn't know where she was. She opened her eyes and tried to focus on the room. Had she been asleep? She didn't know what was happening. Something cold was being poured onto her body. Whiskey. The smell was sickening. They were still here. They didn't care that she was so battered she passed out. They didn't care about anything and their cruelty knew no bounds. One of them was licking the liquor from her breasts and the others were encouraging him. She couldn't see his face. She knew there were three of them and she could tell by the voices they were all in the room, but she didn't know which one of them was on top of her. It was incomprehensible, but they were beginning all over. It wasn't possible. How long had she been asleep? Minutes? Hours? She was trembling from the cold room and the sticky liquid on her body, but too weak to move otherwise. Completely helpless, she couldn't fight back. She couldn't speak. All she could do was lay there while they brutalized her. Now, they knew she was awake. Her tears were silent and they laughed while she cried, asking why she was crying when she should have been enjoying the party. The whiskey made them more ruthless the second time. She was sick, but her body was becoming numb. Maybe that's how it was when pain could no longer be endured. If only death would take over. Maybe she'd die now. She wanted to die. The room was spinning crazily and she passed out again.

Her head was throbbing and it was hard to open her eyes. One eye was swollen almost shut. A ray of sunlight shot through a hole in the dirty window shade and she held her hand in front of her face to lessen the harsh glare. She was alive — barely. She remembered where she was and listened for voices. They were gone. She must have been unconscious for several hours. It was morning. She was naked and cold. They left her right where they dropped her, to die, for all they cared. They probably hoped she'd be dead by the time someone found her. She shivered uncontrollably and pulled her knees to her chest in an effort to generate some warmth. It was summer, but the damp old room was freezing. She was in shock. Her mouth hurt and her eyes hurt. She raised up on one elbow and touched her fingers to her lip. It was cut and swollen. When she sat up, a sharp pain in her abdomen doubled her over. Not knowing how bad she was hurt, she was afraid to move. She had to move. She had to get out before they came back to finish her off. Her clothes were torn and thrown everywhere, tiny black buttons scattered in all directions. The lace camisole was in shreds. She rolled off the bed onto the floor beside the dress. All the buttons were gone. She crossed her arms over her stomach until another shooting pain subsided. Holding onto the bedpost, she pulled herself to her feet and held up the dress. It was nothing more than a velvet rag, torn and wrinkled. She managed to get it on, but the back was open from lack of buttons. She ran her hands through her hair. It was sticky from the whiskey and tangled like a rat's nest. She was too weak to worry about what she looked like. Standing up made everything hurt. The sparkling combs were on the floor and when she knelt down to pick them up, she saw blood on the bed. What had those animals done to her? They cut her and ravaged her body. Her throat was caked with dried blood from where he'd cut her. It was a miracle he hadn't slit her throat and bled her to death. She had to get home.

Barely able to stay on her feet, she stumbled to the door and into the hall. Carefully, one foot in front of the other, she started down the stairs. Two flights to go. Fear of confronting them on the steps fueled the panic and she couldn't stop the tears. Each step sent a searing pain straight up the middle of her body, but she kept moving. Sheer terror propelled her forward. All she could think was that she had to get out of this place before they came back to see if she was dead. She was sure they would. Cowards didn't usually kill people though. They'd probably pay some hoodlum to finish the job for them. She hugged the railing and made her way down to the front desk. The clerk didn't seem the least bit alarmed at her bedraggled appearance. He'd seen it before. She was sure of that. How many women suffered abuse here? It was unthinkable that anyone could be so heartless, but he turned a blind eye to everything that went on in the hotel. She considered asking him if he knew the men. Of course, he did. That's why he hadn't intercepted them on their way upstairs and that's why the politician already had a key. He'd been here often. It would do no good to ask. It was obvious this man never saw anything and that's why they'd get away with the crime. What kind of man was he? She gave him Marian's name and address. It was the last thing she remembered.

She awoke in the attic apartment, in her own bed. Marian was sitting beside her, holding her hand. The doctor had come and gone. She was still in shock, unable to speak. Marian was telling her to rest. The police would be there tomorrow to take her statement. She groaned when Marian said that, wishing the police had not been notified. It would be futile to make a report. Everything they said was true. No one would believe her, and she might be the one to end up in jail. The perpetrators of the crime would never be brought to justice. They had too much power and her word would mean nothing against theirs. There was no way she could report the assault. She managed a few words and tearfully begged Marian not to call the police back to take a report. Trying to be convincing, she claimed she didn't remember what happened and insisted she couldn't identify her attackers. She wouldn't recognize them even if she saw them again and she had no physical description to offer the police. Marian listened to her, knowing she was lying. She could identify them alright and Marian knew it. Anyone else would have considered the bump on her head sufficient grounds to believe the amnesia story, but Marian didn't buy it. She knew Rose remembered exactly what happened. That being the case, the police should be notified and the criminals charged with the crimes. She tried to think how she'd feel if she were in Rose's place. Imagining the scene, she knew she wouldn't want to talk about such an ugly experience either. Rape was a taboo subject, not easy to talk about with anyone. It was a woman's ultimate humiliation. She'd been violated with unspeakable cruelty and was suffering so much from the mental anguish that she couldn't even bring herself to tell Marian the whole story. What made them think she could tell a police officer, a man? It was men who had done this to her. No man could understand what she was going through. It went without saying, the criminals ought to be arrested and punished, but the police would ask questions. She could hear them now. "What did you wear to entice the gentlemen? Did you encourage the attack by virtue of your provocative attire?" She had worn a somewhat revealing dress, a bit low at the neckline, but no more than those worn by other ladies at the dance. It was an evening gown, a party dress in very good taste. The police would make it sound as though she were lewd and immoral, a strumpet, dressed to stir men's primal urges and justify their advances. They'd probably view it as a deliberate temptation on her part — maybe even say it was her fault. She got exactly what she deserved. They would fail to understand that, regardless of what she was wearing, those men didn't have the right to assault her. There was nothing Marian could do. She understood Rose's reasons for not wanting to talk to the police and she'd make sure they didn't come to the house in the morning. She'd let Rose deal with it in her own way and she'd be there when Rose was ready to talk about it.

Marian hugged Rose and they cried together. Then, Marian left the room and closed the door. Rose had to get through this part by herself. When she was alone, it seemed the tears would never stop. What in the world would she do now? Even when she recovered, she couldn't go back to work at the theatre. Her employer, a man she trusted, was in on the whole thing. From the beginning, he'd been in cahoots with the swine, knowing full well what he was sending her into. The troll arranged it. He set her up and probably got paid for his trouble. How could he have been so cruel as to allow this to happen to her? They intimidated him. She underestimated their power and control over him and his business. Sooner or later, they'd show up at the theatre and she'd have to look them in the eye. They'd be laughing at her, knowing she could never tell anyone what they did. They'd gotten away with the most insidious, sadistic crime against womanhood and they would view that as some sort of manly achievement. Her only comfort was in believing that one day, their indictment would be in the presence of a higher power. They'd answer for their crime, but not before any earthly judge. Justice would not be served in her lifetime. She couldn't go back to the theatre and she could never face John again. She had to get away from New Orleans and she had to leave as soon as possible.

She forced herself to get up and look in the mirror, recoiling at what she saw. She was covered with bruises from head to toe. Her lip was swollen and the colors around one eye ranged from black and blue to disgusting, mottled shades of red and yellow. She turned away. She couldn't stand to look at herself. Her whole body ached. They hurt her inside too and she could barely walk, but despite the physical injuries, the humiliation of the whole thing was far more painful.

Physical wounds would heal, but the greater hurt would never go away. She climbed back into bed. If only she could die. It would be so much easier than facing the world. She stayed in her room and cried for days. Gradually, the bruises healed and the internal pain subsided. She'd been in her room for nearly ten days. She didn't want to see anyone. She didn't want to talk to anyone. She had to rejoin the human race sooner or later. If she didn't do it soon, Marian would have the doctor back and he'd make her talk about it. She didn't want to do that. She didn't want to tell anyone. Saying the words would serve no purpose other than to force her to relive what she wanted to forget. Reluctantly, she dressed and went downstairs, relieved to find the house empty and thankful no one was around to ask questions. She fixed some tea and walked into the parlour. On the table was a newspaper from a city she'd never heard of. Some traveler must have left it behind. She didn't remember anyone like that coming to the house, but then, she'd been upstairs and out of touch with the outside world for days.

Looking over the front page, she sat down on the sofa with her tea. *The Tombstone Epitaph*. Strange name for a newspaper. The words were references to something having to do with death. She set the teacup down and turned to the second page where an advertisement caught her eye. The ad was a solicitation for hostesses at a new establishment of entertainment. The Bird Cage Theatre. She wondered how it got the name, envisioning it's construction as resembling an actual bird cage. How strange and how ingenious. If it did actually look like that, what was the purpose of such clever originality? To attract customers, no doubt. She worked up a mental image of the place. Intriguing. She read the ad again. It was certainly her line of work. In addition to hostess duties, candidates for the jobs were required to perform on stage. It didn't specify what kind of talent was required, but she could sing a little and she played the guitar. She always fancied herself as an entertainer or, at least, she would like to have been on the stage. She wasn't sure she was talented enough, but she might have more talent than some other applicant. It was worth a try. She wondered how far it was from New Orleans. Somewhere in the Southwest. Arizona Territory. Ann Merrick was from the Arizona Territory. There might still be Indians in the area, but it couldn't be too dangerous these days. According to the newspaper, a lot of people lived there. White men. She read on. Silver had been discovered a couple years back and the mining camp became a virtual boomtown practically overnight. There'd be a lot of money in a place like that. It sounded exciting. She reflected on the name, a strange name for a city — Tombstone. A tombstone was a monument marking a place for the dead. Likewise, the name of the paper included the word "epitaph," a funeral oration or statement made about a dead person. With hundreds of fortune hunters heading for a piece of the silver bonanza, the advertisement reported Tombstone as being anything but dead, and the Bird Cage Theatre was billed as destined to become a very lively place. Even if she didn't get the advertised job, there was a good chance she'd find employment elsewhere in a town that was growing so fast. No need to think about it any longer. She had to leave New Orleans. That's all there was to it. Painful as it was, she'd resigned herself to never seeing John again. She'd never wear the beautiful wedding dress. Marian would save it for Rebecca. Maybe the opportunities her father spoke of were in Tombstone. With all that happened, there was nothing to lose by going. She had to go someplace, and Tombstone was as good as any.

She'd write to John today and tell him she was leaving New Orleans. It wouldn't be easy. He'd want to know why and there was no reason that made sense when the wedding was so close. All the plans were made. Everything was ready. A reason to leave now? There was none that he'd understand. She couldn't bring herself to tell him about the assault. The truth was far too ugly. She never told him what happened in Ireland either, although she knew she'd have to tell him someday. The older she got, the easier it would be, or so she thought. It happened a long time ago when she was sixteen, but talking about it didn't get any easier with the passing of time. The entire gruesome event was still as vivid in her memory as that awful night in the cold mist. Now, she carried another vile secret, more hideous than the first. How could she ever tell him? He'd push her out of his life. She couldn't bear the thought of him leaving under those circumstances. The only thing to do was to say she didn't want to marry him and call off the wedding. She'd have to lie and say she didn't love him anymore, and she'd have to leave without telling him where she was going. She closed her eyes. She'd always be able to see his face, with her eyes closed or in the dark. This terrible event had changed everything and their future together was no longer a possibility. She was convinced he wouldn't go looking for her once she ran away, especially if she said she didn't love him anymore. Maybe he'd forget her and find someone else to marry and for her, their life together would remain only a dream. He was the link in the chain that made her life complete — love. The chain was broken. John Merrick had just become her past. She'd vanish into the southwestern desert and never be heard from again. It seemed an ironic parallel. Just as a tombstone was the marker of a final resting place, Tombstone represented finality for her.

Chapter 4

Oh, for the faith of a spider;
She begins her web without any thread.

JUNE, 1881

The trunk was packed. The bags were packed. Everything was in order for the trip. The Pixie had been a silent helper throughout the process. When Rose broke the news that she'd be leaving New Orleans in a few days, Rebecca ran out of the room. For three days, she didn't speak to anyone. Marian went to Rebecca's room several times only to find the door locked from within and her efforts at consolation met by silence. Rebecca was so much like her mother, trying to suffer heartaches alone and not wanting anyone to see her cry. The morning of the third day, Marian went to Rose's room where the pressing and folding of clothes began. Every item had to be meticulously folded so as to take up no more space in the trunk than absolutely necessary. Conversation that morning was sparse. They did their best to pretend it was a day like any other while each, in her own heart, felt the pain of the impending separation. Rose looked up to see the Pixie standing in the doorway, silent tears cascading down her pretty face. It seemed she was always saying good-bye to someone named Merrick. Rebecca didn't understand why Rose was going away and Rose didn't know how to explain. Her only hope was that one day when Rebecca was older, Marian might be able to make her understand why this had to happen. Rebecca brushed away her tears. Without a word, she joined in the folding and packing, and that's the way it went for the rest of the day.

At first, it didn't dawn on her what day this was. It was just another morning when she awoke to the sound of birds singing outside her attic window. She stretched and yawned, shaking off sleep. She was restless all night and hadn't slept well. She was still tired. Remembering what she had to do today, a wave of anxiety flooded over her. A scent of jasmine drifted into the room, the leftover perfume from the night-blooming flowers made more potent by the warm summer air. She closed her eyes and inhaled deeply. She'd miss that sweet smell every morning before the blossoms went back to sleep for the day. In the heat of summer, she had chills. This was the day she'd say good-bye to the people she loved. She looked around the room. This attic loft had been a very special place — her sanctuary. She'd spent many hours here thinking about John, contemplating their future together and writing to him. This was where the dreams were formed, dreams that would remain nothing more than dreams forever. He was given to her so unexpectedly one summer day and just as suddenly, she was being forced to leave him behind. Fate dealt her a cruel hand, giving her love and ruthlessly withdrawing the precious gift. Time would never heal this hurt.

She dressed in a dark blue suit and hat. On such a lovely summer day, she should have worn white. The somber image of the woman looking back at her from the mirror was a picture of mourning. She was, in fact, mourning the passing of the happiest elements of her life, Ann Merrick, Marian, Rebecca — John. Most of all, John. Part of her had died and she asked herself the same question over and over, never getting an answer. How would she live without him? She adjusted her hat in the mirror. She was ready to go. She looked around the room one last time. She couldn't bring herself to say the words — good-bye. All she could say was, "I'll miss you." She closed the door, leaving the dreams inside. Downstairs, Rebecca and Marian waited by the front door. She walked past them toward the carriage without turning around. If she looked back now, she'd never be able to go through with leaving, and she had to leave. Stepping across the threshold onto the porch, she felt a sharp pain, but not a physical pain, and thought to herself, "So, this is what a broken heart feels like."

Rebecca rode in silence all the way to the depot, holding Rose's hand and looking straight ahead. Marian sat in the opposite seat. No one spoke. No one could speak. Words would only make this time more difficult. They were so much more than friends. They were family. Rose knew if she tried to talk, she'd break down in tears and she knew Marian was thinking the same thing. Neither of them could do that. They had to be strong for each other. She called on Ann. All she needed was enough strength to get her to the station and out of their sight. After that, it wouldn't matter if she cried.

The final moments before boarding were the hardest. Rose and the Pixie faced each other on the platform, still holding hands. Both made feeble attempts at smiles. The Pixie was growing up. Sixteen! Where had the years gone? Rose could still see her the way she looked at ten — almost eleven, perched on the edge of the bed Rose's first morning in the Merrick Boarding House. It was the picture she'd carry in her mind always. Rebecca was no longer a little Pixie. Ever since her mother died, she'd been so much more of a grown-up than a girl her age should have been. On the brink of womanhood, she was turning into a real beauty. She looked more like her mother every day with that beautiful copper complexion and long black hair. She'd changed a lot since the first time Rose saw her. Her Apache heritage was more prominent now that she was older. The eyes were unmistakably Merrick though — steel-blue like John's, inherited from her Irish father. Smart as a whip too. There had never been one minute of doubt that Rebecca would fulfill her dream of becoming a doctor one day. By the time they met again, she might very well be Dr. Merrick. Over the years, she'd mended countless broken dove wings and rescued puppies and kittens from injury. She was a born healer.

The train whistle blew loudly. Time to say the inevitable words. The Pixie didn't cry. She looked directly into Rose's eyes and said, "When next we meet, it will be when you marry my brother. Then, you'll really be my sister. When will you be coming home?" She couldn't know the wedding they had so much fun planning would never happen. More than once, Rose tried to tell Rebecca the truth, the real reason she was leaving, but the words never came. Instead, she lied. She made up some ridiculous story about a long-lost relative in California who was ill and whom she must go and care for. It was such a lame story and she felt stupid for telling it. She'd never been good at fibs and she guessed Rebecca knew she was lying. Here, at the final farewell, she looked into the blue pools staring back at her and felt the girl was somehow offering her one last chance to set the record straight. She almost said it, but stopped herself. By the same token, there was no way she was about to reinforce the Pixie's belief that they would meet again when she married John. That would only serve to complicate the lie. The painful truth was, they would never meet again. She couldn't bring herself to say that either. All she could honestly say was, "I love you, Pixie. Always remember that." She put her arms around Rebecca. Tears were at the edge of her eyes. If she blinked, they'd spill all over the place and then, she might not be able to go. She couldn't cave in now. She kept her eyes wide open when Rebecca let go and stepped back. They were seeing each other for the last time. They both knew it. This was a good-bye of the worse kind. There were no more words to say.

Marian stood by stoically observing the girls' painful farewell. Now, it was her turn, the moment she too had dreaded. She hoped she could hold back the tears until Rose was on the train and out of sight. An old memory came to mind, a memory of another sad parting a long time ago. She said good-bye to someone she loved that time too. They were young then. He was going off to find gold. He never found it. He never even made it to California. All she had left was a picture in a silver frame and memories. She smiled and took Rose's arm and they walked a little way up the platform. Out of range of Rebecca's hearing, they stopped and looked back at the Pixie, standing alone, watching them. She was doing her best to make the leaving easier for Rose. She had her mother's inner strength alright. She'd be a great doctor someday.

They hadn't discussed it since Rose announced her plans to leave Louisiana. In fact, they'd deliberately avoided the subject. Marian had to ask. Rose was prepared for it. What about John? What had she told him in her letter? Did he know the truth? Did he know where to find her? What was Marian to say when he arrived in New Orleans? He was entitled to some kind of explanation. The Pixie would say she went to California. Rose had rehearsed the answer to each question, but now that she actually heard them, her only response was, "Nothin'. Tell him nothin'." John deserved answers, but she had none to give. None that would make him feel any better. None that would make her feel better. She didn't want to hurt him, but she didn't have the courage to tell him the truth. She couldn't lie and say she didn't love him either, so she was going away with no explanation at all. Maybe that was selfish on her part, but right or wrong, he was never to know where she went. Marian hoped Rose would change her mind at the last minute. She tried to convince her to give John a chance to understand. "He won't react the way you think. I know my nephew. He's a compassionate young man, and he loves you. Tell him what happened. When he reads your letter, he'll understand and..." In the middle of the plea, Rose blurted out the truth. "Marian, I didn't write to him. Tell him whatever you want to tell him. Just don't tell him where I went." They stopped walking. Marian couldn't believe what she was hearing. "You didn't write to him? He doesn't know anything about this? He doesn't know you're leaving?" Rose stopped her. "You promised you wouldn't tell where I went. Will you be keepin' that promise?" Marian sighed. "That's what I said, but that was before I thought about it." She searched Rose's eyes for some indication she might have a change of heart. Rose stared back, waiting for an answer. Finally, Marian agreed. "Alright, Rose. I'll keep your secret — if I can."

The whistle blew loudly and a billowing cloud of smoke puffed from the stack, punctuating Marian's promise. The conductor jumped to the step of the nearest car. Holding onto the bar with one hand, he cupped the other to his mouth. "All aboard." Time to go. She hugged Marian and let go quickly. Before her heart had a chance to change her mind, she picked up her valise and walked to the train. The conductor took her bag and passed it inside. She accepted his hand in assistance up the steel steps to the waiting car. At the top, she looked back. The Pixie! Rebecca was standing alone. She wasn't waving or crying. She was just standing there, trying to look grown-up. Rose wanted to jump off the train and run back to the platform. She didn't want to leave. For one brief moment, she almost changed her mind. The conductor told her to take a seat. The train was leaving and for her own safety, she couldn't stand there. One more step. She was inside the car. There was no turning back. Halfway down the aisle, the engineer released the brake and the train lurched forward. Her ankles turned to rubber at the jolt and she lost her balance, staggering like a drunk on wobbly legs. She grappled clumsily for something to hold onto. Her hand missed the back of a seat and the train lurched again, nearly knocking her down. To keep from falling, she dropped into the nearest seat. By the time she landed, the train was picking up speed chugging out of the station. She sat still and caught her breath. At least she hadn't wound up on the floor or in someone's lap. The train was moving faster. The Pixie! She wanted one last glimpse of the Pixie. She moved over to the window seat and pressed her face against the glass. Too late. The depot was half a mile away and fading fast. They were behind her, Marian and Rebecca. John was behind her. Everyone she ever loved was fading into the past.

She faced forward in the seat and straightened her hat, knocked crooked in the landing. Her life was headed in a different direction now; where, exactly, she hadn't a clue. Outside, the landscape whizzed by as the train moved away from the city and out into the Louisiana countryside. In the fields, darkies stopped working to watch the train go by. Some of the children waved. She knew they couldn't see her, but she waved back anyway. Each second carried her closer to an uncertain future. She was as alone as when she came from Ireland with no idea what lay ahead in an unfamiliar land. She wondered if the pain of loneliness ever diminished over time. She rested her head on the back of the seat and closed her eyes. John's face was as clear as if he were sitting beside her. That wonderful smile. She'd never forget his smile. "Ticket, please." The conductor touched her shoulder and the tap startled her. He must have had to ask more than once. "Oh, yes. The ticket. I'm sorry. I was thinkin' about somethin'..." She found the ticket in her purse and handed it to him. He read the destination and shook his head. "El Paso. Long trip." His expression was sympathetic. He didn't know the half of it and neither did she. The first leg of her journey would be easy compared to the ride she'd get out of El Paso. He moved on to the next passenger and she laid her head back. Might as well take advantage of the chance to rest. After El Paso, the trip would be rough going over bumpy roads and sagebrush. Stagecoaches were not famous for comfortable rides and the one she'd get between West Texas and Tombstone was a dandy.

Having occupied her seat initially under emergency conditions, she hadn't exactly made an unobtrusive entrance. Now that the train was moving, she was aware of the other passengers. The car was full of travelers and they probably all watched her come careening out of control down the aisle and flop onto the seat. She was embarrassed, but upon a look around the car, she discovered no one was paying attention to her. Many were talking to their companions. Some were on their way home after visiting the city. Others talked excitedly about whatever it was that awaited them at their destination. They didn't even know she was there. She had no one to talk to. Just as well. This was not a happy time and she was glad to be relieved of the burden of holding up one end of a conversation. Unlike the other passengers who knew what was at the end of their trip, she hadn't any notion what was waiting for her. She could only imagine. She wasn't sure how far it was, but she knew it was going to be a long, hard trip. She wanted to get there and find work and a place to live, anything to take her mind off what she was leaving behind. Starting over, alone in a strange place, was not something she thought she'd ever have to do again. Like a spider spinning the first precarious strands of a web, she had to make a home for herself from nothing.

At the end of the rail, she bought a new ticket, this time from the Butterfield Company, to convert to an Arizona stage line later. The rest of the trip to Tombstone would be dirty and dangerous. She was a little uneasy thinking about traveling through Indian country, but the line assured her it was perfectly safe. The station master was saying something. Four passengers had purchased tickets. There was a limit to luggage weight that could be carried with that many on board. There was a problem with her trunk. It was too heavy. If all four passengers arrived with baggage, she'd have to leave the trunk behind. They'd ship it out on a future run, but there was no guarantee when it would go. Could be a week. Could be a month, or two months — whenever there was room. She tried to explain that wasn't acceptable. Everything she owned in the world was in that trunk. She couldn't leave it behind. There must be a way. The station master shook his head. "Nope. No other way." The only hope for the trunk making the trip to Tombstone with her was if two of the passengers didn't show up by departure time.

She paced back and forth beside the stage, looking up and down the street for sign of the other passengers. The driver emerged from the office. He'd been listening to the conversation about the trunk. He tipped his hat and she nodded back. She watched him. He walked around the coach, double-checked the tack, and spoke softly to the impatient horses, stopping to pat each animal affectionately on the nose and giving each a sweet. Even they were anxious to get going. He looked up at the sky and squinted. Her gaze followed his. The sun was bright and she shaded her eyes with one hand. She couldn't figure out what he was looking at. Not a cloud or a bird in sight. Nothing but blue sky as far she could see. She looked back at the driver. He reached into his vest pocket and withdrew a gold watch attached to a chain. Acting like he was in no particular hurry, he flipped open the case and took note of the time. He rubbed his chin thoughtfully and looked up at some invisible object in the sky again. This time, she didn't follow his lead. He knew she was watching him when he closed the case and tucked the watch back into his pocket. He purposefully positioned his hat with both hands and looked at her. She was worried. If the other fares arrived, she'd have to wait for the next stage rather than lose her trunk. If she left it behind, she'd never see it again. She had to get it on this run. He raised his eyebrows and shook his head matter-of-factly. Then, he pulled on his gloves and winked at her. "Time's up." She smiled. He knew how desperately she wanted to be on that stage — with her trunk. He couldn't leave without giving the other passengers adequate time to get there, but he'd allowed exactly the time required by company policy to wait for paid fares, not a second longer. So far, only one of the three had shown up, and he had only one bag. The driver motioned to the shotgun rider. They didn't waste any time lifting the trunk and strapping it to the back of the coach. While he tightened the straps, he gave her a funny look over his shoulder. It was an expression of painful strain at lifting something of great weight. "Heavy trunk. What you got in it? Rocks?" She apologized and he winked again. She could tell he was trying to get it tied on as fast as possible. She smiled to herself. He was going to make sure that she and her trunk were on this run and he was trying to move out before the other ticketed passengers got there and demanded their seats. Her other bags went up top. She handed him her personal valise and he put it inside the coach. Everything was loaded on. Everything but her. He opened the door and held out his hand. She didn't hesitate. If she wasted any time, the other people might come and her trunk would have to stay behind. She took his hand and stepped up.

The horses were restless. They danced in the harness and the coach rocked. Her knees buckled and she lost her balance. With both hands, he reached for her waist to steady her, but his reach was a little short of the intended mark and he grabbed her behind instead of her middle. He gave her a push and she flopped ungracefully onto the seat. Her hat was knocked sideways and hung from her hair by one hat pin. She blew at a wisp of hair that came loose and fell across her eyes. Seemed she was having that problem a lot this trip. She hoped it was not an indication of things to come. Once she was on the seat, she tucked her hair back in place and repositioned the hat. He waited for her to regain her composure and get herself situated before closing the door. When he was satisfied she was together, he shut the door and checked its security, pausing outside the coach. "Are you alright, Miss?" She looked at him as though he had some nerve asking the question. "Of course, I'm alright!" She just felt like a clumsy damn fool. She didn't say it though. It wouldn't be very ladylike. Without looking at him, she mumbled an obligatory, curt "thank you." Flustered at the manner in which his help was given, she didn't want to look at him. It didn't seem to bother him in the least and he stood by the door waiting for her to get settled. When he didn't move, she snapped impatiently, "Could we please start?" He nodded his head and smiled. He thought she was cute. Sassy, but cute. Brave too, to be heading for Tombstone all alone. He answered as though she'd asked politely. "Yes, ma'am. We'll leave right off. By the way, that strap over yonder is for holding on when the road gets rough."

She looked at the leather loop beside the window and back at him. He was still smiling. She tilted her head to one side a little, like a curious puppy. She hadn't paid attention before, but now that she really looked at him, he had a nice face. It wasn't his fault she was clumsy, and he was trying to help. She might have broken a leg if he hadn't caught her at such a precarious moment. There was no reason to take out her frustration on him. This was a good man. She couldn't help but smile. Truly, she was grateful for his efforts. His hand rested on the window frame. She laid her hand on his and whispered, "Thank you." He nodded and touched the brim of his hat. He double-checked the latch and gave her another wink. It wouldn't do to have her to fall out now. He disappeared toward the front of the rig. The coach rocked when he climbed up top and three seconds later, he was at the reigns whistling and shouting the command. It was what the horses were waiting for and they responded immediately. Like the starting shot at the beginning of a race, the driver's signal set the team to pulling as one enormous muscle of horseflesh.

It was a rather violent beginning. The stage lurched forward and she held onto the strap for dear life. Once they were moving, she dared a peek out the window. They were rolling at a pretty good clip, much faster than she'd expected. The coach rocked and bounced as the driver gave the horses free reign and she prayed it wouldn't flip over. She closed her eyes and asked her good angel to keep it upright. When she opened them, she realized she was clutching the strap and her knuckles were white from holding on so tight. She blew out a breath. This was going to be a very long trip. She had to relax. She let go of the strap and smoothed out her dress. At least she was in one piece. A miracle. Without thinking, she spoke out loud. "Well now, that was a bloody miracle." From the way they were bouncing around, she couldn't help but wonder what kind of shape her behind would be in when the ride was over. She never thought about bringing a pillow to absorb some of the shock of the road.

She realized she wasn't alone. There was another passenger in the opposite seat. She'd forgotten about the one fare who did arrive in time. He was smiling. He must have thought she looked pretty comical the way she came flying through the door with the help of the driver's fanny boost. She reflected on what he saw. With all that had happened, at least she hadn't lost her sense of humor. She looked straight at him and they both laughed. He extended his hand. "Matthew Kern, United States Marshal." She took his hand. "Rose Callahan, ..."

On the train from New Orleans, she listened to talk of Indian raids and dangers that still made the Arizona Territory a hostile country. She inquired of Marshal Kern as to the truth of those stories. Did Indians still present a cause for concern in the country they'd be traveling through? He was an extremely relaxed individual and quite soft-spoken for a policeman. He assured her that she had nothing to worry about. She'd be perfectly safe. More and more people traveled these roads every day and she shouldn't concern herself with fear of Indian attacks. Moreover, the Army had several posts in the area. Indians wouldn't attack knowing the U.S. Cavalry was close by. She knew he was trying to alleviate her fears and she appreciated that. She felt safe with this man. She was sure he wasn't afraid of anything, including Indians. There wasn't much she was afraid of either. Hadn't she crossed the ocean alone with no idea what awaited her in America? She was curious. Did he know anything about Tombstone? He answered with another question. "Tombstone? Is that where you're going?" She detected a hint of concern at her question, but he was quick to cover his alarm, if that was indeed what it was. "Well, Tombstone is a busy place and getting busier all the time. Plenty of people are going there these days. Most of them hope to find silver. You do know it's a mining camp, don't you? Silver boomtown." She shook her head, "yes." She'd read about it. He had an idea why she was going there. Ladies who traveled to Tombstone alone went for one of only two reasons. Either she was a mail-order bride or she was headed for work in one of the saloons or brothels. Somehow, she didn't look to be either type. She asked if he'd be going all the way to Tombstone. His reply was, "Unfortunately for me, no." She was flattered when he implied he would miss her company, but disappointed in his answer. She didn't say what she was thinking. "Unfortunately for her, too." She enjoyed the company of this charming peace officer. His appearance gave indication of considerable time spent outdoors, but he also possessed a certain air of gentility, perhaps sophistication. She liked him a lot. He was the kind of person she'd like to have for a friend, but that wasn't possible since his home was in Oklahoma and she was going to Arizona. Their paths weren't likely to cross again.

Long before they got close to the Arizona Territory, Matt Kern left her. They shared a meal at the stop in Mesilla and said good-bye. He was on his way to Colorado. After that, he'd be going home to Oklahoma. He'd been to Tombstone in the past and future business could take him there again. She hoped that were the case, but wouldn't count on it. She hated to see him go. In fact, she cried watching him walk away. He'd made the trip this far much easier. She only knew him for a couple of days, but when they parted company, she felt like she was saying good-bye to an old friend. He told her he hoped they'd meet again one day, possibly, in Tombstone. She knew he wasn't saying it just to be polite. He meant it.

She was already on board when the new passenger climbed into the coach, a smelly character with a sweat-stained leather hat, badly in need of a bath and a shave. He took the opposite seat and stared at her without saying a word. He made her nervous and she tried to break the tension by saying hello. He didn't speak, even when spoken to. She studied him, thinking that if he did talk, the sound would probably resemble a snarl. One word came to mind. Carnivorous! His stare had a menacingly wild-animal quality like that of a surly, nocturnal rodent about to pounce on some unsuspecting, helpless little bug feeling its way along in the dark. He made her uncomfortable. She was never one to form opinions or pass judgment on anyone until they had a fair chance to speak their piece, but this one was a mongrel of questionable lineage and not to be trusted. She nonchalantly placed her hand inside her purse and felt the tiny derringer. Marian's gardener gave it to her as a going-away gift to provide a sense of security on the long trip. He told her the small gun would only serve its purpose at close range and should be pointed at a vital organ to be effective. Well, this was about as close as could be.

The mongrel suddenly leaned forward and she thought he was going to grab her. She pulled the pistol from her bag and leveled it at his forehead. She braced herself, ready to give him exactly what he deserved if he dared follow through with the assault. He froze. He knew he scared her, but the determination on her face and the clarity of her message told him one wrong twitch of a whisker would be his ticket to eternal damnation. He didn't doubt for a second this petite, red-haired angel would pull the trigger and send him straight to Hell. Without taking his eyes off her, one corner of his mouth lifted in a leering grin displaying brown, tobacco-stained teeth. He jerked his head in the direction of the outside and turned slowly to spit out the coach door. He was disgusting and he made her stomach queazy. She held her position and he sat back in the seat, being careful to keep his hands in plain sight. He wouldn't want her to misinterpret his move and pull the trigger. He finally spoke. "You intend to shoot me,

Missy?" She stared at him. "If I have to." He didn't doubt that she would. "It's a long ride to Bisbee. I'd hate to think we'd hit a rut and that thing'd go off in my face." It was probably two hundred fifty miles to Bisbee and she had to admit she couldn't point the gun at him the entire way. At least he knew she had it, and she'd keep it where she could reach it easily if she needed it. He had a gun too, much larger than hers. The bullets in the belt he wore were each nearly as big as her whole gun. She took a deep breath and lowered the derringer, but didn't put it back in her purse. Instead, she held it in her hand and didn't take her eyes off the rodent. Maybe she had unfairly misinterpreted his move. Maybe not. At any rate, she wasn't about to leave herself vulnerable in the event her first intuitive reaction to his move had been correct. If she had to stay awake and on guard all the way to Bisbee, she'd do it. The guttural tone of his voice resembled a growl just as she expected. "Think you could point that thing at the floor? You might kill me accidental." He was trying to distract her from watching him and pointed to the floor of the coach. Her grip tightened around the little pistol and she squinted her eyes at him the way he'd done to her. "If I shoot you, it won't be an accident." On second thought, should a bump in the road cause her to inadvertently engage the trigger, she noted the trajectory of the bullet would, sure enough, find its mark dead center between his legs. So be it! She'd hang onto the gun. At least it's presence might make him think twice about any sudden moves in her direction. She felt claustrophobic confined to such close quarters with this swarthy, rat of a man who smelled so rotten, and it could only get worse in the heat. She'd be glad when he got off the stage. At the next stop, he did. She was not about to put the derringer away and he decided she was probably just stubborn enough to persevere all the way to Bisbee. It was a little unnerving for him to think about traveling more than two hundred miles in confined quarters with a short-fused, red-headed female with her finger on the trigger of a derringer pointed at his vitals.

When she heard the trip would be dusty and hot, she never imagined how understated those discomforts were. She tried to pass the time by thinking pleasant thoughts. It wasn't easy. Bouncing around inside a stage-coach in hundred-degree heat with sand in her shoes, sand in her clothes, and sand in her mouth, made thinking about anything but a bath next to impossible. Two people boarded the stage halfway through New Mexico. They were going as far as Bisbee. The woman chattered without giving her husband or Rose an opportunity to enter the conversation. She got on Rose's nerves, but she was certainly a more acceptable traveling companion than the rat. She'd have to put up with it all the way to Bisbee, but it was still better than riding with someone she was afraid of. Meantime, she was trying to act like a lady. That wasn't easy either. She didn't particularly relish the idea of traveling through this country alone, but at times, she wished the two people would disappear for a little while, long enough for her to lift her skirt and air the petticoat. Her clothes stuck to her body in the heat, and the sand — the damn sand. It was everywhere.

By the time they got off in Bisbee, her head was throbbing from the woman's constant chatter. She felt sorry for the husband. He had to live with that mouth. After having spent several days and ridden over two hundred miles together, they departed without so much as a word to her. That was alright. She was glad to see them go. Tombstone was only a few miles away. She was almost there, and she welcomed the peace and quiet she'd have without having to share the coach. Finally, she'd be able to stretch out and air her petticoat and ride in a little more comfort with no one else to see. At the stagecoach line office in Bisbee, the station master told her she'd be going on into Tombstone alone. She was looking forward to it. The layover was short, barely enough time to freshen up and have a quick meal. She was dog-tired, but there was a sense of exhilaration connected with the last few miles. A second wind of sorts. She peeked inside. The coach was empty. It looked like she'd really have it to herself the rest of the way. She was anxious to get the trip over. Fresh horses and a new driver were already installed and she was told to get on board. They'd be leaving any minute.

Many miles back, she learned how to climb in without making a spectacle of herself. She held onto the side of the door and made sure her footing was solid before stepping up. When she was safely in her seat, the driver came by the window and informed her they'd try to make Tombstone today. They'd have to stop for horses, but they'd make a fast change. Uphill to the top of the pass, it was slow going out of Bisbee, but once they were over the mountain, the rest of the trip was easy, barring any Indian problems. His nonchalant comment startled her. Indian problems? That was the last thing she needed to hear. No one had mentioned Indians since the train. Where was the cavalry? Marshal Kern said the cavalry was all over the area. The driver shook his head. He didn't know where she got the idea that the calvary would provide a personal escort for her. She frowned and sat back in the seat, sulking at the way he implied she wasn't worth an escort of soldiers. His remark was uncalled-for. She was almost

there. Would a marauding Apache put an arrow through her heart and prevent her from arriving at her destination? Or worse? She remembered
overhearing a conversation on the train. Someone said they only killed the
men. They took the white women captive. In the heat of the day, she broke
into a cold sweat, envisioning herself being thrown across a horse like a
sack of flour and carried off into the hills by a bare-chested red man wearing feathers and war paint, never to see a white face again. God help her!
She put both hands over her face. Her imagination was running away with
her. She was being ridiculous! That was not going to happen. The cavalry
would see to it. Surely, they were close by. She believed Matt Kern. He
wouldn't have lied about something so important, especially when he knew
her concerns. She had to forget what the driver said. She was tired and
anxious to get going. The last few miles were always the longest.

Petticoat and female parts underneath at the ready for ventilation, she
was prepared to enjoy some privacy on the final leg of her journey. At the
last minute, the door opened and a passenger climbed into the coach. She
smoothed her skirt and sat up straight. The petticoat airing once they were
on the road would have been nice, but after hearing about Indians, a traveling companion was a welcome sight. She wouldn't have to face the Indians
alone. Not that the gentleman would be much help in case of an attack. He
was a frail-looking man. He held a handkerchief over his mouth and
coughed often. Obviously ill, her heart went out to him. She forgot about
Indians. He stopped coughing long enough to draw a raspy breath. His
eyes were red and watery, and he was perspiring profusely. The coughing
spell passed and he cleared his throat. She wondered if he needed some
kind of assistance, but didn't know what to do for him. When he cleared
his throat a second time, she realized she'd been staring. She was being
rude. She averted her eyes and felt her face get hot. He wasn't offended.
People often goggled when he had these fits of coughing. He sensed her
embarrassment and apologized for the coughing. He couldn't help it. He
smiled and spoke softly. "What a pleasant surprise to find such a lovely
travelin' companion in my coach." His manners took her by surprise and
she blushed again. She ought to say something. "Good afternoon." It
sounded silly the way she said it. After the way she'd been looking at him,
she felt clumsy. She held out her hand. "Rose Callahan. ...travelin' from
New Orleans." Her voice broke and she cleared her throat. "...to
Tombstone." She stuttered, "...Ar ...Arizona Territory." She felt foolish,
cloddish. They were in the Arizona Territory. She was fumbling for something intelligent to say. He rescued her from the awkward situation. "New

Orleans!" He knew it well. In fact, he'd been there recently. "Charmin' city." He "...originally from Georgia. John Holliday. Your servant, madam, I'm quite sure." He held her hand ever so lightly and smiled. She was impressed. A gentleman. Moreover, a Southern gentleman, and a truly cosmopolitan specimen at that, or so it would seem. The best kind! Even if he hadn't mentioned Georgia, she would have known. His drawl was quite distinct and she'd heard it often when visitors from Georgia came to the Cordon Bleu. This was too good to be true. He was on his way to Tombstone. Actually, he was returning home after a business engagement in Bisbee. She heard the driver give the command to the horses, a familiar sound by this time. His voice triggered a spontaneous reaction and she instinctively grabbed the strap beside her in anticipation of the initial lurch. Mr. Holliday smiled at the way she took hold and braced herself. She was a seasoned stagecoach traveler. He could see that. He wouldn't mention it though. He watched her close her eyes as the coach began moving. A minute later, she took a deep breath and blew it out. A sigh of relief. She was into the grand finalé of her trip.

It was hard for him to speak very loud because he coughed when he raised his voice. Rumbling of the coach wheels over the road made conversation difficult. He said he was certain they would see each other frequently in Tombstone as he was a resident of the town and she was about to become one. That being said, he announced that he was quite tired. If she'd be so kind as to excuse him, he was in dire need of a short nap. She quickly acknowledged his need for the nap. "By all means, rest." He didn't have to ask her permission. "Might there be anythin' I can do? I'll ask the driver to stop for water if you'll be needin' any. Please tell me if I can help." He was touched by her concern. He leaned over and patted her hand. As soon as he sat back, he dozed off. Her heart was filled with compassion. She recognized the symptoms of the disease. Tuberculosis. Poor man. He was too young to be so ill. As far as she knew, the sickness was always fatal. She shook her head as she watched him sleep, wondering how long he'd been sick and how much longer he had to live.

While her fellow-traveler slept, she drifted off, rethinking the tragedy of her own fatal situation. She was nearly twenty-four, past her prime by some standards. Her dream of being married to the love of her life was gone. She never should have gone into the hotel with that man. How could she have been so stupid? The warnings were clear. Why didn't she listen when they would have done her the most good? She'd never forgive herself for such bad judgment. Her little voice tried to help her. She'd lost everything, but no good would come from dwelling on it. What was done, was done. She couldn't change the past. That's why she was here. Memories of time spent with John were painful. They had such glorious plans. How did it all get so crazy? How did she end up alone in this country full of heat and dust and Indians? If only he could hold her one more time. If only she could hear him whisper the words that took her breath away. She closed her eyes. She could see his face and hear the words any time she wanted to, but something was obscuring his face now. The noise of the coach rolling and bouncing over the road was deafening. It drowned out his words. Her thoughts turned to Tombstone. How much further? What adventure or misadventure awaited? What was the Bird Cage Theatre? It certainly couldn't be any worse than the place she left behind. At least she'd never have to see the troll again or the vermin who hurt her and ruined her life. Maybe it was her ticket to a new life, a better life, the one her father wanted her to have in America. Whatever was over the mountain, whether the streets of Tombstone were covered in gold or mud, she'd find out soon enough. From now on, she'd be depending on God to give her the strength she lacked of her own accord to face the rest of her life without John Merrick.

Once again, she was catapulted back into reality. She fell forward and Mr. Holliday caught her before she landed in his lap, her hat knocked askew. She'd had enough of that. She pulled out the pins and yanked off the hat, pulling half her hair down in the process. He contained his amusement at her display of irritation with the hat. Apparently, she'd had trouble with it before. The stage had stopped. Someone opened the door and offered her a calloused hand down. "End of the line." She looked out the door and was greeted by a wide grin. "Welcome to Tombstone, ma'am."

The second her feet touched the ground, she felt like she'd alighted on another planet. It was a sensitivity to some kind of magnetism, as though the town itself had a hand in drawing her closer to it. She took it all in amazingly fast. If she had to, she couldn't put the feeling into words. It was a most peculiar perception of the place — eerie. If she didn't know better, she'd swear the allure was the result of a spell. There was an undeniable attraction here. Bewitching. That's the only way she could describe it. She squinted her eyes to focus on the street. It was dusty and it didn't smell very good. For sure, a far cry from New York or New Orleans, but there were a lot of people around. It was a busy little town. Music and laughter came from... She strained to hear, but was unable to pinpoint any one source. The sounds seemed to emanate from lots of places. The street was noisy and bustling with activity. She was exhausted and dusty and cranky. All she wanted was a bath and a quiet room with a soft bed and two pillows. She looked up and down the street in both directions. The town wasn't as large as she expected. From the newspaper advertisement, she got the impression Tombstone was a regular city. It was nothing more than a dusty, noisy little town in the middle of nowhere, but she was absolutely fascinated by it. The Bird Cage Theatre was on Allen Street. She was standing in the middle of Allen Street, but didn't see the Bird Cage. How far could it be? She was too tired to think about it. She'd find the Bird Cage tomorrow. She listened to the town. It wasn't what she heard or saw. It was a feeling more than anything, and not a good feeling. She could sense the evil in the air.

Someone touched her elbow and she wheeled around, the trip having left her nerves on edge. "Mr. Holliday! I'm sorry. I'm a little tired." He wrapped her arm through his and patted her hand. "I understand, my dear. You've come a long way." He was recommending the accommodations at the Cosmopolitan Hotel. It would be his pleasure to show her the way. It was only a couple of doors down. She started to walk with him, then stopped, remembering the trunk. "What about my bags? My trunk?" It was a miracle the trunk made it all the way there. She couldn't take a chance on losing it now. She didn't want to let it out of her sight. He could see how worried she was. He dropped her arm and went to speak with the stagecoach driver. When he returned, he said her trunk and other bags would be delivered to the Cosmopolitan within the quarter hour. They'd be there before she was checked in. She was worried at leaving it unattended and he assured her that he'd given explicit instructions that the trunk was to be treated with utmost care and delivered promptly with delicate handling. She was grateful for the comfort of a friend in unfamiliar territory, someone who knew his way around and whose word, quite plainly, carried some influence.

Her knees were weak from riding and the short walk to the hotel helped restore circulation. People stepped aside to let them pass and she figured Mr. Holliday must be a highly-respected citizen. At the hotel, she received preferential treatment when he introduced her to the desk clerk and made a point of telling the man she was his friend. "...a lady of notoriety recently arrived from that great city in the South, New Orleans," and he expected the staff to provide her with the best service and most comfortable accommodations in keeping with the Cosmopolitan's reputation as a fine hotel. She did think it a little unusual for him to shake hands with the man behind the counter being that the fellow appeared nervous, but maybe she misinterpreted his actions. For all she knew, they might be old friends or maybe that's the way they did things in Tombstone.

Following the handshake, the clerk informed her the only sleeping apartment available was a suite which included a bedroom, sitting room, and private tub. They required one hour's notice to deliver hot water. He hoped that would be satisfactory and, "By the way, there is no additional charge for the extras or hot water for the bath." Since there was no single room available, he'd give her the suite for the same price as a regular room. That was fine with her. She noticed he glanced over at Mr. Holliday as if soliciting his approval. Another thing that struck her as strange was the fact that the clerk didn't know the price of the room and had to figure it out on paper. When he finally gave her the cost, she was surprised at the moderate price, considering the Cosmopolitan was a fairly well-appointed hotel. If it had been the price of a regular room without a private bath, it was more than reasonable. Knowing the limited funds at her disposal, she wasn't about to argue. She paid for one week in advance, thinking she'd take advantage of the lucky find at the right price. The clerk didn't seem particularly overjoyed with the idea of letting the suite go for an entire week at the regular single-room rate and suggested he needed to clear it with the owner. Mr. Holliday had been waiting patiently for her to sign the register, but it was fast becoming apparent his patience was being tried. He assured the anxious clerk it was not necessary to clear the price of Miss Callahan's room with anyone and if there was a problem, he'd speak with the proprietor directly. It was his contention Miss Callahan would be invited to stay in the suite as long as she desired — at the price charged for the first week. "Ask Mr. Billicke to send a runner when he's available to speak with me regardin' this matter." The clerk was uncomfortable with the suggestion that the owner of the hotel might be consulted about letting the lady have a suite and private bath for the price of a single room, especially since he'd already shaken the hand containing a payoff. He didn't have to think about it long. Mr. Holliday's assurance that the proprietor would let her have the room at a reduced cost seemed more than sufficient and without further words, the clerk passed the register and inkwell across the desk with a pen for her to sign, telling her if she decided to stay two weeks, he'd see to the arrangements. When she was registered and given the key, he summoned his assistant to show her to the suite. She gave her hour's notice on delivering the hot water and turned to Mr. Holliday. "I'll be thankin' for your very kind help. I'd have been lost without your assistance. I'm in your debt." He smiled and assured her the debt was entirely his as he'd been the beneficiary of the pleasure of her company. It was his sincere hope they'd meet again soon. Tired or not, he made her smile. She suggested they might have tea in her apartment sometime being that she did have a private sitting room due to his gallant efforts. When he accepted, it was without the slightest inference that he viewed her invitation as brash or unladylike. It was simply an invitation to tea and he accepted it as such, nothing more. He had all the markings of an aristocrat, a scarce commodity in these parts. Southern men certainly knew how to flatter a woman. That was the one thing she'd miss about New Orleans. He added, "Incidentally, it's Doc — Doctor Holliday." She was embarrassed. She didn't know. She'd been addressing him as Mr. Holliday. He was a doctor! She was impressed. Her first friend in Tombstone was a doctor. That was certainly comforting. Now, she understood why people stepped aside for him on the street and why the hotel clerk was agreeable to providing her with special accommodations at no extra cost. Seemed she'd made the right connection. At least the place had a doctor, and he was her friend.

Chapter 5

TOMBSTONE, ARIZONA TERRITORY – JULY, 1881

Saturday morning. The trip drained her strength. She was exhausted and fell into a deep sleep. She was dreaming. A loud noise crashed into the dream and she awoke with a start. At first, she thought it was part of the dream. Then, she heard it again. It sounded like the roof was falling in. Her eyes flew open and she sat straight up at the second blast. Gunfire, and close by. Dazed, and not yet fully awake, she stumbled to the window and pushed aside the curtain. It was past mid-morning approaching noon and the sun was glaring hot. There was a lot of shouting going on outside. She blinked to get the sleep out and tried to adjust her eyes to the sunlight. A man sprawled face-down in the street beneath her window, a pool of blood spreading under his body and soaking into the dirt. A crowd was gathering. She opened the window and heard someone announce the man was dead. She couldn't believe her eyes. She stared at the lifeless body. In her whole life, she'd only seen two dead people and they both died of natural causes. She'd never been exposed to anything like this, a man's lifeblood literally pouring out of him. What kind of place was this that a man could be shot to death in the street on a Saturday morning? The same feeling when she got off the stage was back. This was an evil, violent place. Had she walked straight into Hell? She sat on the edge of the bed with her arms around a pillow, asking herself if she'd made a terrible mistake by coming. Why hadn't she considered the implications of what she read in the newspaper? This was a boomtown, born of silver fever. She knew that before she left New Orleans. Hundreds of people came here for the silver bonanza with hopes of getting rich and more were arriving every day. Maybe thousands. There was probably a lot of violence here. The killing in the street in front of her hotel might be only the tip of the iceberg. Miners and cowboys and gunslingers. She'd heard stories about the wild West. This town was full of men. It was a mining camp. Was she the only female? A terrifying thought! That couldn't be. There must be other women. She'd find one and ask some questions. After all, there was culture in town. The Bird Cage Theatre was a prime example. The newspaper advertisement said so.

Entertainment! That's what it said. Entertainers were musicians and actors and actresses, and singers and dancers and any number of other theatrical virtuosos. There were probably other establishments of the same persuasion. The advertisement said national headliners were scheduled to play the Bird Cage and if that was true, it must be a theatre of great notoriety. Ladies went to the theatre, so there had to be women here. She wouldn't draw any conclusions just yet. She'd find the right people to talk to. Doctor Holliday would know. She'd locate his office and solicit his help. The consolation of knowing she had a friend was greatly needed, and he was the only person she knew so far. Maybe the shooting outside her window was an isolated incident; an accident, perhaps. There had to be more to the story than the part she saw. It must have been an accident. Those things happened. No one would kill a man in cold blood in the middle of a busy street on Saturday morning! Would they? Even so, it wouldn't be fair to judge the whole town by one unfortunate event and she certainly couldn't afford to dwell on it. She had a lot to do today. She'd been asleep and the blast did wake her rather rudely. Now that she was awake, she was thinking more clearly. She'd give the town the benefit of a doubt — or maybe she'd be on the next stage out. Either way, she'd have the answer as to whether she ought to stay or go by this afternoon.

She started to unpack her trunk and thought better of it. She might not stay long enough to wear everything she brought. She'd unpack only what she needed for one day. Finding the Bird Cage Theatre to see about a job was the first thing to do. The outcome of her interview would determine if the trunk was to be fully unpacked or not. There was a chance she might not even get the job. The mint-green linen was on top of the pile of clothes. She held it up to herself in the mirror. It was the dress she wore the day she met John. She'd kept it all these years to remind her of that day. It seemed so long ago, that summer day he rescued her from a fatal fall on the front steps of his mother's house. It was July, 1876. Five years ago. It seemed like forever now. She drifted back to that summer. The first time she saw him, he took her breath away and she hadn't been able to speak. A leprechaun tied her tongue in a knot. When he looked into her eyes, she stuttered and lost her train of thought. She couldn't get a word out. He must have thought she was a complete fool. She was mesmerized by those blue eyes and his smile. He had an incredible smile and she'd seen a strange light around him. She didn't know what it was, but it never went away. She'd fallen in love with him the first time he smiled at her. Why had she never told him? That was something she'd never understand and it was her deepest regret. He told her many times, but she couldn't remember telling John Merrick she loved him, although she had to have said it. All she could ever hope was that he knew. What would happen to him now that she was out of his life? He'd probably marry some general's daughter. He deserved someone good, someone better than her. She hoped he'd find happiness. She loved him so much that she had given him up rather than cause him pain. She wanted him to be happy, but how would she find the strength to face the rest of her life without him? Each morning, the heartache was worse than the day before.

She held the dress up to herself in the mirror, remembering how John noticed she wasn't wearing anything under the thin fabric as she stood with her outstretched hand in his that day. His devilish smile told it all. She could still feel the touch of his hand. It was time to put his memory away, safe in the most private place she had, the only place that hadn't been brutally ravaged; the secret place in her heart no one ever saw. There, he'd remain until the day she died. She carefully folded the dress and laid it on the bed. She wouldn't wear it today. Memories tied to it were too painful. She'd save it for another time or, maybe she'd never wear it again.

Ann and Marian both said green brought out the color of her eyes. She chose another dress from the trunk, a deeper shade of green. She liked to wear green and she wanted them to notice her eyes today. Ann said her eyes were her strongest feature. She untied the box containing her hats. A hat? Maybe. She tried one on and posed in front of the mirror, tilting her head from side-to-side. The brim cast a shadow on her eyes and covered too much of her hair. The hat was tossed aside. She wanted them to see her hair too. It was another strong point because of the color. Despite the heat of the day, she planned to wear her hair down for the interview at the Bird Cage. When she was completely put together, she surveyed the finished product in the mirror. Not bad, considering the trip she'd made and the ghastly misfortune of waking up to a dead man under her window. Last night's bath and extended sleep had done wonders. If she was able to inspire them with a combination of talent and beauty, she just might get herself a job. She hoped there was a guitar in the orchestra pit, but she wouldn't worry about it unless they asked her to play. If it was a theatre of any consequence, they certainly had a guitar. She looked out the window again. The dead man had long since been removed from the street. She sighed as a memory of the green hills around Tralee rolled through her mind. She remembered the boats at Galway, so pretty with their white sails puffing out in the wind, gliding on the blue-green bay water and in the North, the hills were covered with pink and purple blankets of heather. She hadn't thought about Ireland for a long time. So much of the land was green. The Emerald Isle. Here, there was nothing but dust. Did it ever rain in this godforsaken country?

She walked out of the hotel and stood on the boardwalk. Not a single woman in sight. It was a hot day without a cloud in the sky or so much as a hint of a breeze on the air. Stifling hot. Perhaps the ladies were simply keeping cool inside. She looked up and down the street in both directions. There were only men as far as the eye could see. That was no surprise, of course. It was a mining town. She knew that before she came and miners were men after all. The sun's reflection off the street blinded her and she shaded her eyes with one hand. It was too bright, impairing her view beyond a couple of buildings. She'd have to ask directions. Two women were walking toward her. At last. There were some females in this town. Breathing a sigh of relief, she smiled and politely interrupted their conversation. "I'll be beggin' your pardon, ladies. Might you direct me to the Bird Cage Theatre? I'm told 'tis located on Allen Street." Neither answered. Instead, the two of them recoiled in unison, stepping back with a jolt as if they'd been slapped. They looked her up and down, then took another step back as though she were some repulsive leper they were afraid to approach for fear of contracting a disease. She thought to herself, "What an unfriendly way to greet a stranger, and why?" She didn't even know these women, prim and proper housewives, no doubt. Their facial features became contorted, like they'd sucked on sour lemons. One sourpuss took the other's arm and led her in a wide berth out into the street around Rose. As they passed by, they mumbled something about "...disgraceful ...harlots walking the street with decent folk. It gets worse every day." She looked around. No one she could see looked like a harlot. That was a pretty strong word. She started to ask what was wrong, but stood still as they circum-navigated her. She watched them walk stiffly away down the street, a dupli-cate picture of sanctimonious disgust. She smiled to herself. Curious ladies, indeed. Perhaps the sun was too hot. A few doors away, they stopped and turned around. They were too far away to hear what they said, but she knew they weren't inviting her to tea. What had she said to evoke such a rude reaction? Rude and unfriendly! She only asked a simple ques-tion. All she wanted was directions to the Bird Cage Theatre. She looked down at her clothes. She hadn't forgotten anything — not even her under-wear. She was wearing everything and it was all right-side out. What was their problem with her? Oh, well, maybe they had mistaken her for someone else. She shrugged her shoulders and took a deep breath, turning her attention to the business at hand. Where was this Bird Cage anyway? It couldn't be too far. The town wasn't that big. She shaded her eyes again and tried to see up the street, thinking she'd have to get herself a parasol.

A man walking toward her tipped his hat. At least he was friendlier than the two ladies. She stopped him. "I'm in need of some assistance. Would you be so kind as to direct me to the Bird Cage Theatre?" He looked curiously surprised. "Excuse me, Miss, but did you say the Bird Cage?" She answered, "Yes, that's what I said. The Bird Cage Theatre. By chance, do you know the way?" He asked her again. "Are you sure you want to go to the Bird Cage?" She took a deep breath to maintain her patience. For Heaven's sake! Was she mumbling? Was it her Irish brogue they were having so much trouble with? She thought she spoke pretty plain English these days. It was a hot day and he was an exasperating man. Standing in the sun without a parasol trying to get simple directions was most irritating and her patience was fast slipping away. One more time! In an effort to make her question perfectly clear, she enunciated her words precisely and slowly. "Which way to the Bird Cage Theatre? Please, Sir. Do you know where 'tis?" She didn't understand the silly grin on his face or the way he shook his head and pointed up Allen Street. "Two blocks, other side of the street." She thanked him and crossed the street, muttering out loud to herself, "Well, about time. For a while there, I thought no one spoke English in this bloody town." She walked on, reminding herself to get the parasol, unaware the walk across Allen Street was about to lead her to a place that would retain its hold on her forever.

The town had an unmistakable air of excitement about it, much different from New Orleans, but excitement nevertheless. She noticed it right off the stage. Once she found work, maybe it wouldn't be too bad. This morning's shooting was a matter of bad timing and by now, she'd convinced herself it was more than likely a misfortunate accidental discharge of a firearm. As she walked up Allen Street, something drew her attention. Out the corner of her eye, she saw a man on the opposite side of the street watching her. She looked over at him and smiled. He nodded and returned the smile. She couldn't help notice he was tall and very nice-looking, different from other men passing by. Even from a distance, there was a certain ambience about him. Maybe it was the way he carried himself or the way his clothes were tailored. Maybe it was the way he wore his hat. She couldn't decide what it was, but he was definitely attractive. There was the strangest notion he was trying to tell her something. At first, she thought he said something and she stopped walking, but he just stood there looking at her. When he made no move to cross the street, she began to feel a little awkward, wondering if she ought to speak first. — No. It wouldn't be right for a lady to start a conversation. The only reason she stopped the other man was to ask directions. It wasn't the same. She looked at him again. He was too far away. If she spoke, she'd have to raise her voice for him to hear and she wasn't about to yell at a perfect stranger across the street. What did she think she was going to say anyway? She didn't know him and she didn't make a habit of talking to strange men standing on street corners. She looked toward her destination a block away. The heat must be getting to her. Buying that parasol would be the next thing to do as soon as she finished speaking with the proprietor of the Bird Cage. She didn't know why she was drawn to the stranger. Maybe she was feeling lonesome, but then, she might go so far as to say he was intriguing. She allowed herself a small fantasy and smiled at him one more time before walking on. Although her back was to him, she could feel his eyes watching her, staring through the back of her head. Tiny hairs on her neck stood up, and in the heat, a bit of a chill rippled down her backbone. Who was he?

Her attention turned to the Bird Cage Theatre. She needed to present herself the right way if she expected to have a chance at a job. She quickly rehearsed what she planned to say. Where she worked before. How long. What she did there. She couldn't leave out some important detail they'd be looking for in her resumé. There might not be a second chance, so she had to get it all just right and make a good impression the first time. She hated to say the name of the Cordon Bleu, but it had to be done. After today, she'd be able to leave it behind and never think about it again. She heard the music and laughter from a block away. At the front door, she read the marquis, wondering if she might recognize the name of an entertainer who performed at the Cordon Bleu. She ran her finger down the list. None of the names were familiar. Back to the business at hand. She needed the job. More than that. She had to get it! The money she brought with her wouldn't last forever. She smoothed her hair and brushed at her skirt, and stepped inside. That was all it took. The

Bird Cage wrapped itself around her.

It was incredibly noisy for a Saturday afternoon. Where did all the people come from this time of day? The Cordon Bleu wasn't even open until the dinner hour. A cowboy approached and said something to her. She didn't hear for all the noise and she cupped her hand to her ear to let him know she hadn't heard him. Rather than repeat what he said, he took her arm and tried to maneuver her to the bar. He was very rude. A gentleman would never be so bold as to presume a lady would step up to a bar with him, but she didn't let on that she was offended by his rudeness. Instead, she thanked him politely while at the same time pulling her arm away. In case the proprietor was watching, she wouldn't want to appear unfriendly to the customers. She smiled sweetly and said, "No time to socialize. I've come on a business matter." He looked at her like she'd made some kind of joke and repeated, "a business matter?" She didn't understand why he thought that was so funny. People in this town certainly had strange reactions to the things she said. She looked around the room. It wasn't exactly as she'd pictured it. It was nice, but nowhere near as elegant as the Cordon Bleu and the clientele seemed a little on the rough side. She coughed. A thick cloud of smoke hung in the air and the smell of liquor was strong. She didn't like either one, but at least the people were friendly. Several had already spoken to her. That counted for something. If she was going to work here, she'd have to get used to the smell of cigar smoke and whiskey. She turned back to the cowboy and thinking she was agreeable, he took her arm again. She allowed him to hold it so she could ask a question, but she had to raise her voice to be heard above the racket. He persisted in trying to usher her to the bar. She persisted in resisting. After several inquiries as to the whereabouts of the proprietor and a firm refusal to go to the bar, he gave up and walked away. She made it to the bar alone and showed the newspaper clipping to the bartender. He pointed to a table where three men were seated, saying she wanted to talk to the bald-headed man with the beard if she was looking for work. Walking through the room, she felt like everyone was watching her and their stares made her nervous. She didn't realize how much she stood out from the other girls. She hadn't noticed them, but they saw her. She was different, although not different from the way they might have been at one time. She looked so innocent, like a schoolgirl in her neat, summer dress and long hair flowing down her back tied with a green ribbon. She knew she looked younger than her actual years. That might be to her advantage in applying for work. She was right. The younger, the better. She was an unsuspecting lamb, walking straight into the lion's den.

She reached the designated table and took a deep breath, trying to be calm and organize her thoughts. She introduced herself and in a very businesslike manner, stated her purpose for being there. She was applying for a hostess position. She arrived from New Orleans only yesterday and needed to secure employment right away. She believed she met the qualifications for the job advertised in the newspaper. She had experience. She'd worked at the Cordon Bleu Playhouse in New Orleans for three years and was certain she could do the job if it was still available. She placed the newspaper clipping on the table in front of him to be sure he understood which position she was applying for. Without acknowledging a word she said, he stood up. As soon as he was on his feet, she lost her train of thought. He looked like the troll. If she hadn't seen it for herself, she never would have believed two people could look so much alike. She wanted to shout at him and run out of the place, but she controlled her temper. He wasn't the troll she used to know. He was a new troll. She couldn't allow a display of temper to prevent her from having a crack at the job, so she forced a smile and hoped he believed it to be genuine. He wasn't paying attention to what she thought was important, but he realized right away what he had. A gold mine just dropped into his lap.

He walked completely around her, stroking his beard and looking her over as if she were a horse on an auction block. He took her arm and turned her around so her back was to him. When he touched her, she wanted to slap him. His behavior was insulting, but she stood still until his crude inspection was complete. She couldn't allow herself the luxury of telling him where to go. She needed the work. When he was satisfied with her construction, he spoke. Her back was still to him. She turned her head from side-to-side, her response being more than a little dry. "Might you be talkin' to me, Sir?" He grinned at her obvious irritation with him, but didn't answer, speaking instead to the men at the table. "This one's got some fire! They'll like her. Irish, too." She turned all the way around. He was an obnoxious, rude man, and his conduct was outrageously inappropriate, but she bit her tongue to keep from telling him so. He finally asked if she had something to say. When she started to tell what she could do, he cut her off after only a few seconds. The interview was over and he wasn't the least bit interested in what she had to say. She was done before she started. He was talking to the men at the table and they were nodding and smiling. She tapped him on shoulder. "Beggin' your pardon, Sir, but what did you say?

He yelled as if she were deaf. "You're hired. Start tonight." She flinched, taken aback by the way he shouted at her. Ignoring his bad manners, she tried to tell him the rest. The fact she was hired was good, but didn't he want to know what else she could do? Did he ask if she had any experience on the stage? She meant to tell him she played the guitar and sang a little. Did he even care? Didn't seem to. Everything happened so fast and there was so much noise, she couldn't remember what she said and what she hadn't said. It must not have mattered anyway. It seemed like a funny way to hire someone, without asking whether she was qualified. She got the job. That was the important thing. "Begin tonight." That's what he said, but what exactly was her job? He hadn't been clear on that. What was she expected to do? To wear? On second thought, she wasn't so sure she wanted to ask him.

He motioned to a young woman across the room. She was about Rose's age, very pretty and very blonde with long hair past her waist. She observed the girl's behavior as she floated through the room, seeming to be on fairly intimate terms with a lot of the customers. When several men stopped her and tried to convince her to stay at their table, she laughed and brushed away their advances in such a way as to imply she really would prefer to stay. In passing one man, he rudely slapped her behind. Rose was shocked. What a crude display of disrespect. Had it been her, she'd have let him have it with the closest movable object. She'd never stand for that kind of thing. She watched the girl. The neckline of her dress was cut so low that her breasts bounced visibly above the bust line when she walked and it was no secret she wasn't wearing a corset. The hem of her skirt was considerably shorter than the acceptable length for ladies, displaying her shoes and, of all things, her legs. As the girl approached, Rose felt herself blush. There were other women in the room, all dressed in similar fashion. Suddenly, the word "hostess" took on a whole new meaning. The girl didn't seem to notice Rose's disapproving look, smiling as she offered her hand in a friendly greeting. "Lizette. Most people call me just plain Lizzie." Rose shook the girl's hand and thought to herself, "There is nothin' the least bit plain about Lizzie." She'd met her second friend in Tombstone — by the Saints, a prostitute!

She turned to thank the troll for hiring her. He was gone. She didn't even know his name. Probably just as well. She didn't like him anyway. At least she had a job. That was a big relief. She'd thank him later, maybe. Lizzie was tugging at her arm. "Come with me, Rosie." Rose started to say she really didn't care to be called Rosie, but before she got a word out, Lizzie took her by the hand as an adult would a child and guided her through the crowd. She saw the other girls more clearly now. Would she be expected to dress like the others? Of course not. Hostesses didn't dress that way. She looked again. She'd better face facts. This was a different world than where she came from. It wasn't New York or New Orleans. She shook her head. Who did she think she was kidding? Not herself, certainly. Taking note of her former definition of "ladies," it didn't exactly fit these women. She was sure they were perfectly nice people, but ladies? They were not ladies, not by a very long stretch of definition. She'd have to make an adjustment of the term. Appalled at the public displays of affection with men, she tried not to let her disapproval show. Why did they let men get away with such crude advances? She watched as one girl was pulled onto the lap of a man who kissed her profusely right in front of everyone. More shocking was that the girl seemed to have no desire for him to let her go. Instead, she giggled and put her arms around his neck. Did these women have no self-respect? Why was she even asking herself such a ridiculous question? The minute she set foot inside the front door, she knew it wasn't like any place she'd ever been before. She might have come from another city, but she was no fool. She knew exactly what this place was and she knew what she'd be getting herself into if she stayed. Ann Merrick would turn over in her grave if she could see her now. Ann was probably watching from Heaven at this moment. She felt ashamed. She wouldn't want Ann to think all that time teaching her to be a respectable lady was wasted. The time had not been wasted. Events long after Ann's passing resulted in her being here today. It couldn't be helped. Fate dealt the hand and she had to play it out. Win or lose, this was where she had to be. Destiny was not something she had any control over.

They were on their way to the backstage. He jumped out of his chair when he saw Lizzie and put his arm around her like they were old friends. "Who's the good-lookin' redhead, Lizzie?" Lizette shooed him away with her hand. "Her name is Rose, but you'll get your chance to meet her later." Rose shuddered at the thought that what Lizzie said might be true. Right now, they had other business to attend to. He kissed Lizzie on the cheek and let her go, holding out his hand to Rose. When she shook hands with him, he didn't let go. "I'm Luther Cain, hoisting foreman up at the Sulphuret Mine. Nice meetin' you, Miss Rose. When you're up to takin' company, I want to be first. Don't forget! Anyone will tell you I'm not stingy with my money when it comes to a pretty woman." He winked and pulled her a few inches closer, giving her arm a squeeze with the other hand before turning her back over to Lizzie. He was polite enough about the way he said it, but his meaning was quite clear. She was glad Lizzie had her by the hand again, leading the way up the steps to the backstage. She always liked to go behind the stage where she let her imagination run free. It was an exciting place on the other side of the curtain. On the backstage, Lizzie turned to her. "Do you have something to wear tonight?" Between the trunk and cases, Rose had plenty of clothes. "Of course?" She realized her answer was more in the form of a question. She didn't really understand what Lizzie meant. Lizzie held out her skirt and pirouetted on her toes. "Something more fitting than the dress you have on — like this one?" Rose mimicked the performance and Lizzie giggled. She compared her dress with Lizzie's. Lizzie shook her head. There was no comparison and she revised her answer. "Well then, no. I guess I don't have the right dress." It was easy to fix. Lizzie had a couple she could borrow until Rose could make her own. It was Rose's turn to laugh. "Make my own? That's very funny." She could cook and clean, and sing and dance, and a few other things, but she didn't know how to sew. She'd find a seamstress to make whatever she needed. Lizzie puckered her lips and raised her eyebrows. "Listen, Rosie, you've got a lot to learn about Tombstone. There's no seamstress in this town who'll make dresses for ladies at the Bird Cage. I can promise you that. You're on your own. Smith's General Merchandise sells dress material. If they don't have what you want, they'll get it from the mail-order catalog, or we can go someplace else." She tapped Rose's arm. "You'll learn to sew alright. You'll learn to do a lot of things for yourself in this town." Lizzie saw the worried look on Rose's face and changed the subject. It was time to leave for the day. She'd stop by the hotel in an hour with the dresses. Tomorrow, they'd go to Smith's and buy material. Lizzie would help her make a dress. It was easy once you got the hang of it. She shouldn't worry. The girls at the Bird Cage helped each other with things like this, with everything. They stuck together. They had to.

Lizzie's promise was good as gold. Over time, Rose would learn that Lizzie always did what she said she was going to do. A change in plans was not something she handled well. In exactly one hour, she knocked on the door to Rose's room. When Rose opened the door, Lizzie practically flew in, jabbering a mile a minute, and flopped the dresses and accessories on the bed. She was saying she couldn't stay long because she had some things to do before she went to work. Rose thought it odd that Lizzie was planning to work at night. "When do you sleep, Lizette? You were there earlier today." Lizzie hadn't stopped talking since she came through the door, but she was quiet now, puzzled by Rose's question. "I don't understand." Rose laughed. "You were workin' today when we met. Will you be goin' back tonight?" Lizzie was confused. Her reply had a melancholy tone to it, a dismal reflection of the state of her life. "Yes. I like it there. I sleep when I get tired, but mostly, I spend my time at the Bird Cage." Her smile disintegrated and she looked down at the floor. "It's all I have." Rose recognized a fragility in Lizzie, something childlike in nature, but much more than that, a deficiency in her emotional state of being. Her mood changed very fast. One minute, she was laughing, bubbling over with excitement. The next, she was wistful, staring at nothing as though Rose wasn't there. Like pages in a book, turning one after another, the moods changed rapidly. Her eyes said she was afraid, a rabbit caught in a stampede, and finally, drowning in a wave of overwhelming sadness on the verge of tears. Rose had never seen anything like it before. She changed the subject, hoping to snap Lizzie out of the mental chaos brought on by a simple question. "Thank you for lendin' me these beautiful clothes, Lizette. I'll return 'em as soon as I can get some of my own, and I'll be very careful with 'em." Lizzie was still looking at the floor. Rose tried again. She began sorting through the clothes on the bed, holding up each dress and commenting how pretty it was. She tried to draw Lizzie back. "Let's see what other pretty things you have here? 'Tis very thoughtful of you to do this for me."

Lizzie sat on the bed where she'd thrown the clothes and shoes in a heap. The melancholy seemed to be passing. "I brought shoes to match the dresses and something pretty for your hair to go with both of them. The colors are all good together. I like everything to be the same color." The depressed spirit took flight and Lizzie picked up speed. "Your hair is beautiful just the way it is, but I thought maybe you'd like the combs. It gets hot in the Bird Cage and you might want to pin your hair up. That's what I do sometimes, but mostly, I leave it down." She was babbling, but Rose didn't dare interrupt. The outfits were complete and Lizzie was right. Everything did match in color. All Rose had to do was put one on. She was sure they'd fit. Lizzie snapped out of the dismal mood as quickly as she'd entered it and was jabbering about the mail-order catalog at Smith's and how you could order shoes in almost any color, and silk stockings, too.

Rose held each dress up to herself in the mirror and asked Lizzie's opinion. She wasn't sure she could bring herself to wear either one, but she certainly didn't dare say it out loud in front of Lizzie, not after seeing how easily Lizzie was distressed. The black velvet evening gown Marian made exposed a little of her neck, but nothing like these dresses which were more than a little revealing for her taste. If this afternoon was any indication of the clientele who frequented the Bird Cage, it meant the place would be full of men tonight, in which case, she preferred to cover as much of herself as possible. After the earlier episode, she understood how sensitive Lizzie was. She'd have to be careful not to say what she really thought about the dresses. She kept her opinion to herself. Lizzie liked the green one. If she had to wear one of them, the green was probably her first choice. She thanked Lizzie again for bringing them by and said she'd be at the Bird Cage at eight o'clock.

When Lizzie was gone, she hung the dresses up and stood back to look at them. It didn't matter which one she wore. Neither would cover any more of her than the other, but she couldn't hurt Lizzie's feelings by not wearing one, not after what just happened. She didn't know if she could go through with this. She touched each dress. She guessed she'd probably wear the green one. The material looked like satin — not real satin, but a good imitation. Green was the best color for her. She repeated what Ann said, that green brought out the color of her eyes and called attention to her red hair, but tonight, she wasn't so sure she wanted to call that much attention to herself.

At seven o'clock, she pulled her hair back on one side and held it in place with Lizzie's comb. There were fluffy, black feathers attached to the sparkling comb. As soon as it was in place, something happened to her. She didn't know what it was, but she recognized the feeling as an indication of things to come. She slipped into the green imitation-satin dress. Lizzie was bigger than her and she thought the dress would hang loose. Much to her surprise, it fit like it was sewn to her measurements. The shoes were a match just as Lizzie said and they complemented the dress, although the heels were higher than any she'd worn before, and they were too big. Lizzie's feet were considerably larger. She'd have to stuff something in the toes to keep them on her feet tonight and buy a pair in the right size tomorrow. Thanks to Ann Merrick, she learned to walk in high-heeled shoes, but it wasn't the heels that presented the problem, it was the size of the shoes. Thanks to Ann, she learned a lot of things. Sadly, she had the feeling none of those lessons would apply in the world she was about to enter.

Her back was to the mirror. She was afraid to look at herself. When she did, she took a step back. She was facing a stranger. No longer would she be looked upon as a respectable woman. The response from the two ladies in front of the hotel earlier today verified that. All she had to do was mention she worked at the Bird Cage and those respectable, Sunday-go-to-meeting, Bible-thumping ladies would damn her as soon as look at her. It was a sure bet they wouldn't waste their time praying for her salvation either. They wouldn't walk on the same side of the street with her. The way things were going, that's how it would be from now on. What was done, was done. She was here and she worked at the Bird Cage. She'd ignore what the so-called respectable women of Tombstone said about her. She'd go to work every night and smile at the gentlemen. She could even learn to tolerate the touching to a certain degree. She'd simply ask them to stand back if their advances were improper. That wouldn't be so hard. She let out a long sigh. Easier said than done. It would be very hard. She'd have to put up with a lot and she knew it. To politely ask them to remember they were gentlemen would make them laugh because most of them weren't. That was clear from the sampling of customers she was exposed to earlier in the day. She needed a job and was lucky to have this one, and she'd do whatever it took to keep it. As soon as she saved some money, she'd find a little house and move out of the hotel. It was just a job. How bad could it be? All she had to do was spend a few hours there every night. The rest of the time was her own. This was her home now. If not home, at least, the place she lived, and she intended to make the best of it. She paused at the door, John's memory engulfing her like flames in dry grass. She closed her eyes and whispered, "I love you, John. I'll always be yours."

She left her room at the Cosmopolitan and crossed Allen Street, unaware of the stares. Most women in her profession lived in or near the Red Light District, but she hadn't been here long enough to know. The night air was a welcome relief from the hot July day and she breathed deeply of the coolness. Some unexpected, sweet fragrance made her take another deep breath. In this town of saloons and killings in the street, there was a delicate flower blooming somewhere close by. It smelled a lot like jasmine and reminded her of home. She wondered how many people in this town noticed the sweet smell. Few, if any. She missed the jasmine outside her window in New Orleans. She remembered everything exactly the way she'd left it in her attic room and what Ann said about the place she left behind as a young girl. "Home is something you never forget."

A lot went through her mind during the walk to the Bird Cage. Here she was, in the middle of nowhere, surrounded by nothing but dust and cactus. The newspaper ad said something about the best climate in the country. That remained to be seen. So far, the weather had been hot and dusty. A sudden gust of wind conjured up a dirt devil in the street and blew a cloud of dust in her face. She covered her face with her hands. Too late. A few grains of sand irritated her eye. She made the mistake of rubbing it and felt the cutting. Her eye teared up and she turned toward the building to await relief from the burning. Why now? She didn't want to go to a new job with red eyes. She stood still while the tears did their work. Someone was watching her. At first, she didn't see him. It was more like she felt his eyes. Across the street, he was leaning against a post; the same man she saw earlier. He was more handsome than she remembered. The eye was better. She had to get to work. She glanced in his direction one more time. Who was he and why was he looking at her? It was the same as this afternoon. She almost said something, but remembered the way she was dressed — like a dance-hall trollop. That was pretty funny. She was a dance-hall... saloon girl! She walked on. She didn't have to turn around to know he was still watching her. She could feel it.

At the front entrance, she looked inside. The place was packed. Music and laughter and the clinking of glass told her this was nothing like the theatre life she was used to. She wondered why they called it a theatre. It was a fancy saloon with a floor show. She was nervous about the dress. At least she wasn't alone. The other women dressed the same way. She took a deep breath. She hoped the men who frequented the establishment wouldn't think her to be as free with her affection as the other girls who worked here simply because she dressed like them. She'd make that perfectly clear right off the bat — she hoped. She filled her lungs with the sweet night air. If she could just get through the first night, she'd be alright from then on. There was no reason to be so nervous. She'd worked in a theatre with lots of people before. She looked down at the low neckline of her dress and tried to pull it up a little. The Cordon Bleu was nothing like this. Once again, it wasn't the people that made her nervous, it was the way she was dressed — like a dance-hall trollop. There was no other way to say it and she did work in a saloon. She had to keep reminding herself of that. Realization can be painful, yet enlightening. Ann's words rung true. "Once you know who you are, everything else falls into place." She was beginning to realize who she was, or more appropriately, what she was about to become.

She'd been told to enter by the back door. She walked to the corner and around the buildings to the rear entrance of the Bird Cage. The door was locked from within. She knocked several times before someone finally opened it. Lizzie! Thank God for a familiar face. It was easier already. Before she was all the way inside, the pretty blonde gave her a hug. Lizzie was excited and talking so fast it was hard to pick up every word. It was bound to be a busy night. Payroll for the mines was in and there was money to be spent here tonight. Lots of money! There'd be high-stakes poker and faro games all night long and if that wasn't enough, the entertainment would hold the men here 'til sun-up. Dancers from the French cancan circuit were in town and they put on one hell of a show. Between acts of well-known headliners, Ruby Fontaine and her dancers filled in the gaps and dazzled the clientele with their own tantalizing version of the cancan, among other things. Their risque performance in which they divested themselves of what little costumes they wore, down to the red feathers in their hair and glittering garters holding up fishnet stockings, enticed customers to sit right where they were. Some stayed all night for the delectable pleasure of watching Ruby dance and peel her clothes off. A full line of singers, dancers, comedians, acrobats and magicians were scheduled to charm and amuse a demanding audience, and the ladies of the Bird Cage would be there to offer a gentle diversion from the stage acts and gambling. They'd encourage patrons to lessen the burden of their purses and money belts by buying a more intimate kind of performance offered in private by a soiled dove. If Rose was smart, she'd leave with a heavy purse. Between the gambling and stage shows, a lot of money passed through the Bird Cage. Rose wasn't sure which of the two was the most popular, but since fortunes were won or lost at the turn of a card, she assumed gambling was the big attraction.

Lizzie led her across the floor to a room behind the stage. In the doorway, she ran head-on into another girl. The girl was tall and the collision nearly knocked Rose down. Luckily, neither ended up on the floor. They grapled awkwardly at each other until they were finally steady on their feet. When they confirmed neither was injured, they both laughed. The girl introduced herself as Jenny. "Everybody calls me Silver Dollar Jenny." Lizzie whispered in Rose's ear. "That's because she only takes silver dollars." Lizzie raised her eyebrows in an all-knowing expression. Rose didn't understand. "Only takes silver dollars for what?" Lizzie winked at her. She thought Rose was making a joke. Jenny was another pretty one, very young though. Rose estimated her age at somewhere around eighteen, nineteen at the most. How did the young ones find their way here? What possibly went wrong so early in their lives that they ended up at the Bird Cage? Of course, she'd been asking herself the same question. When Rose spoke, Jenny laughed. "Say something else, Rose. I like the way you Irish talk. It's cute." Lizzie said so too. She was feeling better already. Lizzie motioned with her finger for Rose to follow her. "Come on, Rosie. I'll take you downstairs to meet Ruby and the girls."

Beneath the stage were more rooms. At the first doorway, she saw several scantily-dressed women inside. Believing they were in their underwear, she closed the door. Men were playing cards at a table just outside the room, but they were so engrossed in their game, they didn't seem to be paying attention to the half-naked ladies a few feet away. Still, the door ought be closed. Lizzie stepped in front of her and flung it wide open, calling to the women inside. Rose glanced over at the poker table to see if any of the men were watching. A couple looked toward the room and Rose tried to stand in the doorway to block their view of the undressed ladies. Lizzie maneuvered Rose into the room. "Meet Rose Callahan." One of them put her arm around Rose, gesturing toward the others. "I'm Eva, and this is Annie and Marie, and you'll have to do better than that. Do you mind if we call you Rosie?" She preferred Rose, but they could call her whatever they wanted to. Lizette had been calling her Rosie since they met and she was waiting for precisely the right time to tell her about it, a time when it wouldn't upset her. She didn't like being called Rosie. Eva touched her arm. "Nevermind, we'll think of something." Maybe a nickname to go along with her red hair. It wasn't important now. Sooner or later, she'd get a sobriquet. It was only a matter of time. "Another redhead! Just what we need! Do you have a bad temper?" They all laughed. She didn't know what was so funny, but she smiled anyway and shook her head, no. She wouldn't want them to think her unfriendly.

They were the dancers. Rose felt a little uncomfortable. They didn't have much on and there were, after all, men in the vicinity. At the poker table, the game was heating up and with so much money at stake, none of the players seemed interested in what was going on in the dressing room. She looked back at the women, wondering what kind of dancers dressed like this. She was sure she'd find out soon enough. You couldn't even delineate their costumes as suggestive because they didn't leave anything to the imagination. They were tight-fitting all the way around — what there was of them, and their breasts were pushed over the top in a most precarious arrangement. The bottoms were cut high at the hip as well as in front with nothing more than a string-like piece of fabric between the buttocks. Black fishnet hose adorned with red garters and red satin shoes completed the costume. Her first thought was that the outfits must be terribly uncomfortable. The only saving grace was a very short piece of material resembling a skirt of sorts, possibly four inches in length, but it didn't save much of anything. Their bottoms were essentially bare. She felt herself blush. They wore tall, fluffy, red feathers in their hair and their faces had been painted and powdered. Their cheeks were colored with rouge and their lips were red. They looked more like sad, porcelain dolls than live girls.

Before she could be too shocked, the big redhead stepped forward. She grabbed Rose's hand and shook it. She had a grip like a man — a strong man. "Ruby Fontaine. Welcome to the Bird Cage, Honey." Ruby wasn't exactly a kid, not like the rest of them anyway. She was thirty-five, if she was a day. Exceptionally well-preserved for an older woman, she had the figure of a twenty year-old. She was tall. Six feet, at least. Her legs were long and shapely, but muscular from years of exercise, the legs of a dancer. She told Rose if anyone gave her trouble at the Bird Cage, she was the one to see. From the looks of her, Ruby could, no doubt, handle just about anything that came up. It went without saying, she kept the rest of them in line. If there was anyone she'd never want to tangle with, it was Ruby. By the same token, if she needed help, Ruby was the one who'd come to her rescue. The redhead commented on Rose's fair complexion. At the same time, Rose took note of Ruby's overindulgence with the face paint, as if she'd applied the makeup by handfuls without benefit of a mirror. Ruby lifted Rose's chin to get a better look at her face. "You need some color?" Rose politely refused, explaining that she wouldn't know how to go about applying the stuff. All she ever did was pinch her cheeks to make them pink. Ruby winked and tapped her finger on Rose's nose. With a sly smile, she pointed at Rose and told her to "stand right there." Ruby went to a dressing table and Eva lowered her voice. "When Ruby tells you to do something, you don't back talk her." Rose already figured that out. Arguing with Ruby was the furthest thing from her mind and she didn't move an inch.

Ruby was back in half a shake carrying three silver containers and a small brush. The girls gathered around. This would be one show they didn't want to miss. She handed the two smaller boxes to Lizzie and took the lid off the biggest one. Slowly and deliberately, she rubbed a pad over the powdery contents of the dish, calculating the right amount of the cosmetic preparation needed. Without warning, she puffed it in Rose's unsuspecting face. The shock wasn't anticipated and the girls laughed at Rose's startled reaction. Ruby squinted her eyes and moved in closer, like a cat stalking a mouse. Rose didn't dare move. The redhead carefully smoothed the silky powder on Rose's face. For such a large woman, her touch was amazingly gentle, but Rose imagined how that touch would change for the person who was unlucky enough to be on the receiving end of Ruby's bad temper. She had a handshake like a man and she probably had a punch like one too. Although stories Rose had heard about red-headed women having volatile tempers didn't necessarily apply to her, she had a feeling this redhead was the one about whom such stories were told. When Ruby was satisfied with the face-powder application, she closed the box and traded Lizzie for the next one. Inside the second box was a pink rouge as soft and silky as the powder. She ran two fingers over the blusher powder and applied it gently to Rose's cheeks, spreading it around in circles. That step completed, she stood back to view her work, tilting her head from side-to-side like an artist scrutinizing his masterpiece. Concentrating on the picture, she narrowed her eyes and bit her lower lip. Not quite finished. Lizzie handed her the smallest silver box and the tiny brush. She opened the container and ran the brush back and forth across a crimson lip paint several times, loading it with color. Rose laughed at the funny way Ruby puckered her mouth, demonstrating the position in which Rose was to hold her lips to receive the paint. The girls giggled. Ruby jerked her head to the side and gave them a threatening scowl intended to scare them and they laughed again. They knew when she was kidding, and they knew when she wasn't. It was okay to laugh this time. The big redhead moved in for the final touch, lightly applying the paint to Rose's mouth. The tiny brush tickled her lips and she flinched. Ruby grabbed her chin and told her to hold still. This was serious business. Rose became a statue and the girls held their hands across their mouths to stifle the giggles. When the makeup was done, Ruby stepped back and surveyed the finished painting, nodding her approval.

Lizzie handed Rose a mirror. What she saw rendered her speechless.

She couldn't believe what she was looking at. The feeling was similar to the one she experienced in front of the mirror in her room. A chill ran all the way up her back and into her head and the image in the mirror took her breath away; a revelation of sorts. It made her want to cry. She stared at the painted woman looking back at her, a stranger. Unable to look away, she made a silent promise not to become as hard as the rest of them. She listened to the way they talked. She'd never resort to speaking the rough language of dance-hall girls and prostitutes. She knew that's what they were — all of them. Even the sweet ones, Lizzie and Silver Dollar Jenny. And Ruby. Especially Ruby. She watched the way the tall redhead moved. Most definitely, Ruby! For obvious reasons, they called her Ruby Red. They didn't have to say it, that word decent people couldn't say. Prostitute. She didn't need to be told what they did when they left the stage. Some things never had to be said. If she stayed in this place, she'd be forever branded with the same disparaging title they carried — the infamous "soiled dove." Ladies of the night! She'd hear much worse than that over time. It didn't matter what they were called. The cold, undisputable truth was they were prostitutes, pure and simple.

She raised the hand mirror to her face. She was nearly twenty-four years old. John was out of her life. There was nowhere else to go. Her dreams had fallen apart like an over-bloomed rose, its petals fallen on the ground and scattered to the winds of oblivion. Her life was most likely close to being over anyway. It didn't matter what she did for a living. There was a time when she never wanted life to end, a time when the future was filled with hope and love. Now, she was marking time to the cadence of a drum that was her own heartbeat. Life had become a distance too far to travel alone. Without John, the journey no longer had purpose. Without purpose, there was no life. She was like a mountaineer facing the mountain with no climbing apparatus on hand, the summit hidden far above the clouds, somewhere in Heaven, perhaps, out of reach of mortal man. There would never be a man to love her the way John loved her. He was the solitary love of her life. Her silent prayer was that they would one day be reunited at the summit through some incomprehensible passage in Time, a passage beyond human existence where their spirits would fly together into eternity. She wondered if he'd recognize her. She'd know him instantly.

She remembered her mother's locket around her neck. It was a part of someone pure and good. It was a sacrilege to bring it into this place.

She'd never wear it here again. It wouldn't be right. She handed the mirror to Ruby and thanked her for the makeup. Ruby's eyes softened. She knew the look. She saw it on her own face once. It was a long time ago, but she remembered. She'd never forget that feeling. Everyone viewed her as a hard woman. They'd never know the truth about Ruby Fontaine. They'd never know the pain she tucked away inside herself years ago. She put her arm around Rose. It was the only comfort she could offer. Ruby understood. She didn't have to say it. Rose could see it in her eyes. The girls stood by in silence, all traces of laughter gone. That's all they were — girls. Except for Ruby, most of them were younger than Rose and lonely, just like her. The notorious "Shady Ladies" of Tombstone. She was one of them now.

Chapter 6

"Feathers of red and a wink in your eye,
you knew how to steal the show;
To a tinny piano that Charlie played
you danced and sang while the whiskey flowed.
They whistled and roared when the curtain went up,
and you stepped onto the stage.
They went wild for your dancin'
when they came for romancin'
at the old Bird Cage."

At The Old Bird Cage
ALLEN STREET ROSE

Rose didn't talk when she and Lizzie walked upstairs. The dancers were almost ready for the show to begin and the rest of them were supposed to be out front mixing with customers. Lizzie opened the door and Rose stepped onto the landing next to the stage. She hesitated at the top of the stairs, looking over the room. It was the noisiest place she'd ever seen and the smoke was incredibly thick. She detested cigar smoke. It always choked her. As she expected, there were no women in the room except the ones who worked there. After what she'd seen downstairs, she wasn't a bit surprised to know there were no female patrons. No respectable woman would set foot inside a place like this. In fact, they didn't walk on this side of Allen Street in front of the Bird Cage. Only men came here. The entertainment was strictly for men. Lizzie told her that. Below the stage, a monstrous, black, grand piano stood guard like a sentinel protecting the world beyond the curtain. Two musicians were tuning their violins in the orchestra pit. The piano player was already on his seat, striking keys one at a time for the fiddle players to get in tune. He looked up at Rose and gave her a big smile when he spotted her on the steps. He winked and pulled at his moustache to be funny. He was very young. Just a kid. She wondered how someone his age managed to grow a moustache. Cute. She smiled back.

He was only a few feet away, but he had to shout at the top of his lungs to be heard over the din. He stood up and leaned over the piano, tipping his black bowler. "I'm Charlie. Charles Francis Patrick O'Brien — of the Kilkenny O'Briens, that is." As an afterthought, he added, "...by way of Alabama. They call me Piano Charlie. Welcome to the Bird Cage." An Irishman, but no brogue. Instead, his speech was heavily saturated with the lazy roll and deliberate slowness of the deep South. Everyone was welcoming her to the Bird Cage. It certainly was a friendly bunch. She acknowledged his greeting by wiggling her fingers at him. She'd tell him her name later. No sense trying to talk to him from this distance.

A noise overhead drew her attention. Above the gambling hall and theatre on both sides were small rooms that seemed to be suspended from the ceiling. They were separate, tiny rooms, cribs, barely large enough for two people. Each was occupied by a lady and a gentleman, acting very friendly with one another. At first, she imagined they were theatre boxes, private rooms rented by customers for a bird's-eye view of the stage. Maybe they were the cages that gave the place its name. She noticed them this afternoon and meant to ask Lizzie, but it slipped her mind. She'd seen theatre boxes before at the Cordon Bleu. That place! She shuddered at the name. She never wanted to think of it again. And the troll! The despicable creature! She hoped he'd rot in hell for setting her up. Unbelievable as it was, there was a troll here, but she'd be smarter this time. She wouldn't fall into any traps. From above, the boxes provided a nice view of the stage, but they were different from the ones at the Cordon Bleu. Heavy drapes drawn across some of the compartments were not conducive to watching the show and it didn't take much imagination to figure out the purpose of the little rooms hanging from the ceiling. She looked over the smokey gambling hall. So, this was the Bird Cage Theatre.

In the distance, she heard the faint tinkling of what she thought was a music box. It couldn't be. A music box — here? This place was far too raucous for something as genteel as a music box. She strained to hear it. Strange, she couldn't hear the piano player from six feet away, yet she could hear the delicate tones of a music box drifting across the room. How that sweet melody fought its way to her through the noise, she'd never know. No one else paid any attention to it and she imagined it was playing just for her. The music was incredibly beautiful and she thought about John. She missed him more every day. She felt like crying.

Lizzie poked a finger gently into the small of Rose's back and whispered for her to move on down the steps. The daydreaming ended with Lizzie's prodding and she became aware of the faces in the room below. They were all watching her and their stares made her uncomfortable. She didn't know it, but they'd never seen the likes of her in this town. How long had she been standing there? Lizzie poked her again, a little harder the second time, and it set her in motion. One hand on the railing, she took the first step down the stairs. Every man's heart skipped a beat as the beautiful red-haired girl with the emerald-green eyes came down the steps. No longer cloddish and ungraceful, she walked the way Ann taught her to walk and carried herself like a lady. She was a lady, albeit misplaced by fate. It was a grand entrance. In years to come, this summer night in 1881 would be remembered by those who were there as the night they fell in love with Allen Street Rose.

All eyes were on her as she walked through the room. Her lips quivered from nervousness. They were smiling at her and she tried to smile back, but felt uneasy knowing what was on their minds. Near the back of the room, she heard the music start. Charlie played the fanfare and she turned around. The show had begun. A very animated man on the stage was introducing the first act. The piano played a lively tune. The curtain went up and everyone clapped and whistled. The ladies she met downstairs stepped onto the stage to a roar of applause. To her great relief, they were wearing long, shimmering, silver gowns. She relaxed. So, there was more to their costumes than she originally thought. That was much better. The red satin slippers drew attention to their legs as they were revealed through the side openings of the gowns, slit to the thigh on one side and gathered up in a drape effect. She could tolerate that much. Their movements, however, were designed to tantalize the audience and if not for all the powder and rouge Ruby plastered on Rose's face, everyone would have seen her blushing from embarrassment. They began singing. Rose was impressed with their talent and soon relaxed, finding herself smiling and enjoying the performance. It wasn't so bad after all.

At the end of the song, the audience was on their feet, clapping and whistling again. The piano moved right into the next number. Ruby was at the edge of the stage. The others followed her lead. Rose held her breath. They were taking off their clothes. She was petrified. Everyone was watching the dancers, but she felt conspicuous in the middle of the room. The gowns were off and tossed to the rear of the stage. The crowd was roaring. No wonder. From where Rose stood, the girls appeared to be nearly naked. The costumes she'd seen earlier were in full view — what there was of them. More disturbing was that the women were in full view. Her feet were riveted to the floor. She stood perfectly still staring at the stage. The act that followed was a risque exhibition of feminine charm, obviously appreciated by the male population. Never, in her wildest imagination, had she dreamed that a woman could perform for an audience with such explicit sexual connotations. She'd never even considered a performance like that in the privacy of her own room. She certainly knew what sex was. It was a word you just didn't say. Her great misfortune was to have experienced it's cruelest form. These women were purposefully soliciting the response of every man present. It was disgraceful. She stopped herself. What was she thinking? Fact was, she was thinking in terms of respectability and that didn't apply here. This stuff went on every night. This, and worse. It wasn't a Sunday-afternoon family picnic. Tombstone was a mining camp turned boomtown, full of men and with a shortage of women, and this kind of entertainment was in large demand. It was the Bird Cage Theatre playing to the crowd and she'd better get used to it if she intended to stay. Lizzie was off into the room and Rose panicked when she found herself alone. Ruby's scandalous performance threw her composure completely off balance and she tried to gather her wits, concentrating on removing any trace of shock from her face.

He startled her. She hadn't seen him standing there. He said something, but she couldn't hear above the music. Not wanting to be impolite, she forced a smile. It was weak, at best. She took a deep breath and tried to make the smile a little more convincing. She shook her head, letting him know she hadn't heard what he said. He moved closer. Her heart raced when she felt his breath on her ear. She wanted to run out of the room, but she stood her ground. She remembered Ann's lesson about remaining calm in a crisis. Not sure why she felt his being so close was a crisis, it was the feeling. The sun had tanned his face and turned his brown hair to the color of golden sand. For all his weathered appearance, he was not without appeal. His expression was placid, undisturbed by the stage exhibition or the noise around them. He didn't smile. She was struck by the depth of his eyes. They were the bluest blue. John! The eyes were like John's. No, they weren't like John's. They were blue, but not steel-blue like John's.

His hand was on her arm. She started to pull away, but changed her mind. She stared at the floor, trying to think whether to stay or run. A second time, he waited for her to withdraw. She had the feeling that if she moved away, he wouldn't try to stop her. She looked around the room. Most men were not nearly as attractive as this one or as civil. Truth was, many were vulgar and repulsive. He wasn't forcing her down on his lap and kissing her like some did with the other ladies. In fact, he wasn't being the least bit forceful. His hold on her arm was light, giving her the chance to walk away if she wanted to. When she didn't go, he guided her toward a table where two other men were seated. He introduced his companions. They were waiting for her to give her name. She started to say "Miss Callahan," but stopped herself. Given the circumstances of their meeting, that would sound ridiculous. He pulled a chair out and she sat down. They were still waiting for her to say her name and she was uncomfortable with the way they looked at her. She didn't want them to think she was like the other girls simply because she dressed the way they did and painted her face. Her mouth was dry from the tension when she spoke. "Rose." No last name was required. They probably didn't care what her first name was and she'd already forgotten theirs, but at least she made an effort to be sociable. That's what she was paid to do.

She never drank whiskey in her life. It was being offered. She knew this was part of her job too. She took the glass and thanked him. When she raised it to her lips, the smell was overpowering and she coughed. He patted her on the back and her eyes teared up. She'd never be able to go through with this. She tried again. Determined to get it down, she held her breath and allowed a drop of the liquid into her mouth. As soon as she swallowed it, she choked and coughed again. It burned her throat all the way down to her stomach. She looked at him for help, like a deer sinking in quicksand. He threw her an invisible rope. He moved closer and placed his arm around the back of her chair. He wasn't going anywhere and he wasn't forcing her to drink the whiskey either. Her hand was shaking when she reached for the glass and he pushed it away toward the man across the table. For the first time since she saw him, he smiled. "You don't have to drink it. Jesse will take care of it." He motioned to the other man, then rested his hand on her bare shoulder. It was warm, but his touch gave her chills and set her heart racing. When he moved his fingers over her skin, her pulse pounded wildly, echoing in her head. His mouth brushed against her ear. The moustache tickled and she moved away, laughing out of nervousness because she didn't know what else to do. He pulled her back gently, whispering her skin had the feel of silk and her hair was a blazing fire, drawing him to its warmth. Poetic courtship for a lady of easy virtue. She didn't know if it was his words or the way he touched her that made her shiver.

While he talked, she watched the next table. Lizzie was in a similar situation, except the miner who had ahold of her didn't whisper passionate compliments in her ear. He was rough and his hands were all over her. She caught Lizzie's eye. This was all part of the job. They didn't have to speak to understand what the other was thinking. Lizzie was laughing. When they talked earlier, Lizzie said she liked it here. Watching her friend being mauled by the greasy-handed miner, it was hard to believe that could be true. Rose looked away and shivered again when he touched the back of her neck. She sat perfectly still, clenching her teeth together until the muscles in her jaw cramped. She knew what was coming next. He took something from his vest pocket. The silver dollars made a loud clunk when they hit the wooden tabletop. She stared at the money. Payment for her services! Was this the customary fee? She had no idea what the ladies charged for their favors. They hadn't gotten that far in their conversation. Was she really expected to do this? No one actually told her what to do. She didn't touch the money. She remembered what Lizzie said about Jenny. "She only takes silver dollars." Three dollars was a lot of money.

Jesse hadn't touched the glass of whiskey in the middle of the table. When she looked at it, he slid it back in front of her, offering to replace it with some tea. She shook her head, no, and stared into the amber liquid. Then, she picked it up and held the glass to her lips, slowly inhaling the aroma of the liquor. The smell didn't repulse her like it did the first time. Maybe she ought to have the fortification of a little hard liquor to help her through the rest of the night. She closed her eyes and took a tentative sip. It burned all the way down, but she didn't choke or gag. She took another sip. The second swallow went down easier than the first. The burning sensation decreased. He sat very close and let her take her time with the drink. By the time it was gone, she was getting numb and a bit fuzzy-headed. His arm was around her, lifting her to her feet. The three silver dollars were still on the table. He picked them up and handed them to her. Without a word, he turned her around. She looked up at the suspended cribs. She didn't know how to get up there, but it didn't matter. He knew the way.

The curtain was down between acts. Card games were in progress, music played, and people were laughing and clinking glasses in what seemed to be ongoing toasts for a reason to drink more. Every now and then, a poker chip hit the floor. She felt as though she were walking through a dream. Something stopped her. Lizzie was near the stairs and he allowed them the moment. Neither of them smiled or said anything. Lizzie understood this was the first time for Rose. She wasn't alone. They'd all been there. The first time was the hardest. Starting up the stairs, her feet were heavy and she felt like her ears were stuffed with cotton. He was right behind her, steadily moving her forward. She was walking up the steps, listening to people going in and out through the front door behind her. At the top, he led her across the catwalk and down the narrow corridor. She stopped walking. Down the hall, she knew what awaited her behind one of the doors. This was the way to the suspended cribs above the theatre. She felt his body touching hers. He placed one hand on her shoulder, close to her neck. His fingers squeezed gently and the pressure sent a tingle through her whole body. He was waiting for her to walk on, but she was thinking about something. She didn't even know his name. She asked. Didn't he think he ought to at least tell her his name? He answered her question with another question. Was it really important? He didn't give her time to answer and propelled her forward again. Earlier words repeated themselves in her head. Resignation of Destiny. Halfway down the corridor, he stopped. Still holding her arm, he reached around her to open the door. She went in ahead of him and he closed the door.

The crib was very small. With furniture limited to absolute necessities to serve a specific purpose, there was barely enough room to turn around. Two people were cramped in the confined area and the only way to relieve the overcrowding was for both of them to occupy the bed at the same time. The tiny room contained a small bed covered by a flamboyant red and gold spread with several pillows, and the carpet was a garden of roses underfoot. Beside the bed, a black, oriental table atop the carved feet of a dragon held a slender, glass oil lamp with red and gold crystal pendants dangling all around the edge of a miniature umbrella shade. The final touch, on the wall, a gold-framed portrait of a naked lady, her flimsy drape covering nothing, bespoke the irrefutable intendment of the room. Although a bit extreme for its diminutive size and for all its implications, the overall chinoiserie was exotic. It could have been the boudoir of an oriental princess rather than a temporary crib used by prostitutes. The opposite side was a window to the theatre and he released the ropes holding back the red velvet draperies so they fell across the opening. Noise from the gambling hall below became muffled. He lit the oil lamp and the little room was instantly alive with a thousand invisible, dancing imps reflecting from the swinging crystal prisms. They were in a separate, elevated world near the ceiling. She hadn't moved since they entered the room. He waited, watching her. Again, he was giving her a chance to change her mind. He figured it was her first time. She didn't know what to do. An experienced lady of the night wouldn't be so apprehensive. He didn't take his eyes off her as he laid his hat on the table and his revolver beside the hat. He unfastened his gunbelt and let it drop to the floor. The refracted light from the crystal pendants bounced off the pearl-handled gun, exaggerating the colors and causing the imps to leap and fly wildly across the dark curtain in seemingly perpetual motion.

He hadn't made a move to touch her. He said she was pretty. That wasn't what she was expecting and the compliment made her blush. She smiled and looked down at her hands, clasped and fidgeting with each other. He touched her hair, curling a strand around his finger. He said it felt like spun silk. Then, he said she didn't have to stay if she didn't want to. She could keep the money and they'd go back downstairs and talk. He didn't want her to be afraid of him. At first, she thought she'd heard wrong. He'd already paid for her favors, probably more than was required, and he was offering to let her keep it without giving him his money's worth? She stared at him, dumbfounded by what he said. A man with compassion? She was pretty sure there weren't many like him passing through the doors of this place. He was no straight-off-the-range ordinary cowboy or uncouth clod like the rough-handed, profanity-spewing type Lizzie was stuck with downstairs. Poor Lizzie. She wouldn't be so lucky tonight. Neither would she if she turned this one down. She shook her head "no" and whispered, "I'll stay." He kissed her, first on the cheek, then on the lips. She dropped her hands at her sides and stood perfectly still with her eyes closed. He reached behind her and turned the lock on the door. She kept her eyes closed while he unfastened her dress and when he let it fall to the floor, she stepped out of the pile of green imitation satin. The silky camisole came off slowly, his hands gently caressing her body. He took his time undressing her. Despite the fact that he was paying for her favors, he was doing his best to let her know he wanted her to enjoy the time. She watched the way he looked at her body. He appreciated what he saw. He was easy on the eyes as well. She had to admit she could have done worse by way of a man. Surely, one with his looks and gentle temperament would have no trouble finding a woman, a respectable woman. Why did he come looking for one in a bordello? She knew the answer. For whatever reason, he wasn't able to settle down. Circumstances in his life made him a drifter or something along that line. It hadn't always been that way, but his heart was broken and like her, he'd given up the search for love. She didn't know the details, but the story was on his face. She didn't have to know the details to know they were a lot alike. There was a sadness in his eyes. She wanted to ask if he'd tell her about it, but there was no reason. Before the sun came up tomorrow, he'd move on. After tonight, she'd never see him again. She took the feathered comb out to let her hair down and laid down on the bed. He wasn't in any hurry to get it over with and he didn't take his eyes off her as he turned the lamp flame lower. She'd never been with a man like this. Her only sexual encounters were instances of violent abuse where she feared for her life. This time, there was no fear, no anticipation of pain. He was gentle and passionate and she allowed herself to be swept away in the lovemaking. She knew he felt the same way. It wasn't love, of course, not by any wild stretch of imagination. They both knew that. She didn't even know his name. It was simply a fleeting moment in Time, a moment they both needed and perhaps, in some strange way, it was love.

When it was over, they lay in the glow of the oil lamp. He held her close for a long time without saying a word. Finally, he spoke, whispering he'd never forget her. He'd been quiet, thinking. It took a lot for him to tell her and she knew he said it because he meant it. The words came from somewhere deep inside. She'd never forget him either. It didn't matter that he hadn't told her his name. It wasn't important. After all, they'd never see each other again. He watched her talk. It was important. She wouldn't have said it that way if it wasn't important. He was quiet for few more minutes. "People know me. That's why I can't stay in Tombstone long. It's better if you don't know my name." She didn't understand. Why couldn't he stay? He wasn't a criminal or anything like that. Was he? He didn't answer. She asked again. Was he running from the law? His body stiffened at the question and she knew that was it. He was on the run. His expression told her to leave it alone. No more questions. Before they left the room, he held her one last time in a bittersweet embrace. He was trying to say something else. He never did. A final kiss took the place of words, a gentle kiss, but one without feeling; only a gesture at making the time spent together seem a little less impersonal. He didn't have to say the words. They would never meet again. He picked up the three silver dollars and handed them to her. "I gave the rest to Ruby." Twenty-eight dollars all tolled. Three extra for her trouble. The words were cold and the significance of the money hit home. She was one of them for sure now. She accepted money for sexual favors. She was a prostitute. The word had such a coldness to it, but cold or not, she was one of them. On the landing beside the stage, he moved her to one side and stepped past her. She stood on the stairs and watched him walk away. At the table where his friends were waiting, he poured himself a drink. He threw it down fast and the other men got up. They were leaving. She didn't expect him to turn around and was surprised when he did. It was only for a second, just long enough to let her know he saw her, and he was gone.

Lizzie was at the bottom of the steps. "Is everything alright?" Rose wanted to scream at her, "No! Of course, everythin' isn't alright." She held her temper. Of all people, Lizzie was not the one she was angry with. Angry and ashamed and disappointed. She was all of those things, but only with herself. She smiled at her friend. "Yes, Lizette. Everythin' is fine." Not only was she a prostitute, but a liar as well. She felt conspicuous, as though everyone was looking at her, all of them knowing what she'd done. They were watching her like a pack of hungry wolves. Sooner or later, they'd all come around, shoving their money in her face or down the front of her dress. They'd seen her come to the landing with the cowboy and they knew where she'd been with him. What they could never know was that her initiation into the ranks of the soiled doves was a gentle fall. It had not been a violent leap into the viper pit that was this room. Few men would treat her with a gentle hand as this one had. Fewer would recognize her pain. She wanted to run away and hide her face where the wolves couldn't see. The thought of being near any of them repulsed her and made her sick at her stomach, but she had to hide what she felt. No purpose would be served by crying or working herself into a fit. Prostitutes took men up to the suspended cribs in a constant stream 'round the clock, twenty-four hours a day, every day of the week, and that would probably include Christmas. If they kept it up at the present rate for long, they'd wear the steps thin from traipsing up and down. It was their job and it was hers.

She held her head high and smiled when she and Lizzie made their way through the room. It was business as usual, nothing more. She had to get that through her head if she expected to last here and make a living. It wasn't as if she had any choice in the matter if she wanted the job. She thought about the cowboy. At least he made her first professional experience, so to speak, less painful than any of the others in the room would have done. Future encounters would be far less tolerable. She wasn't fooling herself about that. The ability to block out feeling was already in place. She felt numb inside. Funny, it hadn't taken long. She used to see the ladies of the night on the street in New Orleans and they often came into the Cordon Bleu with gentlemen. She always recognized them because they had a certain look that identified them for what they were, members of the oldest profession in the world. Sometimes, she'd stare at them, wondering how they could do what they did for money. They were nice enough to her, but there was a coldness about them. Now, she knew why. That's how they all got through it. They didn't allow themselves to feel anything. Their bodies were merely tools of the trade. Well, maybe that wasn't entirely true. They managed to cover their feelings well, but she saw the heartaches through the facade of fancy gowns and smiling, painted faces. Despite what anyone thought, she viewed them as brave women and never criticized them for earning a living the only way they knew how. Unlike women who were fortunate enough to have husbands to take care of them, prostitutes were forced to fend for themselves, the only alternatives being begging or suicide, and she gave them a lot of credit for having learned to survive on their own. They hid their private pain from the men they provided entertainment for and from the rest of the world, but they didn't hide it from each other or from Rose. It was the same in this place. Pain was the common bond that held the girls together for the sake of survival. Each night, the walk up Allen Street got a little easier and each night, she added more stones to the invisible fortress she was building around herself to keep out the hurt. One thing she noticed, some nights were harder than others.

Hours in the dance hall and poker parlour were easily passed. Time in the suspended cribs and basement bordello rooms was more difficult and had to be dealt with in a different frame of mind and dispensed with as quickly as possible. It didn't take long to learn ways to avoid at least some of the unpleasantness. By the time most men made the trip upstairs with her, they were pretty well liquored up. She did her best to see to that. While encouraging them to down glass after glass of hard liquor, she sipped cold tea, the amber color of which gave the appearance of whiskey. Not to be outdone by her request for another drink, they too had another. They were clumsy, drunken sots for the most part, sweating and grunting like pigs in a wallow. Luckily, those who were in the worse shape never obtained the necessary anatomical prerequisite for intimate contact and usually passed out before she had to deal with them on a physical level. She learned fast. She'd let them sleep for half an hour and when she woke them up, she'd pretend to be completely exhausted, claiming they'd absolutely worn her out, and convince them they'd had the time of their lives. What could they say? They'd never admit to not remembering a damn thing. If they did, they'd be the laughing stock of their friends when they went downstairs. She had to control herself to keep from laughing out loud when they puffed themselves up like roosters fresh out of the chicken coop. They'd stumble back downstairs and spend the next few hours strutting around bragging about what a good time they had upstairs. All the girls went through it. Each had her share of that kind. Whenever it happened, they winked at each other and figured they got off easy. Men could say whatever made them feel like men. All that mattered to the girls was the money. Stories from the mouths of drunkards didn't mean anything. The ones who couldn't remember whether they'd been beneficiaries of the ladies' favors paid the same price as the ones who did. The only difference was that the girls laughed at them harder than the ones who actually got their money's worth.

It was a little different in the bordello downstairs where she was becoming more in demand with an elite group of gamblers. High rollers didn't usually drink as much as the general clientele because of the big money they laid out in the private, basement poker game. They gambled heavily, but for the most part, they maintained control of their faculties to keep track of the money. Drinking expensive liquor was part of social interaction when there was more money on the table in one run at the game than most men saw in a lifetime. Premium sipping whiskey and good cigars made the game more enjoyable without creating a diversion. They weren't there to get drunk. They were there to win a fortune and they took their gambling seriously. Time in the more spacious and comfortable basement bordello rooms didn't come cheap and for those who could afford it, the entertainment provided by a high-class lady of the night was expected to be the best money could buy. When they needed a break from the game, they put out the money for a softer diversion. In those larger rooms, lavishly furnished with mirrors and full-sized beds covered in good linens and with individual warming stoves for winter, they were treated like royalty, their every whim catered to by the prettier and more experienced ladies. Depending on the beauty of the lady and the services required, prices went as high as five-hundred dollars to reserve the room for an entire evening. At least those customers were sophisticated — most of them anyway, bathed and clean-shaven and smelling of fragrant tonsorial oils. They also expected more for their money, and there was no easy way around providing whatever form of pleasure they had in mind. Rich men often had unreasonable expectations of prostitutes. Money and a dousing with cologne from Paris didn't necessarily mean they were nice men, only that they were richer and sweeter smelling than some sweaty miner who'd been underground for a week. When it came to their demands on a lady, some were preoccupied with quite distasteful perversions, but if a choice had to be made, the ladies preferred big spenders from the private game over the masses that swarmed the gambling hall and theatre nightly and paid much less for a lady's company in the suspended cribs upstairs.

Money for services of a shady lady was paid in advance and Ruby was the keeper of the cash. She kept track of every penny on paper. No one argued with Ruby. She knew exactly what was taken in and she kept everybody honest. At the end of the night, she did the tally, took the house cut and distributed the rest to whoever earned it. If you gave her a dollar, you could be sure you'd get your fair earnings. On the other hand, if you collected a dollar and didn't give it to her, there was hell to pay. Ruby didn't miss a trick and anyone who thought she did was a fool.

It didn't take Rose long to learn her way around town. During the day, she made a point of dressing conservatively and being as inconspicuous as possible when she went out. Of course, that made no difference to the good, God-fearing women in town. When she passed them on the street, they crossed to the other side, sniffing and puffing their contempt. The mere fact she was alive was a constant source of aggravation to them. One afternoon in Smith's, she and Lizzie looked through bolts of dress material. When they decided on the fabric, they stacked the rejected bolts neatly back on the table, ignoring the two women staring at them from the other end of the counter. The last thing they wanted was a confrontation with the two biggest busybodies in town. Like the girls, the other two ladies were there to buy material, but stood back from the table piled with bolts of fabric. They were up to something, but neither of them had the nerve to come forward and say what was on her mind. Instead, they stood in the corner, staring and whispering rudely. Every so often, a hissing or sputtering sound came from their direction, but Rose and Lizzie continued to ignore them. When the girls paid for their purchases, the women approached the counter. They both avoided looking at Rose and Lizzie when they curtly informed the clerk they'd come to buy cloth. Until today, they considered Smith's the best store in town. They'd spent a lot of money there. However, in view of the store's recent preference in customers, they'd be taking their business elsewhere. The clerk politely directed their attention to the neatly-stacked bolts of cloth on the table. The ugly one snorted that she refused to handle the bolts after "those women" had touched them. They were such hypocrites! They went to church on Sunday and professed to be good Christians, but their attitudes were anything but Christian. They thought they were better than everyone else, better at least than Rose and Lizzie. Outside church, they forgot the part about all being "God's children." Did they think they had a different God?

When a pretty little blonde girl about seven years old smiled and said hello to them in the store, her mother pulled her braids and shook her severely. "If you ever speak to those dirty things again, you'll get the whipping of your life." She yanked the little girl's braids again to emphasize her point and screamed in the child's face, "Do you hear me?" The little girl shook her head up and down and squeaked out, "Yes, ma'am." She started to cry and her mother shook her again. Lizzie was furious. She made a move toward the woman and Rose grabbed her arm. "Don't do that, Lizette." Lizzie wanted to give the woman a piece of her mind over the remark about the cloth, but kept her mouth shut. Now, she wanted to punch her in the nose. Rose knew better than to let go of Lizzie's arm. If she did, her friend would get herself arrested for sure. She knew Lizzie would never simply tell the woman off and let it go at that, and her temper would earn her a night in the calaboose. Spending the night in jail would lose her a night's work and cost her a fine to boot. The law did not go easy on local ladies of the evening who participated in scuffles in the general store, or anywhere else for that matter, whether they started the trouble or not. She couldn't deny the woman deserved a lump from Lizzie's fist. Fact was, she'd liked to have given her one herself. She just couldn't let Lizzie be the one to let her have it.

Rose held tight to her friend's arm with both hands while Lizzie strained to get to the woman. It took all her strength to hold Lizzie back. "She's not worth the effort, Lizette. Don't bother about her." She pulled harder. Finally, Lizzie backed off, her fist still clenched and ready to take a swing at the woman. She pursed her lips and scowled, her body trembling with anger. She knew Rose was right. She was used to the name-calling. That didn't mean a thing and it's not what made her so mad. It was the way the woman mistreated the little girl. When Lizzie doubled up her fist, the woman knew she'd lit Lizzie's fuse good. It was turning into a showdown she hadn't expected and she backed up to be in a position to run out in a hurry in case Lizzie decided to hit her. The other lady didn't want any part of a fight with a couple of prostitutes and she was holding the door open, coaxing the mouthy one to leave before there was trouble. Prostitutes had reputations for savage brawling and when they got into a fight, somebody always got hurt. Most of them carried daggers or pocket pistols and those easily-concealed weapons proved lethal to an adversary on more than one occasion. Even to those who didn't frequent the saloons and brothels, it was a well-known fact these ladies weren't the kind to antagonize or goad into a physical confrontation. Many were scrappers who enjoyed a good female brawl and wouldn't think twice about sticking somebody in the ribs with a blade.

Once Lizzie decided to stand down and the open door was within escape distance, the woman resumed her former combative stance. She snorted at Rose's remark like a hog with a mud clod up his nose, then turned on her heel and stomped out the door, banging it hard behind her. Believing she'd been victorious in having had the last word and putting the girls in their places, she stood outside, loudly chastising the store clerk for "allowing whores to contaminate the goods" and threatening to inform the proprietor of the clerk's outrageous conduct in showing preference to prostitutes over respectable customers. "We'll see how long you work here when I get through with you." With that, she took her friend by the arm and tromped off up the street. Although she didn't know enough to shut her mouth, she figured she'd pushed things about as far as she dared and it was in her best interest to leave before Rose was no longer able to restrain Lizzie. She had no idea how close she'd come to getting the thrashing of her life. If Lizzie had her way, the witch would have found herself flying backward out the door and deposited in a most indelicate position in the street. She'd never know that Rose saved her not only from Lizzie's right hook and a broken nose, but a great deal more. It wasn't Lizzie who carried a derringer in her garter. It was Rose.

In her haste to withdraw, the woman completely forgot the little girl, still teary-eyed with a hair ribbon dangling untied from one braid as the result of the shaking. She stood outside the door watching her mother and the other lady walk away, oblivious to the fact they'd left her behind. Most little girls would have skipped happily along to catch up with their mother on a shopping day, but not this little girl. Her face was full of sadness and rejection. She stood outside the store, in no hurry to follow. When she was sure her mother had forgotten about her and was a good distance away, she opened the screened door and peeked inside. She was such a pretty little thing, a few wisps of her blonde hair out of control and clinging to her tearful face. Rose wanted to put her arms around the child and tell her not to cry anymore, that she was sorry her mother was so mean. It was none of her business though, and putting her nose in someone else's family affair could only mean more trouble if the mother found out she'd said anything. Still, she couldn't take her eyes off the little girl. How could a mother be so vicious? One of those good, Christian women, no doubt. Maybe letting Lizzie give her that thrashing wouldn't have been such a bad idea.

Rose made the most ridiculous face she could conjure up, sticking her thumbs in her ears and wiggling her fingers. Like magic, the tears disappeared and the child laughed. She looked up the street in the direction her mother had gone, making sure she hadn't suddenly been remembered. If she was caught anywhere near the bad girls, more punishment would be forthcoming. When she was satisfied the coast was clear and she'd truly been forgotten, she stepped into the store and smiled at Rose. "That was a funny face. My name is Emily Grants." Lizzie spoke for both of them. "I'm Lizette." She pointed to Rose. "...and this silly goose is Rose." Rose wiggled her fingers one more time, then took her thumbs out of her ears when Emily laughed again. Lizzie knelt by the child and took her hand. "Don't cry Emily. We'll be friends, but it'll be our secret. Is that alright with you?" Emily was delighted. "You mean, you'll be my very own secret friends? Can I tell the secret to my brothers? They'd like to be friends too. Mama cuffs their ears if they talk to anyone who works in a saloon, so they won't tell if we're friends." Rose looked sideways at Lizzie, suggesting she didn't like the idea of telling the child they'd keep a secret from her mother. She turned the little girl around and tied the fallen hair ribbon in a bow to match it's partner, then knelt beside Lizzie. She brushed the stray wisps of Emily's hair back. It wouldn't be right to say what she was thinking, how much she'd like to have a little girl like Emily for her own. She'd dress her in calico with lace pinafores and tie satin ribbons in her hair. Funny how some people never appreciated what they had, while another would give anything for that which was taken for granted by the first. "Now, Emily, you can't be deceivin' your mother. We won't be invitin' you tell a lie or go behind her back. Do you understand?" Emily shook her head up and down that she understood. "But can we be friends? ...and William and

Marcus too? Can we?" Rose sighed. It was hard to say no. "Well, I suppose it can't hurt to be friends." That was good enough for Emily. She clapped her hands and a smile lit up the angelic face. Rose stood up and opened the door. "Run along, Emily. Your mother will be worried about you." Emily's smile turned into a frown and she looked at the floor. "No, she won't."

She'd been at the Bird Cage three weeks. This night was like all the others. She came in by the back door and went downstairs to say hello to Ruby and the girls. By the time she went upstairs, the show was about to start. She stopped on the landing to look over the room. Charlie was at the piano and they greeted each other the way they did every night. He winked and she wiggled her fingers at him. At a table in the back of the room, three men talked quietly. She recognized two of them. One was her friend, John Holliday. In the three weeks since they rode the stage in from Bisbee together, she'd visited with him often, including twice over tea in her private sitting room, which she acquired through his influence with the hotel desk clerk, and once at dinner. He stopped by the Bird Cage almost every night to see how she was getting along, his visits having become more frequent lately. He always asked if she needed anything. He wasn't just being polite. He was genuinely concerned about her and if she had needed anything at all, she knew he'd see to it. Every time he came in, he bought a bottle and asked her to sit with him. Well aware of his efforts to keep her occupied in conversation as long as possible, she also knew he paid the house a hefty price for her time in addition to the bottle of premium whiskey or brandy. One thing about Doc, he wasn't the least bit cheap. When the take was split up at the end of the night, part of what he put in went to her. It didn't seem to matter what her job was. He knew, of course, and he also knew how hard it was for her. That's why he did what he did. He never said anything about it though. He just did what he could to save her from having to entertain some drunken miner or cowboy upstairs or high roller in the basement. He was becoming a valued friend. She fancied him as a guardian angel of sorts; a peculiar angel, but a guardian nonetheless.

No one ever bothered her when he was around. She knew why. She'd heard stories about him and his volatile temper. They said he'd killed quite a few men and despite his frail, sickly countenance, he did command a certain respect if for no other reason than the shotgun that rested across his lap. He carried a revolver too, and everyone knew he could and would use it with little provocation. Despite the gun ordinance, he was always armed. He claimed he'd been deputized and had a legal right to carry guns in town, although it was never quite clear by whose authority. Nobody had enough nerve to call him on it for the simple reason he was unpredictable and not a man to be antagonized. They said he could lay down a five-card hand and draw and fire his gun with the same hand faster than the blink of a sparrow's eye. Some spoke to him in passing, but in general, most avoided his table. He also had a reputation for being less than gentle with his equally well-known volatile counterpart, Kate Elder, most unflatteringly known as Big Nose Kate. Kate, on the other hand, had her own claim to fame for outbursts of temper. Some said she was fearless. Others swore she was just plain loco. Story was, Doc slit a man's throat over a card game in Fort Griffin, Texas and Kate busted Doc out of the hotel room where he was being held in custody single-handedly by poking a couple of forty-fives in the sheriff's face. She let all the horses go and set fire to a livery stable to create a diversion, then, calmly walked next door to persuade the sheriff to turn Doc loose when the vigilantes set on lynching him went to put out the blaze. On top of that, she supposedly "borrowed" a couple of horses to get them to Dodge City. All of it was a cross between scuttlebutt and speculation, but if you knew Kate, the story was entirely believable. Rose asked Doc if it was true and saw the devilish twinkle in his eyes when he replied, "Kate loves horses. She'd never do anything to hurt one." Anybody with walking-around sense steered clear of Kate when she took to waving a pistol around, drunk or sober. In all probability, Doc and Kate were a fair match.

By this time, she knew "Doctor" Holliday was not a physician as she originally thought. It was true he'd earned a medical degree — Doctor of Dentistry, but he didn't practice his profession anymore save for an occasional emergency. Too much whiskey attributed to his shaking hands, rendering him incapable of using the instruments of his trade. Everyone knew he drank to kill the pain of his disease and then, of course, he had a new profession these days. The trouble that chased he and Kate into the Arizona Territory only added to the preclusion of his practice. In recent months, his profession had changed drastically. They said he was a gambler and a cheater, and a lot of other things. He had a way with words, a real knack for getting under your skin, and he took advantage of every opportunity to rile an opponent. Some said he was crazy, looking for somebody to kill him to put him out of his misery. Maybe they were right. He was a dying man. He had nothing to lose by starting a fight. He didn't want to die in bed, drowning in his own blood and gasping for his last breath. He wanted to go with his boots on, hot lead from an adversary's forty-five sending him into oblivion in one swift blast. It was only a matter of time before he'd be dead anyway, and not a very long time at that. He'd killed a few men. For all she knew, maybe more than a few. Maybe they deserved it. Maybe they didn't. It wasn't for her to say. Nevertheless, she still accorded him the degree of respect she, and she alone, believed he deserved. Since his initial introduction as John Holliday, she addressed him as "Doctor" until he insisted she be less formal. He said friends ought to be on a first-name basis. His friends called him "Doc." His given name was John Henry, but outside a handful of acquaintances, most everyone called him Holliday or something less than complimentary. She thought that was disrespectful of his position and status, notwithstanding the fact that he didn't practice his profession much anymore. First names were fine and his other friends could call him Doc, but if he had no objection, she'd prefer to call him John. He smiled and said he'd be honored to have her call him John. He told her once he could count his friends on one hand — Wyatt, Kate, Morgan, sometimes Virgil, and always, Rose. Of one, he was absolutely certain. The other four, he wouldn't bet money on.

Although never formally introduced, she knew the second man at the table was Wyatt Earp. Everyone knew him. He was a force to be reckoned with in Tombstone. She'd heard that he and his brothers were committed to bringing law and order to the town, one way or the other. It was good to know he was a friend of Doc's. At least they were on the same side. That was probably to the great advantage of them both. In a showdown between the two of them, it was likely neither would emerge a winner. Neither the Earps nor Doc Holliday were men you wanted to be at odds with. She didn't know the third man. He was vaguely familiar, but she couldn't remember where she'd seen him. She studied him and it finally dawned on her. He was the one who stood across the street watching her walk to work every night. The silver in his hatband caught the light from the chandelier and the flash made her blink and turn her head. When she turned back, he was looking straight at her. His eyes penetrated her in what felt like a silent embrace. Under other circumstances, that sort of stare would make her feel uncomfortable. A lot of men looked at her these days, but not the way he did. He kept his eyes on her as she walked toward him. When she was a few feet from the table, he stood up and removed his hat. He stepped in front of her and she noticed the silver star pinned to his coat over his heart. He was tall. Six feet anyway. When she saw him from across the street, she thought he was attractive, but up close, he was more than that. He was very good looking. The thing that struck her most was how well he was put together and the way he carried himself. Not only was he handsome, he was impressively well-groomed, all in black except for a white shirt. She repeated the thought to herself. He was quite handsome in black. Maybe it was the diamond stud in his tie. It was real. She could tell by the way it sparkled. There was nothing counterfeit or unnatural about him. His hair was neatly combed and his moustache impeccably trimmed. Ann Merrick always said a man who took pride in his appearance probably took pride in everything he did. She was sure that was true of this man. She realized she must have been standing there a long time to take all of that in. He watched her walking to work every night. She knew that. She started to say something. He extended his hand and spoke first. "Virgil Earp. Town Marshal." So, that's who he was. She'd heard the name more than once. His reputation preceded him. "... and you must be the famous Rose Callahan." He was looking right through her, into her mind. She smiled and took his hand. She wasn't so sure about the "famous" part, but she confirmed that she was Rose Callahan. He didn't let go right away. His grip was firm, but easy on her delicate hand. She'd seen the sign on the door of his office on Allen Street. That explained why he stood on that corner every evening. His office was upstairs. He proceeded to tell her that stories about the lovely Irish girl with long red hair and emerald eyes had traveled fast through Tombstone. He'd come to see for himself if the tales were true, and he had to admit, the accolades of her beauty were greatly understated. She smiled as he spoke. He was obviously taken with her. Perhaps, the feeling was mutual. She wasn't prepared for his next move. He raised her hand to his lips and kissed it. There was the strangest look in his eyes. He was looking into hers intently, as though trying to communicate some silent message he didn't want the others at the table to hear. She wasn't quite sure what the message was, but she felt the intensity of its meaning. They could add his name at the top of the list of those who were in love with Allen Street Rose.

Doc was on his feet and, as usual, full of compliments. She could always count on him to boost her morale. "You're lookin' especially lovely this evenin', Miss Callahan." She couldn't help but smile. The man had a gift for saying things. "Georgia devil, born with a silver tongue" is what

Ruby said about him. The best part was he meant every word and she was a grateful recipient of his praise. By the way, did she know Marshal Earp? Wyatt stood up and extended his hand. A light reflecting off his badge made her blink and she hoped he didn't think she was winking at him. He didn't. His expression was no-nonsense, serious. He was the kind who looked you right in the eye, the sign of an honest man. His smile was cordial, but not lingering. Like his brother's, his handshake was firm. That was something else Ann said. You could tell a lot about a man by the way he shook your hand. If it was strong, he was honest and sincere. If it was loose and weak, most likely, so was he. He was polite, although not excessively. He was pleased to meet her and hoped she was enjoying living in Tombstone. He was another handsome one. These Earp men were certainly not lacking in good looks or social graces. He asked if she'd care to join them? She was about to accept the invitation when Virgil linked her arm through his. The move startled her. Looked like he wanted to find out right away if the stories about her were true. He was still staring at her, waiting for her to remove her arm although he held it in a way that let her know he'd prefer she didn't. She would have liked to visit with her friend, John Holliday. A conversation with Wyatt Earp would probably be interesting, but before she could accept the invitation to sit down, Virgil turned to his brother and Doc. She thought he was going to say he was taking her upstairs. "Miss Callahan and I are going outside for a breath of air." That was the end of that. An unexpected turn of events. Without another word, he steered her away from the table toward the front door. She looked over her shoulder at Doc. He wasn't smiling, but he was watching her and he didn't appear to be too happy about her leaving with Virgil. His expression was curious. At first, she thought it was one of concern and she wondered why he'd be worried about her going for a walk with Virgil Earp. Sometimes Doc could be funny — hard to read. Maybe she was mistaken about the way he looked at her. Probably her imagination. She didn't have time to think about it because Virgil didn't waste any time leading her away. On the way out, she caught the looks of the other ladies. They envied her position. They'd give an entire night's wages to go for a walk in the moonlight with Virgil Earp. Lizzie winked at her. Virgil was too busy watching Rose to notice.

The sweet perfume of jasmine, or something that smelled like jasmine, filled the warm night air. Every time she smelled the fragrance, it took her back to the attic room in New Orleans. That, in turn, triggered memories. It was happening again. Here she was, walking in the moonlight with Virgil

Earp, and thinking about John. She'd never walk in the moonlight with John Merrick again. Her life had become so tangled, she wondered if it would ever unravel. She felt the tears welling up inside and she swallowed hard to keep them in check. She looked up at the moon. It was exceptionally bright in the clear August sky and it lit up Allen Street like a giant oil lamp. They stopped walking. He turned and looked at her, her arm still linked through his. For a minute, she thought he was going to kiss her. She didn't want him to do that. She welcomed the opportunity to get outside in the fresh air, but hoped he wouldn't ask for any more than a walk with her. Providing personal pleasure for a local lawman seemed a little cumbersome and awkward. He was saying he was glad he finally came to see her in person. He'd heard a lot about her. She managed a weak smile. That was not what she wanted to be told. She wondered what it was that he'd heard, but didn't dare ask.

She had a bad habit of drifting off during conversations these days and she realized he said something she missed. She tried to act like she'd heard every word he said and he didn't realize she'd faded away while he was talking. His words made her uneasy. "Inside, you turn every head, but you're even prettier in the moonlight." She closed her eyes. She didn't want to hear that either. She was thinking about John and she didn't want compliments from this man, this stranger — this very handsome and exciting stranger. He didn't understand, of course. How could he? He didn't know what was going through her mind as he spoke. He kept talking. He wasn't sure if the moon was lighting up her hair or if it was the other way around. She shivered and he noticed right away. Was she cold? Did she want his coat? He started to take it off. She raised her hand. "No, thank you. I'm not cold." She wanted him to stop talking. She couldn't say it though. He was only trying to be nice. She remembered the way her friends watched as she was walking out the door with him. The girls would slap her silly if they knew she was rejecting praises from Virgil Earp. She changed the subject. "Do you know what flower 'tis that smells so sweet?" He knew exactly what it was. "Cactus. Don't know the name of it. Other cactus flowers come out with the sun. That one blooms at night and closes up in the day. Purely aromatic." He took a deep breath to identify the scent further. "Smells a lot like jasmine. Pretty, isn't it?" She agreed. "Yes, I love jasmine. That's what I thought it was." With the night-blooming cactus flower the topic of discussion, at least he wasn't asking what brought her to Tombstone. She was thankful for that. She wouldn't want to have to explain.

The more he talked, the more she began to understand who he was. A grand stature of a man, tall and of considerable physical strength from the looks of him, he was self-assured as they came. It wasn't just because he was wearing a badge either. It was what he was made of. There probably weren't many with the inclination to stand up to him in a bare-knuckles fight, not sober anyway. Aside from his obvious physical presence, he was a pleasant fellow and he had a way of talking that made her like him right off. When he let it show, he had a nice smile. There was something else, a real gentle side to the man. It was interesting that he knew about the cactus and thought it smelled like jasmine. With all that went on in Tombstone, she'd bet he was the only man who paid attention to the perfume of a cactus flower and knew what it was. For that matter, how many men knew what jasmine was?

A shot rang out, then, several more in rapid succession, bringing their conversation to an abrupt halt. Virgil reacted instinctively at the first blast of gunfire. He dropped her hand from his arm and moved her close to the building. The urgency in his voice was clear. "Stay right here!" His revolver was already in his hand and he ran inside. She stood where he planted her against the building and watched him bolt through the door. Was he crazy? She couldn't "stay right here!" Who did he think he was anyway? Her friends were inside. What if one of them was hurt? She followed him through the door. The music had stopped and people were shouting. Glass was breaking. All hell had broken loose. It was total pandemonium. She tried to see where the center of the commotion was, focusing on the far side of the room. There appeared to be a fight in progress. Two men were being restrained by half a dozen others, but there were so many people in the way, she couldn't get a clear look. She moved closer. Wyatt and Virgil were smack in the middle of it. The two being restrained were shouting obscenities and threats at the Earps as they were handcuffed. Virgil thumped one of them on the head and she heard him say they were under arrest — for murder. She was aghast. Murder? What happened? She pushed through the crowd, trying to find Jenny and Lizzie. Someone touched her and she jumped. They were right beside her, both okay. "Thank God." She breathed a deep sigh of relief and hugged them. They didn't understand why she was so upset. Then she saw them, lying on the floor right in front of her. She saw the blood, a puddle around each man. She'd never seen that much blood. From pure shock, she couldn't move. One was dead, shot through the head, his open eyes still staring at the last thing he saw before he died; the other bleeding profusely from a gaping hole in his stomach and dying fast. A third man was being helped up, blood streaming from his shoulder and down his shirtsleeve, large drops splashing onto the floor when they got him to his feet. Rose stepped out of the way, but he was bleeding so bad it ran down his arm and dripped off the ends of his fingers, hitting the floor in front of her and splattering her skirt. She tried to move back another step, but there were people right behind her pushing to get a better look. More blood sprayed her dress. She was horrified. The scene was gruesome and sickening. She put her hand over her mouth and pushed her way back through the crowd to get to the front door and fresh air. Lizzie and Jenny followed her. They'd seen it before. She hadn't.

Outside, they tried to tell her it was all part of this kind of life. She'd better get used to it. This was Tombstone! People were crazy and they killed each other all the time here. She hadn't seen anything yet. She was amazed they took it so nonchalantly and she shouted at them. "It's not part of life, not normal life! How can you be so insensitive about murder? How can you watch two human lives be snuffed out and not feel any compassion? How can you be so calm about killin'?" They looked at each other, knowing full well what was happening to her. She had a lot to learn, but she had to let out the frustration this once. After that, she'd have to accept it like they said, all part of living in Tombstone. If she didn't, she'd never make it in this town. They let her go on with her angry yelling and waving her hands around. The killers were brought out on their way to jail. She stopped the tantrum and gave them a cold stare as they passed her. Wyatt walked by without so much as a glance in her direction. The dead men were carried out next and she stared at their blood-soaked bodies. Moonlight reflected off the tears streaming down her face. She was quiet. The outburst was over.

Virgil came out next. He was looking for her. When he saw her with the girls, he knew they'd take care of her. The pained look on her face needed no explanation. When the shooting started, he told her to stay outside, but she didn't listen. She followed him and saw what happened and now, she was upset. He knew she didn't understand. She hadn't been in town long enough to understand. He wanted to tell her he was sorry she saw the killings, but he couldn't do it right this minute. He had a job to do first. That came before all else. He'd tell her later. He'd have to explain a lot of things about this place to her later. He moved on with his brother and the prisoners. She looked from Lizzie to Jenny to Ruby like a lost child. Maybe her first impression of this town was right. She'd arrived in Hell.

When she got off the stage, she sensed evil in the air. What she just witnessed was nothing if not the devil's work. Doc was the last one out. He put his arms around her and she buried her face in his coat. She never let anyone see her cry, but she couldn't hold back this time. Her brand of anxiety wasn't easily relieved, not even by tears. He held her and told her to cry it out. He'd stand there with her all night if she needed him. He said he was her friend and as long as he was around, she'd never be alone. She didn't understand what a profound statement of friendship that was coming from him. Years later, she'd remember this night and the man they said had no heart.

Sleep was fitful, abounding with nightmares of ghoulish faces jumping out of the woods at her, startling her into an agitated, semi-wakeful state more than a dozen times. She had intermittent spells of crying and rage and stayed in bed all day. When it was time to go to work, she considered locking the door and pretending she wasn't there when Lizzie or Jenny came knocking. Between the crying and lack of sleep, her eyes were red and puffy. She felt like she did after the attack in New Orleans. Violated. She didn't want to talk to anyone. There were plenty of girls at the Bird Cage. Nobody would miss her for one night. Maybe she'd never go back. Maybe she'd pack the trunk and be on the first stage east. The wild, wild West was not for her. They could have their mining camp and the crazy people who went with it. For all she cared, they could kill each other over the damned silver.

She flopped around in bed for another hour, then, in contradiction to her inner urgings to stay home, took out the red dress and prepared for another night at the Bird Cage. The first time she met Ruby and the girls, she promised herself she'd never become as calloused as they were, but after last night, she had to alter the plan. Doc told her she hadn't seen the last of this kind of thing and there was only one way to deal with it. Forget about it. Pretend it never happened. Build up a resistance to hurtful experiences the way he did. There were many more to come, so if she couldn't do that, she'd better leave this town and forget she was ever here.

She pinned up her hair and painted her lips red. Then, she slipped into the red dress and left the hotel. Walking up Allen Street toward the Bird

Cage, she knew he was standing in the same place he always stood, leaning against the post and watching her. Tonight, she didn't look at him. She looked straight ahead and walked fast. Tomorrow, she'd devote some serious effort to finding another place to live, someplace on the other end of town where she wouldn't have to pass him on her way to work every night. Lizzie and Jenny tried to convince her it was too expensive to be living at the Cosmopolitan anyway, and they said it wasn't safe for her to be there alone. Ever since they discovered where she was staying, they wanted her to move into the little house they shared on Sixth Street a couple of blocks from the Bird Cage. She preferred to live alone. She was used to her privacy. Time alone was all she had with her memories of John. Maybe she'd find a little house away from Allen Street where she'd be less visible and not feel like she was living in a fishbowl, someplace where she wouldn't have to see Virgil every night and feel him looking through her.

After contemplating not going to work at all, she arrived an hour early. No one mentioned the events of the night before. No one talked about the men who were killed. She went to the spot where they died, thinking it ought to feel different there tonight. Nothing had changed with the exception of the floor having been scrubbed and a table placed over the still-visible bloodstains soaked into the wood. Customers who sat at the table over the stains weren't the least bit concerned about what transpired a few hours earlier. It was business as usual at the Bird Cage.

Halfway through the evening, a hand brushed her elbow. She had hoped to avoid contact with customers as much as possible. It wasn't a night for socializing. In fact, she decided it was a mistake to be there and was on her way to tell Ruby she didn't feel well. She was going to her room where it was quiet and she could think about where she'd go when she left Tombstone. That was the idea, to leave Tombstone and go somewhere less wicked and violent, someplace where men didn't kill each other over card games or other stupid things. She turned to decline whatever invitation or proposition was about to be offered and was met with the same penetrating gaze as the night before. Virgil's eyes impaled her heart with the intensity of their message and she felt the compassion. He knew last night's killings made a powerful impression on her and he was there to explain. He took her arm, assuming she'd go with him, but she balked and jerked away.

When he tried again, she crossed her arms and stood her ground. "You assume too much, Marshal. Even payin' customers ask first." Her snippety rebuff took him completely by surprise. The way she was glowering at him made it pretty clear she wasn't going anywhere unless he said the right thing. He cleared his throat and started over. "Miss Callahan, would you care to join me for a brandy?" She looked off in the distance, acting like she hadn't heard what he said, or didn't care. He watched her. She was still upset about what happened last night and she blamed him for it. That was it. She wasn't going to make this easy. He came closer. "Please?" She looked up at him and he pointed to a corner table where two glasses of brandy were already waiting. When she saw the glasses, she started to say something else about his presumptions and he interrupted her. "I'm not going to stand here all night begging you to sit down. If you'd prefer to drink with someone else, all you gotta do is say so." He put his hat on. "I'll be on my way." She didn't want to drink with anyone else, and now she'd lost control of the situation. Virgil just let her know he wasn't going to put up with her foolishness. Without answering, she went to the table and sat down, but when he pulled up a chair, she refused to look at him. She stared into the brandy in her glass. After several minutes of her avoiding eye contact and not talking, he finally gave up and moved his chair back. It was plain to see he was through waiting for her to get over the tantrum. "If you're going to pout like a spoiled child, I'll say good-night."

For the second time, he picked up his hat and stood up. She better say something quick. She felt her face turning red. Maybe she was acting childish. She took a deep breath. It was now or never. "Sit down, Marshal." He wasn't in the habit of being told what do to and not many got a second chance once he made up his mind to quit. She was lucky he wasn't out the door and down the street with the first word out of her mouth. He didn't obey the order to sit, but stood behind the chair, watching her. It was a terrible uneasy feeling having him stand over her that way and she wasn't sure what to say next. To her great relief, he laid his hat on the table and sat down. He was disgusted and it showed. Not the kind of man who tolerated nonsense from anyone, it was a miracle he'd stuck around this long. He was waiting for her to say something. Either she set things right, or he was done with her. She rolled the glass between her hands, thinking about what to say and having a hard time getting the words out. There was a certain amount of justification to the way she felt about the killings of last night. He agreed with her, but he handled it differently. Violence was foreign to her and difficult for someone like her to deal with.

He knew that. When she looked at him, it was an obvious plea for help. She really didn't know how to handle it. He raised his glass. "Truce?" She smiled and clinked her glass against his. "Yes, I suppose so."

There was something that drew her to him, but she fought like crazy to reject any feeling of attraction. Attempts at putting John's memory away had failed miserably and he was still on her mind all the time. No one would ever take his place, not even someone like Virgil Earp. That being said, and whether fortunately or unfortunately, the attraction to Virgil was there. It was purely physical, of course. It couldn't be anything else. She didn't even know the man. Before the shooting started, she'd only had a ten-minute conversation with him. It'd be so much easier if he'd go away. He pulled his chair a little closer. He wasn't going anywhere. He was asking how she was feeling. He was sorry she saw what happened last night, but she had to understand how things were in this town. Life here was unlike any other place. It was a mining town and mining towns were nuts. There were some far worse than this one with no law at all and they were in a state of complete bedlam all the time. At least, in Tombstone, the Earps were trying to tame the lawlessness and keep the crime down. It wasn't going to happen overnight. Law and order were still infants and it'd take a lot of doing before they matured. Silver fever made men crazy. Women too. Sometimes people died in the heat of passion. Sometimes it couldn't be prevented. It was just the way it was. Her eyes flew open and her heart started racing. She was furious at his disimpassioned attitude and she exploded at him, her Irish brogue charged with indignation. She didn't have to understand anything of the sort! Maybe he could justify murder by virtue of Tombstone's dubious distinction as a wild mining town, and maybe he could blame it on silver fever, but she could never pardon such violence against humanity under any guise. It was intolerable and unacceptable, and if he condoned such transgression against mankind, he was every bit as much a barbarian as the killers themselves. She slammed the palm of her hand on the table to emphasize her message. Their conversation was over. He'd have to excuse her. In reality, "they" hadn't had a conversation at all. She'd been the sole orator in a protracted tirade.

She tried to push her chair back from the table. He was calm, watching her with the intensity that defined his character, all the while with one foot firmly planted against the leg of her chair, one arm around the back of it, securing it in place. She tried to move it again. It wouldn't budge. She clenched her teeth and felt the muscles in her jaws ripple from the pressure.

She turned to him, her green eyes flaring with the fire of injustice she felt over the situation. He was unrattled by her outburst and the faint trace of a smile crossed his face. His eyes wandered casually around the room and he took a sip from his glass. She quieted down and stared into her drink. She didn't have to look around to know everyone was watching her make a fool of herself. It was the kind of show they liked to see, the beginnings of a good fight. They were waiting for her next move, hoping she'd pull a dagger or hidden pistol from her garter and lunge at him across the table. She picked up the drink and gulped down a big swallow. She hated the stuff and, as usual, it burned all the way down. She took a deep breath and closed her eyes to regain her composure. Keeping her chair anchored with his foot, he started over, speaking softly so the gawkers couldn't hear what he said. "You alright?" She stared at him. It was unbelievable. He had a goodly amount of patience. No other man would have put up with her ranting and raving like a lunatic. Her answer was next to a whisper. "Yes, I'm alright." However, she couldn't bring herself to apologize. Why should she? She'd said exactly what she felt, all except the part about him being a barbarian. She was sorry for that. "I didn't mean to call you a barbarian. I take that back." He was anything but uncivilized. He was sitting close, so close that his arm around the back of her chair touched her shoulder and sent a shiver through her. With the ice thinned, if not broken, the overall tone changed and they talked quietly. Gradually, the conversation lightened. She had to admit he was a welcome change from what she usually had to deal with. He wasn't like the miners or gamblers. His character was different even from local businessmen and mine executives. He was one of a kind, a gentleman, refined in his own way, intelligent and perceptive, taking in things most men never tried to understand. There was a sensitivity about him, an awareness of gentle things. She remembered how he knew about the cactus and identified the fragrance of its flower with jasmine. She thought it was jasmine, but he knew the difference. He spoke softly, but with purpose. She breathed deeply while they talked. Whatever it was that he put on his face after shaving had a deliciously sensuous aroma, like warm spice and lavender. His smile was genuine. She could tell he liked her more than a little, and despite the fact that his arm ever-so-slightly brushed against her shoulder now and then, he kept his distance.

Later, he walked her home with her arm linked through his. It was three o'clock in the morning, but she felt safe. No need to be looking over her shoulder to see who might be following her. At the hotel, he didn't ask to go up to her room, but said good-night at the door. She thought about inviting him up, but when she saw the desk clerk and everyone else watching them, she kept her mouth shut. They all knew he was married and they knew who she was and where she worked. His walking her home was most likely enough to make them talk. No sense giving them more.

Chapter 7

"Beware of the man with the silver star,
and don't let it start.
I will defend your honor
to the death, my dear,
But I cannot mend a broken heart."

Silver Rose Marie
ALLEN STREET ROSE

He came to see her every night, sometimes accompanied by his brothers or Doc, but more often, alone. He'd buy a bottle to keep the house happy and invite her to sit with him, paying full whiskey price for her glass even though she frequently drank only tea, and often staying until she left work to see that she got home safely. Between Virgil and Doc, she spent virtually no time plying her trade in the suspended cribs or the basement bordello for weeks. As long as they bought the whiskey and dropped money in the till that would otherwise have profited from her private entertainment of men, the house was satisfied. She was grateful for their efforts. When Doc and Virgil were there at the same time, they were civil enough to each other, but she noticed there was some kind of friction between them that they both made a conscious effort to keep under control. She sensed that Virgil Earp and Doc Holliday were not exactly the best of friends.

As time went by, she looked forward to seeing Virgil and the first night he failed to appear, she was visibly disappointed. She became irritated when Lizzie told her to stop pouting and forget him. Jenny told her he was married and she couldn't afford to get attached to him. He shouldn't be there at all. He ought to be home with his wife. She was perturbed at their comments. Considering they provided pleasure for many married men, they had a lot of nerve telling her to stay away from Virgil. Besides, she wasn't attached to him. She liked him. That was all. She enjoyed conversations with him and appreciated the escort home in the wee hours. There was no more to it than there was to her friendship with Doc Holliday. Virgil was always a perfect gentleman. He never asked her to go upstairs and she didn't expect he ever would. He never offered her money for anything. Feeling a sudden need to justify his reasons for coming around so often, she put an emphasis on the "anythin'." He had to be there sometimes to keep the peace. They knew what could happen if a card game got out of hand or a fight broke out. People got killed in this place. It was Virgil's job to keep those things from happening. They were being unfair to him. They looked at each other and then at her. Lizzie shook her finger at Rose. "Just wait. The time will come when he'll ask for more than talk from you. It's no secret Virge has always liked the ladies." Rose lashed out at her friend. "Shut your mouth, Lizette. It isn't like that with Virge and me." Lizzie threw up her hands in surrender, surprised at Rose's sudden defensive posture. "Okay, Rosie. Whatever you say. You don't have to get so uppity with me. I'm telling the truth." Jenny stepped between them, facing Rose. "If you think he's gonna leave his wife for you, you're crazy. When Virge leaves you crying, don't say we didn't warn you." She took Lizzie by the hand and they walked away, leaving Rose standing alone. For the first time, she was angry with her two friends. Their words made her so furious she wanted to slap them. As they walked off, she let her temper get away from her, waving her hands in the air and shouting after them, "It's none of your damn business and I'll be thankin' the both of you to keep your noses in your own dirty laundry." She was so mad, she was shaking. She closed her eyes to compose herself. They were right, of course, and she wasn't really angry with them. They were her friends and it disturbed her to have an altercation with them, especially over a man. Didn't they all agree men weren't worth wasting the powder it would take to blow them across the street? They were only trying to help. Truth? She was mad at herself for having expectations of someone like Virgil Earp, and she knew it. Unreasonable expectations. She decided if he came around again, she'd be too busy to see him. That would put an end to anyone's thinking there was something going on between them.

A day later, the argument with Lizzie and Jenny still bothered her. They hadn't spoken to her since last night. She watched them from across the room, but they wouldn't look in her direction, deliberately avoiding her, and she couldn't blame them a bit. They were right about Virgil and she knew it. As friends, they told the truth because they didn't want her to get hurt. It's just that the truth hurt sometimes. It seemed to be the story of her life. Every time she found something good, there was a fly in the ointment. She wished she'd listened to her little voice when it told her to stay home tonight. All she wanted was to be alone, but she was in the wrong place for that. Coming to the Bird Cage to be alone was like jumping in a lake and expecting not to get wet. Ten minutes after she got there, she found herself in one of those unpleasant situations none of them liked to get stuck with. The miner caught her walking by his table and yanked her arm so hard that he pulled her right off her feet and onto his lap. For the last hour, he'd been trying to stuff money down the front of her dress and she'd been choking on the musty smell of a mine. If he didn't fall down soon, she'd be going upstairs with him. She was trying to ward off his advances by acting silly and encouraging him to drink more beer. Much to her dismay, he was a stalwart fellow with an unusually high tolerance for the grog and even after she thought he'd swilled enough to make three men pass out, he was upright. As luck would have it, he didn't show any signs of weakening and she resigned herself to the inevitable trip upstairs to a crib. Across the room, Lizzie and Jenny looked the other way. Next time, she'd pay attention when her little voice told her stay home.

Somewhere around eleven, Ruby came to the table and told the miner she needed to see Rose, privately. He objected vigorously, and held on tighter, refusing to turn Rose loose. Ruby peeled one hand away, bending his fingers backward in the process. He yowled and let go with the other one. When Ruby pulled Rose off his lap, he protested loudly, saying he'd been working in the mines all week and wasn't going to let anybody stop him from having a good time tonight. He got up and Ruby moved Rose aside with one hand. With the other, she shoved him back in his chair and held him there by his throat. Before he knew what happened, Ruby's knee was planted in his groin. His eyes went wide open. He never expected a woman to be so strong, and he'd obviously never seen Ruby Fontaine in action. She didn't like violence, but she wasn't opposed to a little arm twisting now and then to get her point across. So there was no misunderstanding on his part, she positioned her face a few inches from his. She smiled, but any fool could see it wasn't an exhibition of goodwill. "Patience, friend. You'll have a lady, but not this one." He struggled only momentarily. Her hand tightened around his throat and she applied a little more pressure with her knee to encourage him to quit squirming. She said it once more, slower and plainer. "In case you didn't hear me the first time, sapper, Rose has other business. Understand?" Her message came across loud and clear. Not many resisted Ruby. Although she was still smiling, he figured her benevolence could change in a heartbeat if he put up any more fuss. He shook his head "yes" and sat quietly. When she was satisfied he'd settled down, she let go of him and motioned to one of the other ladies to come to the table. The minute Eva sat herself down on his lap, he didn't waste any time picking up where he left off with Rose. With the situation under control, Ruby patted him on the shoulder. "Have a good time, friend."

Ruby turned to Rose. "Somebody's waiting for you downstairs." Rose's heart fell. She hadn't been there in a long time and she didn't want to go now. Doc and Virgil occupied so much of her time lately, she hadn't thought about what the rest of her job entailed. They'd kept her from a big part of what she was hired to do, but they weren't here to help her tonight. Ruby showed her the money. "He paid in advance. Go on down, Honey. You won't be disappointed." She shook her head at Ruby. How could she say a thing like that? They were all disappointments. She started to say something in protest and Ruby tightened her hand around Rose's arm. She liked Rose, but she was also the boss and fact was, Rose had a job to do just like the rest of them. The first thing she learned when she came to work here was that you didn't argue with Ruby. Rose let out a sigh and Ruby let go of her arm. The big redhead patted her on the back and gave her a gentle, but firm nudge. She took her time on the stairs, imagining what was waiting for her, a liquored-up miner, or worse. Another one with his pants down around his ankles, boots still on and an idiotic grin on his face, waiting for a woman. Maybe it was someone from the big money game. Whoever he was, he had money if he paid for a lady in a room downstairs, in which case, he'd be demanding special attention. From experience, she'd learned influential, rich men often had warped sexual preferences and she hoped this one wouldn't be difficult or favor a perversion. She shuddered at the thought. How did she ever get into this in the first place? When did her life become so crazy? She took a deep breath. Might as well get it over with. When she reached for the latch, the door opened from the inside. She stood in the doorway, staring in disbelief. Virgil!

Her heart sank like a rock to the bottom of a well. She didn't know what to say. She hoped he'd never ask her to do this. It'd been perfect until now, the talks and walking home after work. She considered him a friend. His being here tonight, in this room, would change that forever. She'd been waiting for him all evening and now that he was here, she wished she'd never met him. He must have come in by the rear entrance. It made sense, of course. He'd be discreet about things like this. Anyone who saw him downstairs would keep it to themselves. Players in that game had more important things on their minds than who Virgil was spending his time with in a bordello crib. She stepped inside and he closed the door. The flame in the lamp was turned down low. Red crystal pendants on the lamp refracted energy from the flame, setting free a thousand diaphanous apparitions to collide in their uninhibited dance of light all over the room. The decision was made quickly. She couldn't stay. She turned away from him and laid her hand on the doorknob, but didn't turn it. She couldn't. She was trying to leave, but something held her back. Several seconds went by, perhaps minutes. She wasn't sure. She lost track of time. She looked down at her hand. It was trembling. She didn't resist when he took her hand off the knob and turned her around to face him. His voice was low, almost a whisper. "You don't have to stay. I'll understand." She closed her eyes and he kissed her forehead. There was so much conflict within her. Here was a man she respected and cared for, as a friend. He was married. She could justify a friendship with him, but anything else just wouldn't be right. She'd been here before with other men who were married, but she didn't know them. They were nothing to her. Virgil was different. She opened her eyes. It was so comfortable being with him that she felt like she'd known him forever. She didn't want to misinterpret the feeling. She hadn't known him long, but he'd become an important part of her life. She didn't want to do the wrong thing and lose a valued friend. If she laid down with him, would they be able to preserve the element of friendship that was so important to her? She searched his eyes for an answer. Without hearing it, he recognized the question. He told her he was married. She knew that. He could never offer her the kind of life she deserved, a home and a family, and he wouldn't be so unkind as to make promises he couldn't keep. Her heart was racing. Why did he have to be so painfully honest? Then, he said something so unexpected his words made her dizzy. "All I want to do is love you, but I'll never be so presumptuous as to think it's enough for you." She couldn't believe what she heard. That was probably the closest she'd ever come to hearing someone say they loved her again. Again! A memory from the past surfaced like the sun suddenly bursting free above the horizon in the morning to light up the world. Someone loved her once, but that seemed like an eternity ago. John Merrick was still there, in her heart, on her mind, but only in memory. He was imprinted there forever. That would never change and no one would ever take his place. She looked at Virgil. He couldn't take John's place, but he was all she had now.

The next evening when she walked to work, Virgil crossed the street. She stopped and waited for him. There was something she wanted to say, but he didn't give her the chance. He spoke first. "Can I see you later..." She started to tell him she thought it would be best if he didn't come by anymore, but he finished the end of his sentence "...for a brandy and a little conversation?" She sighed and looked at the ground. She didn't really want him to stay away, but things were more complicated after what happened last night. He was waiting. She let out a big sigh and gave him his answer. "I'll see you at the Bird Cage." He repeated, "See you at the Bird Cage." He stepped aside, tipping his hat as he would to any lady passing on the street. Walking away, she felt his eyes watching her. There was a lot more than just a friendship between them now, although she didn't know what to call it. She couldn't even talk about it with Jenny or Lizzie. It was a private affair, an affaire de coeur, as it were. An affair of the heart. She could go one step further if she dared and call it a love affair except — she didn't love him. She loved John. What was she thinking? They spent entire evenings in conversation, but she only spent a couple of hours in bed with the man and he paid for her services. Well, he didn't pay her directly. He paid Ruby. Same thing. His money was part of what she took home. Was she forgetting who she was, what she was? She was a prostitute for God's sake! A scarlet woman. Lady of the night. It had nothing to do with love. Of course, he did say he wanted to love her. She wasn't sure what that meant. There was a twinge of guilt about the whole thing. He was married and she was still in love with John Merrick, a man who was two thousand miles away and she'd never see again. Virgil ought to be faithful to his wife, and despite the fact that John was gone, there remained a feeling of being true to him. No one said she had to turn away company. Being alone was a self-imposed sentence. Virgil, on the other hand, went home to his wife every night. She was confused. Maybe she was wrong in assuming John wouldn't understand her story. He might have forgiven her. It was too late now and there was no way of knowing what might have happened if she'd stayed in New Orleans. What was done, was done. She couldn't change anything and she couldn't consider contacting him, not after what she'd become in this place. Even if he understood, he'd never forgive her. Thinking about it was making her crazy.

She knocked on the rear door of the theatre. She needed to talk to somebody. No — she just needed time to think. Everything was so mixed up. She had a headache. She rubbed her forehead and knocked again, a little harder. She'd talk to Doc. She already told him about John. He always listened without criticizing or passing judgment. ...or, maybe she'd try to talk to Virgil. Maybe it would help. Maybe it wouldn't. Then again, maybe his curiosity about her had been satisfied last night in the basement bordello room. Maybe he'd never come back. Maybe that's all there was to it. Her head was throbbing. She pounded on the door again, this time more impatiently with her fist. Why didn't they open the damn door? The lock clicked and Eva flung it open wide, nearly knocking Rose down. She reached out to steady Rose. "Sorry, Rose. I guess the hinges are loose." Rose pushed her away and snapped at her, "Why don't you be more careful, girl? You could've killed me." She brushed past Eva and started toward the little dressing room in a huff. Eva stood by the door, very surprised at Rose's shortness of temper. She closed the door and locked it. Rose stopped and turned around. "I'm sorry, Eva. I have a headache." Eva nodded her acceptance of the apology and walked away. She'd have to resolve her feelings about what happened with Virgil, and soon. If she acted that way with any of the other girls, she was liable to get slapped, or punched. She hoped he wouldn't come to see her tonight. As if her life hadn't been complicated enough, now she had to think about what she was doing with Virgil. She spoke out loud. "That's a good question. What in Heaven's name am I doin' with Virgil?"

When he walked in with Doc and his brothers, she was sitting with a customer. She'd only seen the young one in passing on the street. Morgan Earp. Not surprising, he had the Earp good looks. He seemed out of place here. She thought he should have been home with his pretty wife, but she knew he'd been drawn into his brothers' world of law enforcement and business ventures. She knew they owned a gambling interest in the Oriental Saloon down the street and they probably had young Morgan involved in that too. She tried not to look at Virgil and she tried not to let him know she was nervous about being in the same room with him. Jenny and Lizzie spotted him right away. Neither of them had spoken to her since their little tiff, so she wasn't expecting them to talk to her now. She watched Lizzie approach the table with Jenny in tow. Lizzie always took people by the hand. Rose guessed it was part of the motherly instinct. Lizzie might have been a good mother if circumstances of her life had been different, but the chance of that ever happening was not likely. They proceeded to move in on Rose's customers. Lizzie, being Lizzie, shoved Rose out of the way. At first, Rose thought about shoving her back. Then, she realized what they were doing. Lizzie never ceased to amaze her. Jenny was in on it too. She stood up and backed away from the table when Lizzie winked. Jenny whispered three words. "Get lost, Rosie!" She emphasized the "Rosie" because she knew it irritated Rose. This time, it was a play on the way she acted. They were still her friends and she was ashamed for yelling at them. They were giving her a chance to take care of whatever business she had with Virgil and they were making their peace after the little spat.

It went without saying she always liked to see Doc. She walked straight to him. He kissed her cheek, then held her hand while he introduced Morgan Earp and invited her to join them. When he pulled out a chair, he noticed her hands were trembling. She sat down and he whispered, "Are you well?" His question threw her off and she smiled nervously when she answered, "No." She meant to say, "Yes." Right off, Doc knew something was wrong. It was odd that he asked if she was well. She hadn't been sick. Was her discomfort so noticeable he felt the need to ask about her health? Apparently, she wasn't covering it as well as she thought. She said she felt wonderful. He knew better. Doc was more perceptive than most people gave him credit for, and he'd come to know her pretty well. He didn't offer her a drink because he knew she didn't like whiskey, but when she asked for a glass, that did it. Something was definitely wrong. Now was not the time to ask, but he figured it had something to do with Virgil judging from the way she avoided looking at him. Doc reached under the table and squeezed her hand. She could feel Virgil's eyes, but she refused to look at him. From the first day she saw him watching her on Allen Street, she felt his eyes. When she couldn't stand it any longer, she glanced across the table. She was right. He was staring at her and she crumbled. Doc took it all in; Virgil staring at her the way he was, then her trying to ignore him and falling apart the second their eyes met. He saw the sparks that passed between them. It was time to leave.

Morgan was surprised at Doc. He wasn't known for jumping from one gambling hall to another. Where he first lit was where he stayed all night. "What's the hurry, Doc? We just got here. Haven't seen the show yet." Doc patted Morgan on the shoulder and announced that he recalled an obligation to participate in a game of chance. He winked at Wyatt and continued. "I regret I must excuse myself, but the Oriental is waiting, as is a gentleman's full purse which I intend to lighten for him forthwith." Wyatt took the cue and picked up his hat. Probably just as well. It was never a good idea to let Doc get into a card game alone. The accusation that he cheated came up frequently and, as rumor would have it, resulted in his opponent leaving the game by way of the undertaker's wagon. Wyatt stood up. "Maybe we'll tag along — to keep you honest." They laughed even though they knew there was wisdom in the comment. Doc raised his glass toward Wyatt. "Sir, I thank you for your concern." It was a lot more than concern since the Earps owned a gambling interest in the Oriental and that was where Doc was headed. If Doc started something, the furniture could get broken up. Of course, that was the least of the worry. For many reasons, it wasn't a bad idea to keep an eye on any game Doc got into. He turned to Rose, lifting his glass and launching into one of his familiar fond farewell toasts to her beauty and charm. She'd be first and foremost on his mind and in his heart until next they met. She had to laugh at Doc's toasts. She wondered how Kate would view his flowery compliments and public announcements of affection for her. Kate probably was never too surprised at anything John Henry did, but to be on the safe side, it wouldn't hurt to find Kate and introduce herself. She'd never want Kate to get the wrong impression of her friendship with Doc. He drained the glass and bent down to kiss her cheek. He whispered, "Silver Rose Marie, beware of the man with the silver star. I will defend your honor to the death, my dear, but I cannot mend a broken heart." What a strange thing to say. When he stood up, a troubled expression clouded his face, the same look of concern he gave her the night she met Virgil and went outside with him. She'd gotten the message from Lizzie and Jenny too. Why did they all assume she'd get hurt if she continued her involvement with Virgil? Involvement! Up to now, she emphatically denied any such thing. There was no question that she was involved with him and everyone knew it. He was married. She had to remember he wasn't free. Doc left with Morgan and Wyatt, leaving her alone to settle up with Virgil.

He sat across the table, waiting for her to say something. They hadn't exchanged any words. Not so much as a hello. He'd been looking at her the whole time though. When the others left, he moved to the chair next to her. She felt awkward after what happened last night. People were watching. After the tantrum she threw, they were all waiting in anticipation of a new show. Further confrontation with him would be a dead giveaway there was something going on between them. Well, they'd be disappointed tonight. She had no intention of ever creating a scene like that again.

As the evening went on and she realized he wasn't going to ask her to go downstairs, she relaxed. It helped that he never mentioned anything about the previous night either. That didn't surprise her. He wouldn't discuss their private business in the middle of the Bird Cage anyway. He talked about everything else, trying to make her feel more comfortable about being with him. Suddenly, in the midst of talking about the new deputy he'd hired, he asked her how she felt about moving out of the hotel. He didn't wait for an answer. He thought it might be a good idea for her to find a place of her own, a more private and less expensive residence. She'd already thought about that. Living at the Cosmopolitan made her feel like she was in a glass fishbowl with people watching every move she made. A hotel in the heart of town was not designed for privacy and she couldn't walk in or out of the place at any hour without someone stopping to stare. A woman alone who had enough money to live at the Cosmopolitan was a curiosity, but who she was and who she kept company with made her a bigger target for sensation-seeking gossip-mongers. Although she'd become accustomed to disparaging remarks from women who despised her for her line of work — women like Emily Grants' mother, it didn't make passing them on the street any easier. Coming and going from the hotel as she did, there was always someone right there to say something, and if it was Caroline Grants, the encounter was bound to be unpleasant. It'd be worse the first time Caroline or one of her cronies spotted Virgil walking her home from the Bird Cage. If they ever got wind of her relationship with him, they'd be running to his wife to tattle. They'd love to inform Allie her husband was keeping company with the notorious Silver Rose of Bird Cage Theatre fame. Notorious! That was downright funny. It was one of those words usually paired with another such as "criminal" or "outlaw." She never thought of herself as notorious, but she was sure they did. It didn't matter. They could say what they pleased. She couldn't stop them from gossiping, but it would be nice to be out of the line of fire from their sharp tongues.

Virgil was talking about a small house a few blocks away. "You can plant flowers in the yard and sit on your own front-porch swing. In fact, I think a rambling red rose is in bloom along the fence as we speak. Oh, yes, night-blooming jasmine too — the real stuff, climbing up a trellis by the front porch, sweeter than the cactus flower you thought was jasmine." She laughed. He remembered. "If you're interested, I can arrange for you to see it tomorrow. The rent's reasonable and if you like it, you can move in right away." He winked. "Just so happens, I know the owner." It sounded too good to be true. She liked it already, without seeing it. It would be wonderful to have roses in the yard — and jasmine. Those were the two flowers she loved. Hotel living was expensive and she was tired of being ogled. She'd thought about moving out of the Cosmopolitan plenty of times, but never found a place. Maybe this was it.

Living in her own little house would certainly have its advantages, privacy mostly, away from prying eyes and wagging tongues. It was a most appealing idea, but what made him suggest it? She wondered if he thought the time she spent with him in the room downstairs last night entitled him to dictate where she ought to live. Seemed he'd already made up his mind. At first, she was offended by his audacity to conclude he had the right to tell her where to live just because he bedded her one time, and for money at that. She reconsidered. It couldn't hurt to look at the house. She agreed to see it whenever he could arrange the appointment. He said he'd pick her up at four o'clock tomorrow afternoon, and after they saw the house, he'd buy her dinner. She was offended again. He hadn't asked if he could take her to dinner. He told her. Maybe that's the way men were in the habit of treating women in this town, but she wasn't going to stand for it. Once more, she reconsidered her thinking. She had to stop being so easily miffed. She was far too defensive lately and she didn't like it. She never used to be like this, quick to jump down someone's throat without provocation and being put out at every little thing. He didn't mean anything by it. It was his way, and it was an invitation she didn't want to turn down. If she were to reconsider anything, it had to be her own ill humor and earlier decision not to see him anymore. She did want to see him, and he wanted to see her. That was a fact. She remembered what he said last night. He "only wanted to love her." She still wasn't sure what that meant exactly. She wasn't sure at all what love was, but whatever it was that he was offering, she had to take it. It was all she had. He ordered a bottle and two glasses. Cold tea for her. If she was going to sit with him, he had to keep the house happy. There were no special dispensations when it came to money and even Virgil Earp paid full price if he wanted to take up a whole table and the entire evening of a shady lady at the Bird Cage.

When the show was over, Ruby headed their way. Ruby liked Virgil and never missed the chance to say hello. Seemed he was as glad to see her as she was to see him. He greeted her with a big hug and a kiss on the cheek. A very warm reception, indeed. Rose raised her eyebrows. He wasn't that friendly with the other girls. He was flirting with Ruby! If she wasn't mistaken, that was a little pang of jealously she just felt. Rose noticed the money he slipped into Ruby's hand. "I hope it won't be an inconvenience for the house if I monopolize Miss Callahan's attention for the rest of the evening." Ruby didn't look at the money. "I don't see that to be a problem, Marshal." She laid her hand on Rose's shoulder, but she was smiling at Virgil. Rose thought back to Ruby's comment last night when she told her someone was waiting downstairs to see her. She'd made a point of saying, "You won't be disappointed." She wondered how Ruby could have been so sure about that. She watched the way Ruby moved while she talked to Virgil. Did Ruby have some first-hand knowledge about him? She'd never know, of course, because she'd never ask and Ruby wouldn't tell her if she did. She remembered the way Ruby's blue eyes sparkled when she said something else about Virgil once before Rose met him. She said, "I'll get him someday. Mark my words!"

Rose's time obviously having been paid for, Ruby left the table. She watched the big redhead swing her hips as she walked away, unmistakably for Virgil's benefit, and she noticed Virgil watching too. It was easy to understand why men were so taken with Ruby Fontaine. Well-practiced in the art of seduction, Ruby had a come-hither look and a pair of sapphire-blue eyes that charmed men and turned the smoothest talkers into blithering idiots. Tall and beautiful and slinky with a shock of red hair drifting around her shoulders, she looked like some kind of mythical goddess. She had a heart of gold and a devil of a temper. With the strength of a lumberjack behind her punch, arguments were settled fast when she stepped in. Ruby was no ordinary lady. As soon as Virgil said the next words, Rose decided she'd been right about Ruby knowing more about him than she told. It wasn't so much what he said as the way he said it, or maybe it was the smile that gave it away. He said, "Ruby and I are old friends."

Half an hour later, Ruby came by again. "Business is slow tonight, Rose. No reason for you to stick around. You've got a safe escort home, so why don't you go on and leave early?" Rose looked around the room. Slow night? How did Ruby come to that conclusion? The place was packed to overflowing. She turned to thank Ruby, but she was already stirring up excitement at the next table. Outside the theatre, Virgil linked arms with her. Granted, it was nice not to have to walk home alone, but Ruby wasn't entirely right about the safe escort. In truth, walking on the street at night with Virgil Earp was anything but safe. He was a constant target and his life was always in danger from the wild ones — the Clantons and McLaurys, Johnny Ringo, and that crazy Indian Charlie, to name a few. There were plenty of others. It was no secret the Earps had enemies, but despite the ongoing threats, she wasn't a bit afraid. She knew he wasn't either. If they were going to get him, they'd get him. It could be tonight in the dark, or tomorrow or the next day in broad daylight.

She held his arm and they walked down Allen Street toward the hotel. He was glad she'd be living in the house over on Toughnut. He'd visit her there... He stopped walking. ...provided, of course, that she invited him. She laughed. Of course he'd be invited. Wait a minute! She hadn't agreed to move into the house yet. All she said was she'd look at it. She let go of his arm. Maybe he had personal motives for wanting her to live alone, away from the mainstream of prying eyes and gossip. Maybe that was alright. Was she going to throw another fit right here on the street because she thought he was presumptuous? She was losing her temper a lot lately over stupid things. She was doing it again, reacting defensively to his good intentions. There was no reason to be upset with him. He was trying to help her find a better place to live. There was nothing suspicious or devious about him and she was ashamed for thinking he only wanted her in the little house for his own convenience. She did know if she took the house, he'd be more than a casual visitor though. Maybe that would be alright too. Of course, a visitor was all he'd ever be. He already said he wouldn't make empty promises. She accepted that. She had to. One thing she'd always know was that he was honest. Honest? Now, that was funny. He was cheating on his wife and she was an accomplice. Where was the honesty in that? She felt guilty about it, but she needed someone to care about her too, and here he was. It wasn't fair to the woman who waited at home for him. She thought, "Here I go again, feeling sorry for his poor wife, but what about me?" What about her? His wife couldn't know about her. She felt compassion for the woman she'd never met. There was no malice or deliberate intent to hurt anyone. She wouldn't want to cause his wife any heartache, and she believed there was no happiness to be gained from someone else's misery. They'd have to be very discreet. No one could know about them. She realized how ridiculous it sounded. It would be impossible to keep that kind of secret. He said it himself. Stories traveled fast in Tombstone. It wasn't as if either of them was inconspicuous. Everyone knew them both. He was Virgil Earp for Heaven's sake, and she was Allen Street Rose — Silver Rose Callahan, the Irish prostitute from the Bird Cage Theatre. He was the big man with the badge and she stood out from all the rest with her Irish brogue and fiery-red hair, and temper to match if you made her mad.

She looked up at the man beside her. He was strong and handsome, and he had an indescribable charm. Every woman in town probably wondered at one time or another what it would be like to be with Virgil Earp, but they'd never admit it. At least the girls at the Bird Cage were honest. They wondered out loud. All except Ruby. She said she'd get him someday, but never speculated like the rest of them about an intimate interlude with Virgil, and Rose figured out why. Ruby already knew. None of them approached him, not since they knew he came to see Rose, and only Rose. He was an unusual man alright. He lived by a creed most men didn't understand and believed so fervently in the law that he'd lay down his life to defend it. Most people would say Wyatt was the controlling force in the Earp family, but in truth, Virgil was the strong one — and he was married. That fact kept coming back to keep her on the right track. She'd have no unreasonable expectations about their affair of the heart — or whatever it was. She resigned herself to accept whatever each day brought and be prepared for the day he'd tell her he couldn't see her anymore. For now, she'd take whatever time he offered to spend with her and be grateful for it. He replaced her arm through his and pulled her closer to him as they walked on toward the Cosmopolitan. He knew she'd been deep in thought and had a fair idea what she was thinking about. At the hotel, he reminded her he'd pick her up at four to inspect her new house. She smiled at the way he said "your" new house. He smiled too. They both knew she'd be moving in a couple of days. At the foot of the stairs, she looked back. He was still standing outside the door. She'd better get a good night's sleep. Tomorrow, she'd start packing.

She was awakened by a thumping on the door and Lizzie's voice calling to her to get up. She had hoped to sleep late today. Then, she remembered — the new girl. How could she have forgotten? The stage would be arriving today with the newest prospective Bird Cage dove from St. Joe. Lizzie and Rose were to meet her and get her settled in. Lizzie was still knocking. Rose got up and shuffled to the door. "Stop, Lizzie! You'll wake up the whole place." She opened the door and Lizzie flew in, chattering away like a nesting magpie with a cat up the tree. Sometimes Rose wondered if Lizzie's feet even touched the floor. She found herself looking down at Lizzie's feet, thinking how silly it was. She rubbed her eyes and shook her head to get the sleep cobwebs out while Lizzie flitted about the room, talking and waving her hands. Arms and legs and mouth all going at the same time, accompanied by animated eye expressions and a wiggling body emphasizing every word, Lizzie resembled a jointed marionette whose strings were manipulated by a puppet master afflicted with Saint Vitus'

Dance tremors. Lizzie was a whirling dervish, not unlike the Pixie. The Pixie! She missed the Pixie so much. She ought to write to Rebecca and explain why she had to leave and how sorry she was, but not today. The truth was hard enough to think about and more difficult to say. There were voices in the hall and she realized she was standing in the doorway in her nightgown. She closed the door and turned the lock.

Lizzie was pulling clothes from the closet and drawers and throwing them onto the bed. "Hurry up Rosie! Get dressed! She'll be here any minute. You were supposed to meet me at the stage office an hour ago. What are you doing in bed this late? Half the day is already gone." Lizzie was a sweet girl, but Rose was certain God must have been distracted when He made her given the fact that He failed to bless her with anything remotely resembling patience. Sometimes, she could be absolutely exasperating. Rose folded her arms. She hated to be called "Rosie." Lizzie stopped in her tracks, understanding the message and holding her hands up by way of apology. "Okay, I'm sorry — Rose." She stopped moving and stood perfectly still. Rose laughed. She could never stay mad at Lizzie.

With Lizzie's "help," she pulled herself together in record time, though not fast enough to suit Lizzie. Nothing ever moved fast enough for Lizzie. She tapped her fingers impatiently on the table while Rose took an extra minute to adjust her jewelry. "Why do you wear all that silver anyway? It's hot, isn't it? Isn't it heavy with the stones and all? I don't know how you can stand all that stuff hanging around your neck, and all those bracelets and rings..." Rose crossed her arms and glared at Lizzie, her eyes narrowed and her voice ominously calm. She enunciated her words precisely. "I wear it because I like it and that's why they call me Silver Rose. Otherwise, they'd call me Rosie — and you know how I hate to be called Rosie. Anymore questions, Lizette?" Lizzie knew she'd pushed Rose to the limit of her patience for this conversation. "No. Let's go!"

When they left the hotel, Lizzie grabbed Rose's hand to make her walk faster. Rose stopped, pulling away her hand and scolding Lizzie. "For Heaven's sake, Lizzie, let go of me — and slow down! The stage isn't even here yet. Sometimes you drive me crazy!" As soon as the words left her lips, she realized how pointless they were. Lizzie never "slowed down" and it was foolish to expect she ever would. She knew her friend's defense against personal heartaches and inner turmoil was perpetual motion. If Lizzie ever slowed down long enough to really think about her life, the result might be tragic. She knew Lizzie tried to kill herself once. It was no secret the girl was unstable, suffering from dramatic changes in mood, often within seconds of each other. Virgil said Lizzie was like a goose — she woke up in a new world every day. One day, she was like she was this morning, in control of her situation and everyone else's. Other days, she was a lost child without a clue which way to go. Rose had an idea something inside Lizzie created continual chaos and caused her to run like a clock that never wound down. There were doctors who could help people with such afflictions of the mind, but not in Tombstone. She'd been a little too irritated when she shook herself free from Lizzie's tugging and the added remark about Lizzie driving her crazy didn't help matters. Lizzie was about to cry. Rose recognized the look. This was one of those "lost child" times. Without warning, her mood changed drastically. Rose tried to fix it fast. "I'm sorry, Lizzie. I'll try to walk a little faster." Reversing the roles, she took hold of Lizzie's hand, "Come on. We don't want to be late."

They didn't have to wait long. Arrival of the stage always generated a crowd and today was no different. There were people everywhere. Of the four passengers on board, three were men and they got off first. Then, they saw her. She looked like a scared puppy peering out the coach door. The driver helped her down and she smoothed her dress and straightened her hat. It was good to stop riding in the heat and pull herself together. Rose knew the feeling well. The best part about a stagecoach ride was when it was over and your backside stopped vibrating. She looked so proper in a wine-colored suit and hat to match. A banker's daughter maybe. A real lady. She probably answered the same advertisement Rose answered and didn't have any idea what she was getting herself into. Looking at the girl, she saw herself, or what she used to be anyway, before the Bird Cage. She wanted to tell the scared puppy to buy a ticket back to wherever she came from. She looked so innocent. What would Tombstone do to her? Rose thought back to a few weeks ago. Had it only been a few weeks? Hard to believe. Seemed like she'd been here forever. With her hand out and no trace of her thoughts showing, she smiled at the girl. "I'm Rose Callahan. This is Lizette McGee. Welcome to Tombstone." Her own words made her step back, the same words she'd been greeted with a few short weeks ago when she got off the stage. The girl smiled and held out her hand. "I'm

Abigail Treneaux. Abby." She shook hands with both of them and turned to Rose. "Have we met before?" Rose shook her head no. "I don't think so."

He was right on time. Four o'clock. For such a short distance, they could have walked, but he picked her up in a buggy with a canopy. She was well aware of the stares as they drove down Allen Street. She was sure Virgil saw them too. She wondered what kind of gossip would circulate now that he'd been seen driving off with her in broad daylight. It didn't seem to bother him. He wasn't like the rest of the hypocrites who cheated under cover of darkness in a den of iniquity, then put on a display of affection in public with their wives the next day. She had a feeling he wasn't the kind of man who hid anything and if it came right down to it, all he was doing was showing her a house for rent. He stopped in front of the little gray house and it was love at first sight. The fence was covered with rambling red roses in full bloom and she could see the jasmine climbing a trellis off to one side of the porch exactly as he described it. Inside the gate, a rosebush loaded with miniature white roses reminded her of the wild white rose that grew on her mother's grave in Ireland. She smelled the flowers from the street.

She couldn't take her eyes off the house as he lifted her down from the buggy. He unlocked the door and pushed it open so she could walk in ahead of him. It had been freshly painted, inside and out, and the wood floors were polished to such a high luster, she could see her reflection in them. It even had a fireplace. She loved fireplaces. Everything was shiny and clean. The windows sparkled and the room was full of sun. Earlier, she tried not to get too excited thinking about the house, but now that she saw it, she could hardly believe her eyes. It was exactly what she wanted, small and cozy. Perfect for her. She realized she was smiling. Had she also been thinking out loud? She turned to Virgil. She must have been thinking out loud because he was smiling too. "When do you want to move in?" Was it that obvious she'd already made the decision to live here? He put his arms around her. She had to tilt her head back to see his face at close range. He kissed her and she closed her eyes. "I want you to be happy, Rose. I'm going to take care of you." She kept her eyes closed, afraid that if she opened them he'd see the question in them. Had he slipped? Was this one of those promises he said he couldn't make? She didn't ask. It wasn't exactly a promise anyway. He didn't say "I promise," but for the time being, it was good enough. She'd be ready to move in tomorrow.

They went outside and she questioned him while he locked the door. "What about the rent?" ...and how much was the rent? Could she afford it? Who was the owner? Surely the owner would ask for payment in advance. She was excited and talking very fast. He pulled the key from the lock. "The rent's paid." She didn't understand. He explained. "I own the house. The rent is paid. All you have to do is live here." She protested. "I couldn't live in the house without payin' rent. It wouldn't be right. I'll have to pay." She was so excited, she lapsed into Gaelic. "You'll be needin' to tell me how much you're wantin' for the rent and..." He covered her mouth with his hand. "I can't understand that gibber. You talk too much, Rose. Just say thank you and let it go at that." He took his hand away. It wouldn't do any good to insist, and he was right about the gibber. It was a bad habit. All she said was, "Thank you." She wanted to pay her own way, but this wasn't the time to talk about it. He was a lot like Ruby. You had to know when not to argue with him. She'd be quiet for now, but she'd find a way to convince him to take rent money later.

At dinner, they agreed she'd move in two days. He told her to pack and he'd send someone to pick her and her belongings up Monday afternoon. She didn't know how to thank him. She wanted to reach across the table and touch his hand, but people were watching. They had to keep their distance in public. The mere fact they were having dinner together was enough to start the gossip ball rolling. Watching him across the table, it occurred to her this was the first time they'd been together outside the Bird Cage. He'd been around quite a bit lately, but she knew it was only a matter of time until that would change. It wouldn't last forever. She savored every second with him and compared them to heartbeats. You never knew when a heartbeat might stop. They finished eating and left the restaurant. It was a lovely, relaxing time. She couldn't remember when she'd enjoyed an afternoon so much. It seemed her life had taken a turn for the better. It was far from perfect, but Virgil was certainly making it more tolerable. She'd have to work at the Bird Cage, but at least she had something to ease her burden a little. She had Virgil. Well, she didn't really have Virgil. Virgil's wife had Virgil. She just borrowed him for a while and hoped no one would get hurt. She wasn't quite sure what she had, but it was better than being alone. She couldn't call it love, but she had to admit she did feel a certain affection for him. John was still on her mind. She never stopped thinking about him. She'd subtract ten years from her life if she could see him again. Until the day she died, she'd miss him. John was the only one she'd ever love, but he was gone. Virgil was here, and he did say he was going to take care of her. That wouldn't do either. She'd take care of herself. To dare think he might stay forever was a mistake. She knew better than to believe that would happen. She had to remain independent and take their arrangement one day at a time. If she didn't expect anything, she wouldn't be disappointed when he went away, and she had no misgivings about the inevitable.

He didn't come to the Bird Cage that night. Doc came — with Kate. Wonder of all wonders! She finally met Big Nose Kate. She didn't want to slip and call her that though. She guessed Kate knew who she was by now. News traveled pretty fast in Tombstone and Doc was spending a fair share of time at the Bird Cage lately. It was no secret he came to see her. Kate was sociable enough, a little rough around the edges, but who wasn't? Rose saw the way Kate looked her over when they were introduced. She'd heard the stories about Kate's bad temper and had no desire for Kate to ever be angry because she thought Doc stopped in the Bird Cage too often to see her. Contrary to what her nickname implied, Kate was not unattractive, although she did have a prominent nose. She was friendly and straight-spoken, and she rolled her own cigarettes right there at the table. She said and did whatever pleased her and didn't give a damn what anyone thought. The fact that she came to the Bird Cage was proof of that. The woman could drink too. After belting down a couple of two-finger glasses of whiskey, she announced she had business elsewhere. Rose guessed Kate's sole purpose for stopping by was to give her the once-over, and she surely did that, but she was satisfied Rose wasn't after Doc. That dispensed with a worry. When they were leaving, Rose prayed Doc would forego his usual farewell toast. If he didn't, Kate might change her mind and rethink her decision about them only being friends. He was smart. He knew better than to get Kate's dander up, although, if rumor was to be believed, he did exactly that on a regular basis. According to everyone who knew them, they fought like cats and dogs, with poor Kate being the recipient of more than one black eye. To Rose's great relief, all he said was, "A pleasure to see you, Miss Callahan. Have a pleasant evenin'." Kate told her to stop by any time. He offered his arm to Kate on the way out the door. Another relief. Doc had a reputation for being more than a little unpredictable and Rose was worried he might say something to deliberately get Kate sideways. When they reached the door, Kate went out ahead of him and he turned around and blew Rose a kiss. She covered her eyes with one hand. He had to do it. She laughed. John Holliday! He was really something. With all they said about him, she never once heard anyone tell that he had a sense of humor.

When they were gone, she told the girls about her plan to move into the little gray house. That was good news to them, but they still worried about her living alone, especially Lizzie, who couldn't live alone. She wanted to tell them she wouldn't be by herself, not all the time anyway, but she bit her tongue. She couldn't tell them she expected Virgil to be spending time there. "Well, at least Virge can see you whenever he wants to now." Rose closed her eyes tight. Leave it to Lizzie to blurt it right out. Rose played dumb. "Whatever makes you think Virgil would want to see me?" Lizzie and Jenny laughed. She was irritated. They thought they were so smart! No use arguing with them. She couldn't fool them and she knew it. Maybe she wasn't fooling anybody. They kept talking, ignoring the fact that they had ruffled her feathers yet again over Virgil. He was a temperamental issue with her and they wisely avoided another confrontation by dropping the subject. They'd see her tomorrow. It was their day off too. They'd come by and help her pack, and when she was moved in, they'd help plant flowers all around the house. They were incorrigible! What could she say? — and what would she do without them?

Although everyone seemed happy about her move, she detected a hint of sarcasm in Ruby's voice. "Virgil must really have taken a shine to you, putting you in that house and all." By the "and all" she meant the special attention he was paying to Rose. "It's not often a man pays the house for the company of a lady for the entire evening the way Virge pays to sit and talk to you." As an afterthought, she threw in an extra little tart comment completely out of character for Ruby. "Of course, Virge has always been partial to redheads." She was jealous and said so — jokingly, but Rose sensed there was more than a little truth to the assertion. Ruby didn't say things she didn't mean. Everyone knew she liked Virgil and more than once, they'd all heard her say she'd get him someday. She rarely said things twice, but where Virgil was concerned, she made her point very well-known. One thing about Ruby, she wasn't bashful and she never held back if she had something to say. She also never moved in on any man claimed by a friend, and that's how she saw it now. To her way of thinking, Virgil was Rose's private domain and it was hands off for her and anybody else who might have had their eye on him. From now on, she'd keep her ideas about Virgil to herself. She said her piece and that was the end of it. She shifted the conversation to the house. She couldn't wait to see it. She'd even go so far as to help plant flowers with the girls. Somehow, Rose couldn't picture Ruby digging in the dirt, but didn't doubt she would.

For the rest of the night, her house was all they talked about. By the time she went home, Lizzie already had the garden planned. "Tomatoes! You gotta grow tomatoes, Rosie. Flowers too. Lot of flowers — the kind we can pick to put in vases. We can buy seeds from Smith's and the feed store sells them too, all different kinds." Rose imagined them all digging in the dirt. Hell's flowers — planting flowers! ...and tomatoes. She didn't know why the idea struck her so funny. After all, they were just ordinary women who liked to do the same things other women liked to do. That's what was so funny about it. They were not "ordinary women."

The next day was Sunday. She used to go to church on Sundays, but no more. Not since Emily tried to talk to her a couple of weeks ago. As in Smith's the day she and Lizzie were buying cloth, Emily's mother yanked the little girl's pigtails and shook her so hard a ribbon fell from her braid. The child was in tears in the churchyard and all because she said hello to Rose. Rose felt terrible. She never wanted it to happen again, so from then on, she prayed in her room, sure it didn't matter to God where she said her prayers. She tried to go to church. He knew that. The handful of good, Christian women in Tombstone let her know, in no uncertain terms, that whores had no place in the house of God. After the service, the minister stood on the church steps listening to Caroline Grants and her cronies call Rose a whore and tell her she wasn't welcome in their church. He never said a word. He just turned his back and went inside. She opened Ann's Bible and read for an hour. When she was done, she rested her head against the back of the tall rocker and closed her eyes. Memories always came back at times like this, keepsake remembrances of the people she loved most in her life; her father and the mother she never knew, Ann Merrick, Marian, Rebecca. John. Most of all, John. She missed them all, especially John. The pain of losing him never subsided. If anything, it got worse with time. She wondered if he ever thought about her these days and prayed God would take care of him.

She didn't have to work tonight. That was another good thing about Sundays. She soaked in a hot bath scented with lavender until the water cooled down. The smell of sweet oils in the tub reminded her of the first night she spent at the Merrick home in New York. Ann poured the soothing oils into the water and she remembered her wonderment at the silkiness of her skin when she dried off. After the bath, she opened the window in her room. It was a pretty morning. Not too hot. She brushed her hair until it was dry and took her time getting dressed. She enjoyed the peace and quiet of Sunday mornings. Now, for the packing. She opened the trunk. Peace and quiet abruptly ended. She could tell by the knock who was at the door. She opened it right away to lessen the possibility of other late sleepers on the floor being awakened by Lizette's impatient pounding. She promised to help with the packing and Rose should have known she'd show up. Lizzie always kept her promises, thus, ending any chance for a quiet Sunday.

By Sunday evening, everything was packed. She was so excited about moving, the thought never occurred to her that she had no furniture, no bed, not even a chair to sit on. Tomorrow, she'd have to see what she could find in a hurry, a bed, if nothing else. The rest she'd get later. She started a list of things she'd need to set up housekeeping, everything from dishes to blankets to food for the cupboards. She'd lived in a hotel and eaten at the restaurant for so long she'd forgotten what it took to keep house.

She didn't know the two young men who came for her trunk and boxes Monday afternoon, but she knew Virgil sent them. They gave her the key to the house and carried her things downstairs, carefully loading them into a waiting buckboard. An hour later, she was standing at her new front door. The grass had been trimmed and the roses pruned. Trailing runners of the jasmine bush had been intertwined in the trellis to help it hold on as it crept upward toward the roof. Since she came to town, there'd only been a couple of small rain showers and she wondered where the water came from to keep the grass green. There might be a well around back, but she hadn't noticed the first time she was here. Knowing Virgil, he probably had it hauled in by the barrelful. It might very well be the neatest house in town. She placed the key in the slot and opened the door slowly. It was exciting. This was her house — her home. She was glad Lizzie hadn't promised to come with her today. She didn't want to share this moment with anyone.

Expecting to find an empty house, her mouth fell open and she dropped the key. She didn't even hear it clatter on the wooden porch. It looked like someone already lived there. Was she in the right place? She must be. The key opened the door. Not wanting to intrude if someone had moved in unbeknown to her, she tapped on the door. "Is there someone here?" When there was no answer, she stepped inside tentatively, looking around for sign of an occupant. It was beautiful. There were lace curtains at the windows and roses in the carpet. Around the edge, the polished wood floor framed the carpet like an artist's floral painting. While the boys carried her trunk and cases in, she walked gingerly from room to room as if walking on eggshells, afraid of shattering the dream by putting her feet down too hard. In the kitchen, a bouquet of freshly-cut pink and yellow roses filled a glass vase on the table, and a copper teakettle on the stove was so shiny it was almost too pretty to use. The black iron stove was brand new. She ran her hand across the griddle. It was just like Ann's and she remembered her first day in the Merrick house when she wondered if she'd ever have a house with lace curtains and a cast-iron stove. She heard a small chirp and looked up. Hanging from the ceiling was a white wicker cage with two tiny blue birds cuddled side-by-side on the perch. He thought of everything! "Will you need anything else, ma'am?" She spun around, startled by the voice. She'd forgotten they were there. The boys were finished bringing in her things. "No. Thank you." She fumbled in her purse. She had to give them something for their trouble. One held up his hand. They'd already been paid. Of course! He would have taken care of that too.

When she was alone, she turned toward the bedroom. There had to be a bed in there. He wouldn't have forgotten something for her to sleep on. He certainly hadn't forgotten anything else. She approached the room on tiptoe, giggling at the way she was acting, and peeked around the corner. She couldn't believe it. The rest of the house was a dream, but the bedroom was beyond a dream, a room straight out of a fairy tale. The white grapevine bed trimmed with brass was a work of art, and the comforter looked liked a big white cloud intricately embroidered with pink flowers and lace all around the edges. She ran her hand over it, thinking what a beautiful piece of work it was. Many hours' worth. It was very soft. A down comforter... "made from the feathers of a goose's behind." She laughed out loud remembering Ann's description of the comforter.

"How do you like it?" She hadn't heard him come in and she nearly jumped out of her skin. Overwhelmed with discovering so many treasures and realizing the magnitude of his generosity, she started to cry. There were no words to describe how much she liked it, or how she felt. She was overcome with emotion and he put his arms around her while she cried. When she stopped sniffling, he gave her his handkerchief. "I didn't mean to make you cry. If you don't like it, I'll send it all back." He was kidding, of course. He knew she was crying because she was happy. She burst into what he called her gibber, talking so excitedly that she threw in an occasional word in her native language. "I don't know how I'll ever repay you for all of this. Everythin' is lovely, and I know it must've been very expensive. I can't believe you did this, Virge. ...and the little blue birds. I'm goin' to call them Romeo and Juliet. You must let me pay..." He held up his hand to stop her blubbering. "You don't have to pay for anything, Rose. It's a gift, not a loan, and I think Romeo and Juliet are fine names for the birds. I just stopped by to make sure you got your things moved in alright. I can't stay. It's Monday and I have work to do." What he really meant was, it was daylight and he couldn't be seen there too much during the day. She was disappointed, but this was how it would be. There'd be lots of times when he couldn't stay, or couldn't be there at all.

He snapped his fingers and opened the door. "I almost forgot." She was puzzled. What could he have possibly forgotten? He'd thought of everything in the house right down to a vase full of roses on the table and a couple of parakeets to keep her company. He went out to the porch and when he came back, he handed her the puppy. A few days earlier, she'd helped a young Apache boy when some cowboys were picking on him in the street. The boy took quite a beating from the bullies, but managed to protect the dog. When it was over, he gave her the puppy for saving his life. Living at the hotel, she had nowhere to keep a dog, so Virgil took him home. "Little Bear!" She hugged the little gold ball of fluff and he licked her chin. "Thanks for keepin' him, Virge. I hope he wasn't too much trouble." She looked the dog over. "He's grown a bit." Virgil patted the pup's head and laughed. "More than a bit, I'd say. He'll be a big dog before you know it. I've been working on making him mind. Teach him right when he's young and he'll come in handy for protection when you're alone. No trouble though. Just eats everything in sight." She laughed. He kissed her and told her to keep her derringer under the pillow and the doors locked. He'd be back later to see how she and Little Bear were getting on.

Her role at the Bird Cage was changing. She was being asked to sing more often lately and she never went to the suspended cribs or the basement bordello rooms anymore. Whenever it looked like she was getting herself into a sticky situation, Ruby pulled her away. The last time she was downstairs, she was with Virgil. She still danced with customers and sat at their tables, but whenever they reached the point of wanting to buy her favors, something always happened to get her out of it. On nights when Virgil wasn't there to take her home, he sent someone to make sure she got there safely. He was keeping his promise to take care of her. On her nights off, he came to the house after dark. She wondered where his wife thought he went, but she never asked him. They never talked about Allie, and that was fine with Rose. There were other things to talk about. Keeping the peace during turbulent times and performing city administrative duties was a full-time job, and he was juggling a lot of other things as well. There were the Earps' business ventures and family responsibilities — and his wife. Then, there was her. She wondered when the man found time to sleep. She knew he came to her to escape the rest of life's pressures. He never said it, but she knew he needed her, and she tried to provide an escape for him in the private world of the little gray house. It was her escape as well as his.

Chapter 8

"Throw down your guns, boys," Virgil yelled,
"or take a .45 to hell."
Six-shooters blazed and belched hot lead,
and in thirty seconds, three men were dead.

Gunfight at the O.K. Corral
October 26, 1881

She could see the commotion on Allen Street from a block away. When she reached the corner, people were running in every direction. She asked someone what was going on. Word was, the inevitable confrontation was about to happen. The Earps would settle things once and for all with the Clantons and McLaurys. The cowboys were about to take a big hit if Virgil had anything to say about it. She looked up and down the street. Where was the Sheriff? What was he doing to stop this craziness? Someone was bound to get hurt. Across the street, three men walked out of Hafford's — Wyatt and Morgan and Virgil. Her heart pounded wildly. He saw her standing there, but didn't stop. He shook his head at her and kept walking. His eyes sent the message, "Stay where you are." They were all armed. Virgil was carrying a shotgun and two revolvers. Panic gripped her as soon as she noticed the rawhide strings tied to Virgil's leg, securing the holster in place for fast removal of the long-barrel .45. The second gun was stuck in his belt. He was ready for a fight. He crossed the street with his brothers. Doc met them on the corner. They stopped and talked to him for a minute and Virgil handed Doc the shotgun, exchanging it for the cane Doc was carrying. Doc concealed the shotgun under his coat and they didn't waste any more words. The four of them headed up Fourth Street, walking like they were on a mission and prepared for a deadly clash. The way they walked made her more anxious about what their destination might be.

She stopped another man, urgently tugging at his arm. "Do you know what's goin' on? Where are they goin'? What are they doin' with all those guns?" He scratched his ear and pondered the questions, looking thought-fully after the four men walking up Fourth Street. "Well, ma'am, looks t'me there's one hell of a fight brewin' and from the direction the Earps and what's his name there — Holliday, just lit out, probably gonna be out back of the O.K. Corral. Tom and Frank McLaury been holed up over at Dexter's with Ike and some of them Clanton boys for quite a spell. Could be a couple more cowboys in there with 'em. The lot of 'em been drinkin' a mite heavy all day and Ike had a run-in with the Marshal when Virge broke up an argument between him and Holliday. Buffaloed Ike up side the head out there in the street once today, the Marshal did, and took Ike's gun away from him. Ike got hisself a goodly lump from Virge takin' a pistol to his noggin. I heard tell, the Marshal locked up one of the McLaury boys' guns along with Ike's. There's a bunch been sidin' with the Clantons agin' the Earps and I promise, they ain't up to no good congregatin' over yonder. 'Course, Ike ain't partic-ular' big on nerve when he's alone. Good at shootin' off his mouth to cause trouble, then leavin' the fightin' to somebody else. I'm figurin' they'll be headin' the same way over to the Corral any minute." The man paused to scratch his beard and pull the strap of his bib overall straight on his shoulder. He shook his head in bewilderment. "Ain't never seen old Virge so fired up. He's plumb mad. You can tell by the way he's bein' so damn quiet and squintin' them blue eyes of his. I could see it clear over here. He's mad alright. If'n you ask me, we'll have some buryin' to do this time tomorrow. More'n one, I reckon. I'd lay money on it." She looked at the men, nearly a block away already, then back to the man she was talking to. "Maybe they're goin' to talk to Mr. Clanton." He spit on the ground before philosophizing on the situation further. "Well, if I's to be just talkin' to settle somethin' peace-ful-like, I believe I'd smile — act a touch friendlier. Wouldn't be tying down no Colt revolver to my leg and handin' out buckshooters to crazy damn fools like Doc Holliday. Didn't see no smiles on them faces over yonder, did ya? Na, they ain't a goin' to jawbone with Ike Clanton and his bunch. They're goin' on to shoot themselves some sidewinders."

She looked back up Fourth Street. So, it was finally happening. They all said it was bound to be this way, sooner or later. The ongoing power strug-gle between the Earps and Clantons and McLaurys was well-publicized, but she never thought it would come to a real showdown. Virgil tried to reason with them time and time again, but they weren't reasonable men. Wyatt tried too. Peaceful negotiation was out of the question and they were through trying. One thing she'd learned about Virge. He had a lot of patience and he'd try more than most men would to settle things peacefully, but when he'd had enough of talking and knew he wasn't getting anywhere, he moved pretty quick to do whatever had to be done. That's what he was doing now.

Across Allen Street was the O.K. Corral. The old prospector said he thought they were headed for the Corral. They were walking up Fourth towards Fremont, to the back gate. She watched the way they walked, looking straight ahead, each stride full of purpose and determination. Doc was carrying the shotgun in plain view. They weren't sneaking around for some surprise attack. They were right out in the open and they knew what was going to happen. They had no intention of trying to disarm anybody. Virgil would say it once and when Ike and his boys refused to turn over their guns, there'd be no more talk and only one way to settle things. Off to her left, several men walked out of Dexter's Livery Stable and crossed Allen Street. When they entered the O.K. Corral, panic hit again. It was Tom and Frank McLaury with Billy and Ike Clanton and four other men. Ike was shaking his fist and waving his hands in the air and talking loud. There was big trouble in the works. Virgil and his brothers and Doc were outnumbered two to one. The Earps and Doc Holliday were still walking, going for the other side of the Corral, and no sign of the sheriff anywhere in sight. As they approached the corner, Virgil switched the cane to his right hand, an indication that he didn't plan on drawing his gun right away. He was going to try and talk to them one more time. The cane was in his gun hand. She hiked up her skirt and ran after them. Somebody had to stop the insanity.

At Fremont, she ran around the corner with no thought to the danger or what might be waiting. She saw Ike trying to talk to Virgil. Virgil yelled something at Ike and pushed him away. Ike ran. The sound was deafening and she jumped back against the building with her hands over her ears. Two shotgun blasts roared through the air, followed by an agonizing scream of pain. It went on for half a minute, non-stop gunfire and several more painful cries as the bullets found their mark. The air was filled with the acrid smell of burned powder. Then, they were out in the street. She saw him fall. He was lying in the dirt, blood seeping through his pants at one knee. At the same time, another man stumbled up the street and around the corner, bent over with both arms holding his stomach. His clothes were bloody and he was crying. He was young, just a kid as far as she could make out. Somebody yelled, "Tom don't have a gun. He didn't fire a shot, but he's sure enough dead over here. Been murdered in cold blood." It all happened so fast. There were a lot of shots fired in only a few seconds. People were running every which way in the confusion. She turned back to the street. "Virgil!" He was clutching his shattered leg and his face was twisted in pain. She started to run to him, but stopped when she saw the woman. Close to the building, she stayed in the shadows and watched. His wife? It must be Allie. She'd never seen Allie Earp before. Amazing. Allie had red hair. Not as red as her's, but red nevertheless. She and Allie were about the same size too. She remembered what Ruby said about Virge being partial to redheads. Allie was on her knees beside Virgil, crying and cradling his head in her arms. Doc knelt beside him, wrapping his belt around Virgil's wounded knee and cinching it tight to control the bleeding. They were trying to help him sit up, but he was in a lot of pain. Rose felt helpless. She wanted to be with him. She wanted to change places with the woman at his side. Virgil touched his wife's face and Rose felt a twinge of jealousy. She realized her fists were clenched tight, her fingernails digging into the palms of her hands. She was standing in the shadows a few feet from Virgil and when they lifted him, he saw her. Allie held his arm and the message in his eyes was clear. She stayed where she was. She wouldn't go any closer. There was no reason for his wife to see her. Gossip-mongers like Carolyn Grants had most likely filled Allie's head with all kinds of sordid stories and there was a better than good chance Allie already knew about her husband and Silver Rose. That being the case, why did she stay with him? She must love the man an awful lot to know he had a mistress, a prostitute at that, and still want to be married to him. On the other hand, maybe she didn't know. It was better that Allie didn't see her. She watched them carry Virgil away, wondering how bad he was hurt and when she'd be able to see him.

In the middle of a silent prayer for Virgil, someone touched her arm. "Abby!" Abby saw Rose running toward Fremont Street and followed her. She watched the whole thing. She saw Rose start to run to help Virgil, then, stop when the other woman showed up. She knew why Rose was there. She knew all about them anyway. Everyone knew. You couldn't be around Lizzie and not know. For that matter, you couldn't live in Tombstone and not know. She saw the way Virgil looked at Rose when they carried him away, his eyes asking her to stand back so his wife wouldn't see her. Rose was very worried about him. Abby held her hand. "Don't worry, Rose. He'll be alright. He's a hard man to bring down. Come on, I'll walk back to the house with you and we'll talk about it over some tea." Rose pretended not to understand what Abby meant. "Talk about what?" Abby looked at her sideways. "Stop it Rose. Isn't it about time you quit pretending? What are you going to do about Virgil?" There was no point denying it any longer. "You're right. Guess I need to decide what I'm doin' with Virgil, don't I?"

A close friendship was developing. The girls at the Bird Cage were her friends, but Abby was different. She was a special friend. They were both different from the others. Sensing a connection neither of them could explain, they felt like they'd known each other forever. In the weeks that followed, they spent a lot of time together. Rose had time on her hands now that Virgil hadn't been around. Since he got shot, she hadn't even seen him in town. Doc said his leg was better, but he'd probably walk with a limp for the rest of his life. She wanted to see him, but he hadn't been able to come to the house. She was worried. Doc was a friend, but she needed a woman to talk to. There were some things she just couldn't tell a man. She and Abby became each other's moral support. Neither had a family. All they had was each other. They shared their private heartaches during long talks on the front-porch swing of the little gray house. She told Abby all about John Merrick — and Virgil Earp. Abby had her own tragic story. If fate hadn't been so cruel, they'd both be living happier lives. A year ago, neither of them would have guessed where they'd be today. One thing they knew was that they had a similar rendezvous with destiny — the Bird Cage Theatre.

A month had passed since the gunfight at the O.K. Corral. She hadn't seen Virgil at all since he was shot. It was two days after Thanksgiving. She came down the stairs just in time to see him walk in. He used a cane now. The bullet had done some permanent damage and he had a hard time walking even with the cane. She watched him move slowly to the corner table where he always sat. He looked tired. The injury had taken a lot out of him and he walked like an old man. She felt like crying, but she knew he didn't want sympathy. She took a deep breath and went to the bar for two glasses, one whiskey, one brandy, and delivered them to the table. When she set the drinks down, he started to get up and she heard him groan. He'd never complain even if it hurt like the devil, so a sound like that slipping from him meant it did hurt like the devil. She laid her hand on his shoulder. "Don't get up. I already know you're a gentleman." Times past, she sat across the table. Tonight, she took the chair beside him and pulled it right up next to him. She asked how his leg was healing. He said it was better. She tried to think of something to talk about. She couldn't think of anything. He did the talking. He wanted to thank her for keeping her distance the day he was shot. He appreciated her discretion. He didn't want to hurt Allie anymore than she'd already been hurt.

He apologized for not having been able to visit her since the shooting. She understood. He didn't have to explain anything. He wanted to come to the house, but he thought he should ask first after having been away so long. She smiled at his somewhat shy request. He'd never asked to visit her before. In fact, he was in the habit of showing up at all hours before he got hurt. "It's your house. You can come to visit whenever you want to." He made a point of correcting her. "No, it's your house." Tomorrow was Sunday, her day off. "Would it be alright if I stop by tomorrow evening?" That was to be expected. After dark was about the only time he ever came to the house. She laughed at the idea he'd ask at all, and he asked twice. His expression was very serious while he waited for her answer. At first, she thought he was joking when he asked if he could come to call, and she laughed again about his asking. "I've waited a month to see you." He was staring into the amber liquid, turning the glass around and around, but never picking it up to take a drink. As she watched him, she felt strangely sad. He looked sorrowful sitting there, lost in thought, like he'd just said goodbye to his best friend. His question wasn't funny anymore. She stopped laughing. He was moody. Quiet. She touched his hand and he moved it away. His rejection sent a hot poker right through the middle of her stomach. He was acting very strange. She answered the question. "Of course you can come to the house. I'll be there." That was all he needed to hear. He got up and leaned on the back of the chair for support. The leg hurt worse than he'd admit. He hadn't touched his drink. He'd only come by to ask if he could see her tomorrow and now that he had his answer, he was leaving. She started to walk with him to the door and he put up his hand to stop her. He didn't even say good-bye. She choked back the tears as he limped away. He was a strong man who normally walked with such resolve. One thing she always noticed about him was the way he walked, like he knew exactly where he was going. It was his attitude, the way he carried himself, that set him apart from the rest. He knew who he was and most people didn't test him. Tonight, he walked slowly, guardedly, with a cane no less. She sensed evil in the air from the beginning, the first day she came here. This town destroyed people. It was a terrifying thought, but true. Tombstone was destroying Virgil and this injury was not the end of tragedy for him. She didn't know why she thought that, but the feeling was an ominous prediction of things to come. She saw him in shadow, a black cloud overhead blocking out the sun, soon to rain down a storm of monstrous calamity on Virgil Earp.

As soon as the last traces of pink and gold sunset were transformed into night, he knocked on her door. When she opened it, he pulled the bouquet from behind his back and handed it to her. "I'm looking for the famous Rose Callahan." She laughed and took the bouquet. She noticed how careful he was about putting pressure on his knee. He couldn't walk very fast these days. She watched him. She felt so bad about his leg. The cane made him look older. Maybe it wasn't the limp or the cane at all. Maybe it was the way he lived, or maybe it was Tombstone. She swore the town did this to people. Since she saw him at the Bird Cage last night, she sensed he was different than he was before he got hurt. Sad. He didn't talk much. He didn't kiss her, not even on the cheek. He just held her hand for a long time. Around midnight, he said he had to go. She had the strangest feeling she was about to see the end of an era; if not an era, at least a chapter in their lives. It was a sense of loneliness creeping in around her like the mist settling around the bogs; that old feeling of being in mourning.

She walked with him to the door, reminding him to come by any time he had a mind to. In case he'd forgotten, it was his house. He repeated the words he'd said the night before. "No, it's your house." She started to dispute what he said and he held up his hand for her to stop. "This isn't an argument." As if having suddenly remembered something, he reached inside his coat and pulled out an envelope. He handed it to her and said it again. "It's your house, Rose." She took the envelope and turned it over in her hands. He waited patiently while she decided what to do with it. Finally, she opened it and removed the paper. It was some kind of legal document. A deed — the deed to the little gray house. She folded it up and put it back in the envelope, shaking her head. She held it out to him. There was no way she could take it. He'd already been far too generous. He pushed her hand away. "You have to take it." She looked at the envelope. "Why?" He didn't answer. She knew why. The magnitude of what he was doing overwhelmed her and she couldn't speak. He'd already done so much and now, this. There were no words to express how she felt. After having been so gloomy, he was smiling. "I own other property. I don't have any need for this place. You do. It's important for you to own a house — this house. Do you understand?" She understood owning land brought with it respect. Tears were so close all she could manage was a whisper. "Thank you, Virgil. I don't..." He touched one finger to her lips. She didn't have to say anything. He knew how she felt.

She never asked when she'd be seeing him again and he never committed to a time when he'd be back. She knew the day would come when he wouldn't be back at all. She just didn't want to hear him say it yet. It was what she'd been afraid he was up to ever since she saw him last night, but at least he wasn't saying it. On his way out the door, he gave her the same words of caution he always left her with. "Keep your derringer under the pillow and the doors locked." He didn't kiss her good-bye this time. He left without another word, waiting outside the door until she locked it.

More than a week went by before she saw him again. When he came to her door, she had the same uneasy feeling as the time before, like a hundred butterflies were trapped inside her stomach, all fluttering at once. She invited him in and asked if he wanted tea. He said yes, then went to sit on the sofa. He seemed preoccupied, a long way off in thought. She asked if something was bothering him. He said his knee hurt a little. That was all. She knew it was more than just the leg. She asked him again. "Is there somethin' the matter, Virge? Somethin' I can do to help?" He started to answer, but didn't finish. She asked a third time. "Why are you upset? What's disturbin' you?" By the way his jaw flexed, she could tell her persistence was irritating him and he was trying not to lose patience with her. She always did that. They'd talked about it, but it was part of her character, a habit she hadn't been able to change and probably never would. Not much discouraged her when she was determined to get an answer. He understood her story and thought it remarkable so many heartaches hadn't daunted her tenacity. To the contrary, the kind of things she'd been through that would have changed most women and made them commit suicide had the opposite affect on her. They made her stronger.

Most people couldn't read him, but she'd come to know him pretty well and always knew when he had something on his mind. He finally told her someone took a shot at him a few nights earlier. That was why he'd stayed away from her house. He was concerned he might be followed and he didn't want to involve her in his business. She couldn't believe what he said. "Business? Someone shot at you? ...tried to kill you? ...and you call that business?" She thought things settled down after the gunfight. Apparently not. He and his brothers and Doc had been acquitted of murder charges filed against them after the killings of Tom and Frank McLaury and Billy Clanton, but it was foolish to believe that was the end of it. Ike Clanton had declared a vendetta against the Earps to even the score, and he wouldn't let it rest until either they were dead or he was. How could she not realize his life was still in danger? The Earps were constant targets and there'd always be somebody wanting to take them out. That would never change.

He was exceptionally quiet, as he was the last time she saw him a week ago. He was deep in thought when she returned to the parlour with tea. When she set the tray on the low table in front of him, he was staring off into space, unaware of her presence. She touched his shoulder. He jumped. That wasn't like Virgil. Now, she was really worried. Things must be much worse than she imagined. She sat down beside him and held his hand. "Listen to me good, Virge. I don't want you to stay away. Comin' here is the only relief you have from this damn town. I'm not afraid of anyone, not Ike Clanton or his brother and their passel of threats put together — none of it, and I'm tellin' you right now, you're to come here whenever you've a mind to." He watched her talk and heard the fire in her voice. "I won't be lettin' a band of bloody hoodlums tell me who comes to my house. Their shenanigans don't scare me a bit." She made her point. She wasn't afraid of anything. He'd seen proof of that plenty of times.

She and Abby planned to spend Christmas Eve together, starting the dinner fixings. The rest of them had to work. She'd have a houseful on Christmas Day for dinner. They'd be in and out all day long being that they worked different hours, and they'd be elbow-to-elbow in the little gray house, but they'd all been invited. No one who worked at the Bird Cage would be alone on Christmas. Those who had disagreements with each other had to make their peace in her house that day. She and Abby would cook the dinner. Ruby volunteered to bring the pies. That would be interesting. She never pictured Ruby up to her elbows in pumpkins and pie dough, but Ruby claimed she baked the best pumpkin pie in the world. Virgil would be with his family. She didn't want to think about it. Something else at this time of the year was painful too. Memories of John.

If he'd gone home for the wedding at the end of the summer, chances were the Army wouldn't give him leave so soon after to spend Christmas in New Orleans. He'd probably be spending the holiday in Washington with strangers. She wondered if he missed her or hated her after all these months. Running off the way she did, she couldn't blame him if he hated her. And what about Rebecca? She might never understand any of it, forever believing Rose deserted her. Life dealt a cruel hand, but there was no use agonizing over something that couldn't be changed. The past and everyone who was part of it was better forgotten. If only that were possible. Although she gave up thinking about family gatherings a long time ago, the people she loved would never be forgotten. It was as Ann Merrick said. "Home is the one place you never forget." The girls at the Bird Cage were her family now and Tombstone was home.

Thinking it was Abby arriving early with her hands full, she hurried to answer the door. It wasn't Abby. He held out a small white box tied with a red ribbon. She could tell he'd made the bow himself. "Merry Christmas, Rose." She took the box. "Merry Christmas, Virge." She never expected a Christmas present from him. In fact, she didn't expect to see him at all tonight or tomorrow. She should have known he'd have something for her. They sat on the sofa and she untied the bow, slowly lifting the lid and enjoying the suspense of the moment. It was a ring, a gold ring with a delicately-carved rose, its stem wrapped around the circle of gold. Set in one leaf was a tiny green stone — an emerald. She stared at the box, hardly believing what it contained. He took the ring out and slipped it on her finger. When he did, he noticed the bracelet around her wrist was silver. All her jewelry was silver, except her mother's gold locket. "I'm sorry. I've made a mistake. Your silver jewelry... That's why they call you the Silver Rose. I should've remembered. I should have had the ring made out of silver." She held her hand to the light, moving it from side-to-side so the emerald sparkled. "No, you shouldn't have. Gold is for special things. It's beautiful. I'll never take it off. I'll wear the rose ring forever." He stood up. He had to go. It was Christmas Eve and the family was waiting. He only came to bring her the gift. She tried not to let her disappointment show, but she never liked to see him leave. He couldn't stay, of course, and she could never ask him to, especially not this night. His smile was unusually sad and he looked at her for a long time before opening the door. He was trying to say something. She thought he was going to change his mind and stay. Before he left, he kissed her and held her tight. When he let go, she saw a tear in his eye. Whatever he was having so much trouble saying never came out. There was a feeling of sinking, losing her footing. At the last minute, she started to ask him to stay a little longer, but he spoke before she got the words out. "Good-bye, Rose." It took her breath away like a punch in the stomach. He never said it before. Every other time when he left, he told her to keep her derringer under the pillow and the door locked. He didn't say it tonight. This time, he said the two words that cut deep and she knew he really meant good-bye.

It was the last time she saw him. Four days later, Virgil Earp was shot crossing Allen Street in front of his office. One bullet went through his body. The other one nearly ripped his left arm off and did some severe, permanent damage. Surgery the next day resulted in the removal of his elbow joint and several inches of bone loss. He was crippled for life.

Having justified doubts about the enthusiasm of Johnny Behan to pursue the suspected shooters, Virgil swore Wyatt in as U.S. Deputy Marshal to do the job. It was no secret Sheriff Behan sided with the cowboy faction, and even after Ike Clanton's hat was found near the scene, Virgil knew Johnny would never hunt Ike down anymore than he'd go after the other four suspects he'd been keeping company with lately.

When Doc came to give her the news about Virgil's injury, he said it was very bad. Recovery was going to be slow and Virgil would never be the same. He was lucky they didn't have to take his arm off, but he'd probably lose the use of it. She swallowed hard. It was terrible news. With that in mind, she figured it might be a while until she saw him. She could be patient. She just wanted him to get better and... Doc interrupted her. "It's more than that, Rose Marie. He doesn't want you to see him the way he is. He's changed." She was frustrated. "I can overlook his infirmity, whatever it might be. It doesn't change how I feel about him. Will you tell him that for me?" Doc sighed. Getting the real message across to her was going to be very difficult. "Yes. I'll tell him."

She passed the message to Virgil through Doc, wishing she could make him understand it didn't matter. She could overlook anything that might be wrong with him. Problem was, Virgil couldn't get past it. He didn't want her to see him crippled. His return message was, if she needed anything, all she had to do was let Doc or Wyatt know. He'd always help her. He cared for her, but he could never let her see him the way he was. She sent him another message. They were friends. Friends didn't turn their backs on friends in times of crisis. She cared about him and she didn't want him to stay away. Again, he answered by letter, saying they'd always be friends, and more. She had to remember that, but his condition prevented him from visiting her. He couldn't come back. She had to try to understand. He told her he'd think of her often and he'd be there to help with whatever she needed. His letters frustrated her. She tried to talk to Doc. Couldn't he convince Virgil to see her? If she had a chance to talk to him face-to-face, she could make him understand it didn't matter to her if he had no arms at all. Doc listened patiently. When she stopped talking, he pulled a chair around to face him and told her to sit. Reluctantly, and still pouting, she sat down. He held her hands and spoke in such a low voice she had to be quiet to hear him, tears of utter frustration running down her cheeks. He told her she had to try to understand Virgil's position. He was not the same anymore. She didn't care. She pulled away and jumped to her feet, waving her arms and crying while she stomped around the room expressing her anger at the unfairness of it all. She hadn't let her temper get out of control since the night Virgil tried to talk to her in the Bird Cage about the two men who were killed there. Doc was quiet while she threw the tantrum. He knew her story. He knew about John and the reason she left New Orleans. He knew how difficult life in Tombstone had been until Virgil came along and took care of her. She was different from the other women at the Bird Cage; a fish out of water, trying desperately to fit into a new kind of life and knowing all the while she didn't belong. He knew all about her relationship with Virgil. He'd made life a little more bearable for her and now he was gone. It wasn't hard to understand why she was upset.

Doc never believed Rose and Virgil loved each other, not the way Rose loved John or the way Virgil loved his wife, but he knew they needed each other. He was right about that. Virgil had Allie and his family. Rose had nobody and it was hard for her to face knowing she'd seen the last of Virgil. The Earps were considered better-class folk than ladies of the night and gamblers who spent their time in brothels and gambling halls. They were gamblers too, but their business ventures and the fact they were lawmen with money made the distinction between them and gamblers like Doc Holliday. They got away with throwing their weight around because they had money, and money meant power. They also had the power of the law behind them. Rose and Doc were part of the other class, and Virgil lived somewhere in between the two worlds. A family man by day and full-time peace officer, he was a frequenter of saloons and gambling halls and the home of a prostitute by night.

Allie Earp was a good woman and she put up with a lot from Virgil and his brothers. It was no secret Virgil liked the ladies, but the stories were scattered and faded quickly as his one-night flings were left behind. No one paid much attention because it was always temporary, never more than a little time spent with a lady of easy virtue to pass part of an evening. He wasn't the only man who did it and it was nothing personal. Stories about his time with Rose Callahan were different, more permanent, and not so easily forgotten. Rose never doubted that Wyatt disapproved of his brother's relationship with her, but she figured he didn't say much until he realized it was taking the form of a long-term arrangement. Given the stories she'd heard about his influence in the family, she wouldn't be surprised if he'd finally come right out and insisted Virgil end the affair. Allie was Virgil's wife and even though she and Wyatt had their share of disagreements, when it came to family, the Earps stuck together. She was sure that was a big part of the pressure on Virgil to stay away. His recent injury was not the real reason he wasn't coming back. It was a convenient excuse.

Rose still had Doc and Abby and Lizzie and her other friends, but there was something missing. She never meant for Virgil to replace John, but he had become an important part of her life that was hard to let go. He'd helped her survive the day-to-day heartbreaks that never left her. The link in the chain that was her life was still missing — John Merrick. No one would ever fill the empty place in her heart where John belonged, but Virge kept her from being lonely. He made her feel needed and he made her smile. He put his arms around her when she was feeling bad, and he made her feel safe. He understood who she was and why she was here. Things just wouldn't be the same if he didn't come back. Doc watched her drift off deep in thought. When she looked over at him, more tears streamed down her face. Why did things always turn out wrong? Why had all this happened? Why had she gotten involved with Virgil? Doc knew she didn't really want him to answer. He held her hands. "Remember what I told you, Rose Marie. I will defend your honor to the death, if need be, but I cannot mend your broken heart." She remembered. She remembered what they all said. They told her not to have anything to do with Virgil. His injury wasn't the reason he stayed away. Why didn't he tell the truth? Why didn't he just say he didn't want to see her anymore? Doc tried to console her. That wasn't it. Virgil did want to see her, but the situation had become too complicated for him. Family pressure made it impossible for him to continue seeing her. He would have been gone sooner or later anyway. She always knew that. She used to tell herself she was prepared for the day when he'd leave. She just never expected it to come so soon. They hadn't even said good-bye. She thought back to Christmas Eve. He said good-bye. She recognized his message then, but didn't take it at face value. Even if he hadn't been shot, he would have left. He was saying good-bye on Christmas Eve as best he could. It hadn't been easy for him either. Painful understanding of the truth was written all over her face. Nothing Doc could say would make her feel better; not holding her hand, not words. Nothing. He wished something would come to him, words of comfort. Reminding her about his warning to stay away from the man with the silver star would only make things worse. There was nothing to gain by bringing it up. It was too late. Her heart was already broken. He kissed her hand. "I'm sorry."

Chapter 9

*"A faithful friend is a strong defense, and he
that hath found such a one hath found a treasure."*

Maude Adams

She stood in front of the music box for a long time, playing the song over and over. The melody was mournful, and it got sadder every time she heard it. She thought about John and wondered how she ever managed to leave him behind. None of it made sense now that she'd had time to think. She underestimated his capacity for understanding. The rapes hadn't been her fault. He'd have known that. She threw away her future with him because she felt guilty about something not of her doing. It was wrong. She made a terrible mistake in leaving and it was too late to set things right. Loneliness and despair never left her these days. If only she could turn back the hands of Time and ask for a second chance. Time! Time had become her bitter enemy.

She hadn't been able to eat or sleep for days. Lizzie nagged her to eat more. She was developing a cough. Abby told her to stay home and get some rest. Ruby insisted she was too skinny and had to pull herself together. She'd been warned about Virgil. No man was worth making herself sick over. Their hearts were in the right place and they were trying to help, but they didn't understand what it was like to be left alone. She felt like crying all the time. The weather turned cold and it rained several days in a row. She walked back and forth to work in the rain, oblivious to the wet. When she didn't show up for work, Abby got worried. It wasn't like Rose not to be there every night. The next morning, she went to Rose's house. When her knock went unanswered, she turned the knob and pushed. The door swung open. Rose never left her door unlocked. Virgil had drummed it into her to keep the door locked. Abby called out, "Rose, are you home?" No answer. The house was unusually cold and damp. There was no fire in the fireplace nor any sign of one having been there in a long time. Rose hadn't even boiled water for tea. The stove was cold. In the bedroom, she was horrified at what she found. She ran to the bed and laid her hand on Rose's forehead. Rose was burning up with fever, too weak to speak and having trouble breathing. Abby could hear the rattle in her chest with every draw of air through the congested lungs. She shivered from the damp chill and covered Rose with an extra blanket, pulling it up around her neck and tucking it in under the mattress. Rose needed the doctor, but before anything else, the house had to be warmed. Abby placed a scoop of wood shavings in the fireplace and lit the pile. When they took fire, she arranged the logs on top and fanned them to bring up the flames. As soon as she was sure the fire was burning strong, she ran all the way to the doctor's house, praying he hadn't been called out to the mines. She pounded frantically on his door and when he answered it, she broke down in tears. All she had to say was that Rose couldn't breathe and he was out the door with his bag, pulling on his coat as he ran.

Abby sat quietly while the doctor held a stethoscope to Rose's chest and listened to the rumbling in her lungs. He lifted her eyelids and asked Abby to bring the lamp closer. When he finished the examination, she watched the muscles in his jaw tensing as he placed the stethoscope in his bag. He didn't say much, only that it was very bad. Abby was worried. "How bad?" He took a deep breath. If Abby was going to be the nurse, she'd have to be told what to do and she ought to know the truth. Rose's lungs were full of fluid and he was surprised any air was making its way through the congested passages. In fact, it was a wonder she hadn't suffocated already. While he talked, he moved Rose to an upright position and told Abby to pile the pillows behind her. Breathing would be a little easier if she wasn't lying flat down. Abby knew Rose was sick, but the doctor said her condition was grave, one of the worse cases of pneumonia he'd seen in a long time. His face was grim as he wrote down the prescribed medicine on paper for the pharmacist to mix. He said to make sure Rose stayed warm and drank plenty of liquids. Some broth or soup would be good, and as much water as she could take. He took an amber bottle from his bag and told Abby to pour a spoonful of the medicine. Then, he held Rose's head back while Abby fed it to her. Rose sputtered and tried to spit the thick syrup out, but he made her swallow, rubbing his fingers gently on her throat. One more spoonful. Once the medicine was down, she went straight back to sleep and they arranged the pillows to keep her propped up. The doctor closed his bag. He'd done all he could.

In the parlour, he talked while Abby helped him on with his coat. "I think you should prepare for the worst. Rose is very sick. I'm not sure that she can get over pneumonia this bad." He paused to button his coat. "There are some other things that disturb me, the way she's lost so much weight for one, and the spot of blood on the pillow. Do you know if she coughed that up today?" Abby shook her head. She didn't know. She didn't remember hearing Rose cough since she found her. The doctor continued. "If she gets over this, I want to see her for a complete examination. Apart from the pneumonia, she has all the symptoms of tuberculosis. It wouldn't surprise me to find out she's got it, what with all the time she spends with that good-for-nothing, Holliday, and him hacking the way he does. I hear he sits with her for hours over at the Bird Cage and I guess he visits her here at the house sometimes. You'd be wise to cover your own face if she starts to coughing. The disease is highly contagious, carried on the air when they cough, you know. Some still call it white plague because once it gets started, it can spread like wildfire and infect a whole town. Closed in with her, it wouldn't take much for you to get it by breathing the same air. Fresh air lessens the risk of contracting it. Open the windows and doors and air the place out every day when the weather is cool the same as when it's warm. You've got to look out for yourself. A little fresh air will be good for her too. Keep her warm and away from drafts. If she is suffering from tuberculosis, a cold draft will only serve to complicate the pneumonia. The sad thing is, if she lives through the pneumonia, the consumption will kill her eventually. How long she's got is anybody's guess. It depends on how far along the disease is and how she takes care of herself. If she makes it through this, another round of it will do her in." His words and the tone of his voice frightened Abby. "She'll get well, won't she?" He took a deep breath and touched Abby's arm. He knew she wanted him to say everything was going to be alright, but he couldn't lie. "Don't get your hopes up. If you want the truth, it'll be a miracle if she lives. Even if she does get better, if she's got tuberculosis, her days are numbered. It's a killer. Once they get it, they don't live long. It eats up a body. That's why they call it consumption and it's why Doc Holliday looks so sickly and thin." Abby could hardly believe what he was saying. Rose might die! He patted Abby's shoulder. "Keep her warm and try to get her to drink warm liquids. Make her some soup. She won't feel like eating for awhile, but she might take some broth. She'll need sustenance if she's to get her strength back. Soup's the best thing. Give her the rest of the medicine in this bottle. It won't be easy getting it down her, but you have to make her swallow it if there's to be any chance at all. Two spoonfuls four times every day. You'll need to get over to the pharmacy for more of it, but what's in here will last until morning. I'll look in on her tomorrow. In the meantime, if she gets worse, come and get me."

When the doctor left, Abby covered Rose with another blanket. He said to keep her warm. She sat on the edge of the bed watching Rose sleep and listening to the labored breathing. It was the worse sound she'd ever heard, a death rattle. How could this be happening? She should have paid closer attention to the warning signs. Rose had been getting noticeably weaker lately and coughing a lot. They'd all talked about how thin and pale she looked, but nobody did anything. Why hadn't she done something to help sooner? At least there was medicine to give her now that the doctor had come and she knew what to do. She had to make sure Rose didn't die. She pulled the blankets up to Rose's chin and went to the parlour. The fire was warming the house and the chill was gone. She stirred the glowing pieces of the first wood and put another log on. The house had to be warm and that meant keeping the fire going. What else did the doctor say? "Keep her drinking liquids. Anything — water, soup, as much as you can get down her." That's what he said. She checked the kitchen. The cupboards were empty. From the looks of things, Rose hadn't been eating much. She went back to the bedroom. Rose was still asleep. After making sure the stove fire was started, she put on her coat and headed for the market, running most of the way. When she came back, she was lugging two sacks of food. She'd never been much of a cook, but she was determined to feed Rose. It was only a matter of time until Jenny and Lizette came around and they were both good cooks. As soon as they found out about Rose, they'd help make sure she got fed. She stared at the chicken she bought. Her mother used to say chicken soup was the best thing when you were sick, but her mother wasn't here to teach her how to make it. How hard could it be? Probably not hard at all for someone who knew how to cook. She wished Jenny and Lizzie would come by soon. Jenny's chicken soup was the best she'd ever tasted. Without the slightest idea why, she washed the bird and dried it. She took a deep breath and turned her eyes upward. God would have to give her the recipe for the chicken soup. She picked up the chicken and tears rolled down her face.

She didn't know where to begin. Crying wouldn't get the soup made though. She wiped the tears away and dropped the bird into a pot of water on the stove. It was a start. She'd figure the rest out as she went along; she ...and God.

Abby hated to wake Rose up to give her the bad-smelling medicine, but it couldn't be helped. She imagined the stuff tasted every bit as awful as it smelled. Still, she had to follow the doctor's instructions and make Rose take it. Rose fought her all the way and the first spoonful went all over her nightgown. The second one hit Abby in the face when Rose batted the spoon away. On the third try, she managed to get the spoon in Rose's mouth and the foul-tasting syrup went down. While she was still making a face at the unpleasant taste, Abby snuck in another spoonful and it went down too. Finally, the effort exhausted Rose and she collapsed back onto the pillows. Abby plugged the bottle and sat on the edge of the bed to clean up the sticky mess. She rubbed at the stain on the front of Rose's nightgown with a wet cloth and spoke softly. "Now, see what you've done, Miss Rose? You've got it all over both of us." Rose looked up at Abby, her eyelids heavy. She was still burning up. It was the fever. It had to be brought down.

Abby set a bowl of cool water on the bedside table and began alternately dipping a cloth into the water and laying it across Rose's forehead as she slept. She kept it up for hours, changing the water often because the heat from Rose's face warmed the cloth and dipping it took the coolness out of the water.

Throughout the afternoon, she stirred the soup which, with the help of a little salt and an onion and a few other things she'd thrown in, really smelled like soup. When she sampled a spoonful, she was amazed how good it tasted; every bit as good as her mother's and Jenny's. All day, she'd been afraid to leave Rose for more than a few minutes and once, when she returned to the bedroom, she thought Rose stopped breathing. She panicked and made Rose sit up, shaking her and yelling at her to keep breathing. Rose didn't open her eyes as she gasped wildly for a breath, but after several terrifying moments, she finally coughed. The coughing helped and she began to breathe better. Then, she was asleep again. Abby rearranged the pillows and blankets and returned to the rocker to resume the vigil, only leaving for a few minutes now and then to stir the soup. Tomorrow, she'd feed Rose a little of the broth. By morning, she had to be better.

The rain continued all through the night. Large drops pelted the house like millions of tiny stones falling from the sky. Abby sat in the rocking chair beside Rose's bed, afraid to sleep in case Rose needed her. She picked up Ann Merrick's Bible from the little table and began reading. The passages made her cry. That night, she prayed harder than she ever prayed before. Thunder rocked the little gray house and lightning lit up the room from outside. She kept the fire going and the blankets tucked in. Every hour, she woke Rose up and made her drink as much water as she could swallow and at the prescribed times, she got two spoonfuls of the bitter medicine down her. When Rose gagged on the medicine, poor Abby felt like she was torturing her dearest friend, but she was determined to have that miracle the doctor said it would take to keep her alive. She did what he told her to do and she sat up all night, working on a miracle.

Rose opened her eyes. The curtain was pulled aside and the morning light, though darkened by storm clouds, hurt and she pulled the blanket over her face. Rain was still falling in torrents. She'd been lying flat down and it started the coughing. Abby heard her from the kitchen and rushed into the room. She made Rose sit up until the spell passed. Rose tried to fall back onto the pillows and Abby struggled to keep her upright. "You have to sit up, Rose. You have to breathe. You've got to get well. I made you some good soup and I want you to drink a little of the broth." Rose closed her eyes. She was very weak, but the fact she talked at all was a good sign. "Leave me alone, Abby. Let me die." Abby was furious. "I didn't sit up all night to let you die." She cleared off the little table and moved it closer to the bed. She left the room and Rose heard pots banging in the kitchen. When Abby came back, she had a towel and a pan filled with steaming-hot water. She set the pan on the bedside table. A strong, oily aroma filled the air. Rose's eyes were open and she was wrinkling up her nose at the smell coming from the pan. Abby watched her. If she could smell the oil, it might mean she was breathing better. Maybe the medicine was working. As soon as the doctor came by, she'd go get the bottle refilled at the pharmacy. When she lifted Rose up from the pillows, she was like a limp rag doll, and fell back flat as soon as Abby let go of her. Abby was tired and lack of sleep was wearing her patience thin. She moved Rose's legs over the edge of the bed. Rose kept trying to lay down, but Abby held her tight. "Stop being so mulish. You can lay down in a minute, but first, you have to do as I say." Rose started to cry and the crying provoked a coughing spell. When it was over, Abby covered Rose's head with the towel and told her to lean over the pan and breathe the vapors. Rose gagged on the smell and turned her head away. "God, Abby! What is this stuff? It smells rancid. I can't breathe. Are you tryin' to kill me?" The determination in Abby's voice was fierce and she pushed Rose's face toward the pan of water. "It's not rancid and I'm not trying to kill you. It's creosote. It'll open up your lungs. Now, breathe." Rose turned her face away from the steam and her foot kicked the little table, nearly dumping the pan of hot water over. "Why don't you leave me alone? You don't understand. I want to die." Abby steadied the table and pushed Rose's face down close to the water, irritated at Rose's obstinance. "Damn it, Rose! Breathe! You are not going to die." Abby sat on the bed next to her, waiting for her to inhale the vapors. There was no getting out of it. She didn't have the strength to fight Abby's resolve. With the towel over her head to trap the steam, she leaned over the pan and took as deep a breath as her congested lungs would allow. The intake of air brought on another fit of coughing. Abby held onto her until it passed. Her eyes were red and watery and it was clear she was suffering. Abby's voice softened. "One more time. Breathe!" Rose was too weak to argue. She inhaled twice more. Tears streamed down her face as she took the steam in. Breathing at all was painful, but taking deep breaths the way Abby wanted her to do was much worse.

When she was sure Rose had taken in as much of the creosote vapors as she could stand, Abby moved the table away. "That's enough, for now." She gently patted the perspiration from Rose's face with the towel. Sweating was another good sign. It meant the fever was breaking and that encouraged Abby to press forward with the doctoring. "Open up!" Rose looked like she was in a drunken stupor, trying to focus her watery eyes on what was coming next. The spoonful of medicine was poised in front of her mouth. It smelled worse than the creosote and she wrinkled her nose. No use putting up any more fuss. Abby would get it down her, one way or another. She opened her mouth and Abby dumped the thick syrup straight in. It was bitter, but she swallowed it, making a terrible face at the bad taste and sticking out her tongue. "It tastes like poison. I think you're tryin' to kill me." She looked sideways at Abby. Abby smiled. At least Rose was talking and the fact that she was being a little cantankerous was an even better sign. She fluffed the pillows and laid her hand on Rose's forehead. She was cooler. The fever was down. "Tell me, how would you know what poison tastes like?" She adjusted the blankets, tucking them across Rose's chest and bringing her arms out. With the fever broken, she wouldn't keep her so tightly covered. She supported Rose's head with one hand and held a cup of water to her lips with the other. "Take a sip." Rose closed her mouth tight and rolled her eyes suspiciously at Abby. Abby laughed. "It's only water. It'll kill the taste of the medicine and help keep the fever down. The doctor says you've got to drink lots of liquids." Rose rolled her eyes up at Abby again and sipped the water. "Mmm, I never thought water could taste so good." Abby was smiling. "Good girl. Now, you get some soup." Rose was suspicious. "Soup?" She wasn't so sure Abby's soup would exactly be a reward for taking the medicine. She took a deep breath and there was no coughing. A sharp pain cut through her chest when she breathed in, but went away when she exhaled. She could feel a change in her breathing. It hurt, but it was tolerable. She was weak, but didn't feel as sick as when she took to her bed a couple of days ago. Maybe the creosote and medicine were working, or maybe it was Abby's stubborn perseverance to save her. And she thought only Irishmen were so hardheaded.

She watched Abby straighten the table. "I never knew you could be so mean, Abigail." Abby threw the towel over her shoulder and picked up the pan of water. "Well, now you know, and you'd better get used to it because I'll be bringing in the creosote again in a little while. You have to take in the vapors every couple of hours, and when the doctor comes by, I'll be going for more medicine." Rose made a bitter face at the mention of the medicine. Abby smiled at the response. "I'll bring you some soup." She disappeared around the corner and Rose laid back against the pillows. She had a delayed reaction to the last thing Abby said. "Soup?" Abby was surely trying to kill her? First, creosote, and now, Abby's soup? Abby couldn't cook a bean without burning it.

Abby sat on the edge of the bed tucking a towel under Rose's chin and giving an order. "Open up." Rose kept her eyes closed. Abby wasn't fooled. "I know you're awake, Rose. Open your mouth and drink this." Rose opened one eye. Another spoon was poised in front of her mouth. No use putting up a fuss. If she didn't drink whatever was in the spoon voluntarily, Abby would get it down her. She opened her mouth and Abby poured the warm liquid in. She swallowed, pleasantly surprised at the truly excellent flavor. Both eyes were open. "Good soup." She opened her mouth again, like a baby bird waiting for the next bit of food to be dropped in. Abby obliged and fed her another spoonful. She only got a few down before she had to sleep again, but even a few swallows was an accomplishment at this stage. It wasn't much, but it was good enough for Abby. She set the bowl on the little table and wiped a dribble of soup from Rose's chin. The doctor said, "Get whatever liquid you can down her. Some soup would be good." He said it would take a miracle to keep Rose alive and she'd worked all night for that miracle. She pulled the blanket up and felt Rose's cheek. It was cool. The fever was gone. Abby kissed her on the forehead. "You are not going to die, Rose Callahan."

Chapter 10

"She's only a bird in a gilded cage,
a beautiful sight to see.
You may think she's happy and free from care;
She's not, though she seems to be.
'Tis sad when you think of her wasted life,
for youth cannot mate with age.
...And her beauty was sold, for an old man's gold;
She's a bird in a gilded cage."

A Bird In A Gilded Cage
Arthur J. Lamb and Harry Von Tilzer

Tombstone was growing. With a seemingly inexhaustible mother lode of high-grade silver ore, the mines ran twenty-four hours a day, every day. As work shifts changed, a constant stream of miners went back and forth between town and the hills. To accommodate the demand for entertainment, the drinking and gambling establishments — not to forget the brothels, kept up the pace, and the Bird Cage Theatre was the most audacious of them all. It's popularity escalated and it soon gained a reputation as being an intrepidly-daring and wild night spot. The place never closed. You could get into a game of chance at any hour of the day or night, and when you were tired of cards and whiskey, or needed a softer diversion, there were always the ladies. You took your chances in more ways than one every time you went there. If the man across the table accused you of cheating, or if he just plain didn't like your looks, you might be looking down the cold-steel business end of a Colt .45, or worse. Bloodstains on the floor were testimony to flaring tempers whose short fuses had been lit more than once over a card game or a woman. Everything was a matter of luck. If you were unlucky at cards, you could be just as unlucky upstairs in a suspended crib if the soiled dove whose company you chose spent time there with a customer who left her with whatever he'd been scratching. You might end up with the same unpleasant itch in your britches. On the other hand, you could win big downstairs in the high-stakes poker game that changed players, but never stopped, and your run of luck might extend to the room adjacent to the game where especially-talented, high-priced ladies of the night plied their trade. Chance was the name of the game at the Bird Cage — any game, and you could be a big winner or a big loser. It all depended on whether or not Lady Luck took a fancy to you.

Although the Bird Cage drew national headliners and sophisticated performers like Lotta Crabtree, Eddie Foy, and young Lillian Russell, it was a well-known fact the show was geared for the male population. Ruby's high-stepping dancers brought the house down when they shed their outer costumes and left little to the imagination. You could hear the whooping and whistling a block away when she put on a performance that drove the men wild with excitement. Women — respectable women, never went to the Bird Cage. They wouldn't be caught dead on the same side of the street. They condemned it as a den of iniquity. The devil's playground. Opinions differed, of course, depending on which side of the door you were standing on. Overall, they were right. It was a bordello with a floor show and gambling. A stone's throw from the Red Light District, it was a haven for everything from sophisticated, high-rolling gamblers to tinhorns, drifters, miners, local businessmen, and a variety of lost souls, all looking for a grand old time. If you fell anywhere within those categories and you had a pocketful of money, you could get just about anything you wanted any time of the day or night; whiskey, gambling, entertainment, fighting, and women. The Bird Cage had it all.

Rose hadn't worked for more than a month. The doctor said it was a bloody miracle she was alive. She had Abby to thank for that. Abby never gave up on her. She'd kept her warm, fed her, made her take her medicine and breathe the creosote oil vapors until she regained her strength. The Bird Cage was a little drafty in March, but she needed to work. The money she had wouldn't last forever. Her ribs ached from all the coughing and she was weak. The pneumonia had taken her strength and left her looking like a bag of bones. She was tired all the time. At twenty-five, she looked and felt like an old woman. Ruby watched her draw a shawl up around her shoulders. Since the sickness, she was always cold and no wonder, she didn't have an ounce of fat on her. They'd all told her to stay home a little longer, but they were wasting their breath. She had a streak of Irish stubbornness a mile long and she'd set her mind to going back to the Bird Cage. Every night, she showed up for work intending to stay through her hours and every night, she went home early because she didn't have the strength to sit up for more than a couple of those hours. By the time the four-block walk home was made, she was so tired she could barely climb the two small steps and unlock the door. Many mornings, she awoke to discover she had all her clothes on and had been sleeping on top of the covers with no recollection of laying down.

It was early. The whole night was ahead and she was tired already. She couldn't seem to recover from the sickness. It had taken a lot out of her and the cough never went away. The syrup the doctor gave her helped a little, but it didn't get rid of the cough. She never mentioned the traces of blood on her handkerchief every now and then, but she had her suspicions about it even before the pneumonia. When the doctor examined her after the sickness, he told her what it was. He said the right thing to do was to avoid coughing in a person's face because the disease was carried on the air and they could get it from her if they breathed contaminated air. She kept the handkerchief ready and covered her mouth with it every time she coughed. By rights, she probably should have stopped working in a place with so many people in close proximity to one another, but she reasoned there were a lot of folks already infected with the consumption. Miners passed it among themselves by virtue of confined quarters in which they worked under the ground and the dampness down inside the mines contributed to the spreading of the killer disease. Could be, she caught it from one of them in the first place. She'd certainly been close enough to some of them. Then, there was Doc. She knew he had it from the minute she met him. They'd spent many hours together during some of his violent coughing spells. Whether it was by breathing bad air from him or a stricken miner, she'd never know how the disease came upon her, but it wasn't uncommon and plenty of people had it. No, it didn't matter whether she was there or not. Chance was, if they were bound to catch it, they'd catch it down in the mines or up top from some miner who didn't have the good sense to cover his mouth to confine the spreading of the disease when he coughed. It was all around them. For her to give up her only source of income because she was sick wouldn't make a difference one way or the other in lessening the risk to other people catching what she had.

She felt a chill and decided to get a brandy. She couldn't take a chance on catching cold so soon after the pneumonia. If she got sick again, Abby wouldn't be able to save her. Nobody would. On her way to the bar, she noticed two soldiers at a table, conspicuous in their uniforms among the civilians. They nodded when she passed their table and bid her a good evening. She smiled and said she hoped they enjoyed themselves. Waiting for her brandy, she only half paid attention to two more soldiers leaning against the bar. The taller of the two had his back to her. The bartender passed the glass of brandy across the bar. "Here you go, Rose. I warmed it a little, the way you like it." She thanked him and started to leave when the soldier closest to her turned around. When she saw his face, the glass slipped from her hand and hit the floor, the brandy splashing onto her dress and the soldier's uniform. Neither of them seemed to comprehend the accident and stood staring at each other like they'd both just seen a ghost. She couldn't believe her eyes and he was as astonished as she was. He stared at her, not convinced that what he was seeing was really there. "Rose?" The sound of his voice triggered the recall. She would have known his voice anywhere, even without seeing his face. She couldn't speak. It was the front porch of the Merrick house all over. She felt faint and reached out for something to hold onto. He saved her from falling as he did that summer day in '76. She was looking straight at him, but not believing it was really him. Either she was dreaming or the medicine was finally making her see things, except, he wasn't fading away. She whispered his name, thinking that when she did, it would break the spell and he'd disappear. "John."

He was holding tight to her waist. Unlike the day he saved her from falling backward down the stone steps of his mother's house, she wasn't embarrassed or flustered by his arms around her. She whispered his name again, staring at him as though he were a ghost materialized from some distant memory intentionally forgotten. It wasn't a dream and he was not a ghost. John Merrick was right in front of her, plain as day. The look on his face was evidence that he was as stunned as she was. In a room full of people and activity, they were alone, oblivious to the noise and their surroundings. They were in the park and the band was giving a concert. He drew her close and she rested her head against his chest. His heart was pounding. She never thought she'd hear his heartbeat again or see his face or feel his touch, but here he was. His arms tightened around her and she closed her eyes. If it was a dream, she wanted to remain asleep forever in his arms, and if he was a ghost, she'd return with him to whatever spiritual element he came from. The touch was the same as she remembered, strong and gentle all at once. It was him alright. She couldn't believe it.

He moved her away a little, just enough to look at her. He had a moustache now, but his smile was still the same. She always thought his smile lit up the world. His eyes seemed bluer than she remembered — and he was taller. That couldn't be. Had it been so long since she'd seen him that her memory played tricks on her? Maybe it had something to do with the uniform. Maybe the boots he wore made him appear taller. She studied the man. It was none of those things. He was tall. She'd forgotten how tall. She thought she remembered everything about him. The light she used to see around him was still there. That hadn't changed. She wondered if anyone other than she ever saw it. She meant to ask his mother if she saw it, but never got around to asking. She was drifting back to New York, five years ago. All the memories came rushing back. Except for the moustache and the uniform, he hadn't changed at all. The elements were out of perspective. He was still the same. It was she who had changed. She remembered where she was, who she was, painfully aware of the revealing cut of her neckline and the style of her dress, and the paint on her face. The makeup felt suddenly greasy and heavy. What must he be thinking, seeing her this way? Panic took her as she realized his eyes were searching hers for answers to all the questions she hoped she'd never be confronted with. She'd run away from his questions before he had a chance to ask them in New Orleans. It wasn't fair. She'd always known that. She'd been a coward, running off like she did. He deserved so much better. At this moment, she wished a great hole would open in the floor so she could sink into it and disappear from those incisive blue eyes, powerful magnets pulling her to him as they always had. There was no hole in the earth into which to escape from the inevitable truth she must tell and the pain of telling it. A combination of surprise at his unexpected appearance and the thought of telling him the truth made her stomach constrict and a sharp pain below her rib cage doubled her over. She crossed her arms over her stomach. She felt weak. The room began to spin around her and she thought she was spinning with it. She lost her balance and he caught her before she fell.

He was holding her up and she was looking down at the floor. The room came to a dead stop, but she couldn't bring herself to face him. She closed her eyes, hoping that when she opened them, he'd be only a figment of her imagination, but the sound of his voice told her she wasn't imagining anything. He spoke softly. "Where can we talk?" His words were a mere whisper, but they reverberated like the dynamite she'd heard so many times echoing down from the mines, detonating inside her head. Her heart was racing and she was out of breath. She wanted to run, but he was holding on too tight. He'd never let her go without hearing the truth. The sense of panic intensified. She owed him an explanation, but where would she find the words. Her eyes flew open and she started to tell him to go away and never come back. Something stopped her fiery retort. A comforting hand rested on her shoulder. The soft whisper of an unseen, friendly spirit seemed to be breathing a reassuring sense of peace into her, extinguishing the fire of retaliation for what she misconstrued as an attack, and telling her to calm down. She imagined the attack. It was nothing of the sort. All he said was, "where can we talk?" A calm settled over her and her breathing slowed. Her heartbeat returned to normal. She pointed to a small table in the corner and he told his fellow-officer they'd meet in the morning at the Army office.

When he reached for her arm, she drew back and faced him squarely, narrowing her eyes like a strict nanny about to convey alternatives to her young charges. She crossed her arms and spoke as if he were a complete stranger. "I work here. You'll have to buy a bottle if you'll be wantin' me to sit with you. House rules." She was certain that bit of information, coupled with her nonchalant attitude, would cause him to turn on his heel and leave without another word. Instead, he showed no reaction to her announcement. While she waited for his response, he just looked at her. Her heart began racing again, wondering what he was thinking and what he'd do next. He'd never seen her take a drink, but then, neither had he seen her in a saloon, dressed to please the men and painted up like a China doll. All the way across the country, he tried to prepare himself for whatever he might find. He wasn't sure what to expect, but he'd been told lawlessness ruled in the mining camp turned bonanza boomtown and it wouldn't be like any place he'd ever been before. They were right about that. This was not his mother's home or New York or New Orleans or any civilized city. This was another world and she'd been changed by it. This was Tombstone. He'd heard it was a wild and wicked place and he tried to picture it in his mind. He told himself he'd be ready for whatever he found and shock wouldn't be an element to be dealt with cold. Despite that preparation, he never expected to find her like this. What he saw went a long way beyond imagination. She was no longer the innocent eighteen year-old girl in a mint-colored summer dress, albeit without proper underwear, who captured his heart the first time he saw her skipping up the steps of his mother's home. She still captured his heart, but it was different this time. The innocence was gone. There was no mistaking the change in her. She wasn't the Rose Callahan he knew before Tombstone took her. He acted unaffected by her appearance and circumstance, responding to her spiel about "house rules" with an equally indifferent question. "Brandy or whiskey?" Without blinking, she answered, "brandy." If he was stunned, he covered it well, showing no reaction when he ordered the bottle and two glasses and laid the money on the bar. Holding the bottle in one hand and the glasses in the other, he raised both and motioned in the direction of the table. She took a deep breath and led the way, a forgotten thought coming to mind as she walked. Resignation of destiny. No matter what happened, she was ready.

Rose stared at the grain pattern in the wooden table while John poured the brandy. He drank his down before she ever took a sip from her own. She looked over at his empty glass, but not at his face. She didn't remember him ever taking a drink before. In days gone, she was never at a loss for words when she was with him, but she couldn't think of a thing to say to him now. He poured more brandy for himself and she rolled her glass between her hands, causing a little of the liquid to slosh over the side. It was sticky and she licked it off her hand without looking at John. In a Merrick house, she'd never have had such bad manners. In a Merrick house, she'd never have been drinking brandy. She didn't have to look at him to know he was watching her. He and Virgil, the two of them always stared right into her head and saw the words before she said them. There was that old familiar feeling he knew what she was thinking. He was waiting for her to look at him. She remembered his tenacity. He'd sit there all night if he had to — waiting. That was the other thing. They both had patience with her. She'd never understand it. John was waiting to hear her explanation. She searched for the right words to begin the story, but when she opened her mouth, nothing came out. He expected her to start the conversation, but it wasn't that easy.

The voice startled her and she jumped, nearly tipping over her glass and once again spilling a little of the brandy. "Shame on you, Rose Callahan. Keeping this handsome gentleman all to yourself and not even a word to him. You know better than to treat a customer that way. Where are your manners, girl?" She didn't have to see the face. There was no mistaking Ruby's voice. It corresponded to her size. Ruby saw what she liked and as was her style, didn't waste any time moving in. Her hand was out in greeting and she was turning on the charm thick as honey. "Welcome to the Bird Cage. Haven't seen you here before..." She ran her fingers up his sleeve, counting the stripes. "...Captain." She was impressed with his rank. "I'm Ruby. You can guess why they call me Ruby Red, but I only tell the rest of my secrets in private." She winked at John and gave him a little nudge. Her smile and suggestive movement of her body were intended to send him an unmistakable message that she was available if he was interested. The communique couldn't have been clearer if she'd said the words. Ruby wasn't the least bit bashful and her aggressive advances and seductive inferences threw most men into a stutter. Not so this man. Even her best efforts wouldn't rattle him. His manner was quiet and smooth and his next move was predictable. Rose knew exactly what his repartee to Ruby's advances would be. He didn't move as fast as she expected though and as a reflex, she glanced across the table. He hadn't taken his eyes off her, waiting for the precise moment when she'd give in and look at him. It only took a second, but when their eyes met, they both knew the barrier she'd been trying so hard to maintain between them had been breached. He smiled and pushed his chair back. His timing was perfect and he didn't miss a beat. With no indication of what just transpired between himself and Rose, and responding to Ruby's advances as though she'd said good-evening like a lady, absent all the seductive signals, he stood up and graciously accepted her outstretched hand. "I'm Captain Merrick. A pleasure to meet you, Miss Fontaine. I know a Fontaine family in New Orleans. Old friends of my aunt. By chance, would that be your family?" Ruby was surprised by his question and her smile was apprehensive. "No, Captain. I come from Mesilla. That's New Mexico Territory — a long way from New Orleans. Truth is, Fontaine is a variation of my family name — for purposes of the stage, you understand." It wasn't like Ruby to feel the necessity to offer an explanation for anything and she was ill at ease knowing she'd done it. The conversation was quickly getting away from her control and Rose could tell Ruby would just as soon drop the talk about her family name.

He was taller than Ruby and had to look down when he spoke to her. If Rose didn't know Ruby better, she'd swear John was causing some degree of discomfiture and making her nervous. The way he carried himself projected self-confidence and power, something Ruby didn't run into often with men. Those were the qualities that attracted her to Virgil. Holding her hand and smiling at the big redhead, he awaited her next comment. Ruby was speechless, gaping at John with her mouth open. It'd been a long time since a real gentleman treated Ruby like a lady and her reaction was appropriate under the circumstances. Rose couldn't help but smile, wondering if Ruby realized her mouth was open. She never thought she'd see the day any man could render Ruby speechless. He affected Rose the same way the first time she met him. John had always been a perfect gentleman, in the truest sense of the definition. In keeping with his nature and upbringing, as well as his status as an officer, she'd not have expected anything less from him. He'd be polite, but by introducing himself as Captain Merrick, as opposed to first name only, he sent Ruby a clear message. He wasn't interested. The handshake was polite, but transient. He let go of her hand quickly without obvious indication he was in a hurry to drop it and asked if she'd care to join them for a drink. After extending the invitation, he glanced over at Rose. Ruby didn't miss a trick and she saw the electricity that passed between the two of them. The second message came across loud and clear. Rose didn't say it, but she didn't want Ruby to sit down. Not this time. Ruby was no fool. She understood both messages. She whispered to Rose, "He's the one, isn't he?" The look in Rose's eyes confirmed her suspicion and Ruby quickly dispensed with the awkwardness that would have followed had she pursued her advance on John. In typical Ruby fashion, she rested her hand on his arm. For purposes of preserving her reputation as a woman who always got the man she was after, she had to make it look like she was rejecting his proposal although she initiated the advance. She spoke loud enough for all to hear. "Another time, Captain. Another time." She winked at him and left the table.

Rose watched her walk away. So did John. Men always watched Ruby. She mesmerized them. She was something to watch. Everyone agreed on that. Even the girls said that for a big lady, Ruby really knew how to get her sashay going. Rose watched Ruby glide through the room, thinking about the unspoken understanding that existed between the girls when it came to men. Most of them anyway. That included Ruby. Invisible, proprietary bounds had been set tonight. If he came here again, Ruby would be sociable, but she'd never approach John the way she did tonight now that it was clear he was special to Rose. It was the same way she acted with Virgil when it was known he was there to see Rose, a kind of covenant between Ruby and Rose; an acknowledgement of claimed territory that Ruby would never trespass into even if she thought about it. By the same token, the fact that Ruby was interested in both Virgil and John did not escape notice. It didn't come as any surprise that she was attracted to John. Ruby had an eye for quality and recognized John as a cut above the rest. Aside from his good looks, he had an indescribable ambience and charm and his overall manner emanated a combination of strength and gentility. He was different from other men. She remembered thinking the same thing about Virgil. She studied the soldier across the table, in a way, a stranger, though she knew him better than anyone. It was an odd feeling, uncomfortable and sad. She felt like crying. He was more handsome than she remembered, getting better with the passing of years. She'd never met another man like him anywhere. The only ones in this town who came close to paralleling his sophistication and style were, possibly, the Earps, but even that good-looking bunch couldn't compete with him in physical appeal. She felt a twinge of guilt as the Earp name came into play. She couldn't think about Virgil with John here. It wouldn't be right. Sooner or later, she'd have to tell John about him, preferably, later. Before she did that, she had to deal with the immediate crisis of explaining why she left New Orleans right before the wedding. There was no easy way to tell the story, and beginning was the hardest part.

They'd both been trying to think of what to say to break the ice and Ruby had given them a reprieve from the awkward silence, but Ruby was gone. She was across the room and their attention was drawn back to each other. Rose lowered her eyes to the untouched glass of brandy. She heard him sigh. He'd been watching her trying to remain composed and having a hard time of it. John decided to make it easier at the same time she was finally able to get a word out. As luck would have it, they began simultaneously. They laughed and then, the silence was back. Each waited for the other to say the first word and after another clumsy pause, they both started to speak at the same time. They laughed again. She stared at her hands resting in her lap, turning them over to inspect the palms. This was the man she once felt a part of, still felt a part of, and she was having a devil of a time coming up with anything to say to him. Words would simply not come out. He'd have to start the conversation. She couldn't do it. He watched her staring down at her hands, waiting for him to go first. It was as if they'd met for the first time, yet known each other forever. She closed her eyes. Why did this have to be so hard? Her thoughts were interrupted when he spoke and she was surprised at his choice of beginning. He complimented her jewelry. "I never knew you liked silver. The blue stones are particularly beautiful. Turquoise, aren't they?" It was a strange way to start the conversation, but at least the door was open. Her hand went to the piece around her neck and she rolled one of the stones between her fingers. Before she realized it, she was talking.

It had always been her favorite, the first one she owned. The necklace was made of thin, silver strands on which several of the blue stones were strung. She explained the stones were a rare turquoise, found only on the other side of the mountain in Bisbee. All the pieces were given to her by the Indian boy, Nalanche. "A friend." She hesitated before continuing with what she apparently believed was a necessary explanation. "He's only a child." She felt the need to clarify the fact he was just a boy, an orphan, in fact. "He's alone. 'Tis a hard thing to be alone in this country. He has no family, only me and Little Bear. But then, Little Bear isn't so little any more either. I told them he'd grow into those feet and I was right." She laughed at something she thought was funny and he listened, wondering if she realized what she said. He had no idea what she was talking about. "Little Bear?" Maybe that was yet another Indian child, with big feet perhaps. She repeated everything. She didn't want John to misinterpret her relationship with the young Apache boy. Strange, indeed, considering he found her in the Bird Cage and knew what she did for a living, that she was concerned about him misunderstanding her association with the boy. Why she felt the need to explain at all was beyond him. John nodded his understanding, although he hadn't a notion of who the boy was or what Rose's connection was with him, and "Little Bear" was a complete mystery. She was babbling, switching back and forth from English to her native language, mostly from sheer nervousness, but he remembered she used to do it a lot when she had trouble getting her point across in English. Despite the education she'd received from the Merrick women, she still had the problem. It was one of the reasons he loved her. Some things never change. Maybe that was good. She went on for another minute with what Virgil referred to as her gibber, lapsing into Gaelic every now and then when she couldn't find the right word in English. John smiled and waited patiently for the rest of the story. When she looked at him, she realized she was gibbering and stopped in the middle of a thought. After a deep breath and a sip of brandy, she began the story, from the beginning.

The boy was about fifteen. At least, that's what Ruby said. It was hard to tell his true age. A month after she arrived in town, a commotion erupted in the street. There was shouting and a lot of dust being kicked up by the horses. At first, she thought it was just another of the frequent, minor skirmishes that occurred when men got a little too much whiskey under their belts, but when she got closer, she saw that several men on horseback had trapped an Apache boy within a circle, yelling at him and poking him with a stick, accusing him of stealing food. They were shouting obscenities about his Indian heritage and maneuvering their horses in such a way as to make him jump back and forth to avoid being trampled. One wielded a whip and struck the boy, knocking him to the ground. As he went down, she noticed he was clutching something close to his chest and when he fell, he drew his knees up and protected the small object in his arms by wrapping himself around it. Still holding tight to the bundle, the Indian scrambled to his feet and one of the cowboys reached down and got hold of his hair. Unable to keep his balance, he stumbled and tripped as the cowboy dragged him through the dirt, twisting and pulling his hair. He never cried out as he struggled to regain his footing. In their preoccupation with laughing and shouting out shameful references to his ancestry, a subtle move went unnoticed by the attackers. She saw the boy shift what he was carrying to one hand and pull a knife from his belt with the other hand. Before they realized what he was doing, his arm swung upward, the blade finding its mark and slashing the hand that held him. Blood spurted from the cut and he was released. He jumped back as far as he could, still protecting his tiny possession, only to be slammed into the dirt again by the flank of a moving horse. He fell forward, but even with the impact of the fall, he managed to roll and hold onto whatever he was carrying. He was on the ground when another crack of the whip caught him. Blood streamed from his head and he laid still in the dirt with both arms wrapped around the object. She thought he was trying to hang onto the food they said he stole. If he was that hungry, why didn't they leave him alone? He couldn't have taken much. The package was so small, she couldn't see what it was.

Their cowardly behavior infuriated her and she picked up a rock and hurled it at the cowboy with the whip, striking him hard on a shoulder blade. He let out a yip when the stone hit him, and the sharp blow to the sensitive bone nearly knocked him out of the saddle. From the sound of the crack, she got him pretty good with a solid hit and the stone might have broken something. He reigned up his horse and turned on her, his face twisted in a painful grimace, a curse on whores exploding from his lips. She'd seen pictures of the devil in books and the contorted expression on this man's face was so hateful, she thought she was laying eyes on Satan himself. She blessed herself hurriedly with the sign of the Holy Cross, just in case. The devil was holding the whip that struck the boy down; no ordinary braid of leather, but rather a cat-o-nine-tails, designed to inflict unbearable pain and death. He would have killed the boy with it if she hadn't come along and thrown the rock. About the time the idea of what might have happened to the boy occurred to her, the devil let out a wild whoop and dug his heels hard into the horse's sides, splitting the air with the cracking of his whip in the advance, his mind set to trample her into the dirt.

She never remembered what happened next. To this day, she didn't know how she managed to get out of the way of the galloping horse; why she wasn't dead. She recalled how, as the horse was bearing down on her, she had the distinct impression that something moved her out of the path of the oncoming animal. She said it felt like two strong hands lifting her away. She didn't remember jumping out of the way or running for safety, and she didn't remember seeing anyone close enough who would have pulled her back. Many times since, she considered the possibility it was no earthly hand that carried her to safety when the horse went racing by. It wouldn't be the first time she'd been saved from a brutal death, by her good angel perhaps. Later, she asked some of those who were there that day what happened, but no one had any recollection of how she escaped death. They were as amazed as she was that she was alive. It was as though they'd all gone to sleep for that few seconds. Time stood still. No one saw a thing. Nobody remembered her getting out of the way. The best she could get from one fellow was, "That's a stunner alright. Don't know how's come you ain't dead. No reason I can tell." One minute, horse and rider were headed straight for her. Next thing she knew, she was kneeling on the ground beside the injured boy. The time in between was blank.

The young Indian struggled to get to his feet, but the last blow stunned him so severely he couldn't stand up. The men restrained their animals in a circle around Rose and the boy. When she saw how badly he was hurt, she stood over him, shaking her fist at them and calling them cowards for striking down a defenseless child. If she'd had a gun, she'd have shot the lot of them. The stone she'd thrown at the one with the whip was nearby. She picked it up and challenged them, daring them to come after her.

Her intervention was completely unexpected and they all stood still, not quite sure what to do with her. No one ever came to the aid of an Indian, especially not a woman. And there was no question she was a woman, a small one at that, facing six armed men on horseback with nothing more than a rock in her hand. They'd never been up against anything like her and were puzzled as to what their next move should be. They stared at her in disbelief as she stood in the circle, shaking her fist with the rock in it and spouting fire and brimstone like a Sunday-morning preacher all fired up by a full-house congregation, condemning them to burn forever in the inferno of Hades for their cowardly actions. Her red hair picked up a glint from the sun and her eyes flared like a mountain lion defending her cubs under attack. They'd never seen a woman so mad as this one and she couldn't remember ever having been so angry as she damned them over and over. Thinking she fit the description of Lele, the mystical avenger of the weak they'd heard the Indians tell about — the winged woman with hair of fire and courage of a bear, they began to wonder if there wasn't something of truth to the legend. Picking on the Apache boy was turning out not to be such a good idea. They never expected a little redhead with the temper of a wildcat to come along and spoil their fun. No question about her position though. She wasn't afraid of them and she was ready to take them on one at a time or in a bunch.

Lizzie would say they were in a pickle. If anything, that was an understatement. None of them knew what to do. They looked back and forth at each other, waiting for one of them to make the first move. When they realized she wasn't about to back down voluntarily and let them leave on their own terms, every one of them got a little fidgety. Ridiculous as it seemed, fact was, she had the upper hand. Of course, they couldn't back down either. If they did, they'd be the laughing stock of the Arizona Territory. They traveled together like a pack of wild dogs, but when the game was too big, they looked to the one with the whip to handle the kill. Any other time, he'd have puffed himself up and accepted the opportunity to be the loudmouth, bully spokesman for the group. This time, he wasn't so sure he wanted to be the leader of this pack of mangy curs. He would have welcomed a little moral support from those who followed him, but they were dumping the mess right at his feet like a pile of stinking, hot manure, fresh from the horse. He'd have to figure out how to get around the mess without getting too dirty. Not wanting to make the decision alone, the devil spoke up. Curling his whip and hanging it on the saddle behind him, he asked if he ought to shoot her, his question directed at anyone who wanted to answer. Much to his dismay, his question died on the wind. He looked from man-to-man for some kind of sign that he wasn't alone in his thinking the only way out was to cut her down. No one answered and he shifted uneasily in the saddle, looking around for reinforcements he knew wouldn't be forthcoming. One-by-one, they looked away from him and over the building crowd. None of them had any inclination to shoot a woman — not in broad daylight anyway.

He was in a real predicament because he'd asked the question about "cuttin' her down" and got no answer. What made it worse was that he tried to run her down once and failed. He was still trying to figure out how that could be. One minute, she was right in front of him and the next, she was gone, clear over by the Indian a good twenty feet away. He'd never know what happened. All he knew was that he'd backed himself into a corner real good and it was a standoff between him, loaded for bear, with enough weapons to hold off a small army, and a tiny woman with a rock in her hand. Still, the odds were not in his favor. Nothing he could say would turn it around either. He took off his hat and scratched his head. Everybody was waiting for him to make the next move. Maybe the idea of a .45 slug between the eyes would scare her enough to make her turn tail and run. At least then, he could say he backed her down, and he might not have to shoot her. It was worth a try. The longer she stood there with the rock in her hand, the more foolish he felt. He had do something before the crowd started heckling him.

For lack of a better idea, he pulled his revolver and leaned slowly forward, resting his elbow on the saddle horn for balance and closing one eye to take a bead on her. He was counting on making her believe she was about to die to intimidate her. She didn't budge an inch. If anything, his pointing a gun at her fortified her position, only serving to make her more obstinate. When he pulled back on the hammer, she raised her hand, threatening to throw the stone at him. He cringed and clenched his teeth together. The tension was too much and his eye began to twitch and water. That was the end of his options. Now, what was he going to do? She could have made it easy by walking away. Easy for him anyway. Just his luck to get something like her to face off with. If he had his druthers between dangling from a rope with a mountain lion on the top end and a fire burning up from the bottom, and her, he had to think he'd take his chances with the wildcat and the fire. At least he'd save his dignity. The way things were headed, she wasn't about to let him come away with any part of his dignity or anything else if she could help it. Damndest thing! She just plain wasn't scared. There had to be another way. He lowered the gun and rested both arms across the saddle horn. Beads of nervous sweat glistened on his forehead and he wiped them away with his coatsleeve, looking up at the sun and hoping anyone watching would think the heat of the day was the cause of his sweating. Another stream of water trickled down his forehead into one eye. The salty drops stung like crazy, but he tolerated them and didn't wipe them away for fear someone would think he was weak — or worried. The burning in his eye was nothing compared to the discomfort he felt with the situation in front of him entirely out of control. To say the least, it was a bad stroke of luck running into the little Irish cyclone and he began wishing he were somewhere else.

Women minded him because they were afraid of him, but he'd underestimated this one. She was nothing like any female he'd ever seen in his life. Here he was, pointing a gun at a woman with a rock in her hand and she was calling him a fool and a coward. What was worse, there wasn't a thing he could do about it. It was darned humiliating. Might have to shoot her to shut her up. Of course, if he did that, it'd prove her point. He was a coward — and a fool. To top it off, she'd probably get her wish. He'd burn in hell. He let out a big sigh, rubbing the stubble on one side of his face, then the other, pondering the dilemma. He was stalling, trying to figure a way out that wouldn't leave him looking like a bigger fool than he already was. He had an idea. He'd just shoot her.

Pretending the sun was too bright again, he squinted his eyes and looked around. The gun was still in his hand and he raised it, pointing it at her head this time. He bit his lower lip. No telling where the Marshal was this time of day and the law in this town wouldn't take kindly to killing a female. Might even get hung for it. Then again, which was worse, getting hung or being laughed at for the rest of your life?

The onlookers who cheered the cowboys on when they cornered the boy were quiet. She clenched her teeth and stood her ground defiantly, the rock still in her hand. Then she heard him. The cowboy heard him too. He didn't turn around, but he became very uneasy knowing who was behind him. It was Virgil, telling them their fun was over and the crowd to go about their business. Virgil walked between the horses into the circle where she was standing over the boy, the hand holding the stone still poised in the air. He pried her hand open and took it from her, looking down at it in his own hand. He thought to himself, "Only a damn fool, or someone who hadn't been in this town long, would call out Frank McLaury armed with nothing but a rock to throw at him. Grown men who were good shots didn't do it if, for no other reason, than the unpredictable nature of the man." Never thought he'd see the day. He knew Frank had to feel like the biggest fool in the Territory right about now. It'd be almost funny if it wasn't so downright idiotic. He couldn't believe she'd squared off with the odds dead against her. Fact was, he couldn't believe she wasn't already dead from stupidity. Blind luck. That's all it was. Blind, jackass luck! He looked over at her and she was staring at him, the blaze of indignation burning wildly in her eyes. When she was fired up, her brogue was thick as molasses in winter. "Well, Marshal. Are you goin' to arrest these criminals?" She was fearless, an outraged defender of the helpless, fighting for something she knew was right and willing to give her life in it's defense if necessary. An honest-to-goodness Joan of Arc. No wonder the cowboys were dumbfounded. He'd never seen anything like her either. His thought was, "too bad she wasn't a man." He needed a few more good deputies as tough as her. He had all he could do to keep from smiling when he started to answer her question. "We'll see..." She stamped her foot indignantly and interrupted, stepping up to him and shaking her finger in his face. He moved his head back a little to avoid being poked in the eye. She snapped at him, talking louder and louder the madder she got. "What do you mean, you'll see? The only thing you'll see to is the arrestin' of the milk-livered cretins. Do your job, Marshal, or give me that gun you're carryin' and I'll do it for you." He gently pushed her finger away from his face and held onto her wrist, leaning close enough so that only she could hear what he said. "Miss Callahan, you're making matters worse. You settle down or I'll have my deputy escort you over to the jail for a night's free room and board. Do you understand?" The tone of his voice left no room for doubt that he meant what he said. Her body stiffened obstinately and she pressed her lips tight together in acrimonious acceptance of his message. The green eyes flashed defiance, but at least she was finally quiet.

With the wind blowing her hair around and the sun behind her shining through the wild strands, she looked like some kind of ethereal apparition. From the crowd, someone shouted the Apache boy had stolen food and ought to be punished. The others chimed in, their nerve fortified by strength in numbers, and the whole crowd was soon yelling. A single shot ripped through the air and the sound bounced back and forth across the street like a ricocheting echo in a canyon. The gunfire silenced the mob. Then, a voice beyond the circle repeated Virgil's message. "Excitement's over, boys. Go home or spend the night in jail." She looked between the horses and saw Wyatt and his younger brother, Morgan, with her friend, John Holliday, all with guns drawn. Virgil gave them a chance to speak up. "Anybody see the boy steal anything?" There wasn't a man among them who wanted a confrontation with the Earps and Doc Holliday. When no answer was forthcoming, Wyatt spoke again. "I can't arrest him without evidence he committed a crime." He waited, searching the crowd for sign of a witness. "Speak up!" Still, no one came forward to point a finger at the boy. He figured as much. "If you got nothing to say, get on about your business."

Gradually, the crowd dispersed, grumbling as they went, disappointed that was the end of it. The cowboy still had his pistol in his hand. Without turning around, he knew there were three guns pointed at his back and Virgil had been keeping an eye on him from the front. There wasn't much danger of him pulling the trigger with all that firepower concentrated on him. Virgil was holding the horse's bridle. Now that he had Rose's temper under control, he could deal with the next thing. His voice was low and calm. "Holster that weapon easy, Frank. You had your fun. Time for you and the boys to be on your way. No need for anyone to get hurt. I'd appreciate it if you'd go peaceful and let this be the end of it. If you do, I won't be taking anybody to jail. Sound alright to you?" Behind him, he heard Rose start to sputter her objection to his diplomacy and he raised his hand to shut her up. The situation was still hot and he didn't need any help from her to fuel the fire. While Frank was deciding whether or not to take the Marshal up on his offer, the others didn't need to be told twice. One-by-one, they turned their horses around and headed south out of town. Frank smiled nervously at Virgil who was giving him the cold stare of a rattlesnake just before the strike. There was no smile on Virgil's face. The Marshal had given him a way out. Nobody would think less of him for putting away his gun by order of Virgil Earp with all those guns aimed at his back. If he made the wrong move, it'd be his last, but he was still trying to save whatever might be left of his dignity after he'd made an outright fool of himself, or better said, after Rose made a fool of him. His shoulder was throbbing from the clout he'd got when she threw the rock at him and he was having a hard time steadying his hand. Even if he pulled the trigger before Virgil showed up, he never would have hit her. His hand was shaking too bad from the pain, or maybe partly from the situation he'd found himself caught in. At that point, he made what was probably the smartest decision of his life. He holstered his gun very slowly so as not to give any false impression of the movement, muttering something to the effect that "...weren't no woman worth gettin' hung for." His words trailed off at the click of a hammer locking back behind him and he decided he'd said enough. He'd pushed his luck about as far as he dared for one day. He wasn't opposed to taking risks, but even the best gamblers played it smart when it came to knowing when to fold. It was time to throw in his cards. Punctuating his final remark by spitting in the dirt, he let one last, contemptuous glare fly at Rose. Once he felt like he'd had the final say, he turned his horse south with the rest of the cowboys.

It was then Rose realized the incident had been observed by a lot of people. No one raised a hand to help the boy. No one came forward to help her either, a defenseless woman against all those armed men on horseback. She was disgusted with all of them. She turned to the stragglers and gave them a dose of her leftover indignation. "You're all cowards. That's what y'are — the whole damn bunch of you. Cowards!" She scooped up a handful of dirt and threw it at them, following through by waving her hand in a sweeping motion that covered the crowd so they knew none was excluded from her anger. "You ought to be ashamed of yourselves. Cowards!" About that time, she went into her gibber, rattling off several words in Gaelic and back to English. When she spit on the ground to accentuate her contempt, that took even Virgil by surprise. He was about to tell her to settle down again, but changed his mind when she spit. She was really something. Pretty funny, but he didn't dare laugh. He decided there was no harm in letting her throw a fit now that the real danger was gone. Besides, she was right. Not a man among them stepped forward to help him in a fight either, even when he'd asked. They complained about the crime in town, but left it up to "the law" to keep the peace. He'd experienced a little of that righteous indignation himself more than once with the good citizens of Tombstone. He could see the fire in her eyes burning like crazy when she called them cowards, over and over. There was something about her stance there in the middle of the street. With hands on her hips and a scowl on her face, the way her brogue put an accent on the words gave terrible emphasis to their meaning. If anyone could make them feel like cowards, it was her and it was obvious her animated revilement did exactly that. Some looked at the ground and some looked away, but none of them looked her in the eye. Her tirade wouldn't let up and they wanted to get as far away from her as fast as they could. It was a tongue-lashing they wouldn't soon forget. When the street cleared out, the tantrum subsided. One thing Virgil knew for sure. He'd never want her to be that mad at him.

She turned to the boy, still lying in the dirt and clutching his possession, as yet unrevealed. He'd taken quite a beating. Virgil helped him stand up and Rose let out a groan when she saw his face. It was bad. Blood from the gaping head wound ran down his face and onto his shirt. He was scratched and dirty and bloodied knees showed through the holes in his pants from being dragged through the street. When she tried to brush him off, he pulled away and when he did, she saw what he'd been so intent on protecting, a tiny dog — a puppy the color of gold. She smiled. She probably would have done the same thing if she'd been in his place. There was something very strange about him. She couldn't quite put her finger on it, but he was a most unusual boy. She wasn't sure why that thought came to her except she felt a calmness that seemed to enfold her as she stood beside him. All the anger was gone, replaced with a sense of peace. She watched the boy stroke the puppy to comfort it. He knew if he let go of it during the attack, they would have killed it. He was a lot like her, ready to defend it to the death if necessary, and he almost did just that. The puppy whimpered a little and he held it up close to his face, speaking softly to it in his native language, petting it and quieting the small cries. The poor little thing must have been half scared to death. It was a wonder it didn't die from sheer fright. He rubbed it's head and when it calmed down, quite unexpectedly, reached out and handed it to Rose. He pushed it against her chest, indicating she must accept it. She looked at Virgil for help. He shook his head. "No use arguing with him. Apaches are a pigheaded lot. You might as well take it because he won't take no for an answer." She argued anyway, that she couldn't take it. She had no place to keep a dog. She lived in a hotel.

The puppy was awful cute. She rubbed the little black nose with the tip of her finger. He closed his eyes and pushed his nose against her finger for full benefit of the rubbing. "He is a pretty little thing, isn't he? Soft." Virgil looked away, pretending not to be the least bit interested in the dog. He tried to act like something caught his eye up the street. The crowd was gone, his brothers and Doc too. He heard what she said, but didn't acknowledge her remark about how cute the pup was and he continued to look up the street when he spoke. "If you don't take it, the kid will sit outside the hotel and he'll follow you everywhere you go. Somebody might think he's bothering you and he's liable to get hurt again. Some don't need much reason to shoot an Indian. If you want my advice, you'd best take the dog and save everybody a peck of trouble." She'd been watching Virgil intently while he talked. She looked at the boy. She certainly wouldn't want him to get hurt again and she didn't want to cause anyone trouble. He hadn't made a move to withdraw the gift, still holding the puppy out to her, determined that she take it. Virgil shaded his eyes from the sun, waiting for her to make up her mind. He was getting a little irritated. "You just got yourself a dog, Miss Callahan. Take it, so we can all go home."

With no other option available, she took the quivering little ball of fluff from the boy and held it under her chin. It nuzzled close to her and she giggled when the soft fur tickled her face. "He loves me already." Virgil looked away again, trying to appear disinterested. He whispered something under his breath. "Women!" She heard what he said. "I beg your pardon, Marshal?" He took off his hat and smoothed his hair, wishing she hadn't heard. "I didn't say anything." He put his hat on and looked up the street, deciding he'd better keep his mouth shut, especially since her hearing was so good, and hoping she wouldn't start another argument. Lucky for him, her attention shifted back to the dog. She lifted the puppy to view its underneath just as Virgil turned back and saw what she was doing. "Miss Callahan! Do you mind? This is a public street." Lowering the pup, she raised her eyebrows, pretending not to understand that he meant she might have been a little more discreet about checking the private parts of the puppy in public. She batted her eyelashes at him and feigned innocence. "We'll need to see if he's to have a boy's name or a girl's, don't you think?" He didn't answer. She'd do as she damned-well pleased anyway, no matter what he thought. She held it up again and announced the pup was, in fact, a boy. Satisfied as to the determination it was a male, she ran her fingers through his fur and looked him over. "He seems fit. For such a young one, he's very strong. I think he looks like a little bear. What shall we call him, Marshal?" Virgil patted the pup's head and ran his hand over it's back. "Call him Little Bear." She looked at him sideways, not quite sure if that was a sincere suggestion or a bit of sarcasm directed at her. She decided it was probably a little of both. She turned to the Indian boy for approval. "Do you like that name? Shall we call him Little Bear?" The boy nodded his agreement and she held the pup to her face again, gently rubbing her nose against his. "Well then, 'tis settled. You are my Little Bear, but from the size of your feet, I have a notion it won't be long before I'll be changin' your name to Big Bear." Holding one of the tiny paws in her hand, she laughed at her own joke, but stopped when Virgil didn't laugh with her. She fluttered her eyelashes at him and he finally broke down and smiled.

An earlier thought returned. She had no place to keep the dog. Living at the Cosmopolitan, the management would strongly object to her having an animal in her room. She turned to Virgil, but before she could say it, he raised his hand to stop her, anticipating what she was about to ask and shaking his head in resignation. Without another word, he took the pup out of her hands. She smiled at him. "Thank you, Marshal." He didn't answer. Instead, he turned the puppy onto its back and held it on one arm like a baby and scratched its stomach while he spoke to it ever so sternly. "I don't care much one way or the other about dogs. Let's get that straight right off. You'll have to behave yourself if you're going to live with me. There are rules, you know. I won't tolerate a bad dog. There won't be any barking at night or hole-digging in the yard." The puppy looked up at Virgil with his brown eyes open wide as though paying close attention to the admonition that he'd be living in the street if he was a "bad dog." Virgil continued the one-sided conversation. "Understand?" He waited a couple of seconds for an answer though obviously not expecting one. He said it again, this time, shaking the puppy gently to be sure there was no doubt in it's mind about the rules. She smiled when Virgil asked the question, emphasizing his message with a scowl, as if the dog could understand the importance of the directive. She mocked his sternness with an, "Oh, I'm sure he understands every word you say, Marshal. A small suggestion, if I might make it? Keepin' him in the house might eliminate the barkin' and hole-diggin'. Not that he'd think of it, of course. Don't you think he's much too little to stay outside? He'd be afraid in the dark all alone, and we wouldn't want a wolf to get him at night, would we?" She forced herself to hold back the smile. Virgil didn't move his head to look at her, only his eyes. He knew she was making fun of the way he laid down the law to the dog, and her suggestion about keeping the puppy in the house was really more than a suggestion. She was telling him what to do. He cleared his throat and shifted the puppy upright to one hand, looking at her like she'd made the dumbest remark he'd ever heard. "There aren't any wolves in Tombstone." He meant business, or so he tried to make her believe. "He'll mind, or he'll be in the street." She knew better. There was not a shred of doubt in her mind that he'd keep the dog inside.

She only met Virgil Earp a week earlier, but she'd learned a lot about him. Beneath the surface seen by most people and beyond the austere countenance of this serious lawman was a soft heart. She had a feeling that not only would the puppy not be outside, but he'd probably be sleeping on Virgil's bed. She was still trying to keep a straight face. "I'd be grateful if you'd keep him for a little while, just until I find a place to live where I can have him. I don't expect he'll be much of a burden. He's very small and I'm sure he doesn't eat much. I'll take him as soon as I can. 'Tis only a temporary arrangement for your keepin' him. I'll start lookin' for a house right away and..." Virgil raised his hand, indicating she could stop babbling. It was an annoying habit. She never knew when to stop talking. He already said he'd keep the dog. He rarely smiled and she didn't expect one from him now. The tone of his voice didn't change. "You'd better. I don't have time for dogs." There was a mischievous twinkle in his eye when he added, "Take him soon, or I'll be turning him out to the wolves." That was the end of the conversation. He turned and walked away, leaving her standing in the street with the Apache boy. His back was to her, but she could tell by the way he lowered his head and moved his arms that he was petting the pup and talking to it, probably saying he was sorry for being so gruff, or chuckling about her thinking a wolf would get him at night. It wasn't long after that he moved her into the little gray house over on Toughnut Street, and Little Bear with her.

With it settled that Virgil would take care of the dog, she turned her attention back to the Indian boy. She tried not to let him know she thought the cut looked bad. "You need to have that wound tended to right away. I'll take you over to the doctor's office for some stitchin'. It won't take but a few minutes." He shook his head, no. She persisted. "You have to get it tended to. It needs cleanin' and sewin' up, and medicinal salve to keep out infection. It's too big a wound to let go without closin' it." She thought about taking him to the hotel to clean him up, but she knew they'd let her have the dog in her room sooner than they'd allow the Indian upstairs. She finally convinced him to follow her to Nellie's back door. She didn't know the woman, but the miners called her the angel of the camps and Nellie Cashman had a reputation for never turning away anyone in need of help. Rose wasn't sure if that included Apaches, but as soon as Nellie saw the injured boy, the question was answered. She cleaned and dressed his wounds. Rose knew the iodine scrubbing of the deep cut in his forehead had to burn like crazy, but he showed no sign of pain. He sat perfectly still and never made a peep while Nellie cleaned and stitched. She clipped the last thread and gently covered the wounds with a soothing ointment and bandages. When she finished wrapping his head, he stood up. He hadn't spoken to either of them during the tending to his injuries. He removed the small leather pouch that hung from his waist. The stitching was very pretty, and it was sewn with a few small, colorful beads. He handed the pouch to Nellie. "Good medicine." She tried to tell him payment wasn't necessary. By now, Rose knew how it went. "You have to take it, Nellie. 'Tis important to him that you do. I'll explain it to you later." Nellie rubbed her fingers over the soft leather and delicate beadwork. "It's lovely work. I shall keep it forever as a special treasure. Thank you... I don't know your name."

She could see he was pleased with her acceptance of the gift. He answered. "Nalanche." She repeated his name. "Nalanche. A strong name. A name for a chief." She knew what the significance of the medicine bag was; not medicine as she practiced the healing art, but rather a talisman to be taken quite seriously, the Indians' symbol of luck and positive spirit forces. Apache good medicine meant something important that represented good spirits chasing away evil ones. There was a stone or animal bone or some little thing protected within the medicine bag that was symbolic of good luck and more, something to be treated with respect in order to gain the benefit of its power. However, the contents could never be revealed to her or to anyone. She would never open the bag to see the icon inside. She pulled the drawstring tight and tied it in a knot, acknowledging that she recognized the importance of keeping the bag closed so as not to allow the good medicine to escape. Nellie had a way about her — a kindness. Rose was glad she brought the boy to her for doctoring and now that she'd seen the woman, she knew why the miners called Nellie an angel. She was Irish.

Satisfied the medicine bag was secure with Nellie, he turned to Rose. He hadn't thanked her for saving his life. Not in words anyway. To his way of thinking, the puppy was only the beginning of repayment. Out in the street, he saw her looking at the silver ornament he wore around his neck. While Nellie cleaned and bandaged his wounds, Rose asked him where the blue stones in the necklace came from and he pointed in the direction of the mountains towards Bisbee. He took off the necklace and placed it around her neck. She remembered what Virgil said about the Indians believing if you saved a life, the one you saved owed you his. She didn't see it that way, but she reasoned that by accepting the necklace and the puppy, he wouldn't feel obligated to her further. She didn't want him to believe she owned his life. She had enough trouble taking care of her own. Accepting the necklace indicated repayment of any debt he thought he owed her, so she thanked him and promised to wear it always. That should have been the end of it, but fate had a different idea about how things were to go.

It wasn't an end at all, but rather the beginning of what she'd come to know as an incredible link with not only a mysterious Apache boy, but a connection with a world unto its own. He'd become her teacher and guide as she learned to understand the connection, stepping across the threshold of Time into the world of spirit winds to experience a revelation of the ancient one the Apaches knew as Coshani — past, present, and future; a passageway to the other side the Indians called the crossover.

From the day she helped him, whenever she walked beyond the town limit into the desert in the evening, Nalanche followed her. The first few times, he didn't speak to her and he kept a substantial distance between the two of them. She turned often to say something to him, but he didn't seem to want to talk. On the way back to town, she expected to see him in front of her on the trail. He was gone. A few minutes later, she'd look back and find him walking behind her. When she reached the town, he always disappeared and she could never figure out where he went. He was an elusive spirit, appearing only when he believed she was in need of his protection. She decided that was what he was doing, protecting her. Despite her acceptance of the dog and silver necklace with the blue stones, he didn't believe the debt was repaid.

During one of her walks, she went a little further than usual beyond the noise of the town. When he called out to her, she turned around, surprised he'd said anything at all. Other nights, the only sounds she heard came from the town behind her and echoes through the hills of water pumps and hoisting chains where the mines never rested. Closer, tiny desert wrens flitted among the creosote bushes and cactus before bedding for the night. She waited for him to catch up. When he came near, she noticed his injury had healed well, thanks to Nellie. Only a faint trace of a scar remained in the scarcely-visible, jagged shape of a broken arrow in the middle of his forehead. She smiled and held out her hand to him. When he stopped, she expected him to disappear as he always did. This time, he didn't leave and she was even more amazed when he took her hand. He looked at their clasped hands for a long time and she could see the muscles in his jaw rippling. He acted like he was daydreaming or far away in thought. There was a curious feeling of kinship, a sense of peace. She felt protected in his presence. Then, she realized what it was that made her feel that way every time she was near him. It was a light that surrounded him, the same light she saw around John, and it gave her a sense of well-being. He was a strange boy. For someone so young, he never smiled and there was something about him that made him seem old beyond his years.

His eyes were on the necklace she was wearing, the one he gave to her at Nellie's. She wore it all the time. This evening, he had another present for her, a bracelet, silver with more of the blue stones. She asked if there was a name for the style of the jewelry, what it was called. He said only that it was "Apache silver." As far as she knew, Apaches didn't work with silver, but that didn't mean it was true. They'd been in this country long before the white man and the silver was always here. The Indians might have figured out a way to process it before the white man ever knew. It was talk she'd heard that they stole whatever they got their hands on, but she didn't think this boy would steal anything. In the street that day, it was discovered he hadn't taken the food he was accused of stealing. All he had in his arms was a puppy. Whether he stole the jewelry or made it himself didn't matter and she decided not to ask where he got it. Instead, she fastened the bracelet around her wrist and raised her arm for a closer look. It was beautiful, delicately etched with Apache symbols and inlaid with the blue stones. She turned to thank him. He was gone. She looked around in every direction. It was as if the desert had swallowed him up. He disappeared and she didn't hear him go. The sky was red and gold. It'd be dark soon. She didn't look behind her as she walked back toward town. There was no sound of footfall on the gravel behind her, but she knew he was there protecting her.

She was never alone on her walks. Nalanche was always there. She took Little Bear and he ran with the boy. They made her laugh with their running and jumping and silly games. The longer she watched them, she began to understand what first appeared as games were much more than play. They were acting out something purposeful. They belonged together. Try as she would, she was never able to get her message across to the dog. Whenever she gave a command, he cocked his head from side-to-side and wagged his tail. Then, he'd run off as though she hadn't said a word. Despite the affection he showed for her, she couldn't get him to mind. On the other hand, he seemed to understand every word Nalanche said and obeyed the boy's commands. If she told Bear to do something, he invariably did something else, but the boy could give an identical command and Bear obeyed every time. She'd never understand how that could be. Whenever it happened, Nalanche would tell her how smart Bear was. She'd look at the dog and shake her head. "Nalanche says you're a smart one, but you can't prove it by me. You never listen to me." Nalanche's explanation for Bear's failure to pay attention to her consisted of one word. "Squaw." Her response was, "Takes a man to say somethin' like that. You and Virgil."

It had nothing to do with her being a woman and she insisted it was much more than that anyway. She swore there was a secret language only the boy and dog understood and she was not privy to it. It wasn't English or Apache, but something else. Something secret. He could talk to the animals. That's all there was to it. Whatever it was, they had a unique bond that drew them closer together with the passing of time. There was a link between her and the Indian boy too, a connection that defied any logical explanation. She didn't understand it, but she knew it existed. The feeling grew stronger the more they were together. She always thought Ann Merrick was an angel. Perhaps Nalanche was an angel sent to protect and guide her through the desert and the life she was living. He gave her more silver and blue stones, and she started wearing all the pieces together. The girls at the Bird Cage didn't understand why she did it. Silver was heavy, hot, and uncomfortable, but she wore every piece. Before long, they took to calling her Silver Rose.

John sat quietly while she talked about her young Apache friend and the puppy who hadn't been a little ball of fluff for many moons. The identity of Little Bear was no longer a mystery and he knew she was talking about a dog. She'd been right about the size of Little Bear's feet. He'd outgrown the "Little" part of his name months ago and she called him Bear now. She lost her train of thought about the silver jewelry and began rambling, telling how she'd been intrigued and saddened at the same time by Nalanche's story about his family.

When the white soldiers came, they killed many Apaches, including Nalanche's father. He said it was good that his father died because he wouldn't have been able to bear the disgrace of being taken prisoner by the white soldiers, knowing the land no longer belonged to the Apache. More soldiers came and herded what was left of his people like cattle, tethered by ropes, and took them away. Many suffered great hardship at the hands of the white man. As his father lay dying with the white soldiers rounding up the people in camp, he told the boy to run into the desert. Nalanche asked his father how he would live in the desert alone. He was only a boy and had not learned the ways of a man to hunt and find water. He was afraid as he held his dying father's hand and hid the tears so not to let his father see his fear. Otahe replied that the son was as brave as any warrior in the Apache nation, and the wisdom of his ancestors was within him. The Great Spirit would show him the way to live if he believed it so. There would be a sign — a guide. He would recognize the guide and know what to do and he would not be alone in the desert. His father and his grandfather would be always near and he needed only to call their names and they would come on the spirit winds to lead him. His father closed his eyes and spoke no more. Otahe, the chief, was dead. The white soldiers came closer and the boy knew he had to hide to keep from being taken prisoner with the rest, but he didn't know where to go so they wouldn't find him. He asked for guidance from the spirits of his father and his grandfather who had gone before to the crossover. He faced the wind and called their names as his father had instructed him to do. "Otahe. Tehanache." He heard the voices on the wind telling him to run and not be afraid, that they were with him. He left his dead father's side and raced out into the desert, not knowing what awaited him, but trusting the wisdom of his father.

The boy ran fast, his feet flying over stones and cactus. He didn't look for a place to hide, but kept running far out into the desert, believing the words of his father as truth and knowing he would be shown the place of shelter when the time was right. Far from the encampment, he stopped running and called out again to his father and grandfather. A warm wind came up and the voices drifted around him and comforted him. They told him to trust the animals. He didn't understand. He looked around for the sign his father said he would find to guide him and was startled to see a coyoté nearby. At first, he was afraid she would attack and kill him, but she made no aggressive move. Instead, she turned and began walking away. After a few steps, she stopped to look back at him before walking a little further. She repeated the motion twice, quickening her step to an easy run the third time, all the while looking back at him as she moved. It was as if she was beckoning to him. When she ran without turning back, he followed her. Suddenly, she broke into a dead run and he ran with her, faster and faster. The animal led him to her den between some rocks where she was hiding her pups in a hollowed-out place beneath a thick cover of creosote. She crawled into the hole and turned around to face him. He hesitated, not understanding what he should do next. Then he heard them — the soldiers, not far off. If they held their present course, they would come the same way as he and the coyoté. The dog moved back into the hole and close to one side of the den, leaving a space open just large enough for him to squeeze in. The soldiers were getting closer. He heard the voices on the wind and he knew what to do. If the coyoté attacked, to be killed by a wild creature of the Great Spirit would be a far more honorable death than to suffer the disgrace of being captured by the white soldiers. He crawled into the hole with the dog and laid down beside her and her whimpering babies. She began licking the puppies with a purposeful rhythm until they quieted down. The boy moved close to the animal, keeping the pups between himself and the mother dog to muffle any noise they might make on waking. As if by magic, the young ones remained sound asleep when the line of wagons and people approached. They were so close he could see the looks of despair and sadness on the faces of his people. He wanted to run to them to share their fate or to kill as many of the white soldiers as he could before they killed him, but he remembered his father's words. There was no dishonor in what he was doing. His death would not make a difference and he was to stay in the desert until the others had gone. One day, he'd make things right for his people. He didn't know how, but as he was guided to this place, so would he be shown how to help them. He understood there was a plan for him and it was the reason he was not to run to them.

One of the soldiers walked toward the hole where the boy and coyoté lay together in hiding. If the babies woke up, one squeal would give away their hiding place, but every one of them stayed sound asleep. He was so close to the dog, he could feel her breath on his face. She didn't take her eyes off the soldier as he walked in front of the opening and the boy noticed she stopped breathing. He followed her lead and held his breath. He felt himself become part of the desert with her and they were silent as the grains of sand around them. The soldier never knew they were there. Someone called to the soldier and he went back to his horse, telling the others about the coyoté tracks he found, but making no mention of moccasin prints in the sand. The boy and dog didn't make a sound as the wagons passed by with the sad and broken remnants of his tribe. This day of silent tears would be the last time he cried. When they were gone, he climbed out of the hole and looked back inside at the coyoté and her pups, now wide awake, squealing and pushing through the warm belly fur to find the life-giving milk of their mother. She laid on her side looking at him as her babies nursed. He knew what happened. She was the guide his father told him about. She was sent to save his life. He petted her head and she let him touch her. Outside the hole, he looked around in the sand and traced the route he'd been running. In his hurry to find cover, he'd forgotten to cover his tracks that would give away his hiding place to the soldiers. He searched all around the den, but found no footprints of a man in the sand — only those of the dog.

After that, they hunted together and the coyoté taught him the ways of the wild creatures. One night, he called to her to go on the hunt with him. The excitement was not in her that night and she made no move toward the hunting grounds. Instead, she laid down at his feet. It was time to say good-bye. He knelt beside her and they stayed close until the last crimson traces of the sun were gone to the other side of the world and darkness fell upon the desert. When he stood up, she stayed on the ground and did not look up at him. He touched her head and ran his hand over her coat. He spoke to her in his native language and called her sister. He thanked her for being his guide and said they would meet again at the crossover when he joined Otahe and Tehanache in the place of Apache spirit winds. That night, he went alone knowing when he returned from the hunt, she would not be waiting for him. Her pups were grown and gone, and the time had come for her to find her mate for the next season. The male coyoté kept his distance while the boy was there, but he'd been calling to her every night lately. Now that her teaching of the boy was over, the wild ways were calling her to fulfill her purpose and it was not possible for her to stay with him any longer. She taught him well in the time they were together and because of her, he'd survive on his own. There was no sadness at their parting for each believed in the circle of life that never ends. They would forever be part of each other, creatures of a different kind, joined by a spiritual bond that few of his species ever knew. Peace.

When the dog was gone, Nalanche lived alone in the hills until gradually, he moved closer to the white man's town that was beginning to grow. He watched from a distance as more people came to the place that belonged to the Apache, defiling the hills and disturbing sacred land. He saw the first mines open and the buildings go up. It was foreign to him, the way white men lived. He didn't know what the things were that made so much noise in the hills beyond the town, but they disrupted the serenity of nature with their clanking and moaning. He didn't like what they were doing to the land and he hoped they'd go away. It was at the edge of the town that he found the gold puppy, nearly dead from starvation and thirst. He nursed the fragile little body back to life and by the time he ran into Rose, the pup was fat and fluffy.

She lost track of time talking about Nalanche. His story of survival with the wild coyoté was amazing and she never tired of it. He'd become like a brother to her and she held a great affection for him. John had been sitting quietly throughout the story. She apologized for rambling. It had always been a habit of hers to talk too much. She was also stalling, trying to avoid the subject they'd sat down to talk about. She only meant to tell him where the silver jewelry came from. He finished his brandy and poured another. Then, he started talking. He was sorry he'd been away so long. He would have liked to come home more often, but the Army had a different plan. Although he'd been in the Army for more than three years, he was still in the early stages of his career as a military lawyer. The government assigned him a heavy caseload that rapidly increased, burying him in work. He was trying to earn recognition for his accomplishments and had succeeded beyond his original expectations. He understood how difficult it had been for her to wait, never sure when he'd be able to come home. Whenever he did get there, she didn't complain about the duration between visits, but concentrated instead on the time they had to spend together. She supported his career efforts and she was a never-ending source of encouragement to him. When he went home and found she'd gone away, he realized the career had dominated his life and he'd taken her for granted. He'd been so absorbed in his own acquisition of success that he failed to take the time to acknowledge hers. He was pleased with the air of sophistication she'd gained and he noticed what an extraordinary lady she was, but never mentioned it. He was sorry for not having been able to participate in the wedding preparations, but he was looking forward to the day when they'd be married. When she went away, he knew he'd neglected her. He was here to set things right and hoped she'd forgive his thoughtlessness.

As he talked, it became clear what he was doing. He was apologizing! He thought it was his fault she left New Orleans. He was blaming himself for her running away. She laid her fingers against his lips. "Your assumptions are wrong, John. My leavin' wasn't your fault in any way." He was puzzled. "Then, why did you leave?" There it was. The question she never wanted to answer shot through her like a bolt of lightning and she blurted out the answer. "I had to leave." As soon as she said it, she wanted to retract it. It was no explanation at all. No matter what she told him, the fact remained she was living in circumstances beyond his understanding. She was doing it again, thinking he couldn't understand. How many times had she thought if she'd told him the truth in the first place, he might have understood? If she had, they wouldn't be here. He came all this way to find her and she could no longer deny him the truth. "This isn't a good place to

talk. I'll tell you why I left. I'll tell you everythin'. Wait for me." She left
the table to talk to Ruby. When she returned, she was ready to leave. He
could walk her home. They'd talk there.

By this time, she was sure John's arrival in Tombstone was not accidental. She'd heard about the military trial to be held at the new courthouse, but
never considered he might be assigned as the government's prosecutor. The
only other way he could have found her was if Marian told him where she
was, but Marian promised not to tell. She held John's arm as they walked
toward her house. In front of the Oriental Saloon, she noticed the darkened
figure of a man in the shadows and a glint of something shiny in his hand —
the silver handle of a walking cane. It was dark and she couldn't see him
clearly, but she knew who it was. He saw her too and he knew who the soldier was. They didn't speak; two silent spirits passing in the night, their
presence known only to one another.

At the house, she saw the way John looked around. She knew he was
wondering how she could afford the house and furnishings. She was thankful he didn't ask. If he did, she'd have to tell him everything. Truth was
the one word that stuck in her mind. She was about to tell the truth about
everything, but she didn't want to start with Virgil. That would come soon
enough. John sat at the kitchen table while she made tea. He always sat
with her in the kitchen at his mother's house when she made tea. Her back
was to him as she poured hot water into the teapot. If only she could turn
back the hands of the clock to that wonderful place and time when life was
simple and happy. She'd do things different if she had another chance.
They'd be in their own kitchen making tea tonight. She'd be Mrs. John
Merrick and none of the events of the past few months would have happened. She placed the teapot and cups on a tray and they went to the parlour. Now, came the hard part.

Since she stopped him from apologizing in the Bird Cage, he hadn't
said much. He was waiting for her to tell him why she left New Orleans.
If he'd been wrong in thinking she left because he put off the wedding so
many times, she needed to tell him the real reason. She couldn't postpone
the inevitable conversation any longer. He sat in the chair, she on the sofa.
She poured his tea and stirred in a spoonful of sugar. When she passed the

cup to him, he smiled. "You remembered. I like a little sugar in my tea." She remembered a lot of things. That's why this conversation was going to be difficult. "How did you find me, John?" He drank some of the tea and set his cup and saucer on the table. Then, he leaned forward, clasping his hands and resting his arms on his legs. He stared at the roses in the carpet for a minute. Then, he sat back and crossed his arms. "I think you'd better start at the beginning, Rose. Why did you leave New Orleans?" He was right. She was the one who had to answer the questions, not him.

She took a deep breath and started talking. He listened intently while she told the story, beginning with her terrible ordeal in Ireland when she was sixteen. At first, she tried to pass over part of what happened in New Orleans. To simply say she'd been attacked was not the truth. She could tell by the way he looked at her he knew there was more to it. She told him everything and as she talked, she felt the weight of the world lifting from her shoulders. He'd probably go away for good when he knew the whole sordid story, but at least when it was over, she'd know she finally did the right thing. He didn't interrupt while she talked and when she finished, he stared at her. "Why didn't you wait for me? Did you really think I'd believe it was your fault? They had no right to hurt you. If you had told me, they would have been arrested and I would have seen to it they paid for their crime." She could hardly believe what she was hearing. He didn't blame her. He understood she'd been the victim, not the perpetrator and what's more, he would have gone after the ones who hurt her and made sure they were prosecuted. She made a terrible mistake by not having more faith in him and she complicated matters by running away. There was no way to go back now that she worked in a saloon, and worse. She had to tell him the rest and that would be the end of it.

"I'm sorry for runnin' away. I thought I ran because it would save you the embarrassment and pain of knowin', but I guess I was tryin' to save myself." She hung her head. "I can't ask you to forgive me." He moved to the sofa beside her and held her hands. As in times past, his touch sent a wave of excitement through her. She always felt he touched her spirit. He was doing it again. Tears were close. She studied his face, slightly lined around his eyes from being in the sun. His mother and father would be proud of him. He was every bit the success his mother said he'd be, and more. Her thoughts turned inward. She was a failure, a prostitute. She could never expect him to forgive that. His voice interrupted her thoughts. "There is nothing to forgive. What happened wasn't your fault and I understand why you left, but that was then. This is now. I love you, Rose. Nothing will ever change that." She had to make him understand. He had to know what she'd become in Tombstone. She tried to explain and he stopped her. "There's no need to say more. We can't change the past. We can only go forward from this time." He knew why she left New Orleans and he knew the kind of life she lived in Tombstone, and it didn't matter? He could forgive everything? She tried to tell him what she did for a living. She had to be sure he understood. Again, he stopped her. He was not a fool. What was done, was done. It was time for a new beginning.

If she was going to tell the truth, she had to tell him the rest. She had to tell him about Virgil. He'd think she'd been too quick to strike up a relationship with another man. She accepted some very large gifts from Virgil. The house and all the furnishings. Money. Special consideration was afforded her at work because of her involvement with him. She had protection around the clock because his men watched out for her. She'd been right about their inability to keep the clandestine affair secret for very long. There wasn't a person in Tombstone who didn't know about them. How could they not know? He visited her at the Bird Cage. He walked her home. He went to her house at night. She lived in the house he owned and he paid for everything, including dinner at a restaurant once a week and her account at Smith's General Merchandise. Despite the fact he no longer came to the house, she knew the reason she was treated different from other ladies who worked in the gambling halls and brothels was directly attributable to his influence. Women in town still snubbed her, but they'd become less vocal in recent weeks. She could pretty much go anywhere these days without running into the conflicts she encountered during the early days at the Bird Cage. She was met with a tolerance other ladies of the night did not enjoy. In fact, there were times when she felt that tolerance bordered on respect. She remembered how she laughed when she overheard a conversation in which she was the subject of discussion. They said that because of her association with Virgil Earp, she'd become a "respectable whore," an obvious contradiction of terms. Nevertheless, the statement was apropos.

How could she explain her involvement with Virgil to John? More than anything, Virgil had been her friend, the one person she could tell everything to. He made her life easier. He arranged for her to be watched over and protected when she walked the streets at night on her way home. Many times, she'd seen the men walk around her house, checking the yard and the street. They were his men. She never worried about intruders or vandals who terrorized the homes of other prostitutes. Her house was always safe from trespassers. Although she still worked at the Bird Cage, she didn't go upstairs anymore and she didn't have to put up with men crawling all over her. Her time was spent downstairs in the gambling hall. She talked with customers and sang more often on the stage. That was all Virgil's doing.

She liked to sing the Irish love songs and lullabies and she was learning some of the new songs. Charlie could play them all. He couldn't read a lick of music from paper, but he could play anything. She was fascinated by the way he knew which keys to strike. It was fun to sing when Charlie played the piano. He had a special touch, an affection for the instrument. Sometimes, they shouted for her to sing and when she did, the place became quiet as a cemetery. When the song was over, there wasn't a dry eye in the house. Grown men wiped away a tear, then roared their appreciation for her ability to stir such deep emotion in them. She never thought she sang very well, a little off key, but they loved to hear the Silver Rose. Thanks to Virgil, she'd become a celebrity of sorts. He'd done a lot for her. She didn't know how she would have survived without his help. He'd been her lover too, but they were not in love. Not the way she and John were in love. They provided an escape for each other from the rest of the world and the times. It was going to be difficult trying to explain that to John.

They talked late into the night. She did most of the talking and she didn't leave anything out. When she finished, he was quiet. Maybe she'd said too much. She didn't want to hurt him by telling him about her involvement with Virgil, but if she was to clean the slate, it all had to be said. She watched him stare at the carpet the way he did earlier. Now that she'd bared her soul, he might not be so willing to forgive her. There was more to forgive than when she started. A lot more. He was quiet for a long time, the impact of her story painfully evident, her words like a dagger piercing much more than his heart. She was sure his next words would be good-bye.

"It seems I owe Marshal Earp a debt of thanks." What was he saying? Again, she underestimated John Merrick. What man would forgive so unconditionally? He listened to every word she said. "I don't care what you've done, Rose. For years, I've been saying I love you. Were you not listening? Did you not understand? Or have you been through so much that you've purposely forgotten? Have I waited too long? Did you simply give up on me?" She started to answer and he interrupted. "Whatever the reason, it's behind us. I don't blame you for anything. There is nothing to forgive. The past is the past. I want you to go away with me after the trial." She didn't know what to say. After all she'd said and done, he still wanted her? Maybe he was the one who didn't understand. He kept talking. "I thought I'd lost you forever. Thank God, I found you." That brought up the question again. "How did you find me?" The serious look disappeared from his face. He moved closer and wiggled his eyebrows the way he used to do when he teased her on the porch of his mother's house in New York. He still had the roguish twinkle in his eye. She listened carefully as his mouth touched her ear. He whispered, "It's a secret." She closed her eyes, shaking her head with the realization that some things never change. Despite all that happened, he still had a sense of humor.

They lost themselves in the passion of the night, oblivious to the world outside and all things that went before. His kiss was gentle at first, then, more passionate. His touch produced a surge of energy and warmth that enveloped her. The feel of his skin against hers took her breath away. She closed her eyes. When she opened them, she was met with the steel-blue of his eyes, like the sharp blade of a dagger, penetrating clear through to her soul. He never looked at her. He looked inside her. She stopped breathing. Time stopped as their bodies moved to the rhythm of music only lovers hear; slowly at first, like willows swaying together gently in a summer breeze. Sensations intensified as the momentum and power of their passion increased, taking her to a height she'd never experienced before. She felt as though she were floating. She was overwhelmed with a sense of spirits embracing somewhere above the physical confines of human contact, in a dimension beyond anything known to mortal man.

In the midst of a wild place, a fragile space exits in Time for those who love; that space where memories are imprinted on two spirits, merged as one, never to be erased by mortal man or Time; the space that rests in the hand of God alone and is, therefore, untouchable by any other element. Where love overcomes all else, Time cannot erase the memories that love has made.

Many times, she wondered where the place was that the spirits of her father and mother lived, where the spirit of Ann Merrick lived. She knew such a place existed. She'd felt their presence often. She couldn't see them, but they were near. More times than she could remember, she thought about the place she drifted off to when she was a young girl in Ireland when the camp fires burned low. She never knew how she traveled there, but it was always a feeling of being lifted out of the body that sat by the fire. She wasn't sure if it was a dream, but she'd seen herself sitting by the fire as she flew away. She'd gone to a place of golden light and peace where she ran through meadows of soft grass in her bare feet, leaving earthly cares far behind. Something carried her there and she never resisted when she felt the gentle hand on hers, the hand of Annie Callahan perhaps. She always knew if she met John Merrick beyond this life, she'd recognize him. After this night, there would be no mistake in recognition. She'd know him anywhere; in the dark, with her eyes closed; in the life beyond. Their spirits had merged to form a connection that could never be severed. Long before he ever held her hand or kissed her, she felt the tie with him. She always had the feeling she'd been searching for him. When he reached out to save her from falling on the steps of his mother's house, the word that kept flashing through her mind was reunion. It was the strangest thought. She'd never seen him before that day, but the energy he directed into her when he touched her and kept her from falling was nothing less than familiar. She often thought about what it would be like when he finally made love to her. Now that he was as close as he could be, in the most intimate expression of love, the same thoughts were flying past her mind's eye, messages of recognition. Once again, it was the feeling of having been with him in another place and time.

They were exhausted. She awoke in the dark. A small stream of moonlight illuminated his face as he slept. She pulled the comforter over him. Looking at it, she recalled Ann's description of its construction — a blanket made from the feathers of a goose's behind. It was still funny and she put her hand over her mouth to keep from laughing out loud. He looked so peaceful in sleep. When his lips quivered, she wondered what he was dreaming. She turned her eyes upward and thanked God for bringing him back to her. She didn't deserve him. She suddenly felt cold. With all the love in the room, there was an ominous chill in the air, a sadness that surrounded her. She tried to push the feeling away. The room was dark. The moonlight was gone. She'd forgotten about Bear. He was where he always was at night, on the floor beside the bed. She tripped over the furry pile and he yipped. She got down on her knees and hugged the big dog, whispering she was sorry for stepping on him. She tried to be very quiet climbing back into bed. She looked at John. He was still asleep. At least her clumsiness hadn't wakened him. She breathed a quiet sigh of relief and closed her eyes. His arm was around her and she whispered she was sorry she woke him. He whispered too. "I love you, Rose. I'll always be yours."

Morning brought not only a new day, but a new beginning. When she opened her eyes, he was sitting in the rocking chair beside the bed, sipping his coffee. She stretched and inhaled deeply. The coffee smelled good. He set his cup on the bedside table. "I thought you were going to sleep all day." She'd been in the habit of sleeping most of the morning away since working so late at the Bird Cage. He left the room and returned with a cup for her. She piled the pillows behind herself and took the coffee. He sat in the chair. She sipped the coffee and closed her eyes, savoring the flavor. "You never answered my question. How did you find me?" He took a drink from his cup, but didn't answer. She asked again. "Are you goin' to tell me?" She had an annoying habit of persisting until she got what she wanted. It was quite irritating. He looked at her with an expression of complete innocense as if fully expecting her to believe the fairy-tale fib he was about to utter. "A little bird told me." She rolled her eyes up. "And by chance, was the little bird named Marian?" If anything, she was persistent. By the look on her face, he knew she wouldn't drop it until she got an answer. He stalled a little longer by taking another drink. "It's not her fault. I made her tell me." She was quiet. He leaned forward, holding his cup with both hands. "Someone else told me. Do you remember a man you met on the stage? A U.S. Marshal?" She did remember. He left her in Mesilla and went north to Colorado. He continued. "Matt Kern is an old friend. We went to school together in Boston. He decided not be a lawyer and took a job as a sheriff in Oklahoma. Next thing I heard, he was a U.S. Marshal. When Marian told me you went to Tombstone, I thought about Matt because he knew this part of the country. My telegram was waiting when he got to Oklahoma. He wired back that he'd met a pretty Irish girl in Texas and rode the stage with her into New Mexico Territory. As soon as he said she had the most beautiful red hair he'd ever seen and green eyes that sparkled like emeralds, I knew it had to be you. He said she was on her way to Tombstone and it didn't seem right. Shortly after that, I learned about this trial. I applied for the assignment, and here I am."

She dressed for work as usual. John was busy preparing for the trial that would begin in a week. Yesterday, she thought she'd be alone for the rest of her life. Never, in her wildest dreams, did she imagine she'd see John Merrick again. He reappeared as if by magic and today, her life was taking a different direction. All had been forgiven. She'd been given a second chance. After all she told him, he still loved her. She couldn't believe it, but he was here and she was going with him after the trial. In the middle of brushing her hair, she stopped, wondering if the situation had been reversed, if he'd been the one who left and done what she'd done, could she have found it in herself to be as forgiving? She said it over and over. He was an extraordinary man.

John would work long hours for the next few days getting ready for the trial. She went to the Bird Cage at seven o'clock the way she had for months. When she left the house, it seemed dark earlier than usual. The sky was black and heavy with rain clouds. A booming clap of thunder startled her and lightning flashed in the clouds. It made a loud crack when it hit the ground in a sizzling flash not far from the house. She pulled her shawl over her head and quickened her step. It was the middle of March and still cool. When the sky looked this bad, it promised a deluge not far off. A block away, a fine sprinkle of rain began falling. She started to run. As she reached the Bird Cage, lightning crackled again, closer this time. Claps of thunder followed one another, echoing through the hills as they rolled across the desert and slammed into the town. She barely made it to the back door of the theatre when the sky opened up. If she'd left the house one minute later, she'd have been drenched. In no time, the rain and wind grew into a fierce spring storm. Even with the noise inside, she could hear the rain falling in torrents on the building. From the front window, she watched the sudden downpour turn Allen Street into a giant mud puddle. She'd seen these storms before. They came up fast and furious. In a matter of minutes, a thunderstorm of this magnitude would turn the desert into a lake. Unless it passed over quickly, she'd be walking home in water up to her ankles.

They'd all seen her leave with John the night before. Lizzie was the first to find her, taking her hand as usual and rattling off one question after another. "Who is he? How do you know him? He's so handsome. What's his name? Why is he here? He's an officer, isn't he? I can tell by the stripes on his coat and those little gold things on his collar." She would have kept going if someone hadn't stopped her. "Lizzie, let her catch her breath for Heaven's sake." It was Abby. Rose bit her lower lip to keep the smile from coming too fast. All the girls were standing around by that time. She couldn't hold back. "John Merrick. He is John Merrick." No one said a word, not even Lizzie. They all knew about him, but he was like a character in a fairy tale, a figment of imagination. No one ever really expected to see him. She went on. "His aunt told him where I went. He has a friend, a U.S. Marshal from Oklahoma. John went to the university with him. I met him on the stage comin' here. He told John about his meetin' me." No one said anything and Rose threw up her hands. "I can't believe it either." Lizzie was the first to speak. "It's a miracle. That's what it is, you know — a miracle! Miracles really do happen. I know they do and..." She rattled on about miracles until she caught Abby's look. Realizing what she was doing, she stopped in the middle, lowering her head. Abby was the only one who could make her stop with a look. They had to hear all about him, but not right now. Ruby was giving them an evil eye from across the room. When Ruby put her hands on her hips and scowled that way, she meant business. She didn't have to say a word. They got the message. Get back to work. There'd be time to talk later.

Rain continued to fall on into the night, showing no sign of letting up. Rose was sitting at a table on the far side of the room when two men rushed through the door. Out of breath and dripping wet, they went straight to the table where the doctor and his friends were watching the show. They spoke only briefly to him. He was on his feet, grabbing his coat and hurrying to the door. He ran outside with no thought for the downpour, pulling on his coat along the way. The others at his table left their full glasses and dashed out into the rain behind him. She was alarmed at how fast they left. The delivered message was obviously a medical emergency of an extremely urgent nature. She followed them to the front door. The rain was falling in torrents, covering the windows in rolling sheets of water. She could barely see them running down the other side of the street towards Virgil's office. Her first thought was that something happened to Virgil again. She wanted to follow them, but the street was flooded and it was raining harder than she'd ever seen it. She couldn't risk getting wet and taking a chill, not after the pneumonia. She hadn't fully recovered from the last bout of illness yet. She'd have to wait to hear the bad news, and she knew it would be bad.

She didn't have to wait long. The bearer of bad news was soaked, water running off the brim of his hat and dripping on the floor as he stood near the bar making his terrible announcement. He shouted that one of the Earps had been shot. "He ain't dead yet, but he's fast bleedin' out. Doc Goodfellow says he's gut-shot through the back and can't be saved. Blood's flowin' out of him like a river. He's probably in company with his Maker by now." She was overtaken by panic. It was an old nightmare happening all over. Someone tried to kill one of the Earps again. "Which one?" She still couldn't get the name. She tugged at his arm. "Who is shot?" He kept yelling that it was cold-blooded murder and the Marshal was calling for a posse to go after the killers. People began running out into the rain. The man turned to follow the crowd and she held tight to his arm with both hands, shaking his arm and shouting at him. "Tell me! Who is shot? Which Earp?" He pried her hands off and headed for the door. She screamed after him, "Who is it?" On his way through the door, he called back over his shoulder, "The young one. Morgan." His voice trailed off as he ran out into the downpour. She whispered the name. "Morgan." She closed her eyes and breathed a sigh of relief. It was Morgan who was shot, not Virgil. She was ashamed of herself for feeling relieved. Had her heart become so cold that she dared think one life was less important than another? It was this place. Tombstone. It changed people. The town had a spirit of its own. She felt the evil in this place when she got off the stage, and the first morning, she awoke to the crack of gunfire and saw a man dying in the street beneath her window. Tonight, the town had taken another good man. This time it was a real tragedy. Why was it always the good ones? Morgan was one of the good ones. He was young. He had a wife. He had a future, so much to live for. His life was taken away by a bullet, fired by a coward who hid in the dark and shot him in the back.

They said it happened in Campbell and Hatch's where he was playing billiards. He was getting ready to take his shot when the bullet hit him in the side, rupturing his kidney and perforating his spine before passing through out the front of him, tearing a hole in his stomach to conclude its deadly journey. He lost a lot of blood too fast to repair the damage. The rotten bastards didn't even give him a fair chance to fight back. Too many hated the Earps. They had enemies everywhere. She blamed Wyatt and Virgil for this heartbreaking catastrophe, more than likely a retaliation for Morgan's part in the O. K. Corral shootout a few months back. Some said Morgan put the bullet in Tom McLaury's head that hastened Tom's departure from this world. Although Tom didn't have a gun that day, he was smack in the middle of the fracas and Morgan claimed he didn't know Tom was unarmed. When the bullets started flying, he said he was firing wild and never really aimed at anyone. The younger brother would still be alive if they hadn't pulled him into their business. Lawmen. Damn them! She was sick to her stomach. It happened every time. They said she'd get used to it, but they were wrong. She never did. Never would. Death was part of life, but the kind of death doled out in Tombstone, like a bad hand in a poker game, was sickening. It was senseless. Mindless. If she lived to be a hundred, she'd never understand the killing. It would always make her sick. They said it was bad. He was still alive when the news came, but bleeding to death. That was ten minutes ago. He was probably gone by now. She closed her eyes and thought about Morgan. She heard that he had a bad temper, but she never saw that side of him and had a hard time believing it. The few times she'd seen him, he was nice to her. She prayed that he didn't suffer.

Thunder rolled and the wind slammed the rain sideways against the building like rounds of rapidly-fired bullets from a Gatling gun. It was late. She wondered what time it was. Someone touched her shoulder and she turned around. John was beside her, his clothes wringing wet. Before he said the words, she knew. "I just came from Hatch's. Morgan's dead." She braced herself against the tears and brushed at the water on the front of his coat with her fingers. "You're soaked. You'd better dry off before you catch pneumonia. There's a stove in the other room." She turned to lead the way and he stopped her. "You can cry if you want to, Rose." She was so stubborn. "What makes you think I want to cry?" He went on. "I met Virgil tonight. They called him right away when Morg was shot. He told me you thought highly of his brother." There was no use fighting the tears. This was a terrible loss. She leaned against John and cried for Morgan.

The trial had begun. On the first day, Rose saw the Indian boy, Nalanche, across the street. She asked John to wait while she went to speak to the boy. A few minutes later, they crossed over to the Courthouse together and she introduced him to John. When John extended his hand, Nalanche made no move to engage in the handshake, instead, scrutinizing John to determine whether he was friend or enemy. Past experience with white soldiers taught him they were adversaries, not to be trusted. It was white soldiers who devastated his people and killed his father, but this soldier was not white. Except for the blue eyes, he was an Indian — Apache. Rose prompted him. "Remember what I told you, Nalanche." He shook John's hand. John thanked him for looking after Rose and said he was honored to meet such a valued friend of hers. He hoped they would also become friends. She nudged the boy with her elbow to solicit a response. "Rose is my friend. I am pleased to meet you, Sir." John's approval of the boy's formality was obvious. He knew she'd been working with the boy, teaching him manners and to speak English. Her efforts were paying off in both areas. He spoke excellent English and was very polite. He was clean and his hair was combed and he was dressed appropriately for Court in a long-sleeved shirt, buttoned all the way down and tucked into his belt. She laid her hand on John's arm. "Do you suppose Nalanche might sit with me in the courtroom, John? He's very interested in the law you know. He might even be a lawyer himself one day." She fluttered her eyelashes and John restrained a smile. He spoke to Nalanche without letting on he knew Rose set the whole thing up. "Really? A lawyer! I didn't know. In that case, you are certainly welcome to observe the proceedings, Nalanche. After the trial, perhaps you'll tell me what you thought about it." The boy didn't answer. Rose raised her eyebrows. She didn't want to have to nudge him again to make him talk. "Thank you, Sir. I will listen good." John nodded his approval and Rose breathed a sigh of relief. Time spent teaching him hadn't been wasted. John had a funny look on his face and she knew what he was thinking. "Sir?" The boy addressed him as "Sir." An Indian who showed respect for an Army officer. Very impressive, indeed. He'd met a lot of white boys who weren't as respectful as this young man. Rose had done better than he thought. Truth was, she'd probably worked something close to a miracle with the Apache. He wasn't surprised. Nothing she ever did surprised him.

Her look triggered Nalanche's next move. He held his arm for her and John saw the little wink she gave the boy when she linked her arm through his. She tilted her chin up and dusted the air with her hand to wave John on ahead. "Lead the way, Captain." She was good at giving orders. He obeyed and took the first step. His aide saluted and opened the door to the courthouse, so new, the smell of fresh paint and varnish lingered on the air. His hands were full, an attaché in one and a book in the other. He nodded his acknowledgment of the salute, thinking as he walked ahead that the girl with the red hair and emerald eyes behind him had more in mind for the Apache boy than teaching him simple manners. So, he wanted to be a lawyer, did he? Wonder where he got that idea. Amazing how an Apache, at most sixteen years old and not long from the desert where he lived alone for God only knew how long before Rose adopted him, would have decided, all by himself, to be a lawyer someday. How would a boy like that even know what a lawyer was? If he knew any English at all when he first came into town, it couldn't have been more than a few words picked up from traders passing through Indian land. No, observation of this trial was not just an interesting way to pass a morning, nor was it coincidence that found the boy standing across the street when they arrived at the court-house. There was a lot more to it. The entire scene was staged and Act One was about to begin.

Rose brought the boy to the courthouse today with specific intentions, to have him watch the trial. She'd made the decision to educate Nalanche long before John came back and her plan was already in motion. His future had been carefully mapped and every step of the way was planned. The direction he'd take was engineered in a straight line. It was her doing that got him into school over strong objections from the mothers of white children. Caroline Grants led the opposition, but her contention that Indians had no business in school was squelched when Wyatt and the mayor himself showed up at the school board meeting and put Caroline in her place. Nalanche was allowed to attend class. Rose figured the letter she asked Doc to deliver to Virgil did the trick. He said if she needed anything, all she had to do was ask. She wouldn't have asked for herself, but Nalanche deserved the chance to go to school. She recognized the boy's intelligence early on and saw the potential in him to make something of himself. Virgil saw it too. There was something about him that bespoke a wisdom far beyond his sixteen years, and the positive qualities so lacking in human nature among most men were abundant in him. That was apparent by the light that surrounded him, an aura that could only come from within one who was entirely good, the same light she saw around John. He was a lover of nature and a believer in what was right. A gentle spirit. Despite his youth and nonviolent temperament, he wasn't afraid to stand up for what he believed in, a rare quality not found in many men. There were none of the failings or weaknesses she saw in other men either. He was ready to give up his life to save the life of a tiny, helpless creature because he knew it was the right thing to do. If not for his bravery, Little Bear would be dead. Maybe it was that she recognized something of herself in him that day when he was attacked in the street and showed his strength of character in protecting the dog. Maybe they were two of a kind. Whatever the reason, she'd come to love the boy as a brother and she had great plans for him. Today, she'd open a door to the future for one who had heretofore been a child of the desert and a brother to the wild coyoté. He already possessed the inherent characteristics that would make him successful. By watching this trial, he'd see what an education could do for a man who had his eye on the future. What better example for him to follow than John Merrick.

Rose didn't go to work during the trial. John needed the evenings to work on the case and if she was at the Bird Cage, she knew he wouldn't be able to concentrate. He'd be worried about her, so he'd be there every night, taking away from his time to work and rest. It was easier for him if she stayed home. She didn't want anything to jeopardize his courtroom performance, and that meant getting enough sleep. He had to be able to do his job without distractions and convince the jury which way the verdict should go. While he worked at the kitchen table, she watched quietly. She was fascinated by what he did. She always knew he was smart, but she had no idea what he could really do until she saw him in action. He was a dynamic speaker and his voice resonated throughout the courtroom. When he paused to give the jury a chance to think about what he said after making an important point, you could hear a pin drop. She watched Nalanche leaning forward with his elbows on his knees, his chin resting on folded hands. He was listening intently, absorbed in the trial and fascinated by John's presentation. At one point, John turned and faced the spectators to emphasize a statement. He looked straight at Nalanche, holding the position as though speaking directly to the boy and establishing a connection with him. She was sure that's what he was doing. It was no less intense at home with John and his assistant going over the day's testimony and planning the next day's strategy. Nalanche sat at the table with the two lawyers, taking in every word they said while Rose curled up on the sofa with the dog at her feet, equally captured by the drama.

Throughout the trial, Rose was never sure what the outcome would be. John had his work cut out for him. The defendants had witnesses who corroborated their alibi, but John was smarter. He was clever, asking questions designed to catch them in their lies, questions she would have never thought to ask. Before they went to bed, he and Nalanche sat at the kitchen table, talking about the case. The boy had an uncanny ability to understand the process and John encouraged him to speak his ideas. Rose was glad Nalanche was there. Recuperation from the pneumonia was taking a long time and she tired easily. When she needed to rest, John and the boy talked. She'd gotten wet on the way home the night Morgan was shot and taken a chill. Since then, she'd been fighting a case of the sniffles and some congestion in her chest. Worried about getting sick again, she asked the doctor for another bottle of the medicinal syrup she hated so much and was taking it faithfully every day. The odor of creosote oil permeated the house from all the steam pans she fixed to breathe the vapors. She remembered the doctor's warning. It wouldn't take much for pneumonia to set in and next time, she might not be so lucky. She had to be very careful. She shouldn't have been going to the courthouse every day. She should have stayed home and rested, but she couldn't stay away. On the fourth day, she was relieved. The trial was over and it didn't take the jury long to find the accused guilty as charged — all of them. John had performed brilliantly. The convicted murderers mad-dogged him as the verdict was read and he looked them each in the eye, unmoved when the Court passed sentence on them. Their vicious looks and the threats he knew they'd make on the way out didn't scare him. He didn't care who they were or who their friends were who would retaliate after they were hung. The innocent victims who died at the hands of these killers couldn't be brought back, but retribution would be swift. The cowards who robbed a federal bank and killed three unarmed people would hang. If nothing else, the murdered souls could rest in peace and their grieving families would know that justice had been served. John was satisfied. He closed his attaché and his aid gathered the books. When he came through the gates to the spectator section, Nalanche was waiting to shake his hand. There was no longer any hesitation. The past few days in court and the nights of John drawing the boy into the circle of confidence by respect for his thoughts solidified a bond that would never be broken. Moreover, Rose accomplished what she aimed to do by bringing the boy to witness the trial. In less than half a day of watching and listening, he made up his mind. He'd be a lawyer someday alright. All that remained was the education and she'd already started the wheels in motion to that end.

The trial was over and John's orders were in hand for the next assignment. He was talking about California. They'd have to leave in two days. She'd like the ocean. He was excited about taking her. She closed her eyes as he talked. She was tired and not up to making the trip. There would be a military escort taveling with him and she'd be a burden because she needed to rest more often than they'd want to stop. His spirit was high and he talked about the trip and how they'd be married afterward, but they didn't have to wait that long. They could get married tomorrow by the Justice right here in Tombstone. All day, she'd been trying to think of a way to tell him she didn't feel strong enough to make the trip. Even if she made it to California in one piece, there'd be the trip back to Washington, and that was clear across the country, providing the Army didn't decide to send him someplace else first. That would mean a lot of traveling. It wasn't only that she was still recovering from the pneumonia. There was the consumption. She hadn't told him about it. She finally said it — part of it anyway. "I can't go with you. My health is not good since the pneumonia. I'm not strong enough and I'm easily caught in short breath. And then, there's the ...coughin'." She started to say "consumption." She didn't finish the sentence. Maybe it was better left unsaid for now. To tell him about the blood she coughed up and the doctor's diagnosis of tuberculosis would cause him undue worry while he was in California. It could wait until he came back. He didn't say anything for several minutes. Abby told him about the pneumonia and how Rose almost died. He must not have realized how much the sickness had taken out of her. What did she propose they do? He had to go. The Army would court-martial him if he disobeyed orders. The only solution she could offer was that she stay in Tombstone until his California duty was done. He didn't like the idea at all. There had to be another way. She repeated that the trip would be much too taxing on her health. Through the mountains, the weather would be cold and there might even be snow. Breathing that cold air would surely result in more sickness for her and she never wanted to be sick again. He thought about it and finally agreed to her staying in Tombstone on one condition, that she stop working at the Bird Cage. She couldn't continue entertaining men. She let out a big sigh. It wasn't that easy. She couldn't stop working. She had to support herself and... John was adamant. She had to quit. It was absurd to think she could work in a gambling hall and bordello anymore even if all she did was sing. He'd arrange for her to have enough money while he was gone, but she had to stay away from the Bird Cage. She'd have plenty to keep her busy. There was the packing. She had to be ready to go when he came back. She could take her time and rest when she needed to. He figured a month to six weeks should get him back to Tombstone. Then, they'd go to New Orleans for a visit with Marian and Rebecca and from there, to Washington.

The prospect of seeing Marian and Rebecca again brought tears. It sounded wonderful and exciting. She'd like to live in New Orleans, or

Washington, if that's where the Army kept him. It didn't matter as long as they were together. He talked about resigning his commission and setting up a private practice. If he decided to do that, they might go to Tucson. The climate would be healthier for her than New Orleans or Washington. He even suggested staying in Tombstone. The way the town was growing, it could always use another lawyer. The only reason he joined the Army was to please his father, but he'd much rather have been in private practice. He'd kept his promise to his father and served his country the way his father believed every man should. Finding her was not the only reason he was thinking of leaving the military. Maybe it was time to make himself happy. Rose touched his face. "Whatever you decide to do, I'll be with you." His words were apprehensive. "Wait for me this time."

They stood in the road at the edge of town watching the column ride away until the soldiers were out of sight. When they were gone, she turned to the boy. "Do you think I made a mistake? Should I have gone with him?" He started walking and she ran to catch up. She took his hand. Unlike earlier days when he wouldn't let her touch him, he held her hand. "Nalanche, did I do the right thing?" He stopped walking, but looked straight ahead. She had her answer.

When she told them she was done working at the Bird Cage, they gathered around and took turns hugging her and wishing her luck. Luck was an element they knew all too well and she was truly one of the lucky ones. Their lives were like a card game that never stopped. Some days were a royal flush. Other times, you couldn't hit a pair, let alone three of a kind, if you played the game all day and all night for a month. There was no plan or scheme to what they did. For them, in a literal sense, it was wherever the cards fell that determined the events of their lives. She had beaten the odds and been rescued from the game of chance they played. It was rare that one of them was offered a way out, but the way was clear for her. They were still prisoners of circumstance. She was free.

They all talked at once, excited and happy at the prospect of the future that awaited her. Even Ruby couldn't resist joining in the celebration. She grabbed Rose and lifted her off her feet, swinging her around in a circle as a child would swing a rag doll. Rose was embarrassed. Ruby wasn't one to put on a show of affection toward the girls. She let out an unladylike "Eeh Hah" whoop like a cowboy rounding up strays from the herd. By the time she put Rose down, they were all laughing. For awhile, they forgot where they were. It was a time to celebrate the good fortune of a friend. They were her friends. If nothing else, she was sure of that. Like their own, her dreams had fallen like shooting stars, disintegrating on their fiery earthbound path to die. Broken dreams were the reason they were all here. They kept their dreams deep inside, never daring to let them too close to the surface for fear they'd fly away and there'd be nothing left. They lived day-to-day with no thought for the future. How many times had she said the words in her own mind? Resignation of destiny. They were all resigned to their destiny. Her dreams had been resurrected by love and were streaking across the sky, a glowing comet burning brighter and brighter, racing toward the future. Lizzie was right. What happened to her was nothing short of a miracle.

After the initial celebration following her announcement, the excitement died down and the laughter faded. The impact of her good news created a euphoria they were all momentarily caught up in, but when reality set in, the blanket of sad resignation lay over them once again. Rose was about to move on to better things, but their lives hadn't changed. She looked at downturned faces and from Lizzie, tears. Abby hugged Rose. "You know we're happy for you. We love you and you'll be missed." Jenny and Eva were next. They hugged her and tried to smile. She told them she would write and come back to visit. They were quiet. They knew when she left, they'd never see her again. Those who were lucky enough to leave didn't return to the Bird Cage. She was a prisoner on the brink of parole. They would remain prisoners until the silver gave out or they died. They stood in silence, Abby and Ruby each holding one of Rose's hands, like mourners gathered together at the wake of a friend to say a final good-bye. Saying good-bye would not be easy. Lizzie didn't say anything. No one noticed her walking off alone, crying. A couple of hours later, Jenny realized she was missing. No one knew where she went. Jenny decided to run to the house. When she came back, she was very worried. Lizzie was nowhere to be found. She wasn't in the Bird Cage and she wasn't at the house. Jenny had gone up and down Allen Street and couldn't find her. They'd been so careful with her. Someone always knew where she was, but tonight the rule about keeping track of her fell through the cracks and Lizzie slipped away unnoticed. It wasn't like her to go off without telling a soul. She never wanted to be alone. She'd always had trouble dealing with life, getting upset and confused over the silliest things. Silly to other people maybe, normal people, but not silly to Lizzie. What appeared as a small bump in the road to others might look like a mountain to Lizzie, the simple way around it never occurring to her. Whenever things became too difficult, she invented situations to take her away. You never knew what to expect. She was different every day. Virgil said Lizzie was like a goose. She woke up in a different world every morning. In the past, when life became intolerable, she took to hurting herself and even tried to kill herself once. Jenny knew her better than anyone. She lived with Lizzie and her changing moods. "We have to find Lizzie. I'm afraid Rose's news has upset her. She doesn't know how to handle things like this." They all agreed. Someone had to find her before she did something drastic. Ruby was the first to admit it wasn't good for Lizzie to be alone tonight. They shouldn't have let her out of their sight. The rest of them would take care of business. Jenny and Abby would look for Lizzie.

Midnight. Abby and Jenny still weren't back. Rose felt a tugging at her arm. It was Nalanche. Her eyes opened wide in horror. There was blood all over his clothes and hands. He spoke quietly, but there was great urgency in his voice. "Come home. It is your friend with yellow hair, the one of many faces. She is very sick from the tolguacha." She didn't understand. "Tolguacha? What is tolguacha?" His jaw muscles flexed and he narrowed his eyes. "Bad medicine." The way he said it gave her goose-flesh. She squeezed his arm. "How bad?" He didn't answer. "How bad, Nalanche? What did she do? What is the tolguacha?" He took her hand and led her outside. "She has visions of the black bird. The evil one. She sees the dark spirits. They take her mind. She does not know who she is or what she says." Rose's mouth fell open. "You mean she sees things? She took medicine that's makin' her see things that aren't there?" He shook his head, yes. "There is much blood. She is weak." The thought of what Lizzie might have done to herself sent another chill through her. "Blood! Did she shoot herself?" There wasn't time to explain. Much blood meant Lizzie tried to kill herself. That was all Rose had to know. Lizzie must have shot herself or cut her wrists. She'd tried it once before. Rose held the boy's hand and they ran all the way to her house.

Running brought on a coughing spell and Rose stopped outside the gate to catch her breath. Light shone through the windows and they heard voices coming from inside. There was a small black carriage parked in front. It was the young doctor's rig. She went to the porch. What she saw caused an automatic reflex. Her hand went over her mouth. The sight turned her stomach and she felt sick. The floor and front door were smeared with blood and there was more on the steps and porch rail. She walked up the steps slowly, wondering how anyone who lost that much blood could still be alive. It looked like there'd been a massacre on her front porch. Nalanche opened the door and she stood in the doorway. Abby and Jenny were in the parlour. They'd been crying. They came to her and put their arms around her. Jenny sobbed out loud. Rose stood with her arms at her sides, in shock. Voices were coming from the other room. Someone was wailing in the bedroom, then, a pathetic scream like a rabid animal, crying out for relief from the worse kind of suffering imaginable. Rose stared at the bedroom door, listening to the young doctor's quiet voice. He was speaking softly, trying to calm and comfort someone. She pushed Jenny away and moved toward the bedroom. Abby touched her arm. "Don't go in there, Rose. The doctor and his wife are here and they'll take care of her. You can't help her anyway." Another bloodcurdling scream sent chills through her and set Jenny to crying. Nalanche stepped in front of her. She turned to her friend. "My God, Abby. What happened? What did she do to herself?" Nalanche took Jenny outside. Abby put her arm around Rose and led her to the couch. "Sit down." Rose glanced back toward the bedroom. Abby said it again. "Sit. I'll tell you as much as I know. The doctor will have to tell us the rest when he comes out."

They sat together, holding hands while Abby talked. "Nalanche found her in the yard out of her mind, saying crazy things, and bleeding something awful. She was cursing and talking about devils and wild animals eating her flesh. She had a straight razor and she cut her wrists. She sliced her face up pretty bad too." Rose shuddered. Abby continued the story. "Nalanche wrapped her wrists up tight to slow the bleeding. She didn't know who he was and from what he says, I guess she fought him until she finally passed out. Jenny had an idea she might come here. Lucky we came by when we did. We stayed with her while Nalanche ran for the doctor and his wife. They came right away. She lost a terrible lot of blood. The doc said Nalanche saved her life by wrapping up her wrists like he did, but that stuff she ate made her crazy. She doesn't know what she's saying. She's wild out of her mind. The doctor had an awful time sewing her up. I don't think she felt it though, screaming and fighting him the way she was." Abby shook her head. "Losing so much blood, I don't know where she got the strength to fight, but it took three of us to hold her down. I never knew Lizzie was so strong. She spit at the doctor and tried to bite him, but the poor man kept right on sewing. He told us to hold her down tight so he could sew and he talked real nice to her all the while she was calling him terrible mean names and trying to bite him. I never heard Lizzie talk that way before. Anyway, the man's a saint. He's got a lot of patience. He did some pretty fancy stitchery on her too. He's been in there talking to her for a long time and she's calming down. You should've heard her when he first got here. I guess maybe that crazy stuff is wearing off some by now." Rose felt terrible. "This is all my fault, Abby. I should've known Lizzie would be upset when I told her I was leavin'. There was a better way to let her know, a gentler way. I should have taken the time to help her understand. It took her by surprise and put her into one of her moods. I'll never forgive myself." Rose closed her eyes and lowered her head. Abby put her arm around Rose. "Don't blame yourself. You know how Lizzie is. It's not the first time she's done something like this. Anything can set her off. This is not your fault."

Jenny and Nalanche came back inside. The screams and cursing disintegrated into whimpers and the doctor emerged from the bedroom, drying his hands on a towel and noticeably strained from the ordeal. His white shirt was covered with blood. He blew out a breath of relief and stood for a minute looking thoughtfully at the two blue birds. One of them chirped and he touched the cage with his finger, telling them they were pretty. Shaking his head, he finished drying his hands. "I don't know why she didn't bleed to death before you found her. She lost a lot of blood. If it hadn't been for that Indian kid tying the tourniquets on her, she'd have been dead hours ago. He saved her life. I'm concerned she might try it again though. She's pretty upset. Somebody will have to stay with her every minute." Jenny answered right away. "We'll make sure there's someone here. We won't leave her alone." The doctor's expression was grim. "I don't mean just until she heals. I mean all the time, from now on. She's a very disturbed young woman. From what you told me, her mind wasn't right before this. I think it might be worse now that she has an idea she's being deserted by a friend." The girls told him what Lizzie's reaction had been to Rose's earlier announcement at the Bird Cage and he knew why Lizzie went over the edge. What he said made Rose feel worse than ever. He quickly tried to clarify his meaning. "She doesn't have the ability to understand how the world changes, that circumstances in her own life change. She wants everything to remain the same, day after day. Change frightens her. Your leaving is a change. It could have happened over anything. For example, they tell me she always works the same hours." Abby answered. "That's right. Her hours never vary, and she's always there right on time every night. She never misses a night's work either. She wouldn't know what to do if her routine changed the least little bit." The doctor nodded his understanding. "My point, exactly." He turned to Rose. "Do you see what I mean? It didn't have to be something as significant as you leaving. It could have been a simple thing like a change in her work hours." Rose understood. She knew Lizzie and she knew what he said was true. She just wished her news hadn't caused it to happen this time. The doctor kept talking. "She's been hallucinating for a couple hours from the tolguacha. It's a powerful drug. The Indians use it to induce visions during ceremonial rituals. My guess is she took a good-sized dose and it might have done some permanent damage to her brain. You need to make sure she doesn't get hold of any more of it. By the way, it wouldn't be a bad idea to hide the kitchen knives or other sharp utensils — razors or the like." The girls already thought of that. The doctor's wife came out of the bedroom. She was a petite woman in her late twenties. The last couple of hours had been a strain for her too. She smiled, but looked very tired. "You can go in, but please don't stay long. She needs to rest." Rose stared at her. The woman's dress had been soaked all down the front with Lizzie's blood.

They stood beside the bed, Abby and Jenny on one side, Rose on the other. Lizzie's eyes were closed and her face was ashen. Both wrists were wrapped with bandages covering her arms all the way to the elbows. Her face was swollen and bruised from falling in the yard and ugly cuts on both cheeks and her forehead were freshly closed with sutures. The area around the black stitches was red. Her hair was wet where the doctor's wife cleaned the blood away. A tear rolled down Rose's cheek as she brushed her fingers across Lizzie's forehead. Poor Lizzie. She was such a lost soul. Lying there all bandaged up and bruised, she looked more helpless and pathetic than usual. Her eyelashes fluttered and she opened her eyes halfway. Her lids were heavy and she squinted to focus on the people next to the bed. She was too weak to raise a hand. When she tried to speak, nothing more than a small whimper came out. Rose brushed Lizzie's hair away from her face. "Don't try to talk, Lizette. You have to get well. You have to get strong again. Then, we'll talk." Tears poured from Lizzie's eyes. Rose tried to dry them, but they kept coming. She didn't cry out loud, only tears, running down her face to the pillow. Rose kissed Lizzie's forehead. "Don't worry, I'll be here for us to talk when you're feelin' better. I'm not goin' anywhere yet and if I do, you must remember I'll always be your friend, Lizzie. I'll come to visit you, or you can come to

Washington to visit me. We'll never say good-bye for good. We'll still see each other." Lizzie looked up at Rose. "Will you promise to come and see me? Promise?" She was a frightened child. Lizzie's fingers protruded from the bandages and Rose held them gently, smiling at the pleading, tearful face. "I promise, Lizette. I promise to come and see you." Rose's reassurance made everything alright. Was it really that easy? Lizzie let out a broken sigh and closed her eyes.

When John left, she wondered how she'd keep busy now that she didn't work at the Bird Cage anymore. Lizzie was the answer to that. Taking care of Lizzie made the time pass quickly. They talked every day about Rose leaving and every day, it got a little easier. Gradually, Lizzie was accepting it and talked about the visits Rose promised they'd have. Jenny and the girls helped by talking to her. They brought gifts and food, and the doctor's wife stopped in to see how she was doing every day. Nalanche performed his magic tricks while she sat on the porch swing. Never empty-handed, Jenny came every day with a small present, a flower or ribbon for her hair; a tiny, porcelain cat painted with pink rosebuds. She got plenty of attention. Everyone assured her she wasn't alone. When Rose left, she'd still have friends and they'd write letters together and take turns visiting Washington. They knew that while she laughed, it was only a matter of time until the next episode. It was all part of the affliction of her mind. All they could do was take one day at a time with Lizzie and hope for the best.

Rose sat at the kitchen table sipping her coffee and thinking about the way they always helped each other. They did have a common bond, the girls from the Bird Cage. She was going to miss them. Funny how they were labeled wild and tawdry woman of easy virtue; soiled doves, prostitutes — notorious ladies of the night. The bad girls of Tombstone. She smiled. They were all of those things. There was no denying any of it. But they were something else. You had to be one of them to understand. Once you got through the face paint and rough language, there was more to them than most people ever knew. If you were one of them or if you were someone they called a friend, they'd do anything for you. When she was sick, she didn't have to ask for help. They were there, bringing food, taking turns sitting with her so Abby could have a break, cleaning the house, taking care of Bear. Abby! How did she ever get so lucky as to have a friend like

Abby? She wondered how many people in the world had a friend like Abigail Treneaux. She was more than lucky. She was blessed.

Her thoughts were interrupted by Lizzie setting her cup on the table. As usual, she clanked it down hard. Those little irritating habits used to be cause for Rose to scold Lizzie, but it didn't bother her anymore. Lizzie pulled up a chair. "Are you the famous Rose Callahan? I've heard all about you." She was mimicking what Virgil said when he introduced himself to Rose. Rose played along. "Well now, I don't know about the famous part, but I am Rose Callahan." Lizzie laughed. She was being her old self today. It had been a little more than two weeks since she'd attempted suicide. She'd felt hopelessly lost and confused, abandoned by Rose's news. Rose looked at Lizzie's smiling face. This morning, there was not so much as a hint of what might have caused her to feel so miserable that night she wanted to die. It always took a minute to determine Lizzie's state of mind. It changed frequently and without warning, and after what happened, Rose didn't want to say anything to upset her. This time, she was smiling and talking a mile a minute when she sat down at the kitchen table. Rose knew the mood could change in a heartbeat and turn the laughter and gay chatter to tears. Lizzie had regained her strength and her wounds were healing well. She turned her arms over for Rose to inspect the scars. Considering the damage she'd done to herself, the doctor performed a virtual miracle with his sewing. The scars on her face would never disappear completely and Rose said one of her silent prayers that no unkind or unthinking person would mention them to Lizzie. That could be the thing to set her off again. This morning, she was babbling like the Lizzie they all knew so well. Jenny convinced her to go back to the house they shared, so she'd be going home today. In only two weeks' time, she'd accumulated a lot of stuff. Between the presents brought in by friends, clothes dropped off by Jenny, and various sundries and possessions from home, including a calico-cloth cat with green-glass button eyes who Lizzie insisted couldn't sleep without her, Rose's bedroom was getting a little cramped. She'd given up her room to Lizzie and was sleeping in Nalanche's room. She didn't mind at all, but now that Lizzie was going home, she was looking forward to a good night's sleep in her own bed.

Lizzie stopped jabbering and looked down into her coffee mug. The smile was gone. Rose was ready. She was always ready for sudden changes in Lizzie's temperament. By the look on her face, Rose thought Lizzie was troubled about something. It came out the way Lizzie always blurted things out, like an unexpected blast from a double-barreled shotgun. "Can I tell you something, Rosie?" Rose cringed. She remembered all the times she'd scolded Lizzie for calling her Rosie. She couldn't scold her now. Lizzie continued before Rose could answer the question. "I'm grateful to you for taking care of me, but your bed is way too hard. My back is killing me." Rose sat back in her chair. "That's all? My bed's too hard?" She laughed out loud. "Dear me, Lizzie. I'm truly sorry. I wish you'd told me sooner."

Rose watched Lizzie dump three spoons of sugar into her coffee. It was a miracle the girl survived life at the Bird Cage. It was a miracle she'd lived this long at all. Although a beautiful woman, they all looked upon her as a child and because of the illness in her mind, the girls felt a shared responsibility to watch over and protect her, a perfect example behind their reasoning being her recently attempted suicide. How in the world did she come to be a prostitute anyway? Knowing Lizzie and the afflictions of her mind, Rose never understood how such a fragile creature tolerated this kind of life. Maybe it was where she belonged. She got plenty of attention from men and from the friends she made there. Men and women alike said she was beautiful and everyone loved her. She hadn't a single enemy. Unlike the rest of them, she had no talent for the stage, yet the owner kept her on. She couldn't sing or dance or perform acrobatics. She couldn't juggle or do magic tricks. Truth was, her stage performance was quite limited. She was more of a prop than anything else, but the gentlemen did like her. There was never any doubt about that. She was effervescent and talkative and she helped them forget their cares. Rose was embarrassed at her next thought. Lizzie's real talent was probably recognized and appreciated most during her performances in the tiny cubicles above the gambling hall. For all she knew, upstairs, Lizzie's act might border on spectacular. She felt herself blush at the idea. That's why Lizzie spent most of her time at the Bird Cage. Attention. That's what she needed and that's where she got it. If the theatre ever closed it's doors, what would happen to poor Lizzie?

Rose thought back to all the nights she wished there was a way out, all the times she had to put up with the smell of whiskey and cigar smoke and men touching her. She was strong. She had the ability to reason things out. Lizzie was weak. She had no analytical ability, no mechanism in her mind to sort out the complications of life. Lizzie had trouble with simple day-to-day experiences like going to the store for sugar, yet she managed to survive life at the Bird Cage. Rose didn't understand it. The Bird Cage was a world within itself. Perhaps, in a convoluted way, it was Lizzie's escape from the real world. It was her world. There, she didn't have to try to filter out things she couldn't deal with. It was the same every night. Strangely enough, it was a safe place for her. Rose watched Lizzie stirring too much sugar into her coffee and humming softly. At this moment, Lizzie was inside her own private world and had become completely unaware of Rose sitting at the table. Virgil was right. Lizzie was in a different place than the rest of them. Maybe that wasn't all bad.

Lizzie reached across the table and touched Rose's hand. "I'm alright, Rosie. I know you have to go away with John. I understand and I'm not scared about you leaving anymore. Like you said, you can come back and visit or I can visit you in Washington. Jenny says she'll come with me. Won't that be fun? I've never been to Washington." She knew Lizzie didn't really understand, but for the moment, she'd been blessed with acceptance. Any other time, she would have told Lizzie about the "Rosie" thing. She hated to be called Rosie and everyone knew it. Lizzie always said it without thinking, mostly when she was caught up in the excitement of the moment. Lizzie did everything without thinking, but she wasn't excited now. She was calm and appeared as normal as could be. Rose understood it to be Lizzie's personal affectionate name for her. When Lizzie realized what she said, she put her hand up to her mouth. She'd been scolded for it before. "I'm sorry. I forgot. You don't like to be called Rosie. I won't do it anymore. I forget things a lot." Rose took Lizzie's hand in both of hers. "You know somethin', Lizette? I've decided I like you to call me Rosie. No one else can do it though. Only you." Lizzie broke into a smile, obviously pleased with Rose's declaration that only she was given permission to call her Rosie. She got up from her chair and put both arms around Rose in the hug of a grateful child.

When Lizzie moved back home with Jenny, Rose began packing. Her plan was to have everything ready to go when John came back. They'd have to leave for Washington right away. She'd been marking off the days on the calendar until he'd be returning from California and more than two weeks had already gone by. She had to get busy packing and preparing for the trip east. She sent a message to Virgil about the little gray house and furniture. If he wanted them back, she'd take only what she came with and leave the rest behind, including the deed to the property that she offered to sign over to him. She was grateful for all he'd done for her and she would never forget his kindness. His response was delivered to her within a matter of hours, a formal note consisting of only two sentences.

> *Dear Miss Callahan,*
>
> *According to the deed which you hold in your possession, the house on Toughnut Street belongs to you, together with its entire contents. Best wishes to you and Captain Merrick for a long and prosperous life together.*
>
> *Very respectfully yours,*
> *Virgil W. Earp*

At first, she thought his correspondence cold, but what else could he say? He wished her luck and there was no question about his intentions that the little gray house be hers. The first time he told her it was her house, he meant it and he never changed his mind. All the note did was confirm that fact. The more she thought about it, she imagined the note had not been easy for Virgil to write. In the back of her mind, she always thought he cared more for her than he dared say. She'd been over it a hundred times. He hadn't stayed away because he wanted to. He had to. Doc made that pretty clear. In the beginning, it was hard to be alone, and the thought never occurred to her that maybe the going of their separate ways wasn't so easy for him either. If the truth be known, it might have been harder on him.

Packing turned out to be a bigger chore than she expected. In the short time she'd been in Tombstone, she'd acquired a lot of things. As each box was filled and tied up, Nalanche stacked them in one corner of the bedroom. By the end of the second day, she was nearly finished and the boxes had overflowed into the parlour. She sat down with a cup of tea, thinking about what was left to do. Her intent was to get the packing done early and rest for a couple of weeks before making the long trip to Washington. Virgil had taken great pains to furnish the house with things he thought she'd like and now, those pretty things presented a dilemma. Living with them every day, she'd grown attached to them, but because they were gifts from him, she didn't feel right taking them into her new life with John. They'd be a constant reminder to both of them of her past relationship with Virgil and that wouldn't be fair to John or her. The answer to her problem was easy. Abby hadn't been here long and she needed just about every-thing. She was living in close quarters with Jenny and Lizette and really needed more room. It would seem the logical solution was to ask Abby to move into the little gray house. She could be a sort of caretaker and have her own place at the same time. Abby liked the furniture and the rose carpet and the front-porch swing. Abby had been a good friend, the best friend anyone could ask for. If not for Abby's persistence, she'd have died from the pneumonia. When Virgil stayed away, Abby was there. Nights when she talked about John for hours on end, Abby listened. She owed Abby a lot. She'd make a gift of the furniture and swing to Abby and let her live in the house free. Rose would tell her when she came to visit this afternoon. The day she and John left for Washington, Abby could move in. With Abby living there, they'd be sure the house was being taken care of and they could decide later what to do with the property. Maybe they'd come back to Tombstone to live someday. If not, maybe she'd give the house to Abby the way Virgil gave it to her. It was settled. All that was left was to finish pack-ing her trunk and wait for John.

Chapter 11

"I would give all the silver in Arizona
for one more of your smiles."

I'll Be Waiting
ALLEN STREET ROSE

John was to return in a month to six weeks. That's what he said, but a month had come and gone three weeks ago. He was long overdue. She tried to stay busy to keep from thinking about the number of days gone past the date of his anticipated return. She was worried something had happened to him. Maybe the column had been ambushed by renegade Apaches. They still caused trouble on the road. Maybe he was sick or hurt, or maybe the trial in California was taking a lot longer than he expected. If that was the case, he could have sent a wire telling her he'd be late. Maybe his orders had been changed unexpectedly with no time to write or send the wire. There were any number of reasons to explain his delay — or maybe he decided she wasn't worth coming back for. He'd had time to think about everything she told him. He might have changed his mind about forgiving her. She couldn't blame him. She waited one more day and when there was still no word from him, she unpacked everything. The pain began all over, only this time, it was John who'd left. She had to face facts. It looked like she'd be staying in Tombstone, lonely and alone.

Nalanche was going to school every day. She'd taken on the responsibility of seeing to his education and after he sat through the trial and watched John work, he was more enthusiastic than ever about book-learning. His mind was made up to be a lawyer and he envisioned it as being a way to help his people. Many times when she watched him making his letters and saying the words out loud from the reader, she wondered what his mother would think of him. She wondered what his mother had been like and if she could see her son from Heaven. He said she died when he was little, probably four or five judging from the way he described his life at that time, but he remembered what she looked like. His father died in his arms from a white soldier's bullet when they invaded Apache land and killed many of his people. The government sent the rest of his family away to the East and he never saw them again. Years ago, his grandfather told him about his father's sister who went away with a white soldier when she was a young girl. He didn't know where she was today. Not long after she left, his grandfather went to the crossover and his father became chief. His father told him to run into the desert and hide to escape the white soldiers. He ran and was led to safety by the wild coyoté. After Geronimo surrendered, most of the Apaches left were renegades, driven to be so by the white man's persecution, but the boy never joined them. He'd been living by himself in the desert until Rose rescued him from the street attack. Before John left for California, he asked Nalanche to move into the house. He'd feel better about leaving Rose in Tombstone if someone he trusted was there with her. Nalanche was only sixteen, but he was strong and smart, and John trusted him. The boy still felt he owed his life to Rose. No one knew where he slept or what he ate, or even if he slept or ate. He lived off the desert and never asked for anything. When he wasn't in school or in the desert, he stayed close to Rose — protecting her. She tried to convince him that saving Lizzie's life was repayment. He didn't agree. He rejected the invitation to move into the house until John argued it was the best way to watch over Rose. He wouldn't worry so much about her if he knew Nalanche was there. John finally convinced him it was the thing to do and the day John left for California, Nalanche spent his first night under a roof. The next morning, she discovered his bed hadn't been slept in.

The house wasn't very big to begin with and during the two weeks Lizzie was there, it seemed even smaller. Nalanche insisted Rose sleep in his room. Sometimes he slept in the parlour and sometimes she knew he left the house at night when he thought the two girls were asleep, whispering to the dog to stand guard while he was away. She was sure he went into the desert where he'd lived for so long. He'd been a big help with Lizzie. He was quite a magician and he made her laugh with his tricks and illusions, often with Bear's participation as his assistant. Lizzie squealed with delight and clapped her hands in childish appreciation for the entertainment. Rose watched closely, but she could never figure out how he did the tricks. When he finished, she'd coax him to tell his secrets. Lizzie insisted it was magic and Nalanche would stare at Rose when she said there had to be a logical explanation. "Tell me how you did that trick, Nalanche. What is the secret?" His face would be an unreadable stone. He'd look into her eyes and give the same reply every time. "Good medicine, bad medicine. No trick." She never understood what he meant. There were times when even she thought it must be magic. It was without question he did have some special abilities that defied logical explanation. He talked to the animals and they understood. At least Bear knew what he was saying. She remembered the early walks in the desert when he kept his distance behind her on the path. Several times when she turned toward town expecting to bump into him, he was gone — disappeared. She looked in every direction and couldn't see him. The desert seemed to have swallowed him up. A few seconds later, she'd turn around to find him walking behind her. She never knew how he moved so fast and got behind her when he should have been in front. She never heard him walking either. She stopped and listened, trying to pinpoint his location. She never did. When she walked on the road, stones and sand made crunching sounds beneath her shoes. When he walked on the same road, his feet made no sound against the earth. He walked silently, like a ghost whose feet didn't touch the ground. She used to accuse him of being able to fly because he moved so fast. She joked about him being an angel. Now that she knew him better, she no longer laughed about his ethereal qualities. There was no doubt in her mind that he was different. Mysterious. She thought back to the night he saved Lizzie from bleeding to death. The doctor said he didn't understand it. According to his medical knowledge, Lizzie lost so much blood by the time Nalanche found her, he should have found a corpse instead of a living, fighting woman. Did he do more than tourniquet her wounds? Was there a greater power in his hands that saved Lizzie?

She sipped her coffee and looked out the kitchen window. Lizzie was visiting and, as usual, jabbering across the table. She had a way of always showing up when Rose was looking forward to a quiet morning. As Lizzie rattled on, Rose thought about Nalanche. Even when she didn't see him, she knew he was nearby. She called him her spirit protector and when she thought about it, he never once disputed the suggestion.

The money John left with her and the little savings she had wouldn't last forever. Painful as it was, she had to think about once more moving on without him. If he was coming back, he should have been here by now and if the Army detained him, he should have at least sent a wire, a letter — something.

Saturday morning she awoke to the smell of coffee and a gentle breeze blowing through the bedroom window. The coffee smelled good and the air was cool for this time of year. The winds picked up the perfume of the desert and mixed it with the roses and jasmine in the yard. When the combined fragrances drifted into her room, she closed her eyes and took a deep breath. It was better than all the expensive perfumes from Paris put together. She liked the gentle desert wind. Many times, she thought she heard voices floating on the breeze. Nalanche called them Apache spirit winds. He said the spirits of his ancestors rode the winds down from the mountains and across the desert at night and it was their voices she heard. They told of the old ways, before white men intruded into their land and killed the people. He said they told about a great chief from another time who walked the earth today as a man, and who would soon return to them. She thought his accounts of conversations with the ghosts of his dead father and grandfather and stories of ancient times were the equivalent of Irish fairy tales, legends of mythical figures and spirits the Indians believed guided their lives. She had a great deal of compassion for the Indians and she thought it was a shame the government treated them so badly. Sometimes, she wondered if those ancestral spirits Nalanche talked about were getting even with the white man by giving him Tombstone.

She sat on the edge of the bed and ran both hands through her hair. Then she pulled it all to one side and twisted it thoughtfully for several minutes until it became a single, long curl. She wondered where John was. Maybe she dreamed the whole thing and he really hadn't come back at all. The old pain swept over her and she felt the tears coming fast. It had been like a fairy tale. Her handsome prince came back, but unlike the fairy tales where the prince rode away with the princess on a white horse bedecked with gilded trappings, there was no happy ending to this story. He was gone and she was alone again. She put her face in her hands and sobbed. Nalanche was standing next to the bed holding her robe out to her. "He is coming back." She shook her head, no. "How can you say that? I haven't heard from him at all. If he was comin', he'd have been here by now, or he would have wired why he was late." The boy repeated. "He is coming. I made coffee." He dropped her robe on the bed and left the room. He never stayed when she pouted and had no interest in discussing negative ideas. If she kept it up, he'd leave the house.

She put on the robe and shuffled to the kitchen. Nalanche was sitting at the table practicing writing his letters. He didn't look up when she went to the coffee pot and poured a cup. "I'm goin' back to work at the Bird Cage." She sat down at the table, her announcement apparently having fallen on deaf ears. She got no response and he didn't look up from his writing. She patted her hand on the table next to the paper he was writing on. "Did you hear me? I said, I'll be goin' back to work tonight." He kept writing. She waited for his reaction, thinking if she stared at him long and hard enough, he'd have to acknowledge what she said. By the time she finished her coffee, he still hadn't said anything. She tapped her finger against the cup, watching him. Despite having lived in the desert, his complexion was smooth and unweathered. He was a beautiful child. She rearranged her definition of him. He was a child in years only. He was very wise for his years, a man already. Ruby had been the first to say it. In the beginning, she looked upon him as a child, but she'd come to recognize something in him that made her understand it was no longer the case. He knew things she couldn't explain. She believed he knew the secrets of what he called "good medicine, bad medicine." She never knew what he was thinking. He could maintain an expression that was totally unreadable. She had to laugh about that. John said he'd be a great lawyer someday. They'd never know what he was thinking and he could call anyone's bluff. He possessed an inner strength. He was a good boy. A gentle spirit. It was the best way she could think of to describe him. He was tall for an Apache; tall for fifteen, or sixteen, whichever he was. Perhaps that's what made him appear older than his actual years. There was something behind his eyes that bespoke a far-reaching wisdom. She asked him once why he still went into the desert alone when he had a house to live in. He told her he went to talk to the spirits of his ancestors and his father and grandfather, and to listen to their wisdom. Sometimes he stayed out there all night to listen and learn the lessons of the old ways.

When Nalanche asked Rose to trim his hair, she imagined it was because he wanted to be more like John. It was no longer past his shoulders. He bathed regularly and wore a shirt all the time, buttoned and tucked inside his pants. He was up before dawn every morning, running with Bear for miles out in the desert and when he returned, he'd study and practice his writing before it was time for school. He wanted to learn everything. Even now, he was trying to make each letter perfect. It was the way he did everything — just like John. They were two of a kind. She knew she loved him, this boy who had become like a brother to her. He called her "sister." She got up from the table and laid her hand on the back of his head, looking over his shoulder. "That's very good." He kept on writing. He said John would be back. She smiled at that. He never said it, but she knew he missed John too. She wondered if he really believed John was coming. She didn't want him to have false hope. She put her arms around him and whispered in his ear. "I love you, little brother." There was no reaction from him and she started to move away. She wouldn't make him talk if he didn't want to. When he reached back and held her hand, she knew things were right between them. He wasn't angry because she was going back to the Bird Cage, just disappointed, and maybe a little worried.

She'd been back at work for several days. Still no word from John. He was always on her mind, but she'd resigned herself to the idea that he wasn't coming back. She was thankful to have been able to see him for a short time again. He was gone, but at least she'd cleared her conscience and told him everything. Wiping the slate clean didn't make being alone any easier though. She prayed he was safe. She tried to be strong and not let the sadness show. She saved her tears until she was alone. At work, she pretended to be having a good time. She had to keep smiling and do what-ever it took to keep her job. This night was like all the others. She opened the lid on the wooden box where she kept the silver and blue turquoise Nalanche gave her. Carefully, she removed each piece and arranged it around her neck or on her wrist, and a ring on every finger. The girls still laughed because she wore all of it at the same time. She adjusted the last piece. There was something else, one other item inside; a small, white box tied with a red ribbon. She pulled the ribbon off and slowly removed the lid. All of her jewelry was silver. All but this piece. This piece was gold. The rose ring. She hadn't worn it while John was here because she didn't feel right wearing a ring that was a gift from Virgil. The tiny, green stone in the leaf sparkled. She'd forgotten how pretty it was. It couldn't be appreciated if she never wore it. Besides, John wasn't coming back. It didn't matter anymore if she wore it. She slipped the ring on her finger and closed the wooden box.

On her way out, she stopped and looked at him, sitting on the couch with his arms folded, a speller on his lap. "I'll see you in the mornin', Nalanche." She knew he heard her, but he didn't look up from the book. He hadn't had much to say since she told him she was going back to work at the Bird Cage. He'd spoken his piece once about not wanting her to work there and he wouldn't say it again, but he wouldn't try to stop her from going either. There was no need to look back. When she turned the corner onto Allen Street, she knew he was there. She smiled to herself. It was like the walks in the desert. Her spirit protector was always there. He didn't like it, but if she was bent on going back to work at the Bird Cage, he wouldn't let her walk alone. It was the same on her way home, but at night, Nalanche wasn't the only one who watched out for her. Virgil's men followed her. A few times, she thought she saw Virgil standing in the shadows. Twice, she started to cross the street to speak to him and both times, he faded into the darkness.

She heard them giggling as she approached the end of the building. They were hiding around the corner. Like all the other times, she'd have to clutch at her heart and gasp for breath, pretending to be frightened half to death when they jumped out and shrieked at her like a bunch of screaming banshees. When she reached the corner, she began the performance, pretending to look across the street and giving them ample opportunity to scare the wits out of her. She stepped past the end of the building to the corner. Raising her hands to her heart in a demonstration of sheer terror, she reacted too soon. Nothing happened. She stopped and listened. Quiet — Not a sound. She peeked around the corner. The banshees weren't there. Where did they go? They were always in the same place, waiting for her when she walked to work. She was the unsuspecting target of their "surprise" attack and they played the same game with her every night. She heard them giggling a minute ago, but they weren't where they were supposed to be. She looked around the corner. No one there. Maybe one of their mothers finally caught them playing the game with her and dragged them home by their ears. She'd gotten to the point where she looked forward to seeing them, but it didn't look like they were here tonight. It was a bit of a disappointment. She shrugged her shoulders and crossed the street. Little did she know, she was already under attack.

They were stealthy little banshees. She never heard them coming. Silly giggles usually gave them away, but not this time. They'd formed a new war plan. Part of their strategy was silence and the element of surprise. She didn't suspect a thing. They attacked from the rear, all grabbing and tickling her at once. Their plan worked. She let out a scream that set them to laughing hysterically. Emily jumped up and down, applauding the success of the attack. "Did we scare you, Rose?" Did they scare her? Her hands were over her heart as they were every time they played the game. The only difference this time was that she wasn't acting. They really scared her. The scream was a reflex to genuine surprise. "Yes. You scared the stuffin' out of me." Emily clapped her hands, squealing with sheer delight that the newly-contrived attack had been executed precisely according to plan. "Can you play another game with us?" She always left a little early to allow enough time to be properly frightened when they jumped out from around the corner. The first time they did it, she practically had heart failure and they ran off before she had a chance to catch her breath. Anyone else would have reported their behavior to their mother with a demand that they be properly spanked. Not Rose. She had a different plan. A few days later, she saw them coming before they saw her. She hid around the corner and jumped out at them as they came skipping past, completely unprepared for a grown-up to turn the tables on them with their own prank. She scared the bejesus out of them and they thought it was glorious fun. Ever since that night, they waited for her when she went to work and they never tired of the game. If their mothers found out, especially Emily's mother, they knew the punishment that awaited them was of grand measure. They took a big chance talking to a shady lady, and especially so with her. Their mother hated Rose. They knew the risk, but they didn't seem to care. She remembered the incident in Smith's when she and Lizzie were buying dress material. Emily got her haired pulled that time just for saying hello. Rose had to restrain Lizzie from punching Mrs. Grants in the nose, all the while wishing she could have done it herself and regretting later that she hadn't.

She patted Emily on the head. "I have a few minutes. What game do you want to play?" Emily squealed and jumped off the walk. She began drawing squares in the dirt with a stick. Her brother, William, made a disgusted face. "That's a girl game." He threw the ball he was carrying into the air and held up his hands to catch it, misjudging the distance and fumbling to get it when the ball fell to the ground. He picked it up and looked at Rose like it was her fault he missed. She had to think fast. "Since Emily suggested her game first, we'll play that one tonight. Tomorrow, we'll play catch, so don't forget to bring the ball. Does that sound fair, William?" He squinted his eyes at her suspiciously. "Promise? You have to promise." She stuck out her hand to seal the deal. "I promise. We'll play catch tomorrow." That was good enough for him. They shook on it. He'd wait for tomorrow. She hoped she'd remember to wear lower-heeled shoes for the game of catch that awaited her the following evening because William would expect her to run after the ones she missed. Try as he would, his aim was not very good and he hurled the ball with admirable enthusiasm in every direction but toward the intended catcher. At nine, concentration and coordination were not skills he'd perfected yet, so in order to play the game with him, you had to be willing to chase down the ball nearly every time he threw it. Of course, he'd never admit to it being his fault when the pitch went wild. Every time she missed it, he'd shake his head and roll his eyes up in disgust, blaming her failure to field the ball on the universal male rationale that justified her weaknesses — she was a girl! The fact that she was a grown-up lady didn't seem to matter to William. If she was going to play the game, she had to understand there were no special concessions made for age or gender and there were no apologies for his misaimed throws either. Ten minutes of chasing down William's unruly pitches tired her out. Needless to say, the games didn't last long.

Emily was finished drawing her squares in the dirt. "You go first, Rose." She handed Rose a stone. She'd drawn more squares than usual, the last of which was some distance from the starting line. Rose knew that by creating extra squares, Emily thought she could make the game last longer. Rose pretended not to notice and took careful aim with the stone, tossing it onto the furthest square. Then, she lifted her skirt and began hopping through the squares, first, on one foot, then two, then one. She made it to where the stone landed in the far corner, stood on one foot, lifted her skirt with one hand to see the stone, and bent down to pick it up with the other hand. No easy task. The object of the game was to then turn around and jump back through the squares without touching any of the lines separating the squares. She made it all the way up and back. Next, it was Emily's turn. She tossed the stone and jumped through the squares. Rose had to get to work. When it was her turn, she threw the stone onto a square and started hopping. She picked up her stone and turned to make her way back to the starting line. On the turn, she pretended to lose her balance and put both feet down where she was only supposed to have one on the ground. Her foot smudged a line and she hung her head, feigning disappointment at losing. "You win, Emily." The little girl consoled Rose's loss by holding her hand and repeating what Rose told them many times. "It's only a game. Having fun is what's important." It was time to go. She lifted the hem of her skirt and hopped through the squares one more time, just for fun. This time, she didn't miss a square. Of course, it was too late to win because the game was over. Emily applauded Rose's efforts. "See, I knew you could do it, Rose." William's scowling face gave away his suspicions. He knew Rose let his little sister win. Rose winked at him. "Don't forget the ball tomorrow, William. I'll be ready for that game of catch." He got the message. He wouldn't tell Emily he knew Rose let her win. She was back on the boardwalk and waving to them. "I'll see you tomorrow. Run home now. It's gettin' late. Your mother will be frettin' about you." She blew them a kiss.

As she turned toward the Bird Cage, she heard what she thought was the cry of a wounded animal. It wasn't an animal. It was a woman's high-pitched voice, one she'd heard before. She'd recognize that screech any-where. Mrs. Grants! That good Christian woman who punished her daugh-ter for talking to Rose at church on Sunday and pulled the little girl's hair to be mean. She knew Emily was in trouble. Emily knew it too and stood with her hands at her sides, looking down at the ground. Tears were already streaming down her cheeks in anticipation of the punishment she knew was heading straight for her. William and their little brother came to stand with their sister. Rose watched the woman stomp across the street toward the children. Their friends ran for home, leaving Emily and her brothers stand-ing side-by-side in the street waiting for the unavoidable castigation to fall upon them. They held hands. Daily abuse from their mother taught them there was strength in unity. Rose thought they looked like little Christians thrown in the arena, waiting for the lion to attack — and the beast was on her way.

Mrs. Grants was furious. She grabbed Emily's braids and pulled with such force that the three children lost their grip on each other's hands. Emily began to cry. Marcus, the smaller brother, wasn't more than six. He tried to explain. "It was only a game..." His mother slapped him so hard the blow carried him backwards and he landed several feet away from where he'd been standing with his brother and sister. He was stunned and sat on the ground staring with a blank look on his face. Unlike his sister, he didn't cry. He rubbed his face. William helped his brother up and Mrs. Grants turned her anger on Emily. She shook the little girl so violently it made the child dizzy. Emily stumbled and nearly fell. The only thing that kept her on her feet was her mother yanking on her hair. She screamed in Emily's face. "How many times do I have to tell you to stay away from the whores?" Emily stopped crying and pursed her lips defiantly. "She's not a... what you said, Mama. She's nice and she's our friend." The woman's eyes flared. "How dare you sass me?" She pulled the braids again with one hand and raised the other one in the air above Emily's head. Emily closed her eyes and braced herself for the forthcoming blow, her reaction indicating that she'd been through it many times.

Rose couldn't believe what she was seeing. She jumped off the walk and ran toward them, shouting for Mrs. Grants to stop. Someone else got there first and grabbed the woman's hand on the downswing before it struck Emily. The force of the restraint took Mrs. Grants off balance and she turned on the person who had hold of her arm. Her face became more hateful when she saw who stopped her. Nalanche. An Apache! She hated the Indians. She closed her eyes and took a deep breath, putting as much force as possible behind an earsplitting scream designed to shatter window glass a block away. He let go of her arm. Rose ran between Emily and her mother, moving Emily behind her skirt. The angry woman forgot about Nalanche and wheeled around, hissing a threat at Rose. "Let my daughter go or I'll have you arrested." The threat was without merit or impact, like a rattlesnake coiled for attack and rattling, but absent fangs with which to inject the deadly venom. Delivery of the threat didn't scare Rose and Mrs. Grants' presumption that it did was soon dispersed. With Emily hiding behind her skirt, Rose took a step forward. "Caroline, if I ever see you strike this child or pull her hair again, I will personally break your arm. Make no mistake about my meanin'." Caroline Grants' eyes were wide and her mouth was agape, her body rigid with anger. She was a gangly woman with an exceptionally long neck. Quite homely, if truth be told. Rose thought Caroline resembled a goose who suddenly stopped honking and extended its neck to listen when it heard the fox approaching.

Caroline had earned herself a reputation for being an habitual retailer of scandalous and, more often than not, inaccurate dirt she dug up in her dogged effort to have her nose in everybody's business. She circulated rumor without so much as a passing thought that her prattle, and expansion of it as she went along, was hurtful to the people she gossiped about. Today, her tale-carrying caught up with her and she was being confronted by the person she'd talked about the most. She'd been overhead many times saying how she'd relish the chance to tell the redheaded Irish whore a thing or two — Marshal Earp's private whore. This was her golden opportunity. Rose waited. She and Virgil had seen Caroline stroll past the house in the evening many times when she had no cause to be there after sundown. She was always up to something, sneaking around to spy on them and believing they wouldn't notice, like an ostrich with his head in the sand. Why her husband allowed her out alone at that hour was a mystery. They speculated that maybe Tom Grants would not be entirely aggrieved if his wife met with an ill fate and disappeared on one of those outings in the dark. She'd gone out of her way snooping into Rose's business and starting the gossip ball rolling right through the middle of town, pushing it every chance she got to make it pick up speed. Rose was sure Caroline had given Virgil's wife an earful about them.

She was still waiting for Caroline's response. "Is there somethin' you'll be wantin' to say to me, Mrs. Grants?" The woman didn't answer. She was looking for Nalanche. He was gone. She turned back to Rose. She wasn't much older than Rose, twenty-eight maybe, but the angry, hateful look on her face aged her by thirty years and she looked like a mean, old woman. Rose had seen the same expression before. Now, she recalled when. It was her first morning in town. She stopped two ladies in front of the hotel to ask directions to the Bird Cage. She remembered thinking they both appeared to be having a case of the vapors when she told them where she wanted to go, and she thought the two of them were going to faint dead away right there in front of her. One of them was Caroline Grants. The idea of having to speak to Rose repulsed her and she spat the order out. "You keep that heathen savage away from me." Emily peeked at her mother from behind Rose's skirt. "He's not a savage. He knows magic." The veins in Caroline's forehead bulged. Rose watched them pulsating, thinking to herself that Caroline's head might explode any second. Her face was as red as a tomato and she was sweating. She reached for Emily. The little girl ducked behind Rose and Caroline grabbed for her again. Rose raised her hand for Caroline to stop and shook her finger at the angry woman. "I think that's about enough. I want you to promise you'll not punish Emily and the boys for talkin' to me. They were only bein' friendly. They haven't learned to hate yet. 'Tis more than I can say for some folks." Mrs. Grants couldn't believe it. This whore... was telling her to promise...? She started sputtering. "How dare you tell me to..." Rose was calm and there was no quivering in her voice. "Caroline, if you don't promise, I'll take Emily to the Marshal's office right this minute and I'll tell him you're beatin' your children. I can tell you he'll not be pleased to hear it. Judgin' from your public regalin' of my association with Virgil Earp, you do understand my word carries a certain amount of credit there with the Marshal. Are you given to wonderin' which of us he'll be believin'? He might throw you in jail." Caroline knew Rose was right. She'd better think about her predicament, and it was a predicament she was in at the moment. She'd shot off her big mouth a lot, but she really didn't know the extent of Rose's connection with the Earps or anyone else for that matter. She'd been out of line with some unkindly words about Nellie Cashman too after she discovered Nellie and Rose were friends. When she got wind of it, Nellie went to see Caroline and put a stop to her mouth. Rose always wondered what sweet-tempered Nellie said to shut Caroline's flap.

Today, her gossiping came back to haunt her as it did when Nellie Cashman heard about the malicious rumors and unkindly references she was making to Rose and Nellie's shared nationality. She couldn't take a chance the Marshal would be upset enough to actually put her in jail. That would be intolerable. She didn't want to end up on the wrong side of either Virgil or Wyatt Earp, and she wasn't sure how much influence Rose might have with them. William had his arm around his little brother and Emily was behind Rose. If Caroline expected to take her children home, she'd have to do the right thing. Otherwise, Rose might follow through with her threat to take the kids to the Marshal. Caroline would die if he put her in jail. She pointed her nose skyward. "Alright. I promise. Emily, it's time to go home." She held out her hand to her daughter and Rose guided Emily out from behind her skirt to face her mother. "Emily, I want you to tell your mother you didn't mean to dis- obey her and you will not do it again." The little girl started to protest and Rose held up a finger to her lips in a gesture that meant for Emily to say no more about it. Emily didn't want to promise any such thing. She didn't understand why her mother so vehemently objected to them talk- ing to someone they liked, someone who never did anything except be nice to them. Rose raised her eyebrows and tipped her head forward. Emily let out a sigh. "I'm sorry, Mama. I was only trying to be friends. I won't talk to Rose anymore if you say not to." She looked up at Rose for approval. Rose lifted her eyebrows again. There was more. Emily continued. "I didn't mean to disobey you. I won't do it again. I promise." She didn't understand why she had to say it. Rose turned to the boys. "William. Marcus. Do you have somethin' to say, boys?" William bit his bottom lip and though clearly lacking the sincerity Rose had hoped for, he said it. "Sorry, Mama." Marcus followed his brother's example. "Me, too." That was as close as they were going to get to a sincere apology. Rose pushed Emily toward to her mother. "Good- night, Emily. William. Marcus. Good-night, Mrs. Grants." She turned around, lifting her eyes toward heaven in silent prayer that she'd done the right thing for the children. She'd hope for the best, but if she found out

Caroline whipped them when she got them home, she'd take them to Wyatt's office tomorrow.

"You should have been a politician, Rose Callahan. If it'd been me, I'd have laid that old biddy out cold in the street. I'd not have wasted my time talking. You can ask Doc about that." It was Kate, shaking her head in disgust and voicing her opinion over what happened. Rose had to admit she shared Kate's feeling, but she couldn't have very well knocked Caroline down in front of her children. "Don't think I didn't want to. A good beatin' might be just what Caroline Grants needs to set her thinkin' straight. 'Tis a shame the way she behaves, and no example for those darlin' children. I'd hate to think the little girl will be growin' up to follow in her mother's footsteps. I'm late for work. I don't have time for fightin' in the street with the likes of Caroline Grants. However, should you come upon the woman takin' out her mean disposition on those little angels and I'm not around, give her a fist for me, won't you, Kate?" Rose shook her fist in the air and Kate laughed. When she reached the front door of the Bird Cage, she remembered Nalanche. She looked down Allen Street. He'd kept Mrs. Grants from hitting Emily, but he was gone now. She wasn't surprised. He always showed up at the right time to help somebody, then, disappear. It was nothing new.

It wasn't quite seven and the place was overflowing with people. She was tired thinking about the busy night ahead. Maybe a cup of the coffee Ruby kept on the little stove downstairs would help. It was strong and bitter, but it would give her a jolt and keep her awake. She laid her shawl on a chair behind the stage. A creaking sound made her turn around and look up at the fixtures holding the curtains. Several sandbags were tied with ropes near the ceiling. When they were lowered to the floor, shifting of the weight raised the curtains. They worried her the way they moved and she made a wide circle to bypass them whenever she walked across the backstage. She must remember to mention it to Abby and the others. She looked up at the bags. Their precarious position was dangerous. If the rope knots slipped loose, the bags would fall. Someone could get hurt.

Chapter 12

"I will defend your honor to the death, my dear,
but I cannot mend a broken heart."

Silver Rose Marie
ALLEN STREET ROSE

With the doors wide-open, a cloud of smoke floated over the room like a lazy ghost. She hated the bitter smell of strong tobacco and the damn cigar smoke, but it went with the territory. It made her head ache and her eyes burn, and it irritated the chronic cough she hadn't been able to get rid of since the pneumonia. Some of them coughed and hacked as they drew the smoke into their lungs. She wondered why, if it caused them so much discomfort, they continued to puff away. She figured it had something to do with what men thought they had to do to publicly reinforce their manhood. She couldn't believe they actually enjoyed it, but then, she'd come to realize men often did things that made no sense to her. Spitting was the most disgusting of their manly habits, and they all did it. She thought she'd have been used to the smoke by this time, but it still gave her a sick headache. A couple of hours was all she could stand before she had to get some fresh air. She headed for the door. A breath of the cool, night breeze always made her feel better.

She ignored the pat on her backside as she squeezed between the men standing by the bar. It seemed more people came in every night. She was almost to the door when she smelled the whiskey on his breath. He was standing over her shoulder. He said something. She didn't want to give him the idea she was interested, so she pretended she didn't hear what he said. He spoke again with his face touching her neck, several days' growth of bristly whiskers scraping against her skin like a wire brush. The shock of the abrasion made her flinch and jerk her head away. She took another step in an effort to increase the distance between them. Too late. His arm was around her before she could get through the crowd and he pulled her back so hard it knocked the wind out of her. He grabbed her and whirled her around, picking her up so that her feet came right off the floor. She struggled to get free, but he was strong as a grizzly and darn near big as one. He was laughing and telling her she was the prettiest thing he'd ever seen. He thought they could have a right-good time upstairs. "Name your price, little dove. I been up there in that old mine for nigh on ten days and I'm ready for some fun. You're just what I want." From the way he smelled, she had no reason to doubt he'd been down in a hole in the ground for more than a week. He hadn't bathed or shaved for several days and then some, probably grabbing a few hours sleep in a tent up in the hills and going straight back to the mine when he woke up. He smelled of layers of old sweat and stale cigars and the unmistakable musty dirt that came from the caverns deep inside the earth. The town was full of it. You could always tell a miner from the covering of damp dust that saturated his skin and clothes.

He was leaning on her. She staggered under his weight and almost fell down. He helped her regain her balance, displaying a repulsive grin that caused her to gag and cough. She knew what was on his mind. A gap on one side of his mouth once occupied by two teeth made his smile that much more lecherous and offensive. Something else. His eyebrows were thick with no separation to distinguish one from the other. They sloped down-ward in the middle and met at the bridge of his nose to form a continuous line of bushy hair. They looked like a long, fuzzy caterpillar caught in a lightning storm, all of its hair standing on end. His eyes weren't quite right either. She tilted her head to one side, trying to identify the discrepancy. They didn't both look in the same direction. The right one looked straight ahead, but he seemed to have no control over the wandering of the left. She wondered what the world looked like through such dissimilar lenses. Perhaps his dysfunctional vision contributed to his offensive nature. From the looks of him, she knew he'd put away the better half of a bottle of whiskey. He'd spilled the other half down the front of his shirt and he stunk to the high heaven. As if the whiskey and need for a bath wasn't enough, he chewed on the soggy end of a half-smoked cigar. He leaned close to her face and the smoke burned her eyes. She blinked to clear them and turned her head to one side to avoid the smoke. He didn't pay any attention to the obvious fact that the smoke bothered her. Instead, he held the cigar in his teeth right under her nose. With his eyes on her, he turned his head and spit a piece of it on the floor. Feeling her stomach turn, she put her hand over her mouth and looked away. He was disgusting. If he kept this up, she'd be sick for sure.

It'd been awhile since she'd run into such an obnoxious character. He could see that his behavior was making her ill and he was noticeably pleased with his doing. She forced herself to look at him. Could be, he was the ugliest and stinkinest man she'd ever seen, worse even than the one who rode the stage with her back in New Mexico. At least she had her derringer handy that time. Here, she had to talk her way out. He was leaning on her again. If he was out to find a woman tonight, he was going about it the wrong way. None of the girls at the Bird Cage would go upstairs with him. The way he smelled, they wouldn't even sit with him for a drink. They were expected to entertain anyone who had the money, but the line was drawn with his sort. Ruby would back her up. She wouldn't be expected to socialize with the likes of him.

The ladies understood miners. They were a raucous bunch, but didn't mean any harm. They worked hard in the silver mines and when they came to town for fun, most had the good sense to get a bath and shave if they expected to buy the pleasures of a shady lady. Many of the red-light brothels advertised their girls as clean, disease-free and "professional" and insisted that gentlemen who desired to purchase the favors of a lady of the parlour house be bathed, without lice, and properly mannered. The saloons and gambling halls had no such "house rules," and a bath and shave were not prerequisites to entering an establishment to spend money, but most of them cleaned up pretty good if they intended to buy feminine company. When they came into town with a pocketful of cash looking for fun, the ladies at the Bird Cage gave them their money's worth. If that had been the case this time, she could have tolerated him. She wished he'd taken a bath.

The longer he stood next to her, the thicker the stench became. His hands were filthy, dirt and grime having permanently stained his skin and settled in the cracks from so long without washing. He lifted her hand and pressed several coins in the palm. She noticed his fingernails were black and she pulled her hand away, dropping the coins. He grinned and squinted his eyes, the cigar still between his teeth. He kept looking up at her while he squatted and felt around on the floor for the coins. When he'd picked them all up, he plopped the money back in her hand, closing her fingers around the coins to prevent her from dropping them again. He moved the cigar around with his tongue and spit another piece out. It hit the floor with a splat. He nodded his head toward the money in her hand. "That enough?"

She didn't look at the coins, thinking to herself, "No amount of money would be enough for this one." She'd be hard-pressed to come up with the right words to discourage him though. He'd made up his mind and said so. He picked her and he wasn't about to be put off much longer. Of course, if he didn't have enough money, that would be all the reason she'd need for rejecting him. Ruby would make that clear to him. She only felt a few coins in her hand, so it was plain he didn't have the required twenty-five dollar minimum to buy a lady's time in an upstairs crib anyway. She opened her hand and looked at the money, about to say she was sorry, but the house set the rates and he didn't have the right amount. She swallowed hard, trying not to show her combined surprise and alarm. The coins weren't silver. They were gold — five of them. Twenty-dollar gold pieces every one. A hundred dollars. That was an awful lot of money. She kept looking at the coins, trying to think of a way to get away from him. If she looked at him, he'd think she was agreeing to his proposition.

He interpreted her delay in answering as meaning it wasn't enough money and dropped one more coin onto the pile in her hand. She still didn't say anything. She couldn't believe he was giving her a hundred and twenty dollars gold to go upstairs with him. It was a hard sum to turn down, but if it had been ten thousand, there was no way she'd be able to let the filthy beast touch her. Her eyes darted from one end of the room to the other. Where was Ruby? — anybody who could get her out of this. She was trying to buy some time by not letting on about the money. He shoved his hand in his pocket. "I got more. How much?" She finally stopped him. "I'm flattered you think I'm worth so much, but I'm very sorry. I can't go upstairs with you tonight. I'm not feelin' at all well. Another time, perhaps." She held out the money, but he made no move to take it back. The smile left his face and his eyes narrowed. He shifted the cigar to the other side of his mouth with his teeth. He stared at her, the wandering eye squinting almost closed, the good one focusing on her. Her excuses were not acceptable. She wasn't going to get out of it that easy.

She looked for a familiar face. Where the devil was Ruby? The big redhead was nowhere to be seen. She was on her own. He came closer, his breath hot and rancid in her face. It smelled like rotting eggs and she shuddered at the sickening stink. His voice was an angry growl. "Don't you know who I am?" As far as she knew, she'd never seen him before, but she didn't want to escalate his anger by saying so. She didn't care who he was. She just wanted him to leave her alone. She shook her head and squeaked,

"No." He barked in her face, blasting her with his rotten breath. "I'm Wild Jack Branch." She thought for a minute, trying to remember if she'd ever heard his name. She had no recollection of it. It didn't mean anything to her. She shook her head again and gave him an apologetic half-smile. His sense of self-importance was offended. Once again, he leaned closer and she felt the heat from his cigar on her face. He puffed on it until his head was engulfed in smoke, then blew it in her face on purpose. The smoke on his foul breath gagged her. She coughed and put her hand over her mouth, on the verge of throwing up. "Mr. Branch, I..." Her voice trailed off when he grabbed her face and squeezed the sides of her mouth, forcing it open. Times like this, she wished she was as big as Ruby, so she could have knocked him silly. He was hurting her and the smoke made her eyes water. With the other hand, he took what was left of the cigar out of his mouth and spit the remnants on the floor near her feet.   He put his face right next to hers, determined to make his intentions clear. "You listen, girlie. I got plenty a'money, and yer goin' up there with me. I like redheads and yer the one I want." He emphasized his message by giving her face a harder squeeze. This was the kind of thing they all hated. When it went this far, there was bound to be trouble. She looked around the room again for Ruby. She needed help fast. Might even be cause enough for Ruby to pull out the pistol she strapped to her thigh underneath her dress. He wouldn't go easy. He grabbed her arm and wheeled her around, pushing her toward the stairs. She couldn't let him get her upstairs. She'd rather die.

Three men came toward them, acting like they had it in mind to intercede. She was relieved. At last, someone was going to help her out of this situation. She started to ask for their help. Three of them ought to be able to handle one man, even one as big and mean as Wild Jack. "Need some help, Jack?" They laughed and prodded each other. It wasn't what she expected. They were his friends. One of them continued. "This one too much for you to handle?" They all laughed again. "She ain't very big." The one who spoke walked around her, squeezing her arm. "Kinda scrawny, ain't she?" She jerked her arm away. The others chimed in, commenting on her small size and how someone as big as Jack shouldn't have so much trouble getting a female her size to mind him.

The cigar was between Jack's teeth and he was moving it around, obviously irritated by their banter. He was looking at her, but he was becoming more chafed with every word they said. He was already boiling mad and they were unknowingly fueling the fire. His teeth were bared like a wild animal and a growling sound rumbled up from deep in his throat. He bit down hard and the burning end of the cigar dropped off, hitting her skirt on its way to the floor. She jumped back and brushed at her dress to be sure no sparks were caught in the material. He spit the wet end onto the floor and curled his upper lip. The other men were laughing hysterically, unaware that Jack didn't share their amusement at his being the object of their ridicule. He watched them as they continued joking among themselves about his inability to control the little redhead, viewing the situation as extremely funny. They failed to see that he was taking in every word and his face had turned beet-red with anger. They didn't know enough to quit. By this time, he was enraged. Her arm was going numb from the way he held it and when she tried to pull away, he squeezed harder, the pressure causing her to cry out. He shook her and yelled, "Shut up. Quit yer damn whinin'." The second before he turned on his laughing companions, she saw the wild, unthinking look of a killer in his eyes. Then, she saw his free hand move. She squeezed her eyes closed and turned her head aside to avoid what she anticipated would be a blow to her own head. Men like this gave no thought to hitting a woman, but as luck would have it, she wasn't the target of his anger. The one nearest Jack's free hand wasn't so lucky. Unfortunately for him, he was laughing so hard that the crazy expression in Jack's eyes went unnoticed. Jack was like a wounded bear on the charge, blinded by rage and out to kill whatever got in his way. Rose opened her eyes in time to see Jack's hand moving away from her. For a big man, he moved unbelievably fast. His capacity for tolerance was next to nothing to begin with and his compadres had pushed him way beyond that limit. They'd made a big mistake making fun of his little problem with Rose. Apparently, they forgot why they called him Wild Jack, but their memories were quickly refreshed.

The big miner's hand moved so fast the one they called Tasker didn't have time to duck. Matter-of-fact, he didn't even see it coming. Jack's knuckles caught the man square on the end of his nose, knocking him into the other two and sending all three sprawling flat on the floor. When the bones in Jack's massive fist connected with the other man's face, the sound was like glass being crushed beneath the blacksmith's iron hammer on the anvil. A river of blood gushed from Tasker's nose and he choked and gasped as some of it ran down his throat. He howled in pain and rolled on the floor, blood streaming through the fingers of the hand he held over his shattered nose and running all over him. No one came to help him. When they saw the damage Jack had done with one blow, every man who might have considered helping Tasker backed away out of Jack's path. He was a raging bull on a rampage, turning toward the others and threatening to strike them. He bellowed at the sniveling threesome cowering at his feet, "Who else wants some of this?" His companions huddled together on the floor, lifting their knees to their chests and covering their faces with their arms as he stood over them ranting like the demented maniac he was. He swore at them and told them never to laugh at him again or he'd kill them. The one named Tasker whimpered and held both hands over his broken nose. Jack gave him a hard kick in the rump. The injured man howled with the infliction of additional pain and Jack thumped him on the top of his head, making him yell again. The more he hollered, the more he got beat until finally, he managed to scramble to his feet and limp away with Jack shaking his fist and yelling obscenities after him. The other two took advantage of the third man's beating and hightailed it out the front door.

He was still holding Rose's hand and she stumbled along behind him as he shoved aside anyone who got in his way. She had to make him stop. She panicked at the thought of what he might do if he managed to get her upstairs. Out of breath, she called to him. "Jack, please stop. You're hurtin' me." She started to cry and he stopped so abruptly that she bumped into him. Patience was not a word he knew and he was still mad from the beating he'd just given his friends. He yelled into her face. "I said, quit yer damn snivelin'. What the hell do you want?" His nostrils flared and his eyes were wild. Simply refusing to go with him hadn't worked and tears wouldn't distract him for long. She decided to use a different approach, but she'd have to talk fast and say exactly the right thing because Jack was out of patience, if any he ever had.

They were at the foot of the stairs when she spotted Doc. He must have just come in and was busily engaged in his usual extravagant spiel to interest an unsuspecting gentleman in a turn of the cards. He didn't see her. Doc was her salvation if she could get his attention. To begin with, she had to convince Wild Jack she changed her mind about entertaining him and was agreeable to the trip upstairs. She put on her sweetest smile and fluttered her eyelashes, speaking in a breathy voice that made him forget what he was doing. She walked her fingers up his dirty shirt to his chin, resting one finger on the wiry whiskers. "I've changed my mind. You're a big, strong man, Jack. I never met a man quite like you." That was the truth. She continued the flattery, holding his interest. "I'd like to get to know you better. Would you mind if we have a drink first? We're in no hurry, are we?

After all, the whole night is still ahead. Are you in a hurry, Jack?" She nuzzled close to his sweat-stained shirt and held her breath to keep from gagging on the stench of his body odor. He thought about it. There were too many questions for him to sort out, and he wasn't used to a woman saying she wanted to get to know him better. In fact, he couldn't remember it ever happening before. He looked down at the top of her head resting against his chest. Most times, he had to drag a woman into a corner and take what he wanted. He never had one go willingly. This was more like it. He smiled his toothless grin. It was plain to see she was crazy about him. He could always use another drink, and she did have a point. The whole night was ahead. Why rush it? He smiled wickedly at the thought of what he could do with her for the rest of the night. A little whiskey might even loosen her up some. He winked the good eye. "I'll get us a bottle." She kept on smiling, keeping Doc in clear sight across the room. "That's a good idea, Jack. I'll wait right here." She gave him a devilish little wink and licked her lips. His eyes were on her mouth, his tongue tracing the same route over his own lips. The ploy worked. He let go of her arm and headed for the bar.

As soon as he turned his back, she went in the opposite direction, straight for Doc's table. She hoped Jack wouldn't decide to turn around and catch her leaving, but he did, and he was madder than ever when he saw her walking away. Luckily, it took him a second to figure out what happened, just enough time to afford her the advantage of a head start. She didn't waste time looking back to see where he was. She had to get to Doc's table fast. She'd be safe there and she knew exactly what Doc would do. As soon as Jack realized she wasn't coming back, he was after her like a duck on a June bug. His long-legged stride closed the distance between them quickly. She squeezed through a tight cluster of people, glancing anxiously over her shoulder to see how close Jack was. She barely made it through the group when he knocked them out of his way. He was only a few feet behind her and she panicked. He was cursing and shoving people aside as he lumbered after her. She knew one good lunge would put him right on top of her. He grabbed for her and managed to pull a few strands of her hair out. She jumped forward. Doc still hadn't seen the chase. She called out frantically. "Doc Holliday!"

Doc looked up from his cards. The smile that started across his face disappeared when he saw the urgency in her eyes and Jack Branch hot on her heels, stretching his arm full-out to catch her and cursing as he went. In an instant, a revolver replaced the cards Doc was holding and it was aimed at Wild Jack's gut. The big miner stopped cold in his tracks and held his hands up in surrender. Rose ran behind Doc's chair. It was a close call. She was out of breath, more from fear of what Jack would do if he caught her than from the mad dash across the room to safety. Jack snarled at him. "I don't have a gun, Holliday." Doc acknowledged the fact with an affirmative nod and smile. Then, the smile was gone. His voice was deadly congenial. "I can see that, Sir. However, as any fool can plainly see, I do have a weapon." He reached back and touched Rose's hand on his shoulder. "I don't believe the lady desires your company any further this evenin'. She's with me." He patted Rose's hand. Jack growled, "The whore stole my money. I want my money." Without moving a muscle, Doc answered. "I'm sure you are mistaken. This lady is not a thief. It would be my guess any money she may have which you claim to be yours, she found. That bein' the case, it would be appropriate to assume she is, therefore, entitled to keep it." The muscles in Jack's jaw twitched and his face became contorted at Doc's suggestion that Rose keep his money. He moved forward an inch and Doc raised the gun, pointing it directly at Jack's heart. If she didn't stop it now, someone was bound to get hurt. She didn't want any trouble. "I have Mr. Branch's money, John, but I didn't steal it. He gave it to me and I'd like to give it back to him." She reached around Doc and tossed the money on the table. Doc didn't take his eyes off the big man in front of him. "I believe you owe the lady an apology, Sir." Jack looked at the money laying on the table. He never said he was sorry in his life, but for a hundred and twenty dollars gold, he'd apologize to the devil himself. He glared at Rose, the contempt in his voice flying in her face. He spit out the words the way he spit out the wet pieces of his cigar. "Sorry." Doc knew that's all he'd get and he motioned toward the money with the gun. "Pick it up." Jack snatched up the coins and stepped back, counting the money. Doc was still holding the gun on him. "I will personally guarantee the lady has returned every penny." He wrinkled up his nose and sniffed. "It would seem there is a foul odor on the air this evenin'. Perhaps your money would be better spent on a bath than on whiskey or women." Jack clenched his teeth and made the now familiar growling sound in his throat. The look in Doc's ice-blue eyes was a dare. He was hoping Jack would make a move toward the table. It would have been his last. Rose rested her hand on Doc's shoulder. "Let him go, John. I just want him to go away." She once heard someone say Doc had a stare that could give a rattlesnake a heart attack. He was concentrating that stare on Jack, and with a loaded revolver in his hand, it was a deadly combination. The congeniality in his voice changed to hostility. His eyes were cold. This was the Doc Holliday people talked about — the man you'd be a fool to cross. He'd as soon shoot Wild Jack Branch as look at him. Doc's voice was icy. Jack had run out of chances. "You heard the lady. You have overstayed your welcome. Get out!" The big miner didn't move a muscle. He was staring at Doc, asking for more trouble than he could imagine. Nobody backed Doc Holliday down. If they tried, they'd lose.

Either Jack was deaf, or just plain stupid. Any fool could see Doc's hackles were up and that was a dangerous sign. Doc eased back the hammer, narrowing his eyes and clenching his teeth so the muscles in his jaw flexed. He was livid. Jack was pushing the wrong man and if he didn't turn around and walk out the door, he stood a better than fair chance that Doc would put a bullet in him. At this range, a forty-five would go clean through and leave a hole in his back the size of Kansas. Doc pushed a little harder. "Sir, you smell like horse manure on a hot day." Rose closed her eyes and let out a small groan. Why was he doing this? The answer was easy — because he was Doc Holliday and he was mad as a hornet rousted from the hive. His card game had been rudely interrupted and Rose was forced to run to him for protection from this fool. He wasn't famous for patience, and particularly not with a jackass like the one standing in front of him. The hand that shook with tremors caused by his disease was steady as he rested his elbow on the table, the gun still pointed at Jack. He was deliberately trying to antagonize Jack into making a fatal move and the way things were going, it looked like the odds were stacked in favor of exactly that happening.

Throughout the confrontation, Ruby watched, waiting to see if Jack would go without a fight. Clearly, that was not going to happen and the only one who stood to gain from Doc killing Jack Branch was the undertaker, and even that was doubtful being that Jack most likely didn't have a friend left who would pay for his burying. It would have been interesting to see the hand played out with no intervention, but better judgment got the best of her. It was time to break it up before the excitement got too much for all of them. Doc had a way of forcing a hand and when he did, someone always paid a heavy price. That was the story anyway. He had a talent for bringing out the worst in people with his descriptive vocabulary and not-so-subtle insults, all accented by the Georgia drawl. In this case, he was waiting for Jack to make the wrong move. The outcome of such action was predictable. Doc was the only one with a gun.

Ruby slapped Jack on the back. "How are you Jack? We haven't seen you around here for awhile." He ignored Ruby and shook his finger at Doc. Before he got another word out, she hit him on the back again, this time, much harder than the first. She had to divert his attention away from Doc. He looked at her like he was thinking of giving her a slap in return for the one she'd given him. She smiled at him, pretending not to see his mean eye. "No harm done, Jack. Why don't you sober up some. Get cleaned up and come on back tomorrow night. I'll make sure there's a special lady here just for you." The offer of a woman finally got his attention. He looked her up and down, then rested his gaze on the low neckline of her dress and the bountiful view it provided. He forgot all about Rose and he forgot about Doc holding a six-shooter on him. He gave Ruby a hungry look that made her skin crawl, but she forced herself to stay close to him, turning her head away for a second to grab a fresh breath.

He wrapped his arm around her waist and pulled her up against him. Ruby grimaced when he showed his tobacco-stained teeth, exclusive of the two that were missing. The whiskey caught up with him and he slurred the words. "How 'bout you, Red? I like big women, 'special redheaded ones. You and me, we'll have a good time, huh?" He rolled his eyes upward toward the suspended cribs. The idea of going up there with him made Ruby wish she'd kept out of it. The thought crossed her mind that maybe she should've let Doc shoot him. She gave him one of her seductive smiles and a wink. "You go get yourself cleaned up, Sweetheart. Then, we'll have a nice, long talk. I like a man who smells good. You understand, don't you, Jack?" She knew he didn't. She took hold of his arm and steered him away from Doc's table. A few feet away, he remembered. He turned around and pointed his finger at Rose. "I'll see you again, little dove, when that mad dog ain't around." He pointed the finger at Doc with added emphasis and Doc motioned with the gun for Jack to keep walking.

When they were gone, Doc put the gun away and Rose sat down beside him. "Thank you, John. I'm sorry I had to run to you like that, but there was no one else around." He started to speak and was overcome by a fit of coughing. She was glad Jack was gone. Doc wouldn't have been able to steady the pistol if this attack hit when he was holding the gun on Jack. It was one of the bad ones, causing him so much distress he was barely able to stay upright in the chair. When the spells came on him violently, all she could do was pray for them to pass quickly. She felt helpless having to sit there and watch him suffer, knowing there was no relief for him. By the time it passed, he was perspiring heavily and when he took the handkerchief away from his mouth she saw blood on it. He coughed up blood a lot lately. His eyes were red and watery. He was suffering so much with the disease, yet he still thought about her. "You be careful, Rose Marie. That one's got a mean streak longer than the Mississippi. Mark my words. He won't let it lie. He'll be back." She remembered what he said when he tried to discourage her from seeing Virgil. "I will defend your honor to the death, my dear." She believed he'd do just that. She smiled and touched his hand. "I don't want you to kill anyone, but I am grateful for your help tonight. Let's hope he doesn't come back." Doc put his handkerchief away. "You be careful. He'll come back and when he does, I'll kill him."

After the episode with Wild Jack Branch, she forgot about going out for fresh air. A couple of hours later, her eyes were burning from the smoke. She did need some air. She wondered what time it was. It had to be at least midnight. She wrapped the shawl around her shoulders and stepped out the back door into the cool evening air. Nightbirds flitted around. The day had been hot and like her, they were taking delight in the refreshing coolness of a summer-night breeze, glad for relief from the day's heat. She looked up at the sky. The moon was straight up and the stars twinkled like millions of tiny fireflies. Just about midnight. She yawned and rubbed the back of her neck. She'd be glad when it was time to go home. Two hours and she'd be done for the night. Lately, it seemed all she looked forward to was a time to rest.

She thought she was alone when a voice from the shadows startled her. "Told you I'd see you again, little dove." In the dark, she tried to focus her eyes. Her voice was tentative. "Who's there?" He laughed and moved out of the shadow of the building into the moonlight. Doc was right. Jack came back, sooner than she expected. He hadn't followed Ruby's advice to get a bath either. Outside in the night air, his body odor was every bit as wicked a stomach-curdling stench as inside the theatre. She glanced at the building, calculating the distance between herself and safety. She'd have to move awful fast to get to the back door. She remembered. They locked it from the inside to keep people like Jack from wandering in. Sometimes, you had to pound on it for quite awhile before anyone opened it. If nobody was close enough to hear the knocking, she might not get in right away.

Then, she'd be trapped for sure. He was moving toward the door. In another minute, he'd be there. She looked for a different route of escape. From the other side of the building next door, she heard voices. She'd have to make a run for the street and it was a long way from the back of the Bird Cage. It was the only way out. Someone would help her, provided she could get that far. Jack was so drunk, she just might be able to outrun him. The other three moved out of the shadows. After the beating he'd given them, she wondered why they came anywhere near him. The path to the street was cut off, her escape route blocked. Absent any options, she decided to try and talk her way out of what was fast becoming a no-win situation.

Big and mean and ugly as he was, and evil-smelling on top of that, it was easy to see why they called him Wild Jack. He swayed a little and took a few staggery steps to one side to keep his balance. With unruly, coarse hair sticking out in every direction from under the brim of a dirty, sweat-stained hat, floppy with age and wear, he looked almost comical. He'd spent at least part of the money on more whiskey and was drunker than when he was here earlier. She started to talk and he laughed, but there was no humor in the sound he made. He pointed his finger at her, his voice angry and sinister. "You think I'm a fool, don't you?" She swallowed hard. She dared not say what she thought. Of course he was a fool. Anyone who backed Doc Holliday into a corner was a damn fool. She tried not to sound as scared as she felt. "No, Jack. I don't think any such thing. I was only..." He bellowed at her. "Shut up." She flinched and backed up a step. She tried to talk her way out of it once and he fell for it, but even Jack wasn't dumb enough to let her get away with the same trick twice. A terrible memory flashed back. It was the old hotel in New Orleans all over again. She had to think fast. Words were all she had. She tried again. "I'm sorry about what happened a while ago, Mr. Branch. I know you were only wantin' to have some fun." He took a step toward her and she backed up, looking toward the street. There were people on the street, but they were too far away to see what was happening. She needed to get someone's attention. If only she'd taken Virgil's advice and carried her derringer all the time. She didn't think she'd need it after the stagecoach trip and although she carried it in her garter for a short time after she first arrived, the small gun had been in her vanity drawer for months. That was funny. Of any place, Tombstone was where she needed it most. She never thought she'd see the day she could kill someone, but if she had the little pocket pistol in her hand right now, she'd shoot Jack dead.

His intentions were clear and he was on his way to fix her good for making a fool of him. If ever there was a call to act, this was time to put on the performance of her life. She mustered all her strength to stay calm, smiling to cover the fear as she spoke. "Why don't we go inside and have a drink." He didn't answer. All four of them were advancing, boxing her in. She was surrounded. Trapped! Too much whiskey slurred his words. "We can have a good time right here in the moonlight." He waved his hand toward the moon and staggered off balance. "I think it's more romantic out here in the moonlight, don't you? Besides, that horse's ass, Holliday, ain't out here stickin' his nose where it don't belong and spoilin' the fun." She was trembling, but if she could keep him talking, she might buy a few more seconds to think. She'd give anything if Doc would walk out the back door. She followed his lead and looked up at the moon. "The moon is lovely tonight." He wasn't falling for her act. He'd been publicly humiliated inside and no amount of talking this time would pacify him. In New Orleans, she'd made the mistake of not trying to get away from her attackers early on. She had to do something, and do it fast. No time left for thinking, she bolted forward and tried to run between them, screaming as loud as she could. She didn't get far. Her short legs were no match for his long strides even drunk as he was. He tackled her and she went down hard, the force of the impact when she hit the ground knocking the wind out of her. She couldn't catch her breath. He sat down on top of her, squeezing out what little air was left in her lungs. He was heavy and he held her down tight. She was helpless. She didn't have enough air in her to scream. She struggled to get some air, clawing at him frantically and scratching his face. He touched the scratch and scowled at the smudge of blood on his finger. It made him madder and he pinned her arms up over her head, holding them together with one hand. "Wanna fight, do ya? Well, you ain't no match for me, girlie. Time you learned some respect."

"Let her go!" The voice cut through the darkness like an echo in a dream. At first, she didn't recognize it. She wasn't even sure she'd really heard it. She was dazed from hitting the ground so hard and her heart was pounding in her ears. She heard the voice again. It was clear and calm. "Get up and turn around with your hands in the air." He was squeezing the life out of her. Lack of air was making her light-headed. His hand moved toward the revolver stuck in his belt. The voice from the shadows was unwavering and ominous. The voice of Death. "It's up to you, Jack. You can live or die. Let the lady go and you walk away. Touch that smoker and you're dead. It's your call." From the shadows, she heard the hammer click back. Jack missed it. The whiskey fogged his brain and dulled his hearing. He was still sitting on her and pinning her hands to the ground above her head. His other hand was suspended over his gun. He'd heard the voice, but he hadn't heard the action on the .44/40 lock into place. He looked down at her, his eyes rheumy and unfocused from overconsumption of alcohol. "How's it a whore like you got so many friends?"

He didn't wait for her to answer. He was clumsy, not fast enough when he made his move. Off to the side, a different voice shouted at him. "Don't do it, Jack!" He ignored the warning. It happened very fast. He let out a high-pitched whoop as the gun cleared his belt. He was in an awkward position to begin with, sitting on her the way he was, and he didn't have enough leverage to get to his feet. His reflexes were bad. He lost his balance, releasing her hands when he tried to steady himself. She wasn't quite sure where the voices came from. They were standing somewhere close by, protected by the shadow of the buildings. He pulled the trigger and fired a wild shot. She opened her eyes and saw the fire and lead belch from the direction of the voices in the dark. The only thought in her mind was that she was dead. From her angle of sight, it looked like the fire was aimed straight at her. The shot roared above the music coming from inside the Bird Cage and the building next door. She heard the thud when the .44 hit him in the back and the sound of tearing flesh and splintering bone that followed as hot lead ripped through his body. The bullet went clear through him and careened over the top of her. A smaller man would have been felled by the shot, but he remained sitting upright on her stomach. Turning to get a look at the shooter, his hand was still raised in the air, drunkenly brandishing the revolver. He moved in a slowed motion like the mimes she'd seen on the street in New Orleans. When he looked down at her, his eyes were wide and glassy and a thin trickle of blood ran out of one corner of his mouth. The hand with the gun wavered and she was sure he intended to put a bullet in her before he keeled over, but he no longer had the ability to point it, let alone pull the trigger. He was a dead man sitting up. The gun dropped from his hand and he fell.

Jack was dead before he hit the ground. She moved her head to one side to avoid being hit when he fell on top of her. He went down hard, his head slamming into the dirt beside her like a boulder dropped to the sand from a great height. If he'd smashed into her head, he would have killed her. As it was, she was suffocating from the dead weight. She tried to roll him off, but he was too heavy. She was getting weak from lack of air and her stomach turned sour at the feel of his warm blood seeping through her clothes. The bullet made only a small hole in his back, but it came out his chest carrying parts of heart and rib fragments with it. She pushed frantically at him and beat on his shoulders, but the crushing weight of his body was too much for her. She couldn't budge him. Panic was growing in the futile struggle to catch her breath. Then, the weight was gone, the pressure on her chest relieved. Someone rolled him off and she gulped in the air. He flopped onto his back beside her and she scrambled to her feet, taking deep breaths to replenish her deprived lungs. She looked down at him. His face was covered with dirt and blood, his unseeing eyes still open. His chest had been ripped apart by the exiting bullet and the wound was oozing more than blood. Pieces of flesh and torn internal organs protruded from the gaping hole and stuck to the outside of his clothes like slimy, raw meat. She turned her face away from the gruesome sight. She felt sick. Voices from the shadows were unclear. She tried to see who was there. They walked into the light — two of them. They were much closer than she thought when Jack had her pinned down, only a few feet away, both with guns still drawn. The fatal shot had been fired at close range.

When they moved into the light, her mouth fell open in disbelief. It was another of those times where she wasn't sure if she was awake or dreaming. It was Wyatt — and John Merrick. Wyatt touched her arm. "Are you alright, Miss Callahan?" Time stopped. She stared at John. She couldn't believe it. Nalanche was right. He said John would be back. He'd been so sure about it, but she hadn't shared his faith. She'd done it again, doubted John's word. He promised to come back, and here he was. Why hadn't she believed? They'd been down this road before. She wasn't supposed to be at the Bird Cage. When he left, she promised to wait for him and to stay away from this place. When he came back, he expected to find her at home with everything packed and ready to leave for Washington. She looked at the ground, her thoughts spinning out of control. She was ashamed she hadn't had more faith in him and worse, that she'd broken her promise. Here she was again, exactly where she wasn't supposed to be and face-to-face with John Merrick. How would she explain it this time? When he was overdue, she gave up on him. She thought he'd changed his mind after hearing her story. He hadn't written and there was no wire advising a delay in his return, so she figured he was gone for good. He was supposed to be back in a few weeks. Why hadn't he sent some kind of word? She felt dizzy. He was there, holding her steady. It was the same old story. He was always there when she needed saving. He put his arms around her and she buried her face in his chest. She'd never understand this man. After so many mistakes, how many chances did one person get?

John was always the first one up. He'd been an early riser as long as she could remember. During the time since he'd been back, neither of them had gotten much sleep. There was a lot to talk about in the daylight hours, and love carried them far into the night. Strange, how she used to suffer from perpetual fatigue, but lately, she didn't feel tired at all. Being around him was exhilarating and she had more energy than she could ever remember having. There had always been something about him that gave her strength. He made her feel alive. This morning, she was the first one up. It was nearly ten o'clock and unusual that he was still asleep. She closed the door and whispered to Bear to follow her. Day in and day out, the big dog's tail was in motion and whatever happened to be close to him got swatted. In the bedroom, he'd thump it against the wall or the bed. Lizzie said it was how he showed his happiness, his way of smiling. He was happy all the time, and why not? He had a better home than a lot of people. She didn't want his happy tail-wagging to wake John up this morning. As it was, when she whispered to him to follow her, he stood in the doorway rapping the wood trim with his tail. Now that she was in the other room and the bedroom door was closed, he was happily trotting across the room to sit beside her. She decided to crochet until John woke up. That way, she wouldn't be rattling around the house and Bear's tail wouldn't be thumping anything if he was lying down. Without thinking, she set her coffee cup on the low table in front of the couch. Bear came to her for his expected hug before taking up his customary position at her feet. As usual, the tail swept everything within reach, including the needlework and her coffee. The cup clinked over, spilling the coffee onto her skirt and the floor. She scolded him. "Bear! Just look what you've done. Why don't you watch where you're goin'?" As soon as she said it, she realized how silly it sounded. He was a dog for Heaven's sake. He didn't understand coffee cups on the table. From the tone of her voice, he knew he'd done something wrong, but wasn't quite sure what it was. He laid down with both paws over his nose and rolled his eyes up at her contritely. Whatever it was that he did to upset her, he was sorry. Her irritation with him didn't last long. He looked so comical with his paws resting on his nose, she had to laugh. When she did, he knew the offense couldn't have been too bad. He kept his paws over his nose, but the tail was wagging. She crossed her arms and looked down at him. "A trick given to you by your two-legged brother, no doubt." She was referring to Nalanche. From the time Bear was a pup, Nalanche talked to him. She was sure they understood each other completely, although there were times when she didn't understand either one of them.

She went to the kitchen for something to clean up the spill. When she returned to the parlour, the dog was sitting up beside the couch, but as soon as he saw her coming, he laid down and resumed the position with his paws over his nose. She was wise to his acting. "You don't fool me, Little Bear." He sat close to her while she scrubbed the wet spot on the rug. When she finished, he pawed at the spot. She patted his head. " 'Tis alright. I'm not angry with you. 'Twas an accident. I know that. I should've known better than to leave the cup in your path. You can't be expected to know those things. You're only a dog." He whined at her remark. "Well now, I suppose that's not tellin' it quite true, is it? We all know you are no ordinary dog, don't we?" He whined again and wagged his tail as if to say he was glad she understood that to be true.

The hinges squeaked and she opened the bedroom door a crack, trying not to make any more noise. She peeked in. With the coffee cup spilling and her talking to the dog, she was afraid the clatter in the parlour might have wakened John. He was sound asleep. She figured he had to be awful tired to sleep so late. Bear was right beside her, trying to push the door the rest of the way open with his nose, the tail wagging faster in anticipation of seeing John. She pulled him back and closed the door. He looked up at her and whined, not understanding why she wouldn't let him in the bedroom. "Let him sleep, Little Bear. You'll see him soon enough." It wasn't like John to waste daylight, but his exhaustion was understandable. Before he came back, he completed two trials for the Army in California. While he was away, he thought about what she said. She wasn't in the best of health and traveling would be difficult. He'd been thinking about what Abby told him, how Rose was so sick with the pneumonia, she nearly died. She needed to live in a warm climate. With the California assignments completed, he made his decision. He went straight to Washington and resigned his commission. For a long time, he'd been torn between his father's wishes and his own desires, but he was sure his father would understand why he no longer wanted to be in the military. The Army had been good to Richard Merrick's family, but it wasn't the life for John. He dreamed of having a private law practice, an office with his name above the door, and a library full of his own books beside his father's collection. His plan was to surprise her by coming home without the Army dictating where they went and how they lived. He surprised her alright. It took much longer to get to Arizona than he expected, but he was a civilian now, free and ready to settle down with her and hang out his shingle in front of his own office. They talked about it a lot. Tombstone was growing. The need for all kinds of businesses was increasing and he was a good lawyer. His services would be appreciated and well-paid. He didn't care about having a fancy suite in New York or Boston. He was ready to open his office right here in Tombstone. In time, he could expand and hire other good lawyers. If things went according to plan, Nalanche might be his partner one day. Rose worried that having a wife with what Doc diplomatically referred to as "decorative notoriety" might jeopardize his chance for a successful practice. John didn't see it that way, joking that he might get more business by virtue of the curiosity factor connected with her colorful background. She didn't think it was funny. Besides, it wasn't that colorful, and she didn't particularly want to be reminded of where she'd been.

One more hour went by and John was still in bed. She fixed another cup of coffee and returned to the bedroom with Bear on her heels. He walked slowly, as if trying to be careful not to knock anything over in his travels this time, perhaps mindful of the recent accident with the spilled coffee. Not wanting to be left out, he stuck to her like a shadow when she opened the bedroom door. She couldn't believe John was still asleep. She pulled the curtain aside a little and the sun poured in. In the distance, a few puffy clouds were beginning to pile up. By late afternoon, they'd become a thunderhead. A little rain would be nice, especially at night. She loved to lie in the dark listening to the rain. She sipped her coffee, remembering how he continued with his reasons why they should stay in Tombstone. The weather was good. The town was growing and he'd have plenty of work. Her friends were here. The sunset was beautiful. She laughed at him and all his reasons. "You already said that." He rubbed his chin thoughtfully. "Did I? Well, I'm just ..." She stood on her tiptoes and kissed him. "I know what you're tryin' to do. You're tryin' to convince me we should stay here. You don't have to convince me. We'll stay if that's what you want." He smiled. "That's good. I want to stay." She recognized the old twinkle in his eye. It was always there when he felt a little devilish. He still loved to tease her. She looked sideways at him. "Is there somethin' on your mind? Somethin' you want to be tellin' me? You wouldn't be pokin' fun at a helpless waif like meself now, would you?" He started to give her the old stuff about her not being helpless, but stopped before he said it. "Do you know you always cut the end off your words?" She gave him an exasperated look and blew out a deep breath. "That's not what you're wantin' to tell me — and I don't cut the end off my words. 'Tis your hearin' that's bad, not my talkin'." He smiled at the way she did it again, cut the g's off the end of her words without realizing she was doing it.

There was something else he wanted to tell her. He couldn't restrain his excitement for one minute longer. "I've taken an office on Fremont Street." She figured as much. "I wondered when you'd be gettin' around to doin' it. You've been talkin' about it every day since you came home." He went to the closet and pulled out something wrapped in a heavy cloth. He held it to one side. "Close your eyes. It's a surprise." She obeyed and put both hands over her eyes while he unwrapped the package. "Alright. You can open them." She peeked through her fingers. It was a sign — a very fancy sign, bearing the Merrick family crest above his name, "John Garrison Merrick, Attorney at Law." He was grinning from ear-to-ear. She'd never seen him so excited. "Isn't it beautiful? Nalanche made it for me. Mr. Hampton helped him." She ran her fingers over the sign. It was beautiful, smooth as glass and varnished to a high luster. "Nalanche and I have decided that someday when he becomes a lawyer, I'll make him my partner. We'll have to change the sign to add his name, of course." His expression turned curious. "By the way, does he have a last name?" Rose shrugged her shoulders. "I've never asked him. I think Nalanche is his only name." John thought for a minute. "Maybe we'll give him ours."

She stood beside the bed, remembering how excited he was when he showed her the sign and how pleased he was with the idea of adding Nalanche's name to it someday. Ann used to tell her to be thankful every day for something. This was one of those times to give thanks. Watching John sleep, she said a prayer and thanked God for bringing him back. She'd never know how she got so lucky, why she'd been given another chance at the future with him. She thought about Ann Merrick, the woman she believed was an angel. Maybe Ann guided him back to her. In a matter of days, her life changed and in a few weeks, she'd be Mrs. John Merrick. Ann would be happy about that. Jenny and Lizzie were already working on the wedding plans, not unlike Rebecca when they first announced their engagement so long ago. She thought she'd never see Rebecca again, but it wouldn't be long until they'd travel to New Orleans and the family would be together for a wonderful reunion. She missed the Pixie and Marian. John said they'd make the trip to New Orleans after they were married and when she felt stronger, maybe next Spring. In the meantime, he had his work cut out to set up the practice and have his father's desk and bookcases shipped out. By the time next Spring came around, they'd both be ready for a holiday. Rebecca would practically be a grown woman by the time they saw her again.

She couldn't resist. The day was too beautiful to keep it all outside. She slid the window open slowly to let in the sunshine and fresh morning air. Bear rested his chin on the windowsill with his eyes closed, lazily swishing his tail and taking in the sweet desert breeze. She patted his head. It seemed everyone was happy now that John was back. Many times, she pretended she was in the old, Irish fairy tales her father told by the campfire. She used to dream of being the princess, but with all she'd been through, she'd given up on fairy tales and dreams a long time ago. In order to survive, she had to live in the real world, but things were different with John home. He made her feel like a real princess and the things she wished for most had become very real because of him.

An explosion from the hills interrupted her thoughts. Dynamite signaled discovery of a new vein and the opening of another tunnel. Reverberations echoed down from the mines and when they dissipated, the rhythmic clank of the pumps followed the path of the echoes on the wind. They never stopped. Day and night, they worked to force the groundwater up from inside the earth to keep the tunnels clear. Bigger and better pumps were being brought in all the time. The deeper they went, the harder the pumps had to work to force the water to the surface. She'd have never made a very good miner. She knew she couldn't go down into those holes. The idea of being so far underground terrified her and she thought the miners were brave men. Their lives were hard and the work was dangerous. If the pumps ever stopped, the mines would fill with water until eventually, they'd flood and be forced to shut down. There was always the danger that men could be trapped beneath the ground and killed by a cave-in or, if the water came up too fast, they could drown. She wondered how they lived with that fear every time they went down into the hole; how they slept at night thinking about it. They went down because hope of finding a fortune was greater than the fear of not coming out alive. The search for the mother lode drove them on day after day. She didn't know how many mines were running now, but in the short time she'd been here, several new ones had opened. This morning's blast probably excavated the way along a new vein. She wondered how much silver was in the hills and how many would die trying to get it out. Lately, she thought about the dangers more than ever. It bothered her that John had a little touch of silver fever. He was intrigued with mining and talked about doing some digging himself. Wyatt had some mining interests and introduced John to the owner of one of the larger operations, and he made the trip down into the hole once. While inside, he was shown how they worked the vein and he came home with a memento of his first mining experience, a chunk of silver ore the size of his fist. He kept it on the mantle. After that, he talked about it a lot. She became uneasy when he told her that he and Wyatt discussed the possibility of a partnership in a mine with Matt Kern. Unlike gold which was unmistakable from any other mineral straight from the ground, silver ore didn't look anything like silver. It fascinated him that the black rock with streaks of rust could be processed into silver dollars or jewelry. Thinking about him down inside a cold, damp mine shaft never set right with her and she hoped he'd lose interest once he got his practice going.

John yawned and stretched. She turned away from the window. "I'm sorry if I woke you. 'Tis a lovely day and I was tryin' to let some fresh air in." He held his arms out and she sat on the edge of the bed. Believing John was beckoning to him, Bear ran to the bed before Rose could stop him. In one leap, he landed on top of John. He'd been waiting patiently all morning for John to wake up and he saw the motion of John's hand as an invitation for him to jump on the bed. John laughed and wrestled the big dog onto his back. Bear let out little squeals of delight at the play until Rose ordered him off the bed. He looked plaintively at John for a reversal of the order. John laughed. "Sorry, old boy. I can't help you. She's the boss when it comes to dogs on the bed." He rubbed Bear's head and gave him a little nudge. When the dog was off the bed, he turned to Rose. "You look sad today. Are you unhappy about leaving the Bird Cage?" The question surprised her. She shook her head "no" and ran her fingers through his hair, hoping to change the subject. He could always tell what she was thinking. Being a prostitute wasn't something she planned on and it had been a difficult way of life, but for a reason she didn't understand, she was having a hard time leaving the theatre. Tonight would be her final performance. John agreed to let her stay on for a short time, so long as the work was limited to singing or talking to customers. Anything else was out of the question. Virgil and Doc had both protected her from the harsher aspects of her profession for a while, but when they were gone and their influence of no further consequence, she would eventually have been confronted with the inevitable resumption of her duties as a soiled dove. John's return altered the course of her destiny. The house accepted the proposal and her position changed permanently. A new dove had been hired to replace her and her days as a lady of the night were over. There was no more entertaining men upstairs or down, and socializing with customers at the tables was closely controlled by Ruby. No longer providing specialized pleasure for the gentlemen, her services over the normal spread of working hours were diminished. Tonight, the Silver Rose would say good-bye to the Bird Cage Theatre. Despite the nature of the place, there was a sadness about leaving it. John was right about that. Her friends were there. She'd miss them. She'd miss Doc coming by to visit. Of course, it wasn't as if she was leaving them forever. Since she and John were staying in Tombstone, she could see them whenever she wanted to. Still, there was a strange kind of sadness in knowing tonight would be the last time she'd pass through the doors of the theatre. She didn't mean to get so wrapped up in the place and she couldn't remember when it happened. It just did. Like trying to break free of a narcotic addition, life at the Bird Cage was going to be a hard habit to walk away from. She couldn't explain the feeling, but it had something to do with the reason they were all there, the bond that tied them to each other. She never really wanted to be there, but after all this time, it was hard to leave. She never thought she'd say that. Her future was bright, full of promise. Theirs would remain the same. Maybe the sadness she felt was for them, not herself.

She laid out a plain, gray dress and her mother's gold locket. She thought it more appropriate to dress conservatively, even matronly, now that she was about to become the wife of Tombstone's best lawyer. She smiled at the prospect as she brushed her hair. She'd wear it up tonight. It made her look more reserved. If she wasn't so much smaller than Abby, she'd have given her the other dresses. Tomorrow, she'd take them to the Bird Cage and leave them with Ruby for anyone who could fit into them. It was John's idea for her to wear the green satin for her farewell performance. It had been her favorite. He held it up and said they'd be expecting to see the Silver Rose they all knew, not some demure and proper lawyer's wife. After some coaxing from him, she agreed to wear it one last time. She put the locket away and put on all the silver and turquoise Nalanche had given her, carefully adjusting each piece the way she always did. One more thing.

The rose ring. She'd worn it every night for so long, it was as much a part of her as the Bird Cage. Like the green dress, she'd wear the ring one last time and after tonight, she'd put it away forever. She opened the wooden box. The ring was gone. She always kept it there. She tried to think where else she might have left it. Then, she remembered. She was wearing it the night Wild Jack threw her down in the dirt out behind the Bird Cage. It must have slipped off her finger during the scuffle. She'd never find it now, and maybe it was better not to look for it. Maybe it was meant to stay behind with the rest of the memories of Virgil Earp and the Bird Cage Theatre.

They walked hand-in-hand up Allen Street. She walked slowly, thinking how funny it was that a person's view of life is affected by changes in circumstance. She didn't talk much, preoccupied with her own thoughts. How many times had she walked this way, wishing she could go in another direction? Now, she was trying to memorize every step along the way. A lot happened to her in this town. She glanced across the street at the Oriental Saloon. He used to stand on that corner before she knew who he was, watching her walk to work every night — Virgil. No one there tonight. She stopped and stared across the street for a long time, lost in thought. John finally asked if something was wrong. "What are you looking for?" She couldn't tell him. "Oh, I suppose there's somethin' about takin' this walk for the last time that gives me a little touch of sadness. Can you understand?" Until now, he'd been holding her hand. He put his arms around her. "I understand a lot more than you think, Rose."

They always showed up when she least expected them — the little banshees. They flew out from their hiding place around the corner, shrieking and making scary faces by pulling their mouths out of shape sideways as far as they would stretch and sticking out their tongues. She laughed at the way John jumped at the ambush. They took him completely off guard. She'd been startled too, but not like him. Emily was in charge of the attack tonight and she squealed with delight at the successful execution of her plan. Rose shook her finger at the little girl. "Emily. If your mother finds out you're talkin' to me, she'll be very upset. You did promise her that you wouldn't be talkin' to me anymore." William spoke for his sister. "It's alright. Mama's over in Tucson helping Aunt Viola with her new baby and

Papa don't care if we talk to you. He said so." Rose corrected his grammar. "Doesn't care, William." William happily concurred. "That's what I said. Papa don't care. He thinks you're pretty." Rose rolled her eyes up at John and he smiled at William's failure to understand the correction of his grammar. It was also interesting that the husband of the woman who hated her so much came right out and told his children he thought Rose was pretty. She leaned over and put one finger to her lips. She whispered, "Listen. I'll tell you a secret." The three children moved in closer, eager to hear the secret. "After tonight, I won't be workin' at the Bird Cage anymore. Maybe I'll speak to your mother about our games when I'm the wife of this good man here. Now, run home. 'Tis gettin' late, and we've had all the silliness we can stand for one day." She blew them a kiss and they scampered off, happily anticipating the outcome of Rose's talk with their mother. She watched them until they ran around the next corner. "Oh, to be havin' all that energy." John took her hand and linked it through his arm. "We all had more of it when we were eight years old."

When they reached the Bird Cage, they stopped in front and she studied the building. On the other side of the doors, she knew friends waited to celebrate her good fortune and say good-bye. When she was ready, they stepped inside. John waved at someone across the room, someone she never expected to see again. She recognized him right away. He looked the same as the first time they met on the stage from El Paso. He returned John's wave. When they got close to the table, he held out his hand in greeting to John. The two men shook hands warmly and slapped each other on the back. John maneuvered her in front of him. "You remember Matt, don't you?" How could she forget Matt Kern? He was one of those rare people you counted yourself lucky for knowing. She liked him the first time they met. She wished he could have been her traveling companion all the way to Tombstone, but he'd gotten off early to go to Colorado. He told her he might see her someday in Tombstone, but she never expected it. He said he'd been there before and his business could take him there again at any time. She knew he'd told John about meeting her on the stage out of El Paso and he'd been at least partly responsible for John finding her. She owed him a debt of thanks. He took her hand in both of his. "Glad to see you again, Miss Callahan." She held up a finger to correct him. "Rose. Please, call me Rose. What brings you to Tombstone, Marshal?" He mimicked her and held up his finger. "Matt. Call me Matt." He winked and came close to whisper in her ear. "I was invited to a wedding. I know I'm a little early, but this way, I'll be first in line to kiss the bride." He pulled out a chair for her. "We saved you a chair. You're the guest of honor tonight." Wyatt and her friend, John Holliday were seated at the table along with Kate. Doc blew her a kiss. Some things never changed. She blew one back to him, knowing her friendship with him had been approved by Kate. Tonight, Rose was the princess her father told stories about and her prince was right beside her, holding court, of all places, in the Bird Cage Theatre.

The girls talked about the wedding. John held her hand and smiled a lot. The men teased him about becoming a married man. Doc kept winking at her. People stopped at the table to wish her well and shake hands with John. Wyatt stayed longer than usual. He was pleased that John would be setting up his practice soon. Staying in Tombstone was the right decision all the way around. Tonight was truly a celebration. Somewhere in the conversation, Virgil's name came up. She thought about him and all the pressures he had to endure because of his work and his brother, the man who sat across the table from her. She knew John met Virgil the night Morgan was shot. They did some work together during the trial and John spoke highly of him. He thought Virgil had a lot of guts to do the job he did. She wished he'd come to the party tonight. She was sure he was happy for her and she still considered him a friend. If he came, it might have helped put their old relationship to rest once and for all and they could have parted face-to-face as friends. As it was, she still had the feeling of abandonment because of the way he'd done things. It would have been alright for him to come, alright for her anyway. Whatever there was between them was over, but there was no reason to burn the bridge. John knew about them and she was sure he wouldn't have objected to Virgil stopping by. He'd even said he owed Virgil a debt of thanks for taking care of her. Funny, how men's thinking went. A woman would never thank another woman for taking care of her man. In fact, it was out of the question.

Something else occurred to her. It would have been alright with her and with John if Virgil came tonight, but maybe it wasn't alright with Virgil. From the beginning, she didn't have any unreasonable expectations of him. She always knew he wouldn't leave his wife for her and she didn't want him to. Her feelings for him were not the same as the love she felt for John. It wasn't as if she wanted to marry him and spend the rest of her life with him. He was a friend, a protector. An escape. She identified her feelings for him a long time ago, but maybe he hadn't done the same. On the other hand, maybe he had, and that was the trouble. Why had she never thought of that? Maybe he cared about her more than he let on and that's why he stayed away. She'd never considered that. Or maybe he finally decided Allie deserved better than a husband who slept with another woman. Thanks to Caroline Grants and her cronies, she was sure Allie suffered from the stories about Virgil and his escapades with a prostitute, not to mention, she stood by him through God only knew how much other tribulation. The woman had to be a saint. For Allie's sake, maybe it was better he hadn't come tonight. There was a sudden feeling of closing where Virgil was concerned. In her mind, it was finally done. She pretended not to hear what Lizzie said next — one of those unpredictable blasts of news she was famous for hitting you with when you least expected it and were the most vulnerable. "Too bad Virge couldn't come tonight, but I suppose he's better off in California. Maybe he'll have the good sense not to ever come back." Rose stifled her surprise at the announcement. So, Virge was gone. Now, it was finally and truly over. Abby's hand on her shoulder brought her back to present company. "Why the somber look, Rose? You're supposed to be happy tonight." Rose smiled. John was looking at her and she hoped this was not one of those times he knew what she was thinking.

She was embarrassed at the fuss they made over her. They wanted her to sing. Any other time, she wouldn't have given it a second thought. Everything was different tonight. One last song and then, it'd be over. Lizzie cried when she left the table on her way to the stage and Charlie began to play an Irish song. They applauded when she stepped onto the stage. It was one of her favorites, the one Kevin O'Leary asked her to sing when he came in from the mines. Right about nine o'clock every night, Kevin would show up for his single shot of Irish whiskey and a song. He said she took him home to Ireland and the green hills of Tralee when she sang. He cried every time. It had the same affect on everyone in the room and it made her feel like crying too, every time she sang it. Maybe it was the way Charlie played the music.

When it was over, the room was so quiet you could hear a pin drop. At first, she thought they didn't like it. During the song, she knew she was a little off key in a couple of places. Maybe more than a couple. Maybe they noticed. She felt her face getting hot. She was uncomfortable with everyone looking at her and she stepped back to go behind the curtain. A coin hit the floor and broke the silence. They were on their feet, clapping and whistling. It was the most applause she'd ever received. She looked out toward the table where John and her friends had been sitting. They were standing too, applauding her performance with the rest of the crowd. She waved a final good-bye and blew a kiss out over the room. It was over. Once and for all, she was finished with the Bird Cage. After tonight, she'd never set foot inside the theatre again. She went behind the stage and looked at the props and curtains for the last time. She wanted to remember everything as it was tonight. She touched the curtain and whispered a good-bye.

A clap of thunder shook the building, a fitting accent to mark the end of her time here. Charlie got up from the piano and waited at the bottom of the stairs. When she came down the steps, he hugged her. "That's the best you ever sang. They won't forget the Silver Rose." More thunder, louder the second time. She looked up at the ceiling. The rain she predicted would be here tonight began pounding the roof and she shivered. There was a draft she hadn't noticed before. Charlie rolled his eyes up. "Looks like we're in for a gully washer tonight."

No one was in a hurry to go out in the rain. They sat at the table, laughing and talking into the night. Wyatt and Matt were particularly interested in John's plans for the office. It was painted today and Nalanche would hang up the sign in a few days. He'd sent for his father's desk and his books and as soon as they arrived, he'd be in business. Rose was so proud of him. Doc announced he was John's first client, giving rise to a round of laughter. Rose teased him. "And what have you done to be needin' the services of a lawyer, John Holliday?" Doc sipped his whiskey thoughtfully. His smile was devilish. "I'm sure I'll think of somethin'." She was sure that would be the case. She shook her finger at him and he winked. Lizzie put her arm around John's shoulder and kissed him on the top of his head. "What was that for, Lizette?" She knelt beside his chair. "It's for not taking my Rosie away." She was like a child, grateful for finding a missing, favorite doll. He kissed her hand. "I'm glad were staying too."

In the excitement, they all failed to notice one important development. Matt Kern had pulled another chair to the table and he and Miss Jenny were involved in a tête-á-tête not privy to the other folks at the party. It was clear from the way they looked at each other and spoke softly that the substance of their conversation was not meant for other ears. Matt rested his arm around the back of Jenny's chair and sat close, whispering to her. Every so often, they'd giggle like a couple of kids. Rose overheard bits of Matt's story about the family farm in Iowa. Something about cornfields and pigs, and his father was getting up there in years. The dirt was like gold. Rose thought Jenny looked so fresh and innocent, her face glowing. A strange concept considering Jenny had become a little rough around the edges and a well-known source of entertainment for men at the Bird Cage. Their dialogue was not along customary lines between a man and a prostitute in the Bird Cage. It was a courtship. Who'd ever thought a girl like Jenny would be interested in pigs and dirt? But then, maybe it wasn't so strange. Jenny was what she had to be in Tombstone, but that didn't mean she couldn't be something else. Funny, how falling in love can change a person.

The celebration continued for several hours. Someone said the rain let up. The storm was passing on through. It was after midnight, a good time to go home while there was a break in the weather. There was a good chance of more rain before the night was over. Rose kept a shawl in the dressing room behind the stage. No need to leave it now that she wouldn't be back. She'd run and get it and they'd go home. John stood up with her, taking her hand and kissing her fingertips. She stood on her tiptoes and kissed him on the cheek. "I'll be right back." Before he let go, he raised her hand to his lips again. "I'll wait."

Halfway to the stage, her feet felt heavy, like they were mired in quicksand. She had trouble taking another step. Her knees were weak. She felt a chill and shivered. There was no draft where she stood, but she was cold. She shivered again. There was a perception of something not quite right — an uneasy, aberrant feeling as though something terrible just happened, or was about to happen. Her mind went back to the night when three men were shot a few feet from where she stood. Blood on the floor. Virgil tried to tell her it was the way things were here. Her friends told her the same thing. She'd better get used to it. She closed her eyes and swallowed hard. What on earth made her think of that?

Before she took the first step beside the stage, she heard the shouting and whirled around. They were Wild Jack Branch's friends, the three men he'd beaten bloody; the same three who were with him the night he was killed outside the Bird Cage. They were liquored-up, shaking their fists and hollering at Wyatt. He was on his feet, trying to calm them down. He'd pushed his coat behind the revolver on his hip and one hand rested on the gun. He held up the other hand indicating they should stop and he was telling them to go outside where they could talk about it. He didn't want any trouble and he didn't want anybody to get hurt. If they didn't want to go to jail for disturbing the peace, they best quiet down. They ignored his order to go outside and kept shouting they were here to get even for Jack. They knew who killed him. Wyatt answered them. "I killed Wild Jack because he pulled a gun. He fired the first shot. It was self-defense. There wasn't any other way." The more he talked, the louder they got. They called him a damn liar. That was too much for Doc. He and Matt stood up. Impending danger gripped Rose's throat like a hangman's noose and her heart quickened in anticipation of the trap door opening to snap the rope. She tried to move, but something was holding her to the spot where she stood. People backed away from the trouble site. Some headed for the door. No one wanted to be in the line of fire when bullets started flying. They'd seen it before and with the situation heating up this fast, it was only a matter of time until things got crazy.

The one with a bandage over his nose moved a hand toward his gun. Wyatt raised his voice. "Don't do anything you'll regret, Tasker. Think about it. Jack broke your nose and kicked your ass. Is he worth dying for?" Matt and Doc stood on either side of Wyatt. Tasker clenched his teeth together, waving his hand toward Wyatt and the two men with him. "We got no fight with you or these men here, Marshal. We want him." He pointed at John. Rose held her breath. Why did they want John? He hadn't done anything. They argued back and forth and as she watched, it all became crystal clear. That night — the night Wild Jack was killed, John was with Wyatt. When they came out of the shadows, they both had guns in their hands. They were together. She saw the flash when the shot was fired and she knew exactly where it came from. It came from the gun on the left as she faced them. She remembered. The man on the left was not Wyatt Earp. It was John Merrick. John fired the fatal shot that sent Jack Branch to his eternal reward. Wyatt was a lawman and it had been easier for him to take responsibility for the shooting. It was self-defense anyway, no matter who killed Jack, but it had been easier to say he did it. There were less questions that way. That was it. John killed Jack Branch. Why had she blocked it out of her mind? His name passed her lips in a whisper, "John!" and she started to move toward the conflict. She had to be with him. Piano Charlie's arms went around her. "Stay here, Rose. Let the Marshal handle it."

Wyatt hadn't given up trying to get them outside. He said it again. "You're wrong. I shot Jack. It couldn't be helped. He drew first. It was self-defense. This man here had nothing to do with it." Tasker spit on the floor. The packing in his crushed nose forced him to breath through his mouth, resulting in nasally, pig-like inflections in his voice. Both eyes were blackened and his face was still badly swollen from the beating. His upper lip curled in a sneer and he growled at Wyatt. "It was a forty-four what killed Jack." He pointed at Wyatt's gun. "You're packin' a forty-five there, Marshal." He pointed at John. "He killed Jack Branch. Shot him in the back. We saw him do it plain as I'm lookin' at you and he's gonna pay. You arrest that one for murder or we'll handle it our way." Wyatt was losing patience fast. "No, you won't. This has gone far enough. You can see he's not armed. Now, lay those weapons on the floor easy before somebody gets hurt." They stood their ground. "Wyatt was done talking. "Alright boys, you're under arrest for disturbing the peace and violating the city gun ordinance. I'm impounding your weapons. Matt, take their guns."

John was standing on the spot where she left him. He wouldn't want her in the line of fire and he turned to see where she was. Their eyes met and she knew the truth. His eyes said it plain as words, and the entire event played out in her mind. When the two men stepped from the shadows that night with their guns drawn, only the revolver on the left emitted a trace of smoke. The flash in the darkness came from that gun. John was the man on the left. He carried a forty-four. It was John who killed Jack Branch, not Wyatt Earp.

The next few seconds passed before her eyes like a slow dream and she felt like she had cotton stuffed in her ears. She heard the voices, but they were muffled, dulled by the distance between what was real and what was unbelievable. Matt was trying to talk some sense to them, repeating Wyatt's words. "You heard the Marshal. This man's not armed. Let's not have any trouble here. I'm a United States Marshal. Hand over your guns." John and Rose were still looking at each other, unspoken messages only they understood passing between them. She heard the shot. John's hand went to his shoulder and he wheeled around. She flinched when the bullet whistled past her head and slammed into the corner of the stage off to her left. The second bullet hit him in the chest and spun him around in the opposite direction. He clutched at his chest as he fell, the circle of blood on his shirt already spreading. A dozen more shots rang out in rapid succession. Wyatt and Matt and Doc were fast. The three miners were dead. The room was filled with smoke and the acrid smell of burned gunpowder. John was on the floor, struggling for breath.

She heard Wyatt yell for someone to fetch the doctor. She called John's name and Charlie let her go. She ran to John and knelt beside him, cradling his head in her arms. Doc took off his belt and cinched it tight around John's arm for a tourniquet. Matt was trying to stop the bleeding by putting pressure on the chest wound, his efforts only causing John more pain. John's voice was weak. "I've taken my last walk up Allen Street, boys. Take care of Rose." Matt talked to John as he continued to press on John's chest. "Hang on, my friend. Doc Goodfellow's on his way. He'll be here any second. You're gonna be alright." The fear that he might be wrong came through clear in Matt's voice. He was doing his best not to let John see how afraid he was. John was looking up at Matt, his eyes glassy and his face pale from loss of blood. He was fading very fast. Doc took off his coat and folded it under John's head. Rose wiped the beads of perspiration from his face. He tried to say something and choked on the words. She whispered softly, "Don't talk, my love. The doctor is comin'. He'll take care of you." As soon as the words left her mouth, she knew it wasn't so. She looked over at Matt. He was staring at her. He swallowed hard. He'd been pressing towels from the bar on John's chest, trying to slow the bleeding. His eyes said it all. It was no use. The towels were saturated with blood and his face was an expression of complete helplessness. The wound was too bad and he couldn't stop the bleeding. There wasn't anything he could do. He didn't have to say it. The wound was fatal and John was bleeding to death. He was struggling to get the words out. She held his hand and put her ear next to his mouth to hear what he was trying to say. He could barely whisper, but she heard what he said. "I love you, Rose. I'll always be yours." He gasped with the effort of speaking a few words and she held her own breath. His fingers moved. The whisper was fainter and he no longer held onto her hand. She was the one holding on now. He was dying and he knew it. "I'll see you again. If it takes a hundred years, I'll see you again. I promise." His final word was a barely-audible whisper. "Rose." His eyes were closed. He was gone.

The storm blew in a cold draft when the doctor rushed in, opening his bag as he ran to John's side. When he was summoned, he didn't bother with a coat or hat. He grabbed his medical bag and ran out into the downpour and he was drenched. It was a night reminiscent of the night Morgan Earp was killed. The storm hadn't passed over as they thought and booming peals of thunder once again accompanied the pouring rain like kettle drums in a wild symphony of nature. She knelt beside John, holding his hand. Matt moved away to make room for the doctor. It only took a second to know. He removed the stethoscope from his ears and let it hang around his neck. Then, he ripped John's shirt open a little to get a look at the wound. No need to see more, he closed John's coat to cover the worst of it. This was the hardest part of being a physician, pronouncing a good man dead.

He was the young doctor who took care of Lizzie when she tried to kill herself. He was a kind, compassionate man. "I'm sorry, Rose. He's dead." There was no other way to say it. She looked at John. Why did the doctor say that? It was a mistake. It had to be. He was wrong and she told him so. "You don't know what you're talkin' about. Where's Doc Goodfellow anyway? He was called. He'll be able to help John. He's a surgeon. He knows how to fix these things. We'll wait for him." The young doctor reached across John's lifeless body and touched Rose's hand. "Doc Goodfellow is out at the mines. We sent someone to get him, but when he comes, he can't do anything. He couldn't have saved John if he'd come in my place. I'm sorry." He didn't know what else to say to her. She ignored the doctor. She touched John's face and smiled. He looked like he did this morning when she watched him sleeping. She ought to be able to wake him up by shaking him a little. She smiled and shook him gently. "Wake up, John. The hour is late. We have to go home." She shook him again. "John. Did you hear me? It's time to go." Matt was beside her. "I'll take you home, Rose." She pushed him away and reached for John. Someone else was there and different arms held her. "Nalanche." She smiled at him. "Will you wake John up? We have to go home before it rains." Nalanche lifted her to her feet. She watched as Matt took off his coat and covered John's face. That was it. He was dead. She looked down at her hands. They were covered with John's blood. Her dress was covered with it. Matt had it all over his hands and clothes. So did Doc. It was everywhere. She rubbed her hands on her dress. The blood wouldn't come off. Nalanche let go of her and she moved away, walking backward and staring at the people around John's body. When she reached the door, she bolted out into the middle of the street. Another clap of thunder echoed through town, then another right on top of the first one. The rain began falling harder. In a matter of seconds, she was soaked. The wind came up and blew a stinging rain in her face. She turned her face upward and shouted at God, shaking her fist at Him. "How could you let this happen?" She held up her hands. The rain was washing away the blood.

They carried John outside and she held her hands over him, begging them not to take him out into the rain. "It's rainin'. He'll get wet. Please don't let him get wet." When they moved on, she cried and yelled at them to stop. She was hysterical and began hitting the men. Nalanche stopped her. Another voice was close by and a gentle hand, trying to quiet her down. Abby. "Come inside Rose. You'll get sick if you catch a chill." Rose shoved her and ran after the men taking John away. Nalanche went after her. She fought him, screaming and beating her fists wildly against his chest. He didn't let go and he didn't try to stop the blows. He stood still as she pounded on him as hard as she could, venting the anger only he understood. She was like a wild animal fighting to free itself from the trap. She swore at him and slapped his face, screaming that she'd kill him if he didn't let her go. They were only words said out of desperation and pain and he knew it. He held her while she hit him. There was no one else who could do it. She slapped him again then pulled back, stunned, as if she were the one slapped. In her anger, she'd been striking out blindly. She put her hands over her mouth, realizing she was taking out her frustration on the wrong person. He didn't deserve to be punished for a crime he didn't commit. It wasn't his fault John was dead. He was the gentle spirit she called Brother. She stopped fighting. She touched his face and her finger-tips traced the raised welts across his cheek where she struck him. Her voice was a broken whisper. "Nalanche. Forgive me." He was silent. He understood. John's death was not only her loss.

Bolts of lightning lit up the sky and crackled upon impact with the earth, their sparks igniting creosote bushes whose oil rejected the water and left them vulnerable to fire even in the rain. The bushes exploded in flame and deafening thunder rolled all around them like the galloping hooves of the Biblical horses of the Apocalypse come to trample the forces of evil. The storm unleashed its fury at the moment of John's passing in violent protest of his murder the same way it rained and hailed the night Morgan Earp was killed. The roar intensified with the accelerated velocity of an accompanying wind and the rain became a torrential sea of water falling from the sky, large, cold drops stinging her face like sharp pellets of ice being hurled downward by the great force of a mighty hand. Even the heavens seemed to have become violent on this night of unbelievable tragedy. They were both soaking wet. She buried her face in his chest, sobbing uncontrollably and asking over and over why this happened. At first, he made no move to comfort her. Then, he put both arms around her and rested his chin on top of her head. She felt like she'd been wrapped in a warm blanket. Tears were gone and the anger subsided. She closed her eyes and enjoyed the warmth he generated in the cold rain. She was carried to the valley of serenity she often drifted off to as a child, the place she identified as the element into which one passed after death; the peaceful place where her mother and father lived. He was taking her there, this Apache boy who talked to the spirits of his ancestors.

Down the street, she saw them turn into the undertaker's parlour with John's body, but the compulsion to run after them was gone. Although the rain fell hard, a peaceful silence surrounded them, a most unusual phenomenon for the middle of Allen Street at something after midnight. There was none of the customary music and raucous laughter pouring out of the Bird Cage Theatre. The steady roar of the deluge provided an irenic sedation as it drowned out the voices left behind in the aftermath of death. They stood in the street with the sound of rolling thunder all around them and the heavy rain pelting the puddled street. The bond between them was reinforced as they held onto each other in the presence of what she felt was an absolute strength and power, touching them both and drawing them closer together, sealing the bond. She felt as though John was with them, pulling the two of them closer with his energy. They had become brother and sister. They must always remain so. There was no mistaking the message. Many times, the boy told her she'd understand good medicine, bad medicine one day. He told her there would come a time when she'd recognize the spirits he knew well. She felt it now. He let go of her and she backed away. There was something in his eyes, a look of knowing. She wouldn't run. She saw them. Two men — one on either side of him. From their clothes, she recognized them as Apache. Although they, too, stood in the rain, neither was wet. One was an old man, the black hair of his youth turned white and coarse with Time. It fell around his shoulders. Lines of age and unthinkable hardship crisscrossed his weathered face like the parched bed of a creek long dry. The other was younger by twenty years, but his face carried the mark of Time and his hair showed traces of gray. She started to ask who they were. Nalanche held up a hand to silence her. He didn't turn around or look at them. "They are my father and grandfather. Otahe and Tehanache. It is time for you to know them." She wondered how he knew they were there without seeing them. As mysteriously as they appeared, they were gone. Vanished into the night.

The thunder stopped and the rain changed to a fine mist. The air was saturated with the pungent aroma of the wet desert and creosote, burned when lightning set it afire. In the midst of the town that never slept in the relentless quest for earthly riches and power, a place full of lust and evil, they were somehow alone and isolated from the rest of the world, a world that did not and could not understand who they were. To all who saw them pass by, they were the Irish prostitute and the Apache boy, both designations categorizing them as outcasts from respectable society. No mortal man could understand these two, sister and brother; spirits brought together on the earth at a precisely-appointed moment, one having traveled across an ocean and continent, the other waiting in this place, destined to be connected by an unbreakable link in Time to the past — and the future.

By morning, the rain stopped and the sun was doing its best to dry up the muddy street. A gentle breeze fluttered the lace curtains at the open window, carrying the perfume of the still-damp desert into her room. Everything was rejuvenated and had come alive from the rain. Hummingbirds outside her window suspended themselves by tiny, whirring wings as they drank from the gourd she kept filled with sugar water or fruit nectar when she could get it. Nalanche hung it by a string of rawhide close to the window so she could see them when she woke up every day. She breathed in the sweet, desert air. Bear whined. She hadn't noticed him sitting beside the bed, waiting patiently for her to acknowledge his presence. He'd been neglected last night. Wyatt sent the doctor to give her something to sleep and she hadn't even thought about poor Bear. She felt weak, drained of all strength. She didn't remember getting into bed. Judging from the angle of the sunlight, it was still early. She hadn't slept very long, but it was a deep sleep induced by the medication. She dropped her hand over the edge and it landed on Bear's head. When she moved her fingers, he positioned his nose into her hand to receive the maximum benefit of the scratching and she heard the familiar swish of his tail brushing back and forth across the floor. "Good mornin', Little Bear." She turned to the pillow beside her. The dreadful events came flooding back. John would never rest his head on that pillow again. She stopped rubbing Bear's nose, unaware that he was still nuzzling her hand to keep up the motion. She was reliving the terror of the night before. A picture of John, bleeding, desperately struggling for breath and dying in her arms, was painfully vivid. She was overcome with the same feeling of desperation and helplessness she felt last night, watching his life slip away and knowing she could do nothing to save him. All she'd been able to do was hold his trembling hands and promise to love him forever. His blood covered her dress and hands. She turned her hands over to see both sides. There was no trace of blood. The rain washed them clean.

John was dead, and she'd been right there when Death took him. She should have fought for him. She should have held on tighter. She closed her eyes. It would have done no good to fight. No one could save him, not even Doc Goodfellow with all his surgeon's skill. She remembered how she always felt John's energy flow into her when he put his arms around her. She'd never feel the thrill of his touch again. Their lovemaking had been passionately wild and all-consuming. He had reached through to her soul and drawn it to his own. Loving him was more than physical pleasure. It was a powerful merging of her spirit with his. Sometimes, the feeling had been so strong it made her cry and she'd seen tears in his eyes too. He felt the same thing and said so. When it was over, they held each other close, a gentler form of passion taking them over into peaceful sleep. Theirs was a merging of body and spirit, an absolute connection unseverable by any element, including death.

At first, she thought it might have all been a ghastly nightmare. She touched his pillow. The knot in her stomach let her know she wasn't asleep and it was not a dream. He was really gone. The thought of never seeing him again was unbearable. The real pain had just begun. How long could she endure life without him? When she died, she knew they'd be together in whatever place was beyond this world, but until then, she'd have to learn to get through each day. Her grief would never lessen. She closed her eyes and said a silent prayer that she wouldn't be condemned to a long life. The dog was still nudging her hand. She patted the bed and he jumped up. He laid down beside her and put his head on John's pillow. She hugged him and kissed his nose. He whined and she rubbed the preferred place between his eyes. "You miss him too, don't you? We have to take care of each other, you and me and Nalanche. He'd want that."

Nalanche appeared in the doorway. She hadn't heard him come in and she was surprised to see him this early in the morning. He and Bear were usually out in the desert before dawn until it was time for school. Then, she remembered. This was Sunday. No school today. She looked at the little porcelain clock beside the bed. Eight o'clock. It was later than she thought. "Did you and Bear go runnin' this mornin'?" He nodded his head, yes. As usual, she couldn't read any emotion in his expression. Doc told him he ought to play poker. He had the gift. No one would ever guess by looking at his face what he was holding. Her own eyes were red and swollen from crying. The boy, on the other hand, showed no sign of crying. She wondered how he was handling John's death. They'd become very close. They shared the same heritage. Ann Merrick was a full-blooded Apache. Except for his father's blue eyes, John bore a remarkable resemblance to his mother. There was no mistaking his being an Indian. Like Nalanche, his ancestors had been in this part of the country for hundreds of years, maybe thousands. Her thoughts slipped back a few years to the first time she met Ann Merrick. She remembered thinking what a beautiful woman Ann was, fascinated by the color of Ann's skin and shining, black hair. More intriguing was the story of Ann and Richard Merrick's romance. The soldier and the Indian princess. It was a wonderful story. Strange that she'd think of it now. In a way, it was like their story, her's and John's. Just as they were about to be able to spend the rest of their lives together, the dream was taken away the same way Ann and Richard Merrick's dream was taken when Richard died. She looked at Nalanche. John spoke of giving him the Merrick name. After what happened last night, the boy's name would never be Merrick.

She was familiar with the sense of peace that was part of the remarkable boy. She corrected her thinking. Young man. She knew the tranquility in his voice stemmed from some inner knowledge and peaceful strength no white man could understand. She wanted to understand. She was trying to learn from him and because he believed she wanted to know, he was teaching her the way of the Apache. She remembered last night — the old men who stood by him in the rain. She'd been allowed to see them. He asked them to let her see and they had shown themselves because of him. It was the beginning of understanding many mysteries that would be revealed to her. Nalanche looked at the world in a different way from anyone she'd ever known. He was a mysterious young man, seemingly connected with everything from the dog he talked to right down to the smallest grain of sand in the desert. It came from his absolute belief in spirit forces that directed the life of every living thing. She never thought of a grain of sand as a living thing, but he did. Standing in the doorway with the morning light behind him, he was surrounded by an ethereal glow. It was more than the sunlight that made him look different. It was an unearthly quality of beauty. She'd called him her spirit protector for a long time. After last night, she knew he wasn't the only spirit close to her. Something happened to her when she saw the old Indians. She was being drawn into an element she couldn't identify, yet believed she belonged to.

John kidded Nalanche about his good looks, saying it wouldn't be long before the girls would be standing in line outside the gate to talk to him. It was only natural that a sixteen year-old boy should like girls, but unlike other boys his age whose growing-up process heightened their motivation to flirt in obvious hopes of a resulting intimate experience, Nalanche never gave any indication he was interested. He'd rather practice writing his letters or go running with the dog. She couldn't count the times she'd seen the girls huddled together and giggling when he walked by. Whenever one would muster enough nerve to speak to him, he'd nod politely, leaving them in a giddy, flustered tizzy when he walked away. Part of his mystery was that he never smiled. He wasn't silly and clumsy like the other boys, never teasing or trying to scare them with bugs or lizards. He was quiet and subdued, and always polite. Even the young girls recognized the difference. Occasionally they'd coax him into doing a magic trick and when he was done, the result was predictable. They squealed with delight and clapped their hands. The question was always the same. "Tell us how you did that, Nalanche." They loved to say his name. Like him, it was mysterious, and although their mothers warned them about the dangers of being anywhere near the heathen devils, they were fascinated by the mere fact he was an Indian. For the girls, there was a romance to the mystery and he set their innocent little hearts a 'twitter, but it wasn't only the ones his own age who were drawn to him. He turned more than the heads of young girls. Ostensibly respectable women glanced in his direction when they thought no one was looking. Other women were already appreciative of him and didn't hesitate to vocalize their observations, particularly the ladies who worked at the Bird Cage. Ruby was the first to say what a fine specimen of manhood he'd become, even at his tender age. She always sidled up to him and gave him one of her seductive looks while she squeezed his arm and told him how strong and handsome he was. She teased him all the time, standing right next to him to measure his height against hers. "You're getting tall, boy. Pretty soon, you'll be a match for me." She'd wink at him indicating she meant in bed and he'd just look at her. Every now and then, Rose thought she saw the beginnings of a smile when Ruby kept up her playing with him. "Better lookin' every day. Do you have a girlfriend, Nalanche? I'll bet every little girl in town is crazy for you — and maybe some who ain't so little?" She'd nudge him with her elbow to get a rise out of him. Her observation came across as more of a question, implying he knew the ladies watched him. She was the one person who could get him to smile. Despite her rough edges, he liked Ruby and put up with her teasing. He called her Neha — Fire Spirit. He told Rose about the gentle heart hidden deep inside Ruby, a heart filled with infinite sorrow. Rose remembered feeling an extraordinary sadness as he spoke of a pain Ruby carried within her spirit and she wondered how he knew. Ruby told her about it once, but it was something she didn't share with anyone else, least of all a sixteen year-old Apache boy. It was amazing how he knew the story without being told.

Sometimes, she thought he was not of this world at all, but merely around for the sole purpose of taking care of her. There were many words to describe him. Virgil called him savvy. Lizzie called him Magic Man. In the seven months since the street attack, he'd changed. Rose thought he'd grown some. Maybe, grown up was more like it. Whatever it was, he looked older and there was a prevalent no-nonsense attitude about him that put people on notice he wasn't to be provoked. He wouldn't be intimidated and he'd never take another beating like the last one. Despite his youth and peaceful ways, his general manner and the way he looked them in the eye caused grown men to step to one side when they passed him on the street. Doc said he pitied the man who crossed Nalanche.

In the beginning, John called him friend. Later, they both called him Brother. He possessed youthful strength coupled with a gentle nature and more walking-around sense than men three times his age. He believed the land should be left alone. There was a heavy sadness in his voice whenever he talked about the future and how the white man would kill the land. She didn't know why, but she knew he was right. He objected to the taking of silver and other minerals from the earth for profit. He said it made brother hate brother. He said man should take from the earth only what he needed to live and return something to replace what was taken. Silver and the blue stones made into the jewelry she wore were gifts from the earth that should be appreciated for their natural beauty, but money made from silver was a misuse of the earth's treasure as was the selling of the gift. He was wise far beyond his sixteen years. He carried the wisdom of the ages within him and he'd been given special secrets of life; good medicine, bad medicine as he called it. She called it magic and insight, although she knew there was a lot more to it. He knew about the old ways and he told about the future. He was a prophet. A seer. She didn't know how he acquired such a great store of knowledge, but the source from which it emanated was not of earthly origin. Of that, she was certain. For someone with such great sensitivity and depth of character, she wondered why she never saw him cry. He never displayed any emotion except when he talked about the devastating affect man would have on the earth in years to come. He spoke of man's crimes against nature and humanity as though he'd been given a look beyond the curtain of Time and told in no uncertain terms what the future held in store. His prediction of the mass murder of millions by a man not yet born made her shudder at the very idea that one man could commit a crime of such atrocious magnitude. He said it was going to happen — in his lifetime. He was never outwardly angry or distressed about anything else. Unlike her, he never lost his temper and gave the appearance of being completely at peace. The only time his manner varied the slightest bit was when Ruby teased him or when he played with the dog. When Bear performed some ridiculously funny antic, Nalanche laughed out loud.

She'd never looked upon him as a child. From the day they met in the street when he was attacked by half a dozen men on horseback, she knew he was different from other boys his age. She didn't realize it, but on that day, he knew she wasn't like other women either. She was brave — like an Apache. Most men would never have done what she did, walking into the middle of six armed men on horses and challenging them with nothing more than a stone in her hand. At the risk of losing her own life, she defended him. She got into it without a thought and she'd never know what made her do it. Her actions to help him were instinctive. It was something she had to do because it was right. He couldn't have been more than fifteen at the time, but she felt a power that came from within him even then, a compelling force that gave her the strength to step forward without fear. She'd never been able to put the feeling into words. All she knew was that he was different.

This morning, standing in the doorway of her room with the light behind him, she felt his energy stronger than ever. He was a powerful force. She still couldn't explain it, but the energy he directed toward her was so strong, it moved her to sit up in bed. She'd been lying there thinking about John and how she'd never see him again, allowing the emptiness to consume her. She wanted to die. She wanted to pull the covers over her head and stay there until she withered away to dust. She couldn't stop the tears cascading down her face and spilling onto her nightgown. Nalanche watched her from the doorway. He didn't say a word, but she felt him pulling her away from the feeling of wanting to die. He was controlling her pain. He stood tall and proud. She'd never seen him quite like this and she couldn't take her eyes off him. For months, she watched him do amazing magic tricks. In the beginning, she thought she'd figure them out eventually. She never did. He was too fast. Or maybe speed had nothing to do with it. Lizzie swore it was magic. When she thought back, they were more than tricks. He called it good medicine, bad medicine. He promised to teach her the secrets one day, when the time was right. She sat up straighter. Something was happening to him as he stood there. He was changing. He looked older, like the Indians who stood beside him last night. The features of his young face became lined with age. She felt like a child in the presence of a great warrior, a wise chief. Perhaps the sleeping medicine made her imagine the change in him. She closed her eyes to clear her mind. She wondered what he was feeling in the aftershock of John's violent death. Surely, he felt the loss every bit as much as she did. They'd become so close. Brothers. They called each other Brother. There was a connection between them. Bear was on the bed. She looked away from Nalanche and rubbed the dog's head. When she looked back, the lines were gone from his face and he was the same as he'd always been, but his strength was all around her. There was something else, a presence; a feeling of someone else in the room.

"Did you tell Bear that John won't be comin' home, Nalanche?" His voice was strangely quiet and calm. "He who grieves for one who passes through the crossover does not understand the circle of life." He was talking about her. She certainly didn't understand how this tragedy happened and she couldn't stop grieving even if she tried. Bear whined. His eyes rested on the big dog. "Spirit of the Bear knows where Coshani travels. He knows they will meet at the crossover in the land of spirit winds. My father and my grandfather know Coshani. They speak of him. He has been here many times." Her tears stopped. His words were like an echo. They came from a faraway place — from the past. She repeated the name. "Coshani? Who is Coshani?" There was something in the back of her mind, an old memory she couldn't quite identify. She didn't wait for his answer. "Do you think John is close by? When you went to the desert this mornin', did you see him? Did you talk to him? Is he the one you call Coshani? What do you mean, he's been here many times?" Without answering, he left the room. He didn't expect her to understand. Not yet. It would take time to teach her.

Her heart was pounding. She didn't want to be left alone. She flung the covers back and jumped out of bed, shouting at him, on the verge of bursting into tears. When she thought he was leaving, she became hysterical and stood in the doorway yelling for him to come back, unmistakable desperation and urgency in her voice. "Nalanche! Don't go. Take me with you.

Please, don't leave me alone." She was crying. He stopped, but didn't turn around, waiting for her to calm down. Her hands went over her mouth. She sounded like Lizzie, frantic, out of control. She was quiet. When he was sure the outburst was over and she was listening, he said three words, his message absolute. "He is here." Bear whined and crawled to the edge of the bed. She knelt down and put her arm around the big dog, closing her eyes and burying her face in the deep fur of his neck. When she looked up, her illusive spirit protector was gone. She never heard the front door close when he left. He didn't make a sound. He never did. It was always the same. He seemed to vanish into thin air. She didn't have to go outside to look for him. She knew he wouldn't be there. She knew where he went and she wouldn't follow him. He'd take her there when he thought the time was right, but this was not the time. He'd be going back out to the desert to talk to the spirits of his father and grandfather, and to the spirit of John Merrick, the one he called Coshani. He'd ask them to help her understand. The name sent a shiver through her. Nalanche said the name as if he knew the spirit, as if he'd already spoken to the spirit he knew in life as John Merrick. Coshani. He said Coshani had been here many times. She didn't understand. She went back to the bed and laid down with Bear, whispering the name over and over to the dog until they both fell asleep. Coshani. Coshani.

She awoke to a murmur of soft voices coming from the parlour. Bear was on the bed with his head on John's pillow. When he saw her eyes were open, he raised his head and stretched all four legs. His yawn made a funny sound like a squeaky wagon wheel, prompting a smile from her, and she scratched behind his ear. He jumped off the bed and stretched again, shaking the sleep out. The little porcelain clock said it was nearly noon. Bear went to the door, wagging his tail and looking back at her. He was waiting for her permission to leave. In earlier days, before Nalanche "talked" to him, he would have bounded out the door without waiting for anything. 'Tis alright Little Bear. You can go outside." The dog trotted toward the parlour. In the other room, he was greeted affectionately by a woman's voice speaking to him as if he were a baby. Rose recognized the childlike inflections as belonging to Lizzie, and Bear's tail was demonstrating his pleasure at receiving the attention by rapping against something made of wood. She sighed. She knew Lizzie was there to help, but she'd rather have been alone today. All of her friends would be here before the day was over.

They'd want to help, but there was nothing any of them could do to make things right. They couldn't bring John back. The squeak of the front-door hinges told her someone let the dog out. She closed her eyes and fell back on the pillow. She had to pull herself together and get dressed. People were waiting for her in the other room. The undertaker would be expecting her too. He'd want his money in advance and she'd have to tend to John's funeral arrangements. There was a casket to purchase and she'd have to take some clothes for them to dress him in. It would have to be his uniform. She looked at the steamer trunk in the corner. She'd pressed and folded the uniform so carefully and packed it in a cedar box inside the trunk. She wanted to be sure it was preserved in good shape for the day John would show their children and grandchildren. The sick feeling welled up inside her again and she put both hands over her face. She didn't want to see any of them, the friends who would do their best to console her. It would only make things worse. She wanted to be left alone. "You have lots of friends, Rose." The voice and the arm around her shoulder startled her. "Abby!" No more words would come out. Abby sat on the edge of the bed and held Rose's hands. She felt her own heart breaking as Rose spoke. "I have to bury him, Abby. How am I goin' to do that? How am I goin' to live without him?" Abby had no answers to the heartrending questions. Nothing she could say would begin to stop the pain. All she could say was, "You're not alone. I'll be with you. We'll all be with you and we'll help you get through this." Abby kissed Rose on the forehead. Get dressed. "I'll be in the parlour."

She dressed in blue, John's favorite color. He never liked her to wear black and he wouldn't want it now. She pinned up her hair and placed the single strand of pearls around her neck that he gave her the night he proposed in the park. When she was ready, she walked into the parlour. She remembered how Ann Merrick presented herself in public when her husband died. She called upon Ann to give her some of that strength. Jenny had the merciful foresight to take Lizzie home. Lizzie would have broken into tears as soon as she saw Rose and it would have made this moment more difficult than it already was. Rose wasn't surprised to see who was waiting in the parlour with Abby. They stopped talking when she entered the room. Matt Kern would have been John's best man at the wedding. Tomorrow, he'd be a pallbearer at John's funeral and help carry the casket. She knew Doc would be close. His concern was apparent. Wyatt was there too. She took his arm and they walked out front to a waiting carriage. She recognized the deputy holding the reigns, one of Virgil's men. Nalanche stood by the horse, gently rubbing its nose. She smiled at him. He left the horse and went to the fence to pick a single red rose. When he gave it to her, she pulled one petal off and handed it back to him. Without a word, he opened his medicine bag and dropped the petal into it. She turned to Wyatt. "I know the street is wet, but do you mind if we walk, Marshal?" He looked at Abby. "Maybe you'd like to ride with Matt and the deputy." Abby linked her arm through Doc's. "We'll all walk."

They walked in silence up Fourth Street toward the funeral parlour, Rose holding Wyatt's arm, Abby with Doc and Matt Kern. Nalanche walked alone behind the others and the deputy drove the buggy with no passengers. People stopped and stared. She heard a woman's voice, a familiar, nerve-grating voice. The hateful comment didn't surprise any of them nor did the fact that she said it from the protection of a doorway. "Hmm. The whore's got her hands on another Earp." Wyatt stopped right in front of her. Rose started to remove her hand from his arm but he held it in place, turning toward the woman and forcing Rose to turn with him. The woman's face flushed red and she looked around anxiously for a way out of the soup she'd just thrown herself into. It wasn't the first time she'd been confronted by Rose, but this time was different. This time, she had Wyatt Earp to contend with, a man not famous for patience or diplomacy. She'd finally opened her mouth once too often and backed herself into a corner with nowhere to hide and everyone looking at her. Wyatt's voice was like a quiet roll of thunder. "Miss Callahan has suffered a great loss in the death of her fiancé. Did I hear you offer your condolences, Mrs. Grants?" All the blood drained from Caroline's face and her color changed from flushed-red to white as milk. Her eyes were wide and she was unable to move, the invisible vice of retribution gripping her by the throat. She didn't answer. She couldn't answer. Wyatt waited. Several people stopped to watch. Her eyes darted back and forth; a cornered fox, searching frantically for a gap between the hounds through which to escape. She looked for moral support from the two ladies with her, but they wanted no part of what was coming. Both of them disappeared inside the store and closed the door behind them, leaving Caroline to fight her battle alone. She was so busy delivering her malicious soliloquy about the gypsy whore who cast a spell on Virgil Earp to get him into her bed that she didn't realize the little entourage had stopped right smack in front of her. Now, she'd like to be somewhere else and she wished she could eat those words. It was too late for that. She swallowed hard and made a loud, gulping sound. Something resembling a nervous smile made her lips quiver. Her friends had seen the look in Wyatt's eyes when he heard Caroline's remarks about Rose. Feeling the need to become inconspicuous, they backed up into the store. A wise decision on their part. Wyatt said it again. "Mrs. Grants, did you want to offer some words of sympathy to Miss Callahan?" Rose wanted to move on. In her opinion, this was not the time to face-off with Caroline Grants. Wyatt obviously had a different idea. He thought it was a perfect time to put an end to Caroline's idle gossip and he intended to force the issue.

Caroline's hands were trembling and she fumbled with her purse. She dropped it and looked down at it several times before stooping to pick it up, hoping that when she stood up, they'd be gone. As did her friends, luck had abandoned her this day. Wyatt was holding Rose's hand on his arm, waiting for Caroline's response. Caroline cleared her throat, but when she tried to speak, her voice broke so badly that nothing more than a croak came out. She stared at her hands, her fingers anxiously twisting the string of her purse. She teetered on the brink of falling apart, trying hard hold back the tears. Her eye began to twitch crazily from the pressure of the situation and she realized her whole body was shaking. The ferocity of blustering winds from an ongoing gossip storm about Rose and his brother was diluted to complete stillness by the ominous forecast of Wyatt's public chastisement. That's right. His brother! Whatever in the world possessed her? Why hadn't it occurred to her that it would all come back to haunt her eventually? She wasn't talking about a prostitute's private romance with an ordinary man and she failed to take into consideration the indiscriminate target of her wagging tongue. She forgot who she was talking about. Virgil Earp was no ordinary man. He was someone of considerable notoriety, City Marshal, Chief of Police — and the brother of Wyatt Earp. She'd gone out of her way to turn their discreet relationship into a public spectacle. How long did she think she could get away with it before the family put a stop to it? One thing about the Earps, they stuck together and they were no bunch to take on alone. She'd been so intent on hurting Rose that she never once thought about repercussions associated with spreading rumors about Virgil. Why had she singled out Rose Callahan for such a vicious attack anyway? Rose already bore the burden of the infamous title of soiled dove, lady of easy virtue. Prostitute. Name-calling didn't hurt her. She'd heard it all so many times, it rolled away like water off a duck's back. Everyone knew who she was. It was no secret how she earned her living. She worked at the Bird Cage. Did Caroline think anything she said would make a difference to Rose? They were questions she had no answers for as she stood facing the two people she never expected to confront her together.

Rose was sure Wyatt didn't approve of his married brother's relationship with another woman, a dance-hall girl and prostitute at that, but here he was, walking arm-in-arm with that woman right through the middle of town in broad daylight. There was a message in all of this. The only person who had really been injured by Caroline's hatefulness was Virgil's wife, Allie. Caroline let out a sigh and lowered her head. Why hadn't she considered Allie's feelings? How many times had she run to Allie to report that Virgil was at "that trollop's" house, even as they spoke. "I wonder what she's got that makes him go there. What do you suppose they do for all those hours in that little gray house over on Toughnut? Why, it's disgraceful the way he carries on with that redheaded whore, married man that he is and all. They don't try to hide it. They walk on the street together in the middle of the day, flaunting it. And him, up there at the Bird Cage every night to see her. She's Irish, you know — a Gypsy! Fortune-teller! You know the things they do with their crystal balls. They put charms on men. Spells. They're unchristian. Witches! Used to be, her kind was tied to a stake and burned up to get rid of the devil and all that black-magic hocus-pocus they do. Did it all the time in Salem years ago. If you ask me, they had the right idea about getting rid of her kind back then. She's got a spell on him. Sure as I'm standing here, that whore's got a spell on your husband." She ranted on and on. Every time she ran into Allie, she talked about it. When she was sure Virgil wasn't there, she stopped by the house with more information. Poor Allie. How painful it must have been for her, but she never responded to Caroline's hateful prattle, maintaining her dignity in the face of it, through silence.

Caroline backed up and laid her hand on the door handle. The door behind her was closed tight and locked from within. Thinking it was stuck, she jiggled the handle and pushed on it. It was locked. Why didn't she mind her own business? This wasn't the first time she'd experienced a backwash as a result of her big mouth. She looked beseechingly at Wyatt for mercy. She wouldn't get any such thing from him. His stare was hard and cold as ice. She could tell his patience was wearing thin and she understood she better say the right thing, and soon. If she didn't, she'd get a tongue-lashing she'd never forget, and in front of an audience. If that happened, she wouldn't be fit to show her face in town, and the whole town was sure to hear about it from the two next-biggest gossips who had locked themselves behind the door she was standing in front of. At least she had enough sense to know the consequences of her failure to make things right, and he was giving her the chance to do that. She looked at Rose. She cleared her throat and started over, her voice shaking. "I'm very sorry about the death of your fiancé. Please accept my family's sincere sympathy on your loss." Wyatt was drilling her with a look that made her want to sink into the mud and disappear. She searched his eyes for approval of her efforts. He gave her none. Caroline's offer of sympathy was anything but sincere. He scared it out of her. She couldn't look him in the eye any longer. She turned her eyes to the ground. She didn't know what else he expected her to say. She was about to burst into tears when the woman she'd spoken of so intemperately smiled at her. Rose spoke with the dignity and strength of Ann Merrick, the way she knew John would want her to respond. Her voice was soft and clear. "Thank you, Caroline. Your expression of sympathy touches me." They walked on without further words, leaving Caroline standing in the doorway of the locked store with her mouth open, dumbfounded by the unexpected words from Rose. Her dignity had been preserved by the woman about whom she'd said such terrible things. Now, she owed someone else an apology. There was somewhere she had to stop before she went home today. She didn't wait for her friends to come out of the store. She was on her way to make things right all the way around. She had to talk to Alvira Earp.

Word traveled fast. Everyone in town seemed to have heard about the little procession moving toward the funeral parlour. By the time they got there, two deputies were holding the curiosity seekers away from the door. They'd seen her every day and never paid attention to her, but today she was an attraction, like some sort of carnival freak, and they came out in droves to witness her grief. People stepped aside at the entrance to let them pass, a low murmur rippling among the onlookers. The door opened from the inside and she went in first, Wyatt and the others close behind. She'd never been in a funeral parlour. A strange odor filled the air, something she'd never smelled before; a mixture of cleaning compounds and medicinal salts — embalming fluids. Heavy window curtains blocked out the sun and it took a minute to adjust her eyes to the dim light. She was alright on the walk, but when the door closed behind her, the impact of where she was and the reason she was here took hold.

The undertaker's assistant was animatedly offering his condolences and describing how "wonderfully lifelike the deceased looks," the special features of the casket where John rested. "...finest cherrywood imported from France, lined with real silk." Obviously inexperienced in the sensitive art of dealing with personal loss, the fool had no concept of bereavement and what people suffered on the death of their loved ones. He was simply promoting the selling of the company's products and services. He was a small man wearing a coat at least two, possibly three, sizes too large for him, the sleeves being in desperate need of tailoring as they exceeded the length of his arms by several inches. He kept tugging at his pants, obviously in need of alteration as well and lacking the security of suspenders. Even his glasses were too big for him. They slid down his nose and he was continually moving them back into place every few seconds. He reminded her of a clown she once saw with a traveling carnival show who had to constantly hang onto his baggy pants to keep them up. The clown's efforts turned out to be an exercise in futility when he let go of his trousers to catch a small dog that jumped into his arms. She remembered laughing until she cried at the clown's wide-eyed expression when he realized he'd let go of the pants and they were piled up around his ankles. She hoped this little man wouldn't suffer a similarly-embarrassing disaster. She didn't want to be rude, but the high pitch of his voice and incessant jabbering was grating on her nerves. She closed her eyes. Wyatt observed her annoyance. "Miss Callahan will see Captain Merrick now." The little man stopped speaking abruptly, offended by the interruption. He shoved his glasses higher on the bridge of his nose and pulled his pants up. If not for the gravity of the moment, his appearance would have been laughable. At Wyatt's prompting, he stopped babbling and sniffed irritably, obviously perturbed at being prevented from finishing his speech and elaborating on the extraordinary efforts he'd put into the funeral arrangements.

Rose didn't realize so much had already been taken care of, but she was certain the little man with the high-pitched voice and oversized trappings wasn't responsible for any of it. She was grateful for having been spared the difficult task of discussing the funeral details. Doc must have read her mind. He took her hand. "I hope I was not too presumptuous in makin' the arrangements. I thought perhaps it would relieve you of a painful necessity." She smiled at the man everyone said was so cold-hearted and impassionate. Ruthless. That's what they called him. He didn't go out of his way to help anyone. They'd never understand, but she knew another side of him. "Thank you, John. I appreciate all you've done. I'm sure you made exactly the right decisions." She turned to the undertaker's man, wishing one of the owners had been there to handle the viewing of the body in a more professional fashion. "I'd like to see Captain Merrick." He opened his mouth and Doc pointed his cane toward the curtain separating the entrance from the room containing the casket. "Get on with it." The little man let go another indignant sniff at Doc's perceived rudeness. Holding his pants up with one hand, he yanked on the cord attached to the drape with the other. Rose braced herself as the heavy, black-velvet curtain was drawn aside.

She wanted to walk here to allow herself time to prepare for seeing John, but nothing could have prepared her for this. The shock was greater than she expected. She stood back a few feet from the casket, still holding Wyatt's arm. A dozen candles in tall, silver candelabra at either end of the casket flickered and she could see her own reflection in the warm, red wood. She studied the woodworking. The design had been intricately carved by a master craftsman and was incredibly beautiful. More than beautiful. Exquisite. The cherrywood was highly-polished, with handles of solid silver. Doc spared no expense in seeing that John was provided with the very best. She didn't have to ask the cost to know it was more than she could afford. Doc would never tell her what he paid for it anyway. It was expensive, but it was something he wanted to do. Time was running out for him and he couldn't take his money where he was going. As far as he was concerned, this was money well-spent. She avoided looking at the opening where the lid had been raised. Matt went first. His back was to her, but when she saw him lower his head, she knew he was crying. He stood there for several minutes with his hand on the side of the casket. On his way out, he stopped a few inches past her and reached his hand back to touch her arm. She didn't look at his face. He left and closed the door quietly behind him. Abby and Doc were next. They walked to the casket with their arms around each other. Abby touched John's hand. Then, she leaned over and whispered to him, "Don't worry. We'll take care of her. Goodbye." Doc spoke out loud to John. "I cannot predict that we will meet again, Sir, because I do not believe we are destined for the same eternal reward. However, I will not discard the possibility and I will not say goodbye." His hand tapped the side of the casket as he studied John's face. A few minutes later, he and Abby left the same way they came in, with their arms around each other. When they were gone, Wyatt went to the casket. He paid his respects silently, then went to the door and stood quietly waiting for Rose and Nalanche to take their time with John. The undertaker's man began jabbering. Wyatt took him by the arm, opened the door and threw him outside. When the room was quiet, Nalanche went to the casket. He only stayed long enough to place the medicine bag under John's fingers

— for the crossing.

They'd all seen him. All but her. Nalanche took her by the hand and led her to the casket. When he let go of her hand, he didn't make a sound, but she knew he was gone from the room. She was alone with John. She remembered his pain when he was dying. She thought she'd break down and cry when she saw him here, but there were no tears. Bathed in the soft glow of candlelight, he looked so handsome. Doc had done things exactly the way John would have wanted them. After Nalanche got Rose to bed last night, Doc had come by and asked for John's uniform. First thing this morning, he delivered it to the under-taker with instructions to dress John in it. John's hand rested on the med-icine bag. She knew Nalanche placed something inside the bag for John to carry with him into the next world, something magical to keep away the evil spirits and entice the good ones to stay with him. Good medi-cine. The rose petal from her yard was in the bag. She needed to give him more than a rose petal to take with him, something of herself. She remembered her mother's locket and the strand of Annie Callahan's hair her father carried in it for so many years. It was part of his wife that he kept with him until he died, his good-luck charm; the equivalent of good medicine. She loosened a few strands of hair and curled them around her fingers into a circle. Opening the bag only enough for one finger, she carefully tucked the strands inside. She couldn't open it all the way. Whatever Nalanche put in the bag was good medicine between the two of them — brothers. She wouldn't let the magic out, and when the strand of hair was safely inside, she tied the strings tight and put the bag back under John's hand.

She stayed with him a long time. Tomorrow morning, she'd bury him and she never wanted to forget his face or his voice or his smile, or the way he made fun of her brogue. She hoped he'd never forget her either. He promised to always love her. Somehow, she knew that meant in the life beyond. As life was leaving him and Death closed in, he promised to be with her again. It seemed important to tell her and he struggled to get the words out to be sure she knew. She didn't know how or when, but she knew he'd keep the promise. She promised too. They'd meet again, in a different place and time. She leaned over the side of the casket and kissed him. "I'll be seein' you again, my love." She whis-pered his name. It was a call to him from wherever he might be listen-ing. For an instant, she thought she heard his voice, answering. The words he said so often echoed through her mind. They were so clear, so close. She felt him standing right behind her. She turned slowly. There was no one there; no one she could see, but she was not alone.

Chapter 13

"It's not the way you used to hold me.
It's not seeing your face
even when my eyes are closed.
It's not your laughter or your eyes of blue,
or a song that makes me
think of you.
It's remembering the way you called me Rose."

Remembering The Way You Called Me Rose

This morning when Wyatt came for her, he came alone. The others were already at the funeral parlour. Everyone but Nalanche. He waited outside the house with Little Bear and John's saddled horse. He was wearing John's hat. When she came outside, he took off the hat. He said something to the dog and Bear ran to her, wagging his tail in anticipation of the usual pat on the head. She didn't disappoint him. She told him what a good boy he was. She looked back at Nalanche. He bore a striking resemblance to John. She noticed it the first time they stood side-by-side. They looked enough alike to have been brothers. They called each other Brother.

She went to the boy and horse and touched the animal's nose. It was soft as velvet. He was a beauty and exceptionally gentle; an Appaloosa, strong and fast as the wind. John bought him from a trader in Fort Huachuca before coming to Tombstone the first time. He called him Cash because he paid so much money for him. As far as John was concerned, the horse was worth every penny, and then some. She called him the polka-dot pony because of his spotted coat. She remembered the night John told Nalanche that if he was ever unable to care for the animal, the boy should take him and make sure he was treated well. Nalanche stood close to Cash, rubbing the horse's neck. They seemed to understand each other, the same way the boy and the dog understood each other. She knew he'd been talking to the horse, telling him this was the day. Cash was his now.

After yesterday, she knew people would be watching, but she had no idea so many would come. There'd been other funerals in town, some processions making their way to the cemetery accompanied by a band playing a solemn dirge or, in one case, bagpipes and men in kilts dancing an Irish jig. Those were certainly more entertaining than this one would be, if it was entertainment folks were looking for. She didn't know why this funeral was such a curiosity. Perhaps it was she who was the oddity, not the funeral, or maybe it was Wyatt Earp. They all wondered why he was there, driving a prostitute to the funeral parlour to say her final good-bye.

Their promise to each other lingered in her mind. They would meet again someday. She drifted off with her thoughts, wondering how that would happen and if it did, where and when it would be. In Heaven? Was there really such a place? Nalanche told her spirits lived forever, that they inhabited different bodies each time they returned to earth, but their essence never changed. He was sure about it, but she didn't understand. She turned around in the seat. A feeling of warmth enveloped her, the same as when Nalanche put his arms around her in the rain the night John died. He was behind them, leading the riderless horse, and there was a man walking with him — a soldier. She started to say something to Wyatt, but the soldier was gone. Nalanche spoke to her with his eyes and she heard his message as clearly as if he'd said the words out loud. She knew who the soldier was.

"Is something wrong?" Wyatt was talking to her. She faced forward in the seat. "No, I was makin' sure Nalanche was with us." No sooner had she said it than her thoughts began wandering again. It was not only Nalanche who was with her. Something was happening to her, something extraordinary. First, she saw the old Indians, spirits of two men who once walked the earth in human form. Now, she had seen John Merrick — the spirit of John Merrick. She knew it was him walking with Nalanche. She'd heard about angels and she believed they existed. She always thought Ann Merrick was an angel, sent to rescue her from a disastrous end, and there was the seaman who helped her cross the ocean, Christopher. Somehow, angel was not the right word to describe the people she'd seen. Nalanche spoke of spirits. What else could they be? That's what they were. Spirits. Ghosts of men who used to be here. She was sure of it. They took a different form, but they were still here. She didn't understand how these things could happen, but she knew she'd been given a gift that mortal men rarely received. Many times, she'd gone to a place she identified only as Heaven and if not Heaven, then another place beyond this world. She'd learn more from Nalanche, the boy who talked to the spirits of his ancestors and perhaps, to the spirit of John Merrick. He said he'd teach her when it was time, and the time was near.

She said something to Wyatt about the lovely morning. He agreed it was going to be a nice day. At the side of the street, a man she never saw before removed his hat in a gesture of respect. Another followed his lead, then another. She couldn't believe it. They turned the corner and her eyes fell on a man and woman with three children. The man took off his hat and the woman looked directly at Rose. It was Caroline Grants and her husband, Tom. Rose had seen him many times, frequently, on his way upstairs with one of the ladies in the Bird Cage. She wondered if Caroline knew about his lascivious escapades in the place she called the Devil's playground. Unlike Allie Earp, maybe Caroline had been spared the painful news about her husband's carryings on in that den of iniquity she so openly condemned the husbands of other women for frequenting. She might not have been the victim of idle gossips like herself. Emily and her brothers stood side-by-side, holding hands. Rose blew them a kiss and they sent kisses back to her on the air. Their mother made no move to stop them.

Matt and the others waited in front of the funeral parlour. Wyatt helped her down from the buggy. Off to one side, the undertaker's man stood quietly fidgeting with a button on his oversized coat, a deputy over his shoulder to make sure he stayed that way. Every few seconds, he glanced nervously at the deputy, alternating the pulling up of his pants with the pushing up of his glasses on the bridge of his nose. He'd obviously been told to keep quiet and stay out of the way because the undertaker was here to see to the removal of the casket. He twisted the button one time too may and it came off. He looked at the button, then, over his shoulder at the deputy. At a moment when he thought the deputy wasn't paying attention, he ventured a step toward Rose, his mouth open to let go the first word. Before a sound came out, the deputy had him by the scruff of his neck. His feet were lifted off the ground. His collar was pulled tight and both hands went to his throat in a frantic clawing action to loosen the tension. He gasped as the tightened collar constricted his windpipe. The deputy held him a second longer before releasing his grip on the collar, leaving the little man choking on the sudden intake of air. Rose felt sorry for the pathetic little fellow. His glasses sat sideways near the end of his nose and he barely managed to catch them when they fell. His trousers were slipping too. She couldn't help notice they had dropped dangerously low, but like the glasses, he saved them in the nick of time. She was thankful they hadn't wound up around his ankles like the clown's. He shook his shoulders to make the deputy let go of him, like a defiant child after a cuffing, but the officer never completely turned him loose. He muttered a curse which did not escape the deputy's hearing, something about the deputy's sexual activity with his mother. The deputy lowered his head like a bull about to charge. Luckily, the little man recognized the precariousness of his position in time to retract the insult, raising both hands in the air to emphasize the sincerity of the apology. The pants slipped. With impeccable timing, he kept one hand in the air and rescued the falling britches with the other.

Her attention was redirected when Nalanche opened the door. It was the last time she'd see John in this world. She and Nalanche went in alone. They walked hand-in-hand to the casket. She remembered what Nalanche said about spirits living forever, that the body was only a shell in which a spirit lived while on this earth. She wondered if John was watching her at this moment from beyond the invisible veil that separated the living from the dead, at the gateway to the other side the Apaches call the crossover. Nalanche said she would know the spirit of John Merrick as he knew the spirits of his father and grandfather. She wanted it to be that way. It was the only hope left. There was some comfort in believing his spirit lived, but she wanted to touch him the way she knew him in life. She wanted to feel his arms around her. She wanted to kiss him. She remembered what he said as he lay dying in her arms. "I love you, Rose. I'll always be yours." The words that followed would stay with her forever. "I'll see you again. If it takes a hundred years, I'll see you again. I promise." She promised too, without knowing how she'd keep it. Saying the words relieved the pain a little, or maybe there was more. Maybe, there was a way. John never made promises unless he intended to keep them and he'd find a way to keep this one. Of that, she was certain.

Something brushed against her face. There were no open windows to let in a breeze from the outside, so it was not the wind that touched her cheek. A voice was very close, right beside her. She turned to Nalanche. "What did you say?" At first, he didn't answer and she knew it was not his voice she heard. Then he spoke. "Do not hear with your ears, Sister. Listen with your spirit." She closed her eyes. It was there again, a whisper, "Rose," and the gentle caress on her face. She kissed John one last time, remembering his final word before he died — her name. "I'll be rememberin' the way you called me Rose and I'll be waitin'. I promise."

She took Nalanche's hand and they left the room. At the door, he asked Wyatt and Matt to hold the pallbearers outside while he went back in alone. In a few minutes, he called them in. She waited by the door while the men brought the casket out. Made from cherrywood and silver, it was heavy, and the pallbearers struggled to carry it and lift it into the hearse. Even with six strong men, it shifted a little and they had to work to keep it from tipping.

A man stepped forward from the crowd and held one end of the casket, steadying the heavy box until it was loaded into the Black Mariah. Rose watched him while the casket was secured inside the coach. It was Tom Grants. When she caught his eye, she thought he was going to break into tears. He lowered his eyes and returned to his wife and children. One word said it all. Shame. He was ashamed of the trouble his wife had caused by spreading rumors and he was ashamed of himself for cheating on her, and a few other things. He knew Rose had seen him lots of times at the Bird Cage when he was there to purchase the pleasures of Lizzie McGee or his favorite dove, Claire Dillon. She also knew he gambled away more than a few dollars that would otherwise have been put to good use by his family. All the times she watched him play cards, she never saw him win a plug nickel. He was a lousy poker player and, according to the ladies whose favors he bought, not so good at private endeavors in the suspended cribs either, despite a fair amount of time spent there. Seemed Tom Grants wasn't lucky at much of anything. At this moment, his was a silent plea not to disclose to his wife those escapades, too numerous to mention, with the ladies of the night or the dealers who relieved him of the money he was hell-bent-for-leather on losing. What would Caroline do if she knew her husband spent every spare minute of his time in the bawdiest saloon this side of the Mississippi with some of the wildest women ever to sell their charms in a brothel? And what would she say if she knew about all the stupid bets he'd laid down on a faro table? — family money meant for spending on shoes for his kids. How many nights had he left the house under the pretense of attending a meeting with the church deacons and gone instead to search out the carnal pleasures of the Bird Cage? More times than Rose could remember. No wonder he was ashamed of himself, but today might mark a change in Tom's luck. She'd spare Caroline the colorful details of her good, Christian husband's adulterous activities and reckless gambling away of family money.

She studied them closer, wondering how two homely people like Tom and Caroline managed to have such pretty children. She'd always been curious how they came to be married in the first place, what the attraction had been, and what they were like when they were younger; whether they ever had a loving relationship or if they married out of some necessity or prearranged family contract. Beauty was truly in the eyes of the beholder if ever it was, in fact, beauty they might have seen in each other. A constant storm rained down turmoil and discontent on their lives. All the times she saw them together, Caroline was nagging poor Tom. The man had no pride. He never held his head up, walking along with his head down as though he'd been stripped of his will. Rose suspected he'd conditioned himself over the years to hearing how incompetent and insignificant he was, never doing anything to suit Caroline. His tobacco and pipe store on Allen Street was a thriving enterprise, but not good enough to make Caroline happy. Her constant reminder that he ought to be doing twice as much business and that he was a failure at everything he did had worn the man down. He was like a whipped puppy who learned to do her bidding for the pure sake of avoiding another thrashing. No wonder he looked for female companionship at the Bird Cage. It was the same with the children. Rose didn't understand why Caroline was always screaming at them. They were such good children. The woman wasn't happy with anyone, including herself. She was angry all the time for no apparent reason.

Tom and Caroline stood close together like newlyweds, holding hands. Something had happened to them. Tom put his arm around his wife and Caroline smiled at him. It was the oddest thing. She'd never seen Caroline Grants smile and it was downright amazing how smiling made her look almost pretty. Now, she could understand what Tom saw in Caroline. A miracle must have been dropped on them. It was as if they suddenly remembered they'd been in love once. From the looks of things, they found that love again. After this, she didn't expect to see Tom at the Bird Cage again and she figured the kids wouldn't be wearing shoes with holes anymore either.

She rode with Wyatt behind the glass-windowed coach that carried John's body, wishing all the way that the road weren't so bumpy. They drove to the south end of town, out to the place she and Nalanche had taken so many evening walks. She and John had come this way to watch the sunset from the top of the hill. Yesterday, when she was asked where she wanted him buried, she knew the place. There weren't a lot of trees, but there was one on that spot just big enough to give some shade from the sun and a little shelter from the rain. She stopped there to rest before the walk home many times. You could see forever from the hill, and you could hear voices on the warm desert winds blowing down from the Dragoons and up the other side of the valley. She heard them and so did Nalanche. John liked it there. He said he liked the way the wind whispered and he said it was peaceful. It was the right place to bury him and someday, she'd rest there on the hill beside him.

Nalanche walked behind the buggy, leading the horse with no rider, John's saber hanging from the saddle in a leather scabbard bearing his Army regimental coat of arms. Bear walked with the boy and horse. There was no running today. Even the animals sensed the tragedy and they missed him.

The minute the casket was unloaded, the parson began speaking. He was anxious to get it over with and he talked fast. She figured he was uncomfortable preaching to the company of prostitutes and gamblers, and probably a little confused by the presence of lawmen like Wyatt Earp and Matt Kern mixed in with the unsavories. None of them were part of his regular congregation and she got the feeling he might be afraid of being struck down by the Almighty for being there at all. She didn't go to church because she wasn't welcome. Respectable folk made that very clear, punishing their children to emphasize the point. He said a prayer and a few hurried words about the hereafter and he was gone. Rose was disappointed, but she understood he had something to lose by being there. If the churchgoing population got wind of him officiating at this funeral with so many hell-bound whores and scalawags in attendance, it might cost him a few empty pews on Sunday and empty pews meant empty coffers. He couldn't take a chance on losing money for the church or his own pocket, so he hightailed it back to town as fast as he could get the Twenty-Third Psalm spoke over John. Truth was, the good preacher was as big a hypocrite as the rest of his congregation, and she wondered what they'd say if they knew about his regular visits to the Bird Cage and the church money he spent on ladies who worked there.

It was Matt who said the most about his long-time friend. He told a story about something funny John did when they were in college. Rose smiled at the story. She never heard that one before, but she was glad he was being remembered for his wit and sense of humor. He'd want it that way. She didn't want this day to be morbid. That's why she didn't wear black. She wore a light-green dress. John liked her in that color, the color she was wearing the day they met. When Matt choked up and looked at the ground, unable to go on, Wyatt put his hand on Matt's shoulder and took over. Watching Wyatt speak, she realized she hardly knew the man, yet he'd come forward to help her through this time of immense sorrow as if they'd been friends for years, and as he would have done for any respectable woman in town who lost a husband. Like Virgil, it didn't seem to matter to him who she was or how she earned a living. He'd walked with her, arm-in-arm, right through the middle of town and publicly stifled the town's biggest gossip when he confronted Caroline Grants. At first, she thought maybe he did it for his brother or, if nothing else, because of his brother. Although he hadn't come, she was sure Virgil wouldn't want her to be alone today. The more Wyatt talked, the more she understood he would have done it regardless of her connection with his brother. He did it because he was a decent man and because it was the right thing to do. He didn't say it, but she was sure he felt responsible for John's death. He and Matt Kern and Doc were all armed that night, but John didn't have a gun. They tried to talk the situation down, but talking didn't do any good. Whether they could have changed things by aggressive action when it first started, nobody would ever know. She could see the questions in his eyes as to what might have happened if he'd handled things differently. He looked at her while he talked, speaking directly to her when he recounted John's military accomplishments and how he fought for justice. He said John was a brilliant lawyer, respected by all who knew him. An honest man. A good man. He talked about honor and truth being the foundations upon which John built his life. She expected as much from Wyatt. Then, he took her completely by surprise when he said John Merrick had been fortunate to have had the love of a good woman. He was referring to her, of course. That, she wasn't expecting. He didn't take his eyes off her once and she knew he meant every word; that, and more. He was saying he was sorry, not in so many words, but she understood.

Wyatt's eulogy was interrupted by Doc's coughing. They waited until it passed. It was hard for Doc to stand out in the sun so long, but he was determined to be there. When the coughing was over, they were quiet. There didn't seem to be a need to say more. They stood around the casket in silence, the only sound being the wind blowing down from the Dragoons across the desert. They were stalling. No one wanted to see the box go in the ground. The sun was higher in the sky and the day was getting hotter than anyone expected. Rose knew it was time. She stepped forward and kissed the casket. When she moved back, the men lowered it into the ground and began shoveling dirt over it. She tossed in the bouquet of roses she picked from the yard, wishing they'd stayed better, but the heat of the day wilted them even before they left the funeral parlour. Tomorrow, she'd bring more roses in water and a sprig of jasmine. She should have thought of that today. She watched as the grave was filled with dirt and rocks piled on top of it. It was done quick. John was buried. She wanted to stay, but Wyatt had been so thoughtful in providing a carriage, she couldn't ask him to wait any longer. She'd come back later and stay as long as she pleased, and bring flowers in a jar of water.

Nalanche was a few paces away with the horse and dog. He removed the scabbard from the saddle and carried it to her. She held out both hands and he laid it on her upturned palms. The sword was heavy and it tipped to one side. He steadied it until he was sure she had hold of it. When she held it tight, he let go. A gust of wind started a dust devil to spinning nearby and everyone else covered their eyes in expectation of a blast of sand. They were used to the tiny twisters that whipped the sand up with such force it left your eyes burning and your skin stinging from the irritation. The blowing sand was sharp as fragments of flying glass. Rose and Nalanche watched as the swirling cloud of sand was carried away over the hill, unnoticed by the others who still protected their faces. An unspoken message passed from her to him, the sign he was waiting for. She'd finally done it — passed the message without words, and he knew she understood. Good medicine, bad medicine. Her message was clear. He took off his coat and hat and left them in the carriage. Without further delay, he uncinched the saddle and pulled it off, leaving only the blanket on the horse's back. He carried the tack to one of the wagons and loaded it. Then, he returned to the horse and swung himself up onto its back. Cash tossed his head and danced to one side. He'd been waiting patiently and he knew it was time to go, time to fly with the wind to the secret place in the desert where he often carried the boy who talked to spirits. Sitting on the horse, Nalanche looked like the great chief she saw standing in the doorway earlier, not a boy at all. She had a feeling he had something to do with the dust devil appearing at precisely the right moment to isolate the two of them from the rest of the mourners for the passing of the message. It was the spirit winds he talked about.

The horse seemed to know instinctively which direction to go. She drifted away with her memories and imagination. Watching him ride away with the dog racing along beside the horse, she remembered John describing the exhilaration he felt when he rode Cash. He said he imagined it to be the equivalent of flying. She'd never seen a horse run so fast. She wanted to go with the boy. If not for the obligation of politeness to stay for the others, she would have asked to go. He was free. If she'd asked where he was going, he would have said only that he rode where Apache spirit winds carried him, to the place of the spirits of his father and grandfather — and Coshani. It was hard for her to think of John with any other name, but since his death, the boy spoke of him only as Coshani. He always spoke of spiritual things. According to him, everything was inhabited by a spirit, some good, some evil. There were times she'd study him for an hour when she thought he didn't know she was watching him. He'd be reading or practicing his writing. He looked human enough, but there was something that made him different from other boys his age, different from other men. Sometimes it was hard to remember he was only sixteen. How many times had she caught herself wondering if he was really of this world at all? The first time the thought crossed her mind, she rejected it as absurd, but now that she knew him better, the idea wasn't so easily discarded. His absolute belief in spirit forces and enchanted places made him unlike anyone she'd ever known. He'd fascinated her since the first day she saw him. He moved from place-to-place without a sound. On desert paths where dry brush and sand crunched under her own feet, he walked silently, behind her one minute and completely hidden from sight the next. If she didn't know better, she'd think he really disappeared. Maybe she didn't know better. Her illusive spirit protector. That's what she called him since the early walks when he followed her out into the desert. Good medicine, bad medicine. She didn't know exactly what it meant, but he said he'd teach her. Many times, she'd seen the tricks he did. She paid careful attention, trying to figure out how he did them. They were more than a magician's typical sleight of hand or optical illusion causing a deception in reality not easily caught by the naked eye. Maybe Lizzie was right. Maybe it really was magic. She thought some of it was rubbing off on her ever since she saw the two old Indians the night John died. They were standing in the driving rain, but they weren't wet. She hadn't thought about them for a while. She couldn't explain them, but she knew they were there. Then, there was the silent communication between herself and Nalanche. Now that she thought about it, they'd been doing it all along. She couldn't explain that either, but she was sure it was all part of the good medicine he spoke of.

The wind died down and the dust settled. She'd been daydreaming, holding the saber and looking out over the desert, lost in her thoughts. From the hill, she could see for miles, but there was no sign of them, the boy on horseback and the dog. Not so much as a trace of dust rising from the desert floor in the direction of where they'd gone. Not surprising after all the times he'd disappeared in the desert. There was an explanation, of course. He knew the country well. That had to be it. She turned around. Everyone but Wyatt had gone back to town and she hadn't noticed them leaving. They must have thought her ungrateful and rude. She'd make a point of apologizing later.

Wyatt waited near the carriage while she stood by the new grave, staring at the pile of rocks. It was hard to believe John was there beneath the ground. He'd been so full of life and dreams. Dreams. What a painful word. The dreams were empty now. She sighed and turned to Wyatt. "I don't know how to thank you for all you've done, Marshal." He took her hand. "You just did." The man had suffered his own share of heartaches, and then some. She heard his first wife died when they were very young, during an epidemic of some terrible, killer disease. Story was, he had a second wife, but Rose didn't know anything about her or what happened to her. After that, there was Mattie. She called herself Mattie Earp, but Wyatt never married her. Virgil said the woman was a burden to Wyatt, but he didn't have the heart to send her back to Kansas. What with taking all the laudanum she could get her hands on and the wild ranting and raving that went along with it, the man had to be a saint to put up with her as long as he did. When they first came to Tombstone, he frequently carried her out of opium dens after finding her in a drugged stupor. Eventually, her addiction overpowered her and she became completely dependent on narcotics. Nothing was important to her anymore, not even Wyatt. No wonder he'd fallen in love with Josie. She was a strong-willed woman who suffered from none of the emotional weaknesses that plagued poor Mattie. Wyatt needed somebody like Josie, someone who could not only keep up with him, but stayed one step ahead of him. Josie did that.

More than anyone, Wyatt understood what Rose was going through. He knew how it felt to lose someone you loved to senseless violence. When Morgan died, she sent Wyatt a note of condolence filled with compassion, a thought from her heart. He never forgot the depth of that private message. Then, there was another tragedy in his life. Virgil. Although he never talked about it, she knew Wyatt suffered every time he looked at his brother, crippled for life by another would-be assassin's bullet. He blamed himself for that too, believing he should have seen it coming and found a way to stop it. They had plenty to say when Morgan was killed. Some even said the younger Earp's death was Wyatt's fault. That kind of talk cut deep. They blamed him for dragging his brothers into what they called his private war. They said he was obsessed with being a lawman. They were right about that, but if the truth be known, it was Virgil who convinced the Earp boys to be wearing badges again, not Wyatt.

Wyatt lacked good patience and so did Morgan, both of them ready to solve a dispute by thunking an adversary over the head with the butt end of a pistol sooner than talking it out. The two of them were hot-tempered, unlike Virgil who usually tried talking before resorting to pistol-whipping, but in the end, it was Virgil who called out the dogs of war against the cowboys.

Wyatt tried to keep his family together. Many lambasted the way he pushed his gambling interests to make money with an apparent lack of emotion and total disregard for the human element. Some said he put his money ahead of his family, but that wasn't true. At the same time, they had to admire his determination and fearlessness. He also believed the united strength of the Earp brothers would bring law and order to the town and he was committed to the cause. He received little or no help from so-called concerned citizens when the cowboys stirred up trouble, and he got more than his share of criticism from those uninvolved finger-pointers who insisted the "law" get things under control, the ones who never offered to stand beside him in a fight, but complained when things didn't go according to their liking. They were the same ones who stood by watching a defenseless boy get beaten by half a dozen men on horseback and let a woman stand up to the bullies alone with nothing more than a stone to throw at them. He was a force to be reckoned with and everyone knew it. If you were honest and law-abiding, he respected you, but he despised liars and those who turned a blind eye to responsibility. He did his job with a vengeance and one goal in mind, the prevalence of justice. His commitment to law and order was ferocious. He made no concessions for those who crossed the line and his very name instilled fear in the ones who broke the law. He'd say something once and if he didn't get results the first time, there were no second chances. Unlike Virgil who was, in general, a patient man, Wyatt's nature contained no overabundance of the virtue. With a reputation for rapping heads with a Colt .45, he intimidated many and made friends with few. Not many had been successful in attempts to outwit him, and those who managed to walk away with some partial victory were never able to claim they won the war. He never ran from a fight and like Virgil, he stood up to the worse kind, alone if need be. He hunted them down when they ran, relentless in the pursuit of justice. His vendetta against the ones who murdered one brother and crippled the other was proof of that, and there wasn't a soul who doubted he wouldn't rest until justice was done — one way or another. If you ever saw him in action, the one thing you were absolutely certain of was that you were glad he was on your side.

He was still holding her hand. She was touched by the magnitude of his compassion. "My brother asked me to tell you his thoughts are with you. He sends his deepest sympathy." She knew Virgil had to be thinking about her. He knew John, and she half-expected to see him today, but she wasn't surprised he didn't come. Besides, Lizzie said he was in California. It was probably better this way. Wyatt continued. "If you need anything, send the Indian boy to my office. I'll see to it you get whatever you need." She wasn't sure if that was his own idea or a message from Virgil. She guessed it was a little of both. As long as Virgil was around, help, whenever she needed it, would never be far away.

Abby and Ruby waited on the porch while she said good-bye to Wyatt. When he drove around the corner, she took her time getting through the gate, trying to put off having to talk to anyone as long as possible. They were there to help, but she wasn't in the mood for company. She didn't want to hurt their feelings, but she wanted to be alone. She started to say it and Ruby interrupted. "We wanted to make sure you got back alright. We can't stay, but we'll be around tomorrow. If you need anything, send Nalanche." The girls hugged her and walked off. There was no pressure from them to make her talk. They'd made that part easy. They were the best friends anyone could hope for. She was grateful to have them, lucky to know them. She'd need the comfort of such friends as time went on, but at this moment, she had to be alone.

She had to go inside the house that little more than a day and a half ago was filled with laughter and love. She had to go in, knowing John would not be there ever again. She held onto the porch post and stepped up slowly. When her hand touched the door, loneliness and despair swept over her like a tidal wave. She thought about staying outside on the swing for a while. There was no hurry to go in. No, she had to face it. Sooner or later, she had to face being alone. The hinges squeaked when she opened the door. John was going to oil them yesterday. The house was empty, as she knew it would be. She'd come home to an empty house lots of times, but this was different. Empty took on a whole new meaning today. It wasn't only the house that was empty. It was her. She walked into the bedroom and dropped her hat on the bed. Nights spent in this room would be cold and lonely from now on. Never again would she feel John's touch or know the passion they shared. As the rain rejuvenated the desert, his laughter and love brought new life into this house. She was parched and empty before he came back. He found her and filled her with love. He restored her hope for the future. She loved to hear John and Nalanche talk about how they'd be partners in the best law firm in Arizona. They were making plans for the future. It was an exciting place to think about — the future. They were young and there was a lot to look forward to. So many good things waited up ahead. There were no happy voices here today. It was quiet, still as death itself. There weren't even any hummingbirds outside the window. He took part of everything with him. Part of her died with him. He was the link in the chain that made her life complete. A day and a half ago, at midnight in the Bird Cage Theatre, the chain was broken. Alone in the place they shared so much love, she was overwhelmed with the magnitude of her loss. She closed her eyes and prayed for death to take her to the place it had taken him.

She slept for a couple of hours and by the time she woke up, the day was nearly gone. It was late afternoon. She laid on the bed, staring at the ceiling. There was a lot to think about. She didn't know where to start. She had to decide what to do now that John was gone. She'd have to write to Marian and Rebecca right away. Maybe she should have sent them a wire. Maybe they would have wanted her to send his body home for burial. Maybe she'd been too quick to bury him in Tombstone. It happened so fast, the thought never occurred to her that his family might want him buried in New Orleans. She hadn't written to them since she got here. What would she say after all this time? The first letter and she had to tell them John was dead. It would be terrible news. Rebecca would be devastated. She'd never forgive herself for not going to California with him. They'd have gone to New Orleans or Washington from there and none of this would have happened. Because of her health, he left the Army and decided to stay in Tombstone where the weather was better. It was her fault he was dead and it was too late to be wishing they'd done something different. He was already buried and because he was here, she couldn't leave if she wanted to. She'd have to tell them what happened, but she couldn't think about writing the letter yet.

She felt weak and tired. She hadn't eaten since Saturday night at dinner with John nearly two days ago and she wasn't the least bit hungry. She made some tea and went outside. She sat on the porch swing and closed her eyes. John and Nalanche had so much fun building it — rebuilding it. She came home one day to find the two of them taking the old swing apart, claiming it was in need of repair. In truth, there was nothing wrong with the swing. Building a new one was a reason for them to spend time together. She remembered the porch swing at the Merrick house in New York. They sat there every night the summer they met, listening to the crickets and talking about the future. It was where they fell in love and it had been a wonderful summer. There was another reason for rebuilding the old swing at the little gray house. John built it to look like the one on his mother's porch in memory of that summer. They talked about building a house after they were married and he told her he'd make sure she always had a front-porch swing, no matter where they lived. She drifted off with the sweetheart of her memories. He was holding her hand and laughing, imitating her brogue. She was laughing too and they were dancing in the grass at the park. The band was playing a waltz. He turned so serious that night after the band concert. At first, she thought he was about to tell her good-bye. Instead, he said he loved her and asked her to spend the rest of her life with him. The rest of her life! Contemplating the rest of her life seemed like such a long time then and she said "yes." He gave her a strand of pearls to seal the engagement, the pearls she wore today, to his funeral.

She blinked. Something rubbed against her. Bear was licking her hand. She felt like she'd been dreaming, but it was too real to be only a dream. She was dancing in the park with John and it was very real, not at all like a dream. Nalanche was home. She must have been far away with her thoughts, with John. She was dazed and tired, but she recalled the dream perfectly. It was a strange feeling, like she'd really been with him. She looked at the boy. He was wearing the clothes of an Apache, dressed in a tunic and knee-high deerskin mocassins. A rolled band of cloth across his forehead was tied at the back and a new medicine bag hung from a braided sash, replacing the one he'd given to John. She hadn't seen him dressed this way in a long time. She smiled and called him Brother. "Did you speak to John?" She corrected herself. "Coshani?" His answer was the same as it had been earlier. "He is here."

Two weeks had passed since John's death. The hummingbirds were busily drinking up the sweet nectar from the gourd outside her window. Birds were singing. Bear's tail slapped the side of the bed in anticipation of her getting up to feed him. After his morning run with Nalanche, he was hungry. Some things never changed. When they came back, the boy went to school and the dog was left to watch the house and Rose. It was the same every day. Lately, he had to wait for his breakfast until she decided to get up, noon on some days. She rolled over and found herself face-to-face with him. He licked her nose and she grimaced at the wet greeting. She flopped her arm over the side of the bed and it landed on his head. "I suppose you want to eat." "Eat" was a word he plainly understood and he barked excitedly right next to her ear. She winced and he jumped around in a circle. "Alright, you've earned it. That was a good trick." She sat up and yawned. He barked again. He was hungry and he was telling her so. She covered her ears with both hands. "Alright, alright! I'm gettin' up." She shooed him away with her hand and sat on the edge of the bed, running her fingers through her hair. She'd wash it today — maybe. It always took so long for it to dry. She sighed at the prospect of having to wait for her hair to dry. It was too much trouble to think about doing anything. There were some other things she ought to do today, but she couldn't remember what they were. There was no hurry to do anything. She was becoming terribly absentminded lately.

The dog distracted her from the anxiety attack she suffered the second she was awake every morning since John died. It was back, that overwhelming feeling of being so lost she didn't know where she was half the time. They said it would get easier with the passing of Time, but each day was more difficult to face than the one before. She missed John so much. Every day, she prayed for the day to end so she could go to sleep. Sleep provided the only relief from the pain of missing him and even then, she cried for hours sometimes before she finally went to sleep. Hugging his pillow and remembering the way they fell asleep in each other's arms, she couldn't see how being without him would ever get any easier. Those who said it would were wrong. It didn't get better with the passage of time.

Bear paced back and forth anxiously between the bed and door, barking to get her attention. He was becoming impatient, his bark getting louder and higher-pitched with the increased urgency of his need to go out. The noise made her remember what she was doing and she stood up. What was she going to do? She couldn't remember anything from one second to the next. She couldn't concentrate. Lately, she felt like a tired, old woman losing her mind to senility. She shuffled barefooted to the kitchen, pulling on her robe as she went, the sash forgotten and left behind on the bedroom floor. In days past, she'd never have left her room without brushing her hair and pulling herself together even when she was alone. None of it mattered anymore. Bear barked again, the noise irritating her. "Alright. I said I'm comin', damn it!" Misunderstanding her little show of temper as encouragement, he barked excitedly and ran to the door. She pushed the door wide open. "Get outside. Your yappin's makin' my head hurt. It's too early for noise." It was closer to noon than morning, but she didn't pay attention to time anymore. He ran out and dashed around the side of the house. It wasn't his fault her nerves were on edge. Better fix his food before she forgot. Pouring a cup of coffee, she told herself not to forget he was outside. Nalanche made the coffee every morning before he left for school. He never touched the stuff, but he made it for her. She thought about him as she sipped the coffee. He was so young, but he took care of her. Seemed like it ought to be the other way around. Maybe he was not so young really.

The fire in the stove was out. The coffee was cold and she made a wry face. It was like everything else in her life. She took another sip. It was bitter. She looked into the cup. She never noticed it being bitter before, probably because it was always hot. In the middle of the kitchen, barefooted and robe asunder, with her hair flying wild from lack of brushing, she held the cup of cold coffee with both hands, a habit left over from winter when she put her hands around the cup to warm them on cold mornings. This morning, she was absentmindedly staring at the floor. The cup was cold, but without thinking, she clasped both hands around it.

She was drifting off again, an easy escape from facing whatever the day would bring to remind her of John. Days were passing slowly and memories were painful. There was no meaning or purpose to her life anymore.

Even though she slept a lot, she was tired all the time. She'd hoped to be dead by now, but it didn't look like that was going to happen any time soon. She thought of Nalanche and John talking about being partners in the best law firm in Arizona. John would have made it happen. He always did what he said he was going to do. He intended to see to it that Nalanche got an education. He was going to send the boy to a university in the East to study the law the way Rose had planned. He promised. He would have done it too.

She opened the front door and walked outside, sipping the cold coffee and no longer noticing it was cold. She closed her eyes and breathed deeply of the warm, morning air. Someone called to her and she looked around the yard and toward the gate. No one there. Funny, she thought she heard someone say her name. In fact, she was sure of it. She went to the gate and looked up and down the street. There wasn't a soul in sight. She looked around the side of the house. No one there either. She listened. There it was again, someone calling her name as plain as could be. "Rose." She turned quickly to catch the caller at the gate. No one there. She stood still and listened. Someone was playing a trick on her. That was it. Probably Lizzie. Then, there was a thought that wasn't there a second ago. It was as though someone very close was whispering to her, telling her what she must do next. She understood. She had to follow through with John's plans for the boy. She had to find a way to keep Nalanche in school, to send him on to the university as soon as he was ready. At the rate he was going, that might be sooner than she expected. He'd been working hard at his studies, trying to absorb everything in the books and asking the teacher to give him extra work. The teacher obliged and piled on the after-school assignments and he completed every one of them. Rose was amazed how fast he picked up the reading and writing and arithmetic, much faster than she'd done when Rebecca was teaching her. Of course, she'd never gone to a real school with a real teacher. Rebecca and Marian had been her teachers. It all came so easy for Nalanche. More than once, she'd told him he was smarter than she was and she laughed when he offered to teach her what he learned. He always had his nose stuck in a book and particularly liked learning about other places in the world. When the teacher gave an assignment for each student to pick a country to write about, he chose Ireland.

He was older than the other children at the school and they made fun of him the first day he went there. They learned from their parents to hate Indians, although they hadn't a clue why. When the day was over, they followed him outside, chanting and calling him names. He whirled around and faced them, a small stick in his hand, the element of surprise cutting off their taunting like a fox deciding he had enough of the chase and turning to confront the hounds snapping at his heels. They stopped in their tracks, believing he was about to strike them with the stick. He didn't take his eyes off them as he covered the stick with his hands and when he moved them away, a small, gray dove sat cooing in his palm. He petted the little bird gently and it made no move to fly off. The reaction was "ooh's and aah's" all around. Most of them had seen magicians in traveling medicine shows or carnivals, but never anything like this. A little blonde girl of about eight touched the soft feathers. She turned to the others. "It's a real bird." He laid the bird in her hands and told her she must tell it to fly away. She held the dove close to her face and whispered to it that it was beautiful. When she lifted it skyward, it stayed in her hand. She questioned Nalanche. "Why doesn't it fly away?" He got down on one knee. "You didn't tell it to fly." She understood. She held it up again and talked to it, saying the words he told her to say. "Fly away little dove, and be happy." The bird flew from her hand, soaring high into the air, the children watching its flight in wide-eyed amazement. They didn't tease him anymore and after school, they followed him like a bunch of little goslings running along behind the mother goose, all quacking and chattering at once, begging him to give them a magic trick. Every day, he amazed them with something new and when he was done, the question was always the same. "How did you do that?" The little blonde girl, Emily, smiled at him, certain she knew the answer. "I know how he did it. Magic!"

Why hadn't she thought of it sooner? It was so obvious. She couldn't let his desire to learn go unfulfilled. There was no question about it. She had to do everything in her power to help him get an education. She'd offer to pay his teacher to tutor him on Saturday mornings to help him move along faster. She'd buy whatever books he wanted. To do that, she'd need to go back to work. She had to start bringing in some money again. Her savings was dwindling and if she really intended to send him to college one day, it would take a lot more money than she'd put away. The decision was made. She had to pull the fragments of her life together for Nalanche's sake. He was important. He was her reason to go on. John would want her to do that. In fact, he'd be disappointed if she didn't. She thought about what happened a few minutes ago when she walked outside, the voice she heard calling her name and then, the thought. It hadn't been her own. Someone she couldn't see was making her think when she hadn't been able to remember what day it was.

An idea of what she looked like made her laugh. She shook her head in disgust. She must be a sight. Running a hand through her disheveled hair, she realized her robe was devoid of the sash and the front was wide open. She closed it around herself. How long had she been in the front yard like that? With any luck, no one saw her standing by the gate with her robe flapping in the breeze and her hair tangled and wild, looking like some escapee from an insane asylum. She couldn't remember the last time she ate or took a bath or brushed her hair. She looked down. Her feet were bare. She shook her head at her own absentmindedness and gulped the rest of the cold coffee, puckering her mouth at the bitterness. It wasn't the only thing that left her with a bitter taste. She'd lost track of time, but now she knew what she had to do. Returning to the place where John died wouldn't be easy, but at seven o'clock tonight, she'd be back at the Bird Cage Theatre.

She could hear the laughter and music from a block away. At the door, there were the sounds of glasses clinking and chips being counted and dealers calling for new bets. Girls were giggling and music played. Nothing had changed. Why did she think it would be any different? Because John was dead? That's not the way it was here. It was only different for her. To the rest of them, his life was nothing more than a grain of sand in the wide expanse of desert all around. When the winds blew, sand shifted to change the design of the land and in a matter of minutes, the way it used to be was forgotten forever. That's the way it was with people. When lives ended, they were forgotten, and what they had been was blown away with the winds of Time. He wasn't the first to be killed in this place, nor would he be the last. Men died and life went on for the rest of them as if nothing happened. It was not unlike the first time she saw two men killed here. The next night, she expected it to be different, but no one seemed to remember what happened, let alone care. Two deaths were insignificant in the overall scheme of things. There were no black ribbons on the door. No one mourned their passing or expressed sorrow. The killings hadn't affected them at all. They simply pushed a faro table over the bloodstains on the floor and placed their bets as usual. She didn't understand then and she was incredibly angry that night at the insensitivity of her friends who said she'd get used to it. They'd seen it many times over. Virgil told her the same thing. She remembered how she'd been furious at his lack of remorse. He accepted it as a way of life. He tried to explain life in Tombstone to her and she screamed her outrage at his seemingly casual attitude about the killings. Now, she realized he was only telling the truth. It was the way things were. He and his brothers were trying to change it, but law and order were infants and it could take years for them to mature. If you considered the way things used to be in the early days of the mining camp, they'd come a long way to keeping the peace and in retrospect, Tombstone was actually a pretty safe place to live. At the time, it hadn't been an acceptable explanation. She remembered crying at the senselessness of it all. It was pure insanity that men killed one another over a game of cards or a woman; more often, the former. She was probably the only one who cried for the dead men that night, miners or drifters without families or anyone in the world to care they were gone. She didn't know who they were, but she cried for them. They deserved that much.

A lot happened since that night when she watched a man with a gaping belly wound bleed to death at her feet, one of his friends already dead and the other trying to hold his shattered arm together while the blood splashed on the floor and went all over her dress. It made her ill and she ran outside, retching and crying. It was this place, this town. It was unlike any other in the world. She always had a feeling about this place in the middle of nowhere that she could never explain. It was a contradiction; the one place on earth where Time stopped, yet life went on. It didn't make sense, but it's the way it was. The first morning in town, she awoke to gunfire. Saturday morning, broad daylight, in the street below her window, a man lay dead in a puddle of his own blood, shot for some unknown reason. They unceremoniously carried him off and she never heard a word about what happened. From the day she arrived, she felt the evil in the air, like a fog that never lifted; a rift in the universe surrounded by an invisible, eerie shroud she couldn't identify in earthly terms. Whatever it was, it embraced all who came. In the beginning, she never thought it would happen to her, but she finally had to admit it had a hold on her.

This first night back, the girls were glad to see her. It was what she expected. She was welcomed with hugs and expressions of sympathy and reassurances that she was not alone. Lizzie cried. That was to be expected too. A few patrons offered their condolences, but after the initial formalities, everyone went on about their business. For them, it was just another night.

John Merrick was already forgotten. She stood alone on the steps near the stage, surveying the room and watching life go on below and above, the participants oblivious to her painful observations. A violin was tuning in the orchestra pit. She glanced in the direction of the sound and saw Charlie smiling up at her from his place at the piano. She gave him her customary wave by wiggling her fingers at him and he winked before turning his attention back to the violinist. She could hardly believe she was here. If she was to deal with this place every night again, she must never lose sight of the reason she came back — Nalanche. She'd thought a lot about the day she'd travel to a university in the East to see him graduate, the day when he'd be a lawyer. It was a dream he'd spoken of often, a dream she'd make come true for him. She had it all figured out and nothing would deter her from the plan. Keeping the dream in mind would preserve her sanity in the unbelievable madness of her world.

Abby was beside her, pointing to the stage. "You can't stand here." The show was about to start and they wanted her off the steps. She stepped down into the room, the first step toward realization of a dream. Unfortunately, she'd have to live through another nightmare to make the dream come true. It was alright. She could do it. Music started and the crowd applauded wildly when the curtain went up to reveal Ruby and her entourage stepping onto the stage. All eyes were on the scantily-clad ladies with red feathers in their hair dancing a lively cancan. No one noticed Rose or heard her whisper a prayer for strength. Another night at the Bird Cage Theatre. One step closer to the dream.

Chapter 14

"One more bet I will try, then my silver will buy
the pleasures of Lizzie McGee."

The Pleasures of Lizzie McGee
ALLEN STREET ROSE

There was a magnetism in this universal rift, this place where Time retained its hold on her and all who came here. Riding the stage into the area for the first time, she remembered feeling a strange energy coming from the mountains and desert all around Tombstone. There was something in the air that made her believe she was being watched by eyes without forms. On her evening walks, she'd heard voices and seen smoke from a distant camp fire. Once, after her bout with pneumonia, Jenny walked with her to make sure the exertion wasn't too much for her, unaware of the silent figure nearby watching over them both. She mentioned the voices and pointed to the smoke way over by the Dragoons. They stopped walking and Jenny listened intently for the sounds Rose described. She strained to see what Rose pointed to near the mountains. She finally shrugged her shoulders, turning to Rose with her hand shading her eyes. She studied Rose for a minute, looking for some outward indication of instability or mental collapse. "I don't hear anything and I don't see any smoke." She looked at the ground and back at Rose, trying to think of diplomatic words to express her concern without insulting her friend. Diplomacy was out of the question. The best way was to come right out with it. "You've been through a lot, Rose. Nobody expects you to be your old self this soon after being sick as you were. You're not entirely well yet and I think you need more rest. You're still too weak for these walks. If you weren't so stubborn, you'd wait 'til you got your strength back. You're hearing and seeing things that aren't there." She shook a warning finger at Rose. "You'd best be mindful who you talk to like this. Everyone knows you were out of your head with fever. Some folks might think you've gone foolish if you start telling stories about hearing voices and seeing smoke that's not there. They'll be saying you're crazy." Jenny made her point. Rose bit her lower lip. It was the truth. She'd have to keep these things to herself. No one else could understand, not even this friend who cared about her. She saw the concern on Jenny's face, concern that she might be losing her mind. Jenny was right. It didn't take much to be given a byname in this place, particularly for someone in her profession. They were always looking for something to say about women in her line of work. She wouldn't want word to get around that she was crazy. She could hear it now. "Crazy Rose!" It wasn't a nickname she cared to be burdened with. From then on, she'd never mention what she saw or heard in the desert to anyone except Nalanche.

She touched her friend's arm and laughed. Her laugh was unconvincing and she wondered if Jenny noticed her awkward attempt at conceding she was still a little under the weather as being the problem. "You're right, Jen. The fever did take a lot out of me and I am still a bit tired." She looked out over the desert. From the mountains, white smoke rose from the ground in billowing puffs like cottony clouds gathering together to build a thunderhead in the distance. She wouldn't try to point it out again for Jenny. She watched the puffs drift upward on the warm air and once more, reinforced her friend's opinion that lack of rest was the reason her eyes were playing tricks on her. "Of course there's nothin' there. 'Tis only shadows from the sun goin' down. You know how the heat does funny little wiggly things to the air when it's liftin' up from the desert. 'Twas only the heat risin' from the sand that looked like smoke. And the sounds — well, sometimes the wind makes a whooshin' sound. You know what I mean. Guess my imagination ran off with me." Her laugh was uncomfortable, designed to cover the fib, but Jenny didn't seem to notice. Jenny smiled and shook her head in acknowledgment. "I know. I've heard the wind blowing — kind of whimpering, and I could swear it was a baby crying, if I didn't know better." Rose was relieved. Jenny was satisfied she'd come to her senses and believed Rose's explanation for sounds on the wind and smoke in the distance was reasonable. They linked arms and strolled back toward town. Jenny was in a mood to talk and Rose gave her free reign.

All the way back, Jenny talked about Lizzie's game of hide-and-seek the night before in the Bird Cage with a young man of equally-diminished faculties in the illusive land of common sense. They always laughed when someone offended Lizzie's sensibilities in that area being that, on most days, the affliction of her mind disabled her to where she was incapable of handling even rudimentary problems of life. She wasn't stupid. She was ill, and they'd all come to recognize the difference. She was good-hearted and generous. She loved children. Rose thought if Lizzie could be cured of the illness inside her head, she'd be a wonderful mother. Because of the illness, there was a childlike quality about her that made them all acutely aware of her need for protection and love. She couldn't live alone, so Jenny shared a small house with her. As they walked, Rose looked at the girl holding her arm and laughing as she told the story about the night before. Jenny was pretty good-hearted herself, what with taking on the burden of caretaker for a grown-up person who others viewed as, and more than occasionally called insane. Without Jenny's help, Lizzie would have ended up in an insane asylum or dead, or worse. To Rose's way of thinking, Jenny would one day surely be keeping company with the saints her father used to tell her about, people who sacrificed much in their lifetime for a cause with no expectation of reward or repayment. Jenny was certainly doing that. When Jenny was asked why she took care of Lizzie the way she did, her answer was, "Because I want to." Her reward would not be of this world, but then, she never expected anything. She'd have to wait until she got to Heaven, or maybe that wasn't entirely true. Many times, she said she wished she had a daughter. Taking care of Lizzie might have been the closest she thought she'd ever come to it.

Lizzie! There was no telling when the simplest task might become a monumental obstruction in her path. They'd all seen her break down in tears and lapse into a state of total confusion and distress where she'd pace the floor, wringing her hands and sobbing hysterically at the overwhelming frustration created by having to decide which dress to wear. Jenny was there to console her and help with the decision-making. She always managed to calm Lizzie down. Life was full of obstacles for Lizzie, things most folks took for granted as part of everyday living. No one understood it, but they'd all come to realize it was an illness that had Lizzie in its grip. It was not an illness that produced visible lesions or fever that could be helped with medicine, but rather an invisible demon that dwelled within her and reared its ugly head at the wrong word or, oftentimes, for no apparent reason at all, and just as quickly as it appeared, crawled back into the hidden recesses of the mind to await the next opportunity to inflict pain of an indescribably brutal nature. The cure for the sickness was unknown. Lizzie came to town with a traveling carnival show and stayed at the Bird Cage. Strangely enough, it was the most stability she'd ever known. She felt like she belonged there. There were doctors who were experimenting with treatments for people like Lizzie, but if she went to a sanitarium, she'd have to go alone. They'd heard about those places and they couldn't do that to Lizzie. She'd feel deserted and she'd die there all alone. Besides, she wasn't crazy. She was sick. She'd stay in Tombstone, and Jenny would stay with her because, as Jenny put it, she wanted to.

According to Jenny, the incident of last night found Lizzie in rare form. She'd become completely exasperated with the enamored young man who followed her about the room tapping her shoulder and unintentionally snagging a few strands of her hair in his clumsy pursuit of her attention. She tried ignoring him. She even tried hiding, but there was no discouraging him and no getting away from him. When she had enough, she turned on him, her reaction coming as a great surprise to everyone who knew her. She blasted him with every insult she could think of, using some pretty strong language for Lizzie. Lizzie was prone to emotional outbursts, but she didn't swear. Except for the time she was out of her mind from the tolguacha poisoning, no one ever heard Lizzie talk the way she did last night. Up until the time she hollered at him, he'd been doing all the talking and he wasn't paying attention to where he was going. The unexpected turn of events when she stopped abruptly startled him and he tripped over his own feet backing up, losing his balance and tromping on the toes of the closest person. Luckily for him, the man whose toes were stepped on was of a mild temperament. The man steadied the boy and was thanked profusely for his assistance. When he regained his bearings, he was face-to-face with a markedly annoyed Lizzie. He was quiet as Lizzie, surprisingly, took control of the situation. Everyone who knew her was astonished when she shook her finger in his face, warning him of the consequences of his persistence. Jenny laughed again as she recalled the young man's eyes crossing when he tried to focus on Lizzie's finger under his nose, and how they widened as Lizzie punctuated her threat of bodily harm by shaking her fist at him. He was probably lucky he didn't receive a punch in the nose for his efforts. Jenny was proud of the way Lizzie handled him. Lizzie didn't stand up for herself that way very often, at least not without a friend nearby to back her up if she faltered. Last night, she did it all by herself. It was a good sign, a very good sign.

Any other time, Rose would have shared Jenny's enthusiasm for the story, but it didn't seem that funny today. It was just another episode in the ongoing saga of Lizzie McGee's life. There were plenty of others, the wildest story being about Three-Finger Jim, the faro dealer who was head-over-heels in love with Lizzie. He did his best to discourage other men's interest in her by telling them she was his girl. That couldn't have been farther from the truth. One night, a stranger on Jim's game asked what the lady's name was. Jim told him he was wasting his time because Lizette was his girl. He should have stopped right there, but he kept on talking and made a big mistake when he told the stranger that pretty lady would be his sweetheart someday. The stranger picked up on the slip right quick. "Someday? Then, she ain't your girl here and now?" Knowing he'd caught the dealer in a fib, and finding out Lizzie being Jim's girl was nothing more than wishful thinking, he bedeviled Jim with his next remark. "I'm gonna try one more bet." He plunked his money down on the table and with a hungry look in his eyes, pointed up at Lizzie. "I found lady luck and I got enough silver to buy the pleasures of that beautiful dove for the rest of the night." Leaning over the table in a way that suggested he might have a secret to whisper, he winked at Jim. "Besides, she looks like the kind of woman who likes a man who can hold onto her real tight — with both hands." He was referring to the two missing fingers on Jim's right hand. The stranger threw down his cards and grinned. "She's mine now. What do you think of that, Dealer?" He turned his back to Jim and leaned on the table to look at Lizzie. While he was watching her, the stranger failed to notice that Jim dropped his cards too. A fatal mistake. He didn't pay attention to Jim's hand under the table, and never heard the hammer click back on the hidden Colt forty-five, two missing fingers making no difference in locking back the action on a six-shooter. When Lizzie flew across the stage attached to a wire high above the room, the music got louder. The crowd went crazy, hollering and whistling as she sailed past with arms outstretched like an angel in flight, and when Jim pulled the trigger, the blast from that forty-five just sort of blended right in with the rest of the noise. The stranger never spent that night, or any other, with Lizette. Fact was, he didn't even see Lizzie complete her flight across the stage because he was dead before he hit the floor. Jim laid the smoking Colt on the faro table and walked right out the front door. By the time they discovered what happened and the Marshal got there, Jim was halfway to Sonora, and so was the stranger's money. Nobody ever saw Three-Finger Jim again.

Her thoughts were elsewhere, but she laughed to be polite as Jenny continued with the story of last night's chase. Rose tried to remember what the first part of the story was. Jenny went on. "It was the pot calling the kettle black, if you know what I mean." Lizzie's lecture about her admirer's lack of ability to realize when his consumption of whiskey had exceeded his capacity to hold it gave rise to uncontrollable laughter among those watching the incident. Jenny's descriptive account painted a vivid picture of the fellow's pitiful attempt at eloquence and sincerity as he launched into a discourse on his undying love for Miss Lizette. She walked ahead of him, weaving through the crowd to lose him, but he didn't give up. Undaunted by her evasive actions, he tagged along behind her, speaking the sloppy, broken language of a whiskey drunk. The little game of pursuit soon became the center of attention and Lizzie grew more irritated by the minute. With slurred speech and an occasional, inappropriate, descriptive adjective for emphasis, he proceeded to extol her beauty and charm while at the same time loudly elaborating on his intended activities in the upper cribs that would demonstrate his "love." His description left nothing to the imagination and was met by whoops and whistles from those of more indelicate character at imagining the fulfillment of his objectives should he succeed in maneuvering the pretty blonde upstairs. At one point, he placed his hand over his heart and closed his eyes to emphasize his sincerity, pleading with her to accept his affections, albeit for one night only. With his eyes closed, he was unable to maintain his balance. Someone would steady him before he fell and he'd thank them profusely. Every time Lizzie moved away, he staggered along behind her like a puppy not yet sure of the stability of his own legs, his concept of distance drastically impaired by the workings on his brain of a substantial ingestion of whiskey in a relatively short period of time. Her exit was blocked when someone shoved back a chair and stood up in front of her. She was forced to stop. He paused for a second, a ridiculously-silly grin on his face, success seemingly within his grasp. He took advantage of the opportunity and made an overzealous lunge for his prize, reaching both hands out for Lizzie's derriere. In so doing, he lost his already precarious balance. Before anyone could catch him, and much to the chagrin of the musicians, he plowed headfirst into the orchestra pit. He emerged from the pile of people knocked down by the collision, dazed and entangled in strings. A most disgruntled violinist stared in disbelief at the splinters of his former instrument before casting choleric curses on the young man and smacking him sharply over the head with the remains of the demised fiddle.

Recalling the story was uproariously funny to Jenny and she laughed again, wiping tears from her eyes. Rose smiled at her, but only half-listened as they walked. Jenny went on about the comical event and how everyone laughed so hard they cried. "Lizzie has more men in love with her than a dog has fleas." Her voice drifted into the background of Rose's hearing as they got closer to town. She tried to tell her friend about the sounds and the smoke, but Jenny's reaction had not been one of understanding or acceptance. Instead, there was a concern for her state of mind and Jenny suggested she was hearing and seeing things that weren't there. She knew she wasn't suffering from a fever and she wasn't crazy either, despite Jenny's implication that she might be. Those things were there. She knew what she saw, but the talk with Jenny made her mindful that others didn't have the ability to see and hear what came from another place. She convinced Jenny she was sane, simply suffering from the aftereffect of an illness that would pass in time. If she didn't say anymore about it, Jenny would forget their conversation and she'd keep these things to herself from now on. She wasn't sure what was happening to her, but something in this place affected her in a way she could only explain as mystical, something no one else saw or felt. It'd been that way since she got here; the witnessing of mysterious incidents which, in the beginning, she shrugged off as unusual, but probably having an explanation. Now that she thought about it, the explanations never had been revealed. Jenny stopped talking and was looking at her. Rose hoped she hadn't missed a cue to respond to something Jenny might have said, so she smiled to acknowledge she was still listening. As soon as Jenny resumed the story, Rose blocked out her voice. She did it a lot lately, having discovered a way to go inside herself and escape the craziness around her. During those times, it felt like she had cotton in her ears, and it was happening as they walked. She could barely hear her friend's voice, but there were other sounds that were crystal clear, sounds she knew only she heard. She wouldn't ask Jenny if she heard them. She'd already tried that and found herself having to assure Jenny she understood it to be her imagination. She listened to the sounds of the desert and although Jenny was right beside her, her voice was muffled and distant. Rose rolled her eyes skyward in recognition of familiar voices drifting overhead on the wind. To the east, puffs of smoke from a far-off fire rose in the air, one atop the other.

   She was drawn here by the same element that carried the voices of ones who rode the Pale Horse; those who once walked the earth as mortal men and spoke to the one she called Brother through the veil that separates life and death. The two were much closer than anyone else understood. Nalanche understood the transparency that existed in the crossover and with his help, she was beginning to understand. She witnessed the crossing. She had seen the old Indians. Otahe and Tehanache. She saw the soldier — John Merrick. They had come through the veil and allowed her to see them. She heard voices on the wind and saw the smoke from distant fires.

Standing still, feeling like a sparrow in the eye of a hurricane, she watched the others race through life at breakneck speed. It was calm in the center of a revolving wheel, the outer limit of which was spinning so fast that it made her dizzy to watch. Cards fanned and chips were counted. Glasses clinked together and girls giggled, and the tinkling of crystal chandelier prisms in an evening breeze went entirely unnoticed by all but her. Occasional outbursts of shouting at the win or loss of a hand rose above the music and general din of the place. A few dollars. That's all they were concerned with. Their lives revolved around money and excitement, both inconsequential in the overall scheme of life. She wondered if they had any notion of spiritual things. Of course, they didn't. If they did, they wouldn't live this way. All that mattered was the trivia comprising their superficial lives; a turn of the cards, women and whiskey, a big strike, the mother lode, whatever money could buy, and not necessarily in that order. They never looked beyond material things. What did they think came after all of this? If she asked them, they'd laugh. If she tried to tell them about the crossover, they'd call her crazy. She felt sorry for them because in this life, they'd never know what was truly important.

She was drawn to this place and so was John. So were they all. They saw changes brought on by the passing of time and believed it was a good place to live. They talked about the future and how they'd make things better for their children and grandchildren. They had faith in men like Virgil Earp and the system of justice John dedicated his life to. They were dreamers — castle-builders too far ahead of their time. It would take longer than either of them imagined for Tombstone to become as they envisioned it. They were going to stay here forever. It was ironic the way it turned out. They never realized how accurate their prediction was. They'd both be staying, only not the way they planned. She'd stay because John was here. She couldn't leave him buried out there on the hill alone. There was no going back to New Orleans or anywhere. She was here for the duration, however long it might be.

She surveyed the noisy room from her perch beside the stage. They were oblivious to her watching them. She was alone in a crowd, like a ghost, invisible to the eyes of mortal men, watching them from beyond the veil through which the others could not see. She felt disassociated from them, perhaps by the veil that separates the living from the dead. Although she was still among the living, she perceived herself as viewing life around her as from the other side — the crossover. Things would be different now. She knew exactly how she'd deal with life in this place. She had discovered a way to isolate herself from the rest of them by using the power of her thoughts. Maybe it was more a case of having been directed to the crossing, some of what Nalanche called good medicine. Her thinking was no longer conventional in character. It was of another place. A spiritual conformation.

Her thoughts were interrupted by a woman's voice behind her, giggling, and a man with her. She moved aside and they brushed past on their way down the stairs without acknowledging her and she wondered if her original thought of being invisible might have been right. The shooting of a couple of weeks ago had been forgotten. The woman's laughter was shrill and piercing, higher than other sounds in the room, and her perfume was heavy and overpowering. Rose didn't recognize her. Lately, there was a new face here every time she turned around. John's pain had been forgotten and her suffering for losing him went unnoticed. The Bird Cage possessed a spirit unto itself, masquerading as a site of fun and frolic, enticing them in with the promise of worldly pleasure. Its deception consumed another soul and it emerged flaunting its triumph, unscathed and unpunished for the evil deed. It was amazing how death had little or no impact on the living here. Truth, however cruel, was that life did go on. Business as usual at the Bird Cage — for the rest of them.

They walked out to John's grave every night after supper, Rose and Nalanche and Bear. She asked the boy to teach her how to talk to John, wherever he might be listening from. Even with her life changed in the way she viewed the world around her, it was hard to think in terms of talking to a spirit, a ghost of someone she loved, but she was ready to be with him on whatever level was available. She felt the presence, but was confused. She wanted to know how to reach him and how she'd recognize his message to her. Was it like a telegraph where the receiver of the message couldn't be seen, yet received it? Nalanche asked if she remembered the unspoken message they passed in the middle of the dust storm at John's funeral. She remembered how she had known what he was thinking. She heard him thinking. She wasn't sure how it happened. All she knew was that she felt a power from somewhere deep within her, from her own spirit, reaching out to touch the spirit of the boy she called Brother. He received the message and he answered without words, and she understood his answer. Neither of them had spoken out loud, yet each understood the other. He said, "Coshani listens. He is here." She looked around, but saw no one. She wanted to believe. She wanted so desperately to believe John could hear her. She wanted to be able to talk to him, to his spirit perhaps, the way Nalanche spoke to his father and grandfather. If there was really a way, she could survive life until it was time to meet him on the other side. After having seen the old ones the night John died, she believed a path was laid out for her to follow in search of a realm of vital force and elusive power beyond the reach of human comprehension; a passage to the spirit world Nalanche knew so well. He said the spirits could be summoned and they would guide her. When she rode to the funeral parlour with Wyatt, she turned around to watch Nalanche leading John's horse behind the buggy. It was the second time she saw a man no longer of this earth, the soldier, walking with the boy and his horse; the spirit of John Merrick, there for her to see and know he was still with her. Nalanche said he would not appear as such again and she'd come to know the true spirit of Coshani.

In the beginning, when the boy began teaching her the beliefs and mysterious ways of the Apache, she thought only Indians knew the secret to contacting the spirit world. Nalanche said it wasn't so. He said she must be free to recognize the spirits so familiar to him, the ones he said were everpresent. He believed everything was alive. Nothing ever died. When the body gave out and was no longer of any use, the spirit left it and lived forever in another place. He didn't grieve the way she grieved because he believed John was not dead. He had taken a different form, the form each living thing in this world returned to after death. If that was true, she had to know the form. She had to recognize it and be ready to accept it, whatever it was. She thought back to all the times she went to a place of serenity and warmth when she was a child, the place she thought might have been Heaven. She often thought about where her mother and father had gone, and Ann Merrick. She believed there was a place of peace and beauty where all good people went to be with God when they died, the place she hoped to be reunited with her family and friends known to her in this life; a place without pain or sadness. For as long as she could remember, she called it Heaven. It was where her father said Annie Callahan waited for him, the place where he said they'd all be together someday. He was absolutely certain of it. She imagined it being somewhere in the sky, above the clouds and past the sun. Lately, she had the feeling the afterlife world was much closer, on the other side of an invisible curtain that fell right in front of the living. Some of those gone before had come through to her and she believed she passed over into the element from which they came. She called upon Ann Merrick and her mother to give her courage in the face of overwhelming sadness after John's death. She got the strength from somewhere. She just never thought of the source in quite the same way Nalanche described it. She remembered what he said about grieving because she didn't understand death, that the spirit who lived in John still lived. It was hard to understand and she was unable to stop grieving. She remembered the voices she'd heard so many times during her walks outside of town and the smoke over by the mountains. Nalanche said they were all around. They had always been there, but not everyone was given the chance to see them. He told her to see with her spirit, not her eyes.

She missed him. She'd always miss him. She was human after all. They had known each other in this life and that's the only way she could remember him. She wanted to touch him the way she touched him in life. Nalanche said there would be another time. Not only had they known each other in this life, but in the past as well, and there would be others yet to come. She was confused. Others? Other what? Lifetimes? Sometimes he wasn't easy to understand at all. He told her Coshani listened when she called to him. She had so many questions. "But how will I know he listens? And shall I call him John or the name you know him by? Help me know what to do, Brother." Nalanche faced toward the mountains and held his hands out as if beckoning to friends in the distant hills to come closer. His back was to her as he spoke. "He is as he has always been, Coshani." When he turned to her, he spoke in his native Athapaskan language, a tone to his voice she'd not heard before, lower, older. "You have seen Otahe and Tehanache. They are here. Speak to Coshani. He is here. He has been here before the others." The others? His father and grandfather? She had seen them clearly the night John died. She looked at the ground, turning the words over in her mind. She started to ask him something. He was walking away with the dog and in what seemed like only an instant, they were out of sight. It was always the same. He'd done it for as long as she'd known him. He disappeared like a puff of smoke in the wind, and the dog with him.

She stood alone on the hill looking at the mountains. She closed her eyes and whispered the name into the wind as he had done, "Coshani" — a great chief from long ago. Something told her she was right about the name. Coshani. She knew he'd been a tribal leader long before Otahe and Tehanache. Nalanche was the descendent of chiefs and if she was to believe the voices on the wind, the spirit of the man she knew as John Merrick had once led the Apache Nation. Notwithstanding his features and dark complexion, because of his blue eyes, most people wouldn't have guessed John was an Indian, but in this life he was the grandson of an Apache chief. His mother was a full-blooded Apache and her father was a chief. Rose never forgot that. They all felt the connection and they talked about it many times. It was not inconceivable to think John and Nalanche might be related by blood. When Ann left her family in the Arizona Territory to go east with Richard Merrick, she not only left her father behind, but a younger brother as well. Lately, she'd thought about it a lot and wished she'd asked Ann what her brother's name was. Could it have been Otahe? Was her father's name Tehanache? Was the name John and Nalanche called each other more than just an affectionate designation — Brother? And was that designation so close to being right, there was another word to indicate an actual kinship by blood — cousin?

The boy had been trying to tell her. They chose him to pass on the secrets of good medicine, bad medicine because he was the successor to the magic. It all made perfect sense. What didn't make sense was why she was being allowed to know them. She wasn't from here. She'd come from across the ocean, from another continent and a different way of life. She was Irish. She had no connection to Nalanche's ancestors. Or did she? Old memories came to mind. How could she have forgotten? It was like every-thing here. The place made you forget who you were. She was a Gypsy, descendant of Indians from the Far East and slaves of pharaohs, rulers of ancient Egypt. Over centuries, her father's family migrated across two con-tinents to Ireland. They were as they had always been, restless tribes of nomads wandering the countryside, never settling in one place. They were a dark, mysterious people, much like the Apache in this country. Her ances-tors shared similar mystical beliefs and superstitions with Nalanche's fore-fathers that carried over to this day. Gypsy women still called on spirits for information from the past and predictions to the future. The old woman, Zaida, was one of them — the seer. The adults went to her for advice, but the children were afraid of her. They said she was a hundred years old — a witch with magical powers. They said she kept a devil as a pet and it ate children who ventured too close to her tent. They'd seen it's green eyes leering at them when she carried the thing on her arm. They said they heard it screaming in the night and when first light broke across the bog, there was blood on the ground in front of Zaida's tent.

Rose pushed away the stories as nonsense and she wasn't afraid. She was only ten when she went into the tent and saw the so-called green-eyed devil — an old falcon, spending the last of his days on earth perched on the back of an old woman's chair. Zaida called him Nostradamus. The keen eyesight of his youth was gone and he couldn't hunt anymore. She hand-fed him field mice and bugs she caught for him. He no longer caught rodents and carried them off to a treetop to devour. Instead, he ate his meals on the ground in front of her tent and would have starved to death if not for the kindness of an old woman. When food was offered to him, the scream the children described was not the declaration of a victorious hunter, but rather a mournful cry for lost youth and times past.

In Zaida's tent, Rose had been allowed to see the stone that came from the lost world beneath the sea. She placed her hands around the pleochroic crystal and it turned every color of the rainbow, the vibrant hues pulsating as from a life within the stone. Zaida told her the secrets of the universe were contained within the crystal and she had only to ask to receive the answers. She said Rose was different from the other children, that she had a veil — a special gift she would understand when the time was right. A guide would be sent to show her the way to use the gift wisely, a spiritual power from the universe that would change her life. The old woman placed a magical amulet around Rose's neck, a gold coin bearing the intaglio of a strange figure aiming an arrow skyward — half man, half beast. Before she left, the wrinkled old woman held her hand and told her to listen for the name she'd been known by throughout the ages. Thinking back to that time, she didn't understand what Zaida meant. Questions raced around inside her head. What was the other name the old Gypsy woman said she was supposed to listen for? She'd never heard it. Zaida mentioned the crossover. As a child, she didn't know what it meant. Now, she knew what the crossover was — a passageway into the spirit world. A thought about the crossover had come to her recently. She couldn't remember what it was. Was it possible she'd been here before, in another Time? Perhaps they had met before, she and the boy. Like John, she called Nalanche, Brother.

A gentle breeze caressed her face, a familiar hand. She listened intently, holding her breath to be sure the drum she heard was not the echo of her own heart beating. It was her name she heard drifting on the wind. The voice spoke another name as well, foreign; an ancient name she didn't recognize. Vientoja. The voice whispered, "Sister of the Wind." He was here — Coshani. When Nalanche spoke to her about his father and his grandfather, he said the words in the language of his people. She didn't know the language, yet she understood the words and wondered how that could be. From the hill, she could see for miles across the desert to where the mountains blocked its path. The night John died, she stood in the rain with Nalanche's arms around her. She remembered feeling like she was wrapped in a warm blanket. She had that feeling now, a sensation of being surrounded by a peace she'd never have thought possible in this, her deepest sorrow. The wind rushed past, carrying with it a message of comfort. A door was being opened to her. Barriers moved aside to reveal a gateway to a place Nalanche said would be shown to her when she was ready to know. She remembered the words of the Gypsy seer. Zaida told her the way to use the gift would be shown to her when the time was right.

More questions. Was she ready or did it take some kind of preparation on her part? Was this the time? What determined the time, and how would she know if it was now? So many things she didn't know. The old Gypsy told her she'd recognize the crossover. Otahe and Tehanache had not been there the night John died just for her to see them. They had come for him, for Coshani, one of their own. They were there to guide him through the crossover and she had seen the open gateway. The boy's words came back to her. Again, she didn't understand them at the time he said, "My father and my grandfather know Coshani. They speak of him. He has been here many times." She was beginning to understand. It was the way John would keep his promise and be with her again. One day, he'd come for her as Otahe and Tehanache had come for him. In the world beyond, she would know him as Nalanche knew him, as he had been for all Time. Coshani. Perhaps, in that world, she too would be known by another name, the name she heard whispered on the wind. There would be another time for them in this world as well and she'd recognize him when that day came, no matter how distant in the future. Time would not destroy the memories. If she had to wait a hundred years to see him, or five hundred years, or five thousand, she'd know him. She didn't know how, but she would know him. The boy and dog were back, returning the way they left without a sound.

Looking out across the desert, the view was breathtaking from the top of the hill at any time of day, but in the evening, just before the sun sank beneath the horizon to wake the other side of the world, the panorama transformed into a spectacular kaleidoscope of color. A combination of low clouds and setting sun drenched the far-off mountains in various shades of purple and pink and gold as if some heavenly can of paint tipped over and randomly splashed its contents down the ramparts.

Something moved in the distance and she strained to see what it was. Three horses galloped at high speed toward her, running full-out as though they were on an urgent mission. Vestiges of the day's heat rose from the ground in wavy shafts that made it look like the horsemen were riding through a waterfall. The final remnants of the day's sun reflected off the sand, giving the illusion of a great lake in the middle of the desert. It was not a lake of course. It was dirt, miles of it, and there should have been a lot of dust in the air judging from the speed at which they traveled. She pointed at the horsemen. "Do you see those riders, Nalanche?" He didn't answer. She watched as they came closer. At first, she thought her eyes played tricks on her, but as she studied the approaching equestrians, she could see them plainly. While no ordinary riders, neither did they appear to be apparitions, although the horses were not raising the customary cloud of dust as they raced across the desert floor. They seemed to be riding atop the illusionary body of water. If she didn't know better, she'd swear their feet weren't touching the ground. The thought was absurd, but they appeared to be running on air. She couldn't take her eyes off them. She asked Nalanche again. "Who do you suppose they are? They are without supplies or water as far as I can tell. The only place they can be comin' from is the mountains and they're miles away. No horse can run so fast for such a great distance in the heat. Surely, the poor animals will drop dead if they don't slow down." She was worried about the horses and surprised at how close they were already. They covered the distance in an incredibly short time and kept coming. She was mesmerized watching them approach. "They look like Apaches. There are no saddles on the horses. I wonder why they're in such a hurry. We may not be safe here. They might be dangerous. Renegades maybe! We might ought to get home." She turned toward town and Nalanche touched her arm. He didn't say anything and she looked back over her shoulder to see where the riders were. The three Indians were no longer racing toward her. They had stopped only a few yards away. She was stunned. It was impossible for them not to have made a sound, yet she hadn't heard them coming. Looking past them, there was not so much as a trace of dust in the air from the galloping hooves. Silent riders, their movements causing neither disturbance of air nor impression on the earth as they arrived on what was now clearly defined in her mind as Apache spirit winds. Nalanche told her a long time ago that's how his ancesters traveled. He said they rode the Apache spirit winds down from the mountains every night.

She stood before the riders. She recognized the old ones, Otahe and Tehanache. She shaded her eyes with her hands to see the third one better. Although he was taller than the other two and younger, she had the distinct feeling his true age was much greater than all of theirs combined. Shining, black hair fell around his shoulders and extracted a copper glow from the setting sun. Magnification of the sun's waning light dropping lower to the edge of the horizon produced an illusion of a ring of fire all around him. She was transfixed by the blue stone around his neck, like the ones Nalanche had given her. He'd worn one around his neck for the longest time, same as the one she was looking at now. It was all coming to her. The medicine bag. Nalanche put the stone in the medicine bag and laid it in the casket with John. He said the blue stones were a source of strength and peace. In the beginning, she thought it strange he always put the two together. Not so anymore. The two fit perfectly. One could not be had without the other. A small, leather pouch was tied to the Indian's belt — the medicine bag.

The spirited Appaloosa he rode looked just like Cash. Notwithstanding the distance and lightning speed of their dash across dry country, the animal was not at all winded. Not a single bead of sweat glistened on his coat. Horse and rider moved closer, the horse dancing in eager anticipation of a repeat performance of the race. The sun was lower and she saw him clearly. He was as Nalanche described him, a great chief, riding with others of his rank. As she watched, other Indians joined the three and stood in a long line side-by-side. Like the three, there was no sound and no raising of dust by their horses upon arrival. They were proud men, brave warriors and tribal heralds from the past, come to celebrate a reunion with one who left their assemblage and returned to them many times over. He was the one Nalanche said the spirits of his ancestors told him about when he went into the desert to listen to the winds, the one whose return they were expecting, leader of the Apache nation for all time. He didn't speak to her as the others came to his side, but she felt the power of his energy even at a distance. She looked beyond him. The desert was alive with horsemen, thousands of them. Where had they all come from? There were nowhere near so many Apaches left in all the Arizona Territory. She turned to Nalanche. He was watching her, not at all surprised at the multitude gathering in the desert. It seemed the entire Apache nation, from the beginning of its existence, had assembled to ride with the great chief, Coshani. She finally understood what Nalanche meant when he said Coshani had been here for a long time, longer than she could comprehend. They all knew him many times over and now, she knew him.

He beckoned to her to come closer. She wasn't afraid as she stood beside the horse, rubbing her fingers up and down his face. He was soft as velvet and he nuzzled her hand gently. He was a powerful animal, but he stood perfectly still, careful not to shift his weight and knock her off balance. She stroked the horse's face and looked up at the Indian. He dismounted and stood in front of her. All she could think was that he looked more handsome than she remembered. The moustache was gone and his hair was much longer now. The clothes were different too; soft, deerskin pants and moccasin boots, and a brown tunic tied with a belt of braided leather. Attached to the belt above the medicine bag was a smooth, leather sheath holding a hunting knife. He wore a headband of red and blue and yellow-print cloth tied in the back. A lot of things were different, but there was no mistaking who he was. He removed something from the medicine bag and held it out to her. She took his hand and he placed the tiny object in her palm, but before she could see what it was, he closed his hand over hers. His hand was warm and strong and the energy that passed from him into her was familiar. She'd felt it before. She understood his unspoken message as clearly as if he had said the words out loud, the same way she understood the boy. Before he left, he reinforced the promise. He told her not to say good-bye. They would meet again at the crossing. She was to wait for him — and believe.

They rode away in the direction from which they came, toward the Dragoon Mountains, black with approaching night. Not a speck of dust rose from the desert floor as the three chiefs, accompanied by ten thousand warriors of Time, silently vanished without a trace. When they were gone, she opened her hand so see what the Indian had given her. Still supple and fragrant as the day Nalanche picked the flower, the red rose petal lay in the palm of her hand. The day of John's funeral, she plucked one petal from the flower and gave it to the boy. He dropped it in the medicine bag with the blue stone and left the bag in the coffin with John to keep him safe on his journey through the crossover. It was the sign that confirmed the promise. They would meet again.

The sun was gone beyond the hills, leaving only a faint trace of its earlier brilliance behind, just enough to filter through the creosote and sagebrush to cast dancing shadows over the desert at the prompting of an evening breeze. Coyotés accompanied the dance of shadows, singing their lonely night song, a desert lullaby. It was getting dark and Nalanche took her hand. He wouldn't let her stumble or fall on the loose stones. For the rest of her life, she'd never fall while he was there. She'd come to realize how right she was when she called him her spirit protector. She remembered how they met, how she confronted his attackers with only a stone in her hand. They could have shot her or trampled her to death with their horses, but they didn't. It was a miracle she didn't die that day. When the one she hit with a stone turned on her and spurred his horse directly toward her, she remembered the sensation of being lifted out of the way of imminent danger. They were strong hands that moved her out of the path of the animal bearing down on her. Now, she knew the name of the one who took the form of a speeding horse that day. From his interminable pursuit of all who fell within his reach, she'd been whisked away by those who already knew him by his rightful name — Death. Not by a stroke of sheer luck was she saved, but by design; a plan for them to be brought together, she and the boy. It had to start somewhere to reach this juncture and that day was the beginning. Nalanche never forgot her bravery, and now she understood why the old ones came to her, why they brought John to her this night. It was one of them who lifted her to safety that day; his father, Otahe, or perhaps, Tehanache, the white-haired grandfather. She rescued their son and grandson, a young chief who would not live by the old ways but who was, nonetheless, a chief; one of their own. The old ways were gone. In his life, he would not lead hunting parties to feed the families or warriors into battle to defend their territory. He'd fight a different kind of battle in his struggle to survive as an Apache in the white man's world. His heart was with the old ways, but the world had changed. He knew the secrets of good medicine, bad medicine, and he would use them wisely. He'd teach her to use them as well. He was the guide Zaida told her about when she was ten years old in Ireland, and his father and grandfather were spirit guides who were with her as they were with the boy. She understood a lot of things now. She could go on for as long as she was destined to remain on this earth, knowing the pain of mortal existence was but a temporary affliction. That's why they had come, to show her this life was only temporary. Nalanche would teach her more of the magic — good medicine, bad medicine, until one day, John would come for her as he came today, on a silent horse racing across the desert to carry her away to the place from which he came, on Apache spirit winds. It didn't matter what name he was called by. She'd know him by either name, John Merrick, or Coshani. They were the same.

When she first went back to the Bird Cage, she suffered from feelings of betrayal, once again having broken the promise to John not to go there. It was all she could do. She had to work and the money she was saving was growing to a sizeable sum. She had to earn enough to send the boy to school in the East as soon as he was ready. It was the only thing that was important anymore. Months went by and she never asked Nalanche if he thought John was angry or disappointed because she returned to the Bird Cage. It didn't matter anymore. It was temporary. One day, she'd leave this world behind and when she was gone, chances were that no one would even know she'd been here. She missed John and was looking forward to the time they'd meet in another place, but as long as she was in this world, she had to work. There was no getting around that fact and she was sure John understood. She had learned a lot and viewed life in a different light. She looked at people different too. She spent whatever time was necessary at the Bird Cage, and when she was done, she left that part of her life at the end of Allen Street and went home. At two o'clock every morning when she walked home, someone walked behind her to make sure she got there safely. Virgil's men still looked after her. That hadn't changed. One morning, a drunk stopped her on the street. She told him she was tired and on her way home. She tried to walk away, but he wouldn't take no for an answer. She never saw where the deputy came from. He steered the drunk off across the street and that was the end of it. Any other lady of the night would have had to fend for herself in such a situation. She was lucky and she knew it. She wondered how long it would last. Rumor was that Wyatt Earp was leaving Tombstone. If that was true, she'd be without the protection of Virgil's men who were still on the Earp's payroll, and except for Nalanche, she'd be on her own.

She often thought about what happened on the hill, wondering if it was a dream. In all the times she'd been there since, waiting for them, they didn't come. She looked for them and called their names, but the Indians never returned, not even the old ones and Coshani. Sometimes, she thought she heard voices whispering on the wind, but she never saw them. She called out to John, but he never came. She looked toward the Dragoon Mountains. White smoke from a distant fire floated skyward in a circular pattern and she listened for a voice on the wind that promised they would meet again.

Chapter 15

From the day they met, she and Abby Treneaux were friends, a friendship that grew stronger over time. They were different from other women at the Bird Cage. While the others slept away their days, Rose and Abby spent the time sewing or sipping tea on the front-porch swing. They talked about John and the dressmaking business they'd have as soon as they saved enough money. They'd made the plans and figured out what they'd need in the way of supplies. Nalanche and Mr. Hampton would build the shelves. All that was left was to decide whose name would be first on the sign, "Callahan & Treneaux" or "Treneaux & Callahan, Dressmakers." Lizzie said they ought to call it "Rose and Abby's Needle & Thread Emporium." It was a little long, but they considered the possibility if, for no other reason, than to let Lizzie have her say. Experience had turned them both into better than average seamstresses and they had an idea they could make a good living sewing. A new trade would create respectability and in time, their previous line of work would be forgotten. The way the mines were producing, the growing population included a fair number of ladies. Ladies needed dresses and so did their little girls. There were already women in town who were married to men of substantial means and would be regular, good-paying customers. It was a chance to leave the Bird Cage behind and move into that spectrum of respectability which, until recently, existed only as a phantasm in their minds, a product of dreams. Without husbands to support them, they used to think they were stuck in the Bird Cage forever, but that was about to change. When they opened their door for business, they wouldn't limit their clientele. They'd make dresses for ladies of the night, and if women like Carolyn Grants or the Justice's wife couldn't live with that, they could find another dressmaker. Rose remembered how difficult it had been to get one dress made when she first came to Tombstone. She'd gone to the best seamstress in town to have her measurements taken, offering to pay in advance for the work. The woman served tea and ginger cookies and they were having a delightful conversation, until she made the mistake of telling the seamstress where she worked. The lady dropped her measuring tape, removed the cup and saucer from Rose's hands and curtly informed her that her money was no good in that shop since she did not sew for whores. She didn't mince words when she opened the door and told Rose to get out and never come back. Rose was barely over the threshold when the woman slammed the door. Her luck was no better with the next one.

No matter how successful they might become, she and Abby wouldn't do that. Unlike the good, God-fearing women of Tombstone, they didn't judge anyone by the nature of their profession or their husband's political affiliation, and they'd never forget where they came from. Lizzie warned her what to expect. In the beginning, her feelings were offended when doors slammed in her face. She was turned away from more than one place and finally wound up making her own dresses. The trip to Smith's had been a near disaster that almost cost Lizzie a night in the calaboose. It was her first run-in with Caroline Grants. Lizzie took her to Smith's to buy material that day and it was Lizzie who helped her make those first dresses, which brought another thought to mind. Lizzie could sew with an attention to stitching detail rivaled by none. She made lovely hats too and the millinery was her own design. It was downright amazing the things that girl could do, considering her inadequacies in everyday living. She and Abby talked about it. They might have Lizzie work for them.

Abby missed John too. He'd welcomed her into their home. She was part of the family and she looked forward to being with them through many years to come. They talked about Abby's mother and Ann Merrick, and all the other things committed to the past. She decided to tell Abby about the Indians in the desert and how the one they called Coshani returned the rose petal to her, fresh as the day it was picked. Even if Abby thought she was crazy, she wouldn't tell anyone. Abby listened as Rose told her that she was sure it was John she had seen with the old Indians that day and how they called him by a different name. She told Abby about the legion of warriors who rode with him and how they'd come and gone on the wind without a sound or stirring up a single bit of dust. When she finished the story, there was no laughing or insinuation by Abby that she might be losing her mind. Who'd believe she talked to John and the ghosts of Nalanche's dead ancestors? And, who'd believe she saw ten thousand Indian spirits in the desert — with their horses, no less? She had to admit, the story was pretty far-fetched, sounding like the ravings of a madwoman. Abby believed it. She didn't say Rose was crazy or that she saw and heard things that weren't there. Instead, Abby told her secrets she'd never told anyone for the same reason. She didn't want people to think she was crazy either.

There were occurrences in Abby's life she hadn't been able to explain, but she was certain the source was not of this world. Like Rose, she always thought there was a place beyond this life. She called it Heaven too. For her, there was no doubt that she talked with her mother, dead for ten years. Until now, she'd kept to herself the secret of a ghost who came to her, the woman who died when Abby was nine. She'd been left to deal with a father who drank too much and beat her for no reason. During the most difficult of those years, her mother came to her often. Now that she was older, she knew her mother's death wasn't the accident her father said it was. He said she fell and hit her head, but Abby saw him strike her mother many times. One of his beatings was fatal and Madeleine Treneaux died that day. For the next four years, Abby kept out of his way when he was drinking. When he stayed drunk for days on end, she hid in the coal cellar or ran away from the house and hid in the tall grass of a nearby field. If he found her, he beat her the same way he'd beaten her mother. She was always black and blue. When she was younger, she didn't understand why he hit someone smaller and weaker than himself. Today, she knew he did it because he was a coward. Many times, she thought about getting his pistol and shooting him as he slept. She stood over him once with the gun pointed at his heart, watching him snore and drool onto the pillow in his sleep, the disgusting odor of alcohol on his breath stale and heavy in the room. As she stood there with her finger on the trigger, ready to send him into oblivion, she remembered what the doctor said. Her father was having bad pains in his stomach. The doctor said if he didn't give up the bottle, the liquor would eat up his insides and the pain would get worse. Eventually, it would poison him. She decided to let it happen that way and she prayed for his death to be painful. Instead of blowing his heart out, she wished a horrible death on him by the hand of God and put the gun away.

The doctor was right. The liquor finally killed him. When he lay dying, he cried and told her he hadn't meant to kill her mother. It was an accident. He said he was drunk when he pushed Maddie and she fell down the stairs to her death. Abby stood by the bed, listening to his confession. He was in agony, but she felt neither sympathy nor compassion for his misery. He held out his hand and she turned away, her heart cold as ice. She wanted him to suffer. He deserved the pain. She never accepted her father's apology for the years of suffering he caused her mother and he only confessed to clear his conscience before Judgment Day. That was one thing she was thankful for. He had a real fear of dying because he believed he was about to face the wrath of God. It was only to try to save his black soul that he confessed and begged her forgiveness at the end. Had he not been on his deathbed, he'd have never said he was sorry. She prayed the penalty for what he'd done would be severe. When he was gone, she hoped he took the guilt of his crime with him to whatever punishment awaited beyond the grave. There were no tears at his passing and she didn't attend his funeral. Instead, she went to her mother's grave, leaving the burying of her father to strangers.

She was thirteen when her father died and the next few years were spent in the home of an aunt who took her in because the minister told her it was the Christian thing to do. It was not out of charity or love of family that she was given a place to live and they made her life miserable. She was expected to clean and cook and perform three times the chores of the other children. She was nothing more than a servant, a scullery maid. Resentment of the obligation to have her there and constant reminders that she was a burden to the family drove her to make a plan to get away. When she was sixteen, she began prostituting herself and went to live in a brothel. She soon became a main attraction and the madam demanded a lot from her, taking most of her money in return for a place to sleep and one meal a day. She never complained. She made a plan and kept it to herself. She stayed for almost three years and saved every penny she could manage to hide from the other girls and the madam. One night, she found a newspaper in the parlour and confiscated it, hiding it under her mattress until she could tear out the piece that caught her eye, a solicitation for hostesses by a night spot in the Arizona Territory, a place called the Bird Cage Theatre. She read the ad every day for a month until finally, on the day she turned nineteen, she walked out the door with nothing more than a purse containing her savings and a small piece torn from the newspaper. She rented a hotel room for one day and night and went shopping. She bought a couple of expensive dresses and hats, and a one-way ticket to the town advertised in the newspaper. That night, she slept in the hotel alone and the next morning, she was on a train bound for El Paso. From there, she rode the stage — to Tombstone.

Waiting for the stage, she looked at her reflection in the station window glass. From the way she was dressed, no one would imagine what she was. The day Abby stepped off the stage, Rose remembered thinking Abby looked like such a lady in her wine-colored suit and matching hat with the little feather. She looked so innocent, more like a banker's daughter than a prostitute. Rose considered telling Abby to go back to St. Joe that day, but didn't say it because she knew even a banker's daughter who came to Tombstone for a job at the Bird Cage had her reasons for being there. They believed in the same things, and sharing secrets neither of them told anyone else brought them closer. Sitting on the front-porch swing, they held hands and promised whichever of them took Death's hand first, that one would cross back over to this side to help the other. It wasn't a question of "if," but rather, when. The only question was how the one who was left behind would recognize the spirit visitor. Abby said it was simple. "I'll say your name — Rose." Rose shook her head in agreement. "And I'll say yours — Abigail."

Outside of work and necessary shopping trips, Rose spent most of her time at home. Nalanche was gone during the day at school and except when Abby came by, she was alone, taking care of the little gray house and cultivating the roses in the yard; making a plan for the boy. She isolated herself from everything and everyone beyond the gate. Although she saw the girls every night, she had little contact with them when work was done. In recent months, they'd drifted in different directions anyway. Some left town and others came to take their places. She hardly knew the more recent arrivals. They were a wilder bunch than the original women she'd made friends with and it seemed they got younger and wilder all the time. She had nothing in common with them except the profession they shared and even that had changed for her. She was grateful the younger ones were getting so much attention, like the seductive femme fatale recently arrived from somewhere in Texas — San Antonio or one of those San-something towns. She didn't know one from the other and cared less. Claire Dillon was her name and she was a regular fireball. Even Ruby had trouble keeping her in line. She was a wild one. They said she knew a lot about horses and men. Story was, she could break a bronc or a man in less time than it took to throw down a single shot of whiskey. More rumor was that she had her eye on Frank Leslie. The combination could be a deadly arrangement. Between sips of whiskey one evening, Doc matter-of-factly threw out the comment that it'd be a bloody miracle if somebody didn't get killed before the two of them parted company. He was betting on Buckskin Frank to be the loser. Quite the ladies' man, Rose was more inclined to think an argument would erupt between Claire and one of the other girls over Frank. If Ruby didn't keep things under control, Doc just might collect on that bet. It wouldn't be the first fatal argument in the Bird Cage over a man. She hoped it wouldn't come to that, but she gave up worrying about those things a long time ago. If it happened, it happened. That's just the way things were. She didn't even think about it anymore. They told her she'd get used it. She never thought she'd see the day she'd hear herself say it, but she'd come to accept it as life in Tombstone. It was as Virgil said, "the way things were."

She was spared unwanted trips to the suspended cribs with men. It went without saying that was Virgil's doing and she was grateful for his intervention on her behalf. She wondered how her circumstances would change now that he was gone, and if the latest talk around town was to be paid any mind, Wyatt's leaving might not be far off. Between national-headliner performances, Ruby and her entourage still brought the house down when they danced, Abby still performed her acrobatics, and Rose still sang for them. Lizzie did her no-talent act, flying across the stage and out over the room on a wire as she always had, and men were captivated by her beauty as they would always be. Those things hadn't changed, but the Bird Cage was gaining in popularity and impressive entertainers were making frequent appearances lately. Then, there were the traveling shows. More than one lady answered her calling from the silver-rich, primarily male-populated mining town and stayed behind when the rolling entertainment company moved on. For a lady with the right talents, there was a lot more money to be made in a mining boomtown with a shortage of women than on the dusty road with a carnival full of smelly animals and freaks. One such lady was Josephine "Sadie" Marcus. Wyatt spent quite a bit of time at the Bird Cage when the pretty Jewish girl named Sadie started working there. Sadie was only eighteen when she came to town in 1880 and was involved for a time with Johnny Behan. That relationship became history when she met Wyatt Earp and it also became a hot source of contention between Johnny and Wyatt, contributing in large part to Sheriff Behan siding with the cowboys against the Earps. Sadie fell in love with the handsome and exciting Wyatt, and Johnny would never get her back. You could just feel the heat from their fire by the way they looked at each other. It went without saying, Shady Sadie was Wyatt's favorite.

Tombstone was busier than ever. The town was growing, with two newspapers, a school board and fire department. Thank God for the fire department. Half the town burned twice and the other half would have gone up in smoke both times if not for the combined efforts of firemen and citizens. It was bad, but they'd rebuilt much of it already. Seemed like every time she turned around, there was a new business opening its doors. More mines than she knew the names of had started up and were pulling out larger quantities of ore daily with twenty and thirty-mule trains, one after another, hauling tons of highgrade silver ore to the stamp mills on the San Pedro River ten miles away. They were digging deeper all the time, a quarter mile down in some places. It was unbelievable to think a man would want to go that far under the ground for any reason. A cave-in could trap fifty men and they'd never come out alive. As far as Rose was concerned, no amount of money was worth that kind of risk. A cave-in might not kill them right away. If they were trapped, they could suffocate slowly or the tunnel could fill up with water and drown them if the way out was blocked. She shuddered at the thought of being buried alive or drowning in the caverns beneath the mountain as the water level rose. They knew the risk, but they took it, and all for the silver. They were enchanted by the lure of silver, some claiming they heard the voice of a woman calling to them from one of the mines. Never having found a woman there, the miners were convinced the ghostly echo was the voice of the mine herself.

Water! The mountain was floating on an underground lake. You could hear the pumps running nonstop around the clock, seven days a week, to keep the holes clear of the ever-seeping groundwater that threatened to reclaim the treasure. The deeper they went, the more water they ran into. It was a race against Time and they all knew it. If the pumps ever stopped, the mines would flood and they'd never be able to go back down. If the mines gave out, everyone would leave and Tombstone would become a ghost town. Unlike the rest of them who were afflicted with silver fever and caught up in the boom with no thought to the future, Rose wondered what would happen if it all ended. It was a frightening possibility, but a very real one. She didn't know what she'd do if the Bird Cage closed it's doors. She and Abby could sew, but there wouldn't be enough people left in town to support a shop. They'd have to move up to Tucson or some other city and that worried her. In Tombstone, people had plenty to say about Nalanche living with her, but she didn't care. They kept to themselves and it didn't matter what anyone said. It'd be different in Tucson. If they knew she had an Indian boy living with her, it might be hard to find a place to live. It'd be harder for him too. She might not be able to get him into a school up there. There was a lot to consider in making that kind of move. He was doing well in school. It might be best to stay put a while longer and not worry too much about a change in circumstance just yet.

The mines were running at top production and business was good at the Bird Cage. It could end tomorrow, but she'd cross that bridge when she came to it. Besides, she couldn't leave John buried here all alone. She had to stay, at least for the time being. There was one goal to accomplish before the money stopped coming in or before she died, whichever came first. She had to save enough to send Nalanche to the university. It was her sole purpose in life now that John was gone and she was determined to see it happen. She wanted to have a respectable occupation, but the Bird Cage provided steady money and she needed the money. It was only a matter of time until she and Abby could open their shop. They agreed to hang on a little longer and make the money at the Bird Cage for a few more months. Every week, they both made a deposit into the clay pot under her bed that was their savings toward the business that would give them independence and set them free. They called it their dream pot.

Nalanche mucked stables at Dexter's after school and on Saturday mornings, and when he got paid, he brought his money home for her to add to the second dream pot, the one that would send him to the university. Once a month, she carried their combined savings to the bank. Between the two of them, the money was adding up. More and more, he talked about helping his people and the only way was to get an education. He was working hard to get there and she had to help make his dream come true.

Doc still came by to see her at work, but he wouldn't sit close to her anymore. He covered his mouth with the ever-present handkerchief when he talked to her to lessen the spread of the airborne disease carried by the breath he exhaled. He'd stopped coming to the house a long time ago. His illness was worse and he wouldn't bring it into her home. He was so worried about her catching it that she didn't have the heart to tell him it was too late. She sat across the table listening to him describe the bubbling, hot springs and clear river running through a rocky-cliffed canyon full of pine trees in Colorado, a place of healing mineral waters the Indians believed could cure anything, a place where his tuberculosis could be treated. What he really meant was a place where he could die without giving those who despised him the satisfaction of watching. He usually looked directly at her when he spoke, but this time, he purposefully avoided eye contact, studying a poker chip that he rolled back and forth between his fingers. His feeble attempt at being nonchalant about the trip didn't fool her for a minute. When he told her he was thinking of leaving to try his luck in Colorado, she felt another piece of her life being chipped away. She watched him talk, remembering the stories people told about him. They said he was an educated man, an aristocrat from a good Georgia family, but a man with the scruples of a snake and the sting of a scorpion. He was a gambler, a cheater, and a cold-blooded killer. It wasn't that she condoned any of it. She hated all those things. It just never seemed to matter. She didn't look beyond the fact that he was her friend. She didn't believe the stories anyway. She asked him about it once and all he said was, "You can't stop people from talkin'."

Doc was dying and he knew it. He was trying to break the news to her as gently as possible by implying he was going to Colorado for a combined treatment and vacation, but she knew he was preparing her for the worst. His day of reckoning wasn't far off and when he went to Colorado, he'd be going there to die. She didn't care what his reputation was. In the truest sense, he was a friend, and she wasn't looking forward to the day she'd have to say good-bye to him. His coughing was bringing up more blood lately and she knew he'd be dead soon. She hated to think about him dying alone in some strange place without a friend to hold his hand. Outside of her, Wyatt Earp was more than likely the only other friend he had. It was probably just as well that he went somewhere away from those who would celebrate his passing if they knew. His days were numbered and word was, he'd been particularly provocative in recent days, trying to incite volatile men with loaded six-shooters and itchy trigger fingers into drawing down on him. Given the terminal consequence of his medical condition, she knew if he got the chance, he'd deliberately hold back the speed at which he drew his own gun and allow the other man to put a bullet in his heart. More than once, he'd said that was how he wanted to go, with his boots on and a chunk of hot lead sending him into oblivion for whatever reward or punishment awaited him. Knowing the way he'd lived, he was prepared for either and wouldn't dispute the final hand he drew. If he went that way, they'd never say he was weak, only that the other man was faster. If it happened like that, he could go into eternity satisfied his dignity had been preserved. He told her once that he refused to die in a hospital. He didn't want to drown on fluid in his lungs. He'd shoot himself before he let that happen. One thing about him, he wasn't a coward and he wasn't afraid to die, but he was absolutely terrified of losing his dignity in death. She said a lot of prayers for him, that his ultimate punishment on earth would not be to die in a hospital bed, and she prayed he'd be forgiven for the crimes he committed in this life. Surely, his kindness toward her would count for something when he met his Maker. When she went to the hill, she talked to John and asked him to help Doc at the crossover. It wouldn't be long now.

The creaking made her step to one side. She looked up at the bars holding the curtains, wishing they'd do something about the sandbags. She had to remember to tell Billy about it. He probably didn't know they were loose. The distribution of their weight was what raised and lowered the curtains and they'd been a worry to her the whole time she'd worked here. People were always rushing around backstage with no thought to the danger overhead. She didn't know how much they weighed, but they were heavy. She couldn't lift one. If the ropes holding one of those things broke loose, someone could get hurt. Tonight, she'd warn Abby and the others again and remind them not to walk directly under the bags. She studied the rigging. There had to be a way to secure them better. Abby waved to her from the little dressing room across the backstage. She looked up once more as she walked, making a wide berth around the area directly below the swaying bags. There was some time before they had to begin work and Abby had brewed some of her soothing chamomile tea. They had a cup every night. Neither of them looked forward to what awaited them out front and the tea helped them relax. More than anything, it was an excuse to sit and talk for a few minutes.

They visited longer than usual and were almost done with their tea when the door opened. Ruby stood in the doorway with her hands on her hips. It was later than they thought. "Are you two taking the night off? We've got customers out front you know." They knew. Rose finished the last drops and set her cup down. She gave Ruby an exaggerated smile and squeezed by her. Ruby was no small obstacle to get around and she didn't give an inch when Rose left the room. When Ruby put her hands on her hips, it would have been interpreted in certain circumstances as a threatening pose. She was a woman of formidable proportion and she used her size to intimidate more than one man. When Rose was through the doorway, Ruby looked down at her. "One of us needs to lose a few pounds, don't you think?" She knew which one of them Ruby was referring to, and it wasn't Rose. She weighed all of a hundred and ten pounds, fully clothed and soaking wet. Ruby, on the other hand, probably weighed every bit of a hundred and seventy pounds, bare naked, give or take a few. Rose tried not to laugh. "I'll take that to heart, Ruby." She left the big redhead standing in the doorway of the dressing room and walked toward the steps leading down into the theatre. She'd wait at the steps for Abby. She heard Abby's voice behind her, but kept walking. It was a habit to stand there on the landing before going downstairs. Abby would catch up to her. Moving toward the steps and looking at the floor as she walked, her mind was on some things she had to do tomorrow. She planned to trim the roses and give Little Bear a bath. No easy chore. He was almost as big as her and by the time it was done, it was hard to tell which one of them got the bath. She had to remember to fill the hummingbird gourd too. She noticed it was empty this morning and meant to fill it today. Not the most exciting plans for a day off, but those were the things she did these days.

It happened so fast, like a dream she couldn't remember; a blinding flash in her mind's eye like the exploding powder from Mr. Fly's camera. She heard a voice shouting her name and the next thing she knew, she was on the floor. She must have hit pretty hard. She tried to focus her eyes, but everything was blurry. Pain! She reached for her knee. It was wet with blood. She heard voices, but she was dazed and disoriented. Someone helped her sit up, the pain in her leg intensifying with the movement. There was a substantial gash below the right knee. It was on fire with a white-hot pain and she was sure it was broken. Charlie was wrapping something around it to stop the bleeding. Her head was throbbing. She must have cracked it in the fall. She touched her forehead. A lump the size of a goose egg was already raised up above her eyebrow. Shaken and bewildered by the speed of events and the number of people behind the stage, she looked at Charlie. "Whatever in the world happened? What did I trip over?" She remembered Abby. Abby called to her right before she fell. In the commotion, she'd lost track of her friend. "Where's Abby?" There were people all around. Someone else had fallen. When the crowd parted, she saw a woman lying on the floor a few feet away. She didn't remember what happened. There must have been a collision. With so much activity backstage, they were always bumping into each other. They had to be more careful.

Charlie was holding the bandage tight around her knee and it hurt like the devil. She was still trying to see who was on the floor. She hoped the girl wasn't hurt. The doctor ran up the stairs and right on past her. The bystanders moved aside to make room for him and when they did, she saw who was lying on the floor. She forgot the pain in her leg, pushing Charlie away and crawling toward the lifeless body. The doctor stood up. There was nothing he could do. Rose was frantic. "Abby!" She shook her friend and shouted, "Abigail. Don't you die. You wake up right this minute." She shook Abby again, tears running down her face and falling on the face of the dead girl. Charlie tried to make her listen. "Rose. She's dead." She slapped at him, flailing her arms wildly and screaming. "She's not dead. She's hurt. Where is the damn doctor? Get the doctor." She shook Abby harder. "Abby Treneaux. Open your eyes." Charlie put his arm around her. "Rose. Listen to me. The doc's here. He says she's gone. You gotta stop. Abby's dead." She stopped yelling and stared at the still body. She touched Abby's cheek and whispered, "Abby. Please don't go away, Abby. Don't leave me here alone."

The rope knot gave way and the sandbag moved. Abby saw it begin to drop when she left the dressing room. Preoccupied with other things, Rose forgot to circumvent the area as she usually did and walked directly under the weight at the exact moment the rope came loose from the rigging. After all the times she'd cautioned the girls about that spot, warning to them to keep a safe distance, she was the one who wasn't paying attention at a critical moment. In the dressing room, Ruby had come by before she had a chance to tell Abby to be careful and stay out from under the sandbags. Squeezing past Ruby and joking with her about one of them losing weight, the intended message slipped her mind. The loosened knot held another couple of seconds, barely long enough for Abby to dash across the backstage, shouting the warning as she ran. Rose was somewhere else in thought when she walked under the rigging, completely forgetting the danger and unaware of the shifting weight overhead. She hadn't understood the urgency of the message and when she heard Abby's voice, she stopped right under the slipping bag. Just as she turned, Abby ran into her, pushing her out of the way with such force that the impact sent her sprawling onto the floor all the way to the landing. The rope slipped and the sandbag fell. Abby's neck was broken. She died instantly. It happened again.

Rose was saved, but the Bird Cage claimed another victim.   Abigail Treneaux was dead.

For the next day and a half, she relived the familiar pain of losing someone she loved. This time, it was her dearest friend. She used the money in the clay pot to buy Abby's casket. The rest she gave to Ruby to buy a dress to bury Abby in. Ruby picked out an ivory lace gown, fit for a princess and a gold cross for around her neck. That was the end of the money. The business they'd been saving for no longer seemed important.

Like the rest of them, Abby had no family. If she was buried in the cemetery, she'd be alone, so when the undertaker asked where the final resting place would be, Rose told him to dig the grave on the hill south of town, under the tree beside John Merrick. Once again, Wyatt came for her and Nalanche. He took them to the funeral parlour in the morning and near the end of the day, he drove them out to the hill. He rolled up a blanket and placed it under her foot to keep her injured leg elevated for comfort. He even thought to bring a chair for her to sit on at the graveside service. They followed the Black Mariah coach carrying the body of the sweetest girl any of them had ever known. Except for the clattering of buggy wheels and the grinding of stones under steel horseshoes, there was no noise. They didn't talk. They were in shock over this latest tragedy, the same thing going through all of their minds on the ride to the hill. Why Abby?

Nothing was broken, but the doctor sewed up the gash in her leg and told her not to walk on it for a few days. Wyatt carried her from the wagon to the chair beside the grave. Ruby and the girls came with Charlie and Doc. Poor Doc. He thought so much of Abby. More than any of them realized. He stood quietly as the parson spoke the same prayer over Abby that he said at John's funeral and left in as much of a hurry as he did that day. Doc didn't look up when the minister left. He kept staring at the coffin and before they lowered it into the ground, he rested his hand on it. Perhaps he was telling her he'd see her soon. He kissed the casket and stood at the edge of the grave while the dirt was shoveled in. Rose watched him, certain no one else among the mourners realized what he was doing. Tears rolled down Doc's face and he didn't try to hide them. He just let them fall into the grave with Abby. He loved her. Doc Holliday — the man they said had no heart. If they only knew. When Abby was buried, he stepped over to John's grave. Before he left, he tapped the cross and spoke to John. "With any luck, I'll see you soon, my friend. Very soon."

It was the saddest of days. After the funeral, the others went back to town. Rose waited while Nalanche helped cover the grave with stones. By tomorrow, there'd be two crosses on the hill. Wyatt stood by the wagon. He'd come forward to help her again. No one asked him to. He just came. She studied the man. Few words passed between them, yet he was a friend. Tombstone exacted a great toll from him and his family and his losses were heavy. She knew he'd be leaving soon. They'd be separated by many miles. Once he left, she'd never see him again, but as with Virgil, they'd left indelible imprints on each other, imprints that wouldn't fade or wash away with the tides of Time. When the last stone was in place, she leaned on Nalanche for the few short steps to the cross on the nearby pile of rocks. She kissed the marker on John's grave and whispered that she loved him. Now, there were two waiting for her at the gateway and before long, there'd be three. Doc wasn't far from the crossover.

Chapter 16

DECEMBER, 1889

The old days were gone. The Earps and Doc Holliday were gone. They said Wyatt and Virgil were somewhere in California. Story was that Mattie died from overindulgence in the laudanum and Wyatt took up with the Jewish girl, Josephine Marcus. She'd been Johnny Behan's woman, or so he said. According to Josie, she wasn't anybody's girl, at least, not after the braggart shot off his mouth once too often about his personal affair with the dark-haired beauty. When Rose first heard the gossip, she didn't put two and two together because she didn't recognize the name. Josie Marcus. Then she remembered. They called her Sadie when she was here before. She knew Sadie alright. She had her eye on Wyatt from the first time she saw him. She remembered the way they looked at each other and she suspected they had their own form of unspoken communication. Well, if rumor was to be paid any mind, their relationship passed the silent-message stage and the basement-bordello affair in the Bird Cage a long time ago, and she was neither Sadie nor Josephine Marcus any longer. She was Josie Earp.

She heard Doc was dead. He died precisely the way he hadn't wanted to, in bed with his boots off. She didn't know if that was true or not, but she hoped he hadn't suffered. If he did, she didn't want to know. Saying good-bye to him had been very difficult. She wanted to visit him in Colorado, but he made her promise not to come. Ruby said Wyatt went to see him once and Doc told him not to come back. It was the dignity thing. He didn't want to see pity in their eyes and he hated to have anyone see him dying that way. By the time he left Tombstone, his disease was very bad. He was thin and sickly, constantly wiping trickles of blood from his mouth brought up by the slightest cough. They wrote for a while and then, one day, his letters stopped coming. She thought about him a lot. There'd been some terrible things said about the man when he was alive, and now that he was dead, the stories became greatly embellished. They said he was a ruthless, vile man; a killer with the scruples of a rattlesnake, that being, none. He cheated and lied and murdered men in cold blood, or so the story went, but as far as she knew, nobody ever proved a word of it. Even the facts about the incident in Texas where Doc cut a man's throat over a card game a few years back had been twisted. Kate told her the other man pulled a blade first. Doc just happened to be quicker with his knife when he jumped across the table. According to Kate, it was a clear case of self-defense and Doc never should have been arrested. They said he'd shoot his own grandmother if the mood struck him. Knowing him the way she did, she found the stories real hard to believe. As far as she was concerned, it was all sensationalism, cooked up for the benefit of telling an exciting story. Wherever he was now, he was better off than he'd been on this earth. She'd gone to the hill many times and spoken into the wind, asking John and Abby to meet Doc at the crossover. He'd need some help. Doc said he'd be John's first client. Maybe that's the way it was. She knew if anyone could present a convincing argument in Doc's defense before the highest Court of all, it was John Merrick.

She sat on the porch swing with a blanket over her legs, sipping coffee and thinking about her life. She was thirty-one and staring down the barrel of thirty-two. It was a miracle she'd lived so long. John was dead seven years and Abby had been gone for just a few weeks short of that. Nalanche was in Boston at the university. He'd graduate this year. Hard to believe he was twenty-four. The dream was close to coming true. He'd be a lawyer soon. All the time he was away at school, he wrote faithfully. She knew it had to be a strain on his studies, what with all the extra work he did to graduate early. He was taking classes in the summer at a time when most students went home on holiday. He was so much like John, ambitious and committed to getting his education. He hadn't been home in two years, but when he came back this time, he'd stay for good. He'd taken a new name in his first year at the university. Joseph John N. Callahan. A judge in Boston signed the paper officially changing his name. Nalanche said it was filed at the courthouse and all done legal. He was a Callahan now. Most people would say he was her brother in name only, but they both knew it went much deeper than that. No use trying to explain it to anyone. Nobody else could understand anyway. She thought it was clever the way he kept the N. He retained his Apache name and would use it in future dealings with tribal representation, but for purposes of hanging out his shingle in the white man's world, he'd be known as Joseph Callahan. Her father would be proud to have Nalanche carry his name, but every time she thought about it, she had to laugh. He looked about as much like an Irishman as she looked like an Apache. Of course, her father's name hadn't always been Callahan either. It was her mother's family name Joe took when he married Annie. His family was a dark race whose origin was somewhere in the Far East. She figured he took the Callahan name because fair-skinned, red-haired Annie went with him to live the life of a Gypsy, and that was a concession for what she'd given up to be his wife. He took her Catholic religion too, adding to their persecution as Black Irish.

Sweet Jenny married, of all people, Matt Kern. Guess it wasn't so much of a surprise. It was hard to say which one got swept off their feet first. They deserved each other. A perfect match as far as Rose was concerned. It was funny, at the wedding, Jenny tossed the small bouquet of wildflowers into the air. It would have hit Rose in the face if she hadn't reached out and caught it. Imagine, her catching the bride's bouquet. Of all of them, she was the most unlikely prospect for marriage. Almost immediately after she caught the flowers, she saw Lizzie standing close by, a frown on her face, ready to cry. Lizzie wanted to catch the flowers in the worst way. Rose pretended to fumble and dropped the flowers. Jenny caught them. Rose threw her hands up in the air. "Well, looks like you need to throw them again bein' they've returned to your hands." She winked at Jenny and rolled her eyes in Lizzie's direction. Jenny got the message. The second time, she took careful aim before tossing the bouquet and that time, it landed right in Lizzie's hands.

That was six years ago. Where had the time gone? Matt wasn't a lawman anymore. Deciding it wasn't the life for a family man, when his father passed on, he took over the family farm in Iowa and that's where they were, raising corn and hogs and awaiting the birth of their baby. Jenny wanted Lizzie to go with them. She was afraid Lizzie would do something drastic like she did the night Rose announced she was leaving. Lizzie had been dependent on Jenny for a long time and it wouldn't be easy to find someone to take over the responsibility of living with her. They broke the news to her very carefully when Matt asked Jenny to marry him, apprehensive about her reaction. Lizzie took it much better than anyone expected. There was no outburst or hysterical crying and running away to cut her wrists. They all waited for the breakdown, but it never came. After the wedding, Matt and Jenny left town. Lizzie stood in the road until the stage was out of sight. Tears streamed down her face, but she didn't cry out loud or beg Jenny to stay the way they expected at the last minute. When she couldn't see them anymore, she dried her tears and went home. Believing her pensive mood to be the calm before the storm, the girls kept a close eye on her for days, but nothing happened. She didn't hurt herself or burn the house down, or take to throwing fits. She never took in another housemate either. Lizzie lived alone these days, but Rose and the girls checked on her regularly. No one thought they'd see the day Lizzie would live by herself, but when Jenny moved away, she didn't want anyone there. She struggled with day-to-day frustrations, but she was managing.

So much happened in a relatively short time. So many changes. Except for Ruby and Lizzie, all the faces at the Bird Cage were new. When Virgil left town, there was another change. She knew it would happen eventually. It wasn't that she was treated any worse. She was treated the same as everyone else. She didn't get preferential treatment anymore and when she wasn't singing, she made the trips to the upper cribs or the basement bordello like the rest of them to entertain the gentlemen. Her services were expensive now and she made more money than ever. As soon as Nalanche came home, all of that would end. She might even think about that dressmaking business and if she did, maybe Lizzie would help her. In memory of Abby, she'd call it "Callahan and Treneaux, Dressmakers." Respectability was just around the corner.

It was quiet. Hardly anyone in the place. There was no Lotta Crabtree or Jersey Lily here tonight. Lillian Russell wasn't bringing tears to their eyes with her sweet rendition of "A Bird In A Gilded Cage." No Eddie Foy to make them laugh. No one famous on the marquis out front to warrant the roaring applause that used be heard a block away. Maybe that was it. No interesting entertainment. They'd all seen the local show, same thing over and over. No one seemed to be in a mood to have a good time tonight. Ruby patted her on the shoulder. "The quiet's enough to make you deaf, isn't it?" It was a statement more than a question. The emptiness was eerie. This wasn't the Bird Cage she used to know. Passing a table, she overhead the conversation. Everyone was on the hill. Two pumps at the Grand Central Mine shut down this morning and every available man was there helping to haul up the water by hand. She knew they'd been having trouble keeping the water pumped out. All the mines had the same problem these days. It'd been this way for a long time. Underground lakes were flooding everything past thirty feet and the pumps were working overtime to keep the tunnels clear in a last-gasp effort to bring out a few more buckets of ore. Once the mining operation penetrated the layer of earth holding back the water, the level rose to invade even the shallow diggings, and in some places, miners worked in waist-deep water every day.

They were down pretty deep in some places, a quarter of a mile or more, and the water was pouring in faster than they could pump it out. Six months ago, there was a cave-in when the pumps stopped working at the Lucky Lady Mine. They had double trouble up there. Forty men were down inside the tunnel when the water began to rise. With the pumps out of order and the water level rising, it should have been the first sign they'd gone too far. They kept working, believing it was only a temporary problem. By the time they recognized the danger and the alarm whistle blew, signaling the miners to get up top, it was too late. Only ten of them made it out alive. Despite reinforcement with new timber, old shoring beams were rotting from years of steadily-running water. When a bearing beam snapped and triggered a chain of breaks in the support system, the walls caved in. When they got the pumps going again, the flooding was out of control. Once the water level reached a certain point, the pumps were no longer effective. The mine was flooded beyond hope. Thirty men, trapped more than half a mile below the surface, drowned with the biggest silver strike in history at their finger-tips — the true mother lode. There was no way to clear the tunnels and bring out the bodies, so they boarded up the shafts and the Lucky Lady was abandoned.

She remembered what Nalanche said about the mining. He disapproved of taking minerals from the land for profit. He said it made men hate. Brother against brother. He was right. The greed turned them against each other and made them lose sight of all remnants of human kindness and compassion. She'd seen it happen over and over again. There'd been more killing during the boom years than she could remember, and all because of the frenzied search for silver. He said that when you took something from the earth, you were supposed to give something back. They took everything and returned nothing. The earth finally claimed the payback of the debt and the Lucky Lady Mine gave testimony to it. Thirty men died with a dream, buried with the richest vein of high-grade silver ore ever found, sixteen hundred feet down in God only knew how many feet of water. She listened to the men talking. They were having the same problem up at Grand Central right now. Too much water in the hole and the pumps weren't working. She prayed there was no one inside the mine. They'd gone way below the water level and pumping was probably a waste of time. They'd never clear the tunnels.

The water ran throughout the tunnels, submerging them, reclaiming the unexcavated treasure. One-by-one, the pump houses shut down and the hoisting works quit running. There were no more ore buckets to lift to the surface. No more mules hauling wagons between the mines and the stamping mills on the river. The screech of iron chain being dragged across steel hoist supports to lift the loaded ore buckets up through the shafts used to grate on her nerves like Chinese water torture. The irritating grinding sound echoing around the hills kept her awake many a night. There wasn't nearly so much of it anymore. Gradually, the rhythmic thumping and clanking of the pumps was fading away. It wouldn't be long until the hills would be silent as they were when Ed Schieffelin first discovered the mountain of silver. Miners who couldn't find work at open diggings packed up and left, heading down to Mexico across the Sierra Madres or out to California to catch another kind of fever. Some went north to the Yukon Territory. They were all following the same dream, a dream of a different color. Gold.

Only a handful of mines were still operating. Businesses closed and people moved away. The mines were everything to the survival of the town and without them, some businesses couldn't exist. Many were dependent on supplies and services purchased by the miners. Men who worked in the mines supported the gambling halls and brothels. They spent a lot of money on whiskey and the pleasures offered by ladies of negotiable virtue. Saloons began closing their doors. Buildings that once bustled with the activity of daily business were boarded up and deserted. The streets were quieter. The excitement was gone. Those who stayed depended on what was left of the mines to make a living. Some hadn't gone down far enough to get flooded out yet, but they would eventually and when they did, that would be the end for them. A few shored up their crippled operations and kept the pumps running around the clock. They stayed open despite the threat of flood and cave-in, determined to dig out as much ore as time permitted, every day fighting back the enemy — water, and hoping against hope it would miraculously recede. It didn't happen. They were hanging on until the bitter end, but they knew it wouldn't be long before they'd be closing down the pump house and nailing boards across the entrance to the shaft. They had to face it. The silver boom was over.

Rose sat a table alone, sipping warm brandy. She drifted off, thinking about the way things used to be. In the old days, there was no such thing as a lady sitting alone in the Bird Cage. In the old days, she didn't even drink brandy. Here she was, sitting alone and drinking alone. Funny how, after all the times she wanted them to stay away from her, she was wishing someone would come and sit with her tonight. She sat at this table many times with Doc and Virgil and the girls. She sat here with John a few times too. She even sat here with strangers whose names she'd never know. It seemed so long ago. They were all gone. She pulled the shawl around her shoulders. The weather was changing, getting colder, and bringing with it quite a bit of rain the last few days.

The tapping on her head startled her. It was only Lizzie. Lizzie always patted her on the head. She did it to everybody. It used to irritate her, but over the years, she'd gotten used to Lizzie's little annoying habits, like the way she led everyone around by the hand, and the way she called her Rosie. It wasn't so bad. It was just her way. Rose gave up letting things like that bother her years ago. Lizzie sat down beside her. She was more nervous than usual, drumming her fingers on the table to the rhythm of a tune only she heard. She was trying to say something, but having a hard time beginning. Rose gave her a little nudge. "What's on your mind, Lizzie. Might there be somethin' you're wantin' to tell me?" Lizzie nodded her head, yes. She was trying to hold back the tears. "I'm leaving the Bird Cage, Rosie. I'm gonna have my own place, my own parlour. There's some girls who say they'll work for me. I think I can make more money that way. Things haven't been so good around here since the mines started closing down." Rose knew exactly what she meant and she knew Lizzie was looking for approval. "I know you'll be just fine, Lizette. I'm sure you'll be havin' a grand business." She touched Lizzie's hand. "Don't be forgettin' your friends when you get rich. Come 'round to see me now and then." Lizzie smiled and gave her a hug. That was all she needed to hear. Rose watched her walk away. Lizzie hadn't done great since Jenny left. She managed to live alone, but there'd been a few times where things were a little shaky. Lizzie had been hitting the laudanum pretty heavy lately and everyone knew it was only a matter of time until she did something crazy again. All they could do was hope it wouldn't happen any time soon and be ready when it did.

On the walk home, she looked around. Things weren't the same anymore. She remembered Allen Street the way it was before the mines
flooded, in the days when there was music and people everywhere. There
was a time when she thought it was an evil place, but over the years, that
perception changed. It was a wild place alright, but there'd always been a
kind of magic in the air, something she'd never be able to explain. She
stopped and looked across the street. Virgil used to stand on that corner,
watching her walk to the Bird Cage every night. She could still see him,
the way he leaned against the pole and smiled the first day she walked up
Allen Street to try and get a job at the Bird Cage. It seemed like only yesterday she walked this way with John, laughing and talking about the
future. She could hear his voice, the way he said her name. She'd never
forget the way he called her Rose.

She pulled her coat tighter and held the collar around her neck. She'd
had a chill since she woke up. Come to think of it, she hadn't felt good for
a few days. The chronic cough was worse lately and whenever she caught
a chill or a case of the congestion in her lungs, she couldn't tell if it was a
chest cold or the sickness that never left her flaring up. Each time it happened, she got a little weaker. She hoped she wasn't getting sick again.
The wind was cold and it cut through to the bone. She shivered and walked
a little faster. When she got home, she built a fire and made some hot tea
with honey. Bear laid down at her feet. Better than eight years old, he
wasn't quite as frisky as he used to be. He groaned when she scratched his
ear. She patted his head. "I know how you feel." Nalanche had given the
dog specific instructions about taking care of her while he was away at
school. She smiled, remembering the two of them sitting on the front porch
side-by-side the day he left, the boy with his arm around the dog and the
dog appearing to be taking in every word. She couldn't hear what was
being said, but she knew he was talking to Bear about her that day. The
instructions must have been very clear because when he left, Bear stuck to
her like a shadow everywhere she went. He'd done his job well.

Nalanche was on his way home with a paper that said he graduated
from the university. The doctor said her health was fragile and advised
against her making the trip east for the ceremony. When the official paper
conferring the honor was handed to him, she couldn't be there, but he knew
she was with him in spirit. She was so proud of him. If only John were
here to celebrate with them. She was looking forward to seeing him. Five
years he'd been in the East studying, making the trip home only twice in all

that time to stay for a few days. She knew the only reason he came then was because he worried about her. While he was home, he didn't rest. Instead, he spent the whole time making whatever repairs were needed to the house and stacking enough fire wood to get her through the winters. Five years was a long time, but he was finally coming home to stay. She could hardly wait to give him his Christmas present. Nearly a month ago, she tied it up with a red satin ribbon and leaned it against the wall in the corner of her bedroom where it wouldn't get scratched or knocked over by Bear's tail swishing. Mr. Hampton made a beautiful sign for him to hang outside his office and varnished it to a high gloss to protect it against the weather. She remembered when Mr. Hampton helped Nalanche make the sign for John's office. They even carved the Merrick family coat of arms in that one. John never got the chance to hang it up and she'd kept it wrapped and packed in the trunk all these years.

Chapter 17

"I am here, look yonder to the hills.
...I will not promise love; only silver."

Lucky Lady Mine
ALLEN STREET ROSE

Arlis Hampton was a kindly old gentleman who came to Tombstone from Virginia in '79 with his grandson, Clay. His son was killed fighting for the Confederacy and he lost his son's wife to a sickness not long after. He and his wife took care of their grandson and since she died, it'd been just the old man and the boy. When they heard about the boomtown in the Arizona Territory, they decided to go. Once there, they were no different than anyone else with silver fever. They had dreams of making the big strike and getting rich, and they worked a small claim for a while, but the old man couldn't take the physical exertion. It was too much for one man alone and Arlis was worried about having a stranger come in to work it with his grandson, so they sold out the diggings and the young Hampton went to work for the Tombstone Consolidated Mine. He stayed on the payroll and never missed a day's work, saving his money up until a couple years ago when he switched to another company. His grandfather told him he ought to get himself a wife, but the boy insisted he didn't have time, saying Lady Luck was the only woman he'd ever love anyway. It was just a matter of time until he found her. They laughed about his imaginary love affair with Lady Luck and then, one night, he came home from the hill all excited, telling his grandfather things were going to change for them real soon. To Arlis' question as to how that would happen, Clay said he'd finally met his lucky lady. His grandfather thought he meant he'd found a woman, and about consarned time!

The owners of the mine he'd been working for announced they were pulling out and heading for greener pastures in Alaska. There was a gold-rush there and they offered a job to every miner who wanted to go north with them. When Clay walked into the company line office, they thought he was there to sign up for work in the Yukon Territory. Instead, he asked what they were going to do with the old mine. They said the last ore trains were rolling to the stamping mill that day and lumber was already there to board up the shafts. They'd be shutting down the pump house as soon as the last wagon was loaded in a few hours unless, of course, he wanted to buy the mine. When they quit laughing, he told them to leave the wood out back and keep the pumps running. He'd be back in the morning. They thought he was crazy and laughed again at the suggestion that anyone would think about buying a dying operation. The last thing they expected was to get an offer on what they believed to be a worthless hole in the ground due to flood out any day. He drew his money out of the bank the next morning. Five years earlier, he'd never have been able to pay the price they asked, but now that the mines were flooding, all they wanted was to cut their losses and get out. They never thought they'd get a penny for it. When he dropped his money on the table, they couldn't sign the deed over to him fast enough. They thought he was a fool and they believed they were cheating him, but they took the money anyway. He knew what they were thinking. It was a substantial risk alright. Everybody knew water in the mines was a big problem, but Clay knew something no one else knew.

A day earlier, they'd sent him into the south tunnel, further down than he'd ever gone before. The water was right about knee-deep and creeping up steadily, giving seasoned miners cause to be leery about the rise. Believing it to be a dead end to the vein, the owners abandoned that section, but Clay's gut told him they were making a big mistake. When the rest of them went up top, he stayed down below, chipping and scraping along the tunnel wall. Later, he told his grandfather he could smell the silver. When he couldn't find the edges of the width of black rock and he discovered it ran way past the end of the newly-excavated gallery, he knew what it was. He found that rich vein; rich and wide, running right smack through the middle of the mine and on into the hill. He'd have to work fast. The timbers throughout the mine were weakened from years of wear and water at the depth they'd reached. Before he could risk running full bore, he'd have to spend the time and money to lay in fresh shoring lumber to secure the tunnels. He had the money. Time was the element he couldn't afford to waste. He'd need a good crew and the pumps to hold out — and a little more time. With all the silver that came out so far, no vein was as wide as this one. If he was smart and careful, he could tap into that vein of high-grade ore, and it wouldn't take long to bring enough of it out to make him a rich man. Then, he could take his grandfather out of the cabin they'd been living in and build a real house with a shed for Arlis' tinkering and wood carving. Might even go so far as to give some serious thought to getting himself that wife his grandpa was always telling him he needed.

When he filed the deed, he renamed her the Lucky Lady Mine. Rose had a lot of respect for that kid. All he ever did was work hard and take care of his grandfather. Around town, he had a reputation for being honest and fair, paying good wages and keeping plenty of clean drinking water out at the mine for his crews. If they were hurt or sick, he saw to it they got medical attention and he paid the doctor for tending to them. If they got drunk and ended up in jail, he'd go get them and take them to his cabin to sleep it off. In the morning, his grandfather would feed them and send them on their way and that would be the end of it. Clay would never mention it to them and the same ones didn't often show up twice. Tombstone was his home and whenever there was a need for a volunteer to help put out a fire or ride with a posse, you could count on him to be there. He was a good man. If anyone deserved to strike it rich, it was Clay. In the year and a half that followed, he took a lot of silver out of the mine and he made a lot of money. The water had risen to a dangerous level and he was concerned about the safety of the men who worked for him. When he bought the mine, he knew her days were numbered and he'd already kept it open longer than he planned. He was talking about closing down the operation. He'd made his money and realized his dream, and there was no sense pushing his luck and risking lives out of greed. All he ever wanted was to have a few dollars in the bank and build a house where his grandfather could be comfortable. In just eighteen months, he far exceeded those expectations.

She remembered watching the Hamptons' new house go up. Old Mr. Hampton lived there alone now. When they posted the names of miners killed in the cave-in up at the Lucky Lady a few months back, Clay Hampton's was the first one on the list. One of the pumps broke down and before they could get it started again, shoring timbers collapsed from tons of water pressure. Thirty-nine men were trapped sixteen-hundred feet underground in a subterranean tomb. Clay went down to bring out his crew. Ten men made it to the surface before the rest of the pumps quit running and the mine flooded, but the other thirty never saw the light of day again. Clay Hampton's body was still down there with twenty-nine other miners, the water too deep to continue efforts to bring them up. The Lucky Lady would forever embrace thirty dreamers in a silver-lined, common grave. Arlis ordered the mine shut down and the shafts boarded up.

They didn't know where Nalanche's office would be, but they'd decide once he got home and settled in. At least he had a sign to hang out front. A beautiful sign. With so many people leaving since the mines flooded, there wouldn't be much call for a new lawyer in town. He might want to move up to Tucson where there was more business, but she'd leave that to him to decide. Now that he was a lawyer and they had the same last name, no one would question a brother and sister living together. A lot of things would be easier when he was home for good. A few more days. He'd probably miss Christmas by a day or two, but they'd celebrate when he got in.

She drank the last of her tea and walked into the bedroom with the blanket still wrapped around her shoulders. Despite the misery in her chest, when she climbed into bed, she giggled at the old memory of Ann's description of the comforter — a blanket made from the feathers of a goose's behind. She closed her eyes. She couldn't get sick. Bear was already on the bed, curled up and ready for a snooze. In his younger days, she made him sleep on the floor. She remembered all the times she walked into the bedroom to find him on the bed, and when she caught him, John would pretend he hadn't realized the dog was there. Bear played dumb every bit as good as John. Obviously in cahoots with each other, she was never quite sure which one of them was the better actor, but she was wise to their little game. As soon as she left the room, John let the dog back on the bed. She imagined they had a good laugh believing they'd pulled the wool over her eyes. He and Nalanche. The two of them had a way with that dog. It was only after John died that she took to letting the big dog have a place on the bed and he'd slept there ever since. Fact was, she couldn't remember the last time he slept on the floor. He was big and took up half the bed when he stretched out, and he snored all night. It didn't bother her though. She loved the old dog and didn't know what she'd do when he died. After being so used to having him around all these years, the house wouldn't be the same without him. She rubbed his stomach. "You're fat, Little Bear. When your two-legged brother gets home, you'd better be of a mind to run with him. It'll be good for you to get your old bones movin'." She hugged him, remembering the day Nalanche handed him to her in the street, nothing more than a little ball of fluff nuzzling under her chin. She smiled, thinking how Virgil warned he'd better be a good dog or he'd be living in the street. She knew Virgil would never put the pup out. He was too soft-hearted. Virgil. Whatever happened to Virgil? Last she heard, he was somewhere out in California. She hoped he was in good health and happy. After all this time, she wondered if he ever thought about her. He did a lot for her, giving her the house and everything in it, making sure she was safe, and changing the way people looked at her because of her association with him. For that, and for his friendship, she'd always be grateful. She put her arm around the dog. Whatever happened to her life? She whispered, "I miss you John Merrick. I'm waitin'."

By morning, the sky was gray as slate and the air smelled of a cold rain not far off. They might even get a little snow. She hoped Nalanche made it home before the storm hit. It was Christmas Eve and if he got home today, snow might be nice for the holiday. She just didn't want him to have to travel in it. She thought about another Christmas Eve — 1881. It was exactly eight years ago tonight she saw Virgil for the last time. He brought her a Christmas present in a little white box tied with a red ribbon and a bow he'd made himself. He gave her the rose ring that night and said good-bye. The ring was gone, lost somewhere in the dirt out behind the Bird Cage. She looked for it a few times, but never found it. Like Virgil and everything else, it was only a memory committed to the past.

Not daring to chance taking a chill from walking in the rain and ending up with pneumonia, she wouldn't go to the Bird Cage tonight. Feeling the congestion building yesterday, she took a couple spoonfuls of the evil-tasting medicine the doctor made her keep on hand for times like this. She poured another spoonful of the stuff and held her breath before gulping it down. When she first woke up, she was hit by a violent fit of coughing that brought up an alarming amount of blood and left her with watery eyes and a sweat that wouldn't go away. The coughing finally subsided, but she felt weak and shaky since it happened. Now, she knew what Doc went through. Even the new medicine didn't help. The disease was too far gone and it was all a game of waiting for it to take her the way it had taken Doc. She'd seen what it did to people and death was the only merciful part of it. At best, she figured she had a year. She was ready and there was no fear in contemplating the arrival of Death at her door. If anything, she was looking forward to meeting him and those she loved who waited for her at the crossover. Her Will was all made out and the bank knew who to hand over her money to when the time came. There was plenty of money to buy a library full of law books and furniture to set up the best law firm in Arizona. She bought her casket a while back and Mr. Tarbell was keeping it at the funeral parlour until she needed it. No extra charge for the storage. A long time ago, she set aside the dress she wanted them to bury her in, one she'd had for years — a mint-green lawn, slightly faded with age, but still very fine linen. She saved the dress all this time for a special occasion, the day she'd meet John again. Nalanche was all the family she had and she planned to make her departure from this world as easy as possible for him. The house would be his and the money in the bank, and he'd have to take care of Bear. There was nothing else to do. It was already decided where he'd bury her, beside John and Abby out on the hill south of town. She accomplished what she set out to do. Nalanche had his education and his future was secure. She'd done one more thing she'd put off for years. She wrote a long-overdue letter setting a very painful record straight. Nalanche would see that it was delivered after her death — to Rebecca Merrick. Knowing everything was in order for her leaving provided a sense of peace. At last, she could rest.

Another hour of sleep would do her good. Keeping warm was important and she climbed back into bed. No sooner was she was under the covers when there was a knock on the door. She pulled the blankets over her head, hoping whoever was there would go away, but the knocking continued. The only way to get any rest was to see who it was and send them away. She flung back the covers and pulled a blanket off the bed, wrapping herself in it as she shuffled to the door. It was no surprise who the visitor was. Talking a mile a minute and leaving the door wide open, Lizzie sailed in on a draft of icy, December wind. Rose shook her head. Some things never changed. As usual, it was Lizzie being Lizzie. "Did you hear? Did you hear the news? I can't believe it. I just can't believe they did it. I never thought I'd see the day." Rose had no idea what Lizzie was sputtering about. She closed the door against the cold wind and pulled the blanket around herself, annoyed at being dragged from a warm bed and not overly anxious to have a visitor or hear Lizzie's announcement. Whatever the news was, it better be good. She squinted her eyes and frowned. "Did I hear what?" Lizzie looked at her sideways, surprised at the question. Rose waited. "Lizette, if I knew what you were talkin' about, I'd know as much as you. What is it you're tryin' to tell me that's so blessed important?" Lizzie stared at Rose, noticing the blanket for the first time since she came in. "Why do you have that blanket wrapped around yourself? You look like a squaw. Are you sick again?" Rose was in no mood for Lizzie's jabbering and her displeasure with Lizzie being there was beginning to show. "Yes, I'm sick. Now, will you please tell me what your news is, so I can go back to bed and get well?" Ignoring Rose's obvious irritation with her, Lizzie touched Rose's forehead. "You're burning up with fever. I'll get the doctor." She started out the door and Rose grabbed her arm. "Lizzie, please tell me why you came. I have medicine and I've already taken it." Lizzie was relieved. As long as Rose took the medicine right away when she felt the sickness coming on, she'd be alright. Lizzie blurted it out. "The Bird Cage is closed. I just came from there. The doors are locked. It's closed — forever!"

The news about the Bird Cage closing had come as a shock, like the sudden death of a friend whom you knew had been ill, but wasn't expected to die yet. She hadn't even said good-bye. It was inevitable, of course. They all knew it would happen sooner or later. She just didn't expect it to be quite this fast. She shivered and wrapped her robe tighter. The house was unusually damp and cold. She meant to get up during the night to keep the fire going, but the medicine made her sleep and the fire went out. As soon as she opened her eyes this morning, she heard the rain and felt the damp chill in the air. There were no hummingbirds at the feeder gourd outside the window, only water running off the edge of the roof and dripping on the ground. The tiny birds were keeping dry in the shelter of the overhanging branches of the big sycamore out back. The tree was most unusual for this country, the only one in the area as far as she knew. It was out of its natural element, like the white rose in the front yard that had grown into more of a tree than a bush over the years, climbing all the way to the roof. She always wondered how the sycamore tree got here, brought from another place like the white rose, perhaps, and planted behind the house. Maybe Virgil planted it, or maybe it was carried on the wind or by a bird as a seed. There were lots of birds living in the tree. It provided shelter from heat and cold alike as well as food for a variety of winged creatures. In season, there were holes in the fruit where the birds pecked at it. She tried it once herself and although it was sweet, it had a strange texture and she didn't like it much. She decided to leave it for the birds. Nalanche found the hummingbird nest. He propped a ladder against the trunk so she could climb up to see three tiny eggs no bigger than the tip of her little finger in a nest a quarter the size of a teacup. It was amazing that he found it, hidden among the thick leaves to protect it from the elements and predators. It always fascinated her the way they kept their wings moving fast enough to suspend themselves in mid-air and how their fragile young were able to survive. Both the mother and father fed the babies and took turns sitting on the nest to keep the little ones warm.

She pulled the curtain aside. The sky remained dark and overcast with no sign of the rain letting up any time soon. At least the fire was beginning to warm the parlour. She dropped another piece of wood onto the blaze and left the blanket on the couch on her way to the kitchen. Her chest ached and the chills were worse. Her throat was scratchy and it hurt to swallow. She had no appetite. Why did it always happen when it rained? She probably needed to see the doctor, but going out in weather like this was asking for trouble. She should have sent Lizzie to fetch him when she had the chance. Why didn't she think? Lizzie offered to get him, but she wanted Lizzie to stop her infernal chattering and sent her packing. She started taking the medicine right away when she felt the sickness coming on, but it didn't seem to be doing any good.

There were times when the young doctor stopped in to see her on days like this to be sure she hadn't taken a chill. He was truly a kind soul. She had to smile about the way she viewed him over time. By now, she knew what he could do. He was a remarkable physician and surgeon and she ought to stop referring to him as the "young" doctor and afford him the respect he deserved. It'd been nearly eight years since he came to town and he wasn't so young anymore. The place had aged him considerably. Lately, she couldn't help notice his hair was thinning and there was a touch of gray around the temple. It was a wonder he wasn't white-headed or completely bald by now, what with all the blood he'd seen and pounds of bullets and buckshot he'd dug out of people over the years. He'd patched up many an injured miner and set a hellacious number of broken bones. That wasn't all. A few years back, she came home to a gruesome sight when Lizzie tried to kill herself in the yard. That night, he sewed up Lizzie's wrists and face, and he put up with her cussing and biting and craziness brought on by the tolguacha poisoning. Time with his family was interrupted when there was an accident out at the mines or some crazy damn fool got himself shot over a poker game, and they woke him up in the middle of the night to deliver babies or, on more than a few occasions, a calf or colt having trouble getting itself born. To top all, there was a story about him birthing piglets out at Kanaly's hog ranch. He saved the sow and every single one of her kids and supposedly told Kanaly the pig family deserved better than to end up as pork chops after their ordeal coming into the world. Nobody ever knew whether Chester Kanaly took stock of the kind doctor's wishes and spared those pigs. What they did know was that he never refused to go when he was called, day or night, rain or shine. The man had certainly earned her respect. From now on, she'd simply think of him as the doctor and leave off the word that implied he was green — "young." Maybe he'd look in on her today and she could ask him to prescribe something stronger from the pharmacy. These days, the drugstore had medicine for whatever ailed you. If it wasn't in his bag, he'd go get it and bring it back to her, but for the time being, she'd have to settle for what she had in the house.

She held the amber bottle up to the light. Not much left. Only about a spoonful. She was supposed to take two at a time. Well, one was better than nothing. She turned the bottle upside down to get the last drop out, held her breath and swallowed, hoping she'd poured it down fast enough to be spared the awful taste. She shuddered. There was no way around the bitterness. Medicine tasting that bad ought to kill just about anything. Nalanche would be home soon and he'd fetch the doctor and more medicine. In the meantime, she'd stay warm. She got the stove fire going and put on some water to boil for tea. Bear was scratching at the door. Bear! She forgot poor old Bear. She let him out when she got up and he'd been outside in the rain ever since. She opened the door to let him in and a cold wind swept in with him. The weather was much colder than she thought. If the temperature kept dropping, they'd have snow for sure. It was Christmas and she wished Nalanche would get home today. She could hardly wait to see his face when she gave him the sign for his new office.

There were only a few, small pieces of wood left by the fireplace. The rest was out back and probably too wet to burn after the rain. Why hadn't she thought to bring some around and stack it inside? Until yesterday, there wasn't any need to. The weather had been warm into December and even in years past when it snowed, she didn't remember it being so cold as it was today. She never expected a storm to blow in so much cold and rain so fast. Bear shook the water from his coat, showering her and everything else.

"Bear..." She forgot what she was going to say. She was dizzy and weak. She touched her forehead, then her cheek. It was how Abby and the doctor knew when she had a fever. She felt her forehead again. She couldn't tell if she had a fever or not, but judging from the way she felt, it was probably a good bet that her temperature was up.

Bear was sopping wet and swishing his tail as usual, sending a spray in every direction around the parlour. The next move was predictable. She saw it coming and covered her face with her hands. "Bear! don't..." Too late. He shook himself and water went everywhere, leaving his wet fur parted and standing straight up all over his body. His mouth was open slightly and if she didn't know better, she'd have sworn he was smiling from the sheer pleasure of the moment. If he didn't look so comical, he might have gotten a good scolding. Then again, maybe not. She never could get mad at Bear. Those big, brown eyes saved him from more than one reprimand over the years. Besides, she couldn't blame him for getting wet. It was her fault he got left out in the rain. "Get yourself into the kitchen, you wet dog — and take that silly grin off your face." She pointed toward the kitchen and he trotted obediently through the door. She dried his thick coat with a towel as good as could be and threw a blanket on the floor near the stove. "Lay here until you're dry." She rubbed his nose. "We don't need you catchin' your death of pneumonia. One of us has to stay well to take care of the other one until your brother gets home." She patted his head. "And you know which one of us needs the most takin' care of, don't you?" His tail thumped the floor. He understood she was indeed the one who required the most taking care of.

When the tea was ready, she stirred in a spoonful of honey and went to the parlour for the blanket, once again pulling it around herself. Even with the fire going, the room wasn't as warm as the kitchen. She shivered. The chills were getting worse and her lungs ached. Why hadn't she thought to pick up more medicine and the ingredients for a poultice? And creosote oil? She knew she was supposed to keep that stuff on hand for times like this. Abby used to make the best mint poultice to rub on her chest. Of all the remedies for the pneumonia, it was the one she tolerated best. It was warm and smelled good and within a few hours, it penetrated through to stop the aching in her lungs. It was always the same. Swallow the awful-tasting medicine and fight to keep it down. Then, breathe the creosote and try not to gag on it. Those were the hardest because her stomach was so queasy when this ailment came upon her. The mint poultice, on the other hand, was warm and comforting, and breathing the vapors cleared her head. No use worrying about it. She didn't have anything. No creosote oil and no poultice ingredients, and not much medicine. The kitchen was the warmest room, so she sat at the table wrapped in the blanket. Bear was lying near the stove. She sipped the tea and listened to the rain. Rain had a soothing effect and she liked it, but it made her feel lonely. It rained like this the night John died, coming down in torrents and flooding the streets. It brought back memories of her father, dead nigh on fourteen years. Had it been that long? Seemed like she'd been with him only yesterday, sitting by the fire, listening to his stories.

They were all gone now — her father and Abby. John. Doc was dead. Virgil left Tombstone years ago and she didn't know what happened to him. She heard he owned a gambling hall in California and he was still a peace officer out there. Got himself elected a few times. It didn't surprise her. Virgil was pretty well liked by most everyone, except the desperados he chased out of town or put behind bars. 'Course, he killed a few of them. Virgil was entirely trustworthy and in his stagecoach-driving days after the war, there'd been a lot of folks put their lives in his hands. During that time, Wells Fargo entrusted him with some heavy money shipments. That was really all she knew about him. If she had to say what attracted her most to him, it wouldn't be that he was a nice-looking man or the way he carried himself tall and straight, or the fact that he wore a badge and was fearless. It wasn't even the twinkle in those blue eyes. Of all the things that made him who he was, any one of which was reason enough to like the man, for her, it had to be his kind heart and maybe, just maybe, the boyish smile that gave away his true disposition. Used to be, she didn't think he smiled much, but reflecting back on difficult times, she knew he had a tough job as a lawman in a wild, silver boomtown and he did that job, by God, with an iron hand. He smiled when he had cause to. Come to think of it, he smiled a good deal when he came to the little gray house to see her.

Outside of John Merrick, Virge had the softest heart of any man she'd ever known. Taking the puppy home with him the day Nalanche gave him to her proved what a kind soul he was. Bear didn't spend a single night outside when Virgil had him, contrary to the warning that he'd be in the street if he was a "bad dog." Virgil Earp was a good man and he deserved a whole lot better than he got in Tombstone. He gave the cowboys an ultimatum. They were the ones who chose to shoot it out, not him. After the gunfight at the O.K. Corral that sent Tom and Frank McLaury and Billy Clanton to their final resting place in Boot Hill, did the town thank him for putting an end to the problems with that bunch? They indicted him for murder and suspended him from his position as Chief of Police. That was the reward he got for putting his life on the line. He cleaned up the town and got rid of a passel of desperados, all the while believing in justice and what was right, and did anybody thank him for his trouble? — They shot him and crippled him for life.

She never wrote to Marian and Rebecca after John died. If she had, she might have recovered part of a family, but it was too late for that. It was probably just as well. She wouldn't want them to see what happened to her and she could never leave with John buried here. In her letter to Rebecca that Nalanche would send when she was gone, she told the truth and said she was sorry. She told Rebecca where her brother was buried if she was ever of a mind to visit his grave. By the time Rebecca read the letter, Rose would be buried next to John on the hill south of town. She'd lost everyone she loved except Nalanche. He was all she had left. She went to the window and moved the curtain aside. It didn't seem likely the rain would let up today. That meant Nalanche wouldn't make the stage run from Tucson today or tomorrow either. When she was a child, Joe Callahan told her the rain was the tears of angels. That made her sad. Nalanche said the rain was the Great Spirit's life-giver and she preferred that explanation over tears of angels.

A sizzling bolt of lightning close to the house sliced open another hole in the sky and the water poured through as if a dike broke and freed the ocean to flood the earth. It was raining harder. She looked down at the dog, stretched out contentedly on his blanket by the warm stove. His eyes were closed and his feet were moving, running in his dreams across the desert with Nalanche. She smiled at the way his mouth twitched and he yipped softly in sleep. It would be good for all of them when Nalanche came home. The initial gush of water slowed a little and she watched droplets streaming down the window; tiny bubbles of liquid crystal seemingly joined together by an invisible, delicate filament of nature that made them look like a continuous strand of sliding glass beads. The rain would delay Nalanche's return. Lightning flashed and cannonlike rolls of thunder rattled the little gray house. For a minute, she thought it was letting up, but the storm took only a temporary respite before resuming its furious onslaught. It was really coming down, battering the roof and pelting the window panes so hard she hoped they didn't break. If it kept up, the streets would be a mess, a river of mud before the sun dried it into hardened clay, then back to dust. That would take days. They needed the rain, but she hated the mud it left in its wake. You couldn't walk anywhere after this kind of a storm without sinking in up to your ankles. Once it dried up, dust would blow around. During dry spells, she was constantly sweeping out the dust. She didn't know which was worse, the blowing dust or the mud. Her thoughts were silly. She was grumpy today, complaining about things over which she had no control. It was because she didn't feel well. Tomorrow, she'd be better and none of those things would be worth grumbling about. Another thought — the roof. She had it fixed after the last rain and hoped they'd done it right. In the small bedroom, everything was as Nalanche left it. She never moved anything that belonged to him. Running her hand over the bedcovers, she was relieved to discover they were dry. The ceiling looked dry enough too. No leaks so far. The room was full of his things, but it was empty without him. It was going to be good to have him home. She hoped he'd been eating right and getting plenty of sleep and... Between the two of them, he took better care of himself than she did.

Walking back to the kitchen, she thought about him. He should have been home today, but the rain held him up. The road from Tucson would be very muddy, maybe even washed-out to the point of being impassable. A stagecoach rolling over a puddle that turned out to be covering a two-foot deep hole in the road could throw a coach over on its side or into an arroyo. The line wouldn't risk losing a coach or passengers to an accident like that. Rather than travel in this kind of weather, they'd wait for the rain to stop and the road to dry up some before making the run into Tombstone. Once the sun came out, they'd be back on the road in no time. Depending on when the storm blew itself out, it could be several days until Nalanche got home. The only good thing about a heavy rain was that it replenished the groundwater supply to her roses, especially the white rose out front that grew taller and stronger every season. She never cut it back and the last time Nalanche came home, he built a heavy trellis to support it. He'd be surprised when he saw the way it had climbed above the trellis and onto the roof. It was beginning to look more like a tree than a bush. Everyone said they'd never seen anything like it. She coughed and the spell brought up a lot of blood. When it first happened, it scared her. That was a long time ago. Over the years, it had gotten progressively worse, but she wasn't afraid anymore. If anything, she was amazed that she'd lived this long. From everything she'd heard and read, tuberculosis killed it's victims in a lot less time than it was taking with her. It was a miracle she'd been given so much extra time with the disease so far gone.

Her throat was swollen and hot and the tea she thought would make her feel better hurt when she swallowed. She left the cup on the table and started back to the bedroom. A strange weakness came over her. She had to sleep. The dog raised his head when she got up from the table and she bent down to touch his fur. He was warm. "I think you're dry. Do you want to come back to bed?" He stood up and shook himself, wagging his affirmative answer. There were three things Bear liked to do — run, eat and sleep, and not necessarily in that order. He was into the bedroom ahead of her. She felt dizzy and reached for the wall to steady herself. The room was spinning. She couldn't remember feeling this bad since the first time she was sick and Abby took care of her. Abby. If only Abby were here. She'd know what to do. Abby always helped her get well. She laid down on the bed and pulled the covers to her chin. She was freezing and there was a crushing pressure in her chest. It was becoming harder to breathe and every time she coughed, there was blood on her handkerchief, heavier and darker than the time before. Bear jumped on the bed and curled up beside her. He sensed there was something wrong. She felt so alone and afraid. Everything was spinning and the feeling frightened her. She'd never be able to stand up as long as the spinning kept up. Where was Nalanche? She needed him to come home. They'd both been through so much, but all the hard work was about to pay off. He was going to be successful. She knew it. The present tied with red ribbon leaned against the wall in the corner of her room. She could hardly wait to show him the lovely sign Mr. Hampton made for his office. Of course, they didn't know where that would be yet, but they'd know soon enough. Imagine, her brother, a lawyer. Brother. She couldn't remember when she didn't call him brother.

She hadn't been sick for a long time. Not like this. Why now, when he was coming home? She had to sleep. She had to feel better when the rain stopped and he got home. She and Lizzie and Ruby had a party planned for him to celebrate his graduation and homecoming. It was important that she be well for the party. They had so much to talk about, so many plans to make now that he was a lawyer. She was so proud of him. John would have been proud too. Memories of John came flooding over her. After all these years, she still missed him. They were wrong, those who said the pain would lessen over time. It went deeper with every passing day. Sometimes, she felt close to him. Other times, she didn't know where he was. During those times when she felt he was far away, she thought he must be with Nalanche, helping him learn about the law; guiding him one step closer to the dream. She whispered, "I miss you, John. I'm waitin'."

She tried to focus her eyes in the dim light through the hazy glow that filled the room. It was like trying to see a candle through the fog that rolled across the desert from the Dragoons every morning in winter. The figure beside the bed moved slowly and the voice was muted by some kind of indiscernible, translucent barrier. At first, she couldn't make out what was being said. Gradually, a man came through the barrier. He was smiling. The doctor was rolling down his sleeves and putting on his coat. He was leaving. "How are you feeling, Rose?" She tried to answer, but the fever had taken her strength. It was too hard to speak. He patted her hand. "Don't try to talk. You need to rest. That's all you have to concern your-self with. Rest, and I'll be back tomorrow." She tried to ask him a ques-tion, but nothing came out. He blew out the candle and pulled aside the curtain to let the sunlight in. Before she could get a word out, he left the room. So, he did come by to look in on her. She knew he would. He was a kind man, always thinking of others before himself. She liked him. He was a good doctor. He saved Lizzie's life, and he tried to save John. She tried to think, but her thoughts wouldn't come together. When did he come? She didn't remember letting him in. What was the day? She was confused. At first, she thought she asked out loud. "What time is it?" No one answered and she realized it had only been a thought. The rain had stopped and the sun was pouring through the lace curtains. After being in a dark room, the light hurt her eyes. The woman by the window was smil-ing at her. With the sunlight behind her, it was hard to tell who she was, but... "Abby?" It was Abby. She blinked and tried to focus on the woman. It couldn't be Abby. Abby was dead. Drifting in and out of a half-sleep, she wasn't quite sure of anything. Her thoughts were fragmented and float-ing. It had to have been a dream. She dreamed about Abby a lot and some-times the dreams were so real, she didn't know if she was awake or asleep.

She must have slept all night. The weather cleared and the sun was out. She dreamed about snow. The Gypsy seer, Zaida, said to dream of snow was a message from the herald of Death. For three nights in a row before she turned eighteen years, she dreamed about her father standing in a field of heather in the falling snow. He died on the eve of the fourth day. It must have snowed on Christmas, but she wasn't sure. She thought she'd been standing in the snow. She remembered the weather turning cold, but as far as she knew, it hadn't snowed. She was too sick to go out. She tried to sit up and couldn't. She'd never felt so weak, unable to raise her head. Bits of conversation from the parlour filtered through. What were they saying? Two days? That couldn't be right. The fever was so high she'd been unconscious for two days? Nalanche found her when he came home last night and went for the doctor. If it was true, it meant the dog hadn't eaten for two days. She couldn't remember the last time she fed him. Everything was a blur. She couldn't remember anything. She'd lost track of time — something she was supposed to do. What was it? The last thing she remembered, it was raining. At least, she thought it was raining. Maybe it was snowing. She could have sworn she was in the snow. Now that she thought about it, it was more like she saw herself standing in the snow, but that was crazy. Maybe she dreamed the whole thing. She listened to the voices coming from the kitchen. "The dog acted like he hadn't eaten in a week. He was starving when Nalanche got here." She closed her eyes. Poor Bear. If what they said was true, he must have been so hungry. She started to cry, thinking of him staying with her and having no food. If Nalanche hadn't come home, Bear would have starved to death because he never would have left her side.

What they were saying finally struck her. Nalanche was home? She was aware of someone else standing beside the bed, but everything was out of focus. Her mind wasn't working right. She squinted to see the person next to her. He sat on the edge of the bed and held her hand. Gradually, she began to make out his features. He was tall and dark and he had a moustache. He was wearing a white shirt and black tie. He looked so familiar, but she couldn't quite figure out who he was. She managed a whisper. "John? Is that you, John?" He looked so much like John, but it wasn't John. "Nalanche." She started to cry and the crying made taking in air more difficult. Her breathing was labored, each breath rattling painfully inside her chest. He laid a cool cloth on her forehead. She was burning up. The fever was worse than any time in the past. It was hard to breathe, harder to think. She was so tired, it was a fight to keep her eyes open. "When did you come home? We have a party for you. We need to find Lizzie and Ruby. I don't remember..." A few words exhausted her and her voice trailed off. He spoke softly in his native language. "You must rest, Sister. I will not leave you." She understood the words spoken in the language of the Apache. The sound of his voice was peaceful, soothing. He placed a small, leather bag in her hand — a medicine bag. She held it near her heart. The light that surrounded him was more defined, brighter than she'd ever seen it. Her spirit protector. He was surely that. He kissed her cheek. In all the years she'd known him, he never kissed her. It was a farewell kiss. One of them was leaving. He didn't say good-bye. She just knew. She felt the same warmth the night he put his arms around her in the rain in front of the Bird Cage the night John died. It was all so clear. She knew which one of them was leaving. It was Abby she saw by the window. With her eyes closed, she could see the soldier smiling and reaching out his hand to her. She took his hand and the image changed. The one they called Coshani took his place. They were one and the same. She was at the crossover.

A peaceful feeling came over her and she was surrounded by a golden light that moved with her. She was standing on the hill, watching circles of smoke from a distant fire curling skyward and listening to the drums; not her own heartbeat this time. Familiar voices drifted past, calling her name on the wind. They seemed so close, much closer than other times when she heard them. She looked out over the desert toward the mountains. She was waiting for someone. They were there. Riders on the wind, racing across the desert and heading straight for her. She watched as they came closer, anticipating the arrival of the one she'd waited so many years to see. It wasn't what she expected. There were only two, leading a riderless black and white Paint. The one they called Coshani was not with them. The horse was for her and they beckoned to her to come with them, but she couldn't go. Not yet. She promised to wait for him twice before and both times, she broke the promise. He helped her at the crossing and said they'd meet again. He told her to believe and he'd come back for her, but she must wait. She didn't see him now, but she knew he wasn't far away. It was the test and she would not fail again. This time, she'd keep the promise to wait for him. She had to wait.

Chapter 18

"Ruby, Ruby, it's sad, but true;
The grand old lady has aged.
Allen Street will never be the same
without the old Bird Cage."

At The Old Bird Cage
ALLEN STREET ROSE

When the last of the mines shut down, they all thought the place would become a ghost town, but by some unknown quirk of fate, it survived. They called it the town too tough to die, and for good reason. A lot of the old buildings were gone and some had been boarded up and abandoned. The Bird Cage Theatre was one of them. She stood at the corner of Sixth and Allen Streets, a sad reminder of days gone, a lonely ghost from the past. Thirty years later, she was like a woman who'd lost the beauty of her youth. She was old; old and neglected, in a state of disrepair. Her walls ravaged and stained by years of abuse from the elements, a faded sign out front barely readable anymore was all that remained to tell the world what a grand lady she used to be. Broken-out windows that once reflected light from glittering, crystal chandeliers were covered with wood to keep out birds and bats. Some said they still heard the music of a tinny piano and a crying fiddle coming from behind the rundown walls, and the old chandeliers were blazing away inside in the middle of the night when the place was all locked up and nobody there. They swore ghosts of old gamblers still played poker and a lot of money changed hands across the faro table at midnight; that others still participated in wild carryings-on with painted women in the suspended cribs and basement bordello. Truth was, the old lady was silent now, secrets of a bygone era safe within her walls. There was a lot no one would ever know about the Bird Cage Theatre, plenty that would never make the history books.

Most of them were gone, moved away or dead and buried over at Boot

Hill or in the city cemetery west of town, some with markers, some without. A few of the old faces were still around. For one reason or another, there were some who hadn't been able to leave. Rose was right. The place had a hold on all who came, and some never did break the grip. There were lots of stories passed around, but in thirty years, a lot was lost in the translation. Then, of course, there was a certain amount of embellishment added as they went along and exaggeration of the facts was not uncommon. You never knew exactly how much of it was true and how much was conjured up by imagination. Everyone insisted their version of events was the right one. Most of it was pretty close to the truth, but there were a few things they couldn't have been more wrong about — like the Irish prostitute from the Bird Cage and Doc Holliday, for example. Anyone who said it was more than a friendship just plain didn't know the truth. There was no sparkin' going on with them, only a friendship between two people who understood each other. Since the players weren't around to tell the story the way it really went, you had to search between the lines to figure it out. Sometimes, you had to take the stories with a grain of salt. Those who had been there in the old days and gone inside the Bird Cage during the time when the silver boom was in full swing told some hair-raising tales of what went on behind the doors of the wildest honky tonk west of the Mississippi. Between the music and gambling and killings, not to forget the women, it had been a darned exciting place. Never a dull moment when the Bird Cage was open, and it was open 'round the clock for more than eight and a half years. The doors never closed and the games never stopped, or so they said. It was a mighty long poker game down in the basement with outrageously high stakes — a thousand dollars to buy in. Some walked away with a fortune. Some didn't walk away at all.

They wouldn't want their wives to know, but for some, it was an affectionate reminiscence when they talked about the bad girls of Tombstone, known in their day as soiled doves. They were a colorful group alright, a reference that applied to more than the paint they wore on their faces or the red feathers in their hair. There were stories about all of them, each version more garish than the one before. They smiled when they talked about the women — those notorious shady ladies of the night. Some of them had been there and made the trip upstairs with Silver Dollar Jenny, or Diamond Annie, or the wild one, Claire Dillon. They remembered the beautiful blonde, Lizette. Anyone who'd been there could never forget her. They said she was the prettiest one of all. When she left the Bird Cage, she had her own place for awhile. Hired only high-class ladies to work for her. A shame she got so deep into the laudanum. Ended up killing herself. They liked the big redhead too. Her name was Ruby. Ruby Fontaine could hold her own with any man, whether it be in a fistfight or the bedroom.

...and then, there was Rose Callahan. They said she came from Ireland — a Gypsy. She had fiery-red hair and a temper to match, and eyes the color of emeralds. With a passion for silver and the blue turquoise that came from over in Bisbee, she earned herself the name of Silver Rose. Story was, she had a wild fling with Virgil Earp until Wyatt put a stop to it. Seemed she had another man too, a soldier or somesuch thing. "Army lawyer, I think." That was it. "Ran some big government trial over at the courthouse. Won the case and a dozen desperados swung right there in the yard for their trouble. Come to think of it, if memory serves, he left town for awhile and when he came back, he wasn't wearing a uniform anymore. Gave it all up for the little Irish prostitute." No one seemed to know much about him or if he really managed to hang a dozen men for a crime none of them could remember. All they knew was, "He got shot in the Bird Cage in '82 in retaliation for the murder of some crazy miner. Wild Jack some-body-or-other." One of them recalled a showdown between Jack and that rabid killer, Doc Holliday, over the redhaired Irish girl. "Saw the whole thing. Yep. If you ask me, she was Doc's girl on the side. You know he went runnin' to her every time him and Kate had a fight." None of them wanted to let on they didn't know about it, so they agreed that was the case and acceptance provided fuel for the rest of the story.

The storyteller tilted his chair back against the building and touched a match to the tobacco in a well broken-in pipe, drawing several drafts of air into the bowl and through the shaft. When it was burning to his satisfac-tion, he took a couple of deep puffs before settling the pipe in one corner of his mouth. The fire went out as soon as he stopped puffing, but the story continued. "Why, I remember one time Doc came in with his coat hanging loose over his shoulders. Couldn't get it on for all the bandaging. He pushed Kate around once too often and the old girl shot him. Would've killed him if Wyatt Earp hadn't been there and took the gun away from her. I heard tell, Doc Goodfellow had one hell of a time sewing him up, and George had a lot of experience with gunshot wounds. He was mighty fine doctor, but that was a bad one. Kate was madder than a stepped-on rat-tlesnake and she wanted to blow Holliday's head off. He's lucky her aim was bad from too many belts of whiskey and all she managed to hit was his arm." The storyteller interjected a few editorial comments. "Can't say I blame her much. He was a real sonofabuck. Don't know why she stuck with him and put up with his skulduggery as long as she did. Kate was a fair-lookin' woman and could have done a site better than a no-account tin-horn like him. Never knew how he managed to live as long as he did either, always looking for trouble and all. Somebody should've put a slug in him years ago. Had a strange kind of luck over his head, that one did. Won a hell of a lot of money at cards, cheatin' mostly." They'd heard the story a hundred times, but they reacted as though it was the first telling. They'd shake their heads in confirmation, regardless of whether they knew the stories about Doc's hell raising to be the truth or not and then, they'd get right on with the next story.

John Henry Holliday was a fascination for all of them. The ones who knew him, or had at least known who he was, would have crossed to the other side of the street to avoid contact with him. They were scared to death of him, and rightly so. He was like a stick of dynamite with a fuse so short it was barely visible, and a match constantly burning within kissing distance of the wire, ready to set him off in the blink of an eye if he didn't like the way you looked at him. He'd shoot his own grandmother if the mood struck him. That's what they said anyway, to make the story that much more sensational. Once in a while, they said something about him that made it appear they knew him on a close, personal level when, in reality, they didn't know him at all. He had a lot of enemies and just being around him made you a target, so they stayed as far away from him as they could get. None of them even considered a friendship with the man when he was alive, but now that he was gone, there was something about the excitement that went with the territory — an imagined association with the notorious Doc Holliday, that gave them a certain status to say they knew him. Human nature was funny sometimes.

Outside of Wyatt Earp, Rose Callahan was more than likely the only friend Doc Holliday ever had. Kate stayed with him, but she didn't like him much toward the end. Nobody knew why she stuck it out as long as she did. Two of a kind, maybe. It was a very strange relationship the two of them had. A little love, and a little hate. Most of the time, you couldn't tell which was which. They didn't know what he did to finally run her off, but one day, Kate up and left him. Some folks said she witnessed the gunfight at the O.K. Corral and that's when she decided to leave. According to one story, Kate was in love with Doc and when she saw how close he came to getting killed that day, she'd had enough. She didn't want to stick around

and see him die. Virgil didn't have any use for him, and Doc made no bones
about there being no love loss between the two of them. They tolerated
each other only because of their common tie with Wyatt Earp. Everyone
thought there'd come a day when Doc and Virgil would have their own
showdown, but luckily for both of them, it never happened. Still, when the
chips were down, those two stuck together. Look what happened at the
O.K. Corral. Without each other, neither one of them might have come out
of that mess alive.

They said Doc warned Rose to stay away from Virgil, but she didn't
listen. "Tried his darndest to keep her from seeing Virgil Earp. Jealousy!
If you ask me, that's all it was. Pure and simple. Doc wanted her for
himself. That was plain to anybody who had eyes. Plenty of times, he'd
buy a bottle of whiskey — not the cheap stuff either, and sit with her in
the Bird Cage, and they'd talk real low. All night sometimes. Nobody
bothered her when he was around except that one time Wild Jack tried to
say she stole his money. Doc put an end to that real quick. He pulled a
gun and gave Jack ten seconds to clear out. When Jack stood his ground
and Doc went so far as to lock back the action on that Colt .45 revolver,
everybody cleared out. I thought Jack was a dead man for sure. The only
thing that saved him was the long-legged redhead... What was her name?
Ruby Red! She was a tough old gal that one. Got right in the middle of
it and sweet-talked that crazy-fool miner into leaving. Disappointed the
hell out of Holliday that he couldn't shoot Jack right there. A few hours
later, Jack's luck plumb run out. Somebody put a bullet in him out behind
the Bird Cage around midnight." The storyteller didn't recall whether
Doc was still inside when it happened. "Why Rose took a shine to such
an ornery rascal is a mystery, mean and sick like he was. Always thought
she was real nice. They were an unlikely pair. Come to think of it, they
never did figure out who killed Jack. I think Holliday done it. Wyatt
Earp said he done it, but Jack's friends didn't buy that. They said the
Army lawyer done it. That's why they shot him at the Bird Cage that
night in '82. I heard tell, the lawyer weren't carrying a gun. Always
thought it was right peculiar how all them lawmen just stood around
when it happened. Seems they ought to been able to do somethin'.
There's a whole lot more to it than we'll ever know. Mighty suspicious.
Mighty damn suspicious."

"She took in some orphan Apache kid, the Callahan woman did.
Word was, she sent him to some highfalutin school back East. There was

somethin' fishy about all of that. She was always so secretive. Kept to herself a lot. Lived alone in that little gray house over on Toughnut — the one with the rose tree out front. Virgil put her in there. The fact he was married didn't stop him from keeping the Irish prostitute." There was plenty of gossip. "My wife knows all about it from the woman who lived next door to her — Caroline something. Guess she knew the Callahan woman pretty good." They all knew the house. "It's empty now. Nobody livin' in it. Can't get nobody to live there cuz' it's haunted. She died there, you know. Some say you can still hear her cryin' in the night. Can't swear to it, but chance was, she caught that awful disease Holliday had. She died of a fever or consumption, one of those things, right about the time the Bird Cage closed down, and the Indian kid moved up Tucson way. He's a doctor or lawyer or somethin' these days."

Stories about Rose exhausted for the time being, the storytellers shrugged their shoulders and went on with another subject. Most of them worked in the mines at one time or another and had a hundred tales to tell about their experiences. There was a difference of opinion as to exactly how much silver came out of the hills before the mines flooded. Thirty million? Sixty? A hundred? It was pure speculation what the actual dollar amount was by the time the last mine shut down and the final tally was on the books. Like everything else, no one really knew for certain. Everybody had their own idea about it, but they all agreed on one thing. Any way you looked at it, they found the mother lode. That was a fact. Too bad the water stopped them from taking more of it. They'd have all been rich today if they'd had a little more time.

They never tired of recollecting the exciting characters and events of the time; Doc Holliday, Big Nose Kate, John Ringo, the Clantons and McLaurys, Wyatt Earp and Josie Marcus. The list of notorious folks was endless and so were the stories. They talked about high rollers like Bat Masterson, Luke Short and Diamond Jim Brady who bet big money on the high-stakes poker table in the basement of the Bird Cage where you had to place a minimum bet of a thousand dollars just to get into the game. A lot of money in those days. A lot of money today. They said famous newspaper mogul, Randolph Hearst, frequently participated in the game. "...and the whiskey. Why, it ran like a river." One more thing. The ladies! "Weren't no finer beauties than those what danced and sang sweet songs at the Bird Cage Theatre." The storyteller elbowed the fellow next to him, implying that the singing and dancing might not have been the main reason they went to see the girls at the Bird Cage. What they wouldn't give for the old days to come back around for just one night.

It was human nature to recall the sensationalism of an exciting time in history. They remembered the thrill of heading for the silver bonanza back in '79, and how they were intoxicated by the exhilaration of the very real possibility they might get rich. It all depended on the luck of the draw, and each and every one of them was a gambler in his own way. They could still see the town as it was in the early days, a wild mining camp with no rules and every man for himself. When the Earps rolled in to get a piece of the gambling action and Virgil became Chief of Police, things changed and lawlessness took a turn. He was motivated to keep the peace because he had family and business interests to look out for. He didn't put an end to all the crime, but the situation greatly improved while he was around. A friendly sort with a warm smile and firm handshake, there was something in those blue eyes that warned you wouldn't want to get sideways with him. He had a way about him that let you know he could be your best friend — or your worse nightmare. Under his hand, Tombstone actually became a relatively safe place to live in spite of the fact that it was a boomtown with the usual accompaniment of saloons and brothels and that it attracted more than its share of a bad element. They recalled the gunfight at the O.K. Corral and gory details of young Morgan Earp bleeding to death when an assassin's bullet struck him down in Campbell & Hatch's Billiard Hall. Surprisingly, Tombstone's heyday was not filled only with accounts of violence and gloriously-wild and wicked times in the saloons and gambling halls. There was a gentler side of the town. Nellie Cashman, for one. The woman did a lot for the miners. In fact, she helped anyone who came to her. She was a kind soul. A healer and friend to every miner. Maybe an angel. "She was a friend of the Irish prostitute, weren't she? The one they called the Silver Rose?"

Someone pulled out a pocket watch and noted the time. Getting late. Time to pack up the reminiscing and head home for supper. Before they left, they remembered one more thing. It was what they used to say when they left the damp earth of the mines and headed for town on Saturday night to spend a week's pay on a pretty woman and, "in case she weren't so pretty," enough whiskey to overlook her shortcomings. It had become a tradition of sorts to say the words. It was all they had left — that and the stories. Even though the grand old lady at Sixth and Allen Streets was quiet now, they still said it every time the yarn-spinning session was done. True stories, every last one of them. They'd tell you so. "...and that's the dead truth." It had a nostalgic ring to it, something they'd never let go of completely — an affectionate recollection of a once-beautiful woman they all loved. A sad reminder of the past. They parted company and went their separate ways, not wanting the others to see a tear generated by a special memory. They'd meet at the same place tomorrow to continue the recording of history, as they saw it. Heading for home, they called over their shoulders to each other, familiar words from younger days, days they thought would never end. Long after they were dead and gone, the words would echo down from the silver mines to the stamping mills on the San Pedro River, and up and down the length of Allen Street, whispered by the ghosts of yesteryear. "See you at the Bird Cage."

Despite the passage of time and the never-ending cycle of the elements, rising and setting of the sun, phases of the moon and changing tides, disturbances of earth and sky, in thirty years, the view from the hill hadn't changed. Thirty years had streaked his black hair with highlights the color of the silver that gave life to the town, the ore they use to bring forth from the earth not far from the spot on which he stood, piled high in a mountain of mine tailings as a reminder of what happened there. When she died, he gave her a small, leather bag to take with her to the crossover — the medicine bag containing a single, blue-turquoise stone. He had known when she was leaving and he went with her to the edge of the crossing, giving her over to those who waited to help her to the other side. Otahe and Tehanache were there to let him know she wasn't afraid and she'd have a safe journey through the crossover. They understood how much she meant to him. He'd seen the woman, Abigail, at the window in Rose's room the day she died, and he saw Coshani take her hand and lead her into the light. The presence of so many from the spirit world that day was significant. Not all who left this life received that kind of help through the passageway and his heart was at peace knowing she was with them.

At the funeral parlour, he made the undertaker leave the room and when they were alone, he laid all of her silver jewelry with the blue stones beside her. Around her neck, he placed the strand of pearls John gave her the night he proposed. He closed the casket himself to relieve the undertaker of the burden of temptation on seeing the jewelry. Today was only the second time he'd been back since he buried her in the winter of '89. Two years later, he brought the dog back and buried him beside her. With a single, blue-turquoise stone tied in a leather band around his neck, Little Bear traveled safely through the crossover to meet her on the other side.

He listened to the voices on the wind and answered them in his own Athapaskan language. He lived in a white man's world now, but he never got caught up in it. He never forgot the old ways. He still went into the desert alone and spoke to the spirits of the old ones gone from this world many years ago. To all who saw him, he appeared an integral part of the world as it was today. An old, hand-carved sign hung on the wall of his office in Tucson. Formerly posted outside, it was chipped and weathered. The sign on the door was different today. He had a couple of partners and the practice was successful. One of the best law firms in Arizona. He'd been at it for thirty years and was thinking of retiring to work exclusively on Indian affairs in the Southwest. Arizona was no longer a territory having joined the union seven years ago. When it became a state, he had hoped the government would help improve the quality of life for the Indians, but things moved very slowly to that end. Despite his efforts and those of others concerned with the sad plight of the Indians, things were still not good. He might make some progress in their favor, but overall, there would be no significant changes in his lifetime. He didn't have to come all this way to tell her, but he knew she was watching him; listening. He hadn't talked to her the way he talked to his father and his grandfather in a long time, but he knew she was with him. He also knew she was here, in this place that held her for so many years, the place she'd been unable to leave after John Merrick died. He called to her and she answered as he knew she would. She stood beside him on the hill and called him Brother, and told him they would meet again in the place of spirit winds. When he reached the crossover, she'd be there with Otahe and Tehanache, and his brother, Coshani. She was still waiting for the promise to be kept. There was unfinished business here, but that too would be resolved in Time.

The two wooden crosses were nearly hidden by overgrown creosote and cactus, the names obliterated beyond recognition from close to forty years of windblown sand and rain. He thought about replacing them, but after today, he'd never come back to this place and no one else cared they were here. He knew who they were; the man who called him Brother — John Merrick, and a pretty, brown-eyed girl from Missouri named Abigail. It wasn't something he'd ever forget. The name on the other marker was as clear as the day he placed the stone at the head of the grave thirty years ear-lier. The message on the stone was simple, the way he knew she would have wanted it. "Rose Marie Callahan, 1857 – 1889. "I am the Silver Rose."

Chapter 19

BISBEE, ARIZONA – 1994

From the minute he came to the door, she knew this was no ordinary weekend trip, and he was definitely no ordinary man. He was unique, different from anyone she'd ever met. He viewed life a lot like she did. He hadn't said much, just enough to let her know he shared some beliefs she found difficult to discuss with other people. As he loaded the suitcase into the truck, she got the same feeling she had the previous weekend when they went hiking. She still wasn't sure what happened that day when he took her home. She kissed him on an impulse, something she hadn't done since she was sixteen. An image of some forgotten time flashed in her mind's eye and she remembered feeling like she'd been propelled backward in a tunnel faster than the speed of light. In a week, she hadn't recovered from it. She only met him a few months earlier, but there was the overpowering sense of having known him before. She watched him as he drove, trying to identify what it was that made him seem so familiar. She was doing her best to disguise her excitement when, if the truth be known, she was trembling inside like a schoolgirl on her first date. She'd be embarrassed if he knew what she was thinking.

The trip took about four hours and for the entire duration, she imagined what his touch would be like under intimate circumstances. She stared at the road ahead. If he could read her mind, he'd probably have turned around after the first ten miles. She glanced over at him, hoping she hadn't been thinking those deliciously-wicked thoughts out loud. He was smiling. Did she say something that gave her thoughts away? He didn't say anything, so she must not have let it slip out. Since she accepted the invitation to spend the weekend with him, she'd worried about what would happen once they got to a hotel. Three days. Two nights! She hoped she'd survive it. What a ridiculous thing to be thinking. She was forty-nine years old for heaven's sake. She wasn't some naive kid who'd never been to bed with a man. It was just that it had been so long and she'd made a conscious decision to be alone for the rest of her life. It'd be easier that way. Caring about someone brought too much grief. She didn't want to go through it ever again. Here she was, thinking in all the wrong terms. She was thinking too much. She always did that. It was a weekend. One weekend. Nothing more. A chance to get away and have some fun with a nice guy. When it was over, she'd be going back to Denver and would never see him again. She had to be careful. She'd been avoiding him for six months and couldn't break down now. The attraction was strong. She probably shouldn't even be with him. She turned toward the window so he couldn't see her face. She couldn't believe the ideas that were going through her head. Where did the preconceived notions about what he expected come from? She was being entirely unfair in presuming what he expected. Truth was, he didn't expect anything and she knew it. It was expectations of herself she was questioning, not his. She always placed more demands on herself than others did. She was her own worst critic. ...but, he was in such great shape and she was so... ...out of shape. She'd been over this a hundred times already. Just relax and have some fun with him — for three days, and two nights!

He was more than a nice guy. She knew that the first time she met him. He was one of those rare people who possessed all the qualities of one who strives for perfection and succeeds. It was the light, an aura that surrounded him, and it was what caught her attention in the first place, something from within that was reaching out to her and telling her it was safe to be with him; something reassuring that said everything would be alright if she took the chance. She knew what it was because she'd seen it near two other people in her life. The colors were defined and bright, an indication of the kind of person he was, a significant designation of one who was capable of great things. A sign of power and connection with spiritual elements. She was well-aware that no one else saw it. Maybe he didn't see it himself when he looked in the mirror. She was no expert on the subject and she had no idea why she felt the way she did, but something was telling her there were capabilities within him that had barely been tapped, perhaps even of a psychic character. He was much more in tune with things of a spiritual nature than he realized. In time, she believed she'd find out she was right. It was all pretty deep thinking about someone she barely knew and there was no clue what brought on that train of thought. Again, it was a sense of some obscure knowledge about him that she couldn't bring into clear focus in her own mind. She sat back in the seat and for the first time since the trip began, relaxed. She was looking forward to spending three days with him — and the nights. Could be, Tombstone was going to be more interesting than she anticipated.

Four hours flew past and before she knew it, they were in Bisbee, Arizona. The road led them along the east rim of the Lavender Pit Mine, an extraordinary copper-mining operation. Opened in the mid-fifties and closed twenty years later around 1974, it was mind-boggling to think about the tons of dirt and ore carried up from the depths of the pit by truckloads in that length of time. From the looks of it, she thought a project of that size should have taken twice as many years. Chills ran up her spine when she looked at the terraced grooves along the inner walls, imagining the dangerous job of excavating a hole that size and working on the narrow ledges. Before they started digging, there was a main highway with homes and businesses on either side that ran right over the top of what was now a nine hundred-foot deep, mile-long canyon.

Standing on the edge of the pit and contemplating the work that went into it, she lost track of previous concerns over what would happen once they were alone in a hotel room. The wind was blowing and it was a little chilly standing on the edge of the precipice. There was an old feeling from days past, teetering on the edge of a cliff above a raging river, no life jacket available and the rapids up ahead. She took a jump when she moved to New Mexico and it hadn't worked out. If nothing else, the change of scenery had been good for her. She was about to jump again and there was a lot at stake this time. No life jacket. No parachute to break the fall. She had to get it right. She drifted off, lost in thought about what it was like in the days when there was activity here with steam shovels moving dirt around and trucks hauling she couldn't guess how many tons of ore. The sound of heavy, earth-moving equipment and diesel engines roaring and nerve-grating echoes of jackhammers breaking up the rock bounced around the rock walls of the open pit. The old mine seemed to come alive around her — the place as it was thirty years ago. Unless you wanted to come away deaf, you would have had to worn earplugs to work around all the machinery noise when the operation was running at full production capacity. Mining was a dirty and dangerous way to make a living. A fleeting picture of men hammering at a wall of rock under the earth raced past like an old-fashioned reel of film spinning wildly out of control. It wasn't a picture of more recent-day mining operations, but more of old-time prospectors with handpicks and shovels, digging out the rock a little bit at a time. It was an uncomfortable feeling. Unsettling. It passed.

She had the strangest notion she'd been to this place before — not this pit, just the place, the town. Bisbee. The mine wasn't familiar at all, but the general area was more than a vague memory; something about the way it smelled — the hills, the multi-colored layers of rock from a variety of mineral deposits. A picture was on the verge of coming into focus, but never did. It was like a name you'd known your entire life and said a thousand times; on the tip of your tongue, but all of sudden, you drew a blank and couldn't say it if someone offered you a million dollars to remember.

She felt like the road should have been different. There had been a road over the top of the mine before they began digging, but it wasn't that, although odd she thought about something not there today. She had another picture in her mind of horses and wagons and people traveling across the route. Something else. Maybe there'd been an entirely different route a long time ago. There it was again, that feeling of a connection with something from before her time, further back than she could remember. The thought kept repeating itself over and over, like a phonograph needle stuck on a crack in the record, unable to move on. It was eerie. Spooky! She'd never been here before, yet she recognized something about the hills or... That's where it stopped. She didn't have the faintest idea what it was. Imagination? She didn't notice him step behind her. The second he touched her, the feeling came back. Déjà vu. She couldn't shake it. When he wrapped his arms around her, the windchill disappeared and she felt warm, protected. Like the time he held her at Dripping Springs, there was a rush of energy coming from him and it was an old, familiar feeling — arms that held her before. The idea was crazy, but there was no pushing it away. Considering what she knew about him and the aura around him, maybe it wasn't crazy at all.

Except for indoor plumbing and telephone lines, Bisbee probably hadn't changed much in a hundred years. It was an interesting little town, so full of history you could feel it in the air. A town of hills with very little level roadway, most streets were on an incline, in many instances, a steep incline. She wondered why, in a time when travel was by horse or on foot, they built a town where it had to be a substantial physical effort to get from one place to the other. Anyone could easily have a heart attack walking up the hill to get home, especially in the heat of summer, or slip and break their neck in winter. What happened here a hundred years ago, or before, when there were only Indians in the hills? Although she didn't know the history of the area, she felt it closing in. Maybe it was an imprint left behind by those who passed through a hundred years ago that she was picking up — something from another time. There were probably all sorts of famous people who came this way, a diversity of travelers of dubious distinction. The mode of transportation was either stagecoach or horseback in those days and a journey through this country would have been slow going and very rough. Buildings more than a hundred years old were still standing. The only difference was the people who passed in and out of the doorways. With the exception of modern-day vehicles on the streets and utility lines overhead, Bisbee gave every outward appearance of still being the wild, wild West. It wouldn't be surprising to see cowboys with spurs jingling on their boot heels, packing Colt .45's and riding horses chosen for distance and endurance according to the time. Perhaps, a nattily-dressed gambler, decked out in fashionable black bowler or silk top hat and looking quite dapper with a diamond horseshoe pin in his tie, come to try his luck at cards in one of the houses of chance, a hazardous endeavor at best. His name might have been Bat Masterson or Diamond Jim Brady, or a Georgia gentleman dentist by the name of John Henry Holliday. Seemed there ought to be buckboards on the streets and horses tied to hitching rails, and ladies in long, calico dresses carrying parasols. There was something missing today. Camera-toting tourists in shorts and tennis shoes were out of place.

The flavor was unquestionably yesteryear, an antique town in the middle of modern-day 1994. It was one of those places you'd heard of where you truly felt like a Time traveler. Walking through the streets, one place in particular was a curiosity. There was no one around, nothing exceptional about it, but she had a peculiar sense of it having been a center of activity. There used to be horses and lots of people. She could smell the animals. It sounded so preposterous that she wouldn't even think about saying it out loud. There were horses here once, and people who were on the move. She stood on the spot and thought about what might have been. The street wasn't busy, yet she felt like she was in the middle of a flurry of activity. It had been a popular gathering place where things were always in motion; a saloon or maybe a stage stop. Maybe nothing. She watched him when they walked past the spot. He didn't say anything, so she didn't mention what she felt. They walked all over town, but that one location stood out in her mind. They passed it a couple of times and she felt the same way every time. There were some shops, catering mostly to tourists; nothing to indicate her sense of recognition was warranted, but when they left, she couldn't stop thinking about it.

The Copper Queen Hotel was a charming place with its mahogany staircase and turn of the century decor. In its heyday, it had to have been an elegant auberge. She walked around the lobby while he checked in. In 1902, when the Copper Queen was built, her grandmother was a young girl, sixteen; married two years later in 1904. The hotel reflected the style and grandeur of the era and reminded her of her grandmother's house in New York. She was little then, but she remembered everything about the house, including the red mahogany furniture and hand-embroidered flowers on the dining-room chair seats. Even as a child, she thought the crocheted lace doilies on the arms and headrests of the parlour chairs were beautiful. They were a carryover from years long past, from the era of the Copper Queen, and before, some of it handed down from her great-grandmother. When she was little, she used to pretend she lived in the time when her grandmother was a little girl and believed she knew what it was like back then, in the 1880's. What made her think of that? Funny how something like seeing this furniture could trigger an old memory. Not many took the time to notice wonderful old pieces of the past. Everyone moved so fast these days, preoccupied with getting somewhere in a hurry and never stopping to see the best things. It must have been an exciting era, the early days of the Copper Queen, and the preceding twenty years or so. There was a romance and style about the time that had never been duplicated and would never come again. The idea that those days were gone forever made her feel like crying. She heard a rustling and looked up toward the second-floor land-ing. It wouldn't surprise her if a ghost in a long, flowing dress with a lacy Queen Anne neckline and bouffant sleeves walked down the stairs. Nothing would surprise her in a place like this, not even a lady from another time in history, but there was no one on the landing — not that she could see anyway.

They were on their way upstairs and she wasn't nearly as worried about what the night would bring anymore. She'd come to terms with the fact that she couldn't change the direction of fate. Resignation of destiny. Something like that. Whatever happened, happened. That's all there was to it. She wasn't going to worry about expectations on either side. There were none from her side anyway and she was certain, none from his. She liked being with him and if the truth be known, she was content to enjoy his company and conversation if that's all there was. Anything else would be icing on the cake she already knew was sweet. She wasn't going to think about who was in shape and who wasn't. It didn't matter. If an intimate encounter was meant to be, he'd accept her the way she was. If he hadn't intended it to be that way, he wouldn't have asked her to come in the first place. Now that she was finally settled in her own mind, she was ready for whatever happened. Well, if she were to be completely honest, she had to admit she was a little nervous. She'd get over it. This was going to be a wonderful night — a wonderful three days.

She awoke with his arms around her. She couldn't remember a more spectacular morning, ever. She was right about the night. He dispelled the last remaining fragments of apprehension about spending the night with him. He was a true romantic. He thought of everything including candles and wine. Music from the saloon downstairs drifted up to their room on a warm breeze. It couldn't have been more perfect. His lovemaking was passionate and all-consuming. He carried her away like a bird in flight, free and happy. It had been something she'd never felt before, something she'd never forget as long as she lived; the most powerful emotional episode of her life. She perceived herself as disconnected from her body, floating somewhere above consciousness, experiencing the passion on a higher level. They touched something in each other that transcended any physical sensual experience. She had no words to describe it, but he did. He called it a merging of spirits. There was an unexplainable connection with him that defied the laws of science and Time itself. It was the familiarity thing again. She felt like she'd known him forever.

By noon, they were on their way over the mountain to Tombstone. As far as she was concerned, they could have stayed right there in Bisbee. She was content to walk through the streets looking at the old buildings and contemplating life as it might have been in the town a hundred years ago. He held her hand the whole time. She couldn't remember the last time someone just held her hand. During the night, she woke up several times and his arms were around her. The truly incredible thing about it was that he was still there in the morning. She had to smile, recalling words to an old song that described how he made her feel — like a natural woman. He actually cared what she got out of it. The men in her life were selfish and only interested in themselves. It had never been love. Actually, there had been one, but he belonged to someone else. That was twenty-five years ago. Love was something she'd given up on. It wasn't possible to identify what she felt, but it was definitely more than just a physical experience. The longer she was with him, the more she understood the reason for the aura. She kept reminding herself it was only a weekend — one weekend, but her little voice was telling her to pay attention. There was something else. It was a faint whispering in her ear, barely audible, but more than that. A growing sense of confidence and trust was getting stronger. A day would come to trust him with the deepest, most private secrets in her heart without fear of rejection or ridicule. Unusual feelings for only having been with him a few hours. For now, there were all those obstacles to get around, all the walls she'd built to prevent vulnerability and safeguard against heartache. Opening her heart wouldn't be easy, but when the time came, he'd be the one to tear down the walls. He'd be the one who would listen and care. A long time ago, she barricaded the route to her heart with the intent of keeping it sealed forever, the way ancient Egyptians built the pyramids with precision and secured passageways to the tombs of pharaohs to protect them from vandalism. She didn't think she'd ever say it, but the ramparts were coming down — one stone at a time.

There was one thing that bothered her a little. No, that was wrong. It bothered her a lot when it happened. The night before, in the heat of passion, he called her by another woman's name. "Rose." The intensity of the moment was high and she was carried away with it, forgetting the name until this morning when he was in the shower. She laid in bed, watching the ceiling fan turn, wondering who Rose was. Given the kind of man he was, it was inconceivable that he'd slip and call her by another woman's name, at an intimate moment or any other. If what she'd learned about him thus far was correct, he was more considerate than to permit an insensitive slip of the tongue. He wasn't someone who said anything without careful consideration to the consequences of his actions. In light of that, it struck her as being very odd that it happened at all. At first, she was offended and even considered asking him to take her home. She thought twice about saying so. It could only be that thing she hated most about relationships — jealousy, and this wasn't exactly a relationship. It was a weekend, nothing more. He didn't owe her anything. Her reaction was ridiculous and unwarranted. She had no right to be upset and she wouldn't allow herself to have an emotional upheaval over it. Jealousy was a useless, destructive, human frailty and she discarded it years ago. She wasn't about to let it interfere with what was turning out to be a great weekend with someone she wanted to spend the rest of it with. Nothing would make her cut the time short or ruin their plans, least of all, a childish reaction to a slip of the tongue. She was sure that when he made love to her, he wasn't thinking of anyone else. Still, she was curious. She thought about asking him who Rose was. The smart thing was to let it go. Rose might be a sensitive issue and she didn't want to bring up a subject that could produce an undesirable result, a premature return home. Before he got out of the shower, she'd let it go and was on to thinking about better things, the rest of the weekend.

In Tombstone, she waited in the truck while he checked into the motel, watching the hummingbirds hovering around feeders that hung under the building eaves. They were fascinating little creatures. Outside the truck, something startled her and she looked out the window. No one there. It felt like someone tapped her on the shoulder. She got out and looked around. Must have been the wind. Imagination. Something probably reflected off her sunglasses and she mistook the movement for that of a person. Maybe a leaf floating by on the wind. She looked around again. There wasn't anyone near the truck or in the driveway. On the road into town, there'd been a sense of being pulled along, a need to get there. For lack of a better description, a sense of urgency. She didn't know why. They were in no particular hurry and, if anything, she wanted time to slow down. Once they were inside the Tombstone city limits, there was an odd sensation of settling in, a feeling of comfort. Coming home.

The room wasn't ready. They'd have to kill an hour before they could get in. He drove into town and parked under one of the few shade trees at the north end of Allen Street. He had a cooler full of everything they needed for lunch, so they made sandwiches and sat on the tailgate. It was mid-September and the weather was perfect. Most people would have gone to a restaurant. Not him. He thought of everything and he had a knack for making the simplest things fun. The tailgate picnic was better than lunch at the Ritz. There wasn't one thing about him she didn't like, except maybe, being called Rose. She smiled about that. It wasn't important.

Walking the streets where Wyatt Earp and Doc Holliday once walked, it occurred to her that she knew absolutely nothing about Tombstone. It wasn't a place she'd ever had any special interest in or knew anything about, but now that she was here, she kept thinking something was different. Different from what, she didn't know. She wondered what it had been like over a hundred years ago, living in Indian country miles from the nearest city. When the thought came, she felt like she knew ...and the clothes women wore in those days; long dresses with collars up around their throats and shoes that laced up way above the ankle. No air-conditioning or frozen ice-cream bars! Summertime in this part of the country must have been absolutely miserable. It was bad enough today in shorts and barefoot sandals. She started asking questions. "Why did the early settlers come here? Why would anyone want to come to this place in the middle of nowhere to begin with? What was the attraction?" How did they bring in food? And how did they preserve perishable items without refrigerators? What did they do in a medical emergency?" He laughed a little when she said it. "It was a city. There were businesses, grocery stores, doctors. He explained. Silver! That's why they came — for a mountain of silver." She didn't want to appear ignorant, but she didn't know that.   She always thought Tombstone was just another place where pioneers stopped on their way to California. Wyatt Earp and Doc Holliday lived here. Come to think of it, she really didn't know anything about them either, only their names and a few minute bits and pieces. Oh, yes. Boot Hill was here, wasn't it? ...and the O.K. Corral? Everyone knew about the gunfight at the O.K. Corral. Well, that wasn't entirely true either. She'd heard about it, of course. Wyatt Earp and...? She wasn't sure who participated and she'd never known the details about why the fight started in the first place.

She didn't know people still lived here. She expected to find a ghost town full of hundred year-old deserted buildings with broken-out windows and decaying wooden wagons, gray and pitted from the elements, leaning to one side on rusted wheels. She thought there'd be old saloon doors banging in the wind and gates of livery stables warped and falling off their hinges. She anticipated stickery bushes of dry tumbleweed blowing around dirt streets where the air was once full of dust stirred up by horse traffic. She was embarrassed for not knowing more about a place in American history. He, on the other hand, knew quite a bit about it, but then, he said he'd been here a few times. Actually, what he said was, he'd been coming here for years because he felt drawn to the place. He wasn't sure why, but he had to keep coming back.

Something in the air seemed to be closing in around her. They planned to spend the weekend in the mountains of Ruidoso, New Mexico, but a local festival filled the hotels and he couldn't find a room. At first, she was a little disappointed to discover he'd decided on Tombstone because she didn't think there was anything of interest here. Now that she was here, she knew there was a reason they couldn't get a room in the mountains. That was a strange thought. Had to come? Is that what it was? The only answer she got was, "Yes." They had to come; for what reason, she didn't know, but one thing she was sure of was that it was all part of some predetermined plan — a rendezvous with destiny. The deeper they got into this trip, the more she believed that to be true.

They parked at one end of town and started walking. Looking at the old buildings and thinking about what took place more than a century ago, she had a notion of something very peculiar. It was much stronger than what she felt in Bisbee. There was a permanence about this place. She didn't understand the feeling, but she knew she was part of it, the permanency. Houses built in the 1880's were still standing. It was amazing to think they'd lasted so long, but they'd weathered well and people still lived in them. With a population of about fifteen hundred, it wasn't a very big town. Even more remarkable was that a place this size earned such notoriety and became so famous, famous enough to draw tourists a hundred years later — a million and a half of them every year. Apparently, there'd been a lot of excitement crammed into a few short years in history. They went through the old courthouse and walked around the gallows in the jail yard. They read about a specially-constructed gallows in the yard where several men swung at the same time for a robbery and murder in Bisbee. It was eerie standing on the spot where they were hung, and for the flash of a second, she pictured the bandits dangling from the ropes around their necks. Maybe the ghosts of the hanged men were still there, haunting the old halls of justice as retribution for their crime, shackled forever in the courthouse and jail yard. From his first visit, Mike said the courthouse held a fascination for him. He went there every time he visited Tombstone and spent a lot of time inside the old building, wondering what was pulling him in. It was all part of the draw for him, but he never understood why. He kept going back, hoping one day he'd get an answer. She felt it too, but not for herself, for him.

There was a local celebration going on, an annual event. Helldorado! They heard shots and spotted a cowboy firing a rifle into the air. He was drawing attention to an outdoor show that was about to begin, re-enactments of gunfights from the old days. It sounded like fun, so they stopped to watch. Halfway through the show, she wrote a name on a piece of paper, put it in her purse, and forgot about it. When the show was over, they walked around town doing the usual tourist things, looking in the shops and stopping off at Big Nose Kate's for an iced tea. What an unflattering name for a woman to have to carry around. Big Nose Kate! Kate had been Doc Holliday's lady. When they left Kate's, she heard someone call her name. It came from across the street. She stopped a couple of times and turned around, but there was no one there. Imagination was getting the best of her. The town was stirring emotions, feelings of what it might have been like back then — in the 1880's, and she was caught up in it. He was holding her hand as they walked up Allen Street, talking, and unaware of her earlier feeling of a meeting about to take place; a precisely-timed rendezvous with destiny waiting half a block away. What happened next was the beginning of an incredible experience, a series of unexplainable phenomena that would change her life. All she'd ever be able to do from this point on was tell the story exactly as it happened to her. It'd be up to whoever heard it to draw their own conclusions.

Chapter 20

"It's not the Arizona moon,
        or the music of an old-time piano tune
        that takes me back to the place where love still grows;
It's not a summer day that keeps me warm,
        or the rainbow at the end of a storm;
It's remembering the way you called me Rose."

Remembering The Way You Called Me Rose

The Bird Cage Theatre was built in 1881, a hundred and thirteen years before she went there. She heard the music before they reached the front door, an old-time piano and fiddles. There was something about the building... She looked up at the sign. "Bird Cage Theatre." It was an historical landmark, but she didn't recall ever hearing the name. As soon as she was inside, she was in a vacuum. Voices were muffled. Distant. She heard them only briefly before they faded away and she was alone. The old music box in the corner was pulling her toward it. She went directly to it and touched it. There was a coin in her hand, but she couldn't remember where it came from. She dropped it in the slot and heard it clank down through the internal mechanism that started the metal disk in motion. The instant the music started to play, she was overwhelmed with a terrible sense of sadness and loss, as if someone she loved just died. She couldn't stop crying. Everything seemed to be moving away and she was catapulted backward in a tunnel at high speed, increasing the distance between her and everything around her. She was talking to someone, but she didn't know who it was. The place was full of people. Many of the faces were familiar, but she couldn't make out what they were saying. At first, she thought they were dressed in some kind of old-time costumes. Then, she realized they weren't costumes. She was there — in that time. An arm was around her. A friend. Although the touch was comforting, nothing relieved the pain of loss. She pulled away from that person and ran out into the street. It was raining very hard and she was crying hysterically.

When she opened her eyes, she felt confused, like she'd been dreaming, unable to remember what happened before the dream. It was the music that triggered the dream. She was standing in front of the music box and it had stopped playing. A terrible sense of mourning engulfed her, but she didn't understand why she felt so bad. She characterized the feeling as immense sadness, grief of indescribable proportion; the way she felt when her best friend died thirty years ago. Worse than that. She looked over at him. He must have been standing next to her the whole time. It had something to do with him. Crazy as it sounded, he was the reason she felt this way. For a minute, she thought he was someone else. There was no logical explanation for it, but she knew it was because of him, or whoever she imagined he was. They'd been having fun. Why, all of a sudden, did she feel like crying? She almost said it. "It's you. This feeling of sadness. It's got something to do with you." She held back. She was dazed and disoriented, like she'd bumped her head too hard. Maybe she blacked out. She wasn't tired and she couldn't blame it on stress or feeling ill. She felt fine. The whole thing was bizarre.

They were standing near a wall that divided the barroom from another part of the building. She knew it didn't used to be there. She asked someone who worked there about it and was told the construction was original. She knew better. They were wrong. The wall wasn't there when the theatre was open and she knew it. She made a mental note of it. She didn't know why it was important, but there was a need to verify it. The room on the other side of the wall was full of antiques and artifacts from all over Tombstone, a ton of historical treasures crammed into one room. There was everything from baskets to tools to a collection of old musical instruments and vintage guns. It was a wonderful museum. The old fixtures and gaming tables were still there. She looked up at the little compartments lining the upper part of the room on either side. They appeared to be theatre boxes, but there was something about them that bespoke another purpose and she felt like crying when she looked at them. She walked toward the stage, passing over one spot where she felt cold. Panicky! The hair on her arms and the back of her neck stood straight up and she was covered in goose bumps. She remembered what her grandmother used to say about that kind of feeling. Either someone walked across your grave or you were touched by a ghost. Something tragic happened on that spot. She knew it. This place could very well be haunted — if you believed in that sort of thing. What she felt wasn't something to joke about though. At first, she thought she'd mistaken the feeling. She re-evaluated her anxiety. It was more than anxiety. She had it right the first time. Panic! An absolute tragedy occurred on the spot that made her cold, generating a feeling of total help-lessness following the event at the time it took place. She felt the inten-sity of whatever terrible occurrence caused the panic, and it all had to have happened over a hundred years ago. She couldn't stop it then and there was no changing it now. That was the strangest part, knowing she was somehow involved with whatever it was that happened in another time — sixty years before she was born.

When she saw the stage, she was overtaken by a different set of emo-tions, recognition and relief. All she could think was, "It's still here." She didn't know what "it" was. She zeroed in on the old curtain, faded and shredded with age, but still there, hanging in the same place as it did more than a hundred years ago. People must have been starved for entertainment in a town like this, so far from civilized theatre. But this hadn't exactly been what you could call civilized theatre. This place had been wild. She didn't know where that idea came from. She climbed the stairs and touched the torn curtain. Feeling the material made her shiver. In one of those ephemeral, cerebral flashes of something resembling memory, she heard what sounded like Saturday night at the busiest casino in Las Vegas — con-versation and laughter, glasses tinkling, cards shuffling, poker chips being tossed onto a pile of other chips, and music. Piano and violins. She stared at the old wooden stage, concentrating hard to see what was causing the activity and movement that caught her attention a second ago. The room was full of smoke — the unmistakable odor of cigars. Walking up the steps beside the stage, one word came to mind. Homecoming. It was a strange concept, but that was it, déjà vu all over again. The intensity of the feeling was growing. She knew this place. It was familiar. She moved to one side to let a woman pass her on the steps, the dizzying fragrance of cheap per-fume overpowering, strong and heavy. She wrinkled her nose at the smell and turned around to get another look at the woman, wondering who in the world would want to wear such an offensive scent. Beyond the steps and the landing was the backstage. She looked behind the curtain. Was she losing her mind? There was no one there, yet she distinctly heard the rustling of petticoats and footfall on the wooden steps — and smelled the perfume. Petticoats? Nobody wore petticoats anymore! The place was getting to her. First, the music box and now, a ghost passing her on the steps, wearing petticoats and strong perfume? Maybe she needed to lie down. From the landing, she looked out over the room below. She coughed. Cigarette smoke always made her ill and she covered her nose and mouth, but it wasn't cigarettes she smelled. The place reeked of cigars. A thick cloud of smoke filled the room from a lot of cigars being puffed at the same time and she went behind the stage to get away from it.

There was that feeling of something tragic having happened here too, on the backstage. Without knowing why, she made a wide circle to avoid walking across one particular spot, looking up at the rigging or, where the rigging used to be. She sensed danger. Death. There was nothing here to indicate a potential hazard, just another feeling, but it was a strong one. The old theatre itself was affecting her.

The wall was covered with pictures of famous entertainers who played the Bird Cage between 1881 and 1889; Enrico Caruso, Lillie Langtry, Eddie Foy, Lillian Russell and Maude Adams, among others. Impressive company, indeed. It was hard to believe they'd come all the way out here to perform in the middle of nowhere. This must have been an important stop on the theatre circuit in those days to draw such a distinguished entourage of national headliners. She stopped in front of Maude Adams' picture. She couldn't stop crying. Again, no explanation for it. She'd never heard of Maude Adams, but here she was, standing in front of a picture of an actress from more than a hundred years ago and crying. She was drawn to the picture, captivated by it. Maude's sophistication was evident. She was an exceptionally pretty, young woman, very stylish and, according to the write-up in the old newspaper clipping under the picture, quite talented. Looking at her was like finding a rare photograph of an old friend, a picture misplaced for a number of years and unexpectedly retrieved from some old trunk in an obscure corner of the attic.

There was no question the place was affecting her, making her feel she was supposed to stay, that she belonged to it, as opposed to it belonging to her. It was as if someone was whispering, trying to jar her memory into recalling something from another time. Even the catwalk was oddly familiar. She didn't know why she called it that. It was a bridge connecting one side of the building to the other to afford access to each group of suspended rooms and the narrow corridor behind them running the length of the the-atre. At one end of the corridor, she heard someone calling to her from the other end. It wasn't exactly that she heard a voice. It was more a sense of something drawing her in, pulling her back to a place she'd been before. For safety reasons, the entrance was boarded up and she peeked between the slats. Something moved in the shadows beyond the boards a few inches from where she was standing and scared her so bad she almost fell down the steps. When she recovered, she pressed her face against the wood and stared down the hallway, trying to detect movement. Nothing moved. It was perfectly still. Not even the air-conditioning stirred a piece of old wallpaper or curtain. The stillness was eerie. She could have sworn there was someone walking down the hallway. In fact, she was sure of it. There was a man up there. She saw him.

They went downstairs and played the music box again before they left. The same thing happened. She was overcome with a devastating sadness and she couldn't stop crying. During the time the music played, she experienced another loss of vision and consciousness, only it wasn't like fainting. It was more of a dream. She was still on her feet and this time, she was dancing. It was not a modern dance, but rather an old-fashioned waltz, and the man she was dancing with was wearing clothing of another time. The music was different from anything she'd ever heard. She was wearing a dress with a long, full skirt. The man was in uniform, an old Army uniform. They were laughing. It was the same place, a different time.

When the music stopped and she opened her eyes, the thought was the same as the first time she played the music box, knowing Mike had something to do with what was happening to her. He kept asking her where she went. She couldn't answer because she didn't understand what happened. She didn't know where she went. As soon as the music box started to play, she was thrown into the dream. It wasn't really a dream the way dreams occur during sleep, but she didn't know how else to explain that she was seeing things from what appeared to be the past. He was part of it and he felt something too, but didn't understand it anymore than she did.

The next thing she knew, they were across the street from the Bird Cage. He moved to one side to avoid something, the way you'd duck if a bumble bee flew at your face. She didn't see what it was. She went blank. She didn't know how long it lasted and she couldn't remember what happened afterward. He said something about being run into. As near as she could recall, it was, "Something came from the Bird Cage. Whatever was after you, bumped into me." She wasn't sure if she heard right. Then, he said when he turned around and looked at the doorway of the Bird Cage, for a split second, he saw her wearing a green dress, a period dress in the style of the 1880's. She looked at the theatre. There was no woman in a green dress standing in the doorway or the street, and she wasn't wearing a green dress from another era, but something was after her alright. Something was absolutely tugging at her, trying to maneuver her back inside, and she was having a devil of a time resisting. She belonged there — in the green dress maybe.

She didn't want to leave the Bird Cage. Something, or someone, had gone to a great deal of trouble to convince her to stay. From across the street, she felt the pulling and she had to fight the urge to run back. Even after they went to the motel, the draw was strong. It was a compelling notion that she was supposed to go back to the old theater. She hadn't felt at all like a tourist there. That she belonged and the tourists were intruding in her town was more like it. He said it was that way every time he'd been here. He never felt like a visitor. For hours, she tried to recover from the overwhelming sadness, fighting uncontrollable fits of crying, completely out of character. She couldn't shake the feeling of devastating loss. It came in waves and when it did, she broke down in tears. The thing that bothered her most was the gap in memory. He said that as they crossed the street, she suddenly turned around and at that moment, he felt that something coming from the direction of the Bird Cage brushed past him. He told her that she wheeled around in the street and said, "Even my car is here," implying that, perhaps, something belonging to her in the present was there with something from the past. They had driven his truck. Her car was in New Mexico, but in front of the Bird Cage Theatre was a car identical to hers. Same model, same color, same year. She never remembered saying it and she didn't see the car. She was in an accident once where a truck rear-ended the car she was driving and the collision propelled her car forward, smashing it into the vehicle in front of her to produce a double concussion. At the moment of impact, she didn't feel a thing and she never remembered the crash. Everything went blank. That's the way it was now. She felt like she'd been in an earthquake, coming to after the fact and standing on the edge of a giant fissure in the ground, unable to remember the cataclysm that caused it to fracture right in front of her.

It was frustrating, but try as she would, she couldn't remember everything that happened right after they left the Bird Cage. Moreover, she didn't remember a lot of what happened inside the place either. Events were fragmented. Unclear. She recalled being there, pieces of it anyway, but not the entire visit. When he told her about it later, she had absolutely no recollection of certain parts. They talked about it and he asked her if she remembered what happened when she played the music box. He played it on previous visits and knew the song went on for about a minute, enough time for the metal disk within to turn one complete revolution. When she dropped a coin in, the music kept going. Ten minutes. He said another person came by to look at the music box as it played. She never saw that person. He said an employee opened the belly plate and tried to turn it off. It kept playing, even after the spring was wound tight. She didn't see that person either. She was oblivious to everyone around her, and the music box kept playing, despite efforts to stop it. She didn't remember any of it. He said the music eventually stopped and they went through the museum and behind the stage. She remembered that and seeing the picture of Maude Adams. She had no memory of anything else in the Bird Cage.

The second night with him was more exciting than the previous night in Bisbee. She wished they could have stayed longer. The weekend was going by much too fast. They'd be leaving soon, but there was something she had to do before they left. She had to go back to the Bird Cage. Whatever was calling her wouldn't let go until she walked up Allen Street and went inside one more time. Despite the absence of any real explanation for the black-out and inability to recall her own behavior, she tried to convince herself what happened was simply the result of being caught up in the history of Tombstone and insisted the occurrences of the day before would not repeat themselves. He said her explanation of yesterday's bizarre events was wrong, that she "went somewhere when the music box played."

First thing in the morning, they walked up Allen Street to the Bird Cage. The instant she stepped inside the door, she was in a vacuum. Adjacent noise disappeared and she was in a different place. She recognized it as entirely detached from the world around her — another place in Time. She wasn't sure how it started, but the music box was playing and she was carried away. There were voices and music, other sounds she didn't recognize. She felt like she was dancing again with the man from the day before, only this time, he wasn't wearing a uniform. He was clearer than he'd been yesterday. There was someone else with her too, but she couldn't see who it was. For some reason, she thought the second person was a child or a young man. He was very close, there to give her comfort. Just like the day before, she didn't know what happened. She felt the terrible pain and couldn't control the tears. Something awful happened in this place. She knew it. Someone died here. More than one person. There was a third presence. She thought it was a woman holding her hand, a gesture of help from a friend. Later, Mike told her the music box wouldn't stop playing. Efforts to wind down the spring to turn it off failed the same as the day before and it wouldn't stop. During the extended play of the music, he said he put his hand on her neck. Her pulse was racing at an extraordinarily high rate. She didn't remember any of it. He was convinced the music box propelled her into a different element and resurrected memories of another Time. It was the vehicle that triggered the beginning of her transportation into the past. Something or someone was waiting for her at the Bird Cage Theatre. They were expecting him too. Perhaps, spirits of those who passed this way before had been waiting for both of them for more than a hundred years. It was the rendezvous with the destiny she'd been thinking about, but hadn't understood until now. A door had opened to them, a gateway to another era and another place in Time; a passage to another dimension, and it was only the beginning.

She didn't go back to Denver. Going down the list, there were plenty of reasons not to go back. For openers, she'd never done well in winter there. The slightest cold resulted in a problem with her damaged lung. Fighting the traffic on snow-packed, icy streets to get to work or the grocery store was nothing to look forward to and it was only a matter of time until somebody slid into her car. It wasn't as if there was nothing to keep her in New Mexico. Things had changed since her initial decision to go back to Colorado. She had a new life. Winter was right around the corner and she'd be going back just in time for the first snow of the year. Not an exciting prospect. Then, of course, there was Mike; this wonderful man who captured her heart after she was so sure it couldn't be done. Who did she think she was kidding? He was the main reason she decided to stay. There was a time she wanted to be alone. Not anymore. Something always interfered with her pursuit of happiness and she never followed her heart. If she didn't do it this time, she'd never know what might have been. Slowly, but surely, the walls were coming down. Colorado would be there if she changed her mind, but right now, Denver might as well be on the moon.

For weeks after they came home, she tried to explain away what happened to her in Tombstone as having been caught up in the history of the place, a romantic notion about what it might have been like to live there during the great silver boom in the 1880's. Gradually, it became more than that. It was a powerful force making her think there might be an underlying reason behind what was going on because she was unable to put it out of her mind. She was haunted by a recurring dream that she was standing in the street in front of the Bird Cage in the rain, crying. She dreamed the same thing over and over and every time she awoke from the dream, she was crying. It was the way she felt when she played the music box. As time went by, more pieces were added to the dream. A giant jigsaw puzzle was falling into place where objects began to take shape as each tiny area was filled in. At first, events seemed to be mixed up, out of sequence. Nothing made any sense. It was the equivalent of watching a bunch of different scenes from a movie, each disconnected from the others. She couldn't figure out how it all went together or what the story was. She started writing down the pieces of the dream. Every time they said good-night, she joked about going to sleep. Before they went to bed, other people brushed their teeth, took a bath, and went to sleep. She brushed her teeth, took a bath, and went to Tombstone. She laughed about it, but never really felt it was funny. It was taking over her thoughts. She wrote everything down that she remembered from the dreams, each bit of information becoming more important to remember as time went on. Mike encouraged her to keep writing. She wrote about people who lived there and events that transpired more than a hundred years ago as clearly as if she'd seen it all yesterday.

The name she wrote down the first day they were in Tombstone was Rose Callahan. The name meant nothing to her then. Lately, it was more than just a name. She felt a connection with the name — with the person. She knew what the woman looked like; petite, red hair, fair complexion, and green eyes. She knew what that woman felt, her thoughts. He surprised her when he said something about Rose Callahan. It was uncanny the way he described her. He said she had red hair and freckles and a fair complexion. There was another person she'd been writing about, a man by the name of John Merrick. He said something one time that really threw her. Among the things she'd written about John Merrick was a description of how he was shot, first in the shoulder then, through the chest. She believed the chest wound was fatal and he died in the Bird Cage Theatre. She pinpointed the exact spot where he died. It was the area that made her cold and panicky. When she ran her hand over the floor on that spot, it felt wet and sticky.

Blood! She was uncomfortable there. Before she told him, Mike said he thought John Merrick was shot in the chest.

Her thoughts went back to the ride to Tombstone when she was watching him drive. An idea about him having some special metaphysical abilities crossed her mind then and she didn't have a clue why she believed it, but she also remembered thinking he was stronger in that area than even he realized. He said something else one night that she wasn't going to mention, but finally asked him about calling her Rose the first night in Bisbee. He said he didn't call her Rose. She heard him say it. When she persisted, he told her what happened to him that night. He said there were a few minutes where he couldn't remember her name. It was all coming together. She knew who John Merrick was — in the 1880's and today. The more she thought about the series of events, the feeling he had something to do with what happened to her when the music box played, the dreams and unexplained phenomena, knowing about a place she'd never been before — everything, the more she was convinced he was the man she was writing about, John Garrison Merrick. In the Bird Cage, he was standing beside her when she thought she was dancing with someone from another time. Now, she knew who Rose Callahan was. Past lives? Incredible to consider, but even more incredible — to pass the same way again together.

She wrote about Ruby Fontaine, a long-legged, red-haired fireball who worked as a dancer and prostitute at the Bird Cage Theatre. She wrote about a blonde prostitute named Lizzie who suffered from a psychotic personality disorder that would probably be diagnosed today as a combination of paranoid schizophrenia and manic depression. There was another woman too, a very special friend, Abby Treneaux. The name alone was enough to make her wonder about the significance of the story. Her best friend died nearly thirty years earlier. When they were kids, they made a pact. Whichever of them died first would come back to let the other know she wasn't alone. They established a code word they'd both recognize if either of them found herself face-to-face with the other one's ghost. She hadn't thought about it in years. It surfaced in the story and she didn't realize the connection until an initial proofreading. The word was Abigail!

Another mystery was Maude Adams. She cried when she saw Maude's picture on the wall of the Bird Cage. There was a Maude Adams in her family, an actress who began her career in the 1880's, and the Kiskadden branch of the family seemed to be the connection.

As she got deeper into the story, descriptions of people and events from the 1880's became more detailed. Many weren't in the history books, but she was sure they'd been there in that place and time. She wrote about Virgil Earp and John Holliday. Personal things. Information only a close friend would know. She wrote about a rose ring made of gold, lost in the dirt behind the Bird Cage in 1882. She knew it was still there and she wanted to go back to look for it. Finally, three months later, they couldn't wait any longer. They decided to go back to Tombstone after the holidays. There was something about being there right after Christmas that was significant. She didn't know why she felt the need to be there at that specific time, but it was the same feeling they'd talked about often — had to be there.

The night before they left, she woke up a dozen times, each time speaking into a tape recorder. In the morning, she listened to the tape. Nothing made any logical sense; a bunch of riddles. She didn't discard any of it, making a list of items to investigate in Tombstone. Some of what was on the tape was, "Find the house with round windows," "Watch your step," and "Look for the silver rose." Last, and most bizarre was the message, "Look for a 2 and 3 with nothing in between."

Mike picked her up early in the morning the day after Christmas and she read him the things on the list. With no idea what any of it meant or what they were looking for, they headed for Arizona. They didn't take the scenic route through Bisbee and they didn't stop. They drove straight through to Tombstone and when they got to town, he went directly to Sixth Street. No reason to be in that particular location other than it seemed important to be there. He drove up and down the street a couple of times, stopping at one point in front of an old house. They both noticed it, but never figured out what the attraction was except that it had a small, round vent on one side. At first, she thought it might have been the "house with round windows," but decided it wasn't what they were looking for. There was something important about it though. They were drawn to it and felt they might have known who lived there at one time.

A block later, they were at the corner of Sixth and Allen Streets — across from the Bird Cage Theatre. It was raining and she felt as though she were walking into the dream she'd been having for three months. The same things happened. As soon as she was inside, she was swept away. The music box made her cry. She felt like someone was beside her, holding her hand. The room was smokey. There were "No Smoking" signs inside. It was an old building full of hundred year-old artifacts, many of them dry with age. No one had smoked in the place since it was boarded up in 1889, and no one would dare take a chance of a burning cigarette ember igniting the old curtain or an ash dropped on the dry, wood floor catching the place on fire, but every time she went there, the room was full of smoke. She smelled smoke and she saw smoke. They'd taken pictures on the previous trip. When she was choking from the smoke, she snapped a picture. The developed photograph showed the theatre where no one had lit up anything in more than a hundred years — filled with smoke.

The first time they were there, he took pictures behind the stage when she was looking at a picture of Maude Adams. He said while he was focusing on her, something made him step back and move the camera up. He didn't hear a voice. It was more of a thought that he was supposed to do it, something directing him to point the camera at an upper corner of the room. The day the film was developed, he left a note on her desk. It said, "Do you believe in ghosts? I have a picture of one." — He did! There was no conventional explanation to what he captured on film. Even a confirmed skeptic couldn't dispute there was something very unusual in the picture, an apparitional image of what appeared to be a woman with long hair in the upper corner of the backstage of the Bird Cage.

She stood in front of the music box as during the trip three months earlier. The last time she played it, he was behind her. That time, she heard him say, "Play the other coin." He insisted he didn't say any such thing, but she was sure it was his voice she heard. She remembered that now. This time when he told her to play the music, she was listening. She recognized his voice and she heard him clearly. He said, "What are you waiting for? Play the music." Later, he denied having said it. In fact, he'd been on the other side of the room. It couldn't have been him. He was too far away. She insisted. Someone said it. When the music stopped, her shoe scraped across an object on the floor and she picked it up. It was shiny, silver — a heart with a silver rose in the center. There were the chills and the hair standing up on the back of her neck again. It was one of the things she'd spoken into her tape recorder the night before. "Look for the silver rose." The impact was significant. She was so stunned by seeing it that she barely reacted, but if ever she had any doubts about the story she was writing and the source from which it came, they vanished with finding the silver rose.

Later, she told him about something that occurred at a specific location on the backstage. The year that stuck in her mind was 1882. A girl by the name of Abby Treneaux died there when a sandbag used to raise and lower the curtain fell on her. The girl had come from a small dressing room on the other side of the backstage and ran across the room to save someone who was standing under one of the weights. She pushed the other person out of the way just as the sandbag fell. He told her that during their first trip to the Bird Cage, when he felt something was prompting him to step back and move the camera to take a picture of the upper corner of the room, he was standing on the exact spot she was indicating Abby died in the freak stage accident. The resulting photograph revealed a ghostly figure near the ceiling. The strange figure appeared to be a woman with long hair, but whatever or whomever was in that picture was still a mystery.

They spent a lot of time driving around town, but never found the house with round windows or anything significant involving a 2 and 3 with nothing in between. They'd resume the search during the next trip — and there would most certainly be a next trip.

A few months later, she contacted a man who knew the town well, Tombstone City Historian, Ben T. Traywick. An authority on the area, having spent many years studying and researching Tombstone's history, Mr. Traywick was an author, movie consultant and long-time resident of the town. She told him what happened to her in Tombstone and she told him the story that was coming out of her experiences. She told him she'd been searching for evidence of Rose Callahan's life, but hadn't found any trace of her. He said, "Just because you haven't found her, it doesn't mean she wasn't here. Women couldn't vote in those days, so even if she was a resident, her name would not be on a census record. Only registered voters were included on the city census and only men were registered voters."

From the first time she set foot inside the Bird Cage, she knew the wall wasn't there when the place was built. Even after employees claimed it was all the original building, she knew the wall didn't used to be there. For six months, she'd agonized over that one fact because she was convinced she was right. He said she was right. The wall was built much later, when the place was reopened nearly fifty years after flooding of the silver mines caused miners and businesses to move out of town, closing the doors of the Bird Cage Theatre on December 24, 1889.

When she told him she was writing many things she didn't understand and wondered if she ought to continue with the story, he said, "You will travel through this world only one time. Don't leave it wishing you had taken an alternate route." He told her to write everything down and not to leave anything out, even if it didn't make sense at the time or seemed preposterous. He told her that answers become available when we least expect them. She told him about the house with round windows and on their next trip, he took her there. — An answer, when she least expected it. During the previous visit, they'd driven up and down every street in town looking for the house, but never found it. For the past six months she'd thought about it, certain it was there, but not knowing where else to look. It was there alright and now that she found it, she discovered it was more significant than she imagined. He introduced her to a man who was also an historian and preserver of history, someone with extensive knowledge and love of the Bird Cage Theatre — owner of the house with round windows and owner of the Bird Cage Theatre. It was then that more of what she'd written was confirmed, information she was sure was true, but had no way of proving until she met him.

She had written that Rose Callahan arrived in Tombstone in the summer of 1881. Everything she'd been told indicated the place opened in December, but she was positive that Rose came to town and went to work at the Bird Cage in the summer. There was no doubt in her mind that Rose arrived in July of 1881 and there had to be a way to prove it. A fancy, cherrywood bar made in the East didn't get there as planned in the summer when the theatre was ready to open, so the grand opening was postponed until December. However, that didn't delay the gambling hall and theatre opening for business. They built a temporary bar and opened the doors. In those days, drinking establishments, gambling houses, and brothels had to be licensed to do business. At last, there was conclusive evidence that the Bird Cage was open when she thought it was in the summer of 1881.

The Bird Cage was located at the corner of Sixth and Allen Streets in the heart of the Red Light District. The owner gave her a copy of the City License issued by the Tombstone Tax Collector's Office to the B.C. Red Light District for "License on the business of House of Ill Fame, 6th & Allen S.W." The license was signed by John Clum, Mayor, and Wyatt Earp,

Deputy Marshal. The license was dated June 17, 1881. She was right again. The Bird Cage Theatre was open when Rose Callahan rode the stage into Tombstone in July of 1881. More answers, when least expected!

The trip proved more rewarding than she ever dreamed. By the time six more months passed, the story had turned into a book. She wrote graphic details of events and painted vivid mental pictures of people who were not in the history books. Accounts of daily existence of ordinary folks who lived more than a hundred years ago became commonplace on page after page. She told about old-fashioned medicinal remedies from the oil of a desert plant she didn't know and identified a poison derived from another plant used by the Indians to induce visions during ritual ceremonies. She called it by the Indian name, not knowing what it was — tolguacha. It wouldn't be until a year later that she stumbled across the plant in an outdated, dog-eared, agricultural textbook from the 1930's. When other sources failed to turn up any reference to the plant, a friend offered his father's old ag books as a last resort to identify the illusive, botanical mystery. There it was — tolguacha. A poisonous plant, indigenous to Southeastern Arizona, and noted for it's narcotic and hallucinogenic properties. It had a modern botanical name, but the Indians called it tolguacha.

She wrote about the freak accident that killed Abby Treneaux on the backstage, and a rose ring that was lost in the dirt out behind the Bird Cage in 1882. The owner of the Bird Cage said he remembered reading something about an accident that resulted in the death of a woman on the backstage. He found old documents and letters in steamer trunks forgotten in the basement when the place closed and people left town in a hurry in 1889. Among the papers was a handwritten note that talked about an accident behind the stage where a girl died.

There was more incredible information. Fifteen years earlier, he found something in the dirt behind the Bird Cage Theatre — a gold, rose ring.

At midnight, they went into the Bird Cage and turned out all the lights. She sat in a wooden gambler's chair beside the old faro table where Doc Holliday might have played the game over a century ago. The room was pitch dark. There were no windows in that part of the building and the "wall" blocked out light from the street. Ten minutes after they sat down, a light traveled across the stage, stage right to stage left. It never reappeared during the rest of the time they were there.

Her chair was pulled sideways. The unexpected, sudden jolt startled her and she let out a yip. She moved the chair back and concentrated to regain her composure. A few minutes later, someone ran a hand over the top of her head. She reached back to catch whoever the prankster was and felt all around her chair to touch someone who might be close by. There was no one around her chair. In the two hours that followed, her chair was moved eight times and by the time she left the theatre, her hair looked like she'd been in a wind tunnel.

A woman in a blue dress in the style of the 1880's stood on the steps next to the stage. She watched the woman walk down the steps and stand behind one of the four other people who were in the room. The woman placed her hand on the left shoulder of that person. When asked if she felt anything, that person said there was someone standing behind her with their hand on her left shoulder. Later, a man wearing a knee-length coat and western-style hat stood in front of her, so close that his boot touched the toe of her shoe. She could see him clearly and he held out his hand. She wasn't sure if he was trying to give her something or if he wanted her to take his hand. At the time, it didn't occur to her that the room was in total darkness, yet she was able to see him when she couldn't see her own hand in front of her face. She said, "Take a picture of whatever is standing in front of me." The flash went off and whoever had been there dropped something on the floor before he vanished. She didn't hear the object when it hit the floor, but Mike did. What she heard was a man's voice saying, "Don't do that."

The developed photograph revealed a shadowy figure in front of her, reaching out to her, exactly where she said it was. The interesting thing was that for as close as the figure was to her, she never heard the object he dropped when it hit the floor and rolled, but someone else did. When the lights were turned on, a dime was discovered a few feet away on the floor. In another photograph taken before the appearance of the man, the floor was visible. There was no dime or anything else on the floor in that picture. It was an ordinary dime, or — maybe not. Mike had a theory that if she'd held out her hand and accepted the coin, it wouldn't have been a dime at all, and the ghostly figure in 1880's-style clothing would have given her the object he intended her to have. She wished she'd taken what he was trying to give her. Now, she'd never know what the true object might have been. Of course, there would be another chance.

In the year that followed, she found over two hundred dimes.

The last day in Tombstone, they stopped to look at an old house on Toughnut Street. They'd passed it on prior trips. More than the house on Sixth Street, this house had a peculiar attraction. Standing at the gate, the sense of familiarity took over and she felt sad and happy at the same time. It was abandoned and hadn't been lived in for a long time. Mike said the house affected him every time he drove past it and he thought about stopping several times. Another of those curious attractions that neither of them had been able to explain. She wanted to stay. She said it felt like home. Lace curtains, yellowed by time, hung at the windows and an overgrown rose tree at the front nearly hid the little gray house. You almost had to be looking for it to see it. The yard hadn't been kept up and the place was in a serious state of disrepair. She stood at the gate for a long time, a familiar feeling creeping over her — the same as standing in front of the music box. She recognized the house. Without going inside, she knew what the layout was. She'd been there before — a long time ago. She was sure it was the little gray house she'd been writing about and she knew if she went inside, it would be exactly as she described it in the story.

She'd been looking for three graves together. They made two trips to the cemetery, trying to find a marker engraved with the name "Rose Callahan." A couple hours of searching up and down the rows of granite tombstones and wooden markers in the hot sun led to a dead end. Rose wasn't there. They'd have to resume the search in a future visit.

The next trip, they spent a day walking through the hills around the small mines. Driving out the south end of town, she felt like they were getting close to something important. She was looking for a tree. Trees of any size were sparse in the hills around Tombstone, and after more than a hundred years, the tree by the graves might not even be there anymore. Nevertheless, she was certain it was the area where the graves were located. From the very beginning, she'd written about Rose taking evening walks this way and it was the direction they went when she buried John and Abby. She was sure it was where Rose Callahan was buried as well, on a hill south of town. Now, there were three places that affected her, the Bird Cage Theatre, the little gray house, and the hills.

They drove up Toughnut street again and stopped to look at the old gray house. Around back, the steps were gone and the door was wide open, swinging on rusted hinges and falling apart from age. When she went inside, the feeling of having been there before returned. The floor plan she'd drawn nearly a year ago before she ever saw the house was correct. In the story, she wrote about roses in the carpet. Mike pulled up the layers of linoleum, laid down one on top of the other over the years. At the bottom, remnants of an old floor covering, though faded, were still visible. The pattern — roses! The house had been added onto over the years, but the layout she drew was the original house. An odd thing happened when they left the house. Two men walking up the street called to them, asking if they wanted to buy the house. Coincidentally, one was the owner, there for only that day. He came down from Tucson and just happened to be there at precisely the same time they were there from Las Cruces. For the first time since they began driving past the property, she looked at the address on the house — "203." The impact of the discovery was like the day she found the silver rose on the floor in the Bird Cage. She just found the last thing she dictated into her tape machine over six months earlier — "Look for the 2 and 3 with nothing in between." Once more, an answer when she least expected it. It had to be the little gray house she'd written about. She was sure she'd found it, the house where Rose Callahan lived and died more than a hundred years ago.

In Bisbee, they went to the courthouse to look at the old deed books for Cochise County. At the top of a page, they made another discovery — a name; someone involved in a real estate transaction in Tombstone in the 1890's. The name was Emily Grants. The little girl in her book was Emily Grants, and she would have been in her twenties at the time of the property sale in the deed records. What was the chance of finding that name in a Tombstone property transfer during that period in time? It was too perfect to be a coincidence.

Six months after Mike first took her to Tombstone, she wrote a song for him. She called it "Allen Street Rose." It was about what happened to her when she played the music box at the Bird Cage and what she had come to believe was the story behind the song. Over the next year and a half, she wrote and recorded ten songs on an album entitled, "Allen Street Rose." Like the rest of her experiences in Tombstone and the story she wrote as a result, the music was of an origin she couldn't explain. She couldn't read or write a single note, but the songs came to her and she sang them and played them on the guitar and piano. The music was never written down on paper because she couldn't write music. It was all in her head and she played the instruments by ear. When questioned about how she did it, she couldn't explain because she didn't know. All she knew was that she could play the music. It was like the story about Rose Callahan. Somehow, the whole thing was given to her by an unexplained source and she stopped trying to figure out where it came from a long time ago. Two years after the story started, they were playing her music in the Bird Cage Theatre in Tombstone and the only thing she could think was, it was where she was supposed to be — then, and now.

She prefaced the album with a narrative, written the way she saw it:

"Her story has never been proven as history, not yet anyway, but that doesn't mean she wasn't here. They say she came from Ireland. A Gypsy. She had fiery-red hair and a temper to match, and eyes the color of emeralds. Her name was Rose Callahan. She came to Tombstone in 1881 and worked as a singer and lady of the night at the wildest honky tonk between Basin Street and the Barbary Coast — the Bird Cage Theatre. Story was, she might have had a wild fling with Virgil Earp, and some say she was a friend of the notorious, Doc Holliday. Flooding of the mines marked the end of the great silver boom and sealed the fate of the Bird Cage Theatre forever. On Christmas Eve, 1889, the doors were locked, closing a chapter in Tombstone's history. It was the end of an era. At night, she still walks the streets of the town too tough to die, searching for the love she lost over a hundred years ago. They say ghosts of old gamblers still play faro at midnight, and you can hear Rose Callahan singing to the music of a tinny piano and a cryin' fiddle. She lived and died in Tombstone, and they called her the Silver Rose."

There is a philosophy behind all of this. That is, of course, if you believe these kinds of things. There are those who have converged on this place to be together again after a very long separation in Time. Some traveled great distances to be here and some have been waiting for Rose, or the spirit who was known as Rose Callahan, all this time at the Bird Cage Theatre.

Rose Callahan and John Merrick had unfinished business when his life was cut short by a forty-five caliber bullet. After he was gunned down in the Bird Cage in 1882, they had to wait more than a hundred years to finish what they started. Have they returned in this lifetime to do just that? Has he kept the promise he made to her when he died, that they would meet again?

There is a little house on Sixth Street, still standing after all these years. Was it where Silver Dollar Jenny and Lizette lived?

What about the little gray house on Toughnut Street? Did Rose live there? And, is it where she died in 1889?

Is the rose ring found in the dirt behind the Bird Cage the same ring Rose lost there — the ring Virgil Earp gave her on Christmas Eve, 1881?

Do we recognize friends from the past, albeit with different names and faces this time? Abby Treneaux? Ruby Fontaine? Nalanche? Virgil Earp? — A tall man with blue eyes; his hair has turned to white.

Is Rose still singing at the Bird Cage?

Have we passed this way before?

There are a lot of stories about the Bird Cage Theatre, mysteries that have never been explained, tales that make you stop and think about the existence of ghosts; spirits of those who passed through these doors between 1881 and 1889 during the heyday of the most exciting silver boomtown in American history and who, after more than a hundred years, might very well still be here.

A perfect ash, carefully rolled off the end of a good cigar was found on the floor near a high-stakes poker table in the basement. Beside the ash, an expensive gambler's match, finished with a special lacquer to make it burn long to get a cigar going, the kind used by high rollers like Bat Masterson and Diamond Jim Brady; a match not made these days, quite rare — a collector item worth a lot of money. Not the kind of thing someone would strike a fire to and throw away. The match had been burned.

The other thing that made the discovery so strange was that the floor was swept clean and the door was locked. Fifteen minutes later, when the door was unlocked, the cigar ash and burned match were found. No one was in the building between the time the floor was swept and the time the door was unlocked. No one has smoked a cigar in the Bird Cage since 1889.

~~~ There have been numerous citings of an old-time stagehand, wearing a visor and carrying a clipboard, walking across the stage; stage right to stage left, then disappearing.

~~~ A woman has been singing in the Bird Cage, her voice heard for over fifty years, but she's never been seen. There's a new voice singing in the Bird Cage today — or maybe it's Rose Callahan singing there again.

~~~ A large, heavy table blocked the door to the gambling hall and theatre, preventing entry from the front of the building, moved there by some powerful, paranormal force during the night.

~~~ The unexplained, sudden appearance of a valuable poker chip, part of a set where all the pieces had been located except one, this one having been missing for years and found, quite unexpectedly, in plain sight on a gaming table in the middle of the Bird Cage. Story is that over time, the same poker chip mysteriously moved from one location to another without human assistance, including from a bank vault to a locked desk drawer.

~~~ A woman wearing 1880's-style clothes was observed on a security camera, looking into the old wine cellar that extended under the building from the basement. She went through the opening and into the cellar with it's original dirt floor and relics of the past. When the observer investigated the area, she found the opening to the wine cellar covered by iron bars secured by a padlock. The bars weren't loose and they did not swing open freely to allow entry to the wine cellar without a key. The woman had gone through the grate and entered the wine cellar — and vanished without a trace. Was she looking for something she left behind in 1889? An old steamer trunk, perhaps? Or a letter written about a friend who died in a backstage accident in 1882? — A letter that was never mailed?

~~~ A man dressed in clothing of a bygone era was seen standing on the steps beside the stage. He was told the Bird Cage was closing for

the night and he had to leave. He left, but not by the front door or the back. There was no other way out. If he was hiding, he was darn good at it because he was never found inside the Bird Cage Theatre.

Perhaps there are ghosts inside, unable or unwilling to leave for reasons only they know. With all that happened there, it wouldn't be surprising to find out they've stayed for over a hundred years. Stories about the Bird Cage are endless and so are the unexplained and unsolved mysteries. It was the location of sixteen gunfights, and better than a hundred and forty bullet holes riddle the old girl's walls as visible evidence of wilder days. There are a few slugs in another old girl as well. The painting of the famous belly dancer, Fatima (later known as Little Egypt), still hangs on the wall of the Bird Cage in the same place since 1882, in no worse shape for the six bullet holes and a couple of knife slashes in her canvas.

Lots of famous people came to the Bird Cage, exciting people, not the least of whom included Wyatt and Virgil Earp, Doc Holliday, the Clantons and Johnny Ringo, and high rollers like Bat Masterson, Luke Short, and Diamond Jim Brady. When he wasn't playing poker in the thousand-dollar-a-seat buy-in game downstairs, publishing mogul, Randolph Hearst worried the faro bank more than once by placing heavy bets expected to be covered by the house in the event of his winning. Let's not forget those wonderful entertainers whose talent and personalities graced the gilded stage; Lillie Langtry, Eddie Foy, Enrico Caruso, Lillian Russell, Lotta Crabtree, Maude Adams, and Josephine "Sadie" Marcus, the likes of whom will never be seen again on any stage. The list goes on. No wonder the ghosts of yesteryear want to stay.

In 1882, the "New York Times" described the Bird Cage Theatre in no uncertain terms as "the wildest and wickedest night spot between Basin Street and the Barbary Coast," and during the eight and a half years she was open, she lived up to every bit of her colorful reputation. She had plenty to offer every miner, cowboy, drifter, and businessman who was looking to have the time of his life. When they walked through her doors, they ventured into a world of excitement never seen before or since. Gambling, whiskey, women, and a variety of entertainment to exceed the wildest fantasies — the Bird Cage had it all.

One night, a customer commented that the ladies with bright-colored feathers in their hair who sang as they delivered drinks to the tiny, suspended cribs reminded him of sad, beautiful birds in cages high above the theatre. The sight of them inspired the words to a song, and he wrote them standing right there at the bar. He asked a composer friend, Harry Von Tilzer, to set the words to music. Von Tilzer wrote the music and took the finished piece to the Bird Cage where he played it on the piano and sang it from beginning to end for the customers. When the tune stirred the ladies to crying, he figured the piece was destined for notoriety. The next night, a lovely, young singer by the name of Lillian Russell performed the song on stage at the Bird Cage. The song by Arthur J. Lamb and Harry Von Tilzer launched Lil's career and she sang it all over the country. Von Tilzer underestimated the success of the music. It became one of the most famous and popular tunes of the era. The song? — *A Bird in a Gilded Cage.*

They served the finest whiskey in town at the Bird Cage and the entertainment was unsurpassed; everything from famous funny man, Eddie Foy, to sweet-throated nightingales like Annie Duncan, Irene Osborne, and Lillian Russell, and timeless, sophisticated beauties like the refined British actress, Lillie Langtry, known as the Jersey Lily; and the wonderfully witty and pretty teenage actress who would become famous for the first portrayal ever of Peter Pan, Maude Adams.

The cancan was all the rage and it was performed nightly by scantily-clad, long-legged, and genuinely-French dancers who delighted the primarily-male audience every time those ladies stepped onto the stage. If that wasn't unconventional enough, there were risque performances by other dancers and tantalizing teasers, local ladies mostly, who worked at the Bird Cage as prostitutes when they weren't on the stage, and whose expertise at the art of seduction was so perfected that men became intoxicated simply by watching the show. The outcast daughter of a wealthy and politically powerful Mesilla, New Mexico Territory family, Ruby changed her name to a variation of that of her family's, and answered her calling as a dancer. A tall, gorgeous redhead with sparkling, sapphire-blue eyes and a natural manner that drew men like steel shavings to a magnet, she and her precision-choreographed troupe became a prime attraction in a mining town full of men starved for real beauty. There was none better than Ruby Fontaine and her high-steppers. Their stage acts helped promote good business for the ladies in the tiny cribs suspended from the ceiling or, for enough money, the higher-priced brothel downstairs. If you were looking for the best of everything and you had a pocket full of money, you could have it all at the Bird Cage Theatre.

The stories never stopped. Wyatt Earp met his third wife, Josephine Marcus, at the Bird Cage. She was an entertainer both on the stage and as a high-class, high-priced lady of the night in the expensive basement bordello. They called her Shady Sadie. A picture of her, wearing the famous, extravagantly-provocative transparent dress, hangs on the wall in the basement of the Bird Cage today, close to the private room where she may very well have staged her greatest performances. They say she loved the theatre and performing on the stage, but when she met Wyatt Earp, he became the love of her life — and she became Josie Earp.

The longest poker game in the history of the West took place at the Bird Cage Theatre downstairs in the basement. It lasted eight years, five months and three days, and it ran non-stop, twenty-four hours every day, the entire time the Bird Cage was open — including Christmas. It was no place for penny-ante poker players or amateurs. It was serious business. How serious? Well, if you wanted to play the game, the buy-in was a thousand dollars. Big-money gamblers like Luke Short, Bat Masterson, Diamond Jim Brady and the notorious Doc Holliday turned many a card and placed a fortune in bets on that table.

Chapter 21

> *"Down at Billy's Bird Cage,*
> > *the music flows when the place is closed,*
> > *and phantom gamblers are still placin' their bets.*
> *You know what I hear when I walk down Allen Street?*
> > *I hear the way things were a hundred years ago.*
> *I gotta keep coming back for more;*
> > *You know I think I've been here before.*
> *There's a little of me way back then still in me now."*

> *What Do You Hear When You Walk Down Allen Street?*
> **ALLEN STREET ROSE**

There are others who have come back, not exactly sure why, but knowing in their hearts they are connected to the place. They hear the music and girls giggling when they walk down Allen Street. The inviting sound of cards fanning in a shuffle and poker chips being stacked on felt-covered gaming tables awakens the desire to try their luck at a game of chance. There is a memory they can't quite put their finger on, so they stay because they are compelled to stay in what was once the greatest silver-mining camp on earth. Some things never make the history books and cannot, therefore, be proven as fact. That doesn't mean they didn't happen. It's sort of like the old men reminiscing about the early days, a bygone era they don't want to let go of. They can't let go. No one will ever know if they got the stories straight or not. They told some of it wrong, but most of it was probably pretty close to being right.

Today, there are those who have returned to the Town Too Tough To Die to research and correctly record the history of Tombstone; historians, intent on searching out the truth about the past and preserving its integrity for future generations. They've got the facts about Wyatt Earp and Virgil and Doc Holliday. They can tell you a hundred stories, like the one about Margarita, the tall, dark, Mexican beauty who worked as a prostitute at the

Bird Cage Theatre. Her untimely demise occurred when another prostitute by the name of Little Gertie, nicknamed Gold Dollar, pulled a dagger and stabbed Margarita because she was sitting on Billy Milgreen's lap. The petite, hot-tempered Gold Dollar thought Billy was her man and she didn't take kindly to another woman paying him that kind of attention. Billy was nothing more than a tinhorn gambler who borrowed money from Gertie to cover his gambling debts or stake him at a new game. With no particular sense of devotion to the one who was head-over-heals in love with him, he stood back and watched the two women fight to the death when he could have easily stopped it. Although much smaller than Margarita, Gold Dollar's strength was greatly increased by jealous rage, and the Mexican señorita collapsed onto a poker table when Gertie viciously plunged the wicked stiletto blade into Margarita's side. Poor Margarita bled to death before help could be summoned. She's buried in Boot Hill.

Among the stories, they'll tell you all about the gunfight at the O.K. Corral and paint such a vivid picture of the most famous shootout in the history of the West, you can smell the burned gunpowder in the air. Maybe its the diligent research that produces such accuracy in the preservation and writing of history — or maybe they remember something of the past known only to them.

Spirits pass in and out of this world, meeting one another many times over through millennia. However, it's rare they remember each other in human, earthbound form in the place known as the earth plane. We are protected from the incomprehensible knowledge of what went before until such time as we return to the element from which we came. There comes a time when unfinished business must be brought to a close, and those entities who are concerned with the resolution are brought together for the common purpose of universal peace and harmony. They converge on the predesignated place at the precise moment in Time set for them to reunite. What are the chances that two who once loved as mortals will be brought together again in another lifetime and recognize the reunion? What are the chances we'll meet again as friends or lovers and remember what went before? When the significance of knowing is too important to wait, and it is determined by a higher power that we are capable of understanding, we are allowed to know. At that time, we are blessed with a gift that few receive and we are charged with the responsibility of using the knowledge wisely. The veil that separates life and death is transparent and the fragile curtain that covers the gateway to the crossing is lifted when we least expect it, drawing us through to the other side or putting us in touch with those who dwell in another dimension. When a chance to set the record straight is given to us and so many have helped us along the way, we are fools if we don't take it. The crossover is closer than we think.

Who walks down Allen Street tonight? Wyatt Earp? His brother, Virgil? Maybe that notorious gambler and rumored cold-blooded killer, former Georgia gentleman dentist, Doc Holliday? A long-legged dancer from the Bird Cage Theatre, Ruby Fontaine? The Apache boy, Nalanche? A handsome young lawyer, shot down in the Bird Cage Theatre in 1882, John Merrick? The redhaired Irish girl who waits for the love she lost over a hundred years ago, a lonely ghost from the past? Who is a ghost and who is real? Who's still here, and who is here now who was here before? You know who you are. Charlie still plays the piano at the Bird Cage Theatre — or does he? ...and Rose Callahan is still singing there — isn't she?

You can still hear the music and the girls giggling and the cards being shuffled. When the place is closed, they say ghosts of old gamblers are still placing their bets and fancy ladies of the night provide amusement in the suspended cribs and basement bordello rooms. A smoke-filled room where no one has smoked for more than a hundred years? Reality or imagination?

The answers lie somewhere in the place described so appropriately by a friend who <u>knew</u> it well... "a small town, lying in that area somewhere between Peyton Place and the Twilight Zone!" The final question — "Have we met before? Somewhere in Time?"

See you at the Bird Cage!